THE
TEMPERING

The – Foundry – Book 3

J Fitzpatrick Mauldin

COSMIC
ENTANGLEMENT
M e d i a

www.jfitzpatrickmauldin.com
Copyright © 2025 by J. Fitzpatrick Mauldin

You are more than mere flesh and bone.

You are a universe unto itself.

PART I

CHAPTER 1

As the *Transcendence* burned toward a ring of danger suspended in nothingness, a sensation like falling into an endless pit overcame every part of my being. We were a shard of golden-white crystal-glass, bright as a star against the endless black, screaming in silence. Before us there was a path, a clear means to see this mission through, but the gate stood in our way.

"It's got a lock on us," my copilot, Karianna Torlen, reported, but I already knew it. I could feel the Foundry's instruments reaching out for the ring with their soft fingertips, threads of cosmic light crossing us.

Remain calm, I told myself.

"It's do or die," she went on. *"I don't think they'll be treating us too kind after what happened to the Jevox."*

I could feel her anxiety rise, our minds connected through the integration to the ship, flashes of her running fingers through her raven hair, her eyes narrowed, the bracelets on her right wrist jingling. It was strange to experience, given our current technological entanglement. When she felt something intense and wasn't guarding those emotions, I felt it too.

Remain calm.

My wife, Shelly, put a hand on my shoulder from within our virtual space to steady my emotions as the *Transcendence* burned through open space toward the Wandering Gate. She stood at my side with a determined expression, dressed in a white jumpsuit with a FICSE mission patch on one arm and a UEI patch on the other, looking every bit the specialist who had clawed her way through hell and was tougher for it. The two of us floated in a sea of stars and nebula, no walls, no barriers, ribbons of multicolored light and data swirling around us in a maelstrom, bringing to life a place that at first glance might have seemed empty, our physical bodies protected from G-forces and time as they floated in their Star Spheres.

"It will work," she whispered. "It will work." I knew this to be an affirmation, a plea to the Universe to make it so.

I took a deep breath, not because I needed to breathe—a foolish idea in a mixed reality simulation—but because it helped me to steady myself. It was a human ritual meant to calm, nothing more.

"Are the probes in position?" I asked Proxy, focusing my attention on the swelling gold ring ahead of us. The fingers of my broken hand flexed, the missing digits fading in and out of existence.

The Wandering Gate waited for us. We were closing fast, and it had not begun to fire. Instinct told me we were already in range because I'd felt our weapons go offline. We had already entered what the Foundry called the Inhibition Field, an area of space around any facility where weapons of Foundry-made ships were disabled for safety purposes. Our weapons, not theirs. And if our Foundry-made weapons were disabled at this range, a range similar to the gate's own weapons, it stood to reason we had crossed into the danger zone. This crossing was different than the last one.

I knew that change was inevitable. No matter what we do, no matter how grand the things that we build, something always changes. Growth, decay, death. It doesn't matter if in our minds we have a perfect picture of what is, or what should be—these ideas are mere constructs of our will and desire. We exist in a universe of a billion-billion-billion variables, all in constant flux, forces of gravity, expectation, and intent pulling at one another, shaping and reshaping existence. And as lowly humans, as singular life forms of any species, all we can hope for is to embrace entropy, find beauty in chaos, and adapt as best we can.

The true test of strength is not power, but the ability to adapt.

Humanity had made some stupid choices for generations. I chose to believe it was not spite or evil or anything of that nature that led us here, but rather fear of scarcity. We ruined our world, allowed the idea of an infinitely rising economic directive to rule our cultures, and in the end had no way to escape our decline. Humans had faced their end, but a hand had reached out from the stars offering help, and we had taken it willingly.

The Foundry protects life. Even that of lowly little humans.

The Foundry gives gifts, bringing lowly little humans up to the level of others.

The Foundry watches and waits and tests, looking to see if lowly little humans will make the right choices. And for a time, we did. For a time, we were adrift in this cosmic opera, passive participants, but then we took action, became a part of this grand production, and now . . .

The Foundry wanted us dead.

Change had found us once more. How would we have to adapt to it? Who would we have to become if we were to survive not only the choices of our ancient past, but the ire of the Foundry?

The Foundry protects life.

But did lowly little humans protect life?

The jury was out.

One of the reasons the Foundry destroyed all species-made ships that visited their facilities, breaking them down into their base components before recreating them into something new, was that it gave a supreme level of control over first contact. It allowed this autonomous, universe-spanning entity to set a level playing field for all species it deemed worthy. They were given ships of equal power based within its master calculus, using the same generalized technology. It stood to reason that the weaker species, like humans, were given great weapons, and a strong species less so. But in the end, this stacked everything in favor of the Foundry itself, no matter the gifts. It knew what our capabilities were at any given time. It had made us of its own design. This was why when we finally faced the Wandering Gate, our only means of returning to the other side of the Milky Way, we knew we had a problem.

We'd screwed up bad as a species. We'd left our home, traveled to meet with this grand entity designed to protect life. We'd taken its gifts, and in way of thanks enslaved ten thousand aliens only to later kill them in a fiery antimatter explosion. The "we" was Johan van Niekerk and his group, of course, not my crew. But they were human, and we were human, and the Foundry seemed one to make broad judgments. Johan and his crew had not protected life, and so we too were ones not to protect life. That made us an enemy of the Foundry, to be shot on sight when approaching a facility like this. To be shot with weapons much like our own, both powerful and deadly.

Beside me on the invisible floor, a black tuxedo cat with an orange stripe running down its back rubbed up against my shin, its body vibrating as it purred. "The probes are at your command, Milo. Once we activate them, our cover will last for only a limited time. Statistically, we should have a level of safety approaching the gate."

"*Statistically?*" Lance Brittan blurted out over our ship-wide channel.

While Shelly, Proxy, and I may have been together in my virtual space, the rest of the crew were still present, if only over comms. They were in their own Star Spheres, with their own custom virtual spaces from which to watch these events. But they were not the pilot.

"*I don't like the idea of statistical survival,*" he went on. "*One in a hundred doesn't feel great when you end up being the one.*"

"It is what you will get for now," Proxy replied. "The Foundry's defenses around the Wandering Gate will fire at the probes one at a time, choosing them at what might appear to be random. If we get chosen early, this will be over quick. It should be painless."

"*We're hoping for a bit of good luck then,*" Ada Mitchell popped off next. "*And luck is something I think we've been lacking lately. Anyways, guys, we've run the math a hundred thousand times. There are tolerances built in for a margin of error. So, ask for luck, sure, but it shouldn't be necessary.*"

"A margin of error," Proxy echoed, a pink sort of confidence in its voice.

"*It has to be done,*" Leo Nelson added. "*And what a dramatic and daring plan we have! We've made it this far, right? I think we can go a little bit further.*"

"*I do not like this gate,*" said Frelo, the single Jevox we had brought into our crew. "*We cannot be the same on the other side. The gate, it copies us, breaks us into dust, communicates our atomic template across quantum entangled particles, but this is only information. We are not the same on the other side. Only a reassembled facsimile of the original.*"

James Reed let out a laugh. "*Only choice we got, bucko. Would you rather have been left behind? Your fleet was hot on our tail for quite a while.*"

There was a pause, and then Frelo replied. "*No. I am where I should be.*"

I was thankful the Jevox was with us, while at the same time shocked they had stayed after all that had happened. Harper had caused the death of ten thousand of their people when she forced the Prole Genascara's antimatter reactor to go critical. Several times I had asked Frelo why they had remained with us after such a heinous act, and they gave no good answer. They had stayed for their own reasons, and I only hoped those were noble.

"I have said many prayers," Hy Nguyen told the crew. *"All the gods and Gods, low and high, are with us."*

"And the Universe," Xuan added, piggybacking off her husband's sentiment. *"Hope we made good enough."*

"Less than three billion humans still alive," said Renata Cox. *"No other option. It's Earth or bust."*

Earth, or bust . . .

"Bruv, 'dis all bare buki," Chevelle agreed. *"Crazy strange, like a bad trip, innit."*

"The worst kind of hallucination," said Leo. *"Though that can sometimes be the best inspiration."*

"Truth is inspiring enough," Dante Vasquez said, and Emilia, his wife, grunted her approval.

"I hate not being able to fight," Renata, our one true military crew member, went on in a low growl. *"I feel blind with both hands tied behind my back."*

Leo let out a laugh. *"Are we talking about things we should be afraid of? Or a good time? You tell me."*

"Shut up, Leo," Ada said. *"Just shut up."*

"What? I'm just kidding."

"It could be either," Renata conceded.

"You see, Ada? It could be either."

Ada let out a sigh in a way that only she could, like a massive bellows being pressed down one millimeter at a time. *"Not for you."*

"Cut the chatter," I spat back at them, my tone a little too harsh. I knew they were just trying to calm themselves by processing it all out loud, checking off lists, making jokes, but it was messing with my Zen.

We'd had months of subjective time to consider this moment as we traveled away from Yuven back to the Wandering Gate, but there was something about those final moments before it all hits the fan that always brought this out in people. "Look guys, Karianna and I need to focus. If something goes wrong, we've got to adjust quick."

"No ting," Chevelle said. *"We quiet, boss."*

"Thanks."

They're nervous, Karianna spoke directly into my mind. *We've been in some tight spots, but this is mostly outside of our control. We've been closed out from the sweet,*

sweet goodness of this entity. The Foundry does not want to allow us any more progress. We have to be strong for them. Have to be strong.

I responded to this with a sense of agreement, if not words. This was the time to put on a strong front, even if it was fragile. As their leader, I had to believe we had a chance to succeed. Johan had been stopped, if not how we had wanted, and now we were on a new mission.

FICSE Mission: Version 2.0

Step 1: Survive passing through the Wandering Gate.
Step 2: Find the Isopteran home world and recover the pulsar map printed on the golden disc from *Voyager.*
Step 3: Go back to SOL and see if we could undo the damage humanity had done to Earth with our gifted Jevox terraforming technology.

It was a tall order to be sure, but if there was something the events of Yuven and the lead-up to them had shown me, it was that I wasn't alone in this. I was never alone. I had people who cared about me. Talent who followed me with a common goal. Friends I could trust.

"Deploy the probes," I ordered.

Proxy bowed its feline head. "As you wish."

Within my virtual environment, a constellation made up of 244 blue lights appeared, forming a misshapen sphere around the Wandering Gate. Each of the false stars flashed once, producing a burst of light, then gave me a short heart attack as dangerous sensor data fed back. Their signals received by our ship, the points of light were no longer markers for the near-invisible probes, but copies of our massive starship. Thank the Universe these probes were doing their jobs, fooling Foundry-made instruments, including our own, into believing hundreds of *Transcendences* were making a break for the gate, not just one.

Our ship was no tiny vessel, even in this infinite theater, its body stretching out to 1,150 meters in length. Seeing copies of us from the outside, and so many at that, reminded me just how big we really were. Space made scale difficult. My first ship, the *Fidelas,* had been big, tall as a skyscraper and reminiscent in shape of the Shard in London, but once Karianna's vessel, the *Reverie,* had merged with mine after the attack with the dragon, we had grown.

Taking the same basic shape as our original vessels, the *Transcendence* was a jagged, crystalline spear tossed through a flattened diamond, its hull gold with white, and white with gold. It bristled with weapons, arrays of energy beams, antimatter cannons, kinetic rail guns, and piezo-electric spatial compression launchers, as well as fighter bays, with a hull protected by a swarm of mercury-like nanomachines that acted as a shield. Seeing more than two hundred of us diving toward the center of that portal was pretty damn awesome. It made me wish that this illusion was more than just that—but a true armada at our behest.

Karianna urged me to increase acceleration, and so I did, and in tandem, the rest of the probes followed suit. We drew up the Mercurial Integumentum, our defensive barrier of nanomachines, forming it into a deflection wedge at the forward end of the ship. Our sensor phantoms mirrored us in perfect parity.

The defenses of the Wandering Gate came to life, power readings blossoming from its ring.

"Here we go," Karianna called over the open channel.

"Sixty-seven thousand kilometers to the gate," Shelly reported, her eyes narrowed, fingers locked together before her.

"If things go sideways," I told them. "I'm launching your Star Spheres through the gate. You'll have at least a small chance someone like the Melcorin will pick you up in time."

"We're not retreating," Ada responded, her voice hard as steel. *"We've got payback to get. We've got a mission to finish."* I knew how she felt. She too had a personal vendetta wrapped up in this mission.

Karianna and I braced ourselves for the searing pain that might follow the onslaught of the Gate's weapons. I supposed it was good and bad news here, being that the Foundry had defenses on a scale we had never faced. Chances were that if it hit us, we'd be split in half at the first blow. No pain to be had, just nonexistence.

The Foundry opened fire.

Beams of pure, white light lanced out from the ring, cutting at the phantoms of the *Transcendence* in random patterns. Proxy had been clever enough to make these phantoms appear as if they exploded when they were hit, rather than just vanishing, if the probe's vicinity was struck and not the probe directly. This aided the grand illusion. The Foundry defenses at the Wandering Gate could fire each of their twelve, massive Para Lux arrays once per minute, meaning that they could eliminate a probe every five seconds, which was why Proxy had deployed 244 in all. This gave us time— at least statistically.

"Approaching gate maximum entry velocity," Proxy said, its tail flicking at the invisible floor. "Ninety kilometers per second, relative. Probe destruction rate holding steady."

"Backing off on drive," Karianna called back.

Shelly swallowed, her face placid. "Twelve minutes to gate insertion. Feels like an eternity."

"Shit. I wish we could go faster."

"Steady now," I started. "If our current rate of destruction holds, we should have more than enough probes to cover our entry."

"Margin for error," Proxy added. "But that can change. Our chances of being hit increase with every probe destroyed."

"Thanks for the encouragement, Proxy," Karianna growled. *"At least Chinchillette is being positive about this."*

"As we are both networked together, Captain Torlen, I can assure you it is not. We are realists."

"Geez. You're no fun, Proxy."

The Transcendence plunged toward the opening of the gate, probes matching pace, forcing the constellation to collapse on itself like a toy Hoberman sphere. To our starboard came a brilliant flash of white light, a simulated explosion, and then five seconds later, one just below us. Proxy's illusion was convincing. Karianna and I could even feel the heat on our skin through the ship's instruments.

"That was a close one. Those were only a few rows away," Shelly said. "Do we speed—"

"No," I cut her off. "We've got to hold. If we fall out of line, it might pick us off."

She wrung her hands and put on a fake smile.

The gate's assault did not slow. It continued in the Foundry's methodical, evenly paced rate, probes winking out. We could do nothing from our position but hold our breath and wait.

"Eight minutes to entry."

"One hundred and ninety-six probes remaining," Ada said, checking over the numbers. Karianna and I didn't need her constant reporting; we could feel the probes on a base level as part of our eyes and ears, part of our

perceptions, but if it made them feel better— *"Wait,"* she said. *"What was that? Something's wrong."*

I reached out my arms, focusing my attention on what I believed Ada had seen. Sections of the Wandering Gate along its golden ring that had previously been dark began to glow. Nine points of light began spewing radiation across the spectrum.

"What is that?" Proxy asked, surprise in its voice. "This is not part of the specs."

"What?" I asked. "What is it? What are you seeing?"

"I cannot be sure, but there appears to be a secondary defense system I was not aware of. Kinetic weapons. They were not there before—it's as if they were constructed at our approach."

"You have got to be kidding me," Lance said. *"Did it detect a severe threat, and just . . . grow new weapons for the hell of it?"*

"Rapid nanoconstruction," I grumbled. "We should have considered it. The Foundry does this all the time. Why not now?"

"They're firing," Proxy said.

Probes began disappearing at an alarming rate. While these new weapons did not seem as powerful as the twelve massive Para Lux arrays that were part of the gate's technical specifications, they fired fast, and often. Proxy fought to keep up, attempting to make the illusions remain when the probes were hit in different sections with the accelerated slugs. The defenses of the Wandering Gate tore our illusion apart like a toddler with tissue paper. Instead of a single probe every five seconds, we were losing three or four in that same time.

One of the kinetic rounds struck the wedge of our MI, and I felt my teeth chatter as our systems recoiled. The barrier might have absorbed the impact, but it was bright and loud and left a gaping hole in the defenses before us.

"I'm having a hard time calculating this," Ada said. *"Shelly?"*

Shelly flicked her fingers at open air, working through calculations and sheets of numbers. "I'm trying to count it out, but they're firing too fast. All I know is we're running out of time. Five minutes to entry. At this rate, we'll run out in just a couple minutes."

This was not going well. Our constellation was forming gaps.

"What's the upper limit on the entry velocity?" I shouted to Proxy. "We've got to move faster."

"Ninety kilometers per second," it replied. "We cannot go faster."

"We won't make it at that rate."

"No, we will not. I—"

"Fuck it," Karianna growled, and the ship began to hurl itself toward the gate. *"Burn, baby, burn."*

Energy spewed from the rear of the *Transcendence*, our drive plume hotter than stars, increasing our acceleration by five, ten, fifteen, twenty, thirty, forty, fifty Gs. The structure of our ship groaned under the pressure. Alarms informed us that our bodies, even within the Star Spheres, could not keep this up forever.

Normally, Karianna's brash actions would have made me angry, but in this moment, she was right. This was the only real solution, no matter what Proxy said. We just had to hope this gate was a little more tolerant and the posted limits were more suggestions rather than a hard line.

The illusion of the probes was beginning to falter, our screen of protection thinning. They traveled at different rates now, some slower, some faster. I didn't know why this was happening, and there was no time to ask Proxy. Kinetic slugs struck our hull, and pain vibrated throughout my body. Karianna and I began working different sections of the MI to protect us from what we could, reforming it by drawing on the nanovats when shattered.

"Two minutes," Shelly reported, her voice urgent. "Milo, we're down to thirty probes. We're not going to make it."

"The hell we aren't," Karianna groaned, and the ship pushed just a little bit faster.

"Twenty probes left. Our chances of being hit are increasing exponentially."

"Fifteen probes."

Come on. Come on.

"Ten probes."

The *Transcendence* rocked as several projectiles slammed into us. A shot from the Para Lux array grazed the hull, leaving a gash near our aft end that was twenty meters long and four meters deep. More alarms. Antimatter storage damaged. Weapon systems went offline—not that we could fire back.

"Thirty seconds."

"We're gonna make it," I said, and began repeating this as if doing so would make it truer. "We're gonna make it. We're gonna make it."

The last of the probes exploded just as we reached the angle at which the gate could no longer fire at us without putting itself at risk. We were safe from the Para Lux arrays and rail cannons, but we were going too fast.

The Wandering Gate swelled around us, encompassing the cosmic horizon till there was nothing else. We struck the near-invisible surface of the gate, and it accepted us.

I closed my eyes as we plunged into its influence, reality crinkling around us like a sheet of paper crushed into an infinitely dense ball.

There was no way to be sure if we would emerge on the other side at the same incredible velocity we had entered, and so I braced myself to make the drastic maneuvers necessary to avoid colliding with the fields of ice that orbited along with Cynosure on the other side. I waited, hoping for the best. I took a breath, then realized something wasn't right.

As I opened my eyes, the alarms hadn't triggered. I found that we were not within the Lignos system as we had expected to be. There was no ice here, no Cynosure station, no gas giant below. In fact, there was no darkness of space. We were surrounded by light of every wavelength in the spectrum, existence a nebulous collection of diffuse matter and energy stretching out as far as our instruments could reach.

This was not our universe.

There were no exits, no doors, no pathways, just an endless expanse of color and light and chaos.

We were alive, yes, but . . .

But . . .

Where in the hell had the Wandering Gate sent us?

CHAPTER 2

While instincts had us—or at least had me—under the impression that we were screaming forward at over 130 kilometers per second, I had no way to be sure. The *Transcendence* was shooting through a soup of matter full of color and light, yet there were no gases or liquids that were thick enough to halt us from doing anything. There were no fixed points in space; everything around us was in flux.

"What the hell is this place?" Karianna asked, her emotions a mix of anxiety and awe through the integration. *"We are not in normal space-time."*

"No," I replied. "We are not. Proxy?"

My cat closed its eyes and raised a paw to its face as if it was done with this shit. "You entered the entry point exceeding the recommended velocity limit."

"And?" I mused, glaring down at it. "What should that matter? We had no other choice."

Proxy's reply was cold, "Design specifications are put into place for a reason, Milo. The Foundry cannot alter physics. The universe has laws."

"Is everyone okay?" I called out, and one by one, the crew checked in. Everyone was nervous, understandably so, but alive. Vital signs may have been good, if elevated, but hearing their voices was better.

Shelly spun around at my side to get a good look at the strange space in which we had found ourselves. From the look on her face, I could see she was thinking hard.

The intensity of light around the *Transcendence* increased, swelling to some kind of undefined crescendo. It came from no particular location, but from everywhere at once.

"I think we're about to pass through something," Karianna said.

And everything went white.

An instant or an eternity later, impossible to say, we appeared in the same space, screaming toward the same inevitable location, not location. We checked in. Everyone was still alive, but we were no closer to getting out of wherever this place was.

Ribbons of light danced around us, their colors and patterns entropic. My eyes burned from looking at them. They were beautiful, but the intensity of color seared my virtual retinas. I knew I wasn't really seeing this, it was just the Foundry's interpretation through the instruments of the ship transmitted to my brain, but it hurt.

"We've got to get out of here," Lance said. *"We went too fast. Passed a kind of speed limit. Do we need to slow down? Change direction?"*

Ada replied, *"Without knowing where we are, any direction could be detrimental. Do the instruments give us anything?"*

"Not really," Karianna said. *"It's mostly noise. This light, the colors, I don't think any of this is being represented like it really is."*

"Call for help?" Xuan asked. *"Maybe Melcorin in this part of space, they help us out. Lead us to the exit."*

"This isn't a where," Hy said.

"You aren't a where!"

"Shit," Lance said. *"The light. It's building again. It's bright. So damned bright."*

And he was right. I could not just see it but feel it in my everything. We were again passing through something, though I had no idea what that something was. Chaos. Infinite energy. Pure concept, untethered intentions. I attempted to readjust the angle of the *Transcendence*, but without any fixed reference points like stars, it was impossible to tell if it had worked. Even the ships gyros, which helped orient us based on angular momentum, seemed not to be functioning as designed.

"Cross—" Proxy began, but was cut off as everything went white.

We reappeared once more in the same space, the colors slightly different this time. Where everything had been mostly red and green before, it was now blue and yellow.

"Check in," I ordered. I found it increasingly difficult to tamp down my anxiety by the moment. Everything was wrong, and I worried this was just the start.

Shelly was standing beside me. She reached for my hand and sighed, her eyebrows crashing the center of her face in intense thought.

"Hy, and Xuan Nguyen, here."

"Mitchell here."

"Nelson, here."

"Torlen, here."

"Young, here."

"Cox, here."

"Frelo, here."

I waited a moment for Lance to call in. Nothing.

"Brittan, are you there?"

Still no response.

"Lance!"

I scanned the ship for his vitals and got nothing in return. His Star Sphere, or where it should have been, was a blank spot. Not destroyed, just missing, the space empty as if it had been cropped out of the picture of reality.

"Lance?" Shelly whispered, her eyes fixed on me. "Where did he . . ."

"Not good," Leo started. *"Not good, not good at all. Where is he?"*

My face went hard. "Everyone to me. Now."

The remaining crew appeared in my virtual space without delay. They knew that in a situation like this, we needed eyes on each other at all times. Foolish as it might be, we felt a sense of safety in numbers. Lance was missing, and we had no idea why or how. There was a monster in the house, and it had started eating us.

After seeing who all had appeared, Shelly let out a long breath. Even if he was an asshole at times, Lance was important to this crew, and I had begrudgingly come to like him. He was a talented project manager, as well as my best fighter squadron leader. He was always a counterpoint to my lines of thinking and had helped me achieve several breakthroughs over the years. We were weaker for his absence. Was that intentional? Was the Foundry screwing with us? We were on the outs, targeted to be destroyed for not keeping our end of an unspoken bargain.

"Where did he go?" Shelly demanded. "Is he . . ." She let the question hang.

James stepped up next to my copilot and put a hand on her arm. "You okay?"

For once, Karianna did not shrug away from his touch. She moved as if to speak to him but kept her mouth shut, tapping him on the hand in an unusually tender gesture.

Chinchillette, Karianna's version of Proxy, appeared next to my tuxedo cat. Standing as high as my knees, the rodent resembled a giant chinchilla, with a set of huge, radar-dish ears and a mouselike shape, but it was easily fifty pounds instead of a few ounces, and had a pair of beady eyes as large as closed fists. It looked to Proxy, who looked back at it, the two having an inaudible conversation we were not privy to.

"Proxy?" Shelly pressed. "Tell us."

The two Foundry proxies turned to us and shook their heads at the same time.

"We do not know," Proxy reported.

Chinchillette gave a shrug. "We are not sure where we are."

The group began to chatter, voices raised, filled with emotion. Everyone was not just anxious but scared. This was bad, really bad. Did physics here work the same?

"Who's next to go?" Leo asked, rubbing his tattooed arms. "I don't want to go. I don't want to go."

"No one is going anywhere," I said, but maybe a moment too soon.

In the colorful chaos around us, light began to brighten once more. We knew what this was. The duration between the cycles seemed to be lessening.

"We've got to come up with an idea," Ada said quickly. "Whatever this is, there has to be a way out. There—"

Everything went white.

When we appeared once more, I patted my body down with my palms, checking to be sure it was all there. No missing arms. No missing legs. Shelly stood before me, but her expression was not one of relief, it was one of horror.

"Chevelle," she said, reaching out. "She's gone."

I spun around to look, counting our group to be sure. Shelly was right. The South Londoner was no longer here. Karianna made a quick scan of the ship and reported that her Star Sphere was missing too, as well as large portions of the diamond-shaped center of our ship. The sections had not been ripped away—they appeared to have been edited out of existence along the neat lines of a twenty-meter-long rectangular prism.

"We're next," Leo spluttered, taking a step back from everyone.

"I don't know what to say," Hy mumbled. "Maybe they are not gone. Maybe somewhere else? Maybe relocated? Not dead."

"Possible," I replied. "But where, and how do we find this out quick enough? How do we get them back? I need ideas, team, ideas."

Leo swallowed. "We broke the gate."

"No shit," Ada spat back at him, extending a finger and poking him in the chest. "Of course we broke the freaking gate. God damn it. Alex would know what to do about this. He was always smarter than me. He would know how to fix this."

"We did what we had to," Karianna said, but she didn't seem convinced.

"Let's think clearly," James started. "What's the trigger? The light, yeah, and it's getting more frequent. But what is this machine, what does it do, how does it work? We should start there."

"It's a gate," Leo said.

"Yes, a gate."

"It takes us apart," Hy supplied. "Then stiches us back together."

James sucked in a breath. "Is there a transmitter in this thing?"

"I don't think so."

"No," Ada said. "No transmitter. It's quantum entangled."

"Whatever that means," James said. "Just another science term thrown out by people who have no real understanding."

"The gate reads your molecular data as it is disassembled on one end," Proxy began, "processes that information and communicates it to the other gate by a series of quantum entanglements, photon pairs that spin in tandem over vast distances. On the other side, the data is reassembled in the order in which it was taken apart."

"This is bullshit," Renata said. "I can't fight this. I can't fight it."

"I knew the gate was dangerous," Frelo said, their constellation of eyes blinking wildly. "I warned you. Ceruleans have traveled through and come back. They are never the same."

"And were they being chased by energy weapons? Did they piss off the Foundry?"

They flexed a multijointed arm, robes billowing. "No."

"There's got to be something in that," James said, rubbing his chin. "Mom always told me to approach any problem like a puzzle. That's all this is. I think we have all the pieces. We just need to look at it from a different angle. Anyone?"

Karianna gave him a shy look, uncertainty clouding her mind.

Shelly was nodding. "It's what I've been trying to figure out. Why would going so fast do this? Or was that even the cause? Is this a defense system?"

"Like in a computer?" Ada mused while picking at the paint on her chipped fingernails. "Like antivirus, antimalware, or something like address space randomization for overflow."

"It's happening again," I said as the space around us brightened. "We will make it, everyone. Look at me. We will make it."

Their faces did not reflect the confidence I hoped that I portrayed.

Everything went white.

"Hy?" Xuan called when we reappeared. "Where are you? Where are you? Hy? Hy!"

We were back, and yet we had again been left with one less person than before. Another section of the ship was missing, but oddly enough, I still had control of our systems. This made no sense.

"Hy . . ." Xuan collapsed to her knees and began to sob. "No. No. No."

Ada went to Xuan's side and threw her arms around her, burying her face in the woman's chest. If I'd had the time to process it all, I knew my heart would have been broken, but I couldn't. We had to focus on solutions and fast. None of us were going to make it out if we didn't do something and quick. We had some of the smartest people in the universe aboard this ship. There had to be a solution.

Shelly's right hand was balled into a fist, knuckles pressed to her bottom lip in thought. She was shaking, clearly upset but not willing to give in. "Lovelace?" she asked, evoking Ada's nickname.

"Yeah?" she said without letting go of Xuan. "What is it?"

"Think with me. If you were a galaxy-spanning entity, and you had built gates to hurl people across light-years in an instant like this one, first scanning them, then taking them apart, then putting them back together, why would you have a speed limit?"

"Well . . ." She considered this for a moment, eyebrows crinkling. "I might do it because the rate at which I could scan something was limited. I might not want to miss anything. Taking people apart molecule by molecule, atom by atom, would be a tricky process, I would think."

"So, you would have a maximum safe scan rate. And if those scans were not completed in time, what might you do with all the matter, all the data, you collected? Let's say it fell into a place of flattened space-time."

"Thinking from the standpoint of a machine, as far as we understand?"

"Yes."

"Umm. I'd have some sort of overflow that elemental data might be stored. If the entry point to the data systems were overwhelmed— Oh, shit."

Shelly nodded, slow. "Oh, shit."

"Oh, shit!"

"What?" I asked, my heart skipping a beat. "What is it? You know, don't you. You know."

"A hypothesis," Shelly said, drawing a quick diagram in the air. My virtual environment obliged the effort. She started with a blue ring and then drew a red line shooting through it. "You've got an object traveling at a high velocity into the ring. The ring is designed, as Proxy stated, to have an upper entry velocity. The reason being, the system is designed to accept only a limited amount of data per second, or nanosecond, or on whatever the heck scale it uses to measure time. That fixed amount of data, while under the posted limit, is scanned, broken down, and reassembled in Lignos." She drew a line being broken apart within a circle just past the gate. "Follow me?"

"So far."

"This machine has temporary memory like any other, though of course its memory is far more expansive than anything we've ever seen. It's caching, which for one of our human devices maybe could hold terabytes of data; this one might hold maybe 10^{10} petaflops of data. But big or not, it could get overwhelmed. When that caching buffer gets full, it dumps the data to the next level, and the next level, and so on. So instead of us being copied once, we're copied multiple times, our data is spread out. It's going where it has to go because we've pushed the capacity of the quickest memory available." She had drawn a series of boxes at the end of her chain of doodles. Now she was drawing curved lines out from the boxes, bouncing off their tops from one to the next.

"Oh, shit," I hissed, finally understanding. "Oh, shit."

"Right?"

"I'm not following," Leo said, his hand outstretched. "What's going on?"

I put my palms on my face. "Bro, we're stuck in an overflow buffer. This isn't real space because, well, we're literally inside of computer processes. Question is, how are we still conscious? This doesn't make any sense."

Shelly shrugged. "That kind of stuff is all metaphysical. I have no hypothesis for it. You're the one who made contact with the Universe, not me."

The why of this could be debated another day, and there was only one pressing question in that moment. "Alright, it's a good theory."

"Hypothesis."

"Okay. Hypothesis. How do we get out?"

"Well . . ." Ada said, letting go of Xuan and standing. "If we can push the data back through the original ports, allowing it to be processed to the other side at a slower rate than we entered, it should guide us out. Though, I have no idea what level of, if any, data corruption could happen because of this."

"Proxy?" I asked my companion. "Anything?"

It shook its head. "This is beyond my understanding."

"Comforting."

"That said, Miss Mitchell's theory has merit."

"How do we push the data back?"

Shelly twisted a finger in the air. "Turn around. Go back the way we came. When you do, move at a slower rate. The reason I think we're accelerating is that the engines are still burning, right?"

And to my surprise, they were. We were still accelerating. How had Karianna and I missed that? The better question, why did that even matter in a place like this?

I looked to my copilot, and we nodded at one another.

"Engines are off, not that it makes any sense that this would work. Now how do we turn around? How do I know we are headed back in the right direction? Can't we just stay here, and eventually the gate will work through the buffer and process us the right way?"

"It might," Ada said, her hands raised, palms out. "Or it could purge the data completely due to the error. If I were designing this system, that's what I would do with unwanted information. That's all we are at this point."

There's no fixed locations, Karianna mused within my mind as she felt through the ship's systems. *What do we do?*

We have to find something, I thought back. *What about the colors? Each of the rooms, or sectors, or levels, they all have a slightly different quality to them.*

But that doesn't give us direction.

"Uhh, guys," Leo said, pointing ahead. "It's happening again."

And he was right. The space was brightening, colors blooming around us. I closed my eyes to shield them from the intensity.

"I don't want to go," Leo said. "I don't want to go."

Everything went white.

When we returned from the brink, I took inventory of all who were here. Leo was still with us, but . . .

"Shelly?" I called, spinning around. "Where are you? Shelly? Shelly!"

I frantically scanned the ship, searching for her Star Sphere, Karianna's presence with me. As we reached the room where Shelly should have been, we found only empty space. She was gone.

"I don't—" I whispered.

Ada held out a hand, her eyes trembling and moist.

"No. No . . ."

Milo. Karianna spoke in my mind, anxiety and empathy communicated along with her words, everything becoming a jumble of emotion. *We have to get out of here. If she's right . . .*

I know. I know. But where the fuck do we go? Tell me which way we need to fly. She knew . . . You have to know.

I don't. I mean . . . Her thoughts stumbled over one another. *If we . . .*

"Guys," Leo said, taking hold of my arm, fingers gripped tight. "We can't stay here like this. You two are doing your weird being quiet and not talking to anyone thing. What do we do? This is all freaking me out."

Karianna, we've got to pick a direction! I shouted back at her through the integration. The anger I projected was hot. I knew it wasn't fair. *Any direction.*

I know. I know.

My wife is missing. She may be dead. We're all about to be erased forever. Where do we go? You're the impulsive one.

Yeah, but not all the time. I can't make decisions. I'm just a loose cannon, it's what I do best.

Bullshit.

Milo, I don't know what we should do. I don't know where to go. I just know if she's right, we have to pick a direction.

I had to keep my cool. In times past, I had plunged myself into despair when circumstance had pushed me to the edge like this. I couldn't do that now. I had to tell myself she wasn't dead, not really, she was just out of reach.

Then an idea blossomed in my mind, though it was about as flimsy as wet newspaper. I shut my eyes and did everything I could to push the world away, wondering if I could reach at least a portion of that meditative state in which I touched stars. Would that even work here, not really being within the universe?

Everyone around me was shouting at one another. Karianna tried to speak to me, her fear bleeding over into me, but I pushed her away. This was our last moment. We had cut the engines and saved some time, but we had seconds before this sector of memory was passed. I'd be damned if I'd let Shelly go and let us all die.

I blacked out my thoughts and sought direction in the void.

Though I could not meditate as deeply as usual with this many distractions, namely the near-infinite data that pushed into me from the Foundry's instruments, I felt something. It was no more than a thread from a giant tapestry in the vastness of black, a piece picked at and dangling from where it hung on the walls of eternity. I reached for that thread, fumbling with my mental fingertips. It was hard to grab, as if it were being blown by an invisible wind. Every time I leaned toward it, the thread receded. Again and again and again I was rebuffed. I couldn't catch it. Without it, we had no way to escape, no way out.

You don't have to grab it, Karianna said through the integration. *Hold on to it, Milo, I can follow.*

What? I asked, but the effort of my response nearly broke my concentration.

Stop. Don't speak. Don't think. Listen to me. I can see it, focus on that. See where it goes.

Through her, I felt the *Transcendence* begin to move, though in what direction, I could not be sure. We were traveling, surely, and that had to be the exit.

As we accelerated in a new direction, the thread became steadier, moving ever closer to our position. I couldn't reach its end, couldn't pull at it, but we didn't need to. All we needed was to see where it had come from. We needed to close in on its source, the reality from which we came from, and not fall deeper into the depths of this machine's circuits.

Faster and faster we went. While it was a pitch-black void where I had placed my mind, Karianna experienced a tunnel of color and light.

Everything went white.

We moved swifter, though not nearly as fast as when we had entered this gate.

Bright colors.

Everything went white.

My body began to feel ever more whole. The thread drew out into a straight line, thicker by the moment.

Bright colors.

Everything went white.

Anticipation swelled in Karianna's heart, her emotions infectious, a thrill only brought about by riding to the edge of existence and screaming at death itself.

Bright colors.

Everything went white.

Our sensorium tilted.

We were pulled apart and put back together, hurled a thousand light-years across the Milky Way into a black sky populated with more familiar stars, the *Transcendence* having burst from the other side of the Wandering Gate whole.

The golden Cynosure floated beneath us, our masses orbiting a swirling red gas giant.

We had made it.

We—had—made—it.

Thank the Universe.

Karianna smiled at me through the integration. *Good job, partner,* she said. *Good job.*

"Call back," I said in a panic, checking on everyone. My virtual environment had returned to normal. As far as I could tell, everyone had been placed back in their own virtual spaces unharmed.

I spun to face Shelly, taking hold of her hands to confirm this was real. She was here, really here, and alive, and unharmed. She smiled at me in a smug sort of way, and I threw my arms around her. Relief flooded my body, making my legs weak. Virtual environment or not, my eyes were blurry and I just wanted to collapse.

"You were right," I whispered in her ear.

She chuckled in response. "I always am."

"Here," they started calling back.

"Here."

"I'm here, asshole," Lance said, which made me laugh. "Where the fuck did I go?"

This went on for several moments, until everyone was accounted for.

"Time to go," Karianna called as we detected several defensive systems around this end of the gate powering up. *"I think we've overstayed our welcome."*

Our engines roared to life, burning us away from these familiar sites, putting distance between us and anything Foundry-made or controlled. Our next destination lay before us, though we had a small problem with that. Despite my visions, despite what I had already seen in my mind, none of us knew the location of the Isopteran home world other than that it was on this side of the gate. And for us to find our way back to Earth, for us to complete FICSE 2.0, we needed to find our way to the termites' hive.

The pulsar map to Earth was on Nest, which was on this side of the gate.

But where, oh where, was Nest?

CHAPTER 3

We escaped the Foundry's influence and moved the *Transcendence* to the safety of a Lagrange point on the other side of the Lignos system. Comm traffic was thick, which was to be expected. This was the location of one of the Foundry's Cynosures, after all, which meant it was always busy.

For now, the threat of attack from the Foundry's installations or anyone else was minimal, though that in itself did not solve the problem we had at hand.

"How do we get there?" Karianna asked, standing beside me at the front of the War Room, the crew seated and looking up at us. "How do we get to Nest?"

In order to make things easier, or hell, just to give us a break from being plugged into machines, we had all disconnected from our Star Spheres and met in person. The War Room, as we called it, was not a necessity but rather a human luxury. It was a disclike space thirty meters across, with five-meter ceilings, its white walls inlaid with gold lines. A table that was a sort of broken circle sat at its center, reminding me of a horseshoe in shape. A hologram floated in the middle of the table, showing the crew where we were in space, as they each leaned back in their respective chairs, a collection of refreshments on the tables before them—coffee, tea, small cakes, chocolates, even a few sandwiches. No one needed this food—the Star Spheres had been feeding us well—but we had evolved to eat with our mouths, not our veins, and this was always a boost not just to our physical well-being, but to our mental state.

Being out of the sphere was nice. It was nice not having all that noise in my head, not feeling every strong emotion Karianna experienced on top of the millions of instrument readings the ship gave us. I was sure Shelly appreciated it. I knew it was weird for her that this connection was part of the deal, being able to feel what another woman was feeling at nearly all times. It was weird for me too, but it had been the only real choice. Both Proxies had assured us that there was no way to pilot a ship of this magnitude long-term without using both of our minds and faculties to do so. I had my doubts, but who was I to say? I was no expert on how this technology worked.

"As you all know," I started, "the Foundry is not the friendliest toward us right now. As they see it, we do not protect life. To be honest, I can understand why. And so, we need to figure out how to get the navigational data to reach Nest without approaching anything Foundry-made. As we've talked about before, somewhere on the Isopteran home world, there is a room, and its interior is shaped something like a nautilus shell. In this room there is a platform, and upon it lies part of the Voyager probe, a pulsar map printed on a golden disc. We can use this pulsar map to cross-reference stars and find our way back to Earth. To my knowledge, it is the only way."

"Can't we just celebrate for two seconds?" Leo asked, looking frustrated, his body still keyed up from recent events. "I mean, we did just survive one of the most challenging situations we've seen yet."

"We are celebrating," Lance said, reaching for a mug and taking a sip of something hot and frothy. Milk clung to his beard, and he wiped it off. "Take what you can get."

"Personally, I could use a vacation. Some unbidden debauchery."

Ada slapped him on the back of the head. "You had decades to sleep."

He rubbed at the spot, a scowl on his face. "You are so mean."

"Hey, Kitty!" James called. "Why don't you just tell us the way? Pretty please? That would make this whole thing easier."

"Thank you for asking nicely," Proxy replied, its tone cordial. "I wish it was within my ability. I know the data is somewhere on this ship, or in the greater network I have access to, but it is blocked from me. I cannot give it to you because of the rules. We have talked about it."

"Not even for a can of tuna?" He waggled his hand as if he held an imaginary can in the air.

"I do not require food."

"Meh. Worth a shot. What can you buy the cat who has everything?"

"And this room we're after," Renata asked, sitting up in her chair. "You know of it because of your *visions*."

"Yes," I said, frowning. It was in the way she had said the word. "They are more than visions, but it's hard to explain."

"I know we've talked about it before," Lance cut in, "and it's not that I don't believe you. Look, I mean, sometimes I don't get it. It's just . . . You are an honest guy, no doubt, but this is hard to grasp."

"It's not magic, if that's what you think," I told him. "I can't tell you what it is, but there is something out there, a kind of cosmic frequency I've learned to tune in to."

Shelly was sitting at the end of the U-shaped table. She gave me a frustrated look in sympathy, then turned back to observe the crew. She believed me, and that was enough so long as our mission was a success.

Leo raised his hands and gestured around us at the ship. "No telling what the Foundry did to your brain, man. Put you on a whole other spectrum, and like, shifted your perspective. Maybe it just made you more open to something we all experience. I mean, if the Universe is this collective consciousness, and it's not magic, then how does it work? What if the soul is just a piece of that nonlocalized consciousness existing in some quantum cloud and we're just nodes in the network interfacing it. During meditation, you're connecting to a different part of the network that maybe your brain wasn't designed to connect with. Or maybe it was that things just have to be real quiet and we get caught up too much with living."

We stared at the artist, a bit taken aback. I knew he wasn't empty-headed, and had some good thoughts from time to time, but . . .

"Maybe you're not as dumb as you look," Ada said, giving Leo a confused look.

He shrugged at her response. I half expected him to make some sort of flirty comment at her, that being his MO, but to his credit, he didn't.

"It's a good theory," Shelly commented. "The data we have supports it."

"Still feels like a bunch of BS," James said. "No offense, Milo."

Lance lifted his Barcelona futbol club coffee mug in a gesture that reminded me of a shrug, though he did not drink from it. "Come on, we'll be risking our lives on a vision. A potential hallucination."

"Lance," Karianna began, her expression changing, arms crossed, eyes narrowed. "I assure you, these visions are real. We could not have escaped the buffer without his vision. I felt what he saw, weird as it sounds. I experienced it on a bone-deep level. And if it's not real, or it's not what Milo thinks it is, I promise it's something. What that something is, I have no freaking idea, but it's tangible. We were there."

Shelly stood, her expression hard. Like Karianna, she was tired of this line of questioning. "Listen, everyone, if Milo says it's real, it's real. So that leaves us in the following situation. We have to get to Nest. We cannot approach Foundry facilities. How do we get the map?"

"I'm just glad we didn't fucking die in that gate," Lance added, then took a bite of his roast beef and cheese sandwich on plain white bread, coffee mug still raised in his other hand.

Xuan and Hy exchanged a look but said nothing.

Though it hurt not to be believed outright, I could understand the skepticism. What I had proposed, and why, was a little crazy. There was no rhyme or reason to it either. It wasn't like I'd been granted the ability to conjure fire or tell the future so I could do a few parlor tricks and prove to them it was legit. It was all happening in my head, and not something I could summon up at will. Unless they were me, they couldn't fully understand. They would have to take it on faith.

"Okay," I said after some time, "where do we get the coordinates? Ideas, anyone? Proxy?"

"It is likely that other species are in possession of them." Chinchillette spoke up, and I spun to look at it. "The Isoptera have not been quiet since crawling up from their gravity well. They do, however, seem to be obsessed with humans over other species."

"What are you saying?"

"Humans are an ideal food source for them, whereas other species are not, or at least, not as much."

I felt a cold chill run down my spine. Humans as food.

"We saw Isoptera on Cynosure way back when," James said. "Y'all remember that?"

Lance nodded. "I remember. They were different though, wore robes and didn't cause trouble. We steered clear. Perry almost ran into one that day he was headed to the Exchange. Never seen him so freaked out in my life. He was pale as a ghost. That was just a few days before we met the Kabosai."

"We saw them too," I said. "Esteban and I. They weren't aware of us being there."

"So maybe they trade?" Chevelle offered. "Go 'ere, make a few deals."

"Makes sense," Shelly said. "Maybe some of these trade partners are friendly then? Maybe they visit their home world."

"Bet Melcorin don't visit."

"I think you're right."

"There's a good chance this Cynosure has what we need," I said. "But we can't approach the city without being attacked. Proxy, what about the data hub on Creatus? We found a bounty of information, maybe we can pull that from its memory banks."

The cat shook its head. "There are defenses on that planet you were not aware of. The downed battlecruiser your people used for salvage was the result of Foundry weapons. Though it might be possible to get past these emplacements, they are far more substantial than the Wandering Gate's."

"Anywhere we go, the Foundry will be ready to stop us," James said, pushing a piece of rainbow birthday cake around on his plate with a fork. "If they'll attack us at any approach, what can we do?"

I rubbed my face with my hands, massaging my temples and closing my eyes. Everyone remained silent for a time, eating and thinking. A few half-hearted ideas were thrown out, but nothing got us around the primary challenge. The Foundry would kill us if we came too close. It was bigger, meaner, and more well equipped—which was all part of its grand game.

After some time, Frelo stood, their head cocking to the side. It was an expression I had learned meant that they were nervous or uncertain. "There is no other way through this situation that I can see. And so, I will go. I am not human. They will treat me differently."

Karianna piped up. "Where are you going?"

"The Foundry will not protect or allow humans near any of their facilities after what happened when your Harper made the choice to kill over ten thousand Jevox. I cannot claim that I am not angry. Though, I have spent time with all of you and understand your intentions. I know you tried to avoid bloodshed as much as possible, to undo the damage your Johan caused, damage he caused out of fear. I know that the crew of the *Transcendence* has protected life, and this is good enough for me, if not for the Foundry.

"All of this is to say, I am the only one on this ship who is not human. I can warn the Foundry of my approach, go to Cynosure, find the information we require, and return safely."

"But how will you find it?" Ada leaned forward. "Cynosure is a big city to explore alone. Without your enclave . . ."

Frelo winced. Ada had touched on an old pain. "I was, and I am, a Cerulean. I will find a way. I have information on me, data that some might want. I believe someone will have what we require in exchange. Instinct tells me we are not far from our destination."

"Same here." I licked my lips and narrowed them into a line. "Are you sure, Frelo?"

"Can we trust them?" Karianna asked, pinging my implants, though thankfully without the emotions of the integration tagging along.

"I think so."

I turned to Shelly, who didn't need equipment to read my mind. She looked to Frelo, who stood beside her, then to me, before closing her right hand into a loose fist, signaling resolution.

"Can you do this?" I asked Frelo again. "We don't wish to put you in harm's way."

Frelo raised their hands in a shrug, gesturing like one of us humans only with more joints. "It is my duty to see the terraforming equipment is used. We cannot put that to waste. You have what is required to save your planet, if only you can find the labor to put it into practice. It is only right I do my part. I will procure the coordinates."

"Thank you," Shelly said, placing a hand on the Jevox's back as they sat down again. "Thank you."

I closed my eyes for a moment and found myself back in that strange place, the nautilus room, the plinth with the golden disc leading back to Earth, the floating icosahedron of black metal beside it.

They called to me.

A way home.

A terrible choice.

"Look," I said, bringing the conversation to a close. "I know not everyone buys the visions I have, and this whole cosmic frequency I keep being able to interface with, but it did just get us out of the Gate's buffer. It helped us sync with Johan's velocity and arrive in Yuven at the proper moment given time dilation and special relativity. The pulsar map leading back to Earth, it's on Nest. We just need a heading. Please believe me. I have never lied to any of you, and you have always trusted me. So, trust me again."

"Fine," Lance said after a couple of seconds. "It might be total bullshit, but I'm with you. Like I've said before, you're honest, and real or not, I believe you believe it's real. I trust you, even if you are an asshole."

"Likewise," I told him.

CHAPTER 4

Frelo made their preparations, gathering food and other supplies for the trip. Proxy assisted the Jevox in fabricating several data storage devices as well, full of choice information it thought might be valuable in the Exchange. It contained some human items, such as music, movies, and books, as well as the plans to several Jevox terraforming devices that had likely never been seen this side of the Wandering Gate. There were star charts as well, though they carefully excluded places like 75-DFX or JV-01, in order to protect the fledgling humans on Novae and the Jevox home world, Rix. I gave Frelo instructions on how to avoid the Jalek, a sort of crime boss on Cynosure, who, as a Jevox, they might want to avoid meeting considering that its people once attempted genocide on Rix. I hated the fact that it was almost certain the Jalek knew what we required, and could help us get it, but that was not a route we needed to take. That was a closed road.

Though it had been who knew how many years, I asked Frelo to look up an old friend while they were there, Gi'Vor, one of the spiderlike Eiprin we'd once met. I had a feeling this old friend of Esteban and me had passed due to time, but you never knew with other species.

Frelo tossed everything they needed into a backpack and boarded one of the Swift Shuttles for Cynosure. They did not know how long it would take to complete this mission but assured us they would not waste time. That left the rest of us on the ship, waiting and hoping for the best. I felt I could trust Frelo, as did the rest of the crew, but it was dangerous for anyone to go alone. We had no other options, though. We were sending an alien by themselves, an alien that by the nature of their culture and biology was never alone. At its smallest social group, Frelo would be one of five, and yet here they would be alone in a sea of intelligent biodiversity. I hoped that they would be okay.

As the *Transcendence* was not traveling anywhere, and we expected the Jevox back sooner rather than later, Shelly and I opted to remain out of our Star Spheres to exist for a time as normal humans. We slept in a real bed within our quarters, decorating the space to our liking, and had our meals alone in the kitchen nook or in the galley with the rest of the crew. Disconnected from the integration of the ship, and more importantly, Karianna's constant emotional feed, things were better between Shelly and me.

For the past few months of subjective time, there had been tension between the two of us, a variety I wasn't sure would be so easy to resolve. A distance. Shelly had withdrawn from me in some ways, keeping sleights and hurt feelings to herself. We had gotten in spats over stupid things like cleaning up our quarters, or how we organized shared data folders. How she had taken to having a few too many glasses of wine alone in the evenings while I was meditating, and how I was checking out while she was telling me something important she had learned in one of her books about the Isoptera or another species. But being disconnected from the Star Sphere, along with the ship's higher functions, made it all better.

"I don't like fighting with you," I told her what felt like every day.

She would hug me, put her head on my shoulder, and reply, "I don't like fighting with you either."

We got up. We ate. We walked. We spent time together. We laughed. We played. We made messes. We cleaned up.

It was nice to play house again. It felt natural. It felt right.

In the same vein, Hy and Xuan spent a great deal of time together, bickering and making up in a constant cycle. They were the quintessential old couple who seemed as if they had been with each other since the dawn of time, even if they weren't that old, reminding me of my parents in so many ways. Arguing over how to remember past events, the right way to make a meal, or the rules to some game they used to play. They had no interest in ever fixing this, either. The arguments were the relationship, a strange way they showed one another that they cared enough about their life to have strong opinions about it.

Watching them interact made me miss my parents. I often had dreams of Dad and me on our motorcycles in Montana. Mom giving me ice cream when I had a breakup. There were so many days I found myself reaching for her final messages, but I couldn't bring myself to play them. Math had told me all I needed to know about what had happened to her. Too much time had passed since we left. While I had remained young, the result of time-dilation, hypersuspension in the Star Spheres, I knew she had to have become old and brittle and . . .

No. Not today. She wasn't gone. We weren't doing this.

Karianna kept to herself most of the time. Of all the crew, she was the least social, which was something I hadn't noticed as much until now. Thinking back, she had had few friends on Novae. Though she had spent some time with James, and I assumed some other people from the *Brilliance*, she was mostly either alone, or around me. With our connection unplugged, I found her seeking me out often. She would interrupt my meditation time, not with anything important, just wanting to talk. I always listened to what she needed to say, and we would part ways. Whenever I left, and it was always me who ended the conversation, she appeared dejected, her posture limp, as if she were a balloon and all her air had been let out.

"Always freaks together," she often said, rubbing her mechanical arm with her fleshy one, her many bracelets jingling.

And I would agree. "Always freaks."

James had taken notice of these deepening mood swings and tried to spend time with her, bring her treats he knew she liked and encouraging her to hang out with the others making art or watching movies, but she refused, always telling him that she was too busy.

"You know she likes you," Shelly said one night while we were lying in bed, her cheek against my bare chest.

I shook my head. "No, she doesn't. It's just as a friend."

Shelly sighed. "Maybe to you, but not for her."

We didn't have the time or space for drama like this. We had a mission to complete.

Outside my Star Sphere, I spent some time strolling around the ship, becoming familiar with what it looked like as just another human. Our Proxies had outdone themselves in this re-creation. As they had been in the *Fidelas*, the halls of the *Transcendence* were wide, ceilings vaulted with plenty of open space, which made the interior cathedral in nature. Long catwalks crosshatched the many decks, each visible from one another except for at the center of the ship, where the remnants of the *Reverie* had been brought. There, everything was close and thick and tight. It felt strong and sturdy, brutalist and comforting. Everything was made of either gold with white, or white with black, sleek lines and smooth edges, glowing with a sort of luminosity that came from within, not without. Despite its many rooms and chambers, there was still enough open space that you could have parked several copies of the International Space Station within.

I came across Leo's studio on the third level near the aft of the ship. Hearing light music and voices, I paused at the door and peered inside, curious, snooping just a little bit. It was a captain's prerogative. Ada and Leo were alone, Leo painting something colorful and abstract, Ada sitting on a stool staring through the floor into space.

Shelly and I hadn't been the only crew members wanting to unplug for a bit. Leo had moved back into his studio, where he spent most of his days painting. He had been working on several scenes from our journey, as well as several stream-of-consciousness abstract pieces. To our surprise, most days he was accompanied by Ada, which made Shelly deeply uncomfortable. Ada had just lost her husband at the hands of Johan's choices, and Leo had a track record of sexual conquest around emotionally compromised women. Though, from what we had seen so far, their relationship had remained surprisingly platonic. I was sure there were moments that may have been a little more, but Leo was behaving, and Ada seemed grateful for his company. He painted as they talked and drank coffee, laughing, sometimes crying.

"I should be better," she said, raising her hands to cover her face. "Alex would have known what to do."

Leo paused, took a curious look at his picture, and set his pallet and brush down on a table nearby. He drew a stool over in front of her and sat, arms relaxed on his legs. "What do you mean?"

"Alex always had the answers. He always knew what to do. We didn't work out because I was too hard on him. He was a brilliant, bright star in this universe. And yet, when he would have an idea, it consumed him like a fire burning him from the inside out. He became unavailable, not physically, but mentally. His mind would get so wrapped up in his thoughts it was like the rest of us weren't even around."

"And you took this as a sleight?"

"It made me so angry. I would do the same to him in those moments, find somewhere else to be, find something else to do. Alex would climb out of his reverie with some brilliant discovery, and I would be gone. It didn't mean I didn't love him. I just couldn't put my life on hold every time he had an idea. And he had a lot of ideas."

"You ever talk about it with him?"

She chuckled at that. "Talk about it? How would we do that? No, Alex didn't like talking about feelings. They got in the way of his logical processes."

"Everyone has feelings," Leo said, meeting her eyes. "Even those who are cold and logical. Do you doubt he loved you?"

"Never." She shook her head. "Never in doubt. Even after we split, he would bring gifts by my quarters. Little treats. Encouraging notes. I would randomly find bits of code or answers to problems I'd been working out appear on my hand terminal. He was always watching. Always hoping. Always seeking a path back to my heart. But I let him down.

"We need him on this mission. I need him. There's a hole in my chest that can't be filled without him. I just want to stop hurting. Every day I wake up, I believe for an instant there's a message from him waiting on my hand terminal. I get excited. And when there isn't anything there, reality hits hard. I feel the knife pierce my chest all over again. I see their ship reduced to a cloud of dust over and over and over, a nightmare on repeat. All this because of Johan. All this because of Frelo. My sweet Alex is gone because of them. And me? I am a poor imitation. A poor reflection. The universe is worse for having lost him. I am worse for having lost him. If I had been a better wife . . ."

Leo reached out and took hold of Ada's hands, squeezing her fingers gently. He said nothing, just sat there. She waited a moment, looked into his eyes, then threw her arms around him and began to sob. I didn't stick around; it wasn't right to. Ada was hurting and she needed to talk. She needed to process her pain. While Shelly had been there for her, this was different. I couldn't say that it was better, but it was different.

I closed my eyes, projecting my thoughts out into the universe. *Alex . . . if you're out there, Ada needs to know it's okay. She needs to know you made a choice and that you knew what that choice meant.*

Days later, we received a signal from Frelo. They had reached Cynosure, found the information we were after, and successfully traded for it. We had the coordinates we needed to get to Nest, as well as rough tactical data on what we might expect to meet in way of resistance. They were returning to the *Transcendence* without incident. What a gift.

I asked Frelo about our Eipren friend and if they'd been able to look them up.

"Gi'Vor is as you feared," Frelo replied over our channel. *"Time has taken them."*

My heart sank at the news. "I see."

"Yes, though you might be interested to know Gi'Vor's offspring now run a large trade operation out of the Exchange. I told them of you, and your lost friend. What did you call him? A Spaniard? Must be like a Crimson. They told me of stories Gi'Vor shared of two brave and noble humans who lost their companions and would stop at nothing to find them and save them."

"They said that?"

"They did. Your story inspired them to never give up, even when odds are against you. It is a good story."

"Yeah, but you don't know all of it. There are details that make it more complicated."

"I do not need to know it all. Neither do they. Time tends to change stories, each telling sanding off the rough edges of details until you have nothing but a smooth nugget of the truth. The important parts, what need they fulfill in others, those live on to inspire. Gi'Vor was better for having met you. His offspring are better for him having met you. Take joy in this."

Frelo was right, but that didn't mean I had shed my guilt over what I had been manipulated to do. The Jalek had forced me to become a villain, and I had chosen survival. I had chosen my people. Truth didn't make regret any less painful.

"Be careful heading back."

"See you soon."

CHAPTER 5

The information Frelo returned to us was not encouraging. While the Isopteran home world, Nest, was not that far in cosmic scales from our current position in Lignos—9.65 light-years away—it might as well have been a thousand. The tactical data attached to the coordinates outlined the potential resistance we might be forced to fight through. This resistance included thousands of starships, and while most of them would be logistical, there were plenty of warships. Most of the Isopteran vessels were of their own make, capable of traveling between stars well enough, but would be nothing on their own against the *Transcendence*. Trouble was, it was reported they were in possession of seven Foundry-made vessels. Some were as small as Johan's stealth ship, others up to the size of the *Fidelas*. If those ships persisted in their home system or were deployed elsewhere, we did not know. Bad news.

Finished with our diagnostic tests, Karianna, Shelly, and I had met the Jevox near the docking bay and moved into a private room.

"This is the most up-to-date information?" I asked Frelo, licking at my cracked lips in thought.

They lifted their right hand and gestured over the storage device we previewed the information on, the multiple joints between the elbow and shoulder, elbow and wrist turning my stomach. I knew it was natural for Jevox to be like this, but everything in me said that arms weren't supposed to bend this way.

"Yes. The Liowin merchant I did business with retrieved this data on their last visit to Nest. Though seventeen years, by your measures, is a long time. It is quite possible they have moved the larger ships in their fleet into different systems."

Karianna held the mobile data device, using her thumb and forefinger to scan the map. "That's a lot of damn ships. No way we won't be seen."

"Can we hide from them?" Shelly asked. "We've done similar things before. You were able to stealth the ship for a time against the Kabosai, right?"

"That was the *Fidelas*," I replied. "The *Transcendence* is too large. Same reason we couldn't hide our approach to the Prole Genascara."

"What about stealthed drop pods? We talked about using those once. Could they work on Nest?"

"Possible," Frelo commented, "though the Isoptera have been starfaring longer than humans. Yuven was not populated, and still, the Life Changer had its own means to prevent collisions. On Rix, we have defenses to protect from space debris, comets, and asteroids. Stealthed or not, this drop pod would likely be seen by orbital defense systems once it was close. It could be destroyed."

"Is there anything extra we're missing? Anything more specific tactically?"

"This information came from a trader," they said. "Not a warlord."

I nodded at that. It was a fair point. A trader wouldn't need to know things like patrol routes, weapon yields, crew compliments, and other military capabilities. They just needed to know how to get there and get back safely. If we had asked for market-specific information, it was possible there would be something valuable.

"I'm curious," Shelly piped up. "What did you trade for this information?"

Frelo's five eyes blinked in sequence, starting at the top and working around clockwise. "I traded several terabytes of human entertainment. Hy called them sitcoms. I believe this batch was recorded in the 1990s and early 2000s AD by your calendar."

"Sitcoms?" Karianna's eyebrows raised. She began to chuckle under her breath, sounding as if she had lost her mind. Shelly, to my surprise, was not immune to this humor and laughed along. "Humanity saved by sitcoms. That's fitting."

"I don't get it," I said. "What are sitcoms?"

Karianna and Shelly looked to one another, tightening their lips to hold back more laughter. Unable to, they burst into a fresh peal.

"What?" I demanded, pointing a finger at one, then the other. "What the hell is this thing you two are doing?"

Shelly patted me on the back and smiled. "You're too cute. You can fly a hyperadvanced ship across the cosmos, fight dangerous aliens, and navigate through alternate realities, but you haven't ever watched *Seinfeld*, or *Everybody Loves Raymond*."

"*Fresh Prince*?" Karianna added.

Shelly gave my copilot a funny look. "That's a good one."

"*The Office*?"

"No. I never could get into that one."

"No laugh track is kind of weird?"

"Mmmhmm. Oddly enough, I did like *Arrested Development*, though."

"Not my thing."

I frowned at the two of them before sucking my teeth. It annoyed the absolute hell out of me when people did this. But in that moment, I was far too embarrassed to ask what they were going on about. Sitcom sounded like a military term, like sitrep. If sit rep meant situation report, maybe sitcom was a situation commander? No? I was stretching, even if the Fresh Prince did sound like a historical military leader.

"So, what are we going to do?" I asked, distracting from my stupid gap in knowledge.

"Set a course?" Karianna suggested. "We'll have years to figure it out. Isn't that our strategy by now? Always head to the next destination, figure it out on the way? Keep moving forward. I know staying here won't help anyone."

"You're right. It won't."

"Frelo," Shelly said, "did you inquire about the location of Earth? Just so maybe we can bypass all this?"

"Yes," they said, a hand reaching up to touch their face. "No one knows of Earth. Few know of humans."

"I guess that's good and bad," Karianna said.

"Alright." I took the mobile data device from Karianna, thumbing through its information, absorbing it all over again. "Here's what we know. This is what a merchant saw years ago. Ships could have left, new ships could have arrived. Good news is that we know where to go. Bad news is, can we even find our way down to the planet?

"I need to sit on this. Let's not leave yet, give the crew a few more days out of their tanks. Now that I know more, I think my meditation will be more productive. It's just like the gate's buffer. Before we knew what it was, I didn't feel there was any way to get to that place."

"Does that cosmic frequency have a time lag?" Shelly asked.

I scratched at my chin with my prosthetic hand. "You know, that's a good question. I think no, but I can't honestly say. Lag or not, more information is better."

"I'll let the crew know what we learned," Karianna said. "In person. You do what you have to do. We'll tell them to get ready to leave."

"Good." I paused, put the storage device under my arm, then turned to Frelo. "Thank you. You didn't have to take the risk of going to Cynosure, and yet you did. Thank you."

The Jevox stared at me, their eyes blinking in sequence, saying nothing in response. I wondered if they were like the Eiprin. Did they not know gratitude? Did they not know how to say thanks?

Our group disbursed, Shelly going along with Karianna to speak with the crew. For myself, I headed for the forward end of the ship to my quiet room so I could meditate on all we had seen, taking the data device with me.

Though the interior of our ship was under constant flux, having the ability to reconfigure rooms to fit our needs with nanomachines, this particular space had changed little since we left JV-01. The room was simple, open. An observation window faced into space, and a collection of colorful pillows was laid out in a circle in the center.

I settled into place on top of a pillow half as wide as my bed and crossed my legs. After shaking out my hands and taking a few deep breaths, I rested my wrists on my knees and closed my eyes. With a command from my neural implants, I turned down the lights and started up some gentle music. It was something calm, instrumental, hypnotic, allowing my mind to drift rather than to focus on the meaning of words or any melodies too complex. The music I'd settled on this time was something I'd dug up a while back out of Esteban's personal collections. The idea that my dear old friend had liked this song, maybe used it to calm himself when he was headed into battle or to process tough choices he had made as a soldier, gave it a positive energy. I could use that energy.

"If you're out there, old friend," I whispered, "it sure would be nice if you said hello. Wouldn't mind some advice from time to time. Hope you and Dad are having a good time."

I chuckled at myself. I wasn't communing with spirits. This wasn't some sort of séance, but then again, maybe it kind of was. Who knew what ghosts or spirits really were? I had communed with the Universe, talked to everything in all creation at the end of time. As Leo had mentioned his thoughts around the soul, our consciousness, and it being located in an unlocalized quantum cloud, I wondered if it really was that crazy to think I might be talking to spirits.

Allowing myself several moments to push those distracting thoughts away, I calmed my heart and began.

"You are a star, a wave of light," I whispered, thinking back to my time with the Melcorin. "Breathe in. Breathe out." And I did, stating the words before taking the action, falling into a rhythm. "You are a mote of creation, a spark of the Universe. You are the tiniest piece of reality, and yet you are reality unto itself. *Breathe in. Breathe out.* A single point of light. *Breathe in. Breathe out.*

"Death and rebirth. *Breathe in. Breathe out.* Let everything go. In this moment, there is nothing but this moment. *Breathe in. Breathe out.* You are eternity. You are a blip. *Breathe in. Breathe out.* Be the flash of a dying star, a flash of fusion begun. *Breathe in. Breathe out.* Life synthesizes, renders entropy into beauty. *Breathe in. Breathe out.* Focus on the light. Follow it."

Physical reality began peeling away.

Unlike being within the digital processes of the Wandering Gate, here, in the real world, in the right environment, with the right focus, and no distractions, it was easy to find that thread. My mind wandered across the cosmos, traveling from distant stars and supermassive black holes without names, numbers, or designations, to more familiar places: a rock on the other side of this system where Omar was buried, the halls of hyperadaptive quarters in a city of gold and white with bright lights under a glass dome of stars made to look like Captain William's memories. I could see a distant colony populated with humans, growing and thriving, a pillar of light reaching into the heavens at its center. I could see a fleet of Jevox burning away from a star system full of asteroids and debris, its people angry that so many of them had been lost in an antimatter implosion.

Earth was woefully absent in my visions. Sure as hell would have made things easier if it had appeared.

I focused on the information we had been given. It appeared that the more I knew about the state of a place, the easier it was for me to find when I meditated.

Planet Nest. System designation, IT-22. Yellow giant star. Seven planets. Two containing active, diverse biospheres, only one populated by sentient species, a world enveloped by storms with crimson jungles covering its surface. Isoptera came from this dark place, those human-size insects reminiscent of termites complete with wings. A collection of hive minds persisted there, their thoughts dominated by Queens, organized into broods. Driven by insatiable hunger, and . . . and something else. They were driven by something else, I just couldn't quite capture the idea, its slippery edges difficult to take hold of.

It was the second planet from the star: A home world, its orbit, both high and low, filled with traffic, transport ships, war ships, fixed orbital emplacements. It had never known an apocalypse; its dinosaur analogues had never been wiped out. It was oxygen rich. The insects were able to breathe through their skin, growing to extraordinary size given such resources, and then their Queens . . . their Queens did something.

What did their Queens do?

Thousands of ships waited for us. Far more than I had been expecting, their presence blocking our approach. There had to be a way through the gauntlet, a way for us to reach the surface of this red-and-black world without incident.

Within its jungles I found myself in a cave, a labyrinthian set of cramped tunnels, and at its terminus, a room shaped like the inside of a nautilus shell, the open space dead, abandoned. Our prize sat there waiting on a plinth, waiting for us to come and claim it: a golden disc made by humans with something else beside it, something the crew did not need to understand. A device I hoped might never be used.

"A path. A path. A path," I repeated to myself, focusing on this idea. We had to find a way around the patrols, onto the planet, and into this room.

The Isoptera were a hive mind, but not like the Jevox. The Jevox were one entity in thought, connected by a bioelectric adhoc network, but they were not one in emotion. As for the Isoptera, best any could tell, they were one in direction, but only by their queen's will. There were many queens, and these queens fought, hated one another, they . . . they believed they were . . . what did they believe? Why could I not see?

Fractures. Chasms. They did not work together. They traded for mutual benefit but actively fought to undermine one another, asserting dominance within their broods.

An idea came to me. A way through.

It didn't matter if I knew the why. I knew the what. If only—

My concentration was shattered when a sharp ping hit my implants. Nest vanished and I was left in the dark. I was about to curse under my breath before I realized what was going on.

New messages had arrived from Novae.

My breath caught. The music stopped.

"Proxy?" I cautioned, cracking my eyes open.

The feline construct appeared from the shadows of my meditation space. "Yes?"

"Why are there just now new messages from Novae. We've passed through the gate. It's not possible they just reached us. Is it?"

A pause, Proxy staring up at me, its eyes gleaming.

"Proxy?" I urged. "Talk to me."

"I am sorry," it started. "I did not think you needed the distraction at the time. We received them a few weeks before reaching the other side of the Wandering Gate. I kept those notifications silent."

I rubbed my face and groaned. "I don't know if I should be mad or not."

"It is my job to protect the pilot."

"I know. I know."

"Are you going to watch them now?" Proxy asked, a paw rubbing at its face, teeth gnawing at its front claws. It purred and spun around, tail flicking.

It was a good question. I was on the verge of something important, the start of an idea, a way for us to reach Nest, but that moment had passed for now. We would find a way through the Isopteran patrols. There was no way around it; I had been actively avoiding these messages.

I checked the log.

New messages aside, there were some relatively old ones I had not watched. Messages I'd been active in avoiding because I had known what they would mean. We had been gone a long time. Novae was likely not the place we remembered anymore—in the best ways, I hoped. And yet, this seemed the right moment to put it all to rest, even if it broke my heart.

"It's time," I told Proxy. "I've been running away for too long. I have to know."

"I thought you might," it said, stretching its body. "Is there anything I may get you?"

"No. But if you would." I reached out with my damaged hand, the remaining three fingers gesturing for it to come. "Will you sit with me?"

Proxy made its way over to my lap without hesitation, curling up in a ball, its body vibrating against me. I rubbed its spine and scratched at its belly, the volume of its purrs multiplying as if it were in an echo chamber. It was warm on my legs, comforting. I wanted to be alone watching these messages, given what they might mean, but at the same time, I didn't want to be alone. Pets had always been good for moments like this. So had friends. Proxy was something of both, and yet so much more.

I sucked in a deep breath, my chest swelling, then let it out. "Okay. Play the messages, starting with the oldest first."

"As you wish."

A video began, its drone camera view following Mom through a field of rainbow-colored edge blossoms on Novae, skies overhead blue and clear, dotted with the closest thing they had to birds. She grinned as she walked down the path, the lines and wrinkles of her face more apparent than last I remembered, but she looked good, she looked healthy. I immediately recognized where she was going but could not bring myself to speak of it. What good would it do? He wasn't coming back.

"It's a beautiful day here," Mom said, rotating the camera around to show the expanse of colorful fields with the colony of Novae in the distance. "I am sure he loves it here. Your father always loved nature. It was that love that meant we met. Did you know Captain Williams and him were friends? Or at least buddies who might have a few drinks together. They would sit on the upper rim of the Second Arecibo Observatory's dish and watch the sun set, sipping on whatever they could get their hands on. Rum, mávi, pitorro, whatever it may be. They were surrounded by the sounds of the forest and the stars above.

"That's where I saw him for the first time. He was loud, obnoxious, and, well, funny. Your Dad never lacked a sense of humor. He always dreamed of what was up there, and from a young age, but . . . I'm not sure he ever could have imagined this was how it would go. I miss him. I miss you. I trust you are well. It may be hubris, but I think my choices have served us well. And you know what? You're my child, *meu lindinho filho*."

She made kisses at the camera. "Think of us, and tell your wife hello. I miss her sweet face."

The video ended.

Bracing myself, I started the next, not waiting.

"Milo!" Mom's face was immediately on camera, older than last time, but she looked happy and healthy, cheeks full, eyes relaxed. My heart swelled and I smiled. She didn't seem nearly as heavy in spirit.

"You won't believe it," she went on. "Yes, yes, Perry has his little bar, but we actually have a restaurant in Novae, not just a mess hall. Emilio and his team have been collecting recipes from anyone and everyone. We've been writing them down, recording them, and then figuring out how the local ingredients might can make them. He says it's for culture and science. I say he's tired of eating stone bison shit like the rest of us."

The thought of stone bison sausage made me wrinkle my nose. We were not natives to that planet. Our biology did not agree with that gamey fare.

"With the right spices, they've managed to make a *Feijoada* stew that I swear *sua avó* could have cooked. *Mamãe* was quite the chef, and making food here we've got to be as creative as us *malucos* and *malucas* in the *Favelas*. So rich and tasty. Strong, salty, but not spicy, black beans and pork taste. I've included the recipe in this message. I'm sure Proxy can make it for you. Might not be all the same, but good enough.

"Hope you're eating well, son. Wish you would write."

The video ended, and my stomach growled. I swore I could smell the stew from the recording. I narrowed my eyes and peered down at the cat in my lap, but it pretended not to notice me. Was this Proxy's doing? All these sensations. Was it making me smell the food? It would be on brand.

Several short videos played in sequence, updates on the colony itself, Mom not part of them but rather people like the Speaker, my friend Mary, or one of her staff. So much had changed. No longer were they struggling to meet basic needs. Apartments and freestanding homes were being built, some square, some topped with domes; official roads and streets put into place. They had running water, and power twenty-four seven, security from the sawtooths and all the other creatures that went bump in the night. Perry's bar, Invictus, remained crowded most nights, and events at the cultural center were hosted weekly. Marissa, for her part, wrote several more pieces of music and started a school for the children to learn how to write and play.

Seven hundred colonists.

Seven hundred and fifty.

Eight hundred.

Eight hundred and fifty.

They were living in paradise. It was a dream to behold, and my mother, and Mary, and so many others were behind this remarkable outcome. Earth might be in peril, but somewhere beyond the stars, humanity lived on. This idea gave me hope.

The next video began, a view from outside. It was raining, not hard, but steady. Mom was under a familiar tree at the end of a trail, Dad's grave marker beside her. Water ran down her face. Her eyes were puffy. She was shivering in the cold, not wearing her jacket. I wanted to reach through the message and demand where she had left her slicker.

Mom closed her eyes and rubbed them with her palms. "I still can't believe he's gone. The man drove me crazy for thirty-eight years of my life, with his stupid jokes and his sloppy science. That stupid band he always wanted to listen to."

Thunder cracked overhead. Mom looked up.

The video ended. Proxy nuzzled against my hand and licked my palm with its rough tongue. I scratched it behind the ear and swallowed down my razor-studded heart.

Several more updates came, but these were shorter, their time stamps less frequent. Mom didn't send messages in this time block. She knew we weren't coming back, not quick enough for her at least. And now, with the Foundry seeing us as an enemy, I didn't see any way we could make it back through the gate again even if we tried. It would be wise to our ruse now.

I felt a pang of guilt for not writing her, for not sending her regular updates on our mission. It was something I should have done, but what would it have mattered? How would it have changed their circumstances?

They knew they were on their own, and because of it, they had worked together as humans hadn't done since Çatalhöyük or Uruk at the dawn of civilization. They had built something good and real. Something to be proud of. If they had known our mission details, would that have just held them back? Would they have faded away with a false hope that we would fix Earth and take them back, only to have us fail and never return?

I didn't know. I was just trying to avoid my guilt.

The queue was getting thin, only two videos remaining. I knew what was coming, but I didn't want to face it. For me, it had been a year since we left, maybe two. I wanted to believe that was all it had been for them, for her . . .

The video began in a dark room with a long, wide bed flanked on either side by a battery of equipment. I could hear the rhythmic beeps of her heart, the whirr of pumps and machines. Mom lay at the center of the frame, her body propped up by a stack of pillows. She looked old, older than I had ever thought I'd see her become. Her face was wrinkled and ashy, her once raven-black hair now a collection of salt-and-pepper curls. Her dark face had collected tags of skin, and her lips looked dry. She was thin and frail, infirmary sheets hanging off her like loose skin.

My heart tore in half, starting from the top and splitting in two. My stomach churned, and I couldn't breathe. Proxy pressed up against me, burying its head and purring.

"Life is never what we expect," she began, her voice fragile. "We put plans in place, and we do everything we can to see them realized. Plans are good, dreams and hopes are good, but at some point, you must surrender to fate. Life is a river rushing through the cosmos. You cannot hope to change the direction of the river, and it might even be dangerous to cross, but if you can swim in the right direction, you can go so many places. See so many wonders. Do good things."

Mom paused for a moment, then smiled wide. She had never been one to express joy all that often, and with the challenges in her life, that had not changed. She had been focused and hard, determined to see the mission through, but her time on Novae had changed her for the better.

"Milo," she whispered, her voice rattling like paper, "I want you to know that I am proud of you. The mission we forced you to be part of . . . we were selfish for what we did. I hope you can forgive us. And I hope you can see that maybe something bigger was at play. Our mission may change, but our purpose remains the same. Your dad and I could not stand by and let humanity go into the dark. We succeeded. Now, you have taken up our mission, and whatever changes may come, I know you'll do what is right.

"You are a Hughes. You may not be perfect. You will make mistakes. You might even be forced to make impossible choices. Such is the burden of leadership. But you will never give up and you will always do what is right in the end. Our hopes are with you. Tell your wife that I miss her sweet face. Be happy. Touch the stars, *meu filho lindo*."

The video came to an end.

It was the last time I would ever see my mom speak. The last time I would hear her words. I wasn't sure how to feel. She was gone, there was no way around it, and I felt a tremendous amount of guilt for not saying more. There was never enough time, was there? Something was always left unsaid. The Universe had been right. Life did not want to come to an end, be that individual or a collective consciousness. We had a need for the Foundry and the function it served.

Mamãe, I said in my mind, eyes squeezed tight.

Another short update arrived, but Proxy did me the favor of reviewing it and parsing the most important pieces of information. I'd seen enough for now. Enough for a lifetime.

I remained in silence, Proxy nuzzling up against me, attempting to calm my heart. After some time, I realized I had been holding my breath, and because of this I hadn't been able to tell that my face and shirt were wet with tears.

"I miss her already," I mumbled. "I've always missed her."

Proxy turned its head to look up at me. "Milo, if you are right, if Leo is right, and the Universe is all around us, aware and waiting, then she is not gone. She is part of that place you make contact with. She is with you, Milo. In your heart, and within the fabric of space and time."

I picked the cat up and squeezed its body, my face against its soft fur, the missing fingers on my left hand awkwardly squeezing. It vibrated against my cheek.

"Mom is with us," I whispered. "So is Dad, and Esteban, and Mary and Perry, and everyone else."

"They are with us."

"And you know what? If we have an army, then there's nothing that can stop us. We can do this."

"Yes, we can."

I sat Proxy back in my lap, brushed the moisture from my eyes, and took a deep, shuddering breath.

"Music," I said aloud, and the hypnotic swells and rhythms started once more. My eyes squeezed shut, pressing the salty drops from their edges.

I whispered, "You are a star, a wave of light . . ."

CHAPTER 6

My eyes closed in the Lignos system, afterimages of Shelly's face and the gleaming city of Cynosure in the distance locked in my mind, then opened once more nearly ten light-years away in IT-22. Nineteen years, four months, six days, had vanished in a flash. But what did any of that matter? We were no longer tied to the same timescales as our human counterparts on Novae, or even Earth. We were somehow above that, above time itself. At least for now.

We had made the crossing between these two systems, opting to remain in hypersuspension during transit unlike many of our other great crossings. The crew had learned to work together, and so we did not need to take the time we had to prepare. All of us had accepted the fate of what was before us as we made for Earth, and the plan we had cobbled together in order to get past their patrols could not be initiated till we arrived. This was the last obstacle on our way home. We wanted it over.

IT-22 was as we had expected. A yellow giant system with seven planets, the second from their star a roughly Earth-sized rock covered in storms, the rest a mix of smaller rocks and gas giants with many satellites and planetoids. Normally I would have marveled at these many worlds, studied their orbits and lifecycles, compositions and weather, but not this time. The part of me that was my dad, the excitable astronomer, would need to rest for now. The part of me that was Mom, always focused on a single goal without distraction, was the part I needed to channel.

Instruments revealed a host of ships with passive scans, the system giving off flurries of intense radio transmissions, but no neutrino signals. We held at the edge of the cosmic forest, which was populated by bloodthirsty insects, their hive, their haunt, clear before us. While we had expected a large concentration of ships around Nest, we hadn't expected so many would be spread out among the system. This worked to our advantage. Even if the alarms sounded, there was no way they could mount a full-scale defense without more time. Distance would require them to recall ships from the extremities of IT-22, which could take weeks, when we only needed days to break in and get out. Time to go surgical.

Despite the challenge, I knew we could do this. We had a plan. And, according to Lance at least, I was also lucky. So, there's that.

"We're capturing signals," Shelly reported, appearing beside me in my virtual space, fingers flicking furious across a virtual hand terminal. "Ada, you up yet?"

"I am," Ada called back over an open channel.

"Meet in our room? We can start analyzing these signals and work out a plan. So far, I see a few challenges, but I think Proxy can help us work through it. There's a solid carrier frequency. Encoding looks simple enough."

"Sounds good. I'll make coffee."

Shelly turned to me and gave me a hug and a kiss, then vanished, leaving Proxy and me alone in a sea of stars.

"You going to help them?" I asked the cat, bending down to scratch it behind the ear.

"I am already helping them," it reported, its body vibrating. "Unlike you flesh and bloods, I can be in more places than one."

I smirked at the smug little cat. "Good point. Do you think this will work? The plan that is?"

"We have survived far more dangerous plans."

And that was true. We'd pulled off some shit I thought would never have been possible. Shelly and Ada were two of the smartest people among our crew, so if they had a plan to get past these Isopteran ships, then I had no doubts it would work.

Out of nowhere, a series of fingers ran down my spine as if someone had tickled my back. I glanced over my shoulder. There was nothing here in my physical space, but I knew what this was. Karianna was thinking about me, if not consciously.

Hey, what are you doing? I asked over the integration, our minds drifting closer to one another.

Karianna shuddered. *What?*

That thing. That touch. That felt weird. Please try not to touch me like that. Felt like a ghost walking over my grave.

The tingling sensation ceased, and a touch of wounded pride came back. *I—em—sorry. Didn't mean to. I was fumbling around in here. And I think the saying is a rabbit running over your grave.*

A rabbit, a ghost. For a guy who grew up on a starship, they're all abstractions. I paused for a moment, collecting myself. *So, umm . . . How are you?*

I'm good, she replied, brightening in her mood, her heart rate slowing. *Weird question, real quick.*

I took a mental deep breath. *Yes?*

Do you ever have dreams when in suspension?

This was a question I asked myself whenever we emerged, but I still wasn't sure if I had a clear answer. I always woke up feeling as if I'd dreamed the entire time, but there was nothing in my memories to connect it with. *I don't know. Maybe?*

I had a dream.

What was it about?

Well . . . it's not something I ever talk about. Something that not many people know.

I leaned into our conversation, deepening the connection between us. I felt the swirl of emotions in her belly rising, the fear, the anger, the insecurity. *You can tell me if you want. I won't tell anyone.*

The tempest of emotions within her calmed for an instant, allowing me to see her essence through the storm, but then its swirling waters began to boil.

Okay . . . Just doing some thinking. Look, Milo, you aren't the only one who lost their dad. The mutineers at the Foundry facility from the Brilliance *. . . they . . . well . . . They murdered Captain Kwon, forcing Rowan and his team to go head-to-head. My dad got killed protecting me, ensuring that I did what needed doing at the time. He wasn't just hit in the crossfire. He stood between me and a madman. The official report from the event was that Rowan's fire team fought the mutineers back and left them stranded on the Foundry facility. This is true, just with less gory details. Lots of death. And that day, I became the pilot so we could stop the leader of their mutiny, Justin Wiggins.*

Sorry about your dad, I didn't know it was during the mutiny. Though, to be honest, I had suspected.

You wouldn't, she replied, thoughts scattered. *I told everyone who was there that day not to talk about it. It was a shit show. Then Rowan got in with Johan and . . . anyways. I miss dad. I dream about him sometimes, nothing weird, it's just, he was, he is, important to me. I dream about when we would go on hikes in the virtual environments. About how he and I would watch old TV and make fun of stupid-ass cultural references that were so freaking outdated. How we would ramble on about cheesy horror games on our hand terminals or which of our food analogs were the worst. All my life since I was a little girl, he was my best friend.*

Her mood brightened. *Oh! And speaking of food, get this one. We had a competition for a while, just the two of us, where we would try to find the worst combination of flavor pastes and protein substrate.*

I found myself smiling at this. *That sounds like a ton of fun.* And for a moment, I was a bit envious. It had taken the end of everything for my dad to have real time for me. *What was the worst combination?*

Oooh, that's tough. Red spices and chicken squares were supposed to be really good, but they weren't. Chocolate and pineapple, disgusting, tasted like dirt. Peanut butter and bacon strips were another I remember, but that one was actually kind of good.

She paused, considering my question.

Now I remember what it was! It was what was supposed to be a kind of oyster sauce and we mixed it with salmon discs. It tasted like what I imagine a dead sawtooth left out in the sun for a week eaten sushi-style without wasabi might taste like. It was slimy, pungent, and somehow sticky.

Hah. That sounds terrible.

It was fun though, she replied, shaking her head, bright colors surrounding the two of us within this connection.

There was a pause.

Mom was long gone, out of my life when I was a kid before we left Earth. In the end, I was left alone. Dad was the only one who ever got me. Really got me. You know?

I do, Karianna. I do.

The storm within her belly froze, winds dying down. *I know, Milo. That's why I like you.*

Excuse me? The way she said *like* triggered something in me. My hands shook.

Nothing, she replied, laughing under her thought to play it off. *That's why we're friends.*

I attempted to refocus her line of thinking. *You having dreams about your dad a lot?*

Maybe. Dreams about him and how there's someone . . . never mind. It's not important.

I took in a breath. *I think it is.*

She shrugged it off.

Tell me.

Shelly chose that moment to reappear in my virtual space, forcing Karianna's deep connection to retreat. Our conversation was over for now. I wondered where it had been going. It broke my heart that she had lost her dad similar to how me and Shelly had both lost ours, not by an unlucky accident, but by ill intent. So many of us had lost our parents. But how could it have been any different? That was what this mission was, parents and kids, parents and kids with very few brothers and sisters and only a sprinkling of grandparents.

Shelly raised a finger, her expression determined, proud and confident, if not totally pleased. "We got it."

I nodded. "Will it work?"

"If it doesn't, we have no idea what could. All I am going to say is we're about to fuck them up."

I put a hand over my mouth in shock. "Language, Miss Perfect. Language."

"It's Mrs. Perfect, thank you very much." She tapped me on the shoulder with a fist. "I didn't get married for nothing."

"Karianna," I called over the open channel as if we hadn't just been talking.

"Yes, Cap?" she replied, her voice chipper. *"What's the orders?"*

"Get the crew ready. We're about to go headlong into the storm."

"Batton down the hatches, maties!" she said, then cut off.

I made a gesture, unlocking my virtual environment. "Ada, join Shelly and me. Let's get into position. We'll park the *Transcendence* in a spot among a series of high albedo asteroids. That should make it hard for them to spot us. From there, we're going in by Swift Shuttle. As for the rest, it's your plan. Get ready to deploy it."

"Damn right," Ada replied as she appeared next to me, bumping fists with Shelly.

The crew prepared for the mission ahead. As had become our protocol, not everyone was going with us, but many were. As the one with the cosmic vision, the map of memory markers in my head, I would be leading the mission on the ground. James, Lance, Renata, Leo, and Xuan had agreed to be my fire team, each of them armed with real weapons this time, not stunners. We were strapped with body armor, though not powered suits given how much those could hinder our movements in tight spaces, and each of us had a SAG tactical rifle. These rifles carried medium-caliber armor-piercing rounds in high-capacity clips that Proxy assured us would cut through the termite body armor. While we had no intention of engaging the Isoptera if possible, with stealth and misdirection key, we needed a way to protect ourselves if we got pinned down.

Aside from them, Shelly refused to stay back on the ship and let me go without her, and by extension, so did Karianna. I didn't like the idea of taking both pilots down onto the surface and putting them at risk, but Proxy reminded me that it took two of us to effectively pilot the ship. If either one of us was lost, it wouldn't matter anyway. I thought that sounded like an exaggeration, but after what had happened at the Wandering Gate, I would take its word for it. And as for Shelly coming along, well, she just didn't want to let me out of her sight. She didn't want me to vanish to fate.

This left Frelo, Ada, Hy, Chevelle, Dante, and Emilia behind to watch the house. If we died, they might be stuck here, but at least Proxy could keep them comfortable and hidden for a long time. We vowed not to let that happen.

Carefully, we moved the ship into position, hiding it in the shadow of a bright asteroid some twenty AU from IT-22's star. The Isoptera were not masters of stealth like the Melcorin, and so finding a path between their ships this far from the center of the system was simple enough when we had the ability to map out many of their trajectories.

We boarded the Swift Shuttle and wished our remaining crew luck, leaving Ada in charge.

"We are a go to deploy the signal," she said over our short-range communications channel.

Submerged in my Star Sphere, with the rest of the mission crew locked in their seats—including Karianna, much to her chagrin—we exited the *Transcendence* and started to drift toward Nest.

"Do you have a lock on their communications network?" Shelly asked Ada.

"We're locked and ready," she replied.

"Time to see if this works. Deploy the package."

"Done."

A burst of three signals escaped the *Transcendence*, then all was silent. I burned ahead, setting us on our course, the jagged, diamond-shaped shuttle slicing through the darkness. Given the background light the asteroids produced, there was a good chance no one could pick up our drive signature for quite a while, not that that should matter soon.

"Getting pingbacks," Shelly reported. *"Signal has been received and something is happening. Ada, they're taking the bait."*

"Hell yeah."

"The second and third fleets of cargo ships coming from the fifth planet believe they are under attack."

"As planned."

"Ships are inbound to protect them, but the cargo ships believe these are the attackers and are burning hard to run away."

"Com chatter is stupid. I can't understand half of it, even with the translators, but we kicked the hive and they think the boot is their own."

"How in the hell did you two do this?" Leo asked. *"I mean, I know you're both crazy smart, but . . ."*

"We found a flaw in their communications network that Proxy helped us exploit," Ada replied with excitement. *"It seems that since they have certain patterns in their speech that change between broods, a marker among their clicking, and they generally have trust in official communications, their signals are not hardened against attacks. There's no security encryption, none. All the hives can hear each other's communications at the same time. For them, however, they can only really understand those communications sent by someone within their brood, of which we found four distinct linguistic patterns."*

"So, how did you fake them out?"

"With the help of our Proxies, we copied the speech patterns of different broods, and we took a guess. We convinced them one of the Queens was making a power move and attacking the others. They really don't like each other much."

"You pulled a disinformation campaign?"

"We sure as hell did. And it was easy, too easy."

Proxy cut in, "They will adapt, just like the Foundry. This ruse will likely never work again."

"Doesn't need to," Ada said, sounding pleased with herself.

A path was opening down the center of our trajectory through the system, ships breaking in all directions to take up defensive postures against threats that did not exist. My instincts from my meditations that the Queens and their broods did not trust one another appeared to be accurate. Yet despite this lack of cooperation, they had achieved much. They were a starfaring species, numbering in the tens of billions, and from the look of it, they did a better job than us lowly humans had until now. At least they sort of got along.

We approached a fleet of ships burning away from us, and I was able to get a good look at the Isopteran designs. They looked to be somehow organic, black and green and brown, surfaces slick and reflective as if made of something that had been grown, not built. They weren't like the Pentaray, or the Dragon, but these ships weren't exactly made of metal either. From passive scans, their internal systems appeared to contain titanium, steel, and aluminum, but their hulls and other finer systems were something else. The shapes of the craft were irregular, craggy like rocks but slender, their lengths far exceeding their height or width. Some of the ships had strange arrays hanging off of them, connections of rigid tunnels dragging with them sacks of materials, maybe gasses. Others were winged lumps with pincers at their forward end, masses stretching out from between three and six hundred meters that appeared to be escorted by inverted, root-shaped craft with fronds trailing behind them. We weren't close enough to get a good look at anything, and we did not plan on it.

"Proxy, do you know what their technology is built around?" I asked from within my personal environment. "For us lowly humans, our electronics are silicon-based semiconductors. Our ships, aluminum alloys, sure. But this?"

The cat shook its head. "It is hard to say without samples. This is not a typical material, whatever it is. The Foundry network will not tell me."

"Hmm. That's interesting."

"I am sure you will have the opportunity to learn more soon enough."

"Unfortunately, I believe you are all too right."

The fleets pulled away from us without incident, chasing toward or running from phantom threats. Damn, we were getting good at spoofing systems.

We approached Nest, a dark globe of storms with little of the surface visible. Two moons orbited the Earth-sized planet, each cold and lifeless, uninhabited. Orbital defense platforms ignored us as we made for a gap in their screen. We were a ship under power, and friendly or not, that meant we were not going to crash into their planet and cause a cataclysm.

The plan was working. Shelly and Ada were geniuses.

A few hundred thousand kilometers from our orbital descent, my instruments went red. I spun around, looking to our starboard side, and what I saw turned my blood cold.

Appearing out of the bright backdrop of IT-22 came a ship as long as a skyscraper was tall, its tower-like, golden hull striped with white, its surfaces bristling with weapons. It was an awesome and terrible sight to behold, ornamented with ostentatious Baroque designs, with columns and arches and friezes made up of insectile forms. It was the one ship that might be immune to the trick we had just pulled, a battleship of great power, gifted to a race of scavengers by the Foundry itself.

"Oh shit!" Karianna blurted over the open channel. *"Milo. What—"*

Chatter exploded, arguments over what to do next. Everyone was freaked out, and rightfully so, but what was there to do. What options did we have? At this moment we were drifting toward Nest, little more than a shuttle headed to the surface, but if we made to run, this massive battleship would squash us, no question.

"Calm down, everyone," I said, raising my hands even if they couldn't see me. "So far, it hasn't attacked."

"But it's headed toward us," Karianna said.

"It is. But everyone remain calm. Let's think this through."

"We can't run," Shelly said.

"No," Leo agreed. *"We can't."*

We drifted to within just a few thousand kilometers of the ship, its position holding between us and the surface of the planet. It was clearly posturing, but it wasn't contacting us. What the hell was its play?

"Milo," Proxy said, stepping up beside me on the right. "Do you trust me?"

I blinked down at it. "What are you asking?"

"Trust me, Milo." Proxy made direct eye contact. "Trust me."

And of course, I did. We'd never have made it this far otherwise.

Proxy took my lack of response as agreement, then faced forward. Several tense moments passed in which the crew continued to discuss the situation over our open channel. I tuned them out, focusing on whatever it was Proxy was doing.

After nearly a minute, which had felt like an eternity, the grand battleship turned and began moving into a higher orbit, none of its weapons having powered up. It was getting out of our way, leaving.

The crew went silent.

"How did you do that?" I asked, but this time, I used the open channel. The crew needed to hear.

Proxy rubbed against my leg and purred. "Their Foundry-made ship was in a low-activity state, their pilot on the surface somewhere. Before an alert could be raised to call them back, like I did often with you on Novae, I spoke with its Proxy."

My eyes went wide. "You what?"

"Yes. I told their Proxy we did not intend to harm the pilot. It believed me. As Proxies, we exist to protect the pilot, to protect life. It chose to listen to me, for now."

I shook my head. "It defied its pilot and listened to the word of a possible threat?"

"Do we intend on attacking that vessel with our Swift Shuttle's weapons?" Proxy asked. "Do we intend on finding the pilot and killing them?"

"That would be a no," Karianna replied. *"That's a huuuge bitch."*

"Then I have not lied," Proxy stated, matter of fact. "Let us not break our word. The rest of their ships are busy for now, and this one will stay quiet unless its pilot returns. Do be quick."

"We plan on it," I replied.

Shelly sent me a private message over our implants, text only.

Shelly: *What is the Foundry's game? It fights against us, and yet, Proxy helps us.*

Me: *Different sides of the same system of control? Maybe we're not irredeemable.*

Shelly: *I'd like to believe that.*

We reached the upper atmosphere without further incident. The Isoptera were busy, and the one ship that might stand in our way had been convinced to ignore us. Our shuttle descended, the black of space fading, replaced by the bright wash of friction and particle ignition as we aerobraked. The additional oxygen concentration meant that for a time, we must've looked like a fireball screaming across the sky.

This lasted for only a few seconds before we slowed our velocity and began to glide down through the clouds. Our landing zone was obscured by a thick storm ceiling between our current position and the ground. I flew us by instruments, no visual confirmation, Proxy scanning everywhere for dangers, other aircraft, mountains that we might collide with. We were clear.

Emerging on the other side of the clouds, the Swift Shuttle burst from the low ceiling and slowed further. This was when we got our first real glimpse of Nest.

Due to the persistent storms, the world was dark, with very little sunlight, but it wasn't raining. The air was damp, and the winds were high, blowing at more than fifty kilometers an hour, forcing me to constantly readjust our approach as the wind gusted. The ground before us appeared to be rocky and dusty, crimson basins streaked with striations of black. This planet teamed with flora. Everything was hot, the temperature 105 Fahrenheit.

As far as I could see of the world curving over the horizon, there were no cities, no villages, no major industry, just forests of red and murky green plants dotting the banks of narrow rivers. This world, this region, was dark, hot, humid, and yet somehow also dry and dusty. It was not on my list of vacation destinations. It was a pure hellscape. A vision of infernal nightmares. A home to demons who sought to devour souls and torture for all eternity those foolish enough to enter their domain.

"There," Proxy said, pointing its head at a position on my interface. "By that shoreline. We can hide the shuttle in the jungle flora so you can then go on foot."

"Lovely," I said, swiping a hand up to clear my view. "Putting her down. Let's go get what we came for."

CHAPTER 7

By the time I was out of my Star Sphere and dressed, everyone had already slipped on their body armor and collected their backpacks and rifles. They were waiting for me by the shuttle's exit like a bunch of nervous teenagers amped up on too much caffeine.

"Keep an eye on her," I told Proxy, placing my mechanical palm to the hull.

The feline shape twisted its head around and purred. "At the first sign of danger, I will escape. If necessary, I will hide at the bottom of the ocean."

I gave it a scratch behind the ear. "You can do that?"

"Yes. And fast. Without human passengers, this shuttle can accelerate swiftly enough to shear itself in two."

"Wow. Okay. See you when we get back?"

"I wait for you, Milo Hughes." It gave a bow, nose touching the deck, whiskers trembling. "Be careful."

I turned to Shelly, who gave me a nod. "Masks on, everyone. We might have the universal inoculant, and this may be an oxygen-rich atmosphere, but there's no telling what other environmental dangers are in the air."

No one complained.

We found ourselves in a twilight forest made of what could only be considered an analog to trees, just like Novae, though different. It was clear that the evolutionary imperative to grow taller and compete for sunlight to further photosynthesis was universal, whereas the morphology of plants was not. Their stalks were a good twenty to thirty meters tall, and thick, three meters at the least around the trunk, but their leaves or fans or blades or whatever you wanted to call them, which I would have expected to be one natural design, were varied. The trees had several layers of leaves, the topmost of them thick like palm fronds, with each of the following layers getting smaller as they neared the ground. Like the rest of the planet, they were brownish black with stripes of red, other than their dark green leaves, a clear sign of active chlorophyll. The amount of shade this forest provided was incredible, illustrating how efficient these plants were at capturing all available light. Having so little sun on the floor of the forest meant that the undergrowth was sparse, mostly relegated to creepers and small bushes, along with a few saplings of the larger trees. The oddest part was that these trees grew in patterns, not wildly but evenly spaced in rough hexagons, with about ten meters between each vertex.

"Watch where you put your feet," Shelly said, taking a single step forward. Something in the forest floor wriggled ahead of us, catching our attention. "We don't know anything about what is or isn't dangerous on this planet. And no smoking."

"Does anyone in our group even smoke?" Xuan asked, eyeing us curiously. "But why not?"

"You'll catch yourself on fire," I said, raising my weapon and leading us ahead. "This planet is flammable. Very flammable. It has a higher concentration of oxygen than Earth."

"Being on fire would be bad."

"Yes, it would."

We advanced in an inverted V formation toward where my visions had pulled me, our group sweating profusely from the heat. I was at the front, Shelly on my right, Karianna on my left, the rest spreading out with Leo at the rear. The deeper into the forest we went, the more of this alien environment we became aware of, and none of it was good. James, Lance, and Renata were the calmest, while Xuan and Leo seemed a bit nervous, eyeing anything that made the littlest noise. Karianna and Shelly remained quiet. I was having a hard time reading either of their states of mind. The forest was loud, the noise of screeching and whining and chittering creatures persistent, so many calls and cries it was hard to tell one from another.

We listened. We watched. We pressed on.

Roaming the forest were a diverse collection of unwelcome monsters. There were giant, centipede-like insects as large as anacondas, which were scary enough in their own right. Then there were fibrous membranes made of vines on the ground that wrapped around our boots to keep us in place, as if we'd stepped in glue. Not to mention what Xuan quickly dubbed the "tree spiders". They were difficult to describe; these particular nightmares moved like monkeys in the treetops, throwing themselves from limb to limb. They were roundish in shape and did not appear mammalian, though to be fair it was hard to be certain as swift as they passed through the canopy, their flowing tentacles lashing to the floral branches as if they were threads in a web. Their skin shone in the pale light of this world, the same muted colors as the rest of this hell, and as they moved, they made no sound. I had no doubts they were armored and had teeth as sharp as daggers, or maybe they were poisonous.

I had a good feeling if any of us tripped and fell, we might struggle in place while the local wildlife sucked out our eyes and burrowed into us.

"This will make a terrifying painting when we get back," Leo said, pushing a plant away with the barrel of his rifle. "Despite it not having people around, there's certainly a Hieronymus Bosch vibe to this place here."

"A who?" Xuan asked.

"Hieronymus Bosch. He was a Dutch painter from the fifteenth and sixteenth century. Everything he painted was straight up terrifying. Demons. Surreal objects and people. Strange plants and places. Death and damnation."

Something long and wiggly fell out of nowhere onto Karianna's shoulder before it began to scurry over to her chest. She twisted around, nearly clocking Leo in the face with her backpack as she spun.

"Eww, eww, eww. It's going to eat me." She let go of her rifle, its mass swinging at her side by the strap, almost slamming me in the hip. The insect crawled around in circles as she tried to brush it off. "Have I mentioned how much I hate nature?" Karianna growled, shaking her hands in disgust. "I really, really, really hate nature. Get it off. Get it off."

"I second that," James said, calmly stepping close and picking the insect off her chest before flicking it off into the trees. He checked her over to be sure it was the only one. "Why are we here again? Maybe this is the wrong planet? The occupants are bastards."

Karianna gave him a nod by way of thanks, taking a shuddering breath below her mask to clear her thoughts.

Lance groaned. "We're here to follow freak-boy's hallucination."

"Can we hurt them if they attack us?" Renata bowed up. "The Isoptera. Is it safe to shoot them? You mentioned setting ourselves on fire."

"I believe Proxy gave us special ammunition for this mission," I lied, but it seemed probable.

Shelly turned to me and raised an eyebrow but said nothing. What good would it do now? It was amazing we had made it this far. We were no military force, just a bunch of erudite cowboys trying to do the right thing.

"You see that weird, green gunk on everything?" Shelly whispered as she stepped close beside me.

I nodded. "What do you think it is?"

"I'm not sure, but it looks similar to what was on the outside of their spacecraft. I need to take a sample."

With a raised fist, I called for our group to pause. Shelly bent down by a rock and scraped some of the greenish lichen into a metallic sample canister Proxy had provided.

"There's threads underneath," she said, raising a stick with a glob of it on the end. "When I took the sample, it didn't come willingly."

I stepped close and squinted my eyes. "Am I crazy, or does that look like a bundle of wires?"

She deposited the green lump into her canister. "You aren't crazy."

Lance wiped the moisture from his forehead. "We gonna keep moving, or am I sweating my ass off for nothing?"

The forest began to thin, depositing us on a plane of boot-high grass and dirt. I spotted the first of the memory markers from my visions about a hundred meters ahead by a cave that opened up from a mountain slope, its peaks so high they were obscured by cloud cover.

We held for a moment at the edge of the forest, not sprinting across the field, taking a moment to search for threats. Renata, James, and Lance scanned the area with their binoculars.

"Any movement?" I asked, raising a hand to my brow and squinting.

"Lots of grass," James reported. "Lots of grass and crawly things."

Renata lowered her binoculars and shook her head. "Nothing, sir. No Isoptera. No sign of technology either."

"Alright then," I said. "This place matches the visions. I recognize what I think might be a symbol in the rock over there. Let's keep low and move quick since we'll be out of cover. Weapons loose and ready."

We scurried across the open terrain as if the enemy were at our back. Karianna tripped over something and nearly pitched onto her face, but I caught her by the arm. She laughed it off but wasn't amused. The thickening scrubgrass parted as we pushed through it, growing the slightest bit taller until we reached the last five meters before the cave entrance where it vanished all together, revealing level ground covered with vines.

The edges of this unnatural, fifteen-meter opening were formed into place as if by thousands of tiny claws. Around its edges, thick cables led into the dark, ropey shapes covered in the same dark-green lichen.

We scanned the entrance's walls for anything dangerous, traps or detection devices. Nothing appeared mechanical. If they had a means to monitor us, it was not an obvious one.

Xuan kicked one of the ropey cables with the toe of her boot, then bent down and put a hand over it. "Whatever it is, it's hard. And warm, very warm." She stood again and scratched at her hair.

"The side," Lance said, gesturing with a flick of his head. "The strands on the side of your head are sticking out where you touched them."

"What? My hand isn't dirty."

Shelly cocked her head and walked over to Xuan. She inspected the strands of hair on her head, a curious idea having taken hold of her. Xuan raised her hands to Shelly, offering her palms. "Okay, so your hands are clean, but something is playing with your hair. Static electricity maybe?"

Renata removed her hand terminal and stepped over to one of the cables. Its display distorted when she held it close, glitching with scan lines, but cleared as she stepped back.

"That's interesting," Shelly mused.

I kicked at the ground beneath us. The thick underbrush of vines retreated. What I could only call footprints became clear beneath them. There were circular marks in the dirt by the hundreds disbursed before us, each several inches apart, their collection leading into the mountain. Karianna followed my action, checking to see if the marks were solid.

"The mystery can wait," I told the group. "I have a good feeling we're in the middle of a thoroughfare. This looks like the inside of an ant colony, but much bigger. We need to get moving. No telling if they'll come through this place soon. The tunnel curves off to the right. That's our path."

I stepped through the entrance, the interior muted and dark. With the breathing mask on, I couldn't smell anything but recycled air, though instinct told me it would have been damp and moldy if I could have. My team followed after me, not saying a word.

After about two dozen paces, the light from outside wasn't enough for us to advance, and so we were forced to click on the lamps attached to our weapons and aim them at the floor.

As was the case with the entrance, the tunnel appeared as if it had been dug out rather than occurring naturally through the movement of water and time. The floor was level, leading me to believe it was meant for not just foot traffic, but also vehicles. On our left and right, the green cables continued, glowing occasionally along our path but not enough to see by. These organic growths also looked too intentional to be natural.

Karianna stepped up beside me. "How far do we need to go?"

I shook my head. "I have no idea. I only know it's this way. Into the unnatural cave, tunnel to the right, through the big room, and into the maze. On the other side of the maze, there will be a room shaped like a nautilus shell with a plinth at its center. That's where we find the Golden Disc."

"Alrighty, so what do your instincts say?"

"Far, but not too far. Maybe a few kilometers, I don't know."

She sighed and looked around the cave, aiming her light at different spots. "At least I don't see any crawlies in here."

"I'll be here to pick them off it they show up," James said, sporting a big dumb grin, though I could only see it in his eyes given how large the mask was.

She looked away from him in mock disgust.

We kept a steady pace, moving ahead through the tunnel, and as we did, I felt Karianna drift closer. I cut my eyes at her, and she smiled in turn.

"Crawlies or no, I feel safest where I am," she mumbled.

Shelly gave her a hard look, and I picked up the pace, putting a bit of distance between the two of them and me.

Leo squeezed through the group and hurried up beside me, his voice low enough that no one could hear. "Dude . . . you are aware what's going on, right?"

"What?" I frowned back at him. "Nothing's going on."

He let out a single chuckle. "Look . . . the middle can be a fun place, but it can get you in trouble big time. Speaking from experience."

"I'm not in the middle of anything."

"Right . . ." He gave me a curt nod and stepped back. "Not in the middle."

After some minutes we reached a fork in the tunnel, the path on the left bleeding with a pale, yellowish light.

"Flick them off," I ordered with a wave of my hand, leaving us in darkness. We remained quiet while we waited for our eyes to adjust. The soft light ahead began to intensify.

"Do you hear that?" Xuan asked. "Movement."

"Skittering," Karianna whispered, her body giving an involuntary shutter. "I should have stayed on the ship."

Lance gestured to Renata and James with his free hand. They fanned out, poking their heads down the opposite tunnel before going ahead. I tiptoed after, weapon raised, finger resting on the safety.

"Hey," Lance whispered. "Psst. We're here. Well, we're somewhere."

I took a deep breath, cautiously approaching his position. The walls slid back as I curved around the corner, my vision assaulted by an open cavern full of bright lights. Up until that moment, I had thought this was all a good idea. I didn't feel the same anymore.

CHAPTER 8

Where the tunnel ended, a great city of dirt and rock began, sprawling out before us in organic lines and rows with no apparent rhyme or reason. We had found ourselves at the edge of an open chamber several hundred meters high, and who knew how far across, filled with pale brown towers covered in openings that could have been windows or doors. The shape of the towers was rounded but irregular, everything bathed in the amber light of the many ovoid sacks dangling from high up on the cathedral ceilings. The Isoptera numbered in the thousands, their termite forms crawling up and down the many structures, wings beating furiously, though not for flying. I had sudden flashbacks to the *Vasco Da Gama*, when Esteban, Deidrick, James and I had made first contact with this species. They were insects tall as humans, their skin black and brown, shiny and armored, with eyes large as dinner plates and razor-sharp mandibles protruding from the bases of their oversized heads. While it seemed they were excellent climbers, we had seen them walk on two feet aboard our ship and on Creatus, which happened to be the case for those here on the ground level.

Thank the Universe they had not yet seen us. This tunnel was small by comparison, and the nearest structures were less populated by Isoptera. We scurried behind a series of rocks to get out of sight.

"They're just as ugly today as they were back then," James whispered from right beside me. I'd been so focused I hadn't noticed him sneak up on me. "I just want to burn every one of these fuckers. Can we nuke them on the way out?"

I shook my head. Though that would have been a great option, we didn't have the weapons in place to do so. Just like I had reason enough to hate Johan for what he had done to Dad, James had to hate these creatures for what they had done to his mother.

"Just try and keep it together," I told him. "We'll get our revenge another day. Any action now will only complicate things."

James didn't seem satisfied with this, nor should he have, but he cleared his throat, then spat on the ground. "Fine."

Like it or not, this place was a memory marker in my vision. We had to make it to the far side of this colony chamber to get to the maze, though at the moment, I wasn't sure how.

"If we go in there," Karianna said, pointing at the towers, "they'll see us. I don't see an easy way through."

"Then how about around?" Leo asked. "Maybe there's some tunnels like these that we can sneak through. We can use them to stick to the extremities."

"Maybe. But we don't have a map. Not a detailed one, at least."

And she was right. This was stupid. I had a vague impression of where we needed to be, and that was all. Stupid. Stupid. Stupid.

"Look at those," Lance said, gesturing toward a series of roundish structures that appeared to connect to some of the buildings. "Whatever those things are, the ones they touch don't seem to be as busy. Maybe they're another kind of tunnel. Unlike the towers, they've got that same greenish look the surface has."

"I think it's their technology," Shelly said, and the group turned to look at her. "Think about it. The colors on their ship. And the plants in the fields. I'm just speculating here, but the forest grew in neat rows, capturing all available sunlight. Maybe that's how they generate electricity. Maybe, whatever this green stuff is, that's how they power it all."

"We didn't see anything like this when they boarded the *Vasco Da Gama*," James said. "They had some really advanced weaponry. Those grenades terrify me."

"Maybe this technology isn't what they use off planet. Or maybe they had Foundry devices as well. Isoptera are scavengers, yeah? No telling where they got the equipment."

"I guess."

"So, their technology," I ventured, "could be based on something organic."

"Precisely."

"It would fit with how the planet looked from the air. That begs the question, could they be tracking us?"

"If they are," Lance replied, "they sure as hell aren't acting like it."

Renata pulled herself from the edge of our cover, and I could tell from the look on her face that something had happened. "We need to move. Isoptera are headed this way."

"Shit," he growled.

I scanned the area for options, spotting a path on our left that curved around the chamber. "Let's go with Leo's idea. Maybe we can work our way around the outside. I don't see any way we can go back and find a tunnel leading around this area without getting so lost we'd be trapped here forever. Stay low and out of sight. Move quick. This way."

We snaked our way along the edge of the chamber, running from one rock formation to the next, careful to stay out of sight. The chamber was much dimmer this far from the center, but I had a feeling the Isoptera could see well enough in the dark. Sweat poured off my brows, not just because it was a million degrees in here, but from the anxiety over prying insect eyes. If they spotted us, things would go bad, and quick. I hadn't anticipated stumbling into a colony. From my visions, I thought we'd be sneaking around back alleys, not running through the middle of Times Square on New Year's Eve.

Five times we found cover and sprinted to it. The only way for us to track our progress around this massive space was by the amber sacs hanging from the ceiling at its center. The Isoptera went on with their tasks, skittering around the buildings, walking up and down the streets. Whatever fake conflict we had given them in orbit had not seemed to matter to this section of the hive. It was all: *Hey, how are you? How's the family? What's for dinner tonight?* Business as usual.

As we approached one end of the chamber, we started to see Isoptera walking on all eight legs carrying smaller, wriggling termites on their backs which were the size of large dogs.

"Larva," Shelly supplied. "Has to be. If they're like other hive insects, there should be a kind of hatchery nearby."

"I hate nature," Karianna grumbled.

The more Isoptera we observed while sneaking between cover, the more it became clear that their society possessed multiple castes. Most were of one, similar to what we had first encountered on the *Vasco Da Gama*, but smaller and thicker, with wings that did not reach much past the top of their thorax. The second caste in the hierarchy had noticeably longer mandibles and antennae. These did not carry larvae, or food, or anything at all but a kind of black tube that we knew from experience were energy rifles. Among them, we found an occasional third, these walking on two legs, thorax slender, carapaces appearing soft like skin. These were always accompanied by the soldiers, but at a distance, no Isoptera were making contact or communicating with them.

We continued our dashing advance, methodical in our approach to each section of cover. Our target tunnel was coming closer. I was starting to believe we might actually make it.

A group of twenty Isoptera congregated too close to the edge of the chamber for our comfort, our group squeezed behind a rock. They exchanged clicking sets of words, having some sort of conversation, though we could hear nothing clearly from where we were. Lance and I ventured over the edge of the rock we had slid behind to get a better look while Renata and Leo watched for our next opportunity to advance.

Lance's body went stiff.

"What is it?" I asked.

"They've seen us." He nodded off to the right. "Those workers, or whatever the hell you call them, they've stopped in their tracks. They're turning our way."

James and Renata took hold of our backpacks, yanking us into cover.

Lance was right. A group of the first caste had turned to face us, setting their burdens down on the ground. Each of their antennae worked furiously, twitching as if sending signals. Despite our cover, they had seen our position.

"We've got to move," I ordered. "And quick. I see a tunnel on the other side of those buildings. If we can make it, I have a good feeling the maze won't be far. Something tells me it will be safe."

Lance's face went red, eyebrows crowding his nose, free hand balled into a fist. "What tells you? I mean what, really? I can't believe I'm here. This is bullshit. All of it is bullshit. We shouldn't be here."

"But where else would we get the pulsar map?" Karianna fired back, taking up for me, finger poking Lance in the chest. "This is where it is."

"Based on what real information? For all I know he's been dropping acid, tripping balls, and taking really good guesses."

"I don't know, man," Leo added. "Maybe this is just the Foundry talking to us through his visions. He's making a believer out of me."

Shelly cut a hand through the air as if slicing their objections in half. "We don't have time for arguments. We're here. It's happening." She turned to me. "What now?"

I swallowed. "The tunnel. Fifty meters ahead."

"Then let's go before they all hear about us. Isoptera most likely speak over distances by chemicals. That kind of communication could be quick."

Breaking from cover, our group took off after me as I followed the last of the outside trail. Within the colony, the sounds began to change. Where there was once a gentle hum of skittering monotony, it had become quiet. Isoptera were watching us pass, stunned that there was something in their sanctuary that was not of Nest. I hoped that this stunned state would persist, but no such luck.

Energy weapons began to pepper the walls and floor beside us, their source the soldiers we had seen protecting the special units. I had half expected these Isoptera to take off and run after us, but they hesitated to leave those that they protected.

"We're almost there," Renata said. "Do we fire back?"

"Hold for now," I ordered. "They're still not sure what's going on. I think they're trying to scare us away from those VIPs."

Less than a dozen strides from the tunnel's mouth, that grand idea of mine died. Yes, some were trying to protect the VIPs, and no, they were not pursuing, but it wasn't for the reason I thought. Soldiers in red armor burst from a series of towers near the tunnel. They began bathing our position with weapons fire, the walls and surfaces around us sizzling like bits of meat tossed into boiling oil. We made a break for cover behind a set of towers, one on each side of the street, narrowly escaping being shot. If these weapons were even remotely the same as those used on the *Vasco Da Gama* by the boarding party, then they were designed to melt organic material, to render flesh into a charred paste. I didn't want to relive that nightmare.

Karianna's backpack caught fire, having been hit by a stray beam before she reached cover. She shrugged out of it and let it drop to the ground, reaching in to recover only a couple items, which she stuffed into her pockets.

"Weapons free," I ordered, and my team nodded. They took positions by the edge of the tower, firing back at the approaching Isoptera.

The insects made for cover, but I had no doubts they were working to circle back on us.

"Milo!" Lance shouted. "You sure the maze is safe?"

I nodded. "Yes, it's safe from them. They won't go in there. I know this for a fact."

"Okay." He shook his head. "Then we've got to split up and circle back around to it. Run like hell and confuse them."

"A good plan," Renata said.

"No," I said, "it's not. We stick together."

"If we stick together," Lance shouted between bursts of suppressive fire, "they can take us down easier. It's most important you make it through and back to the ship with the disc. The three of you, Milo, Karianna, and Shelly, go left, we'll go right. Xuan and Leo can hop between buildings."

I narrowed my eyes at Lance. "Who's in charge here?"

"It's just a suggestion, asshole. Not trying to take your shitty leadership position away or anything."

The enemy soldiers edged closer. Xuan had managed to shoot one of them, Renata another, but this was their colony and they had near infinite reinforcements at their disposal. They just kept coming.

Lance was probably right. He was usually right, even if he was a dick about it.

"Split up," I ordered. "Head for the tunnel."

The team nodded their assent, and Shelly and Karianna took positions at my side. I led them away from the others down the left road, cutting through groups of Isopteran workers, doing my best to ignore those who were unarmed. So far, it seemed that they would not take action to stop us, only these soldiers in white. That was good news. I could hear gunfire over our shoulders as we weaved between the streets, a sign that our people were still upright.

At a fork in the road, an Isopteran soldier burst from cover, coming inches from Shelly's face, its mandibles ready to snap her neck free from her shoulders. The insect was so close I couldn't turn or lift a weapon to protect her. Karianna moved into action without an instant of hesitation, her prosthetic shooting outward, fist slamming into its face. Her hand tore through its thin carapace with the speed of a biting snake and the strength of a hydraulic press, ichor gushing from around the gaping wound its impact left. The Isoptera collapsed into a heap as Karianna jerked her sticky hand from the gory hole.

"Eww. Eww. Eww," she said, wiping the dirty prosthetic off on her pants, leaving behind blobs of black and green on her thigh.

Shelly looked at her and took a deep, shuddering breath, but she said nothing. That had been a close one.

The left side of the tunnel was in sight, the sound of gunfire starting to die down. I pinged our companions to check their statuses but got nothing in response. They had gone dark.

"We can make it," I said, but just as we were about to reach the last set of towers before the tunnel, the world flashed white, then went sideways. One minute I was standing, the next, the ground had rushed up to meet my hands and face. I struck the floor like a rag doll, my breathing mask cracking into pieces. A flood of putrid scents rushed in.

Adrenaline flooded me, pumped into my system by the Foundry prosthetic I had been augmented with during my donation. I rolled over, about to spring up from the ground, when I was butted in the forehead with one of the rifle-like black tubes the Isoptera carried.

My head smacked back against the dirt, and everything went hazy. I couldn't get up.

A form leaned over me, a soldier with shuddering black mandibles and twitching antenna. Something was different about this one. Its white armor had red stripes on it, unlike the others who had been pursuing us.

The Isoptera made a series of clicking noises that even in my addled state the Foundry's bloodborne nano machines translated.

"Human," it said. "Yes. Human. You come with us. You come with us."

CHAPTER 9

If there was one thing I had a bad track record of, it was keeping myself from being captured by the enemy of the moment. Thinking back to the start of this crazy journey, I had first been incapacitated by Isoptera on the *Vasco Da Gama*, then later stolen off in the middle of the night by those tiny mammals on Cynosure, the Frendol, then captured by Jevox on Rix and almost poisoned in their faulty suspension chamber, before eventually being knocked on my ass and nearly killed while wearing powered armor aboard the Prole Genascara.

And here I was again, unable to collect my faculties as a group of Isoptera bound my hands and led me somewhere I knew I wouldn't like. At least I wasn't being eaten. Well, not immediately.

As my head began to clear, recalling a mixed bag of facts like my name, where we were from, and what I ate for breakfast, I found that Shelly and Karianna were still with me, arms tied behind their backs. They were alive, if bruised up a bit.

We stumbled forward.

Milo, Shelly mouthed, and I gave her a nod in response.

The Isoptera had taken from us our backpacks, our weapons, and our breathing masks. Who knew where they were. The only advantage we had now was Karianna and my prosthetics, and for now I wasn't sure if they knew about those.

Karianna looked to me, down at my metallic arm, then down toward hers. I shook my head. We were surrounded by a group of ten soldiers in an unfamiliar place. Even if we managed to get free, there was no way we could stab them all in the face before the rest melted us into goo.

I wracked my brain over what we could do. As I was thinking, I received a ping from Shelly over our implants, text only, the message appended with a tag that showed Karianna had received it as well.

Shelly: *Why haven't they eaten us?*

Me: *I don't know.*

Karianna: *Whatever they're planning, I hope it's not worse than that.*

Me: *They called us out as human. They know what we are.*

Shelly: *Of course they do. They have Voyager's disc. Still wondering how they got their claws on it. Did they come that close to Earth? Or did they trade for it?*

Me: *Maybe it was just me, or my head isn't clear. But their tone reminded me of how the Kabosai acted when they found Esteban and me on Cynosure.*

Karianna: *What's the plan? It's clear you don't want us to make a run for it.*

Me: *No. Making a break will only hasten our deaths. We've got to wait for our moment.*

Shelly: *I can't reach the others with all the interference from the caves. I know our implant signals aren't exactly the strongest without a network, but this is worse than normal. We're on our own.*

The tunnel they guided us down was narrower than the one we had entered through, busy with traffic. Workers moved past us on the left, carrying translucent larva covered in dark stripes, wriggling and writhing as they were taken for a ride. These larvae were in varying stages of development, some with large heads and tiny legs, others looking like colorless adult Isoptera. I couldn't say how, but they all looked hungry, and as they passed, their developing antennae turned our way as if smelling tasty, tasty us.

I spotted thick bundles of the greenish-black cables we had seen when entering. This place was hot, hotter than the surface of the planet or the city by several degrees. Were Isoptera cold-blooded? It seemed to me that the warmer it was, the swifter they moved.

While there wasn't much light, there was an occasional sack of glowing amber hanging from the wall like a teardrop. What they cast was barely bright enough to illuminate our feet, but it kept us from tripping when the ground was uneven.

Caught up in the spectacle, I must have slowed, as the Isoptera at our rear prodded us in the back with their black tubes. We picked up the pace. I had no way to tell their moods from the looks on their faces, their eyes emotionless black mirrors, but anytime we did something they didn't like, I noticed their antennae became excited.

"Where are you taking us?" Karianna shouted over her shoulder. The armored soldiers did not respond. "Where?"

She spun around and stopped in her tracks, staring one of them down, fists resting on her hips.

The soldiers paused and cocked their heads to the side as if trying to understand. Then the closest stepped forward, slamming its weapon tube into her stomach like a bat. Karianna doubled over, arms going limp as she let out a muffled scream. Shelly moved to help her up, but several other Isopteran soldiers responded, raising their tubes at her face. She backed off.

"You okay?" I asked my copilot.

Karianna spat on the ground and climbed back onto her feet, a look of pure, determined hate on her face. "Assholes."

They urged us ahead.

Soon the tunnel opened up into a massive, single chamber with a dome more than a hundred meters above. Set into its high walls were hundreds of alcoves that loomed over us like black windows, workers crawling feverishly about them, placing eggs in some, coaxing larva to leave from others.

At the center of the chamber at the bottom of a gentle slope, I saw three indentations with tracts leading into them, each at least ten meters across, with a bowl made of dirt or rock before it that was easily three times as tall as me. The arrangement appeared almost like a dinner setting for giants, the indentations their seats, the bowls their earthenware, each equally spaced.

Shelly steadied me. The scale of it all was dizzying. My feet sweat as if we were about to be interrogated by the secret police of a corrupt government.

The soldiers pushed us toward the middle of the chamber, down a dirt row that ran adjacent to two of the settings to a raised platform at its center. At their instructions, we climbed onto the platform and waited, turning round and round to see what might be next. Everywhere I looked, I spotted the greenish cables, as well as other devices I couldn't call natural yet knew were organic. Lights flickered along the chamber's dome in sequences, scintillating patterns dancing with swirling circles and lines across a matrix of glowing amber sacs.

Shelly looked me in the eyes and swallowed. This was beyond bad.

Workers ceased their operations in the alcoves and swarmed the edges of the chamber, heading toward dark recesses that were impossible to see within. The skittering noises of the chamber went silent as if it had taken an expectant breath.

"What are they doing?" Karianna asked, her right-hand fiddling with something in her pocket.

I was about to ask her what she had when a boom rocked the chamber. The lights above us shifted in their patterns as a sprinkling of dust and rocks powdered our shoulders.

A resonant clicking pattern filled the open space, echoing about the chamber, making it impossible to locate its source. The sound set off a pounding in my ears as my brain attempted to make sense of it.

"Dear, dear, dear, guests . . ." The Foundry machines in my blood translated, having taken longer than normal. "So much to give, how quick can we have?"

Another set of clicks rocked the chamber, this time with a slightly different tone, a bit lower in pitch, more insistent. "Waste time and energy. Much easier way. The next generation requires it. The next generation is hungry."

Shelly raised a finger. "Look."

A groaning, cracking noise filled our ears, and out of the dark recesses came a pair of lumpy, writhing forms as large as juvenile whales. They were ivory-colored giants, with different colored stripes, massive grub-like creatures festooned with rows of slimy tubes that belched pale white eggs onto the ground at random intervals that were covered in mucus.

As I squinted to make out details, I found the body of a typical Isoptera at the front end of the massive sac. Though these termite bodies were far larger than those of the rest of their species, even without the egg sac, these were nowhere near the scale of the rest of their insectile form. These bodies were different, with a dozen legs instead of eight, additional antennae that were hard to count, and four eyes instead of the usual two. While they had many legs that seemed capable of walking on, their bodies had become so fat, so heavy, that they could not move on their own, and so they were carried on the backs of workers as if they rode upon an organic palanquin.

Over a wordless minute, these two massive Isoptera were moved into their respective locations around us, leaving one setting empty.

Shelly took hold of my hand and said a single word as the sacs moved into the indentations where they would come to rest. "Queens."

The clicking continued, this time from the one on our left, its body the largest of the two, with crimson-accented skin covered in bright, blue stripes. "Bring our loves. Let them smell what we have found."

"For the next generation," said the smaller Queen, an albino with red stripes that were just like the soldiers who had brought us here. "We thrive, we survive."

"Save the best. Eat the rest."

Behind us came a parade of fresh Isoptera of ordinary size, these walking upright with robes that reflected the unique colors of their Queen's livery. This caste of Isoptera, clearly different in shape and dress, had bodies unlike the workers or soldiers. They were finer somehow, almost pretty for an insect.

"My loves. My beautiful loves," the Red and Albino Queens said, and one by one these Isoptera approached them, touching antennae to antennae in an affectionate gesture.

"Can you smell the life here?" the Albino Queen said. "These are humans. Humans for you. To make you better."

"The hell we are!" Karianna shouted up at them, and the procession of this new caste of Isoptera stopped. "What do you want with us? What is this about?"

"Human speaks," it clicked. "Its words hurt me, even with tiny machines in my blood to let me smell. It is unnatural."

"You must learn to listen," the Red Queen said. "Not just smell. We smell, but not all smell. Many hear."

"They smell of life," one of the "loves," as the Queen had called it, said. "We will be healthy and strong. May we taste them, our Red Queen?"

"No," the Red Queen replied. "Dear, dear, dear, if you taste just them, what will be for your brothers? Nothing. My drones, you must wait, be patient. We have a male and two females. The male will mate with the females, many times per day. Humans enjoy this activity. They will make us many children, hundreds of them in a few cycles I am sure, and those children will have children. With patience we will fill our stocks and you will all be strong. You will have more than you ever need. This will give us the next generation."

"Uhhh," Karianna said, "I don't think they understand human biology."

Shelly's face went pale. I squeezed her hand.

"Waste of time!" the Albino Queen shouted. "Our gray sister will return from their world with her holds full. We will gorge and gorge until we have everything we need for the next generation. These humans, they will be a snack. A little taste of what is to come, little, little, little."

I didn't like where this was going.

Shelly spoke soft, so only we could hear her. "Okay, so it looks like they plan on eating us either way. I think big red wants to turn us into cattle, whereas the albino just wants to eat us and be done with it. Karianna is right though, they are under the impression we have young like they do, in litters like dogs or cats, not one at a time."

"Neither of these options give us a way out," Karianna said. "I don't think we have long before they decide. What are we going to do?"

I glanced over at the empty indentation in the ground, wondering what came next.

"Milo?" Karianna asked.

"We've got to find our moment," I said. "I'm holding out hope our people didn't get captured. Lance is way cleverer than me."

"I wouldn't say that," Shelly replied.

I gave her a curious look, then focused back on the matter at hand. We had to escape. I had to figure something out. It was my fault we had ended up here.

"Find a way out?" Karianna mused, a hand in her pocket fiddling with something. "Way out."

As the drones finished greeting their Queens by touching antennae, workers began to collect the eggs that had been dropped and deposited them into the earthenware bowls. One by one, the drones disrobed, revealing their naked, glossy carapaces, then climbed into the bowls to disappear among the collection of eggs. Despite our view from this platform, I couldn't say what they were doing. All I knew was it made a lot of noise, most of which sounded wet and sticky and gross.

"I'm going to puke if that sound doesn't stop," Karianna said, looking away, a hand over her mouth.

I turned to face the Red Queen, my back straight, hands balled into fists. "We are not your dinner!" I declared with as much confidence as I could muster. "I am human. I am a Foundry pilot. I demand respect!"

There was no plan here, other than to get their attention and give us time to think of one.

The Queen's antennae flickered at me. "Says the worm," she replied, her clicks nonplussed. "You are what we wish of you to be. Your bodies are perfect for giving our drones the nutrition they require. Within a generation, maybe two, dear, dear, dear, we will have all we need forever. We will evolve again, this is the way of it, this is why Nest is ours. We overcame the others. The Crestane, the Prexal, and the Livester, they never stood a chance in the light of our brilliance. This world became ours. A new generation. Evolve. Perfect. Feed the strong, eat the weak."

"What are they saying?" Shelly mumbled. "Did this planet support multiple sentient species, or did they conquer other worlds?"

Karianna shook her head, her face still pale.

"We will not be overcome," I said, using the Queen's word. "You're just another bunch of killers. I have faced your kind before. You do not protect life. You will not be tolerated."

"Protect life?" the Queens replied, then made a noise I could not understand, nor could the Foundry software. It was staccato, and frantic, its tone twisting, pitch rising and falling, phasing in and out of sync, making my legs quiver and my ears throb.

Were they laughing?

"You speak like the great machine," the Albino Queen said once they were done. "Pretends to help all but does not understand us who are of Nest. We *must* evolve. We *must* expand. There is no option. Only imperative. Foundry did not like this."

"Because you're evil," I started. "Selfish. All Isoptera. You're driven only by hunger, by need. This will not be our end, not for us, not for our species."

"Tiny human," the Red Queen whispered. "Even now your world is being assaulted by our sister and her star chasers. The Albino Queen is right, I must admit. Our sister will return with food for our loves. Food in cold sleep. They will feast on that day. Humanity is ours. Till then, we will sow you, and we will reap you. This starts today."

"Is this true?" Karianna mumbled. "Or are they lying? Are they already on Earth?"

Shelly rested a hand on my shoulder.

"Why are you here?" the Albino Queen asked next. "What did you think you would accomplish? If you have come to kill us, you have failed. Your soldiers have failed. We rank in the tens of billions. We have other sisters. You are but a few."

Karianna reached into her pocket, removing a black cube the size of her palm. I sucked in a deep breath and swallowed at its sight. I'd seen one of these before, though it had been a long, long time. She had to have stolen it when the soldier hit her. And knowing her . . . well, that had been the plan all along.

She moved to activate the spatial compression grenade, which would unleash a new set of events for which we certainly had no plan, but before I could tell her to stop, motion to her that this was a stupid idea, a fresh boom rocked the chamber. The Queens we had been talking with paused, as did the workers attending them. Karianna stuffed the grenade back in her pocket but did not let go.

Out of the dark recess at our backs a shadow appeared, its shape not as large as the Red Queen, but thicker than the Albino. A third Queen was being drawn down a ramp toward the empty indentation, eggs spewing from its pulsing black sack of a body, its white strips wriggling with the motion. It looked at us, cocked its head, then motioned with its arms at the other Queens.

"We are fighting again, both above the skies and below," it clicked, tone high pitched by comparison to the other Queens. "To keep as food stock, or to harvest and be done. Too few options. The Prexal, lest we forget, made our drones strong. Gave us so much life. Yet, we ate even their young. Now, now, now, no more Prexal. They were smart mammals, and when they died we advanced the fungara no more. They had knowledge we did not. They showed us how to make machines that speak to one another, star chasers, weapons. The fungus spoke to them, listened to them. But we? We only smell."

The Albino Queen protested. "We took the knowledge of fungara from the Prexal. Our drones may tell it how to grow. It listens to us."

"We have advanced!" the Red Queen cried out.

"But how much more if we had waited?" the Black Queen asked. "Know, know, know, that we would have been gods."

"But I am a god!" the Albino Queen shouted, its vestigial claws raising, antennae trembling. "My brood is the greatest among our species. Paragons.

My body, a portal into the world from the realm of oblivion. I am the Diamond Queen come again. My brood will never want, and we shall scatter my blessing across the cosmos. All will fall to me. The galaxy will drown in blood. We will feast. Feast . . ."

I looked to my companions for help, eyes narrowing at Karianna as if daring her to use the grenade. She took a step back, uncertain with this choice.

"The Foundry will not allow it," the Black Queen replied, its tone calm, considered. "You think only in death. What of allies? Are we not better off for trade? And how do we have trade if not for me? The Prexal would have made us better if we had not eaten them all. While humans are tasty, and yes, they possess exquisite nutritional value, it is dangerous to treat a sentient species as feedstock, standing them up for harvest. These humans may have friends, and these friends could be called upon to turn Nest into ash if enough of them are killed. They have already burned their bridge to the Foundry, have you not heard? What would stop them from turning the Foundry's weapons they possess back on us to avenge the lost? We should help the humans. Find another source."

We blinked at the Black Queen, confused by her words.

"You wish to be allies?" I addressed her.

"All is possible," she said. "I wish to live forever, and forever is a long time to stand alone."

"No!" the Red Queen boomed, its clicking voice shaking the chamber.

"No, no, no!" the Albino Queen said next. "You cannot do this."

A contingent of guards in dark, glossy armor painted with white stripes like their mother's skin appeared behind the Black Queen. Among them, one was wearing a familiar type of powered armor, though it was of a different configuration given its biology.

"The pilot," Karianna whispered, her hand still in her pocket.

Shelly sighed, her attention focused on the newcomer. "I think she's rescuing us."

The Black Queen's guards flanked the platform, pointing their weapons not at the opposing Queens but at their drones, as well as any remaining soldiers who had stayed behind.

"You threaten us all," the Red Queen clicked angrily, her body wriggling and thrashing, making the ground tremble. "Your star chasers come for mine. For my sisters. You stand against us all."

The Isopteran pilot motioned for us to step down from the platform and follow them. We hesitated for a moment, but lacking a better option, we acquiesced, finding ourselves within the protective ranks of a dozen Isopteran soldiers.

"Go with them," the Black Queen instructed. "We will talk."

"Stop!" the Albino Queen clicked. With an unspoken command, likely pheromones us humans couldn't dare perceive, she instructed her soldiers to attack. The chamber erupted into chaos.

The Black Queen's ranks fell under fire from the combined forces of the Red and Albino Queen's smaller contingent of guards. None of them directed their fire anywhere near the Queens themselves, but the fighting was close at hand, and accidents could happen. The pilot urged us up the ramp to the dark recess the Queen had appeared from, blasts from energy weapons scattering all around us, while the queen herself remained stationary. We hurried after as eggs continued to squeeze out of her body as if nothing untoward was happening, leaving behind greenish-black trails of sticky, gelatinous goo as they wobbled down the slope.

"Quick," the pilot clicked at us, and we did not protest. "Into our Queen's tunnel. To safety."

And that was exactly what we did, the three of us looking to one another, wondering what in the hell had just happened.

CHAPTER 10

We hurried into the tunnel, branching off and out, jogging behind the augmented Isopteran pilot dressed in its own version of the Foundry-powered armor. Once we had made two turns and gone a few hundred feet, the sound of fighting at our backs died down, and we slowed our pace.

"Humans," the armored pilot clicked, raising one of its arms and looking at us. Though it was hard to see through the opaque quality of its equipment, I knew that it was not a natural arm by how it moved. "You are like me. Donation."

I raised my right arm. "Donation."

"Donation," Karianna echoed.

Shelly eyed us all but said nothing.

"My Queen speaks through me," it said. "We are connected to one another. Her sisters do not believe in her path."

"Which is?" Shelly asked.

The pilot paused. "Cooperation. We are stronger together."

Soldiers appeared behind us, and we kept moving, going deeper, delving down another tunnel. I tried my best to map these paths out in my mind, to keep a mental record of everywhere we had been, but I had a feeling we were hopelessly lost without a guide. Nothing of this colony's tunnels felt organized, no markers, no signs, leaving me to wonder how they navigated at all. It had to be an insect thing, trails of pheromones or something of the like.

"She mentioned trade," Shelly said. "You have engaged in trade with other species?"

"Yes. Cynosure, some Isoptera live there. We make exchanges. Materials. Isoptera are not good at everything."

"Like working with the fungus?" Karianna interjected, fingers fiddling in her pocket. "These Prexal the Queens mentioned. That was their specialty?"

It made a series of clicks before the translation software caught up. "The Prexal were of Nest. Dominant species. They tamed this world. Then something happened. We evolved. The Diamond Queen was born, and we became aware. Isoptera overcame the Prexal. We ascended to the apex of Nest but went too far, too quick. Consequences."

"You ate them all," I supplied.

The Isoptera made a trill, then went on. "Yes. Our hunger outpaced our intelligence. We knew they could not sustain us forever, and we acted. We had to seek other means of sustenance."

Shelly waved at the cables traveling the edge of the tunnel. "This is the fungara?"

"Yes. The fungara allows us to make star chasers, smell over distances, grow new food."

Karianna licked her lips and sighed. "Except you don't like food that's been grown? Not big on the vegetarian lifestyle?"

"We prefer meat, but meat takes a long time to grow." It gave her a long look, an almost hungry one by its posture, then appeared to force itself to snap out of it. "Life is more important than wants."

"Uhh-huh," she replied, then turned and cut a finger across her neck in a *we're dead* gesture. I was with her on this. I didn't trust the Black Queen's brood for a minute, but gathering information was always valuable.

"Have you been to Earth?" Shelly asked.

"No. I have not. Only the Gray Queen, her fleet, her brood."

"What does she want on Earth?"

"The same as the Albino Queen. She wants harvest."

"And what kind of progress has she made?"

The pilot's antennae trembled. "This is not for humans to know."

"It's our home," Shelly pressed. "And if your Black Queen desires cooperation with humans, she should share information with us."

"No," it clicked in a low and threatening tone. "You are in no position to bargain with gods."

And there it was, that word again. They sure as hell had a high opinion of themselves. Though, I mean, I guess I couldn't blame them. What notion of religion would they have? Everyone seeks to have understanding. If human women gave birth to millions each, would they not feel a little different about their role in the world? Hell, maybe these Queens deserved the title in this context, even if it made them sound insane.

"Look," I said, stepping up beside the pilot. "We are appreciative for the rescue. We just seek to learn more about what has happened to our world. We have been gone a long time, that is all."

"Then keep seeking," it clicked.

"Okay," I exhaled. "At least tell us where you're taking us."

"To see her loves. To cooperate. Perhaps, exchange."

Karianna shot me a look over her shoulder. "No guarantees, huh?"

"How did you find Earth?" Shelly asked, even though we knew the answer, or at least most of it.

"A disc," it said. "A golden disc now lost to us, but its stars are mapped in our chasers."

"And where did this disc come from?"

"You ask too many questions."

"We are only curious."

"The Prexal were also curious. Very curious. Too curious."

Karianna pinged Shelly and me.

Karianna: *We're being played with.*

Shelly: *Agreed. Something is very wrong.*

I said nothing in reply. The plan hadn't changed. We had to get away. We had to find our people, if they were still alive.

The broad tunnel narrowed into a series of winding paths, these devoid of workers. Along the walls of one tunnel, what appeared to be artwork made of fungara appeared, patterns and lines in varying shades of dark colors. For an instant, I felt my implants glitch, as if they had picked up a signal outside Shelly and my copilot, but it went away.

"In here," the pilot said, waving us into a chamber with a low ceiling. The contingent of soldiers was with us, six in all. "You shall get to know her drones, her loves. They make her eggs bring forth life."

"And without them she does nothing?" Karianna mused, her fingers back in that pocket.

"Without her, they are nothing."

"Sucks to be a guy, I guess."

Within the cramped chamber, there were two dozen drones, like the ones we had seen in the hatchery, but this time dressed in black and white livery. My nose was assaulted with a series of smells I could not describe, none pleasurable, all of which made me want my breathing mask back. The drones sat on benches at the edges of the space, their many arms raised in the air as they worked at tables made of dirt. Upon the surface of these tables were piles of green fungus, which as the drones twitched their antennae and moved their claws, began to respond, shaping themselves into new patterns. Something about this action reminded me of my personal nano machines I used to repair, cut, or fiddle with. Was the fungara a sort of organic nanomachine? And to be fair, weren't all organic cells sort of nanomachines?

The drones showed us little mind.

Seeking options, I searched the chamber for exits. There were three, counting the one we had come through. The six soldiers and the pilot were with us, each armed, but the drones were not. They appeared docile like the workers, even if they were held in high regard.

"We are safe here," the pilot said. "The Red and Albino Queen cannot reach us. Many precautions."

"That's reassuring," I mumbled.

"Now, it is time," the pilot said, turning to face us. "In all good deals there is give, and there is take. You must give, and we will take."

I narrowed my eyes at this, brows furrowing.

It waved an arm at the drones. "My Queen requires of you a sacrifice so that our negotiations may begin. You, primary human, the one standing beside you is a mate, I believe. This other one, the one who has given the donation, is not your mate. Therefore, she may be consumed so that we may begin."

Karianna took a step back, eyes going wide. "Excuse the hell out of me? What did you say?"

"It is the way of it," the pilot clicked in rapid patterns. "Do not be alarmed."

At an inaudible command, several of the drones stood and began to move toward us. The soldiers came up on our rear, pinning us between the two groups. Shelly put her back against mine, watching those I couldn't see.

"Screw this," Karianna growled, looking to me. "Can I get the okay, Milo?" She pointed a finger. "I've been holding back hardcore because you always call me impulsive. Didn't want to get judged and shit. I'm a little self-conscious at times."

"Yes, yes, yes!" I said, throwing my hands up. "Freaking do it."

Shelly balled her hands into fists, her expression hardening.

Karianna raised the cube from her pocket into the air, depressing the button on its side to reveal a series of spiked barbs. She turned to face the soldiers along with the pilot, and grinned. "Suck a black hole, motherfuckers."

The grenade left her fingers and tumbled through the air at the armed Isoptera. The pilot, realizing what the object was, dove for cover. Shelly threw her arms out, catching Karianna and I across the shoulders before we rushed the drones closing in on us.

With a whomp of air, the grenade discharged. We hit the dirt and I spun around, looking at the impact. Like the grenade used on the *Vasco Da Gama*, this one created a miniature compression of spacetime that seemed to take a clean chunk out of reality two meters across and press it down into a ball just a few inches in diameter. Of the six guards in the chamber, one was consumed from the legs up, two were cut in half, and one was left without the arms on one side of its body.

"Get up!" Shelly shouted, scrambling to her feet to recover one of the black tubes dropped by the Isopteran soldiers. As she hefted the bulky gun and spun around, fiddling with its controls to figure out how it worked, Karianna and I sprang into action.

The three remaining soldiers fidgeted with their weapons, but we didn't give them much time. Following Karianna's lead, I used my prosthetic right arm and hand to stab one of them in the eye. Fluids shot everywhere, spattering me on the face and across the chest, making my mouth taste of rot.

Karianna faced down another. This one saw what was coming and ducked to the side. She backhanded it in the thorax, the impact like a hammer blow, forcing it to stumble. The soldier recovered, swinging its weapon at her face, clipping her on the chin. She spat blood and twisted around, ducking the next attack before shooting up to hit it once in the chest.

"I told you guys!" she shouted, fury rising in her. "I hate nature, damn it! I hate nature!"

Once, twice, three times she pounded the soldier with her metallic prosthetic, black blood seeping from the wounds, but they were not enough to stop it.

The third soldier pointed its black tube at us, but before it could fire, its head disappeared in a flash of light. Shelly stood still, smiling now that she had found the switch on the unwieldy weapon. She turned around, content we had our targets well in hand, and fired at the pilot who was making a move to jump us, its armored suit gleaming in the dim light.

Her weapon discharged, having no effect on the armor but leaving the pilot confused and stumbling. She fired again, and again, again, until the weapon would no longer shoot. Was it out of ammunition? Who knew how to tell?

The enemy distracted by her attack, I rushed over and took hold of one of the pilot's legs with my prosthetic, flipping it on its back. Its powered armor compensated, putting it back on two feet at the mouth of a tunnel as if this were nothing.

I took a step back to reorient myself, preparing for its counter.

"How do we stop it?" Shelly growled, frantically pressing the switch she had found. "It won't shoot."

"Hand it to me." I took the weapon and waved it over my head, using its blunt end like a spade on the hard-packed dirt above. Dust fell, but the tunnel did not collapse.

"Come on. Come on." I tried again. More came down, but not enough.

The pilot collected itself and faced me, its posture showing it was readying to pounce.

With a final attempt, the weapon's barrel dug through dirt and rock. Something gave way. The tunnel the pilot was trapped within began to collapse, clumps of dirt and stones falling from the hole I had made. It leapt back, away from the cave-in, and it vanished behind a wall of debris. I wasn't sure how long this would last, but for now, it had no route into the drones' chamber.

Karianna screamed as she withdrew her blood-slick hand from the soldier she had been fighting. Her appearance had turned wild. Unlike the first time she'd done this, she didn't bother to wipe off her hand but instead let its ichor drip onto the floor, her hair a matted tangle, her face a reddish mask of rage.

"Let's go," Shelly said, urging us toward the far exit.

"What about the drones?" Karianna asked, eyeing the docile predators huddled at the far end of the chamber.

"Leave them," I said. "We protect life. Let's just get the hell out of here."

My copilot shook her head as if she were having a tantrum, but then she nodded. "We're coming back for you." She pointed at them with two fingers, tips dripping with the fluids of their dead fellows.

Before the pilot could find a route back to us, we took off running, heading down any and every tunnel before us, no clear direction in mind. We had no idea where we were or how to get back to the main colony; all we knew was that we didn't want to get caught.

We rounded a corner, and our implants began to pick something up.

*"Hello?" I called over our channel, this time using audio. "Anyone out there?"

"Oh, shit," a reply came almost instantly. "Look who the termites drug in."

"James! Dude!"

"You guys alive?"

"Yes. We're fine, after a fashion."

"What happened to you, bruh?"

"Long story. Isopteran queens and a whole bunch of bull. You guys have to be close since we're picking you up. We're coming for you."

We rounded a corner and bowled into both groups of our companions. Lance had his weapon raised, ready to fight. Realizing we were not the Isoptera, he lowered the barrel and smiled.

"Maze?" he asked, nodding to the path ahead.

I grunted while clapping him on the shoulder. "Maze."

CHAPTER 11

We didn't waste time catching up before moving on. I had no doubts that the pilot, along with the combined force of all three Queens, would be after us. Lance took point this time, leading us down a series of tunnels they had come through when looking for us. After we had split up in the main chamber, they had been caught in a serious firefight. Xuan had gone hand-to-hand with an Isopteran soldier, its mandibles taking a chunk out of her right arm, but Renata had acted quick, taking the thing out before patching her up as best as she could. James had burns on his left arm from an energy beam that had come too close, leaving him in pain; I could tell from the tight expression on his face. Most had damaged armor and burn marks on their gear, minor injuries from near misses, but all in all, we were okay.

We kept up a solid jog, our group moving as one, weapons ready, fingers resting on triggers.

"I got your samples," Leo said, handing Shelly the sling with the canisters in which she had stored the fungus. "They got the rest of your gear when they captured you, except for this."

"Thanks," she said, smiling at him. "Maybe we can figure out how this all works."

"You guys had quite a fight from the look of it," I said, then licked at my lips, feeling thirsty. James passed me a canteen of water on reflex.

"And we took a shit ton with us," he said, taking it back when I was done. "They may be many in number, and organized in a way, but damn, they are dumb as bricks."

"How so?"

Lance chimed in between breaths. "We set up several chokepoints—knocked down some rocks or pulled equipment into the path, and they just walked down the middle. When one died, they sent another, and another. If we'd had a fixed machine gun, we could have set it to fire in one place and walked off. So long as it had ammunition, it would have kept killing them."

"It's true, bruh," James said, and Leo nodded his agreement.

"Strength in numbers," Karianna mused. "That's one thing we don't have."

"Speaking of ammo," Xuan started, "we're a bit low. Hope we don't have to do what we did again."

Lance raised a fist at a fork in the road, and we paused. He peered left, then right, then nodded. We started jogging again. "This way. The path should take us back into the colony's main chamber for a minute but dump us out right next to the tunnel leading into the maze."

"So, we'll be exposed for a moment," I clarified.

Keeping up this pace wasn't easy. My heart pounded in my chest, and my clothes were soaked with sweat. I didn't know how long we could go before we'd all be exhausted.

"Yeah," Lance replied. "No other way we could find."

"Alright everyone, get ready to run all out. We've got some serious nasties on our tail."

"More soldiers?" Xuan asked.

"Worse," Shelly started. "We found their Queens. And let's just say, one of the things they seem to disagree about the most is how humans need to be handled."

"Handled?" James asked. "Why don't I like the sound of that?"

"Some want to eat us now, as we expected," Karianna told him. "Some want to eat us later, after we've, uh, had a few babies."

"What?" Leo's eyes went wide. "You serious?"

"Deadly serious," Shelly told him. "The last of the Queens, who sort of rescued us, wants to make a deal but required a human sacrifice to get started."

"And I was not going to be dinner," Karianna groaned.

Leo let out a long breath. "Sounds like a happy family. Remind me not to come to their thanksgiving. I might look delicious, but I don't want to be dessert."

"Ada would slap you for that stupid comment," Lance growled.

"We'll she's not here, is she?"

"Now we know the basics of their social hierarchy," Shelly went on. "Queens, drones, soldiers, workers. A few others. Some time back, one of their Queens forced a leap in their evolution. They called her the Diamond Queen, a kind of divine entity to them now. She gave them the ability to subjugate all sentient life on this planet. A mammalian species called the Prexal, who seemed to know how to use this fungus as technology, was among them. The Isoptera ate them to extinction and are a little sad that they did. They prefer meat, and so they ate and ate and ate until there were no more Prexal."

"And now they have a taste for humans?" James asked.

"Yes. But not just a taste. Humans have the right nutrient mix for their drones. If I am understanding it all, they believe these males having the right food will ensure that the next generations are stronger, smarter, faster, more evolved than they are now."

"Sure can't be any uglier," Karianna added.

James peered at her over his shoulder, eyebrows raised. "Preach."

"You should have seen them, Reed. You know how I feel about nature. They forced us to watch them crap out eggs the whole time. It was disgusting. It sounded wet, and sticky, and . . . ugh."

"That sounds horrible."

"It was."

"If you need to, eh, talk to someone about it later. I'm here. Want to borrow my breathing mask? Yours is gone. We can swap off."

She gave him a narrow-eyed look and pursed her lips. "No. It's got germs on it. I'm not all nasty like you."

"Whatever."

"It gets worse," Shelly continued.

"How?" Xuan asked.

"Nest is home to three Queens at least—there's the Red Queen, the Albino Queen, and the Black Queen. But SOL is host to the Gray Queen. That one possesses a fleet of star chasers, that's what they call their ships, and her mission is to harvest what is left of Earth, put them in suspension, and bring them back."

"Shit," James spat. "Sure we can't nuke them while we're here?"

I shook my head. "No. Not with a Foundry battleship overhead and its pilot somewhere on our ass. Our best bet is to get what we need and run like hell. Maybe we can stop the Gray Queen in SOL, but not the other three. Not today. Go that way, keep behind Lance. Heads down."

The idea of doing nothing pissed me off, but I saw no other options. Even if we hurled a rock at the planet on our way out, they would destroy it, and what wasn't destroyed would hardly affect their subterranean lives.

"Cut the chatter," Lance said, leading us up to an opening. "We're back. Look, through the towers, maybe a hundred feet, there's the tunnel. Idiots don't even have it guarded."

I sidled up next to him and gave him a slap on the shoulder. "Good job. We had no idea how to get out of there."

He shrugged. "I've got a good sense of direction."

"They're a little too confident," Renata said, eyeing the open road before us. "Or is this a trap?"

"Not a trap," Leo said.

"Do we make a run for it?" I asked, and everyone nodded.

Taking Shelly's hand, I turned to Lance. "Let's go."

As a group, we bolted from the opening and took off at a dead run, surprising the workers, forcing them to scurry off into the towers like startled cockroaches.

A quarter of the way to the tunnel, soldiers began to amass. Renata fired at them over her shoulder, forcing them back into cover. We weaved and bobbed, making it hard for any one of them to find a target, hopping over objects left by their retreating workers.

Renata's weapon made a clicking noise. "I'm out."

"Halfway," Lance called, raising his weapon to face a series of hungry soldiers who had leapt from a tower. He, James, and Xuan gifted them a series of rattling bursts from their SAGs, insectile bodies shredding apart, greenish-black fluid painting the exterior.

Shelly squeezed my prosthetic hand.

We crossed the final few feet, taking a few stragglers out as we went before the tunnel's darkness swallowed us.

"Where now?" Lance asked, spinning around, ready to hold off the enemy.

I closed my eyes, orienting myself to this place, my heart drawn ahead and to the left.

"It's this way," I wheezed. "We're almost there."

Karianna took a deep breath and started walking in that direction. "They don't like this maze, right?"

"No. They don't."

"Umm, anyone else curious why that might be? They may be stupid, okay, but they aren't weak. I can almost bet that this is not an irrational fear. They don't seem the type."

"I don't care why they don't like it," James said. "But if they don't like it, I freakin' love it."

"Whatever it is," I said. "We can handle it."

"Handle it," Karianna mused. "Yes, yes. Many termites. Handle it."

CHAPTER 12

Within the tunnel there came a clear demarcation, a change in the quality of the ground, the dirt here broken, less smooth, dark like crude oil covered in paths as old as crumbling parchment scrolls. The Isopteran soldiers that pursued us ceased their efforts, turning on their heels as air pressure gusted around us like it had been forced from a mythical titan's twisted lungs.

What had been wider openings, able to admit two or three workers abreast, choked down into a space wide enough for only one, maybe two if they were squeezed in tight. When I reached out my arms, fingertips brushed both sides. The space was dark and musty, cryptlike. Shelly, Karianna, and I held cloths over our noses and mouths, attempting not to breathe it in. The fungara was present here, but it looked different, the organic technology appearing dead. The impression of a maze was confirmed when we hit the first of the tunnel forks which branched off into four different directions, all of which did not follow the same geometric plane. One tunnel went up and to the left at a gentle slope, another to the right, one pushed ahead, while the final path plummeted nearly straight down.

We gathered as close to the hole as we could, but narrow as it was, most of us had to stand in the tunnel and wait.

"Any idea where to go?" Lance asked.

"Quiet," I replied, then sat on the floor and closed my eyes while they covered our backs.

Our group did as I asked with only a few grumbles. Within moments, it was so quiet I swore I could hear every heartbeat that pulsed in that cramped space.

Universe, show me the way. You opened this thought to my mind. Where do we go? You know the answer. We will protect life.

The ground vibrated gently, and I took a slow breath, trying my best not to choke on the stench. The back of my head began to tingle in a pleasant way, though I wasn't sure why. It made me relax.

A flash of light in the dark.

A line through twisting passages.

"The left one," I said, opening my eyes. I noticed then that Shelly had been playing with my hair, her fingers tickling at the back of my neck. "Felt good."

She smiled back at me in that shy way she did when she was caught being subtly mischievous. "Looked like you were having a hard time."

I clambered back onto my feet and dusted off my hands. "Let's go."

The tunnel narrowed, forcing us onto our hands and knees so that we could crawl through the maze. I tried not to think too hard, but it felt as if the entirety of Nest was pressing down on us. More than once we were forced to stop, remove our backpacks, then squeeze ourselves through spaces not much thicker than our bodies like a party of spelunkers.

I was at the front of our group in one of those squeezes, crawling toward what we hoped was freedom.

"Have I ever mentioned I don't like tight spaces?" James asked, his voice muffled by the tunnel walls and all the bodies. "I mean, I know I was raised on a starship and all, but at least we had spacious hallways."

"I don't like them either," Karianna echoed. "But nature? I like it even less."

"Yeah, nature sucks."

"And yet here we are," Leo said, grunting and groaning as he dragged his belly across the ground. "Blazing across the cosmos from one crisis to the next so that we can restore the natural order on Earth. A bit of irony there, don't you think?"

I paused for a moment, turning back to check on their progress. I couldn't see very far, but I could see James cock his head. Sweat was starting to pour from my forehead.

"That's different," he said.

Karianna chuffed. "Just because we might need mosquitos doesn't mean I have to like them."

I lay on my belly, dragging myself through an opening, mumbling under my breath a prayer that the other side was wider. It was not. Torrid gusts of air rushed over us at random intervals, carrying with them the burning stench of Nest's underworld.

Another fork, five different passages, each as twisty and gnarled as the branches of a live oak tree. We climbed down, went to the left, around to the right, then straight for some time, cycling between hands and knees and bellies. The air grew ever thicker, more pungent, thick with a sting of rot. It was as if death itself had died, and this was somehow worse. The tunnel floors were covered in discarded bits of termite chiton along with flaky layers of dried, whitish tissue. I tried my best to keep them out of my way, brushing them to the sides of the tunnel so the others didn't have to crawl over them. We made a rhythm of calling back to one another over implants every couple of minutes to ensure no one got stuck in a tight spot.

"Glad I ate my freakin' Wheaties this morning," Lance groaned, pulling himself through a gap between two rocks, his long beard catching on a jagged edge for an instant. "Damn, is this even wide enough for the termites?" He brushed his hair down before continuing.

"At one time, maybe," Shelly replied, her breathing labored. "This place feels—it feels old, very old. Maybe Isoptera were smaller before—before the Diamond Queen."

We crawled upward, or at least it felt that way, through a tunnel that had a kind of staircase. Much to my relief, it widened at the end, opening up into a hall. I burst onto the other side and wanted to kiss its putrid floor for the blessed freedom, then thought better of it.

"Come on everyone," I called back into the cramped tunnel. "There's space up here."

Having the ability to stand for the first time in almost an hour, I felt the need to stretch, my back and fingers crackling, before scanning the new space with a hand light Leo had given me. I could no longer touch the ceiling, which was nice, but the sensation that an entire planet was pressing down upon us was becoming oppressive. My lamp caught a twinkling of something reflective up ahead. I took a step forward, curious.

"Everything okay?" Shelly asked, appearing behind me as the rest of our group crawled out of the opening one by one.

I shook my head. "I don't know."

Another step into the dark tunnel, the angle of my light adjusting. I squinted.

"Here," Lance said, reaching into a pocket. With a crack, he tossed a chemical light ahead, the glowstick bright as a magnesium flare, blinding us for a moment. Disturbing shadows appeared along the walls, their lines and angles sharp.

My blood went cold at the sight. Shelly took hold of my hand.

Bodies littered the tunnel before us, mummified Isoptera by the dozens, many holding what I could only describe as crude weapons of stone or steel. Given their twisted postures, it was clear they'd been locked in a pitched battle. The Isoptera had torn at one another, stabbed each other with primitive weapons, some going so far as to self-inflict their fatal injuries.

From the look of it, a kind of fungus had sprung from their skin like alien parasites, forming rigid, arm-length tendrils of a slimy, greenish texture, the tips of some ends letting off a pale, bioluminescent glow. It was almost as if these growths had shot from their inside, splitting the termites apart as it had matured.

"No good," Xuan mused. "This a bad way to go. Kind of things that make spirits stick around forever."

I didn't know what to do other than to edge around the carnage, trying not to touch the potential biohazard.

"What made them do this?" James asked. "This isn't natural."

A good question. A question no one dared answer.

Shelly let out a cough, then another. She put a hand to her chest as if finding it hard to breathe. I went to her side to help her, and she shook it off.

"I'm fine," she whispered. "Place is messing with my allergies."

"But we don't have allergies," I said.

"Samples." She opened a canister, cutting one of the spikes free and closing it. "Proxy and I will analyze it later."

Lance eyed the sealed container. "Is it safe to bring something like that back?"

She shrugged. "I feel it's important."

The carnage we witnessed was not over. In fact, it got worse as the tunnel widened. There weren't just dozens who had died but hundreds upon hundreds in endless heaps of dusty rot. It became clear that this was the reason the Isoptera were afraid to come here. Whatever this fungus was, and it looked very much like the fungara, it had acted as a parasite, forcing them to fight one another and kill themselves.

Shelly coughed again, folding over as the toxic air assaulted her lungs. My hands went prickly with sweat.

"Here," Xuan said, removing her breathing mask and offering it to Shelly. "We trade for a while."

"No. It's dangerous. You need to be safe."

"So do you." Xuan slipped the mask over Shelly's face. She was not taking no for an answer, and I wasn't going to fight her over it.

We pressed on through winding tunnels littered with the dead. There were piles of discarded eggs, rotted but without growths, mounds of food stock and other equipment cast away as if suddenly unimportant.

This went on for what seemed forever, an endless procession of the insectile dead, a macabre tableau of murder and suicide and brutal force. A picture of anger and madness made manifest. I might have hated the Isoptera for who they were and what they did, but this was a gruesome way to go.

Lance elbowed Leo. "Is this enough inspiration for a painting?"

He shook his head. "I don't think I need this kind of inspiration."

Karianna hurried up beside me, her bracelets jingling. "Why is it not bothering us?" she whispered.

I patted my mechanical arm. "Protects the pilot."

"I guess, but the inoculant?"

A good question. Everyone had a level of protection from the Foundry, but why wasn't it working on this? How had whatever was present bypassed that biological defense? Was it not considered to be biological?

We had to move.

I picked up the pace, leading us through several more tunnels and switchbacks till we reached the edge of a large chamber. As I stepped into it, hand light extended, I scanned the room. This was it. Just like the black hole engine I had seen in my visions.

"We're in the nautilus room," I declared, taking a step within.

As I scanned the room with my light, I found it was made of dirt and stone and fungara like the rest of the maze, but with a few exceptions. Its overall shape was cut into a swirling, fractal pattern, like the inside of a marine creature's shell from Earth, its construction reaching up toward the surface in a thirty-meter-high dome. For a moment, it felt as if we were standing within an artist's representation of an ancient cephalopod. It was expansive and mostly empty, other than a sort of bench running along the circumference of the room, shadowboxes set every two to three feet above it, each containing peculiar non-Isopteran items behind sheets of clear glass. What fungara was present gave off a soft glow, though it did little more in the dark than to draw attention to its presence while outlining the room's edges.

I brought my light down to the center of the room and a glint of gold and silver shone back.

"So, this is the nautilus shell." James whistled. "Holy shit, Milo, you keep getting it right. It's so weird, not that I doubted you. Not exactly. Okay . . . maybe I did a little."

"How?" Shelly mused. "How does it look like something so Earth-like, and yet, so very alien."

Leo raised a finger to speak but remained silent.

As I edged toward the middle of the chamber, I nearly tripped over a pair of Isoptera who lay in my way, their tattered robes impaled by spears. A length of metal stuck from one of their heads, its edge glinting in the lamplight. I imagined these two were like the mythical guards who stood watch over the Holy Grail, waiting deep within a dark chamber beyond deadly traps and perilous danger, hoping one day someone might try to take their prize if only so they could prove their life had purpose.

A crash came from over my left shoulder, loud enough to wake the dead. I spun around to face it, raising my fists before me, preparing to fight, my heart thumping in my chest. Lance moved in, his SAG's barrel pointed at the disturbance, Renata at his side, the pair's jaws hard set, fingers twitching just over the trigger. Then they relaxed.

Leo crouched at the edge of the chamber with a sheepish look on his face, focused on a set of bodies that had fallen over. Their rusty equipment was now piled on the floor, bits of scrap coming to a rest.

"Sorry," he said, stepping back. "Just got curious."

"Fucking shit," Lance grumbled, and put his weapon down.

James squeezed the bearded man's shoulders and he shrugged it off. "Calm down, bruh. You're so tense."

"It's here," I told the group, drawing us back to the stone plinth, doing everything I could to ignore the prickles of shock still running over my body. "It's here."

I reached out to touch the golden disc on the right, its diameter twelve inches in all, its smooth side facing up. My fingers explored its etched lines and symbols, its many wave forms, boxes, and bits of mathematical language. It was amazing to think how far this had traveled. Long before the FICSE mission, *Voyager 1* and *2* were the most distant objects from Earth made by humankind. They had penetrated the Oort cloud and were delving the reaches of the interstellar medium. Somehow, their radioelectric generators and early spaceflight equipment had continued to operate decades past their expected mission period. Both were launched in 1977 and yet were in near full operation past the fifty-year mark, with the occasional signal being beamed back to Earth as late as 2031. This golden disc of theirs had been a hope to communicate with higher beings, a set of instructions that we could use to find common language. It had sounds and music and knowledge etched into its gold-plated copper so that it would last for a billion years. Had whoever recovered this understood our meager attempts at communicating? Deciphered the information upon it? And where was it that the probes themselves had gone?

This was a moment of history, one that might be remembered for all eternity if only we survived. A moment worth remembering.

Of all the markings on the surface of the golden disc, a convergence of fifteen lines on its bottom left caught my attention the most. Some were mostly straight, while there were others with bumps and markings. Frequencies.

"It's so small," Shelly said, looking over my shoulder, her eyes wild with wonder. "And yet, so important."

Our group began to crowd the plinth, everyone squeezing in close so they could get a good look.

"This is what we came for?" James mused. "This is the record?"

"Pulsar map," Shelly explained, fingers brushing at the edge of the markings. "With Proxy's help, we can use these lines to determine the general location of our sun. Pulsars have specific signatures, times at which they release bursts of energy. We can triangulate the location of our system with that data and go home."

Home. What a strange word. What did that even mean to us now? The *Vasco Da Gama* had been home. Novae had been home. The *Transcendence* was home. I was starting to think home was just some way to describe where my stuff, along with the people I love, was kept.

"And we didn't have this information on the ship?" Lance cut in.

I shook my head. "No. The Foundry deleted it from our data storage. It didn't want us getting back so easily."

"Suspect."

"Let's take some pictures with our hand terminals before we move it. Xuan, do you have the steel sleeve?"

She nodded, then coughed under her breath, the sound thick with mucus. "Yes, Captain."

"You okay?" I asked.

"Just a little tickle in my throat."

Everyone in the group removed their hand terminals and took a picture of the disc before we slipped it into its padded sleeve. There was no telling what might happen next, but if at least one of us made it out with a copy, we should be able to get home.

"I take good care of it," Xuan said as I slipped it into her backpack. "Guard with my life."

"I know you will."

"Uhh," James started, "what in the hell is this other thing?"

I turned back toward the plinth, my stomach twisting at what remained. It had been there all along, sure, but I hadn't wanted to acknowledge its presence. Part of me hoped I didn't feel its call, hoped that I could leave it here, but it was the missing piece to a bigger puzzle.

I stared at the strange, geometric shape that floated beside the dusty impression of where the disc had been, a twenty-sided polyhedron made of dark metal as wide and as tall as my forearm was long. The device was angular and anything but smooth, its many surfaces covered in a scrawl of lines and symbols, though with no clear way to determine its manufacture. From the look of it, the object was heavy, and not with a mere physical weight. It possessed a supermassive black hole of decision, a fork in the cosmic road, a choice in wait.

Unlike the others in our group, I had a general idea what this was, and of the terrible things it might do, from my brief encounter with the

Universe. It had wanted me to know of its existence, but had given me an implicit warning about it.

"What is that?" Lance asked, taking a step forward, hands reaching to pick it up.

I moved between him and the object, stalling his advance. "I'm not sure. But . . . yeah . . . I think we need to take it with us."

Leo's eyebrows raised, his head cocking to the side. "You serious, man? Take it with us? Something about that thing gives me the creeps. Anyone else with me on that?"

"What if it's a weapon?" Renata pressed. "A bomb?"

"I don't know what it is," I said, "but I can't shake the feeling we might need it at some point."

"Bruh." James gestured to the Isoptera by our feet who had impaled one another. "What if that's the thing that did all this? This alien tech does some crazy-ass shit sometimes."

"It isn't," Karianna said, and slapped him on the back of the head with her fleshy hand.

"Hey! What was that for?"

"For being a fucking idiot."

"An idiot?"

"Are you sure?" Shelly took hold of my mechanical arm before laying her head on my shoulder. Even out of the corner of my eye it was clear her face was turning pale. Time never seemed to be on our side. "It could be dangerous."

"I know." I removed the object from the plinth, its metallic surface cool to the touch. To my surprise, it felt as if it weighed nothing, as if it were empty, just a foam prop on a movie set painted to appear foreboding. "I could use a backpack since I lost mine. I'll carry it out."

"No," Lance said, turning around. "Put it in mine. We'll pack it with some ration sleeves so it won't wiggle around. You worry about getting us out. I'll worry about this thing being radioactive and killing me."

"Okay," I said, slipping it into his backpack and securing it. "I don't think it is."

"Did we get what we came for?"

"Yeah. We got what we came for. Time to go."

"Do we have to leave the same way?" Karianna peered back toward the dark tunnel we had entered, a worried fist pressed against her chin. "I don't like that way."

I narrowed my eyes at the far wall, recalling my visions. "No need. We've got an easier way out."

CHAPTER 13

We left the nautilus chamber behind, exiting through a tunnel on the far wall. I led our group with a kind of forced bravado, having little more than a strong impression to guide us, the details sketchy at best, visions shrouded with few if any memory markers.

Dark paths wound within the planet for what felt like hours, my confidence waning like a dying star. The bodies of murdered Isoptera hindered us for a time, but that soon began to lessen. Whatever had caused this event, we started seeing less of its effect. Unmasked and unprotected, Karianna and I were unaffected. The freak part of us was keeping us safe like it was designed to do, but Shelly and Xuan? They didn't have that kind of protection.

Shelly had to stop several times to cough, so intensely she could hardly stand. She leaned against the tunnel wall, her body trembling, sputum dribbling off her lips. I was powerless and broken, unable to help. Xuan had been sharing a breathing mask with her, trying to be a team player, to help out a friend, but all this meant was that she too was starting to have respiratory distress. Neither was breathing well. Their lungs sounded as if they had been replaced by a collection of dry, crinkly plastic.

We had the golden disc, yes, but if I lost Shelly in exchange . . . what was the point?

Blessed light began to blossom from up ahead of us, and the tunnel widened, swelling to as large as the original entrance to the mountain. On either flank came the rush of water, a hidden set of streams feeding from somewhere underground, meeting with a series of frothy, open channels that led out of sight.

We emerged from the maze back onto the surface of Nest, our group standing upon a vista hundreds of feet above a narrow valley nestled between two mountains with a lake positioned at the center of the basin. Nothing more than a carpet of leaves with a smudge of water at its edge was visible for miles. The weather hadn't improved on the surface from when we descended. The sky was a ceiling made of low-lying, charcoal-gray and white clouds, though there was no precipitation for now.

A mild relief washed over me. I had led us out, though likely it had been on instinct rather than with magic space meditation.

"Would have been nice to know this was here," Lance commented, arms akimbo. "The hell, man?"

"I don't think we could have scaled it," Karianna said, tiptoeing her way to the edge of the cliff, bracelets jingling as she leaned on her haunches. "That's a long-ass way down."

I raised a hand to my ear, not for function, but to signal to the group what I was doing. Shelly looked to me, but her eyes were unfocused, pupils dilated.

"Proxy?" I called out with my implants now that they were free of interference.

"Milo," it immediately replied. *"You are alive! We are pleased."*

"I am. We are. And so are the rest of us, though we have a medical emergency and I'm freaking out a little. We found an exit."

"I have you. I am hidden in a forest a hundred kilometers to the north of your position. What kind of medical emergency?"

"Some sort of invasive fungus has gotten into Shelly and Xuan. They can hardly breathe. They're looking pale."

"I understand. I will reconfigure some of the nanomachines in the shuttle to form suspension caskets to keep them safe in the near term. We can take a better look at their condition aboard the Transcendence.*"*

"Thanks. Can you pick us up?"

"Not from the cliff you stand upon. The rock overhangs are too perilous for the Swift Shuttle to approach. The Isoptera are also aware you are here. They are searching the area. We must dust off quickly."

"Where to then? Where do we meet?"

"Look east of the mountains through the valley. Do you see an opening a few hundred feet across?"

I narrowed my eyes and nodded at the distant brush of color. *"I do."*

"Can you make it?"

"I think so."

Karianna turned to look at me, her face twisted in an uneasy expression. "We need to go down, don't we?"

"Yeah." I pointed. "There."

"Fun."

Shelly let out another series of chest-rattling coughs, holding one hand over her mouth. Her eyes were watering. As she finished, pulling her hand free, blood stained her palm. She tried to hide this detail from the group by wiping it off on the back of her pants, but I had seen it.

"How do we get down?" I asked my copilot.

"You're not going to like it," she replied, then pointed at the streams of water beside us. "Though I have to say, it will be quick."

"Is it safe?" Leo asked.

"Looks safe enough. I can see how it twists around and ends up somewhere at the bottom. Water looks clear. So long as there isn't some sort of machinery along the way."

"Let's toss a pack down first," Lance suggested. "We'll put a spare hand terminal in it. If it reaches the bottom, at least we'll know there's nothing big enough to slice us up."

Renata removed her pack and went over, grabbing a few items before tossing it down the rushing channel of water. The pack vanished. We waited a couple of minutes, then pinged the terminal. It pinged back.

"Good enough for me!" Karianna cheered, and without hesitation hopped into the channel feet first. Frothy bubbles of white water surrounded her, soaking her clothes. She shot over the edge of the mountain, vanishing from sight.

Through our implants, I knew that she was alive, if a bit more excited than normal given her racing heart. After about a minute, she called back.

"Okay," she reported. *"That was . . . Yuck. Next up."*

"Is it safe?" I asked.

"Yeah, it's safe, but you might want to spread out your arms and legs to slow you down, it's fast as hell. Pretty sure it's like an aqueduct or a treatment center of some

kind, shoots out into a pool where the water . . . well . . . they process stuff or . . . you'll see."

I turned to face the group. "Alright everyone, one at a time. Try and slow yourself down."

A queue formed before the slide.

"Be quick about it," Karianna called. *"I see soldiers, but they don't see me, not yet. Send guns first."*

"Soldiers," I said aloud, and Lance cut in line, spinning his overstuffed backpack around so that it sat on his chest.

"Yippee," he said, holding back his enthusiasm. "More bugs to squash." He sat down in the channel and pushed off.

James went next, then Leo, then Xuan.

I faced Shelly and brushed the spittle from her bottom lip with my thumb. "Your turn, love."

She shivered as if struck by an acute chill, her attention focused on nothing. I sat her down in the water and laid her hands across her chest.

"Be careful," I whispered, but she didn't reply. The rushing waters took her.

"I've got the rear," Renata said, signaling with her weapon for me to go. "Okay."

I took a deep breath, lowering myself into the cool, churning waters. The channel was smoother than I had expected, worked from some kind of stone made slick through time like river rock. From this vantage I could see everything in the expansive valley hundreds of feet below. The slide pitched itself off the edge of the cliff, looking as if this would send me careening into open air.

A vivid childhood memory surfaced as I settled into place, one in which I had pestered my parents to go to a waterpark. Big Maui? The Kahuna? Some Polynesian rip off. What I remembered about it was that the park boasted of massive waterslides designed to thrill all who came with their many twists and turns and drops, capable of taking your breath away. I wanted to go so badly, but every time I asked Dad if we could, begging and pleading, he would brush the matter aside by saying we didn't have the money. And then some random day when I asked, his story changed. He started telling me that the place had been shut down because its rides were so intense that some kid had been killed on one of them. Something about the viscosity of the slide and how one of the angles had been designed incorrectly. The kid had hopped into the opening, then gone careening off into the sky and had landed in the parking lot, where they'd broken their back and died. It was for this reason that I never went to a water park in real life or even in a virtual environment. The innocuous story to get me to shut up had left me with a potentially unfounded fear, one strong enough to make me sweat when I thought of it.

"Are you going?" Renata pressed.

Another deep breath. "I'm going," I said, pushing off.

I shot off down the open channel like a human bobsled pushed by a rocket, finding it impossible to say in what directions the slide twisted and turned, but I could sure as hell say it wasn't straight. My stomach dropped as if I had fallen from orbit, fingers tingling, head spinning. One moment I leaned to the right, the next, to the left, my temple slapping at the sides of the channel. I spread out my arms and legs as Karianna had instructed to slow my descent, but this had little more effect than to make me spin around in circles.

My feet faced sky, then I was sideways, the slide too small to fit my body. Three times the channel hit such an angle that I expected myself to go flying over the edge into open sky, but then came back to center.

The valley swelled. The slide straightened out.

I was hurled unceremoniously from its terminus into a brackish, fetid pool heaped with decaying biomass. While the water above had been clean, that was not the case here. Out of reflex, I very nearly puked up my guts as I treaded through piles of dead Isoptera and other creatures I thought best not to identify. My feet could not touch the bottom, and there was a pull, a current sucking me under. I fought against it and moved toward my party who waited for me.

"Here," Karianna said, offering a hand to pull me out. "I told you it was nasty."

Putrid fluids dripped off my wet clothes, chunks and hard bits sloughing off of my gear and onto the jungle floor. "Nasty."

"Which way?" Lance asked, pointing off to the left. "That way?"

I nodded at him while shaking my legs vigorously, attempting to get as much of the decaying biomaterial off of me as I could. "Yeah. That's it."

Shelly looked up at me, her face pained, hand against her chest. I threw one of her arms over my shoulder so we could walk together.

As soon as Renata made it down the slide, we shambled off in the direction of the clearing. Our group spread out in an arc, those still armed near the front. The foliage was thicker than it had been near our initial landing site, and it made the trip slow going. Sticky vines tried to take hold of our boots while other growths blocked our way. Karianna wielded a machete Renata had brought, and using the strength of her prosthetic made quick work of the plants. After close to an hour of grueling progress, we burst out onto a trail that led in the general direction of the clearing.

A rustling came from up the path, and out of the jungle a group of Isoptera appeared.

"Company!" Lance shouted, then took a knee, firing before they had a chance to respond. Bullets ripped into the Isopteran squad, taking two of them out. The remaining soldiers shot back.

We ran. The clearing was just a few hundred feet ahead of us.

"I'm out," Renata called, letting her weapon fall limp on her strap. "No more clips."

James echoed her, "Me too."

Lance let out another burst and his weapon clicked. "Shit."

"Move, move, move," Karianna said, pulling at James's backpack straps. "Not coming back for you."

"Okay, okay," he said. "I don't want to be eaten anyways."

By now I was nearly carrying Shelly. Lance and Renata were helping Xuan limp ahead.

We approached the clearing. The jungle burst wide, permitting angry skies to gaze upon us. Bolts of energy weapons whizzed past, catching sections of the jungle on fire, one shot catching James's pants, narrowly missing his leg. He fell to the ground, rolled over to put the flames out, and sprang back up. We were out in the open and had nowhere to go, nowhere to hide.

"Get down!" Lance ordered, and we followed his direction.

Energy bolts whizzed overhead; our group was trapped. We were dangerously low on ammunition, there was no cover to be had, and two of us couldn't move without help.

Karianna looked to me from where she lay on her belly, her eyes wide, fear vibrating them in their sockets. I could only imagine this was what her face had looked like the day the Starfish overwhelmed us in orbit above

Novae. She kept up a good front most days, with her jokes and bullish attitude, but she was no less afraid than the rest of us.

James took a shot, catching one of the Isoptera in the head. Lance dug through Xuan's backpack and found another clip, joining the fight. We were down to just a few dozen bullets at most, but that wouldn't hold them off for long.

The enemy closed in on us, the collective sound of their clicking shouts like a swarm of angry cicadas.

There came a metallic *click, click, click.*

A whine sounded from the distance.

"Shit," James growled. "I'm out."

Lance reached for a long knife strapped to his leg, turning it around in his hand, ready to fight.

The Swift Shuttle came dropping out of the cloud cover like an angry falcon, airfoils extended, engines screaming, dust kicking up around it in a whirlwind. The Isoptera paused in their pursuit, not sure where to place their attention. Proxy did not wait for an order to assist but turned the shuttle's weapons toward those pursuing and opened fire. Energy bolts ripped through the jungle at our rear, tearing open a gash of green and red, those Isoptera not quick enough to flee bursting into flames.

We didn't stand by and marvel at this destruction, except maybe James, but sprang up and rushed to the landing shuttle, its hatch already opening.

"Aren't you a sight for sore eyes," Lance said, slapping its hull before helping the others board.

Once Shelly and Xuan were secure in the suspension caskets, I dove into the Star Sphere, only having had time to remove my shirt. The crew buckled up. Lance gave the all-clear.

"Hang on," I said as soon as my virtual interface sprang to life.

The Swift Shuttle shot skyward, slamming the crew back in their acceleration chairs. For once, they did not complain or argue about it. Everyone knew we had to get the hell out of here, and fast. We rushed through layers of clouds, turbulent atmosphere and walls of moisture rocking the hull of the shuttle, my vision awash with monochrome.

Everything went black. Then white. Then we burst onto the other side of the chaos, breaking free of the planet's atmosphere.

"Foundry ship inbound," Proxy reported over the shuttle-wide channel. *"Fifteen thousand kilometers and closing."*

"Try not to pass out," I said, ramping up our acceleration.

The Isopteran battleship turned in our direction, a monolith in pursuit, but we were too quick. Their ship might have been powerful, but we were nimble. After several minutes of heavy acceleration, I backed off, realizing that they couldn't catch us. Relief flooded me. My body felt ready to collapse.

Next stop, the *Transcendence.*

Time to get Shelly medical attention.

Time to go home.

CHAPTER 14

We raced back to the *Transcendence*, avoiding patrols and staying ahead of the Isoptera's Foundry-made battleship. Proxy kept both Shelly and Xuan in stasis so their conditions wouldn't worsen, but we knew at some point they would have to be revived to treat whatever this was.

It took several days to make the crossing in our Swift Shuttles, which gave me far too much time to think, too much time to consider the possible outcomes.

What if I lost Shelly to this infection?

She would have been just fine if she had stayed on the ship. Why hadn't she?

Who was I without her?

I was a shell.

Ada, Chevelle, Dante, and Emilia waited for us in the docking bay along with Proxy, ready to assist. Proxy had done its job, preparing an advanced medical suite near the forward end. Chinchillette and it had searched their databanks for anything related to this condition, even pinged some nearby Foundry networks for additional information, and had gotten nothing concrete. Frelo kept their distance, not sure what to think. Lance had drilled them with questions, but the Jevox had reminded us Isoptera were a this-side-of-the-gate issue, and their people knew nothing of them. Hy was frozen with fear, his hands shaking, mouth covered as he incessantly paced. For such a carefree individual, I'd never seen him so scared. I knew the feeling.

"Where are the samples?" Ada asked, and Leo started digging through their backpacks.

"Make sure you're in a cleanroom," he told her. "Get buttoned up first, don't want to breathe it in."

Ada took the canisters. "Okay. I will. I could use some help working them, mind pitching in? I'll be damned if I'm losing two of my best friends."

He tipped his head while pantomiming the action of rolling up his sleeves. "I'm all yours. Lead the way."

They left us to tend to the sick.

Karianna went to her Star Sphere to get us underway. We needed to put distance between us and the enemy, no matter our situation. I knew this would overtax her, piloting the ship alone for a time, but I felt she could do enough to get us to a safe distance.

The suspension caskets were wheeled into a sealed, ten-by-ten-meter glass box of an infirmary room, its interior walls covered in cabinets and equipment I knew little about. Chevelle instructed me to put on a clean suit so I could enter. The suspension caskets were parked into the middle of the room beside Dante and Emilia, lights within the space shifting from white to pale blue to ultraviolet.

"Antimicrobial," Chevelle told me through her plastic hood. "Case there's somethink else the universal inoculant can't handle."

I nodded, my white clean-suit glowing purple.

"Proxy? Got us a drip?"

Proxy appeared on a stool to the left of the caskets. "We do not know the specifics of this fungus, but using our best information we have created an antifungal that will help to slow its progress. We are ready to push it through their bloodstreams. Ada and Leo should have more information for us soon."

"Should we just wait?" I asked. "Wait until we have a perfect match?"

"Wish we could," Chevelle said, pointing to Shelly through the window of her casket. "Reefer box 'ere helps, but it's still growin' up in there. Dis is peak, bruv. Got to move."

"Okay," I said, swallowing. "Fine."

The suspension caskets made a series of hissing and whining noises, then began to open, their lids sliding away to reveal my precious wife and our dear friend.

Chevelle tapped a series of invisible controls before her in the air. A set of robotic arms came out of the ceiling, removing the lids and setting them to the side. Once those were free, a pair of tubes snaked down and came to rest near the sides of the caskets. Peering down at Shelly in that chilly metal box made my heart sink. She was pale, her skin the color of snow. Her cheeks had a slight brownish-green tinge, as well as a texture that hadn't been there before. She appeared to be growing a thin layer of facial hair, like a five 'o clock shadow, but I knew it wasn't stubble. It was the parasite, plain and simple, pushing itself through her epidermis one thread at a time, working to break free.

Dante and Emilia took positions on the sides of the room, monitoring vital signs while keeping an array of shots ready. I hoped they had better medical training than I. I hardly knew how to treat a scraped knee, or frostbite.

"I'll get Shelly," Chevelle told me, putting a hand on my shoulder, "you take Xuan."

"Okay." I swapped places with the south Londoner and reached for the tube hanging beside Xuan. Out of the corner of my eye, I could see Hy pressed up against the window. "What do I do?"

"Place it near the left arm," Proxy said. "The probe will tell you when you are near a vein large enough to work."

Taking hold of the tube with thumb and forefinger, I followed Proxy's instructions. Its tip was pale white but began to glow red as I approached her arm. I wasn't the best with anatomy, but I had studied enough to know that major veins tended to run along the inside of the forearm. In the purple glow of the infirmary, I was able to see a dark line running from the inside of her elbow to the wrist. The probe responded as I came close, glowing brighter, then blinking.

"That it?" I asked.

It nodded. "Gently tap it to her skin. The probe will thread the vein."

And it did just that. Something tiny reached out of its end and pierced her skin, then drew itself close and settled into place. The tube changed colors as it filled with medicine. Under the ultraviolet light, it was impossible to say what shade the fluid was, not that it mattered. Stress makes you focus on strange details.

"How's Shelly?" I asked Chevelle, leaving Xuan to her medical drip. "Did it work?"

Chevelle raised her open hands. "She's being given the medicine."

"What now?"

"We wait. Treat symptoms."

"What? There's nothing else we can do? Come on, there has to be."

"No," Proxy said. "If the suspension had fully halted the fungal growth, we could have waited for the lab results. As it is, we must hope this stops or slows the process. I am sorry, Milo."

"Shelly?" I leaned close to her face, her hand clutched in mine. "Are you in there?"

I waited, and I hoped, but my love did not respond.

"The human body may enter this state when it is this distressed," Proxy went on. "They are not in a coma, far as we can tell. But they are sleeping very deeply. Their bodies are fighting the fungus. So is the universal inoculant living in their blood. It is hard to say who the winner will be."

I took a seat on one of the stools and rested my hooded face in my hands, plastic screen against plastic-covered fingers. This was far worse than when Bellamy had found me half dead on that icy planetoid. I was only looking at losing a hand there, maybe a foot. But whatever this parasitic fungus was, it intended to burst forth from their bodies, killing them before spreading its spores to the rest of us. Whatever it was, it was malicious, and angry, and hateful. Was this a natural fungara response, or something else?

"Their vitals are steady," Dante reported. "This seems to be helping for the time being."

I rolled the stool up beside Shelly. "Universe," I whispered, "don't let her go. It's not time yet. Please . . . Please . . ."

I spent three days sitting by her side in the infirmary, holding her hand, hoping for her to wake up. Hy remained outside the glass, waiting for a change in condition, but slept very little, just like me. Often times Lance, to my surprise, could be found pacing up and down the halls of the ship, frantically combing his beard or playing with his hand terminal while muttering to himself. James tried several times to calm him down, but the two got into fights, and so he gave up. I understood Hy being so upset, but Lance? I didn't think I'd ever seen him like this. He was almost as nervous as I was. Why?

The Foundry machines and drugs were hard at work, attempting to purge the fungus from their systems, but it appeared that Shelly's and my suspicions had been right. This fungara was its own type of nanomachines, fighting against the Foundry's inoculant in their blood as a worthy rival.

Time dragged on.

No sleep.

No food.

I was becoming as weak and as frail as Shelly. She had lost a good ten pounds since being returned to the ship. When I asked Proxy if she would make it, it did not have a solid answer, much as I knew it wanted to give me good news.

Chevelle came in one afternoon, took my hand, then patted me on the cheek. "I got this, bruv. Don't vex me. Get some rest. She going no place."

"But I can't leave her."

"You no eat and get rest, you leave her anyway. If not in real life, then in your mind." She tapped her head.

I let out a sigh and closed my eyes.

"Is okay. Call you if she comes round."

I squeezed Shelly's hand, the clean suit's plastic crinkling, and nodded. "Fine."

CHAPTER 15

Despite knowing she was in good hands, leaving her in the infirmary was hard. Chevelle was right, even if I didn't like it, I was brittle, and if I were to be of any good to her or anyone else, I needed to get back my strength.

As I made for one of the ship's galleys, Karianna spotted me in the hall. She waved an uncertain hand. "Where you off to?"

"Food, I guess."

"Can I join you?"

"I don't think I'll be good company."

"That's okay." Her face twisted, eyes narrowed, expression tense. "If I need to just sit and be quiet for you, I can do that."

I did not protest.

We entered the galley and went to the counter on the far wall, next to the stove and sink. There were shelves with boxes of food and bottles, ingredients for cooking, as well as a selection of wine, hard liquor, and soda. Karianna rifled through the cabinets looking for something to snack on but didn't seem to be interested in anything substantial. She settled on some bite-sized powdered donuts before pulling a short cup of coffee from a machine at the end of the counter.

I wasn't in the mood to cook anything, but I knew I needed something solid.

"I need something comforting," I thought, and Proxy heard.

"I know just the thing," it replied.

A bowl materialized before me on the counter, nanomachines somehow forming into a complex collection of consumables. I had no idea how the Foundry pulled off this little trick, but it had been doing it for us since day one—offering cookies, coffee, wine, and more. It could take our memories, our ideas, and make food nearly indistinguishable from what we might have enjoyed on Earth.

The bowl itself was made of a glossy ceramic, an earthy dark green and brown that knitted itself from bottom to top. It filled with a thick, brownish stew of pork, black beans, and rice. I leaned over the dish and took a deep breath. It smelled hearty and satisfying. It smelled like home.

"What's that called?" Karianna asked, popping another donut in her mouth.

"Feijoada. It's a Brazilian dish. One of the last messages Mom sent from Novae had a recipe attached. She said it's a lot like my grandmother's. Thought I'd give it a try."

"Proxy?" Karianna called, then beside her, a bowl of her own began to appear. "Thanks. Looks great. All I'm eating is junk anyways." She set the donuts to the side and took hold of her bowl. "Let's sit."

We grabbed our food and found a table with two benches, taking seats across from one another.

Despite the fact that its smell summoned my appetite even in this darkened mood, I approached the meal with caution. It had been days since I'd eaten more than a couple bites of anything. I wasn't interested in puking it all back up.

One bite.

Two bites.

Three.

Wait.

I ate without much joy until the warmth of the dish began to fill me from the belly out. It made me think of Mom, of what she might have been feeling when she ate this. It made me think of Dad, about how he never got to have this particular recipe, but then again, what else had he gotten to try before we left Earth? *Minha avó* had loved to cook, and he had loved to eat.

It was weird, that even though we'd had such a challenging life together, I missed my parents terribly. When I was a kid, I was so angry for what they did, how absent they had been, how they had taken me away from all I had known, but as I had aged, I realized that they were just doing what they thought best at the time. If we had stayed back on Earth, there was no telling if we would have lived. Out here, we at least had a chance to make a difference, and a difference we had made. And yet, I had just wanted to be a kid. I had just wanted a normal life. But did anyone ever really get that choice? Besides . . . what the hell is normal, anyway?

Either way, they had loved me, and that was all that mattered. It just took half their lives to say it in a way I understood.

"You in there?" Karianna asked after several minutes of silence. "You look like you're a million miles away."

I took a bite of my feijoada, a spoonful of broth and beans, then sighed. "Lost in my head."

Karianna pursed her lips and nodded. "Plenty of opportunity to do that out here." She scarfed down the rest of her food, let out a satisfied "ahh," then came around the table to sit beside me.

I gave her a curious look but kept eating.

She said nothing, just leaned on her arms, staring off into the distance.

"You ever think about how fragile all this is?" I asked after some time, breaking the silence. "Life. Existence."

Karianna swallowed. "Maybe too much. Good moments are fleeting, you know? Here and gone. But that's maybe good news too for the bad ones. They pass."

"Maybe. But they come with baggage. They stick with you forever." I pushed my bowl away, then pinched the bridge of my nose and felt my eyes water. "Your dad, my dad, Shelly's dad. They're all gone. Mom is gone too, and not because of anything terrible, but just life. I lost my best friend, Esteban, a brother of mine, if only by circumstance. Some were claimed by time, as we all will be, but the others . . . terrible events. I'm not sure one group of people is meant for so much tragedy.

"We came out here to save Earth, and we've lost so many people. Potential snuffed out. Dreams not realized. Some days it makes me feel so lonely I want to quit, finding my heart adrift in an endless sea of despair, weak and powerless, not sure what to do. I relied on all of them for strength, for wisdom. Now . . . everyone comes to me for that same strength. If Shelly goes to meet them, I don't know what I'll do. She is my rock, my pillar. She holds me up. And I put her in danger. It's my fault. Her condition is my fault."

Karianna sidled up to me and took hold of my arm, squeezing. I did not fight her off. I had to be honest that in the moment, it felt good to have human comfort, as fragile as I was. The warmth of her concern penetrated me to the core. I closed my eyes and reached an arm around her. She folded into me, and we held tight to one another with a sort of desperation, her head resting on my shoulder.

"I feel your pain, Milo," she whispered. "I feel your uncertainty and fears in the interface. I don't want to be alone either. I don't know where to go, or what to do sometimes. But not all is bad. The mission didn't end as it was supposed to, no, but we saved humanity. Novae will carry on in secret. And your parents, I know they would be proud of you. You are doing the best you can given what information you have. It's all any of us can do."

I sniffled and drew her closer, muscles aching with a kind of stored-up sorrow like all my emotional pains were wrapped around these fibers and were squeezing the life out of me.

"The universe is so empty," I went on. "And yet, there's so much out there. The gulf between my heart and those I've loved and lost is so vast, so . . . terrifying. Empty."

"Are you sure they are so far away? Because I, for one, believe that they live inside you."

"Just memories. Nothing more. Photographs in my head. Films stuck on repeat."

"No. No. I think it's more than that." She began rubbing my leg with her fingertips. "It's more than that."

We remained there for some time, holding one another, my body stiff as a board, her hand brushing the top of my leg in a soothing motion. I promised myself I wouldn't cry, not today, because if I shed even a single tear, my body might shatter into a million shards of glass that could never be glued back together.

"Shelly is strong," Karianna told me after some time. "She'll make it. So will Xuan."

I licked my dry lips. "I want to believe. I really do."

"We all do. Just know, I feel your pain in my heart. I share your sorrows."

And this was true on more than one level. She was the only person in the universe who truly understood how I felt. When we were connected to the ship, existing within the integration, our emotions blended in such a way that they became one. This was both terrifying and comforting. Part of me felt that the connection was starting to extend beyond the ship, an intuition born of emotional intimacy. It made things weird sometimes, as I wished Shelly and I shared the same connection, but we were freaks together.

"Come on," Karianna said, letting go of me to stand. "Let's go check on Shelly."

Stepping away for a moment had done me some good, allowing me to think more clearly. I checked in with Ada and Leo, who feverishly analyzed the fungara samples. The lab was full of empty coffee mugs and packets of chemical stimulants. They were making progress, not wasting any time, but were not moving as quickly as any of us would have liked. Ada was determined not to give up. She was picking apart every thread of an idea she could for any bit of truth, any solution.

"I will figure this out," she told me, her face hard as stone. "We aren't letting her die."

Shelly and Xuan's conditions had not improved, even with the antifungal drip. Proxy was adjusting it as best it could, trying new variations, but was afraid of pushing their systems too hard and sending them into shock. The tiny hairs on their skin had multiplied, now covering most of their faces and part of their arms. Time was running out and we all knew it. Did we have hours? Days? Weeks?

Though Proxy did not show emotion, I could see its frustration over its impotence. But what could it do to help? It couldn't cure this alone.

We removed them from the caskets to make them more comfortable, transferring them onto beds. The hard surfaces inside the boxes had started to give them sores on their backs, and so Dante and Emilia were turning them regularly to prevent the sores from forming. I remained at Shelly's side, not moving but for the brief time it took for me to get a snack or use the facilities outside the cleanroom. Sleep had become almost nonexistent, forcing me into a state of nightmarish disassociation where I was unsure of time or day. When I lay down beside her and drifted off, any tiny movement or cough would wake me. She coughed a lot.

The drip kept running.

The machines kept beeping.

The fungara kept expanding.

The two had become gaunt, sickly, their faces sunken, skin covered in flakes of brown and green. A hard stem had started growing from Xuan's right shin, the skin around it pink from infection.

We cruised away from Nest, time becoming inconsequential. Every moment became the most important moment of my life, the only moment that existed.

James took a seat beside us, suited up in cleanroom gear, expression slack, face ashen through the plastic window on its headpiece. He put a hand on my shoulder and squeezed.

"How you holding up?"

I didn't have the energy to respond. I was a ten-thousand-pound figure suspended by the tiniest of fraying threads. The slightest tug could snap my lifeline in two, and I would fall, and fall, and fall, until my entire being was shattered on the stone floor beneath me.

"It's not your fault," he went on, and those words vibrated the glass I was made of. "You didn't do this to her."

"Doesn't matter," I mumbled. "She's here, and she's hurting. We don't have time to worry about fault."

He frowned through the window of his suit. "I know. Look man, all this does is make me hate those fuckers even more than I already did. They take everything. They don't care about anything but themselves. They're like chemical robots, bruh, puppets on the strings of crazy-ass Queens. And you know what, one day, they need to pay for this. Whatever this is, it has to be their fault."

I turned to look at him, my eyes blurry but dry. "What do you mean?"

He peered around the room as if checking to see if someone was eavesdropping. "If we ever have the opportunity, we should wipe them out. We need to give them a planet-killing weapon. A visit back to their world by us when it's all over, a couple of those antimatter slugs might just do it. They don't deserve to live."

I blinked at him. Sure, I was angry. Sure, I was afraid. Sure, I wanted to lash out and cause pain to those who hurt me. But I was not going to be consumed like I had been during our pursuit of Johan or take an action like Harper had. I could not become that person. Did that make me weak? Did that make me a traitor to my race? There had to be a way beyond genocide.

"What about our Foundry directive to protect life?" I asked.

He raised his hands and shrugged. "That didn't go so well, did it? They already hate us. Are we forgetting what happened at the Wandering Gate?"

"No. I haven't forgotten."

"All I'm saying is, how much worse can it get? We have to protect our own. Hell, we have to protect others. Maybe killing them will put us back in the good graces of that fucking god machine. Look what they did to your wife, man."

"Doesn't feel right," I said, but I could not explain why. Genocide felt evil, even if those it was committed against were also committing evil. Why was this? They'd brought Shelly to the brink of death, the love of my life . . .

"I'm just saying." James cut the silence. "Losing Mom was bad enough. That hurt, but it was quick. This . . . bruh, this is worse. I'm hurting with you. We can't let it happen to others. I mean, it could have infected you as well . . . Could have infected *Karianna* . . ."

The way he said her name drew my attention. There was a need behind it, a longing I could just make out through the haze of my current state.

I didn't respond, remaining silent with him for some time. Once his boredom peaked, James squeezed my shoulder and let himself out.

I checked in with Ada every few hours, and she claimed to be close to a breakthrough, but there was nothing yet. She was trying her hardest, I knew it, but I needed results. I really wished Mom had been here. She would have figured it out. She wasn't just a biologist, she was *the* biologist, the best of the best. She would've known.

Several days later, I awoke to a noise and found Xuan sitting up in her bed, looking around the room. I got up, doing my best to keep my clean suit from making too much noise. I remained as still as I could, observing her, seeing what she planned on doing. The chunks of fungara now poked out of her legs, black spines that reached out several inches just like Shelly. The skin of her face was hard to see under a layer of fungal growth. Some of her hair had fallen out and her gaze was distant, eyes focused on some unknown place.

"Xuan?" I ventured after some time, but she did not respond. "Are you in there?" I stood and went to her, waving for Dante and Emilia on the other side of the glass. They had stepped out for a moment to get a break and were suiting up to come back in.

I placed my hand on Xuan's shoulder. "Hey. Are you there?"

She turned her head to look at me but stared through me as if I weren't real.

"We've got you. Can you understand me? Can you?"

What happened next came so fast I couldn't react. Xuan leapt up from the table like a predator whose trap had been sprung, ripping the drip from her arm, and proceeded to throttle me, one hand on my throat, my clean suit crinkling. I gasped for air, stumbled back, and crashed onto the floor. She jumped onto me, pinning me in place. I scrambled to get out from under her, and with her body so frail, so weak, it was easier than it should have been.

"What the hell?" I shouted, stumbling back several steps, boots squeaking on the floor.

At the sound of my voice, Shelly rose from her bed. I turned to look at her, and she too had that distant look. Behind me, Dante and Emilia hurried to get the cleanroom doors open, but the air had to cycle first, and that took time.

"Love," I said, raising my hands at Shelly. She got up from her bed, looked at me, then threw herself at Xuan. The two began to tousle, pushing each other around, throwing punches. I wasn't sure what to do. I needed to stop them from hurting one another, but how?

As I approached the pair, hands raised in supplication, they paused, then turned to me. As if coordinated, they pounced, fists flying, arms reaching for anything that could be used as a weapon. Xuan clipped me across the chin with her knuckles, then slammed me in the chest. Shelly came next, holding a tank of some sort of medical gas. She swung it at my head, but I was able to block it using my prosthetic arm. The impact of the tank against metal was so hard it vibrated my teeth. I stumbled back, trying to put distance between myself and them, but they were quick, and I was cornered. Within a few exchanges, I found myself pushed up against a suite of surgical tools we had prepped in case we had to be invasive in removing the fungara. Bottles and boxes fell from shelves behind me, glass containers tinkling and skittering across the floor as I tried to slide out of the way. I couldn't fight back. I didn't want to hurt them.

Xuan and Shelly looked down at the tools as one, Xuan grabbing a scalpel, Shelly a bone saw, and my stomach dropped. I reached for a metal tray, lifting it before me, hoping I could use it to fend off their assault without doing too much damage. But to my relief, I didn't have to. Shelly collapsed first, then Xuan, leaving me shaking in my tattered clean suit with a sheet of metal in my hands.

Dante and Emilia stood behind them with empty syringes in hand, Chevelle at their side. They'd gotten back into the room and been able to use a sedative.

"No," I said, shaking my head. "This can't be the end of it. This can't be."

"We'll keep 'em under," Chevelle said, appearing behind them. "Little sleep, give Ada time."

"They tried to kill me." I took several deep breaths, hands clutching my chest. "Just like the Isoptera did each other. They tried to kill me."

"We know," she said, putting a hand on my shoulder. "We know."

I looked up, eyes dry, and saw Karianna at the window, an open palm against the glass. My pain was reflected in her eyes. She had felt it, hadn't she? My fear. My anger. My despair. It wasn't just sympathy.

Their conditions did not improve on their own. The fungus continued to grow. The level of drugs we needed to keep it at bay was reaching its maximum limit. I was losing hope that Shelly and our friend would come back to us. After what had happened, the crew tried to get me to leave them alone, but I wouldn't do it.

I fell asleep, exhaustion taking hold of me, my head lying on Shelly's chest. If she woke up again, I hoped she might take me this time. Maybe it would be for the best. I had committed crimes against other species. Maybe I deserved this fate.

A series of bangs rocked the glass of the infirmary, startling me from my blackout.

I squinted and peered through the plastic visor.

"I think I've got it!" Ada shouted, banging her fists against the windows of the infirmary, words muffled by the glass. "The Prexel. They're the key."

"What are you saying?" I called back, my voice hoarse, raw as if it had been rubbed with sandpaper.

"It was them. They left a present for their murderers, and we stumbled upon it. I can fix this. I—can—fix—this."

CHAPTER 16

I met Ada outside the infirmary, first making damn sure to follow the proper decontamination procedures so we didn't spread deadly spores around the ship, in spite of my impatience. She waited for me on the other side of the airlock, pacing side to side, hands shaking, eyes wild.

The jets within the hermetic space sprayed me down with antimicrobial liquids before hitting me with several different bandwidths of ultraviolet light. I was given a scan, and an all-clear came through. I stepped out into the hall and took off my hood. Hy hopped up from his place on a nearby bench and rushed over to us. Lance wasn't far behind.

"Finally," Ada said, stepping forward to put a hand on my shoulder. "I—I mean, we figured it out."

I stepped back from her. "Okay, okay. Tell me what you found. Can you kill the fungara?"

She gave a crooked smile and let out a desperate chuckle. "Dude, it's better than that."

"Start from the top. And be quick. I don't have much calm left." I pointed back at our patients. "And I know they don't."

Ada nodded her head and scratched at her tattooed arms. "Right. Leo? Where are you?"

"Here!" he shouted, zipping around the corner with a transparent containment box in hand. "I'll sit it on the bench."

"Great." Ada waved for us to come over. "We had a theory. A theory most of us had some variation of at one time or another, Shelly being the first, of course. The fungara are not just fungi, they are tiny machines."

"Like our nanomachines," I offered, crouching before the box Leo had brought forth. I peered inside to see a lump of fungara sitting at its center, its baseball-sized form knobby and indistinct.

"Yes," she said, pointing to it. "Like our nanomachines, just organic. And, hell, maybe way tougher. The fungara are resistant to vacuum, tremendous radiation, and heat far greater than many conventional materials we might have used on Earth. Toss it in the Sun, and it might get a little crispy, but it won't burn up. Stick it in a hydraulic press, it might twist up a little but won't break. The Prexel, the species we believe was first to discover fire on Nest, were ridiculously smart but had to have been naïve. How they discovered they could manipulate a naturally evolving fungus in this way, I have no freaking idea, but the work they put in was Kabosai-level genius in genetic manipulation.

"Somehow, they stumbled upon how to connect with the internal code of this strain of fungus, reprogram its DNA in specific ways, then send it off to build and execute on tasks. They could make computers with it, communication devices, power relays, and weapons. We know from what you said and what we saw that they even made starships with it. Best part? It's self-replicating. No need for huge, specialized manufacturing facilities. It just needs enough substrate."

"And the right conditions to grow," Leo supplied, then reached into his pocket and removed a petri dish–like wafer. "Watch this." He slid the disc into a receptacle on the side of the box, dumping it out a few inches from the fungara sample at the center. "Here comes the magic."

I leaned in along with Hy and Lance, the three of us so close we were touching shoulders. Ada clicked a couple buttons on her hand terminal, and a series of lights went off in the box, then stopped. The lump of fungara shuddered, followed by a small poof of black smoke, and then nothing.

"Not much happening," Hy said. "How this going to help?"

"Just wait," Leo said, pointing at the petri dish.

Several seconds passed in a pregnant silence, before suddenly something began to appear. A structure was forming on the substrate, knitting itself together and growing into a tower made of greenish lattices. Within less than a minute, it was a few inches tall, expanding out and growing to a size about as long as my hand.

"Spores," Lance ventured. "What shape is it taking? Kind of looks like a 3D printer working without a head."

"It—uh—it's taking on the shape I tell it to take," Ada replied, scratching at the back of her neck. She twisted her head from side to side and pressed her shaking hands against her legs. "God damn. Too many god damn stimulants. I'm about to crawl out of my skin."

"Careful," Hy told her. "Drugs no good."

She frowned. "No time, dude. Did what I had to."

"So, you figured out how to make the fungara grow?" I asked, giving her a sidelong look, taking in her jitters. "How does this help us?"

"That's the thing. It responds to its programming. The Prexel, as we speculate, were none so happy about being eaten to death. Big shocker. And so, they put something dangerous in the code they had created. They did not want the Isoptera to get away with this genocide scot-free."

I blinked at her, understanding. "A failsafe."

"In a way." She tapped on the box. "More like revenge. They put a trap on a reasonable command that changed the nature of the fungara to stop helping the Isoptera and turn it instead into a biological weapon. In nature, even on Earth, there's a kind of fungus like this called a cordyceps. It mostly infects insects, ants and the like, and when it does, it makes them latch onto leaves, bite down in place, then die. It's a survival mechanism for the mycological organism, a way for the fungus to proliferate. The parasitic fungus inside the host body continues to mature, using their body as building material, as fuel, and then one day it bursts out of them, and the spores fly free. Ants are really good at keeping fungus out of their colonies, and so this method of transmission, this adaptation ensured that the spores spread along the ants' scavenging trails. Crazy, right?"

"Zombie fungus," Hy said. "I read about this as a child. Very scary. Gave me nightmares."

"And it should. The fungara is acting like a cordyceps on steroids. That's why the Isoptera avoided the maze. They knew it was infected with something that forced them to kill one another. And once they were dead, it would use that biomass to spread ever further. So yeah, they told the others not to go there, not to feed this death machine. Shelly and Xuan breathed in these spores, but the rest of you? The masks kept you safe enough."

I let out a long breath, taking it all in. "But what about Karianna and me? Ours were broken. We had no protection and we didn't get infected."

She threw up her shaking hands. "Hell, not even Proxy is totally sure, but it has something to do with your donation. Somehow it made your body a poor substrate for the spores to grow on."

I tightened my lips into a hard line, considering this idea. It wouldn't be the first time our donation had protected us from something harmful. The Foundry had ways of keeping the pilot safe, even if it wouldn't share the details. "How do we stop it?"

Ada lifted her hand terminal and pressed a button. The box flickered with a series of colors, and the latticework of fungara forming upon the petri dish collapsed. "Kill code. Soon as I knew how it was forming, I just had to find the right combination to kill it. Had to find the cheat code to drop it dead. Like with the Isopteran communications, encryption is not one of their skillsets, and they learned what they knew from the Prexel. Everything here was pretty much surface, though biomechanical machines were new to me."

"Proxy?" I called, and to my surprise, the cat was already by my right foot, sitting on the floor. "Will this kill command hurt them?"

"I do not believe so," the cat said, rubbing its body up against me. "We will continue to flush their blood along with their cells and soft tissue. They should recover, so long as this works."

I turned to Ada. "It's our best bet, isn't it?"

She nodded. "I know you love her. And we love Xuan. Shelly is my best friend. I wouldn't risk her life unless I was confident we had a high chance of success. I—eh—geez . . . We're out of time. Yes—yes. This is the best I have."

"Then what are we waiting for?"

We administered the fungara's kill command to Shelly and Xuan. As it turned out, the colors the containment box produced were a combination of electromagnetic pulses and multiband spectrums of light. The fungara responded almost immediately, halting in its progress and slowly working back, retreating into their flesh. Several times, this progress caused extreme distress to our patients, forcing Dante and Emilia to take action when their vitals crashed. They were given a series of drugs to stabilize their condition. In the case of Xuan, we once had to shock her heart back to life. I stood on the sidelines and tried not to fall apart. I was a powerless, emotional wreck, but from an intellectual standpoint, I knew this had to be done. Though as it ever did, my heart didn't listen to my head, the two constantly at war.

Leadership, love, friendship, the mission . . . they all required me to do things at times that did not feel right, like swallowing bad medicine. Everything had a cost, and I was tired of paying for it.

This went on for about an hour until their vitals seemed to level off, heartrate elevated but steady, blood pressure nominal, oxygen saturation low but not dangerously so. The Foundry drip kept running, though this time it was purging waste material from the body while nanomachines helped the liver process the tainted blood.

The room underwent a series of decontamination procedures until Proxy assured us it was free of spores. We removed our cleanroom gear, hoped, and waited. I offered prayers to the Universe for assistance and did my best to keep my composure. Shelly was so thin, so frail, so pale. I'd never seen her like this in all my life. She was a skeleton of the woman I knew, her face sunken, her eyes tight and closed, but at least her breathing was regular.

Several hours passed when I would not leave her side, even for an instant. Then, out of nowhere, she looked up at me, her eyes focused on mine, their pupils normal. She was back. Really back.

"Morning, love," she whispered, her voice strained as if she'd been screaming at the top of her lungs for days. "Why do I feel like I've been hit by a truck?"

I scrubbed away my blurry vision with my palms. "Oh, no reason. No reason at all."

"You're lying to me, aren't you."

"Maybe just a little."

I nursed Shelly back to health, feeding her simple foods and keeping her hydrated. Within a few days, we were able to take her and Xuan off the drip, their bodies free of any fungara spores. Neither of them remembered the experience, having blacked out sometime around when we took the waste slides down into the processing pool on Nest. To say I was happy to have her back would have been an understatement. My soul felt as if it had been rescued from the depths of hell itself.

Once Shelly was strong enough to think straight, she and Ada began meeting to discuss the pulsar map data. There was no stopping either of them or their excitement, despite everything. We were in no immediate rush to figure this all out, but they both needed something to focus on. With the Golden Disc in hand, their job was easy.

A few days passed. They found SOL. They found the way home.

I settled back into my Star Sphere, ready to set course, and Shelly did the same, finding it easier to recover from inside its protection. Within my virtual environment, I went to work, pulling up the maps they had created.

"Karianna?" I called out, and she appeared beside us. "We ready to do this?"

My copilot crossed her arms and nodded. "I think so." She turned to face my wife. "Shelly, I'm so glad you're okay." And I could feel that she was genuine in that sentiment, but there was something else. Disappointment? No. And yet, maybe. There was no ill will, but a kind of envy I could not identify.

I pushed those thoughts away. Human minds were strange things.

"Thanks," Shelly replied, not meeting Karianna's eyes.

"He was a wreck."

Shelly chuckled at that. "Oh, I'm sure. He can't do anything without me."

I eyed the two of them but said nothing.

"How's the course looking?" Karianna stepped forward.

In the empty space, I had a map pulled up, a slightly curved line connecting two stars, the destination in the middle of a series of pulsars.

"We've been gone a long time," I said. "From the look of it, Earth is seventy-two light-years from Nest."

"What?" Karianna's mouth went slack. She shook a finger at the map and twisted her head. "You serious? That can't be. Can it?"

"It can. And that places Cynosure around fifty light-years from Barnard's Star."

"Truth is, there's no way to know how long we've been gone," Shelly added. "Not from here. When we get closer, Ada and I have a model to look at planetary alignments and take an estimate of the current year. One thing's for sure, we will not be returning to the SOL we left as children."

"The question begs, how bad do we think it is?" I ventured, pausing in my actions on the map. "Any guesses?"

"Bad, bad," Karianna said. "Collapsed Earth for sure. We saw the Jevox's information."

"Isoptera too," Shelly added.

"But what else?" I pushed them. We needed to look at this from a broader standpoint. We needed to speculate, needed to consider any possibilities. "By now, the Isoptera can't be the only ones to have visited SOL. The secret has to be out. Did the UEI ever successfully colonize other planets? That was the plan, right? FICSE was just one part of the solution, not the entire solution. Void Striders and all that."

Shelly began rubbing at her chin. "There was Mars, for one. Luna base was already being inhabited when we left."

"That the one with the pretty garden?" Karianna asked. "Heard about that when I was a kid. Fancy real estate settlement on the moon."

"That's the place. There were plenty of stations around the system too, though only a few messages near the time we hit the Foundry that mentioned actual settlements. I'm sure there are more."

I frowned. "So what humans aren't down on Earth could be living in enclosures of some kind."

"Possibly for generations. But there's no telling what this has done to them psychologically. Think of how this journey has changed us."

"And we've had it easy for the most part," Karianna mused.

We gave her a confused look in unison.

"What?" she said. "Other than the almost dying parts. The FICSE ships were small, yeah, but they were home. Then we get these big, honkin' Foundry ships. Rich assholes from Earth would have died to go on a cruise aboard the *Transcendence*. This place has great service. Proxy butlers are the best."

"We better be ready for anything," I told them. "Humankind could be friendly and welcoming, or outright hostile. We know we'll be facing enemies of at least one variety. We will do what we do best. Adapt. Overcome."

"Yeah . . ." Karianna exhaled. "That said . . . I'll leave you to it. Ping me when you're ready to go. I'll brief the rest of the crew."

I nodded. "Okay."

She winked out of existence, and my virtual environment locked.

Shelly turned to face me, taking a deep breath before speaking. "We will stop the Gray Queen and gather what help we need to reterraform the planet. And after that . . ."

"After that?" I echoed back, taking hold of her hand. "What after that?"

"What would we have done if we stayed on Novae, Milo?" She squeezed my hands and slid closer. "Things were turning around. I know so many wanted to see the mission fulfilled, but you know as well as I do that in a way, we have already fulfilled it. We saved humanity."

"Fair. I don't know then. What do people do when they grow up?"

"They adult?"

"And what is adulting? We would have started a life beyond this. Settled down. Maybe, I don't know . . ."

"Have a family?" she ventured, her words fragile as threads of glass.

I smiled at that, and for a moment felt very hot and very nervous. My hands trembled at the thought. It was a big decision, one that to be honest, with all the struggles we'd faced, part of me had written off as never being possible. But if we had victory? Could we really do it?

"Yeah," I mused, thinking it through. "A family. We're no longer sterile, far as I know. The treatments should have worn off. But are we ready?"

"I don't know."

"Can I say I'm scared?"

Shelly let out a chuckle, her eyes wide and bright. "Milo Hughes . . . After all that we've faced together, having kids is scary?"

"Hell yes, kids are terrifying." I let go of her hands and threw my palms up. "All this happens to us, but when it comes to them, who knows? We're responsible for so much. Keeping them fed and cared for. Keeping them safe."

She stepped close and put her forehead against mine, her dark curls falling forward and framing my face. She whispered, "Mom always told me, all kids really need is love."

"Maybe. But they need to eat too, right?"

"Of course, silly. But the rest, we'll figure it out. We have to."

"Yeah, yeah . . ." I closed my eyes. "You're right. Hopefully our parents didn't screw us up too bad."

"No more than anyone else." She chuckled. "I can't recall a single person on our crew who doesn't have some parental baggage, but you know what, I think we all turned out okay. We're kind. We're determined. We've put others first."

"We protect life," I said, taking her face in my hands and kissing her on the lips.

"Yes," she said after a long moment. "We protect life."

PART II

CHAPTER 17

When we set off from Earth so long ago, I never thought we would have come full circle, despite the UEI's promise of a return trip. Desperate in our need to understand the universe around us, humanity had built many machines to reach out into the cosmos. We had hurled these quiet, lonely minds into the deep reaches of space, hoping to learn a little more about who we were, where we came from, and what was out there. While we knew that the universe was vast from our paltry observations, and that we were insignificant by comparison, the infinite is truly hard to grasp. As humans, we had evolved to live in smaller ecosystems, to travel by foot only a few dozen or a few hundred miles at most. We might have dreamed of great worlds, full of wonder and beauty, existing far, far away, but our concepts of distance had to be understood by levels, by grades. To fully embrace the infinite could make one go insane, and for this, even the ancient Greeks feared this idea, claiming it to be heresy for them to study. But while the universe might not truly be infinite, as far as humans were concerned, it didn't need to be. As individuals, we could only understand so much.

"Our world is a lonely speck in the great, enveloping cosmic dark," the astronomer Carl Sagan once said about the deep space photo known as "Pale Blue Dot." Funny that the image he spoke of had been taken by *Voyager 1* in the 1990s, by the very spacecraft whose disc now led us back to humanity's cradle. Dad had shown me the image as a kid, talked in length about the great astrophysicist, but I hadn't truly appreciated the gravity of those words until now. In Sagan's famous monologue, he spoke of the whole of human history, all the good and evil, all the triumph and tragedy, existing upon a mote of dust in a sunbeam of light, on a single blue pixel captured upon an image from the edge of our solar system. And it was through this distant perspective, this idea that our problems and our greatness were so small by comparison to all creation, that humanity should ever strive to be better stewards of what we had. It was through this perspective that we should be more kind to one another. That we were rare and precious. That we were a priceless, cosmic treasure.

Yes, since we had left Earth, we now had a viable colony far beyond our host star, but it was likely that the largest population of surviving humans were waiting for us upon that Pale Blue Dot.

I crouched in my virtual environment, staring at that singular point of blue light, image unmoving, the dark void of space enveloping me like a silk cloak. My thoughts settled on Dad, his curious presence, his sharp wit. What might he say in this moment? What excitement might he express? That man would have straight up crapped his pants to be here.

The pulsar map from *Voyager* had done its job. We had found the sun, and we were now sitting at the edge of SOL's heliosphere, ready to go home. While the intention of the golden disc might not have been how we had ended up using it, the foresight of Carl Sagan, JPL, and NASA might just have inadvertently saved us all.

We were going home.

To my right, Proxy sat sentinel, its feline eyes fixed ahead, while on my left, Shelly did the same.

What had befallen our world since we had left?

What wonders and tragedies might we behold?

What friends might we find?

Or, what dangers might be waiting for us?

These ideas turned over in my mind like a nightmarish engine, churning out its own maddening horsepower, pushing us forward. I knew that this made me responsible for not just this crew, but for the hope of our species' future.

You are not alone in this burden, said a voice at the edge of my mind. Karianna was listening to me, if not to my thoughts then to my emotions. *Their hope is our hope.*

Shelly put a hand on my shoulder and squeezed gently, sending a series of tingles down my back. I reached across my chest and took hold of her hand, grasping for her warm fingers, my augmentation a distant memory in this place.

"Wake up, everyone," I called across the *Transcendence*. "Meet us in the War Room. It's time for us to finish this mission."

"You heard him," Karianna echoed. *"Time to thaw out, bitches."*

While we were safely positioned at the edge of the system in freefall, the crew climbed out of their Star Spheres and met in person. Ever the good host, Proxy had a bevy of treats waiting for us that were precisely what each of us craved in the moment. These included cookies, candies, rainbow-striped layer cakes, burritos and tacos and tiny pork sliders, the sweet and the savory, steamy soups and salty broths, hearty potatoes with lakes of gravy . . .

Not to mention the cheese. So much cheese. A spread of cheese great enough that any fromager would have thought they'd died and gone to heaven.

The crew said their hellos to one another, stretched, and each got themselves a plate. It had been 130 years since we had been in this room last, and that time was spent mostly asleep, frozen within our Star Spheres in a state of hypersuspension, other than in a few short incidents where crew members got up for several days at a time to study or paint or just exist, before turning back in.

One hundred and thirty years of travel . . .

Did I dream this time?

Did I see Mom and Dad's faces?

Did I laugh with Esteban?

They would have been so happy to see this place. They would have been so proud to know that we had made it. This was an event so momentous that a bottle of champaign fine enough to celebrate it would have been impossible to make. Tacos were always a good stand-in, though.

We were back in the War Room, and it felt good. This place was real, substantial, with a weight of decisions to be made much, like the Council Chambers on Novae. This was our seat of command for FICSE 2.0, and while I might have been the lead captain, always possessing the last word, I had to remind myself, as Karianna tried to at every opportunity, that I didn't do this alone. We did this as a team. Everyone here had a voice. We, not I, carried the responsibility of our species on our shoulders.

Plates in hand, each found something to drink before taking their seats around the horseshoe table. Shelly, Karianna, Ada, and I stood at the front, with Proxy and Chinchillette nearby. Shelly and her best friend had asked to address the crew, to walk them through what we had learned of SOL since arriving. Scratch the itch of a question we all needed to know the answer to.

Ada addressed the room, "I'm sure by now, everyone's curious how long it's been since we left." She flicked at the air between us, making a blue, holographic map of SOL appear, with one star, nine planets, dozens of planetoids and other notable objects marked upon it. Neptune was on the edge of the left side of the map, with Uranus nearby, Makemake between us and them. On the right side, closer to the sun, were Jupiter and Saturn respectively. Beyond them, Mars, Earth, Venus, and Mercury hugged the center, the inner planets hemmed by a scattered collection of asteroids.

She paused for a moment, and then her tone became thoughtful, distant, as if recalling memories from a lockbox at the back of a secret, dusty library in her mind. "How long have we been gone? That's the question, right? Most of us were kids when we last passed through this region of space. Just a bunch of grasshoppers trying to figure shit out. Some of us were older, sure, but not enough it makes a hell of any difference now.

"I remember like it was yesterday, Mom and Dad taking me to an observation deck on the *Vasco Da Gama*, pointing out into space and telling me we weren't in Kansas anymore. What an understatement."

"And are you from Kansas?" Leo asked, interrupting what was clearly becoming a monologue, one outstretched finger pointed at the map, his tattoos visible in his short sleeves, their images hard to discern in the pale, blue light of the hologram. "I thought your family was from Ohio."

Ada gave him a withering look for killing her rhythm, then went on. "We were passing into the interstellar medium, the point at which solar pressure ended or began, whichever way you were traveling, and whatever dark matter and dark energy was out here had enveloped our solar system like a collection of pearls trapped inside a bubble. They told me that while they held out hope of success, part of them never expected to make it this far. FICSE was a truly wild, and dangerous, and desperate idea.

"Remember, guys, it was Mary Stablecamp, our Speaker, who led the team that developed the fusion drive our ships used. If not for her, and a thousand other people, we'd never have made it. I can't say what this means for every one of you here, but today I am reminded of an old saying . . .

'You can never go home again.' We crossed the gulf of space, and we came back to the start of it all. This is not the home we left. And not all the people here who deserved to see it are here."

"The man has changed," Karianna added. "And so has the river."

Ada's eyes fell to the ground, a pained expression having moved in to replace her sense of self. "Yeah. Change. You could call it that."

"So do you know?" James asked, for once leaving his plate of sweets untouched. "Do you know how long it's been?"

Shelly looked to Ada, Ada to Shelly. They nodded.

"We do," Shelly said, taking a step forward to address the room, hands rubbing one another. "As you all know, there are many factors at play here. The first part of our journey, from SOL to the Foundry facilities, those were long years in themselves. For the *Vasco Da Gama*, it was eighteen years to Barnard's Star. For the *Brilliance*, twenty-two years to Wolf 359. Then each of our vessels were destroyed, through one method or another, assimilated and recycled.

"The *Vasco Da Gama* was attacked by the Isoptera, the crew fought back, and during the battle, many of us escaped to the Foundry facility, where we were shipped off to Cynosure under hypersuspension.

"As for the members of the *Brilliance*, you had a different experience. You were not attacked by the termites, not right off, but fought among one another over control of the Foundry's gift, and in the end, Karianna was the one chosen to give a donation."

My copilot swallowed and rubbed at her mechanical right arm, her bracelets lightly jingling as she did.

Shelly pulled a digital overlay down onto the map, showing a wireframe of orbital paths. "We've been gone a long time. None of us have a wristwatch, or a calendar we can look at. So, Ada and I found the next-best clock. Our solar system itself. Mercury takes eighty-eight days to make an orbit around the Sun—a twenty-hour day, not a Novae day. Venus, 225. Earth, if no one can remember, 365, except on leap year. Then there's Mars, 687, Jupiter 4,333, Saturn 10,759, Uranus, 30,687, and last of all, Neptune, 60,190. With these specific orbital periods, and a general map of orbital alignments from when we left stored on our hand terminals, we were able to calculate the objective time that has passed since we left SOL behind."

The wireframe snapped onto the planets and they began to spin. A number appeared at the bottom—2090. Mission start. As the planets spun, those in the center faster, those at the edges slower, the clock counted up. 2091. 2092. 2093. The construct made a clicking noise as it went.

I stood in awe at their design. The two of them never ceased to amaze me.

"How long were we in hypersuspension after we left the Foundry?" Shelly asked no one in particular. "How long did the *Brilliance* take to reach the Wandering Gate and find Novae? Clearly the Foundry manipulated time somehow, made us travel slower, kept us in suspension longer so we could sync up and be around the same age when we reached our new world. But how much did they manipulate us?"

Tick. Tick. Tick.

2100

2105

2110

The planets turned, the clock counting up. I had made my own mental guesses but couldn't be sure. We'd traveled at close to two hundred light-years in normal space, never exceeding more than a little past half of the speed of light.

Tick. Tick. Tick.

2225

2263

2315

Despite the tension in my chest, the clock did not stop. It ticked ever upward, the attention of the room consumed by its blue light, heady with anticipation. Were we too late? Should we have found a quicker way home?

Tick. Tick. Tick.

2490

2515

2580

The clock stopped.

In the year 2090, at the fragile age of five, I had left the earth behind, not sure if I would ever see it again. Now, 490 years later, I'd come back.

Four hundred and ninety years . . .

CHAPTER 18

"Shit," Lance said after several quiet seconds. He rubbed his face with his hands, massaging at his temples and taking deep breaths. "I knew it had been a long time, but . . ."

"We are still young," Karianna ventured, her voice cracked and fragile. I knew what this tone meant. She was afraid, she was surprised, and yet, this was just what she had expected. "We are still young. We spent so much time sleeping, time traveling closer to the speed of light than they have. No one we know, nothing we remember will remain. Most everything will be dust."

"Not even countries will still stand," Renata said. "No United States, no Russia, no China, no Britain. They all thought themselves so powerful."

"Funny how power works," Leo said, then took a sip of his drink. "Everything is way more fragile than we think. Lead-lined piping and cisterns were what killed the Roman empire, driving their population mad, dumbing them down and poisoning their brains. And for us . . . When Earth switched to clean energy and away from fossil fuels, LindVolt batteries for god's sake, the world almost imploded. America had ultimate, unquestionable economic power for a season from one piece of technology, and because of it, everyone wanted in."

The old soldier's eyes fell, trailing to the ground. "The oil wars."

This made me think of Esteban. He had been there for the second of the two great wars. He had seen and done so much for a man with a heart so kind. What a tragedy that he, or Renata, or any human being, should have to bear atrocities like that, to see doe-eyed children used as walking bombs, civilians and soft targets made into meat shields.

"How 'bout a more practical thought," Chevelle asked. "The UEI in these ends no more? This their place, blud, or did other gangs move in?"

"That's a good question," I replied, finally locating my voice. "I would hope some colonies of the United Exploration Initiative remain, but who's to say? Who's to say the Gray Queen hasn't wiped them all out? We're at least a hundred years late to the party, and the other Queens seemed to think she's been pretty busy in that time."

The room sat in silence for a moment, staring at the glowing map, considering the year displayed at the bottom. Proxy and Chinchillette looked to one another as if communicating but said nothing. I hated it when they did this. It always made me feel left out, like the cool kids were passing notes in class.

"What we saw on the Jevox ship," Lance started, an open hand raised in thought, "you know, the other clock counting down Earth's population. We don't know when that was taken, right?"

"No," I replied. "We don't. Though from what we know, it has to be very old. If you take into account our return trip, and the fact that at best that came from a signal traveling at the speed of light, that information would have to have departed SOL within a hundred years of us leaving. It's old data far as we're concerned. Very old data."

"Shit."

"Yeah. Shit."

"I just hope there's something left to save," Hy said, and Xuan nodded. "Just trying to keep myself together. This all very cerebral at the moment, might be bad when I see it with my own eyes."

Dante stood up and shook his head. "I usually stay quiet, but we can't get like this. We did the best we could, okay? If Earth is wrecked, we'll fix it. We've got the Jevox machines from the Prole Genascara. Right, Frelo?"

The Jevox leaned their head to the side. I watched as they blinked their five eyes in sequence, counterclockwise, starting from the top. "It is hard to be sure from this distance, and with this limited data, but I am a Cerulean. We do not give up easy. If it can be done, it will be done. You may trust that."

I licked my lips and scratched the back of my head. "I do, Frelo."

How did we need to proceed? Did we go straight to Earth? And where was this Gray Queen hiding? We would need to deal with her if we were to be left alone while restoring Earth.

"Milo," Proxy said, interrupting our discussion. "We are receiving a signal."

"A what?" I cocked my head, listening to the ship with my implants, then looked down at the cat. "From who? We shouldn't be close enough anyone can detect us."

The feline scrubbed its face with a paw, then shook its head, whiskers waving. "I do not believe that the source can detect us."

"Play the message."

The hidden speakers in the room came to life, and a series of beeping noises vibrated out of them. I narrowed my eyes, attempting to listen, to discern what we were hearing. For a moment, I thought it was more Isopteran communications, but there were no voices, and even given the translation software embedded in the universal inoculant, no alien language came forth. The beeps went on and on, some short, some long. After a solid minute of this, I started to believe that it might be a repeating pattern.

"Dude, I know what it means," Ada blurted out, her expression unexpectedly bright. "It's a code."

Shelly turned and reached for her hand. "What kind of code?"

"Oh, it's an old one to be sure. Morse code to be exact. Now, as far as what the words actually mean, I have no freaking idea. But I know what the words are."

"Tell us," I demanded. "What does it say?"

She spoke through gritted teeth, hands balled into fists. "Love. Live. Pray . . . Burn. Fall. Ash . . . Anger. Atonement. End . . . It repeats."

Love.

Live.

Pray.

Burn.

Fall.

Ash.

Anger.

Atonement.

End.

Her bright expression, born of discovery, faded into a kind of sick unease, as if she might have swallowed something rotten. She mumbled, "Okay . . . maybe it's not so fun now."

The twice-encoded words made my blood run cold; a hidden meaning living within them like a parasite. As I looked to Shelly, then Karianna, seeking foundation in this moment, it was clear they felt the same.

"Proxy, where is it coming from?" I asked.

The cat purred as it looked up at me, its eyes gleaming. "Neptune. Triton, to be precise."

"You mean Titan?"

"No. Triton. Titan is a moon of Saturn. Triton is not."

Because of course it was. Dad would have smacked me on the back of the head for that one.

"Alright, alright," I said, collecting my thoughts. I gestured with a hand and two lines appeared on the map, one green, one red. "The way I see it, we've got two choices before us. Based on orbital alignments, we can go off to the right, curve around Jupiter, and head for the inner planets. Go straight for Earth. That's the red line. Or . . ."

"Or what?" Lance pressed.

I wiped my sweaty left palm off on my jumpsuit. "We go the other route, follow the green line, blow past Makemake, bypass Uranus, and intercept Neptune. Maybe we can see what this signal is and who made it."

"Could it be a distress call?" Xuan asked.

Karianna looked to me and gave a shrug.

"Maybe," I replied. "Proxy, any way for us to know where the Gray Queen might be?"

The cat shook its head. "Not enough information is available at this time."

"If that isn't the most Foundry thing I've heard all day," James said, his lips curling back. Proxy did not seem amused.

"Vote?" I asked, looking to my team.

"Dangers?" Xuan met my eyes. "What will we face?"

"Hard to say. Could be a radio left on repeat."

James chuckled at that idea. "Could be some crazy asshole's podcast that just kept playing on repeat. What a prank that would be. 'Here's some funny shit, let's make a creepy signal and loop it for when the next group of people pop in. Scare the piss out of them.'"

"I don't think it's funny," Ada said.

Shelly sniffed. "Me either."

He waved a hand. "Whatever."

"We just don't know." Karianna shifted in her footing, then rotated the map, zooming in so only the Neptunian path showed. "Would be a good prank though."

"Thank you," James exhaled, the words twice as long as they should have been.

"But at this distance," she went on, "it's the only signal we're picking up. I feel nothing from the instruments. SOL is quiet. Dead air. Rix wasn't quiet. IT-22, not quiet. Not even Novae was totally quiet. This feels . . . it feels different."

"Might be worth investigating to see what happened here while we were gone," Dante offered.

His wife stared off in thought. "Just might."

"Alright." Lance spoke up. "Screw it. Let's go. We didn't come home to tiptoe around our own backyard. We've got a big-ass stick and we belong here, ghosts or no ghosts. We see what's going on, then go back to Earth and fix all this."

"Hey now, no one said anything about ghosts." James sat up straight, his words a touch distressed. "Are there ghosts out there, Milo? You spoke with the Universe, had a nice little palaver with that thing."

"No," I told him. "No ghosts. Just, intelligence. Less Poltergeist, more Scooby Doo. Always a something behind the mask."

"Not sure if that makes it any better."

"Nice reference," Karianna said, smiling over her shoulder.

"Thanks." I stepped up beside her, looking at the map, my arms crossed. "Anyone else agree with Lance? Should we go head long and see what this is?" There was a pause as they metabolized the information.

"Yes," Renata spoke first. "Neptune."

"Neptune," Leo agreed. "This is a puzzle piece we need."

Ada nodded at him, and from there we went around the room, each doing the same, even James. In the end, only Shelly, Karianna, and I did not explicitly agree. Something didn't feel right about this, but that didn't keep us from wanting to go.

I swallowed at the implications. "Alright then. We go to Neptune. For now, everyone do what you need to do, then get back in your Star Spheres. We've got work ahead of us."

They finished their meals, tidied up their physical quarters, took a little time to write in journals or work on personal projects, then made their way back to the protective spheres. Once everyone was accounted for, all systems green, Karianna and I applied thrust.

The *Transcendence* dove back into the ocean of our home star's embrace, its skin bathed in the same light that had brought us into being. Upon our shoulders we carried the hope of billions, even if they themselves weren't aware that hope was near. The mission would continue, and we would see it through. But first things first. It was time to find out what had happened while the stewards of humanity were away. It was time to get a lay of the land.

How far into darkness had our species fallen?

We had to know.

I had to know.

Once we had reached cruise velocity, I extricated myself from my Star Sphere, claiming I needed to take a walk and do some meditation. Shelly and Ada remained busy enough not to notice my exit, but Karianna was always on my tail. There was something I needed to work on, but prying eyes had to go away for a while, and she was hard to keep away.

I pinged James, came up with some bullshit story about how Karianna was feeling bored and lonely, and told him he should go keep her company. When he protested, saying she might punch his head off his shoulders if he made any of those claims, I encouraged him to buck up and be cleverer in his approach. After our little chat, he was determined to cheer her up, so he wasn't taking no for an answer if she put on that she was too busy to chat.

As James made contact with Karianna, I scurried off, sneaking around the outer decks to the aft of the ship to a secure storage area. This particular room was not only locked but shielded radiologically and electromagnetically, as well as on some frequencies and bands of energy only Proxy understood. It was like a black box room, walls near indestructible, far removed from the outside world, its contents unable to interact with us or be interacted with. It was perfect for what I needed to do.

I entered the Dead Room and locked the door behind me. Something strange was waiting for me on a worktable at its center. My heart rate increased as I approached, my fleshy hand slick with sweat. Since recovering the two objects from Nest, we had left this one locked away, secure and uninspected, hoping it didn't blow up in our faces—or worse. I had received a few questions about it from the crew, as you would expect, but for the most part, it terrified them, and so everyone had tried to ignore it. I knew how they felt.

A floating, obsidian shape with twenty sides remained perfectly still in the cool, astringent air of the Dead Room. Its many faces gleamed in the overhead light, giving off the strange impression that it was regarding me. I had no idea what to call this object, or what it really was. All I knew was that it kind of reminded me of a giant, shiny dice from some tabletop board game. I needed to find out more.

It was important. It was useful. But was it a weapon? Was it our salvation? Or was it merely a device of change? It was strange how perspective gave purpose to these words. Change was change, but someone always got the short end of the stick when it came time.

"You have come for it," Proxy said, appearing beside me.

I gave a start and rested a palm over my thundering heart. My attention had been so focused on the device, I hadn't noticed my cat's approach. "Damn it, Proxy. You scared the hell out of me."

"You should be scared, Milo. You should be very scared."

I took a step toward the device but paused a stride away. "Why? What is it?"

"I cannot say."

"Cannot, or will not?"

"Cannot." Proxy hopped up onto the table and sat down, its nose less than a foot from the object's surface. "What I can say is that it possesses great potential energy."

I inched forward, stepping a little closer, the hairs on my arm standing on end as if I'd entered a field of static electricity. "I gathered that."

In the light of the Dead Room, I saw hardly any more features than had been on evidence in the dimly lit nautilus chamber of Nest. The object was made of some type of dark metal that absorbed most frequencies of light. For whatever reason, red particle bands appeared not to be one of them, revealing faint outlines of texture on the surface when I looked at it from the proper angle.

"I need to know what it is." I leaned forward, squinting at it. "And what it's capable of."

Proxy cocked its head at me. "I know." It paused for a moment as if considering its next action. "In our long sleep since leaving the Isopteran home, I have been watching it. Keeping a close eye to ensure your safety."

"Oh?" I pursed my lips in thought. "What did you learn?"

It turned its attention back to the polyhedral object. "The device is twenty-one inches tall, or 543.4 millimeters, and has a weight of ten pounds under one gravity. This height it floats at is a quantum locked state, set to a central point at its center of gravity. You may rotate it. Flip it upside down or sideways. But upon leaving it alone, the shape will return to this state, the same faces pointing up, in a relative sense, same faces pointing down.

"It is not Isopteran in make, despite the fact that it seems to be employing a similar spatial compression technology as they make use of. Think of the compression grenades you have encountered in combat, yet in reverse. It expands rather than compresses."

"Nasty weapons."

"That they are."

"So, you think this is bigger on the inside? That's what you mean."

"Almost certainly."

"How big?"

"It is hard to say, but I believe it stretches deep into other dimensions. If laid out in a three-dimensional space, it could be as small as an industrial park you might see on Earth, a couple of square kilometers of sprawling machinery like an automobile factory. Or it could be as large as a small moon, thousands of kilometers across. Until it is opened, we cannot say for sure."

"But not Isopteran. Then who made it?" But the truth was obvious. I needed to stop pretending like it wasn't.

The cat let out an audible sigh as if sorry to deliver bad news. "I believe it to be from the Gene Brokers."

I nodded. "Okay. That gives us a few clues. What else do we know?"

"Not much beyond that. It releases no standard radiation, x-ray, gamma, alpha, and so on. Possesses no electromagnetic field, though I see the hairs on your arm are responding as if it did. Despite this lack of measurable energy, I do not believe it to be inert."

I rubbed at my arms, attempting to disburse whatever charge was there. "Why?"

"It's spilling neutrinos. This device casts them out from its core like a small star, though I can't imagine fusion is the cause."

"Then what is?"

"A good question."

I licked my lips and reached out, running my fingers along its smooth surface. With a mental command, I ordered the lights to shift to red.

Symbols appeared on the triangular faces of the device, a perfect script of lines set within concentric circles. While I couldn't read these symbols, those on the upper faces, those near the apparent top of the device, and those on the lower faces were a matching set but for a few small variations. Those on the middle of the shape, however, were different. Each face seemed to have a set of language unlike the others, not just different symbols. It was as if different species had written the script on each face.

"Are these instructions?" I asked Proxy.

The cat blinked and began biting at its paw, cleaning the spaces between. "I believe they are."

"Why can't we translate them?"

It shook its head. "No information is available at this time."

"So convenient."

I turned the shape around, observing what Proxy had mentioned. It spun as if it were a top fixed at this position in open air. I picked it up, walked it across the room, then set it back down. The instant it came within about ten inches of the table's surface, it locked into place.

"Okay," I said, musing, "maybe this is to make it easier to work with. Keep it from becoming damaged in transit. Did it not move while we were under acceleration?"

"Not a single nanometer."

"Interesting." I ran my fingers down its lines, feeling for any hidden switches or panels. My prosthetic fingers, more sensitive than my human ones, detected no imperfections in its surface. "I'm going to try and open it."

"I would not recommend that."

"Why?" I asked, half chuckling. "Think this thing will blow up in our faces?"

The cat narrowed its eyes at me in frustration. "I like existing, Milo."

"Yeah. Me too, buddy." I scratched Proxy behind the ear, and it leaned into me, purring. Man did this cat have the softest fur. Unnaturally soft. "I know there are concerns, but we need to know what this is. I don't think we can do that by looking at it from the outside. If it's designed to be manipulated, then it has to have a way in."

"You're playing with fire," it said, pulling away from my affection.

I crossed my arms and nodded, not disagreeing. Proxy was right, and its job was to keep me safe. This was not smart, but the Universe itself had told me to be looking for it, that much was clear.

"Okay," I said, licking my lips and leaning over the table. "Let's see how we open you up."

Danger or not, I wasn't going to be deterred. More was at stake than just our lives. If this was a piece of the puzzle to save humanity, I needed to know where it fit in.

For the next several hours, I tried my best to open the device and see what was inside, but I had no luck. I tried changing the colors in the room, cycling through the entire visual spectrum, looking for additional signs. No result. I kept feeling for switches, tried touching the faces in patterns. No response. I tapped on it with a series of fine tools, leaning close and listening to see if there was any change in its tone, suggesting something hollow. Nothing at all. It was locked tight, and I had no damn clue how to open it.

I received an angry ping from Karianna, so I slipped out of the room before she could locate me. My distraction had worked, but James had pissed her off, per usual. It was time to leave the device and tend to the ship's immediate needs.

This would have to be another mystery for now, but it was a mystery only safe to share with Proxy. Whatever this was, it was dangerous. I didn't want anyone else having to carry that weight of knowledge, not even Shelly. We had enough problems to deal with beyond worrying over a strange device that was sitting silent on our ship, waiting for its moment to . . . to do what?

Everyone had their secrets, and this one? This one was mine to bear.

CHAPTER 19

We drifted deeper into SOL, inching closer to the ancient star that had sustained Earth for time immemorial. Unlike JV-01, the host star of the Jevox, our sun was no hypergiant, and so it remained small at this distance, not much more than a bright set of pixels set against a black backdrop. At close to twenty AU, we were bathed with little more than 1/400th the light that Earth was. We were well and truly in the dark, and without the *Transcendence*'s instruments, we'd have been a group of stupid, fumbling monkeys. Instead, I felt every cosmic thread that crossed us, every stream of particles. I could stretch and pull on each of them, test their tensile strength, study their very makeup and plot their origins. The quality of our star was different than any others we'd encountered, though I couldn't say how. It was as if it knew us on sight.

While we might not have received any signals other than that cryptic code, as we approached the blue-green ice giant, Uranus, goosebumps pimpled my arms within my environment. It was as if a thousand tiny probes had awoken from their long slumber and squinted their tired eyes in our direction to see if there was anything worth observing. We were being watched, I was sure of this, I just couldn't say how or from where.

I can't explain it either, Karianna thought, her connection within the integration deepening to the point it was as if she were looking right over my shoulder. *You ever walk in the woods on Novae by yourself just to get some air, then out of nowhere, it's like someone's looking at you? You know, from a direction no one lives, all wilderness. Without checking, you know something angry, hungry, and afraid has spotted you. You can't figure out if it wants to meet you, eat you, or just run. That's what I'm feeling right now.*

My reply was flat. *Go for a walk? I thought you didn't like nature?*
I mean, I don't. But who doesn't like a good walk? Some fresh air. A bit of sun.
That's why you always carried a gun.
That's why I always carried a gun.

Shadowy and silent, our engines cold, Karianna and I cruised nearer to Uranus, our course making use of it as a gravity assist on our way to Neptune. Upon its thick clouds of hydrogen and helium, a vast expanse of blue lights danced like thunderstorms viewed from orbit, appearing like gods battling in some unseen arena. I could sense the particles streaming out from our sun, caught in its unusual magnetic field, tumbling downward and crashing into the dense layers of gas, exciting them to the point of brilliance and jubilee. Among its many rings, glimmers of light reflected off of millions of chunks of ice, appearing to us like a distant field of shifting diamonds.

Glimpses and starts of information came from the inner worlds, but I tried to keep my focus ahead. Those places were for later. This signal was for now.

Our massive body swung around Uranus, leaving it shrinking at our backs until it was another tiny dot among a black sea. Neptune took its place before us, looking not much different, if perhaps a little bluer in the visual spectrum rather than green. I reached out to its fourteen moons, holding them in my hand, fingers brushing over their surfaces, feeling at their texture, their shape, their compositions. Some were large enough to be round, like Triton, with gravitational forces strong enough to have attracted heavy materials over time. Others were asymmetrical, oblong in shape like potatoes or river rocks. Many were dark, bumpy, and sharp, their surfaces pockmarked and cratered, made of rock and ice with faint traces of hydrocarbons and cyanides, though the one exception to this trend seemed to be Triton.

I wondered briefly how many humans had gone out this far. At the turn of the twenty-first century, Neptunian travel had only been a dream, given how far away it was. Mars was barely possible, and in the fifty prior years before that, trips to the moon had not been nearly as common as transcontinental flights. And yet, the FICSE mission crew had traveled so far beyond any of their wildest dreams. We had tackled the impossible. Why was it that distance mattered now? Had I taken for granted the ease with which we had crossed the vast emptiness over the last almost five hundred years?

Triton was not like the rest of Neptune's moons. It had enough mass to form into a perfect sphere, with a diameter of twenty-seven hundred kilometers. Though appearing dead from space, with little more than a faint nitrogen atmosphere present, Triton was geologically active, with geysers of nitrogen and seasonal winds. While it lacked a stratosphere like most satellites with an atmosphere, it had a thermosphere that extended above its surface, warmed with solar radiation absorbed by Neptune's magnetic field. It was an odd world, strangely similar to Pluto, suggesting that they had common origins, though I had no explanation as to what those might be.

I shook my head, freeing it from the massive weight of data. Half of this information I had because of conversations with Dad, the other half, the Foundry's systems.

We approached the source of the signal, slowing the *Transcendence* with a gentle burn of the main drive, our ship slipping into orbit above the pale moon.

The beeping has changed, Karianna reported.

I replied to her with a feeling like a grunt.

Shelly appeared beside me in my virtual environment, her arms crossed and her eyes narrowed. "Where is it? Where is the signal coming from?"

"Hard to say," I began, pointing to the satellite. We were floating above the surface of the moon as if we hung from an invisible ceiling upon fishing line in my virtual environment, its craggy gray surface at our feet, the waning, blue crescent of Neptune over our right shoulders. "Somewhere in the direction of the surface."

We scanned the area, which was increasing in resolution by the moment, triangulating the signal.

"Almost there," Karianna said over the open channel. *"Almost."*

Shelly pointed. "I see it. There."

I squinted to look as if that would make a difference. "You've got to be kidding me. Is that . . ."

Karianna finished my thought. *". . . a hand terminal?"*

"Yes."

Proxy flashed into existence beside us, alarmed. "Contact!"

"What?"

"Contact! A ship is rising over the horizon of Triton—two hundred meters in length. I detect powered rail cannons, Para Lux Arrays, and antimatter slug cannons. Working on a better scan."

Shelly whirled on me. "That's a familiar compliment of weapons."

"No way," I mumbled in disbelief. "There's no way."

I spun our view around and fixed it on the newcomer, the image of their ship taking its time to resolve into more than a basic wireframe.

As I waited, a stream of neutrinos crashed into our communications network like a hammer.

We were being hailed.

I took a deep breath and opened the channel, my hands tightening into fists. Karianna reached for the Mercurial Integumentum but did not deploy it. The nanomachines swirled in a ready position near their exit ports.

I swallowed hard and opened the channel.

"Well, hello, hello, hello," said an overtly masculine, baritone voice. *"What do we have here? Do I spy more Foundry creations? How wonderful. Do I spy something familiar as part of this abomination, or is it just wishful thinking? Oh,* Brilliance, *oh,* Brilliance, *do you hide in that crystal shaft before me? Here you are swirling with machines, raising your guard, acting as if danger is everywhere. Why, oh why, would I hurt you? We are but friends. Both taken to the communion of a donation given. More than friends."*

The rhythm, the timbre of his speech, came across as a kind of singsong that twisted my stomach into knots. They were forcing theatrics as if this were all some grand play. It made me feel sick, unsettled, and I was not alone in this discomfort.

At the sound of his voice, Karianna's emotions went wild. Wholly outside of my control, my body flooded with a volcanic heat, making me feel as if my head might pop off my shoulders. This was more than just unease. It was a raw, primal injection of rage and fear, mixing with one another into a chaotic soup of fury served with a tall glass of cortisol. Yes, I was pissed off at the situation, that someone had jumped us, and in something so bright and shiny only the Foundry could have built it, but her emotions in this moment were personal in nature. Intimate.

It's him, she thought, her words direct to my mind. *It's him. I thought he was gone. I thought we had dealt with him. I don't understand. I don't understand.*

Who? Who is this?

The mutineer.

CHAPTER 20

Karianna's story came back to me. She was talking about the person who had led to the death of her father, the death of their captain, the catalyst of her taking possession of the *Reverie*.

Our scan finished, allowing us to see his ship clearly. Proxy's initial findings were confirmed, as were Shelly's suspicions. A two-hundred-meter-long crystal wedge drew toward us, its body slashed with many curves. Unlike the *Fidelas*, the *Reverie*, or even the *Transcendence*, this vessel looked as if it were made of thick shards of arctic-blue glass, its edges streaked with bright, prismatic lines. Where our ships had been imposing in their size, if not their shape, this one appeared predatorial, a beast come to consume all life. Along one of the forward sections of its cool wedge a word was printed in block letters: *Absolution*.

"Milo," Shelly whispered, "that ship is like ours. Its Foundry-made."

"Justin!" Karianna called back over the open channel, her emotional soup cooling into a salty bowl of ice. *"Justin Wiggins. You . . ."*

"Justin?" The man let out a peal of laughter so hard I thought it might shatter someone's ribcage. When he calmed himself down after several seconds, he let out a sigh, then lowered his voice to a menacing whisper. *"You speak of a dead person. I am Veetar Nambrale, a god among mortals. Better than he ever was. I am reborn, Miss Torlen. Reborn."*

"No," Karianna growled. *"You are Justin Wiggins. Weak. Cowardly. A child in a man's body. You are nothing, and no one. A manipulator. An agitator. A murderer. A piece of shit on a stick not even fit to fuel my fire!"*

"I am Veetar Nambrale!" he shouted back, words hurled from his mouth among a cloud of poisonous gas. *"You will cower before me, cower before my power.*

You will not ignore me. I am the return. The second coming. I am here to make vengeance known. Come to wipe the slate clean."

The weapons on the *Absolution* began to power up, their Para Lux arrays crackling with energy. Something about the readings were not right. By all rights, we should have been far more powerful than his ship, and perhaps we were on balance, but these arrays were nothing like ours.

"The ship has been modified," Proxy reported. "It does not follow standard Foundry specifications. This is bad. Very bad."

I turned to my cat and threw up my hands. "You think? How did they do it?"

"Not enough information is available at this time."

I wasn't sure how any of this was possible, but somehow, some way, the mutineer left behind by the crew of the *Brilliance* had survived. And not only survived, but ended up in the possession of a Foundry made ship, one with what appeared to be a modified array of weapons. How, or why, had the Foundry given him this gift?

"I've heard the stories about the mutiny from the *Brilliance*'s crew," Shelly said. "He was a madman."

"I don't think he's gotten any better."

Power reached a crescendo aboard the *Absolution*, and in that same instant, Karianna reached behind her and drew the MI into place. I was so stunned in the moment that I had been unable to react, but not my copilot. Our MI formed into a thick wall of nanomachines just as a series of lancing light flashed out from the *Absolution*. The beams crashed into the barrier, ablating layer after layer of the MI, dissolving billions of tiny machines in a flash of light and heat.

Shaking myself free of my surprise, I raised my arms, rail cannons following, hurling several rounds through the barrier at the enemy, testing their defenses. In that same instant, Karianna formed a pair of pinprick holes in our MI to allow our slugs passage. They struck the *Absolution*'s MI an instant later, though unlike ours, which was wider than our ship and diffuse, theirs was incredibly dense, as if Veetor had formed his barrier in exactly the right locations. The rail cannon rounds did nothing but let out a flash of light as their kinetic energy disbursed.

Systems aboard the *Transcendence* whirred as they reached their highest levels of readiness. They sprang to life in an instant, as if it hadn't been almost two hundred years since they'd seen action. Our nanovats began churning out additional machines, the antimatter slug cannons coming online.

"Shoot back?" Shelly asked, raising her arms before her, palms out. "I know they're close, but I'll be careful."

I pressed my lips into a hard line and nodded. "Light 'em up."

And she did just that, flicking her wrists one after the other as if she were tossing baseballs in his direction. A salvo of antimatter slugs left our cannons, targets locked on the *Absolution*. One. Two. Three. The tightly packed chunks of potential energy closed the twenty-thousand-kilometer gap in a flash. They drew close to him, ready to make their final reaction . . .

Nothing happened.

I felt for the projectiles, could sense where they had gone, but saw that they had sung their way past the effective range of our target without triggering. My copilot fumbled with them, attempting to ignite the slugs manually, but nothing happened. Two seconds passed, then came a flash of light as they ignited out of range several thousand kilometers beyond the *Absolution*.

"That shouldn't be possible," Proxy stated. "How?"

"What happened?"

"We—" it stammered, unable to answer. "I—"

Several more lances of pure, white light shot out from the *Absolution* and crashed into our MI. Karianna was forced to readjust its angle, hoping to deflect some of its energy rather than for us to take the full brunt of its power. I wished we still had the effulgence barriers, but part of me knew they would likely not hold up to a stream of particles this powerful.

"Oi," Chevelle cut in. *"What's the word? This tin can's not gettin' on well. She's spillin' jokes from that wasteman, aight fam?"*

"A little busy."

The heart rates of the crew were accelerated, everyone aware of the shit we had found ourselves in.

Pissed as hell, Karianna was ready to lay it all out on the dancefloor, to use every move she had available to melt his face until we were nothing more than a collection of sweat and sore muscle. She cycled through our weapon systems, searching for ways to increase their power, arguing with Chinchillette the entire time.

"Lance!" she shouted over the internal channels. *"Get out there."*

He called back, his reply uneasy, *"Milo?"*

"Yes. Go. Fighters in vacuum. Get out there."

"*Aye, aye.*"

Fighters poured from our bays, our pilots taking to open space, ten deadly, diamond-shaped strike craft forming two attack wings. They split off from one another, Lance leading the forward group, Chevelle leading their backup. As they closed the distance to the *Absolution*, we began pounding Veetor with our Para Lux array as well as our rail cannons. This forced him to spread his MI into a more diffuse configuration, not just focusing on specific impacts in small areas. Several shots made it through, crashing into the menacing glass wedge, igniting its surface in cascades of scintillation.

"*We'll hit them from the starboard side,*" Lance reported. "*Chevelle, come at them from above. Spread out the formations. We don't want to get wiped out by something that covers a wide area of effect.*"

Our pilots did as they were instructed, scattering in perfect coordination, almost as if they were attached to rails. It was beautiful to see how far they'd come as a group. They rained death upon the *Absolution* not just as individuals, but as a team.

Holes appeared in Veetor's MI, with Para Lux beams, rail cannon slugs, and nuclear sabot rounds making it through from time to time, cutting into the hull of his Foundry-made vessel. We tore at him from the forward end while our fighters swarmed him from all sides, his personal barrier wild in its response.

"*You have surprises!*" Veetor called out. "*This ship did not come with fighters. Can I take it back to the dealership, my proxy? Is this punishment? No. No. I have done nothing wrong.*"

"We're making headway," Shelly reported, pointing to a damaged section of the *Absolution* near its aft end. "I don't know what critical systems might be there, but he's spewing radiation. That can't be good."

"Not for him," I replied, then recalculated our weapon trajectories and fired again, trying our best to keep him off balance, not letting up for an instant, not allowing him to gain any ground.

The sections Shelly had mentioned were already being triaged, nanomachines rerouted to patch the biggest of the holes. Fighting toe-to-toe with a Foundry-made ship was maddening. We had to damage them, him, faster than he repaired. We had to take damage slower than we could repair. It was a game of logarithmic trends played out on spreadsheets using that of the fires of cosmic gods.

The *Transcendence* rocked, a shot piercing our barrier, a burning sensation spreading out from my left shoulder as if someone had stabbed me with a hot knife.

We fired back at one another. Blow for blow.

Slam.

Fire.

Slam. Slam.

My teeth rattled in my head.

Fire.

Slam.

Slam.

Slam.

Karianna? How are we holding up.

He's making the MI hard to maintain.

You need me to take over? We can swap.

No. I've got it. It's fine. Stay on weapons.

The space between our ships was a veritable lightshow of titanic exchange, so much noise from instrument feedback that it was hard to keep track at times.

"Gods, and demons," the mutineer prattled on. *"This was fun, truly, but I am getting bored with this little spat."*

Karianna shot back at him, *"You're just pissed off that you're losing!"*

"Losing? Where did you get that idea? Did it come from the same place as those stupid bracelets of yours? Those jokes you and your father used to make? No, no, no. Little child thief. I am not losing. Just waiting on friends."

Shelly's eyes went wide. "What was that? What did he just say?"

"Uh-oh."

"Milo," Proxy spoke up. "We have more contacts."

I let out a frustrated sigh, my hands shaking. "Shit. How did I know you were going to say that? How many?"

"Sixteen warships."

"Sixteen? You've got to be kidding me."

"They are in formation, burning up from the surface of Triton. Milo, these are not like the *Absolution*."

"What do you mean?"

"See for yourself."

I split my attention for a moment to see what Proxy had meant.

Sixteen bright lights had appeared from a gaping hole on the surface of the Neptunian moon. Black hunks of metal were hurling themselves skyward upon fusion torches, their broad shapes departing a not-so-obvious base kept underground. Their shapes were ugly, black and gray forms, each a hundred meters in length, made of hard lines along a sort of rectangular prism strapped with eight to ten cylindrical engines. They had massive communications arrays that spurred outward at all angles running down their lengths, spherical tanks by the dozens in rows, with trusses at their forward ends connecting hardpoints I could only imagine, as menacing as they looked, had to hold weapons of some kind. At their central cores lay toruses that spun with incredible speed, edges alight with flickering blue electricity. It was clear these ships had not been made by the Foundry. These ships were not Isopteran, or Jevox, or even Kabosai. No. These ships were human, with emblems painted down their length in a high-contrast white, clearly identifying them.

United Exploration Initiative.

"Shut the fuck up, bruh!" James spluttered, having reviewed the feed I was broadcasting back to the crew. *"It can't be."*

"It sure as hell is," Lance said. *"How? How?"*

Chevelle let out a noise of surprise, a kind of oof. *"They don't look like blud, fam. Dis may be their ends, but they not actin' like they wanna cotch. You know . . . chill out witch ya. They're all fired up, ready to brawl."*

Xuan's fighter wavered for a second, almost crashing into Veetor's MI but pulled away at the last moment. *"What do we do?"*

A fresh signal hit our communications array and I let it through. It was another voice, a harder voice, but a saner one.

"Attention unknown Foundry-made vessel firing on the UEI Absolution, *this is Admiral Gabriel Cardoso of the United Exploration Initiative, Remnant Fleet,"* a masculine voice called out, raw and tired, no-nonsense. *"You have entered secure airspace and broken communications silence. With the Clickers and Splicers loose in SOL, it is imperative we do not draw attention to any of our locations. The Remnant fleet cannot be responsible for the hell you call upon yourself from the enemy. You are ordered to stand down, to recall your fighters, and lower your defensive barrier. Comply, and we will speak in a more civilized manner."*

We kept up our assault on the *Absolution*. UEI *Absolution*. What a bunch of bullshit. From what I was seeing so far, Justin was just a little man with a big stick.

"I don't trust them," Shelly mumbled. "Something isn't right. Veetor wants us dead immediately, then these people, his friends, want us to stop so we can talk?"

"I'm with your wife," Karianna said over the onboard channel. *"This feels like a trap."*

"Proxy," I called. "How long do we have before they are in range? This Remnant fleet."

The cat looked up at me, cocked its head to the side, then licked a paw and scratched its right ear. "We do not know their capabilities. It is impossible to say."

"Geez, big help. Thanks."

"Who are the Clickers?" Shelly mused.

"Have you received our signal?" Gabriel called again. *"Please confirm."*

Karianna had had enough. Without approval, she spat back at the admiral, *"We're not lowering our defenses, asshole. Not till Justin screws off. You want to talk? He's got to stop this."*

There was a pause. *"Who? Who Justin?"*

"Veetor Namfuckpants. Your Foundry pilot. Get him to stand down."

"Not doing it," Veetor added. *"Can't do it. They are a threat to all of us. We must take them together, Gabriel. Together. Remember your oath. Remember your obligation to your species."*

"What?" the admiral asked, his earlier confidence slipping. *"Take them on?"*

"We can do it together."

"Nambrale, we must speak with them first. It is protocol. They are human. They came from beyond the system. We must cease this battle and speak."

"But I already know who they are. I know their black hearts. They are from the Brilliance. They are those I spoke of."

"Oh." This statement seemed to tell the admiral all he needed to know. Cardoso's attention came back on us. *"One last chance to stand down, Captain."*

This was a hell of a sticky situation. We had just gotten back to SOL and were already under fire, not by Isoptera or Kabosai or some other alien species come to destroy humanity, but our own, and we had come to save them.

"I can't do that, Admiral," I replied. "I'm sorry. I don't want to fire on anyone. Please, I know you are human. We are human. Don't do this. Veetor is not who you think he is, and we are here to help."

"I know just who he is. An ally against our invaders. He helps us keep what is left of humanity safe."

"He tried to murder his FICSE crewmates aboard the Brilliance!*"* Karianna protested. *"Turned on us and tried to take the gift of the Foundry for himself. How's that for your ally? You want to keep humanity safe? Ditch this dick."*

"I don't understand."

"No. No you don't."

"Admiral," Veetor started up again, this time with less bravado, his tone more serious, as if leaning in on the discussion and looking him directly in the eyes. *"They tell lies. Trust in me. Help me tip the balance in this fight. I will give you all the details once we are safe. I have kept you safe."*

And with that, the admiral's link went dead.

"He has switched off his radio," Proxy reported.

"Shit." We kept up our assault on the *Absolution*, giving Veetor no quarter. He was slipping, the advantage of this engagement ours for now. The holes in his MI were widening. He was making very little ground in damaging us now that we knew his strategy. It was clear he'd never fought against an enemy like us. "Keep our attention on the *Absolution*, pull range. The remnant fleet is confused over who their allegiance is."

"They're locking on us," Proxy stated. "Missiles have left their launch bays. One hundred and nineteen in total. From what I can tell, each are equipped with thermonuclear fusion warheads."

"Shit," I growled, reaching for anything we had that might stop them. "Shelly?"

She nodded, firing an antimatter slug in the direction of the oncoming missiles. Karianna readjusted the MI, making it thinner and wider on the side of their approach, giving the warheads something solid to crash upon if they came too close. A flash of antimatter radiation from Shelly's shot took out several, but sixteen of the missiles made it through. I tried using the Para Lux array to target the others, but they were too small, too swift.

Missiles crashed against Karianna's modified MI, explosions causing them to malfunction and drift off into space as little more than junk.

Two made it past our defenses.

In a flash of searing, white-hot pain, the missiles struck the surface of our skin, igniting. Fusion reactions vaporized the upper layers of several decks on the aft end and along one side of the former *Reverie* at our center. Excruciating pain followed. For an instant, it was as if someone had reached into my fleshy back with a set of fingers made of ragged knives and removed my kidney without anesthesia. I was not alone in this agony. Karianna cried out with me as these sharp fingers dug and twisted and then . . . nothing.

Everything went black.

The world flashed past in fits and starts.

I saw the faces of those I had lost. Dad, Mom . . . Esteban. Omar. Alexander . . . that strange creature at the end of all time . . .

Light fought to creep back in. It was a struggle to recover my faculties, consciousness reaching for awakening, clawing, climbing out of the infinitely dark pit it had been relegated to. We had to keep fighting, but our assault against the *Absolution* had paused. Our MI had collapsed from our pain, and we were defenseless.

"Milo," Proxy said, its nose almost touching mine, Shelly by its side. "Get up. Come back to us. Get up."

It took a moment to realize that I was on my back in my virtual environment, the cat in my face, one paw on my arm. The nuclear explosions had shocked my system.

"Karianna?" I called, but got no response.

"She is fine. Her Proxy is getting her up. We are attenuating the feedback from ship systems as we speak. That was not how it was intended to work."

"It's always hurt, Proxy. But never like that."

The *Transcendence* rocked from the impact of weapons fire; our defensive barrier having fallen. I reached out with an open palm and Shelly helped me up. I attempted to collect the MI's broken pieces. The nanomachines fell through my fingers like dry sand caught in a warm breeze. In this dazed state, I was only able to recover a small portion of the defensive machines, but maybe they would be enough for now.

Alarms sounded all over the ship, our nanovats furiously working to keep up with repairs. The battle had swiftly tipped in Veetor's favor, and that was just one missile.

I did my best to keep up with his renewed assault, ordering Lance and Chevelle to focus on disabling his systems, when another signal pinged our network from an unclear direction, no words, just a request to speak.

Who the fuck now? Karianna thought, and I felt a flood of relief. She was conscious. Thank the Universe, she was conscious.

"Identify yourself," I replied to the incoming call. "This is Milo Hughes of the *Transcendence*. For the love of all that is good, do not fire on us. We have traveled a long, long way, and we have come to help."

There was a delay before we heard a response, the signal quality crackly, full of static, low-fidelity. *"Foundry vessel, this is the overseer of the Free Citizens of Earth, hailing you on a secure channel. Flee this scene and come to us. We must talk."* It was a woman this time, her tone far kinder than the others we had already met. She spoke with a slight accent I could not quite identify, and so as a result, she seemed to enunciate her words with a specific cadence. *"Do you read me? Are your communications dead?"*

"Another group?" Shelly put a palm to her face and shook her head. "What is this all about?"

Karianna growled, *"Everyone's been screwing around with things since we've been gone. They couldn't just get the fuck along."*

"Now, now, hold up," I replied to the caller. "Who the hell are you to give me orders?"

Another delay in response. *"I don't think that matters right now. You're being crushed between two very confused groups of people, and I have no intention of doing the same. This makes us friendly. We need to talk, and that is all you need to know at this moment. My best advice? Make a distraction, break some dishes, do what you must, but get away, and quick. Just don't hurt anyone as you go. You would regret that later."*

Again, none of this was the warm welcome we had been expecting. Isopteran attackers loyal to the Gray Queen? Sure. A few confused humans, almost certainly. But not outright hostility and naked aggression.

I wasn't sure what to do. Should we stay and make our stand against a madman and his misguided admiral? Or, should we see what other screwed-up situation we might have found ourselves in? None of the options were good.

We should flee, Karianna's thoughts fed back to me. *I know I don't normally take this position, but . . . let's go see what this is. Live to fight another day. It doesn't feel right killing the Remnant Fleet, and there's no way we make it out without doing just that. I want that fucker dead, and for so many reasons, but . . . damn it. We have to run. We have to regroup.*

She was right.

"Shelly," I said, turning to her. I waved a hand over the battle theater that surrounded us, explosions and flashes of light filling the space at random intervals. "We're out of here. You know what to do."

She gave me a weak smile, took a deep breath, and nodded.

"Fighters, come back," Karianna ordered.

Shelly reached out into the black of space, taking command of two of the ship's weapon systems, splitting their focus. An instant later, she flung a series of crystalline shapes from the forward end of the *Transcendence*, while in the same moment, slugs of antimatter were cast to the surface of Triton. Before the approaching fleet, or the UEI *Absolution* could respond, waves of electromagnetic energy thousands of kilometers wide cascaded out from a series of piezoelectric spatial compression bombs. These waves were joined by devastating flashes of antimatter ignited in open space. The effect was like that of the brightest fireworks show I'd ever seen, causing my instruments to go dead for a moment in their radioactive backwash.

With our fighters back aboard, I closed my eyes and tightened every muscle in my body, willing the ship to move. It was a struggle at best to get anything to work as it should. Every muscle in my extended body was rigid from our moment of unconsciousness. Karianna joined my effort, and we slipped in and out of critical systems, coaxing them back to life.

"Punch it," I said, and the *Transcendence* began to burn away, hard.

Confused in the moment, systems fried, the *Absolution* and the UEI Remnant Fleet did not pursue. They drifted in whatever direction which they already had momentum, weapons silent, instruments grasping for static. This gave us the opportunity to put some distance between us and them.

After several minutes had passed, I reached out to our caller once more, my heart rate slowing. "What's the address? Where are we going?"

Again, there was a delay before she responded. *"Svalbard & Jan Mayen, Norwegian territory. Can you find us?"*

Though the name meant nothing to me, it sure meant something to my wife. Shelly's hands were held close to her chest, fingers interlaced, a thoughtful smile having blossomed on her face that seemed out of place given our desperate situation.

"The seed vault," she whispered in reverence. "They're at the global seed vault."

CHAPTER 21

We were not pursued.

The *Absolution* and the remnant UEI fleet were left behind in Triton's orbit. However, I wasn't confident if this was because of our distraction, or if it was something else. Now that we had made contact of some kind within the system of humanity's birth, SOL no longer acted like a ghost. Over the next few hours, we received fresh signals and power readings, from everywhere and nowhere. It was clear that our appearance had triggered a series of automated responses, presumably both human and alien. Clickers and Splicers, whatever they were, and a dozen other fragmented factions of humankind, were now screaming at one another across the void.

We had been the trigger.

SOL had awakened.

"Isopteran signals coming in," Shelly reported. "Ada and I will go through these and see what we can find out. Our early estimates are that these are navigational chatter, not much more."

I scanned the vicinity around us with passive instruments, stretching out for five AU, searching for active fungara. When I found none, I turned back to Shelly. "Any idea where the termites are? Where the Gray Queen has her base of operations?"

"Not yet. We'll tell you more when we can."

"Okay. We took quite a beating back there. It will take a couple weeks of subjective time before the damage from those warheads is repaired. That was a close one. They almost took out the decks containing our Star Spheres. So, any heads-up would be good."

"We'll do our best."

"I know you will." I paused for a moment, thinking over the last few days, not those spent in objective time during travel, but our subjective, fleshy time that stretched back to Nest. As a group, we'd been on edge for close to a month, going from one crisis to the next with little respite. Because of this state, Proxy had brought a few matters to my attention. We needed to take care of ourselves, if for nothing else than our mental well-being. "Before you go."

"Yeah?"

"Keep an eye on Ada. I don't think she's been sleeping well."

"What do you mean?"

"I know you don't remember, because you were out of it. But when the fungara had control of you, Ada was determined to save you at any cost. Determined to solve whatever puzzle it was to make those tiny machines stop. And so yeah, she took some measures to get more done, didn't sleep well, if at all, for days."

She blinked as she processed this idea. "Are you saying she was taking stimulants?"

"Yes, and a lot of them. I know she's an adult and all, and it's her choice, but as a friend, it might be good to keep an eye on that. I don't think she could bear the idea of losing someone else so dear to her."

Shelly nodded at this, her expression dark, heavy with the clear weight of long conversations leaden with tears. "She's still pretty fragile over Alexander's death. They were done, but that doesn't matter. They loved each other."

"They did," I said, pulling Shelly into a tight embrace. "Just keep an eye out."

"Of course." She kissed me on the cheek and vanished from my virtual environment, heading off to solve yet another puzzle.

I hoped this challenge wouldn't prove to be too stressful, forcing Ada back to that no-win place. She needed a mental break. We'd all done a few stimulants here and there, pressed through when we needed to, but the rush of dopamine they provided was addictive. It wasn't like cocaine or methamphetamines, I didn't think, but they gave you a rush, a feeling of indomitable strength and a manic, inflated ego that could easily untether you from the truth.

"Thanks, Proxy," I said, scratching the cat behind its ear.

"I protect the pilot," it said. "They are extensions of you."

Several small planetoids and free-roaming asteroids exhibited power signatures within our passive instrument bubble. There were clear signs of active machinery, though when I probed deeper at those closest to us, they seemed to be nothing more than automated systems that had woken up. There were no obvious signs that humans or aliens of any kind were living aboard them, and if they were, they were being sneaky like the Melcorin.

As we drew nearer the center of our home system, the heat radiating from our Sun magnified, exciting the particles penetrating the layers of our flesh, our every senses, warming our frozen hearts. This solar embrace was both reassuring and desperate, as if we'd returned to a long-lost loved one who demanded to know where we'd been, why we had left them, and why it had been so many years. They had seen so much in the time between, been forced to grow up in ways that were not fair, and we had chosen this auspicious moment, when their very existence was on the brink, to return to them. Why now? Why today? Did we not love them anymore?

We were sorry.

We did not mean for it to be like this.

We left to save you, to make you better.

We did not abandon you; circumstance kept us away.

We wanted to come home. Please believe us.

We wanted to come home.

Every step of this final crossing was significant, every asteroid, every rock, cataloged and cross-referenced against records from our passing in the *Vasco Da Gama*. So much had changed in SOL since we left, and yet also so little. The void was peculiar this way, populated with an uneven mixture of chaotic change and timeless monoliths, a broken counterbalance of existence. Some worlds remained untouched as if they were insects caught in amber, while others shifted as easily as sand dunes in a storm.

Mars hung suspended off to our starboard side, its atmosphere swirling with blue lights, a twinkle of silver collecting at several points on its surface. There were colonies present, though whether they were inhabited or not was the question. We let the red world be, curving around the system to an orb of blue and brown, of storms and scars—a place of disease and sickness.

Earth, Karianna whispered within her shaky thoughts. *There's Earth . . .*

My stomach twisted into knots. I could now see what had happened to our home, and the wanton abuse was like being stabbed with a rusty knife. I could do nothing but draw into a ball, knees to chest, wrapping my arms around myself as I floated in my virtual environment alone.

Our instruments began returning more detailed scans of the planet. The first thing I noticed at this distance was the band of lights that trailed along the equator, twinkling, glowing dots of debris en masse that ringed the planet like a collection of twisted silver scrap and gemstones. Among the band were structures big and small, from a few modules strung together to floating industrial parks. I wasn't sure what all these structures were, but they were dense in number, and some of them were alive, letting off coded radio signals and power readings, screaming swift and silent along a low-orbital plane.

Beyond the ring, upon the surface, damage was everywhere, entire continents devoid of any significant signs of life. What were once vast forests reaching thousands of miles had been reduced to empty tracts of desert. What remained of the icecaps—and to my surprise, some was left—could hardly be called substantial. The surface showed signs of gamma radiation along scars in what were once major population centers. These included central Africa, Moscow, New England, and the whole of Ireland. Surface temperatures on average, even in the winter locations of the northern hemisphere, were far above the acceptable range by nearly ten degrees Celsius. It would be a wonder if anything at all was living on the surface.

We'd known that it would be bad, but seeing it, that was something else. The vibrant world we had departed from so long ago no longer existed. And the pain of seeing that first-hand had no words. To use Hy's earlier perspective, this was no longer cerebral. The fall of Earth was no longer an idea. It was before us.

"Your home world does not look well," Proxy stated from below me, its eyes alight with data. "It appears the Jevox's information was accurate, or accurate enough."

My chest was tight as a vice, the warmth from the Sun's embrace fading into not just cold, but an absence of heat. An absence of life. A vacuum. A void.

Shelly appeared and wrapped her arms around me from behind, resting her head on my back. We floated there for a time, breathing our non-air in this virtual place, listening to one another's heartbeat.

"We knew it would be bad," she said.

"For all the pain we've faced, we've been spoiled," I said, my hands shaking, eyes blurry. "It's true, we've been living in luxury. We've had our every need and whim catered to, while on Earth people have been dying by the billions. They've been suffering, killing one another, scraping along to keep themselves fed. And what did they think of us? Did they believe we abandoned them? Left them for dead? We didn't. We tried. We tried to make it right."

She squeezed again, the tip of her nose nuzzling into the back of my neck. "Being honest, most of them likely believe that FICSE took us all. That the Foundry had been hostile, or an accident happened along the way."

"This isn't fair."

"No," she said, squeezing me tighter. "It's not. None of this is fair."

"Milo," Proxy cut in, its eyes rising to meet mine, looking to me with an intensity I wasn't sure I'd ever seen in it. "All might seem dark and desperate, but we can protect life. So long as you live, your people are not without hope."

I was in no fucking frame of mind to consider any rationalities, to listen to any platitudes, but I did know, even in this dark place, that we couldn't change what had already happened. Despite the pain in my chest, the ache in my soul, I had to be the leader. I had to show them we could do what we came to do.

"We need to grab the rest of them," Shelly said, letting go of me and floating around to the front. "They need to see before we get closer."

I hung my head. "You're right. Of course, you're right."

"How's Karianna holding up?" she asked with a wounded expression on her face.

I closed my eyes and scrubbed at them with my palms, clearing my vision. "About the same. Hard not to share the pain when everything is connected through the integration."

Shelly pressed her lips together into a hard line.

We remained ready in case of attack, everyone staying in their Star Spheres as we met within a re-creation of the shared bridge space, a room we'd used often when we were a fleet of two. The space was a long hall made of white walls and white furniture that mirrored the aesthetics of our homes aboard the FICSE starships. Down its center ran an infinity couch, which faced a giant display close to ten meters wide.

There were no snacks. No refreshments waited for us. No one craved anything other than to see what had happened to their birthplace.

As the crew reviewed the data, they were hit with a mixture of reactions. We'd known what was happening, but seeing it . . . well, observation made it real.

Lance, who had been sitting at the end of the couch, shot up and began pacing the room, kicking at storage boxes near the back wall while screaming obscenities. Ada sat silent, gripping Shelly's hand so tight her knuckles were turning white. Leo, sitting beside her, cocked his head to the side in thought. He sketched furiously with his pencil on a notepad, translating the images before us and around us, capturing the emotion of our moment within a tableau of agony.

"We have to remember," he kept mumbling. "We have to remember this moment."

James, for once, didn't move. He had his hands over his face, his breathing labored. Karianna was beside him, her expression cold, right foot tapping against the floor. She kept looking to me, and through our link within the ship I knew she wanted comfort, but that was something I could not give her. Sensing her feelings, James climbed out from whatever dark place he had stumbled within his head long enough to take hold of her hand. She turned away from me, and without looking at him closed her eyes and folded into his arms, where she began to sob. It was not like her to do this. She just couldn't keep it inside any longer.

Xuan and Hy were on the floor on bended knees, crying out wordlessly to God, the Universe, whoever was out there that might listen. As for Chevelle, she seemed to have fallen into a frantic conversation with herself, while Dante and Emilia sat stunned, their eyes and mouths wide.

Renata, of all of us, didn't appear sad, but she was angry, like Lance. She raised a finger at the giant display and shook it.

"Every projection pointed to this!" she growled. "Every goddamned one! Why didn't they listen? Why didn't our leaders have the balls to do something about it? To come to some sort of agreement? Why couldn't they work this out?"

"Everyone was hungry," Dante stated, deadpan.

Renata threw up her arms at him. "No, no, no. Not everyone. *Not everyone.*"

I let the crew do what they needed to in the moment to process their feelings. This was a pain that was not going to be easily pushed away, but if we were to help those who might be left, we had to get to a better place.

Frelo walked before the display, raised a hand, and shut it off. Everyone stared at the alien, saying nothing, our melodramatic lamentations put on pause.

"I mourn for your species," it said, raising its right hand, "as I mourn for my own. We experienced this pain. We experienced this agony long ago. We were forced to rebuild, to renew, to rise from the ashes. If there is any species that has seen what you have seen, and will see, it is the Jevox. Remember what the Gan did to us. They laid waste to our home. Destroyed all we had built, all we had loved. It is for this, I help you. We help you.

"All may seem hopeless, it may seem like the end, but I assure you, it is not. Aboard this ship, we have the seeds to save your species. We have the seeds to undo much of this damage. We have the seeds to start again, if only we can enlist help. Not all hope is lost."

Proxy appeared at the front of the room beside Frelo, its chin raised in a defiant pose. "Not all hope is lost."

Chinchillette winked into existence opposite my cat, its gaze focused on Karianna. "Not all hope is lost."

A heavy silence hung in the air, but even our sobs had been quelled for the moment. While this hurt in ways we could not fully express, we had known this was coming. We knew it had been bad. We knew what our mission had become. Johan had done what he had done because he knew Earth was not going to be easy to fix. Though his means were corrupt, he'd wanted to undo what we had done to our planet, give humanity back their birthplace. It was all any of us wanted, and it was why all of us had ended up on this mission to begin with. My parents had taken the choice from me, but now, given all that I had seen and the perspective I had been given . . . I was grateful.

Not for the first time, I considered how if I had remained on Earth, I could have just been another casualty. And even if I hadn't been, I might have lived an unremarkable life. In this position, I had the opportunity to change it all. To turn back the clock. To make a difference that would save our species.

I couldn't waste that opportunity feeling sorry for myself.

I stood up, fighting for an instant against a weight of sorrow, then wiped my nose clean with the back of my arm, took a deep breath, and faced the group. "Not all hope is lost."

One by one, they dried their tears and cooled their anger. We had had our moment, and there would be others. But for now, it was time to bootstrap.

Lance broke the silence, "We can do this, can't we?"

"Yes," I replied. "Yes, we can. Like Frelo said, we need help."

Chevelle thumbed her nose and tossed back her head. "Ain' never been a challenge I back down off. You have a plan, boss man?"

The others began to rally themselves.

I gave her a nod, then readjusted our collective subjective time reference, allowing several days to pass in just a few seconds, drawing us closer to Earth. The screen behind me came back to life and I turned to face it. Karianna untangled herself from James's arms and came to stand beside me. Her unease, her pain bright through the integration, were like a raw wound on her chest that stung every time air blew across it.

The crew stood silent as we piloted the *Transcendence* the rest of the way back to Earth at an accelerated pace. We slipped past the moon, catching a glimpse of the sprawling Lunar colony below, its domes illuminated by only a few scattered lights, before we rose over its horizon to face Earth. This was nothing like the Earthrise our early astronauts had enjoyed. This was not the expanse that took the breath of Neil Armstrong or Buzz Aldrin. But it was Earth.

Where the upper and lower orbits of our world had once been free of little more than the occasional man-made satellite, they were now broken up into four distinct layers of glittering debris, the most distant starting at 4,800 kilometers from the surface, the nearest, 600 kilometers or less. These bands followed but were not restricted to the equatorial line, chunks of metal, silicates, and rock glimmering back at us, catching the sun's light as they rotated. The Earth now had a ring like Saturn, and though beautiful at this distance, it was more dangerous to navigate than a minefield covered with razor wire. Among this chaotic ring were a plethora of working structures—habitat modules, space stations, empty shuttle docks, factories, and supply depots, many of them painted with a white and black logo stating *HARDYHAB*, along with the flags of a hundred different nations. While it appeared that not many humans were still living up here, it was clear that some were. The question was, did these people ally with Veetor and the Remnant Fleet? Or did they stand with someone else? Maybe the group this woman was from?

None made contact with us.

"We can hide in the debris," Proxy suggested, taking up position beside my leg and rubbing me with its face. "The materials present should hide us."

"Even as big as we are?"

"Yes."

Karianna narrowed her eyes and navigated us around a field of debris into the middle of a series of what appeared to be shattered spaceports currently over Southern Africa. This maneuver was no easy feat given that our ship was over a kilometer in length. Despite all her impulsiveness, she handled the controls with deft fingers.

Proxy prepared the Swift Shuttles and loaded them with what supplies we might need on the surface. When the crew exited the Star Spheres, they got dressed, then retrieved backpacks of food, clothing, water, and a variety of survival equipment, along with our rifles. All we needed to do was fly down to the surface.

Everyone readied to leave the ship but for Frelo, Dante, and Emilia. The three of them stayed behind to keep an eye on the house. I wasn't sure if there was much that they could do if things went sideways, but it felt good to know that someone was up here.

We split up, half of the crew with me, the other half with Karianna, our shuttles detaching from the *Transcendence* to drop to the planet at maximum safe acceleration.

Given what we had just been through, we did not wish to be easily followed, and so we entered the atmosphere much further east than our target. We dove through the stratosphere over the skies of Alaska, twin fireballs gliding west to Norway, the ring of habitations ignoring us. The once icy tundra, a sprawling expanse of vast planes and breathtaking mountains, had become a wasteland sparsely dotted with white, most of its permafrost having melted. While I knew the state had never been densely populated, even at the height of the birthing crisis, what settlements remained appeared to be ruined or abandoned.

I took us closer to the surface to get a better look, keeping us just high enough we didn't have to avoid mountains. There were little signs of life, a few scattered trees, a flock of birds here and there, what might have been a collection of deer drinking by a lake. But no humans. No tracks in the snow. No fires. Just emptiness. Everyone remained glued to the windows, hoping to get a glimpse of something encouraging.

Our route took us over the choppy waters of the Chukchi sea along the northern coast of Siberia. There was little or no ice to be seen, as there should have been. Smudges of black appeared on the horizon, stretching out into the continent. Manmade structures. Minimal power readings.

Karianna followed my lead.

Expansive cities had been erected along the jagged shoreline, thousands of homes made of modular blocks of concrete and steel, reminiscent of the cheap, 3D-printed concrete domiciles major cities were adopting before we left. There were scattered signs that some of them might be inhabited, the occasional pillar of smoke exiting a chimney, animal skins drying on racks atop roofs. Cars of unfamiliar make had been left in the streets, most of them appearing ruined, though some looked serviceable, if old. The densest concentration of homes went on for eighteen to twenty miles, with no humans in sight.

Near the edge of the trash-strewn city, a peculiar aberration made for the shoreline. It was dark and leathery, its form striding down the broken and empty streets on four spindly, thirty-meter-long legs, each with joints that reached above its body like a set of shrugging shoulders. The legs forked into smaller appendages, giving the alien visitor eight points of contact to the ground, its feet pushing forgotten, parked cars aside. Near the top of the legs hung a thick body with a flattened head. It had a single blue eye and antennae maybe ten and fifteen meters in length sprouting from it like whiskers. It plodded at a slow, deliberate pace, pausing from time to time to dig through piles of rubble like an elderly dumpster diver, paying us flyers no mind as we passed.

Like most aliens we had encountered, it was impossible to say if this one was hostile or benign. But whatever it was, whatever its intent, seeing this striding monstrosity making its way down the streets of a human city was deeply unsettling. Knowing that entities other than humans were roaming our world made me tremble.

We left the city and its strange visitor behind, our two shuttles screaming off over the Artic Ocean to our target. It was time to stop sightseeing and do something about all this.

We had survivors to meet. We had a mission to complete.

CHAPTER 22

We skimmed a half dozen feet over the Greenland Sea, midnight-blue skies above. Our Swift Shuttles approached our target from the west, their engines kicking up sprays of water in our wake. We'd swung around the island once known as Svalbard, home of the Global Seed Vault, so that we could approach the ancient mining town of Longyearbyen from the fjords rather than the mountains.

Once we had come within a couple hundred miles of the island, our mysterious caller had given us instructions on where to land. They had detected us with their ground-based installations, and we had not been attacked, so that was a good sign, but from a passing look at the state of things down here, we shouldn't have worried too much. They had no true air defense as far as we could detect. They were just a small, ramshackle city.

Given the weather was clear, I was able to make a visual inspection of our target. Unlike the rest of what we had seen so far, Svalbard, an isolated archipelago in the Arctic Ocean, appeared to be teeming with life by comparison. While the islands might have been a desolate tundra, mostly frozen grasslands, rocks, and snowcapped peaks, they were beautiful in their own way. Mountains populated the darkened landmass, sheltering the valleys and fjords from the harshness of the polar ocean winds, appearing like giants standing watch at night.

Readings showed that radiation levels were within a safe limit here, and that the air was fit to breathe. Whoever these people were, they had made a smart choice in where they'd settled. With all the geopolitical turmoil and climate crises over the past 590 years, they'd been left relatively alone in this isolated place. That gave me a sense of hope.

We began to slow, pulling back from just under Mach One to a little over a hundred miles per hour. Isfjorden, the narrow passage of water that entered the island's interior from the western end, encircled us, displaying mountains along its northern shore, with open fields of low grass on its southern edge. Longyearbyen came into view ahead, a scattered collection of several hundred colorfully painted buildings connected by mostly cracked or unimproved roads. Many of the steel and wooden structures were painted fire engine red, while others were a mustard yellow or a vibrant, royal blue. A few miles closer than the town was our landing zone, a worn strip of concrete hemmed by a few hangers on one side with a short, square tower at the center. This was where our caller had sent us.

Karianna and I did a pass over the airport, taking a quick visual inspection for any dangers, but found nothing more than a few broken commercial aircraft and a lot of snow. Satisfied that it was safe, we circled back and made our approach, initiating our vertical landings at the center of the runway near the tower.

Our engines shut off, and we secured the Swift Shuttles.

I crawled out of my Star Sphere, bare chested, dripping wet, wearing nothing more than my underwear. My partial nakedness was met by Shelly's gaze, a bright smile on her face.

"Hey, beautiful," she said.

I blushed. "Hi . . . ?"

"It's cold up here." She tossed me some pants. "Might want to dress accordingly."

"Yes, ma'am."

We all collected our gear, putting on packs and slinging rifles over our shoulders. I hoped not to make a poor first impression with the caller by showing up armed to the teeth, which was why we had skipped the powered armor suits, but I would be damned if I'd let us get taken by surprise. We had no good reason to trust them other than that they hadn't yet attacked us.

"No one leaves till all of us are ready," I called down the shuttle as I slipped into my clothes, which included several layers of shirts, a puffy coat, a scarf, and a hat. "Lance . . ."

"Yo."

"I'll go first, but let's spread out a little. Lead the group, watch for danger, but keep your weapons low. Let's try not to threaten them."

"Alright. Chevelle doing the same?"

I nodded, then pinged Karianna's implants just to be sure.

"Always wanted to visit here," Hy said, lacing up his boots. Xuan slapped his fingers away, not satisfied with how he was doing it. He tossed up his hands to let her finish the job, looking annoyed. "It is very pretty here. Do you believe the Seed Vault still stands? It was meant for that. To survive catastrophe."

Shelly licked her lips as she adjusted the straps on her backpack. "I sure hope so. Tried to spot it when we came in. Those sorts of resources would go a long way in helping us rebuild Earth."

"I'm not familiar with this vault you keep talking about," Leo said. "What is it? I can take a guess, sure, but I'd rather not look stupid."

"Seriously?" Ada whirled on him. "Quantum smart boy artist doesn't know about the Seed Vault?"

He raised his palms in a gesture of "what the hell do you expect out of me?"

Shelly supplied the answer. "The Svalbard Global Seed Vault was founded in the early 2000s. It was designed to be the ultimate insurance policy for the world's food supply. Within its deep halls, they were able to secure millions of seeds, which represented every important crop and variety available. As cold as it is in the ground here, or cold as it was at least, it makes a perfect environment for storing these seeds. Thick rocks. Permafrost. The seeds are brought here, checked, then sealed in a special packaging to keep them dry. The builders wanted nothing more than to ensure future generations could overcome their challenges, just like what it looks like we faced. Shifting climate. Too many people for the ecosystem to support."

Leo tipped his head at Shelly, then gave Ada a pointed look. "And this place should have survived?"

"We'll see. The island appears intact. That's a good sign."

"Let's go check it out then," I said, making my way to the front of our group, rifle in hand, its barrel pointed at the ground. "Follow my lead."

I raised my right hand, and the door of the Swift Shuttle swished open, allowing a gust of icy cold air to rush in. For an instant, I was transported back to that dead moon Bellamy had rescued me from, hungry and frozen and broken, part of my left hand amputated from frostbite, but I forced that memory to retreat. This place was not the same.

We stepped out onto the tarmac, steam rising from our mouths, the sky above dark but not fully night, the brightest of the stars twinkling down at us. The ground beneath our feet was slick in spots, and wind whipped around us, carrying with it occasional flurries. I gave Karianna a look across the runway. From her expression, we had had the same idea. For the first time since we were small children, our feet were back on the ground. Our feet were back on Earth.

We made for the tower with the slanted windows at its top. This was the most likely structure to be a command center. Karianna and her group followed us in parallel about twenty feet away.

Our crew had been out of the shuttles for no more than a minute when a group of five human beings hurried out of the squat, square tower. Among their company, two were armed with menacing-looking rifles and postures suggesting they were prepared to make use of them if necessary. Clearly soldiers, they were dressed in tactical gear of a variety I didn't recognize, loose-fitting pants and slick jackets with hardened plates of segmented black and red body armor worn atop, all of it fitted together with what appeared to be slender, mechanical augmentations. Helmets with dark faceplates reflected snow light, making it impossible to see the eyes within. Our teams tensed at their presence, the barrels of our rifles inadvertently drawing themselves up to level out. I shot a ping through my implants to the group, asking them to calm down.

While the sight of the soldiers was unsettling, they were joined an instant later by three others who sported no obvious weapons. On the left came a portly, broad-shouldered man with dark skin in what I guessed was his thirties. He was well dressed, in black slacks with shiny black boots, a long peacoat, a pressed white shirt, and a red tie. His dress, paired with his close-cropped hair and a tidy beard, as well as a set of rounded glasses, gave him a look of severe intelligence.

Opposite him was another dark-skinned person, though this one had an indeterminate gender. One part of my brain wanted to categorize them as a man given some of their masculine features, square face, the bend of an Adam's apple, and the gait of their step, but others didn't match that. They wore slim pants with a tailored jacket designed to accentuate curves rather than lines. From beneath layers of wool, I spotted a billowing silk blouse, incongruous to the cold. They had pink-painted nails, a fluffy afro, a series of gems that formed a line from their forehead to the end of their nose, and more than their share of makeup. I found myself having an argument in my head, attempting to categorize this person. Every social map I had available made that difficult. And so, in that moment, I decided not to label them at all. What did it matter anyways? The only label that really mattered was human. This person was human.

At the front of their group was the caller herself, of this I had no doubt. She strode to us with a purpose, her back straight, her blue eyes cold as the mountaintops across the fjord, expression narrowing and as intentional as a razor. A braid of blond hair rested over her right shoulder, unmoving, while her unbuttoned long coat flapped in the icy wind, its hems brushing against her black jeans. She was average in height, over five and a half feet, athletic in a way only hard times brought, and yet her companion in the glasses, as well as the soldiers, towered over her. This did not make her seem any less. The fire she carried in her belly was as bright as a star making planetfall.

It was clear that she had seen terrible things. She had known death and pain. She had faced it all down and told it to go straight to hell. She was too busy with living to be bothered with dying.

Shelly whispered in my ear, "I would not cross her."

And while I didn't respond, she knew my answer.

They stopped some twenty feet ahead of us.

"Foundry pilots," the caller said. "I see you by the way you walk. The intention of your step." She pointed to Karianna, then to me. "The two of you have given a donation."

I spoke up. "We have. You must be our contact. The woman from the signal."

"That's me." She crossed her arms and began scanning our group, looking at each person for an instant before moving on to the next. Evaluating. "First things first, has the Foundry made you mad?"

"What?" Karianna asked, looking to me, then back at her. "Why in the hell would it do that? I need some clarity here. Made us mad? As in like, angry? Or like, crazy?"

"Veetor tells us of this donation process," she went on. "They remove limbs from your body and take a part of your brain, replacing these parts with Foundry machines. We can only assume that his, how do we say it nicely . . . his *disposition* is the result of the donation process."

"No . . ." Karianna said, her voice hardening. "Donation has nothing to do with his brand of nutso. He might be worse than before, he might now have power, but he's always been a bad egg. He's always been crazy, self-centered, hateful."

The man in glasses whispered something to the caller, who then whispered to the one with gems on their face. They were trying to figure us out. I only wished I could hear the discussion.

I raised my hands and took a step forward, closing the distance between our groups. "Look, we're not crazy. The Foundry hasn't altered us in any manipulative way. We just—"

"Step back!" the soldier on the left of their group shouted, raising the barrel of his rifle to level on my chest. Seeing this sudden move, his partner mirrored the action. The caller's unarmed companions tensed, both taking a step back, clearing the lines of sight.

Lance and Chevelle responded without orders, fixing their weapons on the soldiers. The whole situation was fast spinning out of control.

"Woah, woah, woah!" I shouted, waving my arms. "Everyone—"

Chevelle, Karianna, and several others joined the mix, shouting at the soldiers to disarm. One voice carried over them all.

"Order them to put down their weapons," Lance demanded, his barrel switching between being pointed at the soldier on the left and at the caller, his feet shuffling from side to side. "Do it. Now!"

Her voice rose over the cacophony. "And why should I? Why should I take orders from you?"

"Because if you don't, this is going to get real bloody, real quick. We've seen more than our fair share of action. Don't screw with us."

She spat back at him, "Says the man who isn't wearing body armor. Bravery does not become you, goldilocks. We know how this will go. You'll hardly get off a shot before you're taken down. Those exosuits our guards are wearing will shrug off almost anything you can throw at them."

"But not these," Lance said, shaking the barrel of his rifle as he narrowed his eyes at the woman. "Our rifles are loaded with uranium-tipped, armor-piercing rounds, hard and hot enough to melt any material, but that's not the worst of it. Each round also contains a colony of nanomachines that will infect the target and dismantle them from the inside. So even if the shot doesn't kill, the machines will finish the job. How's that for your consideration?"

The caller seemed uncertain for an instant. She moved to raise a hand as if to forestall her people's actions but then put it back down, opting to wait the moment out. She seemed far too comfortable in this kind of standoff. Her unarmed companions looked to one another, debating wordlessly, but made no move to interfere.

None of what Lance had said about the ammo was true, other than it being armor piercing. The rounds were effective enough against Isopteran armor, sure, so we could only assume it would work against these soldiers, but that was about it. I just hoped we didn't have to put that feature to the test.

How the hell had we ended up here? I felt naked without the protection of the ship, without body armor. A bluff was all that was keeping us alive.

"No respect from anyone, anymore," the caller mused. Her right arm lowered to her side, and she made a gesture with her fingers. I watched with fascination as they twitched in a clear pattern, unsure what she was doing. "I'll give you one more chance to back off. You'll come under my protection, I promise, but you must lower your weapons."

"Oh no. Beef-ting, fam," Chevelle spouted back. "Don't be another wasteman. Back off it."

She shook her head. "I didn't understand a word of that. Is it even English? What are you talking about?"

"No worry 'bout me. Allow dat."

The woman flicked her fingers again, and with what I was now certain was a silent command, and something strange happened in the space between us. Out of the cracked and broken concrete of the tarmac, a sheet of liquid I'd failed to notice earlier sprang to life. A mercurial sheen no more than a few atoms thick rapidly formed into the shape of a quicksilver dog, head rising up as high as my hip. It was made of all sharp angles and lines, no eyes, and a mouth full of razor-like teeth. The creature looked as if it was fashioned out of solid sheets of reflective metal formed into chunky, three-dimensional polygons. Before any of us could react, the metallic canine threw itself at me, hurling me onto my back. As I fell to the ground, blue skies and scattered clouds filling my vision, I heard someone scream, though no one fired a shot.

I raised my prosthetic arm out of reflex, protecting my exposed neck with my elbow, but it wasn't enough. The dog, perched atop my chest, reached out with one of its fore paws, and I felt a cold spike press into the skin of my breast just above the heart.

"Ingrid," one of the others spoke, though I couldn't see who it was, their voice deep. "Is this the time?"

My heart thundered, mouth going dry. Everyone paused as a decision was made.

"Lower your weapons," the caller said, her voice taking on an annoyed edge, though it was no less hard. "That means the two of you. Steven. Price. Weapons down. I said weapons down!"

The metallic dog stared at me with its non-eyes, nose inches from mine, its surfaces reflecting back a distorted version of my face. The spiked paw pressed down a little firmer, pain shooting through my chest. I didn't think it had drawn blood, but I couldn't be sure. I suspected that any sudden movement might result in me being impaled through the heart.

I closed my eyes for a moment and took a deep breath, fighting not to twitch.

"There we go," Ingrid said. "That's it. Everyone is friends. Everyone is calm."

Karianna growled. "Get that fucking dog off him, bitch."

I could barely see Ingrid from out of the bottom of my vision given how I was pinned to the ground. She shifted in her posture, raised her right hand, and flicked several fingers. The dog made an electrical whine and backed off, taking up station beside her.

"Would it be okay if I sat up now?" I asked no one in particular, my back still flat against the cold, hard tarmac.

Shelly came to my side and helped me up.

"I am so damn tired of ending up on my back," I whispered.

"But I thought you liked being on your back."

That made me chuckle. "Not like this, that's for sure."

Standing once more, I collected my faculties and assessed the situation. It was still tense, sure, but guns had been lowered. I supposed that was progress.

I looked to Ingrid and shook my head. This was going great. Freaking great.

"Can we start over?" I asked, then took a step forward, then another, extending my mechanical arm in a show of friendship. Her guards fought not to raise their weapons, but in the end, they let me close the distance till

I was only a couple feet away, hand extended. "Hello there. My name is Milo Hughes, first of the *Vasco Da Gama*, then the *Fidelas*, and now, of the *Transcendence*. We come in peace."

"The *Vasco Da Gama*?" The caller's hands covered her mouth. "No. It can't be. That ship is a myth, a legend."

"Oh, I can assure you it's true." I gestured at my crewmates. "We are all of the FICSE fleet, born here on Earth, cast off into the stars as kids. And guess what, so is Veetor, no matter what he says. We've come back to you. We've come home to make a difference, to complete the mission. Your name was Ingrid, right?" I waggled my extended hand, trying to draw attention back to it. It felt awkward leaving it hanging out there.

She nodded in thought, then stared down, considering my extended hand. After a heavy moment of consideration, she took hold. Damn, she had a hell of a firm handshake. "Ingrid Gunderson. I represent the Free Citizens of Earth."

"It's a pleasure to meet you, Ingrid. Especially not at gunpoint."

"Come," she stated sharply. "If you're not here to kill us, then I guess you're here to talk. So, let's talk. You have a lot of explaining to do."

"And so do you."

I turned back to my crew and gestured to them with open palms. They lowered their weapons and adopted more relaxed postures, though I did get several sighs and eyerolls. No one liked being threatened.

Ingrid and her group spun around to leave, the metallic dog still with her but having shifted its texture into something softer, now appearing as if it were made of a hairy ferrofluid rather than the low-resolution polygons from an ancient video game.

She gave us a wave over her shoulder. "The trucks are parked in the second hangar. We'll take them into town. We've got plenty of seats for everyone. You can toss your packs on the roof rack."

"You okay?" Shelly whispered, then felt at my chest with a palm. "I saw your face when that dog thing leapt onto you. It hurt, didn't it? You're not bleeding, are you?"

"Yeah, yeah, it hurt. And no, I should be okay."

Lance sidled up beside me and pointed at Ingrid. "She's got a lot of problems."

"I don't think so."

"Did you not see what just happened? We all almost died."

"Yeah, and?" I turned on him. "We've almost died plenty of times. These survivors have been forced into some bad situations is all. I think she's just being careful."

He scrunched up his face and removed a small comb from his pocket, brushing at his beard to calm himself. "You are way too forgiving."

"No." Shelly spoke up for me. "He's angry. Aren't you, love? But what good does that do the mission? Personal feelings won't save us."

She was right. I was angry. Angry in a way where I feared that letting it out might be dangerous.

"Come on," I said, waving them ahead. "Karianna?"

Her dour face brightened at my call. "Yeah?"

"Ready to go find out what's next?"

She ran a hand through her dark hair, the bracelets on her wrist jingling. "You know I am."

CHAPTER 23

We piled into a pair of square-bodied trucks before making a short trip across the island to the town of Longyearbyen. The engines of the vehicles hummed as we sat shoulder to shoulder, rocking from side to side, taking in the sights. A fork in the road not far from the airport caught Shelly's attention, and she tugged on my sleeve. Winding up a snow-dusted mountain on our right was an unimproved road with a simple metal sign stating *GLOBAL SEED VAULT*. It surprised me that as important as this structure was to all of humanity, the road appeared to have no checkpoints, no guards. It was just a dirt path, a side road that could have led anywhere.

We didn't turn to follow it but kept on along the fjord, passing abandoned marinas and rotted fishing vessels, the snow-covered ground populated with plants I didn't recognize. Some of the flora was black, grasslike, with silver flowers that bore dots I could only guess were yellow berries. Others were stunted trees, maybe shrubs, with flapping, green fronds rather than limbs. I wondered if these were alien transplants from another world or something else entirely. It was impossible to say, as diverse as Earth used to be.

Along the shoreline, a group of shadows plodded away from the town, their silhouettes like those of jellyfish walking upon their tentacles. I shivered at their fluid movements, curious what they might be.

I kept a close eye on Ingrid and the guard through the window to the enclosed cab up front. No one said a word as we made the short trip, not even Leo. We merely took it all in, stunned at the sights. Stunned that we were here. We were actually here.

Longyearbyen was much as we had seen from above, a brightly painted town only a few square miles across, with cracked roadways and motley structures, sparsely populated yet lovingly cared for. Unlike the Siberian settlement we'd crossed in which that strange alien had been exploring, these streets contained a scattering of actual humans milling about. Several other similar trucks were on the roads going about their business, while people wearing backpacks roamed the streets, and in the local warehouse yards, others remained busy stacking crates. The buildings were well-maintained, patched but functional, roads kept clear, and other than the occasional ruined structure, everything was nice. Something about the people living here reminded me of Novae, and that made me ache at the memory of Mom and Dad. It was evident that these people had been living here for a long time, working together, keeping the lights on against the dark. Their town might have been a little run-down and worn, sure, but it was not rubble. It had character and pride.

The trucks approached a steel building surrounded by a twenty-foot razor wire fence. A gate rattled open to permit us access. Soldiers who were similarly armed with plated armor and high-power rifles covered our rear before closing us within. When the truck rolled to a halt, the guard sitting in the passenger seat climbed out of the cab and onto the roof. Ingrid slid out of the driver's seat onto the ground and waved for us to get out.

"Toss down their packs," she called, and the guard began doing just that.

Lance sidled up beside me and whispered, "Pretty tight security here. They've got armored soldiers all over the place. Even a few up on the roof. We're going to be in a lot of trouble if we have to run."

"Let's hope we don't," I said. "Any thoughts on their leader?"

He looked the woman up and down, eyes lingering for several seconds, before popping his fingers, rubbing his hands together, and swallowing down whatever deeper thoughts he had. "I'd keep an eye on her. That's my thoughts."

I rested a hand on his shoulder and squeezed. "I'll leave that to you."

"Come on," Ingrid said. "Inside." The ground beside her shimmered with a flash of quicksilver before the mirage disappeared somewhere within the building. "Might not get much darker out here, but I promise the cold will get you if you're not ready for it."

Shelly bent down, putting her palm to the concrete, and sighed. "Not cold enough." She gave Ada a look, and Ada shook her head as if they were thinking the same thing. Sure felt cold enough to me.

We entered the warm embrace of the building and were forced through a checkpoint of armed guards. They searched us over, took our rifles and promised to return them, then led us down a series of halls filled with offices. The floors were covered in some kind of smooth tile with a speckled pattern, the walls painted a neutral gray and showing signs of wear. Within the tiny rooms we passed, desks were covered in papers beside ancient computers of some kind, empty mugs with a variety of colorful logos left abandoned, trash occupying any place that was left. People worked furiously at these many stations, entering information on the ancient terminals, attention focused on the large, flat displays before them, blue light glowing on their unblinking eyes.

From out of a crowded office shot a round-bellied older man, startling me. He extended a hand in greeting, while his other brushed crumbs off his crimson and black sweater. He smiled wide, scanning our group. My attention was drawn to the dimples on his rosy cheeks.

"Hallo!" he said in a cheerful voice. "I am Oskar."

I looked to Ingrid, who had paused in her step, then took his hand. "Milo. Milo Hughes."

"Very good." He shook my hand, hard, then let go, before fumbling around in his pockets. "You hungry? I have breadsticks. A few rolls." He removed a hearty hunk of tan bread from a sling on his shoulder, then fished in a zippered pocket on his pants for several crumbly pieces of baguette. He offered them to us like a kid sharing candy. "A little hard, but the sticks . . . They make them that way. Tasty with soup. Nadia bakes every week. Take your daily bread. Take it."

I wasn't sure what to do in the moment. None of us were that hungry, having just left the Swift Shuttles, each having taken a quick meal of our own liking. But I worried that not accepting this gift might be received as rude. He seemed earnest in his offer. Kind.

Shelly rushed in to save me. "Oskar, was it?"

"Yes, ma'am. I am Oskar."

She put a hand on his broad shoulder, her slender fingers dwarfed by his size, and smiled. "This bread looks tasty. Really tasty. Nadia must be a wonderful cook. Here's the thing . . . we don't wish to be a burden on your personal resources, and we just ate a big meal. Maybe later?"

Oskar nodded his head, appearing pleased with this answer. He tucked the bread away, leaving a dusting of crumbs on the floor. "Oskar will have more for the children. Nice to meet Milo and friends. We will see each other again."

Ingrid nodded at Oskar's sentiment and snapped her head in a gesture for us to follow.

The passage opened into a public meeting space, the halls from the rest of the building feeding into it from the other sides. At the center of the room, lit by sickly yellowish lights, sat a series of tables assembled in a square, the space within them empty but for a few dust bunnies. Along the edges stood a collection of metal shelves, each level filled to the brim with books of varying sizes and conditions. Shelly inspected them with a curious eye, one finger rubbing across their spines as she read the titles. She walked the length of one wall before remarking on their perfect alphabetical placement, A in the top left by last name, advancing to the right and down and working to Z as they went around the room. Items were placed in gaps between the books, knickknacks and collectables, artifacts of painted glass or clay, small sculptures of humans and animals in garish tones, all organized and arranged by color.

Ingrid gestured at the table with a wave. "Feel free to set down your packs."

The crew turned to me for direction. I nodded. "Where should I sit?"

"You?" She narrowed her eyes. "The question is, where do you believe you should sit?"

I looked at the unadorned tables, nothing more than old, cream-colored office furniture you could have easily purchased when I was a kid from any number of chain retailers. They were made of metal and plastic with locking casters on their legs. "This table has no head. I would say anywhere is fine."

"We are all leaders," she replied.

I sat near the middle of one of the faces of the square. Karianna came up behind me and took the seat to my left, while Shelly settled in on my right. The two of them being at my side like this was starting to be a pattern. I looked to Shelly, then my copilot, thankful for their unspoken support. One steadied my heart, while the other steadied my hand. I could not do this without them.

The rest of our crew filled in beside us as Ingrid and her team took the opposite positions. There might not have been a head to this table, but we posed quite a front, one to another. Ingrid sat directly across from me, the one with gemstones on their face on her right, the man in glasses on her left.

"Tight security," I commented, gesturing to the half dozen guards standing around the peripheries who pretended as if we shouldn't see them. "I promise. We aren't here to hurt you. Took our guns anyways. Not much we could do if we wanted to try."

Ingrid looked to the man in glasses, who sighed and waved them off.

"Better?" she asked.

"Yes. Much."

"Our pleasure," she said with a hint of annoyance.

"Looks like you have a good setup," I said. "The town is in good shape, and the environment here isn't totally wrecked. We came in over the northern edge of Russia, where we found a sprawling city, but few people if any were in sight. Hundreds of miles of ruined buildings and wastes. This is a sharp contrast."

"Russia? There's no Russia. That land has not been Russia for over a hundred years at least."

"That so?"

"What was once Russia is now the Nation of the Siberian Expanse. It is one of the larger human settlements remaining, or at least that we know of. They live this far north for the same reasons that we do. Life is harder to sustain closer to the equator, harder to sustain near the many nuclear events of our past."

"We saw the damage from orbit," Karianna cut in. "Earth has scars all over it."

Ingrid nodded. "This is true. But before we get into that, let me stop being rude and introduce my team." She raised a hand and rested it on the table beside her, fingers tapping. "This smart man here on my right is Dameon Price. Dameon is our resource director. He ensures we are doing all that is necessary to keep us fed and that we have plenty of clean water to drink."

"A hard job," Shelly said.

Lance added, "Especially when people don't want to play nice."

Dameon adjusted his rounded glasses, pushing them up his nose, then raised an eyebrow. "Everyone's job is hard. Everyone has to give more than they get. Everyone has to use only what they need, or they are taking from others."

Shelly leaned back in her chair, crossed her arms, and put a fist to her chin. "We understand."

"Beside me on my left," Ingrid went on, placing a palm over the hand of the person with the gemstones on their face. "This is the kind and beautiful soul known as Priscilla, Priscilla West. She is our spiritual guide, our mystic. While Dameon might work to keep us fed, and safe, Priscilla helps us focus on what good there is beyond our suffering."

"A pleasure to meet you all," Priscilla said, raising a hand and waving to us. "We know that the world is full of broken things, but these broken things are the kindest. They think before they act, unlike those who came before us. And so, for us, the greatest sin is to hurt one another, intentionally or not. We must lead with kindness, for if we do, the Universe will respond with the same."

Something about what she said seemed more than just words, more than just a cosmic faith of some kind. I wondered if she'd seen what I had seen. Been where I had been.

I gave Priscilla a quirky smile. "And we are one in the Universe."

"Yes. Yes. We are one in the Universe."

"We represent the Free Citizens of Earth," Ingrid stated, her hands raised, "a coalition of settlements like those here on Svalbard who, while sovereign in our territories, work together to survive. We share information, make trade when conditions are fair, and do all in our power to keep the candle of humanity alight. With the state of things on the surface, it's hard for us to be as mobilized as we'd like, but since our inception by my grandfather over sixty years ago, we have slowed the decline of those trapped on Earth considerably. I, for one, was born here, and will likely die here one day. We want the best for all.

"There are other groups who operate on Earth, other factions around SOL, but their objectives are mixed. Some want to pretend as if nothing has happened or is happening, living high above the death in the clouds, allowing distraction to dictate their reality. Others see no reason to cooperate and seek only to hurt those who have what they want. Some factions are mostly noble, like the former UEI, though they are unreliable at times. And then, there are the Absolutionist."

"Don't you mean abolitionists?" Leo asked. "I mean, are there slaves here you're trying to free?"

"No slaves," Priscilla replied, her expression deadpan. "No slavers. Though these people might not be much less evil. The Absolutionists are a group who have gained considerable influence in the past five years. They are filled with outcasts, disgruntled survivors, and angry souls, believing that the suffering we endure is meant to pay for the many sins of our species. They are intent on watching all of it burn so that we may be forgiven. According to them, the chosen few who are standing in the end after everyone else has fallen will have had their souls washed clean of our filth. They will then be the ones to start anew. Give humanity a fresh start, free of desire, decadence, hate, and selfishness."

"Oh," Leo said, looking to Shelly and me. "I guess it's too much for some. They just like to watch the world burn."

Priscilla's eyes lilted along with her shoulders, making her appear profoundly sad. "You speak into their truth. I believe they are afraid, like all of us. And this is how it manifests. It is easier to hate than to endure."

"Was the strange signal one of their messages?" Ada asked.

Dameon frowned at this before reaching up to readjust his glasses. "It was. It is one of their calling cards. A mantra. What is it again? Love. Live. Pray. Burn. Fall . . ." He trailed off as if not remembering, Ada picking up the thread.

"Ash. Anger. Atonement. End."

"Yes. That. I would like to think of it is as a metaphor, but I have a strong impression its meaning is quite literal."

Before the conversation turned down a darker road, I introduced the *Transcendence*'s crew to our hosts, working around the table left to right. Everyone was cordial, if a little nervous. We needed this meeting to go well, or at the very least, we needed not to die. I wasn't sure what these people were capable of, be it good or bad, big or little, but I had a suspicion they would be the lead domino. Clearly, they had some sort of influence. They had some level of advanced capabilities, like contacting us from Earth when we were in orbit around Triton. How did Ingrid pull off that little trick? There had been a communications lag, yes, but not enough for standard neutrino channels at such a distance. The speed of light was still the limit, was it not? According to Proxy, the lag at that distance should have been close to four hours one way, but it was instead milliseconds. Something didn't add up.

"Now that everyone has met," Ingrid said, her tone hardening into something more serious. "Why are you here?"

Karianna tensed beside me. She raised a finger and pointed at Ingrid. "Uh, because you called us?"

"Nooo." She drew the word out. "That's not what I mean. Why are you in SOL? Why are you in this system? You say you are of the FICSE fleet, but there is no FICSE fleet, and there never was."

CHAPTER 24

"Never was?" Karianna's nose scrunched up. She turned to face me. "What the hell does that mean?"

"Let her finish," I told my copilot. "It's a valid question."

Karianna raised her hands and threw herself back in her chair. James gave her a sidelong look from where he sat a couple of seats down, shaking his head. She stared back at him, but from this angle, I couldn't see her expression. I could only assume she was glaring at him, her tongue stuck out in petulance.

With a deep breath, Ingrid began, "FICSE is a story everyone was told by our grandparents, who were told by their great-grandparents, who had been told by their great-grandparents, and on and on for generations. A fictional story meant to inspire hope. A fairy tale that on one magical day, humans would appear out of the sky with all the power of the Foundry at their side and save us from the terrible crimes we committed against our species and our world. Five ships were sent off into the void to make contact with the great and powerful Foundry. The hopes of our species pinned upon the crews of the *Brilliance*, the *Revelation*, the *Galileo*, the *Starstream*, and let us not forget, the *Vasco Da Gama*. If indeed these ships were real—and many believe the records are falsified, us included—those people would be long dead after nearly five hundred years. None of our ships were capable of approaching the speed of light in such a way that this would matter otherwise.

"And yet, here we are, here you are. You claim to be part of them. You come to us with a story and possess technology that is clearly advanced. This makes me ask all kinds of questions. Could alien assistance be involved? Sure, we can buy that. It's not the first time. But FICSE? Too convenient. Deus ex machina."

"God from the machine," Leo mused, his words not much more than a whisper. Like was often the case, I was not familiar with this term. Another stupid gap in my education.

"Why believe these stories are false even when you have the records?" Shelly ventured, her tone incredulous. "There has to be a mountain of evidence to support it. Schematics. Communications. Bank transactions. Personal accounts. Crew manifests with our names on them."

"Records? Maybe," Ingrid said. "But no. Beside the fact as a species we're always looking for new ideas to hold us together in the hardest of times, there's one thing I do know. Humans are terrible at cooperation beyond a local scale. Look at this world. It's evidence that we're failures at it. People get selfish fast. People live by their fears.

"To believe in the fiction of FICSE, you have to first believe that the nations of this ruined world, who passionately hated one another, somehow came together and spent trillions of PAEN on a longshot. Nothing in our historical records support this level of species-wide cooperation at any time other than FICSE. If they had, we wouldn't be here now. And to be honest, I'm personally surprised the UEI ever got anything done, even what they have around the system. So, if FICSE is the only time they were able to do it, doesn't that seem suspicious?"

"Our shuttles," I said. "Do their designs look familiar?"

"No. They are not familiar."

"Do you believe they are of Earth, or elsewhere? You called them Foundry-made."

"They are like Veetor's ship, and we have covered the fact that you are using advanced technology. What's your point?"

"Our shuttle is like his, yes. But here's the thing. Veetor came from our fleet as well. What do you believe of him? He's from FICSE. Karianna and several others in our group are from his original ship, the *Brilliance*."

Priscilla looked at Dameon, her voice soft. "He did say us that that was where he's from."

"There is so much about him I don't believe," Dameon said. "He shows up out of nowhere just a few years ago, like you, in the nick of time when we needed help to stand against the Clickers. He calls this timing providence. I call it bullshit."

"It's fair not to believe him, just so you know," Karianna added, her bracelets jingling as she shook a hand in the air. "He's a lying fuck hole."

Ingrid went on, ignoring my copilot's comments. "It's clear he has a vessel of superior technology. He tells us that it's from the Foundry, and that this is what was given in exchange for a donation. For now, we believe him. We have seen his mechanical arm, which he proudly displays. Though this claim to be part of the FICSE mission? How is that possible? It has been centuries. There were other missions that left SOL to follow the pink signal. Other expeditions, far more recent. These seem more likely to be your shared origins."

I pointed at the ceiling. "Our ship is parked in orbit. I assure you that it is of the same make as his, though it is certainly from a different Foundry facility—two facilities, in fact. FICSE is where it started, not where it ended. I know it's been hundreds of years since we left, and we're late coming home, but time gets weird out there. Special relativity. Hypersuspension. Subjective time reference. They all play their parts."

Ingrid crossed her arms and looked at her companions. Dameon removed a notebook from his coat along with a tiny pencil that had been sharpened too many times, ready to write while Priscilla leaned in, eyes wide, fingers rubbing gently at her chin.

"Maybe you should start from the beginning," Ingrid said. "You say you have made contact with the Foundry, as does Veetor. But what is it? What does it do? Who are you? Tell us your story."

I nodded and did just that. Shelly was right. We had been gone a long time, and as such, they had no idea what to think of us or the mission. I had no idea what parts of the story had survived, what had become legend and myth. I was sure many had been waiting for the second coming of the FICSE fleet as if it were a messianic event like the return of Christ, the Foundry's machines returning with us to make right what was destroyed. This story must have brought about a false sense of hope, but then again, it was a brand of hope.

My heart broke at the idea that so many generations had waited for us to rescue them. So many children had lain awake at night, struggling, starving, looking to the sky, praying to anything who would listen for us to come back. If we could have done it sooner, so much bloodshed would have been prevented. So many lives saved.

We walked them through the mission, through our travels from Earth to the Foundry facilities in the 2090s, my crew adding details where appropriate. We went through how many of us here had grown up on those ships, how we had found ourselves as individuals, and how we'd readied ourselves to tackle the world like all children do, then been thrown into chaos when our ships were destroyed. We shared stories about living in the shadows of greatness, anecdotes of parents revered by the world and us trying to grow up to be as great as them. Specifically, Lance spoke of his father, the missions he led into low Earth orbit, the rocket launches and prototype testing, as well as to be born of someone like that and the world expecting you to go further. This resonated with Ingrid, that much was clear.

We told her of the Isopteran attack on the *Vasco Da Gama*, the destruction of our ship, and our travels to Cynosure and beyond.

Karianna told them of the mutiny on the *Brilliance*, of Justin Wiggins, his madness, and how his actions had cost the lives of so many.

We held nothing back about the Kabosai, and how they wanted to use humanity to help fulfill what they believed was the Foundry's mission to protect life.

Ingrid confirmed a suspicion I already had. Clickers were their word for Isoptera, and Splicers their word for Kabosai. Part of the reason for these titles came through their disadvantage in relation to us, something we took for granted. Without the universal inoculant, the people of SOL knew nothing of alien languages. They had no way to communicate, and this had made things worse. How the *Vasco Da Gamma*'s crew, as well as the *Brilliance*'s and *Revelation*'s, had all come to call them Isoptera, I still wasn't sure. It was way too big a coincidence. Aside from that, our having delt with them first-hand seemed to encourage her belief in what we said being truer, if only by a little.

As for technology, it turned out they had seen many things we never dreamed of, such as the nanotech of her guard dog, which was far more advanced than my own. They did not have neural implants like we did. Those arcane devices, as they put it, had been banned several hundred years ago, and their development abandoned for reasons that were obvious, if not explicit. We were unique in this.

We told them of Novae, of the thriving human colony beyond the stars and our fight to come home. We told them of Johan, and the death of so many Jevox, the Foundry turning on us as a result, and of our perilous journey back to Earth.

We had returned, and we meant to make things right.

The room fell into silence as our story came to a close.

"And you believe you can fix things?" Ingrid asked after some time.

"The Jevox seem to think so," I said. "This is their trade, and we have seen it first-hand. Their home world, which was nearly destroyed by a hostile species in a war of genocide, is an engineering wonder."

"I see. So, if we have the knowledge, what will it take to put it into practice?"

"To be honest . . . a lot. We need help. Coordination. Solid, reliable, secure communications. Labor. At least twenty thousand people. Supplies. Raw materials, access to manufacturing facilities. We can't do it all aboard the ship. This project has to be a global undertaking. A FICSE level of cooperation."

She turned to her companions, who leaned close to one another so that they could speak in hushed tones. On my right, I could see Ada and Leo doing much the same, discussing something that seemed important. I pivoted my head left and caught James and Lance looking at a hand terminal, pointing at something on a map.

Shelly reached for me under the table, a palm on my leg, then pinged a message to my implants.

Shelly: *This hasn't gone exactly as we expected. Met with open arms is not how I'd take this.*

Me: *I think we've got a lot of trust to build.*

Shelly: *I think you're right. The world has seen a lot. Humanity has seen a lot.*

Me: *Wish we could have been here sooner.*

Shelly: *We all do.*

"So, we became a legend . . ." Karianna mumbled, her attention focused someplace far beyond the walls of this building. She was lost in her thoughts, the fingers of her left hand absently playing with her bracelets as she wandered the hallways of her mind, trying to figure something out.

Ingrid raised a hand, and our people quieted, putting their eyes back on the Free Citizens of Earth.

"You have to understand, Captain Hughes," Dameon began. "You've been gone nearly five hundred years, and while everything here might be a shock, this is the world we grew up in. Most of us were born on Earth, some not but a few hundred miles at most from Svalbard."

I leaned forward. "May we ask what happened? Are you willing to share with us?"

"As in, how the world ended up like this?"

"Yes. What happened after we left?"

He let out a sigh, twisted in his chair, and scratched his chin, not making eye contact with us. "Wouldn't we all like to know. Record keeping is spotty, as you can imagine. I may be telling too much, but here on Svalbard is a data vault. Much like the seed vault you passed on the way into town, the Artic World Archive is near. This facility was used to preserve data given our remote location. It is underground in a series of old coal mines, both electromagnetically and physically protected by the caves. Data from around the world was kept here in case of cataclysmic events. There is a lot of information in the archives, but as you can imagine, it stopped being updated long ago.

"If you were part of FICSE, that means you left in the 2090s. Things were still pretty good, despite what everyone thought at the time. What we do know is around 2150, things got especially bad. The planet had warmed to such a degree that many of the common crops we relied on, say maize and wheat, could only be grown inside specialized greenhouses. This led to many critical species of animals going extinct, and rampant starvation among humans. Though, despite the hunger around the world, we kept expanding, we kept growing, people kept being born.

"Around 2150, there were close to eighteen billion people living on Earth. Can you imagine how crowded that was? There was constant war, though thankfully we hadn't seen anything in the way of nuclear exchange at that point. I suppose the earth did not care for this imbalance, and as the icecaps unfroze, an airborne virus, Perma-V2z, was let loose. It was worse than any pandemic we'd ever seen before, ancient and unrelenting. V2z caused instability the world over, and as a direct result, at least 40 percent of the planet's population was killed. But that's just where it started.

"Humanity carried on, stubborn as ever, limping and grasping in the dark. UEI's efforts were renewed several times over. Millions had gotten the hell off of Earth. Mars was colonized in earnest. The moon was already well seeded. There were, and are, other colonies around the system as well. Colonies like Aeolia, or those in orbit, of which a few remain, small societies living in HardyHabs overhead. For fifty years we expanded into the solar system, those who had the means going up, those who did not staying down.

"Our records show that this was a time of wonders. Humanity started pushing the bounds of what it meant to be human. We started building absurd machines, testing concepts for faster-than-light travel, warping the bounds of space and time. We started reaching out again, seeking friends beyond our system. And then around 2200, everything went dark. We have only a few records from the years between 2203 to 2395. All we know is that a lot happened, most of which was bad. The debris scattered in orbit was the result of something during that period, the wonder of simple space habitats affordable for all, destroyed, creating a navigational hazard that trapped most of us here on the ground, with the exception of a chosen few called to a distant heaven.

"Then comes 2401, when we were recovering from war. You've seen the evidence, the scars. There was a nuclear exchange between several of the superpowers, if you could even still call them that, but thankfully, whatever defense systems were in place by that time kept the damage to only a few dozen fusion weapons. These bombs were nothing small, mind you, but if the entire world's arsenal at the time had been unleashed, I believe we'd be looking at a smoking rock, not just a shattered ecosystem.

"This recovery is the era in which we live now. A world torn by war, plagued by wandering storms of radiation, an uncertain number of humans still living, the planet's people not much more than a collection of about fifteen to twenty settlements, who take direction from us. We are the Free Citizens of Earth. We do not take orders from those above. What is left of the UEI can rot. Aeolia can rot. The people of Mars can rot. None of them have come to save Earth. They say there are too many of us. They say we will give them diseases and destroy their cultures. They say we should be thankful for the fact that they fight back against the Clickers, giving us the chance to struggle on, but they don't get them all. We are third-world now, at least in their eyes. Let us take the brunt of the evil for them."

"What do you mean, don't get them all?" I asked. "The termites come down here, don't they?"

Dameon chuckled at the use of that word. "Yes. Termites. The Clickers raid our settlements constantly. We believe that their intention is to eat us, but we can't be sure. That's why security is so tight. Most other human groups don't have the means to reach us, remote as we are. But the Clickers can."

"Do you not want us to fix this?" Karianna asked, her voice taking on an edge, frustration ramping up. "What you've experienced, what everyone has lived through, is unconscionable. But we are here to help."

Dameon looked to Ingrid and Priscilla, neither of whom made a move. They remained passive.

"Again, this is our world," he went on, "the one we were born into. Let me remind you of that. It is all we know. Don't take offense if we don't believe your promise and take it at face value. Humanity has seen disease and death, so many plagues and wars that most are now without names. We are still here, yes, and for that we are grateful. But we know it won't last forever. These are the final days of this planet. Aliens have come to pick over our bones like vultures."

"Your journey is extraordinary," Priscilla said, "and your story is one that truly inspires. We are blessed that you have taken us across the stars, given us a window into places we've only dreamed of."

"But we have to protect ourselves," Ingrid stated, standing up, her chair's legs squeaking against the floor. "We can't believe this right now. We can't trust our hopes to this possible fantasy. Give us time."

"Time?" Karianna shot up from her seat, raising a mechanical finger to point at her. "Give you time! Time isn't something you have. Not like we have some magic clock or something, but I don't see people here lasting another generation, especially with the forces that are at play. What about the planet? What about Veetor? What about the termite Queen who wishes to harvest you? You're right about one thing you said, the Clickers really do want to eat you—they believe it makes their boys all big and strong. Ever heard of superfoods? We're like that. Get a big bowl of humans for breakfast every morning and you'll evolve the species into a state of nirvana!"

I put my hand on my copilot's arm. "Karianna . . ."

She shrugged it off and scowled at me.

Ingrid seemed to be turning angry at this response, her eyes twitching at the edges. For a moment, I expected her nanomachine dog to appear, but she kept her cool, if barely. Dameon looked uneasy, but she put a hand on his shoulder, and he froze.

"No, Milo," Karianna's voice cracked. "No! This is fucking bullshit! I haven't suffered through all this pain, suffered all these trials, just to have it thrown back at me. It has to mean something. You hear me? It can't be for nothing."

And I felt the same. We all did.

"Please," Ingrid said, raising her open palms. "Time for a break. I think it's best we all take a respite to process this. May we offer you a place to stay? We have food and warm beds."

Ever the diplomat, Shelly cut in before anyone could make it worse. "I think that sounds lovely. I know I could use some time to my thoughts. Milo?"

"Yes," I replied. "We could use some rest."

My copilot fumed, her face red, hands balled into fists. James took her off to the side and they chatted furiously in hushed tones.

"I will escort them," Priscilla said, making her way around the table to us. "We have quarters inside the compound. You can sleep sounder here. The guards will watch out for intruders."

"Thank you," I said, extending a hand, which she shook. "We appreciate the hospitality."

"We will speak in the morning," Ingrid told us. "Do rest."

CHAPTER 25

Priscilla led our group out of the meeting room and back out into the cold. Karianna was no calmer in the chill, and despite his best efforts, James wasn't helping much, since they both wanted the same thing. Diplomacy wasn't his strong suit any more than hers, but I knew he saw the need to be patient.

Wind whipped around us, frigid gusts slashing us in two, making our breath visible as if we were smoking. The ground was slick, icy in some spots, with small piles of snow scattered around the parking lot. Mountains were on display everywhere you looked, and overhead, the sunlight was starting to dim, though from what we had observed, this place didn't seem to really have a night or day.

We followed her in a line around the back of the building to where the fenced area opened up. The man in the ugly sweater we had met earlier stood by the edge of the property, and a couple dozen children were playing soccer in a dirty field nearby. From the looks of it, the man had wires going into his ears that were connected to a hand terminal of some kind. Headphones maybe?

He danced like no one was watching, his eyes closed, feet sliding. He took one step after another, arms making poses like a body builder. The expression on his face was one of pure joy, unfettered ecstasy, a man just dancing for the hell of it.

"Priscilla," I said, catching up to her. "I have to ask. What's up with him?"

"Oskar?" She looked to the peculiar man and grinned. "We love Oskar. He's a good guy. One of the first to come across the sea with us to Svalbard from northern Europe. He helped rescue me from some bad people."

"I get that. Does he have a role?"

"Oskar is a caretaker for the children."

"And are there lots of children here?" Shelly asked.

"Yes. I'm sure you can imagine, having seen Earth from orbit, we don't have it easy trapped on the surface. While it might be hard to stay alive, fertility, strange as this may be, remains high. But children are born all the time without parents. Many of them die for a number of reasons, including childbirth. From what we have seen, this is one of the leading causes of death in women, especially those outside the established settlements. No professional medical care. And so, many of the children come here because of this. People like Oskar take care of them."

I narrowed my eyes at him, cocking my head to the side. "What's he listening to?"

"Oh, music I'm sure, though I can't say what. He likes all kinds."

"He into Parallax?"

"Who?"

"Never mind."

"Oskar is also into motivational speakers. He likes to check his mindset, and a while back, we found a cache of old audio recordings to give him."

"Motivational speakers?" Karianna's eyebrows raised. "Like those 'you can believe in yourself and do anything' positive psychology people?"

"Those are the ones."

"Alright . . . that's um . . . neat?"

James patted Karianna on the back. "Maybe you could use some of that. Get your mindset straight."

She whirled around and gave him a shove, forcing him to take two steps back, nearly bowling him into Hy. James smiled the entire time, which only made her madder.

"There is still good in the world," Priscilla went on. "I for one believe that you are proof of this. The Universe has seen the good we have done here and rewarded us for it, sending you. I regret that my companions are nervous. I am too. We are tired of being hurt. Tired of being let down. Be patient, I beg of you."

Lance broke off from our procession, inserting himself within the boiling group of children, kicking the white and black ball around the field with them. They started laughing, some clapping. He made a few quick actions with his feet, juggling the ball in such a way the kids couldn't get it back, catching it on the front of his boot, lifting it in the air, bouncing it on a knee, off a shoulder, and back onto the ground. The children, ranging from maybe eight to twelve, loved every second of it. Several asked how he had done it, and he went through the action again, explaining each step.

"Takes practice," he told them. "But it's a lot of fun."

We froze in our steps and watched, letting him hang out with them for a moment and teach them something new, give them a few high fives, maybe tell a joke or two. I had to say, Lance was impressive. I knew he was a fan of this sport from conversations between him and Esteban, but I didn't know he played so well. The kids loved him.

Oskar caught a glimpse of it and smiled. He removed his headphones and hurried over.

"I think we found us a new coach for our club!" he said, waving his hand across their primitive field as if revealing some grand facility. "With this body of mine, I do not make the best futbol player. No?" He put his hands on his belly and shook it.

Lance cocked his head at the man and kicked the ball off to the other end of the field, the children whooping as they chased after. "Never coached before. That's a lot of responsibility. Not sure I'm good enough for it."

Oskar leaned close to Lance, looking over his shoulder in a conspiratorial way, then whispered so loud the entire island could hear him. "The talent pool is not so good. Bar is very low. Dameon coached for a while, but he's too stiff. He is athletic like me, not like you."

"Ahh," Lance replied, nodding.

"Was he like this when you dated?" I asked Shelly.

She shook her head. "Didn't have kids around. Never seen this side of him. It's a good side."

"What does that mean?"

"Nothing." Shelly took hold of my arm and clutched me tight.

Priscilla looked at me and smiled.

"What?" I asked, my response perhaps a bit too hard. "Something on your mind?"

"Nothing," she said, her eyebrows raised as if she knew something I didn't. "Nothing at all."

She led us to another building and walked us inside an open set of barracks, a space meant for function, not comfort. Beds were lined up in rows, and a kitchen and facilities lay at the rear. Wind whistled through a window near the bathrooms each time it gusted against the western side. It was warm here, far warmer than outside, but it was by no means cozy. I had a feeling I'd be sleeping with my coat on.

"Lie down wherever you like," she said. "Phillip will be out front. If you need anything, he will get in touch with us."

"Thank you," Shelly said, putting a hand on Priscilla's shoulder. "You are a good host."

Priscilla gave a deep bow and left the barracks.

"They're jerking us around," Karianna spat as she slammed her backpack down on a bunk, making the mattress springs creak. "We are coming here to offer help, and they're screwing around with us."

Hy took a seat and spoke up. "There has been much pain here. How did we feel when we saw Earth for the first time? Really saw it? That wound is raw."

Xuan sat down beside him and laid an arm across his shoulders. "And they have lived through it."

"Yeah, but come on, bruh," James said, taking Karianna's side. "Can't they see we aren't lying? We clearly have tech they don't. Does that not speak for something?"

Karianna nodded at him. "If there are other settlements, maybe we should find one that will work with us more easily. They're fighting everything we say. They don't believe us. We're a damn fairy tale."

"I think that's unfair," Shelly said. "Hy is right. They've seen a lot of pain. Would you not want to work with someone who is cautious? Not just anyone? This project will be a massive undertaking. We need partners who will not give in or give up easy."

"Like us," Ada echoed.

"Like us."

"Look," I said, raising my hands. "I get that everyone has feelings around this. They've got us under lock and key, for the moment, and that never makes anyone comfortable. So far, though, we have no solid reason not to trust them."

"Milo," Karianna started, "that bitch pinned you to the ground with a dog made out of nano machines. She was going to kill you."

I swallowed at the thought, my left chest burning where the dog had pressed down its sharpened spike. "I'm choosing to believe she was being careful."

My copilot chuffed. "Let's walk back through this." Karianna made a reversing gesture with her hands. "They called us here. Not the other way around. What if they think they can take the *Transcendence* from us? Huh? Did we consider that? Yes, they've been through some shit. That would be a good reason for me to do it. They take our ship, and they'd be kings of this world like Justin."

"But they can't," Ada replied. "There's no way. It's hard coded to both of you, and the few times it has been piloted by one of us, it was limited and under explicit instruction."

"They don't know that."

My hands balled into fists. I hadn't thought of this. How had I not thought of this? I'd been so focused on getting their understanding that I hadn't considered the possibility that they might want to steal our ship. The fact remained that they couldn't take it, but that hardly mattered if we got killed in the process. And yet, something about that idea didn't track. While they might not pass up the opportunity to take a ship like ours, I didn't think that was their intention, or at least not their primary one.

As I processed this, the rest of the room continued to discuss our situation. We needed help, this was clear. But did we need it from the Free Citizens of Earth?

"Okay, okay," I said, raising a hand. The room went silent. "Shelly's right, and I'm not just siding with her because she's my wife. We need to do as Priscilla suggested and be patient. We only just got here, only just learned all that they know happened. It's a lot for all of us to take in, a lot for them to take in. I say we sleep on it. If this cautiousness is how they responded, what's to say another group won't do the same?"

This received a number of nods from the crew. Despite maybe feeling the same as Karianna, most agreed it was best to let logic dictate our actions for now. Cool heads often prevailed.

"I don't see a better way to go at it," Lance said.

Chevelle nodded. "We keep watch. Stay safe. Call the Swift Shuttle down if things get bad?"

"Good plan," I said. "Karianna?"

She crossed her arms and shook her head. I was grateful not to be connected to her through the ship right now. She would have given me a heartful, not just an earful.

"Now that that is settled." I dusted off my hands and gestured to the kitchen at the far end of the barracks. "Who wants to cook us dinner? While they said they'd provide food, I feel safer eating ours. I'm hungry as shit."

"Can any of us even cook?" Leo mused. "I spent my time messing around with paint, not playing in the kitchen."

Ada frowned at him. "Sounds like you need to take on another hobby."

"A man only has time for so much, my dear. I desire to be a master, not a jack of all trades."

"I worked with Proxy before we left," Lance said. "Made sure we had some easy meals. There's prepackaged protein if anyone is feeling lazy, or there's plenty of freeze-dried goods. I can cook, if you like, but I'm not the best at it. I get impatient."

Xuan looked to her husband, who was already digging through his pack.

"Leave it to me," Hy said, rubbing his hands together. "I'll take care of you big babies. Big hot meal, coming up!"

CHAPTER 26

With a belly full of noodles and rice, and a mind turned wild with choices, sleep that night was interesting. I found myself running in circles, replaying the painful events of my past: Dad's murder, Mom growing old, Esteban's final moments. I dreamt about the many who had died aboard the *Vasco Da Gama*, the poor Jevox who had been caught in our power struggle . . . what I had done to the Phantamorph. I dreamt of the billions of people who had held to FICSE for hope, and how we had let them down.

There was so much pain. So much to consider. So much to atone for. Maybe the Absolutionists were right. We had a lot that needed forgiveness.

My dreams were fitful and disjointed, taking me on occasion to the Universe at the end of time, then back to Novae, then Whispering Pines, then the lunchroom on the *Vasco Da Gama*. I saw the Earth from high above, turning from blue and green to brown and gray and lifeless. I saw great machines hundreds of stories high working tirelessly to turn back the tides of collapse, filtering the air, enriching the soil, restoring balance. But they weren't enough. The Isoptera sabotage them. They break. People become willfully ignorant and apathetic.

Hope falls into ruin.

As I floated in a distant place at the edge of the universe, I heard a rhythmic set of knocks too substantial to be part of my dreams. I cracked open my eyes, peeling away my visions, and rolled over to see Shelly looking at me. The barracks were just this side of pitch-black, everyone sleeping from what I could tell. In the back of the hall, Xuan was snoring again, her nasal passages making a noise like sawing hardwood logs. As for the rest, they were silent.

With a racing heart, I whispered to Shelly, "What was that?"

She leaned her head to the door, back arched, arms extended as she stretched. "Someone's here."

"At this hour?"

"If my clock is right, it's already 8 a.m. So, not all that early, at least for them."

"Oh. Well, it's hard to tell this far north."

"They say this is the land where the sun doesn't set. Not entirely true, but close enough."

"Let's not wake the others," I said, slipping out of bed as quietly as I could, not bothering to dress. I paused for a moment as I removed our sheets, catching sight of Karianna flipping over on her bunk, her back now facing us.

In only pajamas, the room was chilly, but not as bad as it had been when we'd gone to bed. Our crew's body heat had been trapped inside the barracks, warming it by several degrees.

Dressed in thin pants and T-shirts, we went to the door and cracked it open, allowing a knife of icy wind and pale light inside. Priscilla was standing before us, alone, bundled up in a puffy coat with a scarf so thick it rose up to her ears.

"Good morning," she said with a slight tip of her head. "I trust you slept well."

"Pretty well," I said. "Is something the matter?"

"The matter?" She shook her head. "No. No. I just thought you might want to go for a walk. I see your team is still sleeping. Why not let them sleep?"

I took a step back and looked to Shelly. She gave a shrug and went to gather up our clothes.

"Be out in a minute," I told Priscilla, then shut the door.

Shelly was halfway dressed by the time I made it back to our bunk, having slipped out of her pajamas and into a pair of thick pants. She'd started shrugging on layers of shirts over the clothes she'd slept in. I did the same.

"We need to know more," she whispered. "Priscilla doesn't seem dangerous. We leave the team here, ping them if we need help. No reason to worry them."

"Okay," I replied, and slipped on my coat. This wasn't the dumbest thing we'd ever done, but it wasn't smart. Logic stated that we should say something to the rest of the crew, that splitting up was dangerous, but I didn't want to deal with the conversations that might come with that. Wasn't I the captain? Did I not make decisions? "Quiet then."

Once we were dressed and ready, we stepped out into the cold to meet Priscilla. The wind had died down, and it was dark.

"This way," she said, waving for us to follow.

Priscilla led us through the compound, past a series of guards, and through a side gate that led off to a trail hemmed by thick snow. In the few hours we'd been asleep, several inches of white had fallen, leaving a layer of unblemished powder resting on everything in sight.

In silence, we crossed the street and approached a tram that led up the looming mountain before us. It was hard to make out its details, but the absence of starlight along its edges made the foreboding shape evident.

"Let's take a ride," Priscilla said, waving us to the tram. "Only takes a couple of minutes. The view is worth it, I promise."

"I bet."

We piled into a pill-shaped gray and red car attached to a long rail. With a soft woosh, the door closed, and the car's interior began to let off a dim glow. Priscilla pressed a button near the front as we settled into our seats, and the tram started to move. The interior warmed rapidly as the engines engaged, melting the snow that clung to my boots, making the rubber floor wet. Shelly snuggled up beside me, taking hold of my arm. For an instant, it felt as if we might be off to go sightseeing like people on vacation, have a champagne toast on some gorgeous vista, but I brought myself back to the moment at hand.

The tram climbed its way silently up the incline, Longyearbyen and the many mountains past it filling the rear window, buildings in the valley a collection of dark forms with random pinpricks of lights.

I turned to face Priscilla. The gems on her face twinkled in the glow of the tram's lights. "May I ask you something?"

"Of course." She crossed her legs and rested her hands on them, the action graceful and curious. "How can I be of help?"

"Ingrid called you a Mystic, right?"

She closed her eyes and lowered her head in a bow. "That's right. I am a mystic."

"Apologies for my ignorance," I said, careful in my tone, "but I had to do some reading up on that title. Our cultural group among the former FICSE crew is different than you might expect. While we might have pockets of religious belief and plenty of philosophy, public religion itself was banned aboard many of the ships in the fleet. Leadership was concerned over divisions. Conflict. Crew held to these doctrines in silence, skipping the Sunday church services."

"I had read of this. The *Vasco Da Gama* was one of those ships."

"We were. And yet we had Catholics, we had Muslims. We had Buddhists. That said, what I found reading up on this was that mysticism is more a philosophy than religion. A desire to become one with God, or the Absolute. So, does this framework fit with your worldview? Or do you believe something else?"

She tipped her head again and waved an open hand. "Close enough."

I nodded at that. "Okay, look, in our time traveling the cosmos, we've seen many crazy things. Most have happened in the physical world, the place we are now, but there are a few events that have happened beyond it. I can't fully explain what they are or how I find myself there, other than being in a kind of meditative state, but something in the way you speak makes me feel you might understand."

She leaned in, her eyes widening. "Tell me about this place you go."

"No," I pushed back. "Not yet. You tell me this first. Have you been to the end of it all. Have you met the Universe?"

Priscilla cocked her head to the side as if considering how to respond. She took a deep breath and scratched the back of her neck. "I have seen something, though what it is in truth, I can't say for sure. It appears to be human, but also alien, a million, billion different things all at once. It never speaks to me, but it talks, recounting the experiences of all life. It protects life, because it is life. It is me. It is you. It is everyone. It is from that place Plato spoke of where perfect, eternal forms come from." She chuckled. "You might think I'm crazy for saying all this. Maybe she's taken too many mushrooms or smoked too much grass? Well, I haven't. Whatever it is though, it's God in a way, but not God."

Shelly put a hand on my thigh and squeezed.

"I believe you," I said. "I've met it. I've spoken with it. The Universe. And no, it's not God. Its words, not mine."

She swallowed, and her jaw went slack. "You've spoken to it?"

"I have. And from what it told me, I believe it created the Foundry."

"What? What does that even mean?"

"It means everything. You have to understand the machine's directive, that the Foundry protects life. This is what it has told us ever since we came into contact with it and the *Vasco Da Gama* was destroyed. It protects life because it wants to experience all there is to experience. We created the Foundry, you and I, and all the species that have and will ever exist. We created it because we fear death. We fear reaching the end of all time, and so if we can delay another subjective day, then we have victory over oblivion. The more life, the more experiences, the more subjective time. It is life's way of taking control amidst entropy and chaos."

Priscilla leaned back on her bench, spine resting against the front window. "That's heavy."

"Yeah, I know. Now, I hope you don't think I'm crazy. I swear, I'm sober, just like you. I swear the Foundry hasn't messed with my head too much."

"He's just as insufferable after the donation as before," Shelly put in.

I frowned at her. "Hey, now!"

She landed a playful punch on my shoulder.

Priscilla chuckled again. "Crazy? No, not at all. I find it funny that this brings so many of my visions into focus. There were missing details, gaps in space and time, and now this . . . I think I understand."

The tram jostled and came to a halt. We had reached the top.

Priscilla stood but held out an arm to keep us from going straight to the exit. "Take a deep breath before you step out. What you see, well, it might make it hard to breathe."

We followed her instructions.

She opened the door and lowered herself into knee-deep drifts of snow. Shelly and I followed after, a weight of expectation and curiosity carried between us.

As we sank into the soft powder of the mountaintop, our eyes trailed up to the sky, and I understood what Priscilla meant. Shelly squeezed my hand. The sky above was alighted with ghostly ribbons of green over a backdrop of stars so bright that I felt for a moment I might be back within my virtual environment. Beneath it all was a field of debris miles in length, dozens of crashed and ruined aircraft impossible to see from above given the snow cover. Here, however, the wind had blown away many of the drifts to make their hollow interiors evident. But this wasn't all. Far in the distance, off to the north, an ethereal tower stretched into the heavens, a massive, cloud-busting pillar shining with blue light.

Wind whipped over the mountaintop, kicking up dusty sweeps of dry snow. We stood in silence, taking in the sight. All was beautiful, and yet unsettling.

"As Dameon said," Priscilla started, "there is a period in history we have no records from. During this era, many machines were built, some of which we have no idea of their functions. That tower in the distance is part of those machines. We believe them to be human made, but honestly can't be sure. No one can approach them, as they defend themselves with prejudice. While the icecaps of Earth might have receded, they remained despite the temperatures around the world. We believe these towers are part of the cause. The structures are cold. Very, very cold."

"And they've been keeping the water frozen," Shelly said, squinting her eyes at it. "Drawing the heat from the air and ejecting it off into space."

"That's one theory. We aren't sure it's true name, but we've given it many, the ice spire, the tower, the afterglow. The water around it reaches temperatures as low as negative one hundred degrees Celsius. And so, we observe it. Whatever powers it, it just keeps going. There are other machines like this around the earth, keeping this world taped together. Who knows how long they will function? They are powered by technology that might as well be magic for us."

I waved a hand before us. "What about this aircraft graveyard?"

She shrugged. "Remnants of a battle. Possibly an abandoned salvage operation. It is hard to say. They're damaged in ways it's clear were no accidents. We've already made use of many of the advanced components to repair or upgrade conditions in the town and on the island but haven't yet had the chance to haul all the metals down to be refined and made into something else. Finding salvage like this isn't hard. Finding anything that still works, now that's a different story."

"Hmmm," I said, nodding. "We saw a creature walking through the Siberian city. It was huge, taller than any of the buildings, and it moved on a set of weird legs." I gestured with my hands, gloved fingers walking on open air.

"Was it black and shiny?"

"Yes."

"We call them Land Striders. We have spotted them all over Earth. There are at least a few hundred around the globe. I would steer clear of them."

Shelly framed the spire in her fingertips if she were trying to pick it up. "Are they hostile? The Land Striders."

"Hard to say. All we know is that things go missing around them. Sometimes people. I want to believe they are curious scavengers from beyond the stars, but some believe they are murderers. Others believe that they are dark angels sent to protect us from some greater threat."

"And what do you think?"

"For now, I hope for good. Maybe no angels, but the enemy of my enemy can sometimes be my friend. Either way, they give me the creeps."

Shelly tapped a fist against her chin in thought. "Alien species are often unknowable. They just don't think like we do."

"No, they do not. The Lattice did not, that's for sure."

"And who are the Lattice?" Shelly peered at me, then back to the mystic.

Priscilla grinned, though it held no mirth. "A conversation for another day."

We stood in silence as a group, taking in the sight, listening to the soft howl of the winds as they whipped across the snowy plains.

Minutes went by, and Shelly couldn't stand the silence anymore. "May I be bold and ask . . . why did you bring us here?"

"I wanted you to see," Priscilla said. "See a little of the world you came back to. This place, this is one of the good ones. This is one of the best. And yet, compared to the planet you left, we are a shadow of the former glory. We have little infrastructure, our population is in decline, despite the children. Disease has not taken a break because we are down on our luck. We try to work with the other powers left in this world, but there is no shortage of people out there who are allied with those who take advantage of others.

"I know this is not news to you. We already discussed it. I just want you to be understanding of my companions' positions. To be transparent, we are afraid. We've been given promises before. Veetor for one. The UEI on several occasions. Then there's Aeolia."

"I heard them mention that place," I said. "What is it?"

"A city. A city that some are called to go to, while others are left to die."

I cocked my head. "Okay? What does that mean?"

"It's not important right now. What's important is that you be patient. Please. They will be slow to come around, but even in our short time together tonight, I believe that you are our salvation. If the machines you speak of will do the work, we can rebuild this world. It might take generations, sure, but at least we will be able to survive."

"They will work." Shelly placed a hand on her shoulder. "As we already said, the Jevox use this as their trade. This is a service they provide for mutual defense. We've seen their laboratories, spoken to their scientists. If anyone's technology can do it, theirs can."

She sighed, turning her attention to the spire. "I believe that you believe that."

"You mentioned disease," I said. "We might be able to help with that."

Priscilla's expression became skeptical. "How so?"

"The Foundry gives everyone a sort of inoculation when they enter regions with mixed species. It's meant to keep us from killing each other with our native microbes. They call it the universal inoculant. It's a colony of nanomachines that live in our blood, capable of killing almost anything foreign. We are nearly incapable of coming down with a deadly virus or bacterial infection as a result."

"But it doesn't cover everything," Shelly whispered, her voice shaky.

I squeezed her hand. "No, not everything. But it might help. I can see if our AI, Proxy, would be willing to share it. I'm sure it would help with many common germs you deal with. Won't protect against radiation poisoning or heavy metals or anything like that, but those ancient viruses, it should fight them off better than any vaccine."

Her eyes twinkled at this idea. "This would change everything. Yes. Yes. Let's see if it is possible."

"No promises, okay? I'll ask."

She grabbed one of my hands and smiled. "Thank you. Thank you."

A sonic boom came from over our right shoulders, rocking the quiet air atop the mountain. We spun around to peer at where it had originated but saw nothing other than dark skies.

"What was that?" Shelly asked.

Priscilla's hopeful demeanor shifted in an instant. She was no longer curious and open, but hard, her back having gone straight as if ready for action. She fumbled in a pocket for a hand terminal, removing one of a different design than the ones we had, and made a call. The person on the other end answered immediately.

"Yes?" she said, and began pacing through the dense snow. "How many?" A pause. "Okay. We're on our way."

"What is it?" Shelly asked as Priscilla stowed her hand terminal.

Her expression betrayed a kind of dread, as if that call had announced a terminal diagnosis. "There's been an incident. We need to get back down the mountain. Now."

Without delay, we hopped back onto the tram and descended the mountain at what I could only imagine was the maximum speed of the vehicle. There were no seatbelts to be had, so we stretched out our arms and pressed against the windows, attempting to avoid crashing face-first onto the floor.

When we hit the bottom of the mountain, we scrambled out and ran to the compound.

Proxy pinged my implants, *"Milo. We detect active fungara near your location. Be careful."*

I pinged back a received reply and grabbed Shelly's arm. "They're here."

"Clickers!" guards shouted from inside the fenced area of the compound. "Rolling out. They're at building 17."

"God no," Priscilla said, and picked up the pace.

"What's building 17?" I asked between shallow breaths.

"That's where the children are."

"Oh shit," I growled. "Can we help?"

"Help? You mean fight the Clickers. What did you call them again?"

"Isoptera. And yes. We've fought them before. Many times. We just need our weapons."

Priscilla seemed to consider this for a moment, then removed her hand terminal and sent a message to someone. "You'll have them," she said.

We ran up on our barracks a moment later. Many of the crew were already outside, dressed and ready, though unarmed.

Lance came rushing through the group, a furious look on his face. He made straight for me. "Where the hell did you go? You vanished."

His tone made heat rise on my back, my skin exploding with prickles of anger. "Does it matter? I am not your kid to take care of."

"We're supposed to stick together," he said, poking me in the chest. "It's the only way to keep us safe. Ensure the mission is possible at all. You snuck off and didn't tell anyone. That's irresponsible."

I pulled him off to the side as the guards mobilized behind us. "I'm an adult. I make my own choices. We had an opportunity to learn more, and we took advantage of it. Now we have another opportunity. We need to prove our worth and trust. This is not the time for us to fall apart."

"Whatever, man. You keep talking about us being a team, but this doesn't feel like a team action. We make decisions together. What if you go off and get yourself killed, what if you get Sh— No, no."

My eyes narrowed. "We'll talk about this later."

He threw up his hands and stepped back. "You know what. I don't care. I'm done. No need to talk about this later."

Karianna sidled up beside me, a confused expression on her face. "What the hell was that all about?"

"Nothing."

Shelly waved at a series of guards who were rushing to us, a metal crate in their hands. "Milo, I think they brought us our rifles."

"Good." I turned to face the crew. "Grab your weapons. We're rolling out with their forces."

There were no complaints at this, not even from Lance. We hopped into a group of trucks and tore across town, the roads clear but for a bit of ice and snow. At the end of a cross street, I spotted what had to be building 17. The brightly colored block of windowed concrete was contained within a compound, high fences and razor wire surrounding it like the main base. We were about two hundred feet away when a rumble filled the air, vibrating through the truck's windows.

A green and black shuttle rose before us, its shape reminiscent of a cicada ten meters in length, transparent wings and all. The form rose straight up, turned east, then shot off into the distance with a deafening boom, roof tiles on the building scattering.

"No, no, no," Priscilla said, pulling us through the busted gate into the parking lot of the compound.

Bodies of fallen guards dressed in armor were everywhere, along with Isoptera. The ratio was not good. There were far more dead humans than dead insects.

Priscilla took off, and we followed after her, our weapons raised, scanning the parking lot for danger. When the mystic stopped, I felt my already sinking stomach dive into a black hole.

The kindly caretaker was lying on the ground, his sweater covered in blood, an open sack spilling bread onto the asphalt, a spent pistol smoking nearby.

Priscilla took hold of one of his hands and began to sob. "Oskar, no. No. No. No."

"They took the kids," Oskar spluttered, choking on his own blood. "I tried to stop them, but they took the kids." His body shuddered once, then twice, and his eyes froze in place, vacant.

My heart stopped.

Oskar was gone.

CHAPTER 27

Priscilla was frozen, unable to take action. Her hand terminal, having fallen on the ground, screen now cracked, was vibrating, but she wasn't answering. A moment passed, and a guard who hadn't been shot put two fingers to the side of their ear, nodded, then rushed over to her.

"Radar has them out over the ocean," the guard told her. "Ingrid and Dameon are on their way now."

"No," she said, resting her head against Oskar's lifeless chest. "They can't have taken them. The boats won't catch them."

I turned to Karianna, who by now had a hardened expression on her face.

"Who's up for some payback?" I asked my crew.

James gave me a dark smile, as did Renata. Lance, Xuan, Hy, and the rest were already checking their weapons.

"Can't let these grubs get nabbed," Chevelle said, raising her rifle into the air. "I say we call down de fire."

"Proxy," I said aloud, but it had already been listening. A roar came over Longyearbyen, and next thing we knew, our Swift Shuttles were lowering down on top of us. The blowback from their exhaust cleared what snow had fallen nearby, leaving the pavement clean.

Priscilla raised her head, hair whipping around so hard I thought it might be ripped free from her scalp. "What are you doing?"

"We're not letting those filthy insects take these kids," I replied. The Swift Shuttles landed with a thump. I turned to Karianna. "I've got a plan."

"How stupid is it?" she asked. "On a scale from one to ten."

I raised my open palms. "A solid eight. I need you to fly empty. Everyone will go with me."

"What? There's not enough room."

"But you'll be in your Star Sphere. You can run them down. I need you to be fast."

She narrowed her eyes for a moment, then took a deep breath and nodded. "It's going to be packed as hell."

"Already making room." And as I said these words, boxes began to fall out the back of my shuttle, along with all of its acceleration chairs. Proxy was already ahead of me, making space for the extra crew. I had no idea how fast I could safely accelerate with these modifications, but we were going to push it. We were not letting these kids be taken without a fight. Oskar, as well as several guards, had died to protect them. That ended now.

"You know I don't like flying," Shelly whispered beside me.

"Don't have to go if you don't want to," I told her. "No shame."

She shook her head while forcing her trembling hands to still. "No, no. I'm in."

"Board the shuttle," I ordered, and we climbed in.

The instant everyone was buckled up, we dusted off in a vertical takeoff, then burned northeast in the direction the Isopteran shuttle had gone. The modified seats Proxy had compiled for our crew were rough, little more than seatbacks and belts strapped to the floor, but they allowed for more space. The crew bore the stress they were being put under with solemnity. For my part, suspended in my Star Sphere, I felt nothing.

The island receded behind us as we struck out over the ocean, engines whining, our crafts slicing through low-hanging clouds like blades. Karianna was at my side and ahead of us, closing the gap to the enemy.

"Slow them down," I said over our ship-to-ship communications. *"Just don't damage them too bad. We don't want them crashing, not yet."*

"They're headed over the pole," Proxy spoke into my mind.

"We'll catch them." A nervous excitement entered Karianna's voice. *"We've got this."*

Thankfully for us, the Isopteran ship was easy to track, both because our instruments were calibrated to detect fungara and because the skies were empty of traffic. There was no sorting it out among a thousand ships like on Rix. It was us, and them.

Distance to target narrowed, clouds and choppy waters rolling beneath us. Soon we could see its shape just over the horizon. It was fleeing the island, clear enough, but seemed to be in no hurry otherwise, traveling at a little over Mach 1. From the angle of its airfoils, it was starting to climb. We would not allow it to reach orbit.

"Time to work my magic," Karianna said, then rocketed ahead.

The Isopteran shuttle chose that moment to break left, then right, a flurry of heat signatures escaping it.

"Missiles!" I shouted over the channel.

Karianna dove back to the ocean, a half dozen roaring projectiles following after her. I flew straight ahead, eyes on the target. Several heat signatures made for us.

"Hold on, everyone," I told the crew, "it's going to be bumpy." We banked to the right, offering our bottom side to the oncoming warheads. A series of point defense lasers located on the shuttle's belly spun up, targeting the threats one at a time, deleting them from the sky like someone making a keystroke within the code of reality.

For her part, Karianna outmaneuvered the missiles, cutting back to the waters below at a steep angle before pulling into a death-defying climb that would have turned my meaty passengers into paste. The warheads crashed into the choppy sea, exploding harmlessly below the surface, shockwaves kicking up little more than a salty spray.

"Did you get them all, bruh?" James blurted out. *"I feel like I counted more."*

I shook my head, as if he could see me do it with me submerged in my Star Sphere. Executing a barrel roll, I dove us beneath the clouds. The single remaining missile followed after us. I was forced to ramp up the acceleration, turn the Swift Shuttle skyward, and climb. I couldn't shake it. These were no simple projectiles; they had advanced flight control systems that allowed them to turn on a dime, even in atmosphere.

"I'm about to puke," Lance grumbled.

A commotion in the back of the shuttle, several "ewws," and retching noises followed.

Ada came on next, her words labored. *"Leo—beat us to it."*

"I'm sorry," he gurgled. *"So sorry—I didn't."*

"Clean—it up—later."

I knew that if we couldn't shake this missile, cleaning up puke wouldn't matter. Proxy worked furiously to take the target out with the point defense laser, but this one in particular was wily.

"Karianna?" I called out. *"A little help."*

I needn't have asked for assistance. Being back in our Star Spheres, we were connected through the integration. She was in my head, and I was in hers. And so, just as the words were escaping my mouth, she rose through the clouds, screaming like an angry bird, her weapons hot. The missile ripped apart, but in the process its payload misfired, exploding at a reduced strength. A shockwave rocked our airfoils, ripping several holes the size of doorways in one. We fell out of the sky like a rock, control vanishing as if the strings of our puppet had been cut. I fought to adjust, to pull up, but we had lost all lift and were tumbling into a stall.

Proxy redirected the internal nanomachines of the shuttle and rapidly stitched together the broken airfoils. I felt my control return, wind catching beneath my wings, then fell back in formation with Karianna, the Isopteran shuttle before us.

"Okay. So, they have missiles," I said over the channel, leveling off. "That's fun."

Karianna growled back, *"You leave that to me."* Her Swift Shuttle let out a roar as it kicked into overburn. The miles between us and the enemy shuttle closed.

I pushed the crew as hard as I could to catch up, going a little over four Gs of acceleration, but I could not close the gap.

Karianna shot up so fast on the enemy shuttle that this time, they could do little to react. Firing missiles at this point would have been as dangerous to them as to her. She rose up under their belly and bumped them with her roof. They listed to the left, then right, trying to shake her, but she was faster. She was in a Star Sphere, and they were just meat sacks. Their velocity began to slow.

Two flashes came from their airfoils, and a set of rigid, iridescent objects flipped past us.

"Did she just clip their wings?" I asked Proxy.

The cat, having appeared beside me, replied, "She did. But not enough to cause them to crash. I believe this is the time to push your advantage."

"Get ready everyone," I called over the shuttle.

We rocketed ahead, pushing just a little faster to close the gap, my passengers groaning at the strain. The giant cicada of an Isopteran shuttle continued to attempt to escape Karianna, but it was no use. She flipped over onto her back and began flying upside down, extending the grapple we had used to rescue the trapped shuttle on Novae to hold them in place, making her extended body into a massive counterweight.

"Here's your moment, dude," she told me. *"Get the fuck on with it."*

I brought my Swift Shuttle in over what looked to be the thorax of the enemy shuttle's form, its wings extended on either side of us. While our shuttle was fast, theirs was almost four times larger. I hoped Karianna's craft had enough mass to keep them steady.

"Proxy," I said. "Can you drive? I'm about to be stupid."

The cat nodded. "I will hold us steady. The hatch will take you to the thinnest spot in their hull."

I unplugged myself from the Star Sphere and climbed onto the deck, my body naked but for a set of dripping underwear. The crew looked to me, confused, but began unbuckling from their makeshift seats. I stepped into a small closet, making use of an emergency environmental suit. The device within this tight space wrapped my body in a kind of clear, plastic-like material, before lowering a helmet onto my head and clicking it into place.

I emerged from the box and motioned for the crew to put on their emergency breathing masks.

"What are you doing?" Shelly demanded of me. "You can't—"

"But I am," I said, and turned to a hatch in the floor.

The air in the shuttle went chilly as the pressure shifted, causing my ears to pop. With a mental command, the circular portal irised open, revealing the hull of the enemy shuttle and a shitload of crosswinds.

I took a step forward and dropped through the hole, holding a vial of quicksilver fluid tight in my right hand. Given that we were thousands of feet over the ocean, traveling near the speed of sound, you would have thought I'd have been snatched away and blown off to my death by the wind. But Proxy had designed this emergency suit with enough aerodynamics and weight that it didn't matter. These environmental conditions were mere inconveniences, nothing more.

I landed with a thump on the cicada's hull, feet sticking to its greenish-black surface like I was a gecko climbing rocks. As I sent a command to the vial in my hand, its contents shattering glass, liquid flowed out from my fingers into a solid, bladelike apparatus as long as my arm. I spun the sharp end around and dug its edge into the Isopteran vessel as if I were slaying some great, mythical beast.

As thin as the hull was at this location, the nanomachine blade had no issue parting the fungara's chemical bonds. The blade sliced into the material like a razor through mushroom caps, splitting its layers with such satisfaction it made me smile.

Ice began to form on my suit's fingertips and around my helmet.

The Isoptera twisted the shuttle around, attempting to throw us from their back, to divest Karianna from their belly, but they had no success. We were locked into place, shuttle underneath, shuttle closing atop. We were coming inside whether they wanted us or not.

A neat, circular section of fungara fell into the enemy shuttle with a thunk. I retracted the nanoblade, reforming it into a filigreed design that ran up my arm. Then I stood from where I had been squatting. Proxy lowered a series of umbilicals down, which snapped to my temporary suit and drew me almost lovingly back inside.

My Swift Shuttle lowered several feet, closing the distance between us and the enemy, and a short metallic collar extended and secured itself between the two points, connecting us to them. I rolled onto my side on the decking, catching my breath, then waved for my team to move in.

"No children through the portal," I said, having caught a quick glimpse through the hole I'd just cut.

"Flash bang then," Lance ordered, and Renata sprang into action, tossing one into the hole.

A bright light came from beneath. Goldilocks didn't hesitate. He hopped into the hole, but as he did, Proxy and Karianna gently raised our three shuttles into the air, drawing the floor up to meet him so that he wouldn't fall as far. Lance landed flat footed, firing in quick bursts as he cleared the room.

Renata went next, then Chevelle, Leo, Ada, Xuan, and Hy. Before I knew it, the shuttle was empty.

Shelly remained with me, helping me get out of the temporary suit.

"You're freezing," she said, peeling away the helmet. "It makes it hard to grab."

I felt for my skin, and she was right. The frost had spread everywhere. "It's cold as shit up here. Close to -35."

From our Swift Shuttle's deck, I could hear a commotion down below. Wind rushed along the hull of the shuttle. Gunshots and screams came from the breach. I hoped everyone was okay. I was positive the damned termites hadn't expected this. They weren't that creative.

I rallied myself to stand, reach for a weapon and go into action, but Shelly shook her head.

"They've got it," she said. "Pilot the ship."

It felt cowardly to take this suggestion, but she was right. We stripped off the last of the suit and I climbed back into my Star Sphere, blessed warmth enveloping me. The instant I connected to the shuttle's systems, I got a message from Lance.

"We've got them," he said. *"They're scared. We're trying to get them out. Chevelle shot what we think was the pilot by accident."*

Our intertangled set of shuttles began to list to the right. I fought to adjust along with Karianna's help, but something wasn't right.

"Get them out, quick," I said, then looked to Proxy.

"Their engines are shutting down," it said. "It could be a defensive mechanism, or the result of no more stimulation to the fungara. The end result is the same. We will fall from the sky."

"Lance!" I shouted back. "Quickly isn't quick enough. Run. Get the fuck out. We might have only seconds."

As the Isopteran shuttle's engines spluttered out, Karianna and I struggled to keep everyone aloft. The cicada was so much larger, so much heavier than both of us combined.

"I can't do this forever," Karianna said. *"The grapple is snapping. My hull is under some crazy strain. It's buckling. How much longer?"*

I checked their progress. Fifteen kids had been taken. Ten were in our shuttle, as was everyone in the crew but for Leo.

"Almost there," I told her.

"Shit, shit," she replied, and I felt a snap translated through the hull of the enemy ship up to my connection. *"Milo!"*

Coupled to the Isopteran craft, we fell. I pulled up as hard as I could, extending our airfoils just a little wider to allow us to glide, but we were falling at several dozen feet per second.

The pillowy expanse of clouds, which always seemed so solid from above, swallowed us whole as violent winds rushed past. It took everything we had just to keep somewhat level.

"Hurry!" I called back into the speakers of the shuttle, making them crackle from my voice. *"Everyone back now! No more time!"*

We were in freefall.

Sixteen thousand feet.

Fourteen.

Thirteen.

"Leo?" I asked.

Twelve.

"They're in! We're in!" he reported.

"Proxy!" I shouted.

The cat nodded. "Closing the door. Disengaging lock."

We gently drew away from the dead weight that was pulling us down to the violent seas below. The cicada fell away, becoming nothing more than a smudge at the edge of my view. I arrested our descent, careful not to kill the crew as I pulled up, keeping my turns and changes in acceleration gentle enough that no restraints were required.

"Did we get them?" Karianna called to me as her shuttle appeared at my side, the two of us bending slowly to Longyearbyen.

"We got them," I said, and looked into the shuttle's cabin through the internal cameras. Among my trusted crew, who looked battered and beaten but alive, were the faces of fifteen wild-eyed and frightened children. They clung to their rescuers, faces buried in shoulders, arms wrapped around them, some sobbing, some still as death. We had done it. We had saved them.

Thank the Universe that not everything we did had an unhappy ending.

"We got them," I repeated to my copilot. *"We got them."*

CHAPTER 28

We returned to Longyearbyen, not bothering to land at the airport but instead on an empty field near the Free Citizens of Earth's compound. As we disembarked, Ingrid, Dameon, and Priscilla rushed out with a dozen others at their side. Kids ran out of the shuttle to be reunited with their parents and guardians, and there was a palpable sense of relief in the air. Watching them hug, get kisses, smile, and cry . . . it made all the danger worth it. These were the people we fought for.

Karianna skipped over and elbowed me in the ribs. "You kicked ass out there," she whispered.

I shrugged off her compliment, trying to act like it didn't make me a little giddy. "Didn't do it alone." We gave each other a fist bump. It was pretty badass.

Damp and cold, but dressed, I made my way over to Ingrid, who was counting the children to make sure everyone was okay.

"You got them back," she said, turning to me. "They're all here."

I eyed the group, then inclined by head. "Fifteen were taken. Fifteen came back. We had to search every bolt hold we could find on the, um, Clickers' ship, but we did it. We've dealt with them before, and my crew is tough."

Ingrid extended her hand, her expression hard but appreciative. "Thank you, Mr. Hughes." And we shook. "Thank you, thank you," she went on. Then, out of nowhere, she pulled me into a bear hug and proceeded to squeeze the air out of my lungs.

I looked over her shoulder to Dameon and Priscilla, who seemed confused at this interaction. Priscilla mouthed to me, *She's not a hugger.*

After several seconds, Ingrid let me go and recollected her typical, hard demeanor. "We are heartbroken at the loss of Oskar. Nothing will replace him. Yet knowing that the children are safe, and that for once we had a victory against the Clickers . . . It might be time for us to talk."

"I thought that's what we've been doing." I looked around at everyone, to Shelly, then Karianna. Neither of them jumped in. "What kind of talk do you mean?"

"Let's assume for a minute you're telling the truth," she began. "Let's say you are not trying to manipulate us. It's a path to make things better, right? Even in this generation. Even for these children?"

"It is," Shelly offered, taking a step forward. "It is."

"Communications," Ingrid said, raising a fist to her chin in thought while pacing. "Labor. And no doubt with labor comes the need for transportation—no way supplies get all over the planet without it. Manufacturing facilities might be busted and need work, but they exist in some of the hot zones around the globe. There's plenty of raw materials out there, we just need to move them."

"What are you saying?" I asked.

Karianna began to vibrate, barely able to hold back her excitement.

"We've been thinking through your short list," Dameon cut in, adjusting his glasses in a nervous gesture. "Considering where we might be able to help close the gaps. In a general sense, we are confident where most of these items may be found. The hard part will be influence and labor."

"And influence aside," Ingrid continued, "you need not just solid communications, but secure ones to coordinate everyone. The most secure and reliable network we can make use of is the Resonator Network."

I blinked. "The what?"

"A remnant left behind by the Lattice, a species of aliens who visited SOL a couple of hundred years ago. It sends signals by resonating a series of qubits over channels we do not understand. It is faster than light, somehow, but not quantum entangled, or at least not that we can see."

"So, is that how you called us from Triton?"

She looked up at the sky, then back to me. "It is, but that node in the network is one of the few we still have control of. We know where more of the nodes are located, and with some negotiations, I believe we can get all we'll ever need. And while we procure these resonator nodes, we might be able to enlist the support of one of SOL's larger, more powerful factions."

"Then there's the shuttles," Dameon added. "We don't have many, if any on Earth. Most of the heavy lifters have either been broken or destroyed. Your personal shuttles are impressive, but they won't do the jobs we will no doubt need doing. Our records indicate that there is a cache of shuttles on an asteroid a dozen or so AU away, at least thirty of them, maybe more. These shuttles are docked within a kind of art exhibition tagged as 'The Grand Gallery.' They were left a long time ago for reasons unknown, but given the design that was used, we believe they should be serviceable. This information comes from the undefined age of wonders we had mentioned, so it could be incomplete, sketchy. It's our best lead."

"Okay," I said, turning to Shelly and Karianna, both of whom were deep in thought. "So, we've got a network to use, we just need to get access. A solid lead on shuttles to do the heavy lifting. You say there is manufacturing here in the hot zones, I am guessing this means they have environmental conditions that are not ideal. We can handle that."

"We just need strong backs," Lance said, appearing at my side, arms crossed. He focused his attention on Ingrid. "What you might not know about the Jevox who created this terraforming equipment is that they work together like a machine. They share thoughts. These devices were designed to work in this way. It's too bad we don't work like them. I've led more than a few projects back on Novae when we were building the colony. Things don't always go as planned. The Jevox ship used to terraform worlds had about ten thousand of them aboard, all highly specialized, working as a single entity to a common goal. As bad as humans are working together, however, we might need three times that many to see it done. But we can do it."

"I agree," Shelly said. "It was a wonder to watch the Jevox work. They are fast, efficient, never wasting a moment or getting bogged down in an argument."

Ingrid looked to Dameon, who for his part gave a shrug.

"You leave a portion of that to me," he said. "Get help from up there. I'll coordinate help down here. If we can offer the other settlements incentives, they will likely fall in line. It's in all of our best interests, even for those not living on the ground. Besides, Priscilla told us of your universal inoculant. If we can make use of that, it would be something to trade."

Karianna popped her fingers and licked her lips, her excitement clear as crystal. "We have a plan, don't we? A real plan."

"I think so," I said, turning to Ingrid. "So, you're in? You ready to save Earth?"

She narrowed her eyes in thought, then looked to the sky, watching as the northern lights danced overhead. "Save the earth?" A chuckle escaped her lips. "What a wonderful place to start. First on the list, however, we need to take a trip." She turned to what I believed was the west, then spun a little farther south. Raising a hand, she pointed to the brightest light in the sky. "Have you ever visited Venus?"

"I haven't," I replied. "Why do you ask?"

"That's our first stop. Time for us to see if that place is truly heaven, or if it is what we've always believed . . ."

My mood soured, unsure of her meaning. "And what would that be?"

"Doesn't matter. When we lack evidence, we create our own narratives."

"Then let's go write a better one," I said, gazing at the distant planet along with her and the rest of my crew.

"Yes," she echoed, "let's write a better one."

CHAPTER 29

Ingrid wasted no time getting into action. Her team swiftly coordinated those from around the island they deemed important to the mission and packed their supplies. They were waiting by our Swift Shuttles in less than three hours. It was clear our handling of the Isopteran attack made a major impact on their opinions of us. Maybe they were afraid that if they took too long preparing, this opportunity might just pass them by. And if we had gone with Karianna's initial feelings in this situation, that just might have been the case. I was glad we had waited. I was glad we had been cool-headed. We had shown up at the right time—too bad that right time wasn't just a little bit earlier. Oskar, along with several of Longyearbyen's guards, had lost their lives to bring us to this place, and that didn't feel fair.

I found myself slack jawed and wide eyed when everyone had gathered. Ingrid arrived with her two companions and a host of twenty other Free Citizens of Earth.

"Uhh, our shuttles aren't big enough," Karianna mumbled beside me in the field where we had landed after our excursion. She fiddled with her bracelets and frowned. "I think we're going to need to take more than one trip up."

"Yeah," I said, addressing my crew.

"Why so many?" Shelly asked Ingrid.

She turned to her people, looking them over as if she were taking inventory. "Can your ship not support this many? Do you not have the capacity?"

"Oh, we've got the capacity alright," Lance cut in, putting himself between Ingrid and me while crossing his arms. "Question is, are we ready for the complexity that comes with such a large group?" He gave her a long, piercing gaze. She did not flinch, as their eyes locked on one another's. "Are they ready for it?"

Ingrid took a step toward him, her attention narrowing to pinpricks. "And just what does that mean?"

There was a growing tension between them, one that made me wonder if they were about to fight, or if they were about to toss about in the sheets. What the hell was going on with them? Why was he pushing back when she was being amicable?

"Are they ready for it?" Karianna mumbled to me and Shelly. "More like, are we ready for it? That's a lot of damn people to keep track of. Can we trust them all?"

"Proxy and Chinchillette will keep an eye on them," I said, but I wasn't 100 percent sure what that might look like.

"At least it won't be quiet," James put in, having appeared from out of nowhere, his backpack slung over one shoulder. "Gets a little spooky around the ship sometimes, you know? Especially when everyone has been dunked in their spheres. Weird noises. Proxy showing up out of nowhere to offer help. I don't like ghosts, remember bruh?"

"There aren't any ghosts." Karianna shook her head.

"I didn't say there were. I said it was *like* there were ghosts."

"Why are you so fixated on ghosts? Stop acting stupid."

James turned to Hy. "Gets creepy, right? Like, when the ship is too quiet."

"I like ghosts," Hy responded.

"You're no help at all."

"Why so many, though?" I ignored my crew and pressed on Ingrid's choice.

She rubbed at her temples for a moment as if annoyed, then forced a toothy smile. "If all goes well on Aeolia, our second target, the Grand Gallery, will include the procuring of shuttles, and we will need pilots. Last time I checked, the models mentioned in our records won't fly on their own. We still might not have a pilot for each shuttle, I know, but we can take trips so long as everything is safe."

And that was fair. Twenty shuttles? Thirty shuttles? How many pilots did she plan on taking with us? Could we even provide a place for all these craft to dock? I needed to check on this with Proxy asap.

"Check them for weapons," Chevelle said, approaching the extras. "Don't need no wastemen bustin' up our ends. Aight?"

"We serious?" Ingrid asked, looking to Dameon. "A security check?"

He adjusted his glasses and gave a shrug. "We did do the same to them. It's only fair. This is their house."

I raised my open palms and sighed. "Look, we aren't trying to tie anyone's hands behind their back, but please, let's at least take an accounting of any firearms. I promise, given the AIs on our ship, you don't want to try and mess with us anyways. It would go bad for anyone who made the attempt. But we want you to feel safe in case something happens. Fair?"

"Fair," Ingrid conceded after a moment's pause, waving at her people to comply.

"Did you pack that dog of yours?" I asked, then found myself rubbing the skin above my heart.

She did not smile, but made a gesture with her right hand, and out of the ground rose a pool of quicksilver, its mass solidifying into a metallic canine made of hard edges and lines. "Might come in handy," she said.

I grinned at her but fought not to shrink back from it. "I have to admit. That thing is terrifying."

The metallic animal looked to her, and she tipped her head to the side, while bending down to pet the low-resolution animal on the head. "Hardly. He's a good little floof."

"Floof?" I chuckled. "Does he have a name?"

"Flicker," she offered, then twisted her hand, ordering the nanomachines to decompile, the canine losing its form and vanishing back into the ground.

I cocked my head as I watched it go. "Is this a common weapon found on Earth now?"

"Weapon?" She chewed at her bottom lip and frowned. "Flicker is not a weapon. At one point we believe they were common enough: Somnium Reconstructs, or dream constructs. Found mine in a ruined city near the former site of London, its capsule fully charged, not broken by time or EMPs during the last war. They were artificial pets, capable of taking on whatever form the owner liked. But Flicker is more. He has thoughts of his own. A personality."

"And a sharp one at that," James said, bumping me with his elbow. "Right, bruh? Sharp? Eh? Eh?"

I rolled my eyes at him.

"Priscilla, Dameon, you coming with us?" Shelly asked, the first of us to notice that they were dressed differently than the rest.

"No," Priscilla said, her tone regretful as she gestured at the city with an open hand. "We are needed here. And we could use some assistance preparing for your return. Would anyone from your crew be willing to stay behind?"

I turned to face them. No one looked excited at this prospect, Xuan and Hy least of all. From conversations earlier that day, I knew the two of them just wanted to go home, or the closest thing we had to it.

"Don't look at me," James said, shoulders rising in a shrug. "I'm in for the action."

Leo grimaced. "You'll get plenty down here, that's already established."

"Hmm." James rubbed his chin, considering the idea for a moment. "No thanks. I think I'm good on that variety."

"And don't look at me," Leo said, stepping up beside Ada. "She needs a sidekick."

"No, I don't," Ada replied with a hint of playfulness in her tone. "I'm okay."

"But we make such a good team."

Chevelle stepped up, forcing herself between the two of them, palms pushing them back. "Oi, pussymouts. I'll stay then. Do what it takes. Need someone smart down here."

"I have a couple more who might want to help," I said. "We'll chat with them when we get up. Let's get a move on."

We said our goodbyes to those on the ground and made our first trip, taking my crew and a few others up to the *Transcendence*, then coming back down to collect the rest. It was a tight squeeze for as many as we had to carry, but we made it work.

After a brief chat aboard the *Transcendence*, Dante and Emilia agreed to swap out and headed down to the surface to aid Priscilla and Dameon. Between the two of them and Chevelle, I felt we had our ground situation covered. I could only hope they stayed safe. There would be no protecting them—they were on their own.

Once everyone was aboard Lance assigned them quarters, showing the Free Citizens of Earth where they would sleep, where to find food, and what Star Sphere was theirs for when, not if, we found ourselves in a bit of action. Like all of us had been at one time, they were more than a little horrified at the prospect of being submerged and linked up to an alien machine, but after Proxy's detailed description of what might happen to them if they didn't make use of it in a combat situation, most of their fears were put to rest in light of ever bigger ones. Leo took them through his gallery and introduced them to a bit of original music from Novae, as well as some of the best places to go on the ship when you needed time alone. Ada gave them instructions on using the network, and with Proxy's assistance, how to build simulators for the shuttles and get a bit of practice in ahead of time.

While we were gone, Frelo had calibrated some of the terraforming equipment based on ground readings Proxy had provided. I offered for them to go down to the surface, but they declined, wanting to remain on the ship for now. Something intangible and profoundly sad resided in their eyes, but when asked, they said that nothing was wrong. It must have been hard being alone. Being so far from home. I just wish there was more I could do as a human.

Karianna, Shelly, and I left everyone to their wonderstruck exploration of the ship, returning to our own Star Spheres, stripping down and submerging ourselves in the delightfully warm fluid. Though I had already been piloting the shuttle from a sphere over the last few hours, this one felt different. It felt like home. It was like a broken-in pair of shoes, its leather stretched into the perfect shape, or a chair that had formed around your body over years of use that felt just right. I didn't see how this was possible, given how this worked, but it was.

"Take us out, Ms. Torlen," I said as our virtual environment came online and Shelly appeared next to me. My attention drifted onto North America sliding past beneath us, its former glory a track of scarred and ruined landscape. I felt a sharp pain in my chest as I peered down at the center of the country, thinking back to my brief childhood upon this rock.

Emotions within me became a jungle, thick and full of danger. Karianna noticed my shift in mood and rushed to my side within the integration, doing what I could only explain felt like putting a head on my shoulder. Caught up in these feelings, I did not push her away.

It's where we were born, she thought.

I turned that idea over for a moment like a Rubik's cube of mixed colors, a puzzle I was not prepared to solve. *Part of me wants to go down and look. See if anything is left in Whispering Pines. See if I recognize the place. Is the school still there? The park?*

You're not alone.

We're capable of it. Wouldn't take long.

Yeah . . . well . . . I don't think we should.

Why? We grew up in different places.

Yes, but . . . those memories. There's no need to tarnish them. It's been almost five hundred years, Milo. Maybe it's best to let those memories live in their own little bubbles. Let those pages, those parts of our story remain unchanged. You can never go home, right? I don't think there's anything to be gained from seeing it ourselves. We don't need more resolve. We don't need more hurt or anger. We know what we need to do.

But was she right? We knew what we needed to do. But that pull of curiosity was strong. What would even be left? Smoking holes in the ground. Dust. Hardly a sign it had ever been. Would I even be able to find it?

Too much time had passed.

Too much.

"You okay?" Shelly tugged on my arm.

I shook myself free of that reverie, the faint smell of old coffee and stale pizza dispersing from recall like vapor. "Karianna? Did you hear me?"

"Aye aye, Capn'," Karianna replied over the open channel, and we began to move, slowly extricating our mass from the glittery collection of debris that encircled the earth.

I focused on our instruments as we pulled away, chewing on my nails as I worried over detecting Veetor and the UEI Remnant Fleet, or if there were more Isoptera to deal with. So far, the scopes were clean, only distant signals were giving us any concern, though something odd brushed across the edge of my perception, like a hair tickling the back of my neck, then was gone. I swore it was as if something had left our ship, but I had nothing to prove this, everyone was accounted for, so were all our fighters and shuttles. After checking with Proxy, who reported nothing, I ignored the impression as background radiation, maybe a solar flare.

No threats appeared. No signals from the habitations floating around Earth. It was as if we were invisible for now, unnoticed, just another shifting shadow in the dark.

Hours passed as everyone settled into place. Shelly had run off for a bit, working on a data project with Ada and Leo, leaving me alone with Proxy. The cat brought me up to speed on what it had learned about our passengers as I held it tight in my arms, scratching it behind the ears. I thought back to Flicker and had to admit that having a non-animal animal as a pet wasn't as foreign as I pretended, but at least Proxy was cute. That thing Ingrid had? It was like an angry collection of razorblades with a will.

Proxy had nothing dangerous to report. The Free Citizens of Earth seemed okay so far; everyone was playing nice, following their leader's rules as well as our own. They had a similar sentiment and disposition as their leader, one of a people who had been through hard times, were not afraid to put in some work, and long ago had been relieved of all but the darkest or most cynical forms of humor. So long as things remained like this, we'd get along fine.

A ping came from Ingrid hours later, surprising me. She had adapted swiftly to her new surroundings, having discovered the shared bridge space while wandering through the network.

I answered her ping, shifting my perspective and appearing before the large display at the center of the room. Ingrid was lounging on the infinity couch, a veritable buffet laid out before her. There sat a tray of various finger foods, tiny sandwiches and fancy crackers, along with a collection of drinks in a variety of colors and glasses. Set to the side was a sampling of cheeses and meats, neatly wrapped and arrayed, some of their thin slices folded like rose buds.

She took hold of a simple, slender glass filled with a translucent, scarlet-colored liquid, then took a sip, smiling at the taste. Instinct told me it was not alcoholic.

"How do they get it so close to the real thing?" she mused, inspecting the vessel in her hand. "It's a drink from when I was a kid. No name, really, we just called it Red. It tastes just like I remember it, sweet with a hint of citrus and cherries."

"I don't believe these recreations are as close as we think," I replied, taking a seat next to her. "The taste, the texture, it all comes from memories. I think the Foundry machines lean into that. They present everything in such a way it tricks our minds into experiencing certain memories. Like the pink signal, it's an emotional override."

She set the glass down and picked up one of the pale triangles of bread and cheese. Were those pimentos? "So, it tricks you into experiencing it? Even if that memory isn't yours?"

"That's the idea. I've had plenty of different foods in here, within a sphere, and on the ship, that I have never eaten or drank while in my flesh and blood."

"How easy this could be to just escape into forever," she said, then put the sandwich in her mouth, closed her eyes and chewed.

I waited for her to finish before going on. A question was burning at the back of my mind, one of many. I only hoped it was related to why she'd called me in here. I did not wait. "So, I have to ask. This colony. Aeolia. You mentioned a few details about it, but nothing major. We know there's something we need there, but I know little about the people and how they interact with the rest of humankind."

She dusted off her fingers and leaned back on the couch, her lips pressed into a hard line, looking to the ceiling as if the right words might be written there. "Well . . . it's a lot to unpack."

"Then let's unpack it."

"Sure. Okay. Aeolia sends their shuttles down to Earth from time to time. Sometimes they come to us, sometimes they go other places. When they arrive, delegates invite chosen groups of four or five to ascend from the desperation of our broken home to a new life."

"*Ascend?*" I mused, rolling the letters around in my mouth. "Is that your word for it, or is it theirs?"

"Their word. And to be honest, we have always believed it to be more than just the physical action of leaving the planet. Friends and loved ones are given a new life, whisked away into the sky with the hopes of something better. I was offered the chance once, years ago, but I declined."

"Why?"

"I couldn't leave everyone behind to suffer. It felt too . . . too selfish. I don't fault anyone for taking their help, but I couldn't in good conscience leave everyone."

"So, they arrive, ascend only a few, and then leave the rest. Why? Why not take more?"

She absently chose a slice of pale colored cheese from the tray, put it to her nose, and sniffed, before placing it along with a thin slice of meat atop a smooth cracker. As she ate, her eyes closed, and she took a deep breath, relishing the taste.

"So sorry," she mumbled through closed lips. "I'm being rude. I shouldn't be eating right now."

"No. No." I raised my hands. "It's okay. Take your time. I know what it's like to go a while without anything good on your stomach, real or not. Food on Novae wasn't exactly tasty, let me tell you. You get tired of eating stone bison sausage when all you really want is some damn carnitas."

Finger raised, she fixed another cracker topped with cheese, swallowed it down quick, and wiped off her mouth.

"Okay, okay," she went on. "So, Aeolia. Why don't they take more? We have asked the same question of them. They tell us there's not enough room for everyone. We can only guess that they invite these small groups when there is a need to replenish some arbitrary population level. Perhaps they are making sure their gene pool is sufficiently diverse. We can't say for sure, but after ascending, we never hear from these people again. One such person is a man named Brian Gray, a companion of mine for many years— a friend, nothing more. I hope to find him, make sure he's okay. If he's still there, still alive, I'm confident he'll help us get what we need."

"We'll find him," I told her. "You mentioned having direct contact with the settlement itself, if inconsistent."

"That's right, but official channels only." She reached for the table, taking up a clear, fat mug with a big handle. The contents of the glass were dark and bubbling, a layer of foamy ice cream on its surface. She held the mug before her in both hands, brows narrowed, lips twisted, appraising its contents. "Their leadership contacts us, or one of the other settlements, every few years to check on surface conditions. To learn what settlements are hanging in, and which ones are not. It is less for trade, or any sort of official exchanges, more for information. And their lack of transparency, well, it leaves much to be desired."

She tipped her mug back, sipping at its contents. "What is this?" She smacked her lips and took a second go. "It's wonderful."

"That there is a root beer float. It's from Earth, twentieth century, made from sassafras root, I think. It was a very popular beverage in my parents' time. The ice cream just makes it better."

"I can see why." She set the mug down, then wiped off her upper lip where a bit of foam had been left behind. "That the white stuff? The ice cream? This might be my new treat."

"We all need something," I said, and a single ball of sonhos appeared in my fingers. I popped it in my mouth, enjoying the sweet flavor of the Brazilian treat. "Do you think they'll cooperate?"

She gave a shrug. "Only one way to find out."

I stood to leave, and as I did, several others appeared in the shared space, Lance among them. He gave me a nod, then motioned around the room, pointing out details as he gave a group of Ingrid's people a tour.

"I'll leave you to it," I told her. "Enjoy your treats."

"Thank you," she whispered, and stood to extend her hand. "I know we got lost talking business, but I called you here to say that. Thank you."

"For what?"

"For this, all of this. For what you did on the surface. Some of this might be fantasy, in its way, but when you have faced what we have faced, you take every opportunity to remind yourself that life is more than survival. Little things make all the difference—a good meal, a tasty snack, a conversation without the threat of imminent death."

"The day is young," I said, shaking her hand.

She nodded at that, a smile quirking the edge of her lip. "Very young."

I retreated into solitude, returning to my personal virtual environment. I needed some time to swim in a sea of stars, an ocean of vacuum. I needed quiet to think, to get my head in the right place for what would come next. Something wasn't right about this Aeolia, but I couldn't put my finger on it. This settlement was not just an enigma to us, but to others living in SOL.

On Earth, people struggled in squaller. But on Venus . . . they *ascended.*

CHAPTER 30

While one mystery was before us, another potentially more dangerous one was still in progress. Recent events had made my research over the Kabosai device from Nest difficult to conduct, busy as it was. But with the next influx of crew and the buzz they had created, circumstance had carved a slice of time out for me. I was taking it.

The ship secure, our destination locked in, I returned to the Dead Room to continue my research. In this bizarre confluence of events, everyone's attention was elsewhere. Karianna was busy with operations and repairs. Shelly was working with Ingrid on a secure connection from Svalbard to the ship. Our visitors were running simulations on the shuttles we planned to recover after our stop on Venus. And the rest of the crew were occupied with Leo, who was hosting an impromptu listening party at the forward end of the ship featuring the works of Marissa Martin.

I was able to move like a ghost, leaving nothing more than a cold breeze and tingly sensations in my wake.

The Dead Room was just as I had left it, its log showing no one had entered since last I visited. It was true that not many people had access to this space, especially our visitors, but there were a few who could enter but hadn't.

The obsidian, polyhedral device waited for me.

I approached it cautiously, waving a hand in the air to shift the lights from blue to red, the symbols upon its surface blossoming to life.

"What are you?" I mused, as I went to work.

My prosthetic fingers slid across every surface of the shape, pressing gently as they went, looking for any give. I spoke to it, searching for universal commands that might open it wide. I went through a similar set of actions as before, trying different bands of light to see if they revealed anything other than the symbols I'd already seen. After exploring every frequency of the visual spectrum, I went into the ultraviolet and infrared range, using a special set of glasses to translate the feedback into digestible information.

All of these ideas were dead ends.

If only we understood these languages, this would be so much easier. I was no linguist, and to be honest, with the Foundry augmentations, I hadn't needed to be. With its help, I could understand almost any language spoken by sapient life, be it clicks, or groans, or a series of clipped, vocal vibrations. But this was different. Either the Foundry was unable or unwilling to translate. How would I solve for that? How would I—

"What are you doing?" a feminine voice called over my shoulder, and I leapt out of my skin, heart shooting up out of my chest through my throat. Flashbacks came from that fateful day on the *Vasco Da Gama* when Esteban and Diederick had found James and I snooping in the combat simulator room.

I covered my face and spun around, attempting to lengthen my shallow breaths and calm myself.

"Damn it, Shelly," I hissed. "You scared the shit out of me."

She let out a peal of laughter, hands covering her mouth as she bent over. "You would have thought you were doing something wrong, freaked out as you are."

"Yeah, umm," I said, sliding to the side, attempting to hide the device with my body. "Not much going on in here. You know . . . just stuff. What's up?"

Shelly crossed her arms and narrowed her eyes at me. Those dark slits, usually wide and inviting, gave me the impression this was not the time to cross her. She reached out a hand and pushed me to the side.

"I should have known, you sneaky boy," she began, taking a step up to the worktable. "What have you figured out?"

I swallowed my emotions and took up position beside her. "You're not mad at me?"

She gave me a withering, sidelong look. "I'm furious you didn't trust me enough to tell me you were trying to figure this out."

"It's dangerous," I started. "I didn't want you to get hurt."

"Let that be my choice. I'm a big girl. I know what can happen."

"I know, it's just—"

She raised an open palm to forestall me. "We'll talk about this later. We don't have much time before someone finds us. The crew is busy right now, but we can almost bet that little puppy dog will come looking for you soon enough."

I cocked my head to the side, scratching at the back of my neck. "Puppy dog?"

"Clueless as ever." Shelly shook her head and rolled her eyes. "So, are you going to tell me what you know?"

"Sure," I conceded, not sure what that look was for. Had she been talking about James? He sure acted smitten around Karianna, following her wherever she went, hanging on her every word. He had it bad.

Another question for another day, I suppose.

I walked her through everything I'd already discovered, which to be honest wasn't all that much. She spent the majority of her time inspecting the symbols, calling up a virtual notepad with her implants to record her thoughts. She shared this information with me in a simplified, augmented reality space, splitting it off into groups, and came to the same conclusion as I had over the central characters, that they appeared to each be of different languages, not just one.

"It appears that the top five and bottom faces of the shape are either amalgamations or some kind of hybrid of words," she began after a long silence. "They share similar shapes, twisting lines like you see on faces fifteen, twelve, five, and thirteen, but also share these sorts of modified runes, which appear on eleven, nine, six, and sixteen, single-stroke characters."

"Why do you think this would be?" I asked. "Why would the Gene Brokers have multiple languages?"

"What do we really know of their origins?"

I shook my head. "Not much. Just that they exist. And everyone seems to know who they are."

"They sought humans out because we were natural, yes?"

"They did." I turned the shape around, its base remaining fixed in open air, spinning like a slow top. "Somehow, natural evolution makes for better base genes. Maybe they're better tested?"

"Then consider this for a moment. What if they themselves are no longer natural?"

"Oh," I said, leaning back. "I think I get where you're going. They were likely a natural species at some point, but they have modified themselves so much with the use of other species, that they are themselves an amalgamation of natural evolution."

"Precisely. Which is where this blending of language comes from. These central symbols could be the unadulterated natural tongues of their gene contributors. Whereas the top, as well as the bottom, those could be a more modern Kabosai script."

"Is it not still different than what we saw on their devices at Creatus?"

"Some, but not that dissimilar. I only wish I had a sample to compare."

"Can you translate any of it?"

"Partially." She spun the shape around to bring face number fifteen before us. "This line here, do you see it?" Her finger rested at the end of a scrawling section of scratching symbols. "If I am correct, this shares a common language to some of the passages in a book I traded for on Cynosure. While I can't be sure what particular species wrote this, the book was curated by a Lyowin scholar. According to them, the closest translation would be 'template.'"

I blinked at that thought. "Like a pattern, or does it mean something else?"

"Yes, like a pattern. A stencil. A mold of sorts. A guide. A set of rules. Instructions. A starting point. It means all those things and more."

"That supports our hypothesis." I leaned in to take a closer look at the words as if being closer would help me better understand. "Wonder what kind of template a machine like this requires. Like, what format or form factor? Is it a file? A disc? A fingernail?"

Shelly began rubbing her neck and let out a yawn. I moved up behind her and began rubbing her shoulders. She groaned and closed her eyes, leaning herself into my grip.

"But how do we open it?" she mused, and I had no answer.

We stood in silence for a time, me pressing away the knots from her shoulders, her spinning the shape around, staring at its faces, looking for something to jog her thoughts loose.

Then, out of nowhere, she tossed her hands up and pushed me away. "I've got it."

"What?"

"There's a pattern on the central faces." She pressed her palms against the sides of her face and chuckled like a kid who'd just been given a sack full of candy—the good kind. "I numbered them, but I got the numbers all wrong."

"I'm sorry?"

She drew my attention to a repeating series of dots and dashes along the edges. "These are codes, Milo. They number the faces, but they appear only on the central ones, not the top or bottom set. Maybe this means that those are the only ones designed to be opened." She turned it around, bringing face fifteen back before us. "Let's open the template."

Speakers in the room came to life as she triggered some kind of command. Noises started at a low, groaning frequency, then began to pitch upward. As we hit a baritone note, the face upon the polyhedral shape began to glow. She tapped out a pattern in the air, and the sound responded, shifting between a higher frequency note and the lower pitch of its constant drone.

The face upon the black shape let out a click, and flipped open, creating a triangular shelf. The sound cut off.

"Holy shit," I said, scrambling back a step or two. "How the hell?"

Shelly smiled at me with a smug sense of satisfaction. "This is why you don't leave me out of things. I'm smarter than you."

"That has never been in doubt."

The interior of the shape was dim, a slight yellow glow coming from within. We peered inside. As Proxy had already surmised, the hole was deep, far deeper than was possible given what we knew of physics. At the end of the deep passage was the source of the yellow light, a sort of docking station in the shape of a pyramid six inches tall. It sat empty, waiting for data to fill it.

"That's the template," she said, and I nodded. "And from the looks of it, this device is lacking one."

"So, where do we get one? And, how is it used?"

She shook her head. "I have no idea. But without it, I would say that this device is little more than a curiosity. Whatever it does."

"That's too bad," I said, resting my fists on my hips.

"What had you hoped it might do?"

I gave a shrug and looked away, feeling so small in the moment, so foolish. "Well, I mean, if this device is in fact a Kabosai device, then we know with a high likelihood what it might be capable of, right?"

"I think so. Genetic rewriting in some way, similar to what we saw on Creatus, but on a larger scale. I would venture to say it might be possible to create one of their designer species with it. Could even be what was used against the Gan."

I focused on the open panel, wondering what the rest might do. What they might be for. "I'd believe it. Question is, do you think it to be all bad?"

"What do you mean?"

"There's something I keep asking myself: Is this a weapon? Or does it have a higher purpose? Let's say it didn't have to destroy all life to recreate it. That might have just been what happened to them, for the sake of the Jevox. What if the life upon its target location, or planet, or whatever . . . What if it could be augmented, not completely rewritten?"

She licked her lips and crossed her arms, staring off into nothing as she considered my words. "I've thought about that. Maybe it could make minor changes to upgrade a species."

"Just maybe."

"And those seemingly minor changes could make a major impact on their survivability."

"Which may be why the Kabosai are as they are. Multiple languages, many species part of them. They are something new, traded, brokered, from something natural. They are, without a doubt, survivors."

Shelly nodded at that and gently closed the panel, leaving the black shape solid once more. "So, this begs the question: if you could upgrade your species, who gets to choose what those upgrades are? How can you do this in a moral or ethical way?"

"I don't know." I raised my hands and started pacing the room. "It would be a monumental decision. One you can't go back from. And of course, it would not change everyone, since it would have an effective range. Pretty sure whoever did this would be forcing it upon a population on some level. I'm not sure you could have a democratic process for something so major. And if you did, you'd be debating for so long, it would likely never go into practice."

"We are not the best at making decisions like that as a species, are we?"

I shook my head and took her hands in mine. "We are not. Ingrid and her team are right about FICSE. It's a wonder we ever made that happen. There's too much tribalism hard coded into humans. Imagine trying to get Veetor and Ingrid to agree on anything, even the color of the sky."

"Not likely." She smiled at me, and her eyes twinkled with something mischievous. "But why don't we dream for a minute? Thought experiments don't hurt anyone. If humans could still be human, but we could solve for some of our challenges from a genetic standpoint, what would that be?"

"Easy ones first." I raised a single finger. "No cancer, for starts."

"No cancer."

"Better ways to regulate our metabolism and cravings would be great."

"Could be important." She started making notes in her augmented space, fingers clicking at empty air. "More efficient muscle development would be useful."

"Agreed, especially in null or microgravity. Mom would appreciate that."

"She would." Shelly paused for a moment as if an idea had struck her. "You know who I have envied in so many ways during our travels?"

"Who?"

"The Jevox. They might have an unusually homogenized social order, but the ability to understand one another's motivations and intentions meant they had no war. They worked together. All the great things they accomplished are the result of this deep communion."

"Add it to the list," I said, nodding.

"Done and done."

"Another great one to add," I spread my arms wide, "radiotrophic cells. Make humans like I was when the *Fidelas* nearly fell at Ph0nx. Soak in all the life given by stars. Like the Jalek."

"You want us to be able to eat radiation?"

I gave an epic shrug. "Would be awesome in space, would it not? If we didn't have cancer and could eat radiation, we'd be supersurvivors."

"Might as well add organelles to our cells that can reverse-metabolize and eat carbon dioxide in emergency situations."

I pointed at her and grinned. "Perfect idea!"

"Is this how it feels to be a Kabosai?" she asked, her tone turning dark.

Those words hung for a while, neither of us sure how to proceed. Her father's death had likely been the result of a Gene Broker experiment gone wrong. This would always be a sore subject.

"We are not Kabosai," I told her, hands resting on her shoulders, eyes meeting hers. "We will never be like them."

She sniffled for a moment, then gave me a weak grin. "I know. But it doesn't matter anyways. There's no template for us to work from, and we need no telling how much power to make this thing run. Not sure if it generates its own. Without those, we won't be doing anything at all. I have a feeling if we were to get this operating without the right template in place, it would do far more damage than good."

"Could even be a planet killer."

"Yeah." She wrung her hands. "A terrible weapon, not killing instantly, but enacting a slow suffering as one is rewritten into a lifeform incapable of proceeding. How terrifying. How painful."

A series of beeps went off, informing us we were approaching a critical time in our passage to Venus.

"Back to work," I said, giving Shelly a squeeze.

"Back to work," she replied, and we took each other's hands, leaving the Dead Room and its enigmatic device to themselves.

CHAPTER 31

As sunlight reflected off the atmosphere of our destination, Venus became the brightest object in space other than our star. If we had been sailors of the ancient world, navigating by the sky upon the winds of an unforgiving sea, we could have easily found our destination with the naked eye.

It wasn't far away from Earth, and despite our gentle acceleration, it swelled, and swelled, and swelled. Fine details, storms of carbon dioxide and nitrogen, resolved into a swiftly rotating, pale yellow haze.

We slipped into orbit around Venus, keeping our distance from the manmade station orbiting some three hundred kilometers above the surface of the planet. Its wings spread high above the clouds. The sprawling hunk of metal took notice of us, less from an instrument standpoint and more visual confirmation, as far as I could tell. Massive as our form was, and with the intensity of our deceleration burn, we weren't any harder to spot than Venus.

A signal reached out from the station over UEI standard neutrino frequencies. *"This is Aeolia control to unidentified craft,"* a flat, deep voice called out. *"You have entered controlled airspace. Please note that as we speak, ground-based weapons have already locked on to your position and will fire if you show any sign of threat. Do you copy?"*

Nervous much? Karianna thought, a touch of wry sarcasm echoing through our link. Neither of us were all that worried about what capabilities these people had, but maybe that was foolish.

I looked to Shelly, who was floating beside me in my virtual environment, hoping for diplomatic inspiration. She gave me a shrug.

"Aeolia control," I began. "My name is Captain Milo Hughes of the *Transcendence*, once a crew member of the UEI *Vasco Da Gama* as part of the FICSE mission. We come to speak with your leadership about the future of Earth."

"Repeat. Did you say FICSE? Vasco Da Gama?*"*

"Affirmative. I know, I know. It's been a long time. We need to speak with your president, your boss, CEO, whoever is in charge."

"In—in charge?" There was a pause. I could only assume they were collecting their stunned thoughts. *"Well, eh, that would be Premier Takagi. But she is a very busy woman, and . . ."* They paused again. *"Do you have lighter transport? Do you have ground shuttles with vertical takeoff and landing capabilities?"*

"We do."

"Okay then. You are approved to approach the city. Leave your starship in a high orbit; we will transmit relative coordinates. As you approach the city, stand by for instructions on channel 662. We will guide you to the correct landing platform. Do not take any aggressive actions or deviate from your flight plan or we will be forced to respond with, um, force! Yes. Force. Do we understand one another?"

They did not seem so certain in their position. Or were they just nervous?

"Dangerous out here?" I paused, letting the words hang. *"You're not the first to treat us this way."*

The signal crackled for a moment, and I was pretty sure that the speaker on the other end had barked a laugh so loud it had caused it to clip. *"Dangerous? Ha. That's an understatement, Captain Hughes. Let's just say that, eh, the Splicers like to play with our best and brightest like toys when they see fit. I'm sure you understand why we are a bit cautious."*

Shelly looked to me, mouthing, *The Kabosai are near.*

Those freaking gene brokers were everywhere. Where were they hiding around the system? Maybe they deserved a visit from us before this was all over. Maybe they would give us answers before they burned for their crimes against humanity.

"We'll play nice," I told control, and that was enough for now.

Having been given approval to approach the city, we gathered up our crew, everyone boarding the shuttles but for the Free Citizen pilots who stayed behind to run training simulations with Proxy and Frelo.

Ingrid waited by my Swift Shuttle, speaking in hushed tones with Lance. The two quieted as I approached, their expressions hard.

"We good?"

She looked to Lance, who said nothing, then turned back to me. "Let me do the talking. We have been in loose communication with this settlement for decades. We have a rapport, after a fashion. Let's not complicate things too much."

I raised my open palms. "Fair enough. You're the boss here."

At hearing these words, Karianna gave me a troubled expression before she boarded her shuttle. I paid her peculiar look little mind and got into my own. Shelly was buckled up at the front of the row of passenger seats. She reached out as I approached, squeezing my fingers briefly. Neither of us said a word, just looked at one another, having one of those deep conversations only life partners were capable of. The content of it didn't matter so much as the connection between us. We were descending into a novel situation, and so we just needed to know we had each other's back.

"One thing," Shelly said, reaching into a pocket and producing a glass vial of mercurial fluid. "You left this in our quarters beside the bed. You might need them."

I smiled at her and took it, slipping the vial into a pocket on my pants. "Just might," I replied. "Wouldn't want to be left out."

Moments later, we descended from high orbit, approaching the yellowish-orange globe. Our instruments alerted us that the station was painting us with range-finding lasers and radar, but there were no sign of any weapons. We plunged toward the surface, two pilots suspended in orbs of fluid wrapped in airfoils, our fleshy loved ones riding on our backs, the settlement coming into view.

What we beheld was a marvel.

The United Exploration Initiative had been formed during a desperate time of human history. We had reached a point at which our technology was sufficiently advanced for us to collect and keep track of the many billions of datapoints required to calculate the systematic decline of our planet, but we were not advanced enough to do much about it. We were like doctors, having the knowledge of how bad a particular cancer was but being unable to synthesize a cure for it. There had been considerable efforts around the world to curb climate change through the use of renewables and electric vehicles, but only in countries with the will and the means. Both the Oil Wars had been sparked by technological disruption, the economy of crude-rich countries collapsing overnight when demand from their biggest importers fell through the floor. America and most of Europe had made the switch to Lindvolt-based power storage systems during this time, and that had had dire, unforeseen consequences.

And yet, despite this shift from carbon-producing energy, there were many other ways we were stressing the ecosystem. The economic disparity between the haves and have-nots was widening with every decade. The world was becoming too populous. New, unknown viruses swept across the planet like wildfire. Nationalist tensions were at an all-time high. And so, world leaders had come together to find a solution. It had started small but grown over time, decades before the Foundry reached out to humanity.

The UEI, in cooperation with entities such as NASA and the ESA, had scoured our system for viable locations that humans could settle off-world. Mars had been "the dream" ever since science-fiction writers of the early twentieth century began writing tales of little green men on a red world. But there were problems with this idea, big problems. Mars did not generate its own magnetic field. Its gravity was too low. The world was desolate, with little atmosphere. It was not an easy place to call a second home. Sure, the Martian dream would eventually come true, in spite of all the challenges, but this was not where ideation ended.

And so another bolder, potentially better idea started floating around scientific circles. Something beautiful, absurd, and downright genius. A plan to live around a planet with a magnetic field to protect against radiation. A planet with an atmosphere, an environment that might be able to be exploited for human use. And as we glided down into the ever-thickening skies of Venus, we spotted the results of these dreams. The results of countless late-night sessions of engineers and astrophysicists who had crunched numbers while chugging black coffee till their pots went empty, then switching to sip barrel-aged whiskey till they passed out, worn pencils falling from their tired hands as they drifted into a drunken oblivion.

The city of Aeolia was that dream, a colony floating high above the fiery hellscape of the Venusian surface, an asymmetric collection of two dozen silver platforms, some big, some small, each strung together by thick, braided cables of an unknown material. The largest of these designs, which numbered six in all, appeared like inverted teardrops close to a kilometer in height, their tapered ends elongated, pointing to the surface, their tops curved into perfect domes covered with rows of windows.

Around the collection of inverted teardrops, floated the smaller of the structures, a sprawling collection of silver and white envelopes that reminded me of airships I'd read about in my youth, dirigible sky platforms capable of cruising high above the surface. Beneath these pockets of steel-wrapped air hung open plates of metal several hundred meters wide, surfaces festooned with buildings no more than four or five stories in height, dense cities in miniature filled with busy streets, spires, and neon lights, their exteriors exposed to the comparatively mild conditions of the Venusian stratosphere.

Short-range shuttles buzzed about the structures, ushering Aeolia's people between the different sections of the distributed city. The closer we glided, the fewer we could see, our arrival sending them scrambling for an analogous dry land.

Quick estimates based on what we could see put the population of the Venusian city in the hundreds of thousands. Here they lived, in spires of light and platforms among toxic clouds, suspended in their own kind of heaven.

It was beautiful.

The silver spires swelled, details sharpening at our approach, the rows of windows running up the curves of the domes filling with faces, surprised citizens of this impossible settlement pointing fingers in our direction. A set of instructions came from the station above, leading us to a spinning disc extending from the central spire. Karianna and I carefully guided our shuttles onto the platform. When our engines went cold, the disc spun us around, drawing us into the structure. Pressure doors closed in a heartless embrace.

"Time to play nice," Karianna said through our communications link.

"Time to make some friends," I replied, hoping like hell it would be true.

CHAPTER 32

I climbed from my Star Sphere, ready to slip into my old clothes and get this whole diplomatic sortie over with, only to be halted by my entire crew. Shelly extended a fluffy white robe to cover my wet body and only offered a shrug when I asked why. I stepped into the main cabin, and to my surprise, the crew were sorting through a series of packages it was clear the shuttle's nanoforge had just finished fabricating.

"What's this all about?" I ventured, pulling the robe tight, my eyes narrowing.

"We have to look the part," Leo supplied, handing me a plastic-wrapped square of clothing. "This here is your size, custom tailored to fit comfortably, but follow the lines of your body. A leader's ensemble."

"Ensemble? I don't understand. Can't we just wear whatever?" I tossed a thumb over my shoulder. "I was going to put the same clothes back on."

"Even though they're dirty? Eww."

"Leo is right," Ingrid insisted. "This place, and its people, believe themselves to be of a higher social position than us, you included, big ship captain or not. We should dress accordingly. I reviewed a series of styles he had designed and found some of the clothes closely resembled what we've seen Aeolians wear before. They're not perfect, but it's an improvement over what we're used to. This should create some level of familiarity with them, breed some good will, rather than us going to see the queen caked in dirt and filth."

A proud smile flashed across Leo's face. "You all know I did a little fashion design back on Novae, right?"

"Because of course you did," Ada mumbled as she snagged her package from his arms. "This better not make me look like a slut or something just to serve some fantasy of yours."

His smile faltered for a moment. Then he shook his head as if attempting to divest his mind of an inappropriate thought. "No, no, no. Nothing too fancy. Nothing too lecherous, my dear. These clothes are a bit more formal than what we've been wearing, that's all. No jumpsuits. No jeans."

You reading this? I pinged Karianna in her shuttle. *They're making you do it too, aren't they?*

I got a groan from her and took that to be a yes.

"It's a good idea," Shelly sighed, tugging on my robe. "Think of it as a uniform."

"I'm not sure that helps."

"A costume then?"

We turned our backs to one another and got dressed, assuming no one would take a peek. I felt so stupid putting these clothes on.

For my part, I wore a pair of fitted white pants, with a white collared shirt and a white jacket that had all sorts of odd angles, its hems and lines accented by black stripes. It was like the concert all over again, monkey suit and all, but instead of being swallowed up in black, I was consumed by white. I was given shoes to match my outfit, puffy white sneakers with open laces that went onto my feet like slippers. How they didn't fall off when I walked, I had no damn clue. It was all comfortable enough, but the net result made me feel like a fancy dinner napkin, not a member of the mythical FICSE mission come to save Earth. The first thing I ate or drank was going to get all over this.

Shelly, for her part, was similarly dressed, though the bottom hem of her jacket reached her midthigh and her shirt was open around the chest, with a plunging neckline that ended a few inches from her navel. The outfit accentuated her natural curves, highlighting her most striking features, of which she had quite a long list. It was a look I didn't get to see on her often, given that we always dressed with comfort in mind, and this was . . . well . . .

"You look nice," she said, adjusting my collar and brushing off my shoulders. "Very regal."

I blinked at her, trying not to let my heart leap out of my chest. "And you. You look, uh, well . . ."

"You can thank Leo later." She gave me a playful wink. "Now listen to me, and listen well. When we walk out of here, keep your back straight, don't talk too fast, and consider every word you say."

"Why the sudden advice?"

"We are dealing with humans the likes of which we have never dealt with before. Be on your guard."

Maybe they were right, and I just needed to check my head. The kind of strength exerted here seemed different than what we were accustomed to. I was grateful for my crew, for my team, for Shelly. They were looking ahead, anticipating challenges I had not foreseen. They were giving me the tools I needed to see this mission to success. Who could ask for more? I had never been in a position where politics or social influence meant much more than how hard you worked that day. In fact, I had avoided such ideas, given how Mom and Dad vehemently spoke out against our hierarchical society on Earth. It was all bullshit, the worth of people stacked like a pyramid made of net worth and popularity. Until it wasn't.

"Seriously Leo?" Ada stepped out from the corner, voice raised in anger, fingers pointing at her chest. "I said, don't make me look like a slut! And here we are, look at me, tits hanging out everywhere."

Leo tugged on his jacket sleeves, his expression neutral, actions calm and deliberate. "And this is a problem how?"

Ada wasn't wrong. The cut of her outfit certainly drew the eyes, though those eyes mostly seemed to be Leo's. I had my own spectacle.

"We ready?" I addressed the crew with Shelly's hand gripped in mine.

Ada rolled her eyes, took a deep breath, then flashed a fake smile. "Looks like we are. Everyone's got their Nelsons on, so we might as well go impress these people."

"Nelsons?" Leo repeated, a finger rubbing at his chin. "I like the sound of that. It's like Gucci. Versace. Vuitton."

"Don't press your luck."

"You do look nice," Shelly commented.

This turned Ada's sour expression around. "And so do you, boo. Love the jacket."

"Now remember," Ingrid said. "Our objective is to get their support for this project. I will find the resonators, don't you worry about that. Milo, and the rest, you go make friends. That's your objective."

I tugged on my sleeves and frowned. "What if I'm not good at that?"

"Then you'll just have to get good at it."

"Alright. Make friends. Get the resonators. Save Earth. Simple as all that."

Ingrid nodded. "Simple as all that." But from her look, I knew it wouldn't be.

We exited our shuttles onto the landing platform, our crew forming a neat wedge with Shelly, Karianna, and me at the front, Ingrid and Lance beside us, the rest fanning out.

James rushed up on Leo and slapped him on the shoulder. "Nice fit, bruh. Lookin' sharp. Your work, right?"

"See? He likes my clothes." Leo turned to Ada, who groaned as she searched for a higher button on her shirt to narrow the open gap on her chest.

The pressurized landing platform was brightly lit and wide open, spacious enough to fit at least two additional Swift Shuttles without any trouble. Its ceiling reached upward at least thirty meters, walls neutral in colors, surfaces ivory and grey and white, gothic features accented by copper lines and blue lights. The style and shapes of the architecture reminded me of the photos I'd seen from the interior of ancient cathedrals like Notre Dame in France or the Barcelona Cathedral in Spain. It was remarkable to think that it was humanmade, not the work of the Foundry or some advanced alien species. It had been put together by a bunch of dumb monkeys poking around in the void.

It wasn't long before we were met by a series of guards dressed in white and gold, their bodies protected by plates of armor like the Free Citizen guards, though these wore no helmets. Their faces were hard, implacable, each of the men sporting leonine manes and faces with smoothy shaven jaws.

I was about to speak, offering them a greeting, when the guards parted without a word. As they stepped to the side, an entourage of four appeared, two women and two men. While each of them moved with a sense of entitlement and pride the likes of which I'd never seen, the woman at the front of their group marked herself as their leader, her very presence demanding attention.

When she spoke to us, her words were like silk drawn across bare skin, "*Bonjoir. Bienvenido. Dobro pozhalovat. Khush amdeed.* Welcome, welcome, welcome to Aeolia, the floating islands, the silver spires of heaven." She gestured with an open hand at the space around us as if painting the sky with her palm. "I am Premier Jadier Takagi. This is my domain."

Premier Takagi was an imposing woman, as tall as me, and lean, but with a solid, clearly defined build. While her features were soft, supple, and youthful, they could not be mistaken for weak. She was not a child; she was one who had the means to care for herself and did so with relish. Her smooth skin was the color of umber, her head clean shaven, clothing impeccable, with a clear intent to draw eyes and project power.

If Ada had felt that Leo's style revealed too much of her own chest, making her appear easy, the premier's outfit was flat-out erotic. It was clear that white was the proper color for this place, a color of purity and cleanliness. Like us, she wore a kind of slender white pants, along with shiny white shoes with tall heels. But for her top, she had only a fitted white jacket, open at the front, nipples carefully obscured beneath a set of notched lapels while her neck, chest, and stomach lay bare. Resting within her cleavage was a fine chain, a tiny, gold, human skull hanging from it with details and embellishments as fine as clockwork. I could not say how, but something was off about the object. It felt as if it were a talisman, not mere jewelry.

While Ingrid had projected a kind of strength and power the first time we met, the premier's was different.

"You have come to meet with me," she went on. "How may we be of service to those from FICSE?"

I found myself stunned in the moment, feet rooted to the ground. Karianna elbowed me in the ribs to snap me out of it.

"Yes, eh, hello. Greetings." I gave a grand flourish, one leg extended, bowing deeply. It felt like the right thing to do in the moment, but as I came back up and caught the premier's confused expression, maybe I'd been wrong. "My name is Captain Milo Hughes of the *Transcendence*. Beside me stands my copilot, cocaptain, Karianna Torlen, and my wife, Shelly Hughes. The rest are my crew from FICSE, other than this fine woman here."

Ingrid made her way to the front, extending a hand. "Premier Takagi, I am the overseer of the Free Citizens of Earth. Ingrid Gunderson at your service."

The premier of Aeolia gave Ingrid's outstretched hand a curious look before shaking it. "A pleasure. What a turn of events, I must say." She pivoted back to me and offered her hand. "I shake hands. No need for bows—this is not Queen Elizabeth's court. No one is cutting off heads for a breach of capricious sentiment or fickle protocols. We are friends in this place. More than friends."

I took her hand and shook it. Her grip was firm. She leaned in, squeezing my mechanical fingers, her eyes narrowing, holding on a moment longer than what felt comfortable.

Then she let go.

"Apologies, I suppose," I stammered, "It's been a long time since we've been around humans other than ourselves. Close to 500 years."

"So it's true?" she mused, turning briefly to regard her cohort. They looked to one another, eyebrows raised, but otherwise remained still and quiet.

It wasn't until that moment that I put any real attention on her companions, given how imposing she was. Now a theme emerged between the two men and the woman who accompanied her. They were each some of the most classically beautiful people I had ever seen, their features statuesque, as if they had been carved from marble or sketched by a masterful hand. They were strong, well-defined, dressed in clothes many cultures might have deemed inappropriate, putting their tremendous musculature and perfect curves on display. The men wore pants without shirts, the woman a sort of dress that slashed across her body, its form wrapping around her hips and shoulders but flowing, covering very little in the way of skin despite the fact it brushed the floor. Their hair was perfectly tousled, curls spilling over bare shoulders, and each carried a faint scent I could only just smell because of my augmentations, one of roses and wildflowers, fresh and curious. They were beautiful human subjects, and they knew it, standing tall, noses turned up the slightest bit as their essence dripped with a kind of power-driven sensuality.

With an effort, I drew myself back to Premier Takagi. "Yes. It's true. We are from the original FICSE mission. We were just kids when we left, but now we're all grown up and a good bit wiser in the universe."

"We have so much to chat about. Come. Come. Let us palaver. Let us offer you our deepest hospitality." She gestured to the exit. "Would you be so kind as to join my consorts and me for dinner?"

From the corner of my eye, I caught Shelly's urgent expression. This was the right move, even if I had no idea how to conduct myself at such an event.

"It would be our honor," I said.

The premier's eyes twinkled. "Perfect."

"Premier," Ingrid asked, bowing her head ever so slightly. "May I reserve this honor for our captains and their crew? I would request leave to seek out an old friend from Earth. He came up the gravity well a few years ago, ascended that is, and I am eager to reconnect with him."

A devilish smile twisted at the corner of the premier's lips. "Reconnect, you say? We all love to connect." She tipped her head. "No offense is taken. My staff are at your disposal. And speaking of needs, after dinner is concluded, we will ensure everyone here is given proper accommodations such that you may repair to your quarters and not sleep in your shuttles. Take your time. You have an eternity before you."

"Thank you, Premier," she replied, then turned to Lance, who approached with Xuan, Hy, and Renata in tow.

"We're going with her," Lance whispered. "We'll see you later."

"Very well," I said, then paused, unable to say out loud what it was I was thinking. He looked to me for a long moment, and from the twitch of his eyebrows, I knew he'd gotten some version of the message I needed to deliver without either of us using our implants.

Be careful. Watch your back.

This left Shelly, Karianna, James, Ada, Leo, and me.

"The six of you then." The premier spun on her heels and clapped twice, and her cohorts followed in lockstep. "Let us away to the grand hall. You have much to see in our fairest of cities. So much to taste, so much to experience. Life is short. Existence is uncertain. Let us not waste this divine gift."

"Proxy?" I pinged the *Transcendence*. *"Do you read?"*

"Loud and clear."

"Keep an eye on us."

"As you say. I am tracking your progress."

CHAPTER 33

Premier Takagi led us out of the pressurized landing platform into a long hallway with ceilings that split in three directions, one going straight ahead, the others to the left and right, following the outer curve of the spire like an inverted pickaxe. Tracing the exterior edge was a series of crystal-clear windows a half dozen meters in height. These thick layers of glass revealed an expanse of roiling, sulfurous amber clouds over Venus. The bars of sunlight cast through their many mountainous faces created a sharp contrast of dark and light.

"Welcome to the Neonteichos spire, capital of Aeolia."

"What beautiful names," Shelly spoke up. "It makes me curious. I feel as if I know them from my studies. Your settlement, is it named Aeolia after the floating island in Homer's *Odyssey*? And Neonteichos, the ancient Greek city?"

The premier grinned at this, and her eyes turned bright. "Good ear. It is indeed. We draw much inspiration from the Greeks. Athenians. Spartans. Olympians. We are, after all, in a place of gods."

"What a view," Leo remarked, his nose a hair's breadth away from the glass. "I have to paint this while I'm here. It reminds me of a work by Albert Bierstadt. The clouds, their depth, the many layers."

"This vista is not even the best we may offer," Premier Takagi said, then waved over her shoulder. "Come. Come. Let us give you a tour."

Shelly gave Ada a look, raising her eyebrows as we followed after.

Neonteichos was full of people, though as we approached them with the premier, they respectfully found themselves scarce, hurrying on their way. Like their leader, they were mostly dressed in white, a few with pops of color on their clothing, faces smooth and perfect, physiques fit and healthy. They spoke in hushed tones, as if they were whispering secrets they wanted no one to hear.

"Hi there," Leo said to a slender, blond-haired woman we passed, his eyebrows rising with suggestion. This did nothing but earn a blank look from the woman in question, as well as a scowl from Ada. "By God, I do like to admire beauty."

"Pig," Ada mumbled. "To leer is not to admire."

"Semantics."

"How in the hell is this place floating?" Karianna mumbled to me. "It's a hunk of freaking metal fixed in the sky. I'm not the best at science, okay, but I know that metal is heavier than air."

"A valid question, Captain," the premier responded, raising a finger. "The atmosphere on Venus is dense. So dense, in fact, that the air we breathe, this oxygen and nitrogen, is perfectly capable of keeping these mighty structures aloft when placed upon the atmosphere's thick layers. You saw the balloon cities on your approach?"

"We did," Shelly responded, and Karianna shrank back. "They were massive."

"Those were the first that the UEI placed here. Simple in their design. The whole of their envelopes, their interiors, are filled with breathable air lighter than the gases in these clouds."

"So, it makes them float?" I asked.

"Of course. And in a mild environment, I might add. Fifty kilometers above the surface, the atmosphere of Venus is sublime."

"Still feels unnatural."

"Unnatural? Perhaps. What also feels unnatural is that over four-hundred-year-old explorers have returned from the deep reaches beyond the solar system to be only in their third decade of life, still so very young. But I digress."

She led us ahead, down the main interior hallway. Its twenty-meter-high arches were gothic in style, with a sharp point at their apex, the passage wide enough to drive a pair of trucks side by side. Upon the neutral surface of its walls, patterns emerged, designs reminiscent of Jevox art, though without the garish spread of color. The longer I stared at them, the more it became apparent that these designs were inlaid, carved into the bulkheads, creating textures and not just lines.

"Welcome to the emotional tapestry we call the Gallery," the Premier offered without being asked. "This section is one of two that exist on this spire alone. The northern and southern hallways are more utilitarian, centers of trade and commerce if not beauty."

Leo pointed to a series of patterns overhead, a set of isometric, crystalline shapes curving inward along the arch. "What sort of machine did these?"

"No machines. It was all by hand."

"By hand?" He gaped. "The detail, it's . . . it's remarkable. Mechanical. Beautiful."

"Yes. It took some time to complete, and much of it was done before my era. I believe they used a kind of plasma torch and lay upon their backs on scaffolds like Michelangelo did in the Sistine Chapel, carving one line at a time, never going back. You see, once the mark was made, there was no erasing it. An apt metaphor for life, wouldn't you say?"

"Remarkable," he breathed, eyes glazing over. "And yes. It is."

"You are an artist, are you not?"

"I suppose."

She laid a hand on Leo's chest for a moment, freezing him in place, then caressed his cheek with her fingertips. "We adore artists in Aeolia. They bring such beauty to our hallowed halls. Such beauty." She turned and carried on ahead.

Leo blinked, not sure what to do. Ada gave him a hard look, but he replied with a stunned shake of his head, his eyes unfocused. The consorts inspected him top to bottom, and the woman in the white dress suppressed a bemused chuckle.

After several paces, Premier Takagi paused beside a series of statues that lined either side of the hall, her consorts taking a step back, giving her space.

I focused on the faceless statues before her, an uneasy feeling settling over me. These statues were human in form, or at least bipedal, each similar in height though not identical, and were made of a reddish stone or crystal of some type, with vertical, pale black striations throughout. They wore, or rather were comprised of, suits of some kind, like a futurist's interpretation of medieval armor, thick and carapacial, their shapes curved with hard edges but sealed tight as if meant for use in the void, their postures held at military attention.

"They are our Sentinels," she offered, "left behind by the Lattice. Beautiful, are they not?"

"Left by the Lattice?" I ventured. "We've heard rumor of them. What's the deal with them? Who are they? Where did they go?"

The consorts looked to one another, then to their premier, but each kept their lips sealed.

"Sore subject?" Karianna pried. "No one seems to want to talk about them. There a problem?"

"No," the premier said, though her posture shifted to betray discomfort. "No. Not a sore subject. We will speak more of them later. Needless to say, my FICSE specialists, they are some of the most brilliant minds in the universe. That is all you should know for now."

She turned away and resumed her route, the consorts following close behind with silent steps.

Shelly placed a palm against one of the statues, then recoiled at the touch. "They're hot," she whispered. "Why are they hot?"

I had no answer for this.

"Well, they creep me the hell out," Ada mumbled. "They have no faces, and yet still, I feel like they're staring at me."

"Ghosts?" James whispered, a finger over his lips.

Karianna rolled her eyes at him.

Among the statues hung paintings of various sizes, some as small as photographs, others several times taller than me, as well as collections of sculptures of people and objects placed upon ivory columns. I recognized some of these works, as did Leo from the way he examined them in awe, ancient pieces of art rescued from a tortured and destroyed Earth.

"Rembrandt? Monet?" He sucked in a deep breath. "Van Gogh. A Jolley? It can't be."

Many other hallways opened up as we pressed on, though these had much lower arches.

She gestured at them with a hand. "On our left are some of our quarters, reaching twenty floors along the curve of the spire's dome, some of which will be assigned to your crew. They are lavish in comparison to Earth accommodations, no doubt. Comfortable. And you will be provided with servants. This is not a place to be shy in asking for what you desire.

"As for the right, there is the Grand Hall itself. We will return to this place for dinner, as they are preparing it now. Ahead of us is the core, as well as the elevator banks leading up to the observatories, or down to the mechanical levels that run this place and keep us alive. Beyond that lies the Simulation Chamber."

"And what is that?" James asked. "Sounds like fun."

Ada nodded at this. "It does. What's it like?"

"Do not fret," the premier stated, a sly smile taking hold of her face. "We will play later. I must confess, much fun happens there. So very much fun."

"Premier, this is all so remarkable," I said, feeling the need to fill this moment with some kind of opinion. "To think that humans built all of this. It's hard to believe."

"We had help, of course, though not as much as some would claim. This is human imagination given form. And what a wonderful form it is."

Something about the direction of this conversation was starting to bother me. We had come down from the sky, landed here in our shuttles, our groups splitting up, and not once had we been asked to declare our intentions. The premier was more concerned with showing us artwork and architecture than anything else.

"Look, I'm sorry," I ventured. "I'm not trying to be rude. This place is amazing, and I know we've hardly seen any of it, but you haven't asked us why we are here. We could be here to do anything. To steal. To pilfer. To murder someone."

"And are you?" she asked, her voice hard as steel, eyebrows raised in accusation. "Have you come to commit crimes in my realm?"

I raised my palms immediately. "No. No. No. But you haven't asked."

"If a tired child or a homeless man were to show up on your doorstep, do you first ask their intentions?" she asked, her tone taking on an imperious quality. "Or do you offer them hospitality? Shelter. Sustenance. Entertainment. I am only keeping you busy, sharing all humanity has done in your absence while we wait on dinner.

"Consider, for a moment, Maslow's Hierarchy of Needs: a pyramid with layers that build upon one another, each layer more abstract than the last. At its base, we have physiological needs: air, water, food. Atop those needs, we have safety. And built atop safety, love and belonging. But that is not where it stops. We build upon that love with self-esteem before, finally, self-actualization."

"What are you getting at?"

"As a good host, as the premier of Aeolia, it is my divine duty to first see that your needs are met. We may speak of your intentions later. For now, we must care for those needs. Unless we have something to worry about in the meantime?"

"No," I said. "Nothing to worry about. We come in peace. We come in friendship."

"Wonderful." She clapped once and pressed her hands together. "Let us continue then."

Shelly took hold of my hand and squeezed, drawing my attention back to the crew. Leo and Ada were enraptured by this place and its staggering beauty, but my left and right hand of life, just like me, weren't so sure.

Premier Takagi's tour did not end. She walked us around the spire, pointing out the finer details here and there, other works of art, the shops along the crowded trade halls, while telling stories of the gardens upon the balloons and imparting morsels of gossip. Her consorts made no move to speak, merely stood by and looked pretty, as seemed to be their function.

The conversations and concerns of Aeolia were so different than those on Earth, or Novae. People were not concerned where their next meal would come from, nor if Isoptera would try to steal their children away. Instead, they spent a great deal of time worrying over minor social infractions, sleights, positioning, status. They sought pleasure and new experiences and were locked in a kind of open competition to have more of them than anyone else. They were obsessed with art, parties of every kind, sexual dalliances, virtual worlds, food and drink and Universe knew what else. They glutted themselves on these things, and yet everyone appeared healthy, fit, beautiful.

How does it all not kill them? Shelly pinged me. I had no answer.

Are these people too soft to work? I replied. *We might be barking up the wrong tree if we're looking for labor.*

This earned a shrug from her.

I sent a single ping to Proxy, checking in, and received an all-clear status report. I was nervous leaving the ship up there. Hell, I was nervous being down here in a novel situation, with new people and unexplored intentions.

Karianna could see what I was doing and patted me on the back, "Chinchillette reports all is good too."

Once it seemed that the Premier had run out of things to say, a chime rang out, echoing down the halls of Neonteichos. We paused in our step, turned to face her, and awaited instruction.

"It appears that dinner is ready," she said, leading us away. "Come now."

The Grand Hall of Neonteichos was just as it had proclaimed itself to be. It was a dizzying expanse longer than anything I'd ever seen used for this purpose, at least fifty meters wide and two hundred long, with a slight curve that seemed to follow the outside edge of the spire. Its ceiling was so high I could have easily flown a Swift Shuttle through the space, if not very fast. Along its center, which was obscured by a cover of roiling clouds, dozens of ornate chandeliers dangled, each as large as one of our combat fighters, their starburst designs exploding from central cores, components made of a glowing red crystal reminiscent of the statues from the gallery. Along its walls were rows of copper buttresses, and between them, arches and faux windows framing what I could only call stained glass, though no sunlight shone through given that we were inside the structure. The remaining surfaces were not perfectly smooth either but were instead covered in textures and patterns with scenes of life in bas relief.

The overall effect was of an ancient cathedral of worship, a place in which God himself might dwell. I half expected to see a throne at its center, but there was none, just an open space with a table about fifty meters ahead that I knew to be large, though from the scale of everything else seemed so very tiny.

"Holy shit," Karianna hissed, running fingers through her hair, bracelets jingling. "It's big in here."

Shelly crossed her arms and looked around. "Too big."

"It makes my feet sweat," Ada added. "Ever have that happen?"

Karianna cocked her head at her. "Your what? How?"

"Have you not ever felt afraid of heights, and all of a sudden, your feet and hands sweated like crazy? Makes you feel like you'll slip and fall."

"Can't say that I have."

"Well, I'm right there with you," Leo told Ada. "It's almost too much to take in. But it's beautiful."

And it was. This entire place was. It left you with an overwhelming sense of how small you were in the universe. We had seen big things, sure, planetoid-sized structures, like those of the Foundry, space stations with cities under domes, great ziggurats with impossible geometry, the colony on Nest, the cities of Rix, but this . . . it felt not just big, but ostentatious. Opulent.

"Is that our table at the center?" James asked while scratching at the back of his head, eyes squinting. "It'll take us like forty-five minutes just to walk over to it."

"And we will enjoy the walk," Premier Takagi declared, leading us onward.

"One way to get in your steps, bro," Leo slapped him on the back.

James mumbled and followed over, "Get in my steps . . . I'll show you steps . . ."

"You have no doubt noticed the many scenes depicted within our stained glass and upon our walls," the Premier began, her tone almost dreamy.

"We have," I said, finally speaking up. "They are impressive."

"They are history." She waved. "Reminders of who we are and what we have come from. From our great founders, the first UEI Void Striders to visit Venus, to the soldiers who fought the many wars to keep this place safe, and the hard-working people who made it a home. Here we mark the arrival of the Lattice, the Great Gap, and work our way closer to this day. Perhaps our own meeting will one day be placed upon these walls. The return of FICSE."

I did my best to mentally record the events presented in order. I felt there was something important here. A history we needed to understand.

"I made similar works on Novae," Leo supplied, but when Premier Takagi seemed confused, he went on. "It is, um, a human colony. Novae is more than a thousand light-years away."

"Humans so far away? How interesting."

"It's a beautiful world," I offered. "If a bit cold, and with some rather aggressive fauna."

"Novae," she said, rolling the word around in her mouth. "It means nova, yes? A rebirth. A newly visible star."

"That's right. Funny how we name planets so literally, isn't it?"

She led us to a rectangular table positioned near the center of the room, a slab of white fixed to black metal, with fourteen highbacked white chairs trimmed in copper set around it. We were assigned seats, with herself at the head, the other end of the table empty for now. I was to sit on her right.

Shelly was beside me, the female consort next, then Leo and Ada. On her left, directly across from me, was Karianna, then one of the male consorts, James, and the other male consort. This left four empty seats, which felt uneven.

Though we had our assignment, something told me not to sit, at least not yet. Premier Takagi had not yet sat. No one said a word as we stood in this awkward silence. Karianna looked to me, gave a sort of grin, then looked to Shelly.

"Ah, there they are," the premier delighted. "Always late."

A group of Aeolians had appeared, though I could not say from where. Three men and one woman filled in the empty seats without asking where to sit.

"My apologies, Premier," the man who had taken the chair at the other end said. He had a deep voice and robust features. "The games were held up for some time, you understand. A rather interesting match. Could not quite tell how it was going to end. So much power. So much will. They just wouldn't give it up. I do love those the best."

"These things happen, Demarcus. Though *games* would be best discussed at another time." The way she said the word drew my attention to it. I wondered what kind of games a people like this would even find interesting. Something told me it wasn't futbol.

"Yes, yes, of course. We have guests?"

"We do. And they are from FICSE."

"FICSE?" His expression twisted. "No, it cannot be. Don't toy with me, Premier." He waggled a finger at her. "Tell the truth."

"It is the truth, so they say. And I have cause to believe them."

He grinned, curious but not convinced, then gestured at the table. "Let us sit then, and eat, and talk. Don't let our guests feel awkward. Be a good host."

"With a heavy subject such as this, we must drink," the red-headed wisp of a woman in their group said, earning a laugh from the rest. She spun around as if looking for someone. "Let us have wine brought immediately. Anything from 2470s. The burgundy would be divine."

The Aeolians drew back their chairs and sat as one, this production practiced and proper in some unfamiliar way, almost Jevox in its synchronization. The crew looked to me for guidance, and I did my best to follow our host's lead as we took our seats. After we settled into place, I noticed that our postures were less consistent than theirs, some of us rigid, some leaning forward casually on elbows.

"Make friends," I mumbled under my breath, and Shelly reached for my hand beneath the table.

I looked to her, and she gave me a slight smile.

"Wine!" the woman at the end of the table shouted, raising her empty crystal glass.

"Yes, please," I said, looking to my own, the anxiety in my chest a baseball-sized tangle of nerves for which this might be the only cure. "Wine would be great about now."

CHAPTER 34

A veritable army of servants appeared out of nowhere, holding bottles made of dark glass. They moved around the outskirts of the table, twisting and turning as if performing a coordinated waltz, pausing beside pairs of guests to present their goods.

"Sir, is this red satisfactory?" a male servant dressed in black and white livery said, rotating the crimson label of a bottle covered in scrollwork toward me. "Veritas 2475. It has a bouquet of red fruits like blackberries, cherries, and a bit of chocolate and vanilla. The tannins are velvety with complex flavors, exotic spices, and cinnamon, with a long and soft finish. Ideal for drinking but will pair well with ragù or a filet."

Premier Takagi grinned at me. "It is one of our most expensive and rare bottles. For the occasion."

I swallowed. "Yes, please. It would be rude not to."

"That it would."

The man reached into a pocket, removing a silver tool. He cut the foil off the top of the bottle with a flourish before twisting the cork free with a muffled pop. One at a time, he poured the wine into our crystal glasses, starting with the premier and working his way down to Shelly, using a white napkin to wipe away any excess droplets on the bottle and the rims of our glasses.

It took everything in me not to reach for my glass as soon as the servant was gone so I could guzzle it down. I was starting to sweat. Was it hot in here?

The servants vanished, music replacing their absence, something soft and melodious, though I could not identify the genre. There were strings, and piano, a kind of soft beat, but no vocals.

I took stock of the table, the fancy place settings with their white porcelain plates resting atop shiny copper chargers, a variety of utensils arrayed around them with uses I could only begin to guess. We each had two glasses, one long stemmed for wine, and another more ordinary one I assumed was for water. Along the center of the table, a series of kinetic sculptures made of white metal sat, their spiral designs spinning in on themselves, creating a kind of hypnotic effect that it was easy to get lost in.

Bread was brought out a moment later, placed along the table in cloth-lined baskets with plates of butter beside them. The dark brown loaves were thickly cut and covered in seeds. The premier reached for a piece and placed it on a small plate set on her right, buttering the bread liberally with an odd-looking knife, though not taking a bite.

After all that walking, I was hungry, and so I reached for the bread, but as I did, the servers returned to us en masse, a flurry filling our empty glasses with water, while others made a presentation of removing our topmost plates before replacing them with bullion bowls filled with a savory soup. It smelled so good, but which spoon did you use to eat it? Why did we have three spoons?

When the hell could we drink the wine?

Karianna looked to me, wide eyed and frozen, as if her bowl contained a serving of eyeballs. The rest of the crew looked just as stuck. Our hosts were talking, but we were unable to respond with more than the occasional grunt.

I watched Premier Takagi and her people with fascination, realizing every movement was a production, this entire meal choreographed. From the way they flicked their napkins before placing them on their laps, to the way they lifted their wine glasses by the stem with their fingertips, only to sniff its contents and not drink, to the way they broke bread without making crumbs. There was a hidden language communicated here that the Foundry's translation software was unable to parse, and if we didn't figure out its meaning, and soon, our intentions would likely never be realized.

My heart thundered in my chest as the fear that we might make a critical misstep filled every empty space in my head, crowding out all reason.

We were here to do what? Make friends? How did I do that? How would I make them like us? I was out of my fucking league. The clothes were hard enough, but this . . . I'd be lucky not to drown, and from a cursory observation, I wasn't sure anyone in our group was doing any better. We didn't eat anything like this on Novae. We didn't eat like this on the *Vasco Da Gama*. We had group meals, sure, but they were buffet style. Everyone got a plate and stuffed themselves. There was no theater to it. Food was practical. Just having it was enough.

Follow what they do, Shelly pinged our implants. *I know only a little from reading about events in history like this. Be polite. Don't chew with your mouth open. Don't touch food with your fingers.*

Elbows off the table? Leo replied. *God, all that I've studied, and this was not among it. What a waste.*

Ada chimed in, *We could use Emilio's expertise about now. He knew all about place settings and proper etiquette.*

Yeah, but couldn't that brand of etiquette have changed over time? James asked. *I mean, they are a different culture than us. Clearly.*

Karianna sighed. *We're so screwed.*

Premier Takagi turned to me, her eyebrows furrowed in consternation. "Is everything okay, Captain? You seem as if you're thinking about something."

"Yes, yes," I insisted, forcing a weak smile. Did she know we were talking? "Everything's fine. Wonderful, in fact. Thank you. You are a gracious host."

"Splendid."

She doesn't know about the implants, Shelly pinged back after a moment, her hands busy buttering bread, eyes down to hide her glazed-over expression. *Ingrid told us as much. They don't use them anymore.*

James added, *That's not a bad thing, right? Gives us an edge.*

Not a bad thing at all, Karianna replied. *But I think they can tell something's up if we're not careful when we use them.*

We waited for the premier to reach for her wine glass, half expecting a toast, but she merely lifted it to her red-painted lips and took a sip. We did the same. It was wonderful, sweet and dry, if a bit tart. Somehow it tasted different than anything the Foundry had presented to us. This was not a memory cleverly played on repeat. This was a new experience entirely. The Foundry had no template for this wine, this glass, this setting. And so that made me think of the templates it did have, how disconnected from the original memories they might be. I considered how much memories themselves changed over time, events once crystal becoming nebulous clouds of images with bright motes of nostalgic emotions floating at their centers. Time had a way of making those ever diffuse, spreading out their meaning until they were nothing but an impression of mist. But this . . . this was no memory. It was life.

"I do hope you enjoy the soup," she said, reaching for a round-headed spoon on the right side of her plate. The way she shifted in her chair meant that the lapels of her jacket came perilously close to revealing her bare chest, not that I was looking. "It is a classic. A take on French Onion. We call it Aenion. Can't say how that ever became a thing. It's simple, and delicious. Quite comforting."

"Is this cheese on top?" Karianna asked, poking at hers with a spoon. "Looks like cheese."

"Provolone, though sometimes we use a kind of Swiss."

"Is it real? The cheese."

"Of course. We have dairy cows on the Larissa Spire. Dozens, though they are smaller than you might expect. Here they are not given the space to grow to their full weight."

Karianna looked at the hunk of white cheese on her spoon, eyes wide. "How long has it been since we've had real cheese? Really real?"

"A lifetime," James said, taking a bite, his eyes rolling into the back of his head.

"Our premier has the best stocks," Demarcus said from his place at the end of the table. "Mmm. Yes. The best. She is most generous with them too."

Everyone took a bite, and I had to admit, it was one of the best things I'd eaten in a long, long time, just like the wine. Having everything we wanted, when we wanted it, or when we had a craving for it was wonderful, but this . . . New memories. Human food, not just something we cobbled together from a world we didn't evolve from that was safe enough to eat. I could get used to this.

"Where are my manners?" Premier Takagi said out of nowhere, sitting her spoon down and patting off her lips with the corner of her napkin. "I have not introduced my consorts or my fellow Aeolians." The three who had accompanied her here paused in their actions and prepared to speak, tapping off their lips as well.

"Where do I begin? Ahh, yes. The beautiful woman sitting beside your wife, Captain Hughes, is Aphrodite. She, like myself, came from Earth."

Aphrodite tipped her head forward, eyes closed. "It is a pleasure to meet you. If there is anything we may do on behalf of our master to make you more comfortable, we wish to do so."

"Master?" I choked on my wine.

"Just a game we play," Takagi replied dismissively.

"The premier gives me purpose," Aphrodite added, her eyes heavy. "Before her, there was nothing. Now there is so much."

See gave a hungry smile in response. "Yes. Purpose." There was a pause as she considered her next words. "Across the table we have Hermes. He is my good boy, my pretty one."

This prompted the shirtless man to blush. "Anything for you. We are here to serve. Allow us to be good hosts. Life is a struggle, and so we wish to ease the pain."

Karianna, who sat beside him, gave him a sidelong look. She did not appear comfortable. I could feel the vibration of her prosthetic foot tapping through the floor.

"There sits the brains of my consorts, Ares. He might not be much to look at, but he is a most accomplished programmer. He manages our simulations with a set of skills that require great technical prowess and artistic creativity. He always keeps them interesting."

I stared at him, eyes narrowed, trying my damnedest to figure out what Premier Takagi meant by "not much to look at." If I had half his abs, I could have been a professional model in the late twenty-first century, or an actor. Hell, maybe I could even have bench pressed the *Transcendence* itself. He was a near idealized version of the male form, a Greek hero, muscular, high cheekbones, smooth skin, dark eyes. Shelly could hide it all she wanted, but I was pretty sure that drool on her bottom lip wasn't from the soup.

"Programming?" Ada perked up. "Would you mind me asking about a thousand questions? I know nothing about where human computer languages have gone since the mission started. I'm soooo curious."

He offered a beaming smile. "Mind? Of course not. Where should we start? F-128+, or Oboediens?"

"Your choice."

"You've pricked her mega-nerd nerve," Leo said, joyfully raising his glass by the stem and taking a sip. "She'll never shut up now."

"Never shut up?" He rubbed at his chin. "I find that acceptable."

"As for our tardy arrivals," the Premier went on. "Bridgett is at the end of the table beside our dear Mayor Demarcus. She may present as male, but she most certainly identifies as female, and her sexual escapades involve anyone who she feels connection with. Don't let her deceive you."

"I am not deceiving," she said with a bite in her voice. The way she had entered the room, the pants, the jacket, its shape square and lacking curves, had made it near impossible to identify her gender. "This is who I am."

"Freedom of expression is ever a right here, I am only explaining for our guests. They are from FICSE, remember? I cannot say what barbaric practices might be common in their closed society."

I blinked, the statement taking me by surprise, hitting me in the chest. I wasn't sure if it was her intent to be rude, but I didn't like being talked down to. For a moment, I thought Karianna might blurt out some nasty comeback, but she only gave me a look, swallowing down her rage. Shelly squeezed my hand before I said anything stupid in my cocaptain's place. Barbaric . . .

Make friends. Right? Make friends.

"Opposite myself," the premier said, waving, "is Demarcus, our loudmouth. He is the mayor of Cyme, another of the spires of Aeolia."

"Charmed," he said, tossing his chin at us.

"Of course there is Richard, an old friend of our group, a man who I swear does little or nothing to contribute to our fair society. Then, we have Joanna. Joanna does even less than Richard and is our resident drunk."

"Drunk?" Joanna chuckled. "I prefer the term *lush*. It rolls off the tongue so much better."

"Of course you would, but archaic, late English semantics do not absolve your liver from damage."

The table was silent for a moment as Joanna leaned forward, her attention focused on me.

"So strange," she said after some time, then looked to Richard, before turning back to me. "You know . . . the two of you could pass for brothers. A Milo and a Richard. You've got almost the same provincial haircut, same doughy eyes, a similar build. I wonder if you are the same height."

She was right, though I didn't want to admit it. It was weird to see some of myself in his look.

"I don't see it," Shelly said. "No offense, but my husband's smile is prettier."

"None taken," Richard replied, his voice deep, nothing like mine. "Of all the idiots sitting at this table, I assure you, I am the least vain among them. Call me trash, I don't care. Doesn't keep me from getting what I want, when I want, and with all the social freedoms we enjoy."

"If you haven't figured it out yet, FICSErs," Joanna went on, her words starting to slur, "Jadier might be the premier of this place, but she's a fucking bitch. She can't say a nice word about anyone. Everyone is stupid or ugly or trite. And you know what?" She paused, lost for a moment, searching her thoughts like someone sorting through a handful of rice grains working to extract a specific one. "We love her for it."

"Pleasure and pain," Demarcus bellowed.

His portion of the group echoed him, "Pleasure and pain."

They're crazy, Karianna pinged us. *Fucking crazy.*

I believe the word you're looking for is eccentric, Leo replied. *And I rather like them.*

No. No. I had the right word.

"Tell me, Captain Hughes," Premier Takagi spoke, drawing our attention back to the front of the table, "and Captain . . . I'm sorry, I did not catch your name."

Karianna sighed. "That would be because I didn't offer it."

Takagi leaned in, expectant.

"Karianna Torlen," my cocaptain said with an edge.

"Of course, of course. Hughes and Torlen, and your fine crew. You must recount to us your tales aboard the FICSE mission. Almost five hundred years have passed since you departed our fair star system, and yet, you look too young to have lived so long. We understand the concept of relativistic travel, so you must have gone a long way for this to make any sense. Enlighten us. Tell your tale."

"It's a long one," I said, reaching for a lump of bread to keep my hands busy. The group nodded.

"And it has some not-so-fun parts," James added.

This made the Premier grin. "Then we should have appetizers brought out." She clapped twice. *"Regale us."*

The bowls were taken away, and more food was brought out. Everyone was presented with a small plate that had a series of savory treats arrayed in a sort of sampler. There was a kind of bacon-wrapped cream cheese with a green garnish, roasted green vegetables, maybe sprouts, a crispy cracker with an orange-colored sauce, and a short cup of pickled fruits. Everything was wonderful but for the fruit, which was a bit too sour for my taste.

We told our story.

Unlike with Ingrid, with whom I felt a kinship, if a tenuous one at first, we left many details out for the premier. We did not know or trust these Aeolians, and so it felt prudent to hold back. I wanted to make friends, to garner assistance, but I moved with caution.

Broad strokes.

Major events.

CHAPTER 35

Several bottles of wine were emptied in that time. The more I drank, the better the food tasted. The more I drank, the easier I found it to drink. The Grand Hall had narrowed down from its great scale to just our table and its current inhabitants, the rest of the ostentatious place now hazy.

"You are like the space adventurers of the old days," Ares said when I had reached a pause in our tale. He raised his wine glass in a flourish, before taking a sip. "Adventurers battling monsters. Exploring new places. Uncovering wonders. I have always loved those stories. They are so inspiring. Telling of heroes rising up against impossible odds."

"Not as fun as you would think when you're in the middle of it," James said. "You ever been chased down by a squad of Clickers?"

"Can't say that I have. Aeolia is rather safe, you see."

"And how again did you say you earned these grand ships of yours?" the premier asked, her tone a bit too pointed. "I'm sure the Foundry does not accept credit."

"Donation," I said, raising my right arm and drawing back the sleeve with the three remaining fingers of my left hand. "At first glance, it appears normal enough, but it's a prosthetic. And so is my left leg."

"An arm and a leg?" Hermes considered, a touch of warm amusement in his voice. "How poetic of the Foundry. It is refreshing to hear that even aliens are aware of drama."

"And its purpose?" Aphrodite asked. "Why take this donation? Seems unusually cruel."

"To better understand human physiology," Karianna offered. "We don't think their intent is like that of the, what do you call them . . . the Slugs? The Slime Balls?" But she knew the answer.

"Splicers," the premier insisted, tapping a finger on her chin. "They are a worrisome species. Hard to locate, hard to be rid of, even here."

"That's too bad." I reached for my drink and swallowed down a long gulp.

"But let us not dwell on all that is bad. Let us focus our thoughts on all that is good, all that is pleasurable in life." She raised a glass. "A toast," she said, her voice once more taking on that silky quality. "To our guests, and your pleasures. May your dangerous journey soon be at an end. May you earn the reward of a job well done."

We raised our glasses to be polite, though I could see the apprehension on everyone's faces. It felt so awkward.

We drank, some emptying their glasses entirely, and so servants returned to fill them. Shelly leaned her head on my shoulder and nuzzled me, patting me on the lap. The world was becoming unsteady, and I wasn't even standing. I needed to pace myself. This wine was strong.

Several conversations had run wild around the table, Ada and Ares discussing base numbers and machine language, Joanna hanging all over James and his nervous replies, his eyes darting back to my cocaptain. He didn't appear to be enjoying the Aeolian's attention, which was shocking considering I thought she was just his type. Hermes and Karianna went on about cheese, though she seemed anything but relaxed. Leo and Aphrodite prattled on about the merits of the art in the Gallery, with random commentary shouted across the table from Demarcus and Richard in support of the shift to generative AI in the late twenty-first century. It was too much to process at once, and with my head already swimming with drink, I was lost, drowning in noise.

"You okay?" Shelly asked.

I smiled and reached for my water. "I'm fine. I just—"

Out of the corner of my eye, Premier Takagi gave her people a look, and in an instant they quieted. The sudden whiplash of frenzied chatter to silence was jarring.

"Now that we are a bit more relaxed," she began. "A bit more familiar with one another and what might arouse our interests, what might stoke the fires within the passions of our souls, tell us, Captain. What are your intentions? Why are you on Aeolia? What do you want from us?"

I took another sip of wine despite knowing I'd had enough, gripping the stem of the glass, then setting it down carefully, trying my best not to let it clink against any of the other tableware.

"We've come to save Earth," I said. "You know our original mission: Foundry Intent, Contact and Save Earth. Humanity went to the Foundry to receive the help it offered, and we've come back. Not everything was what we thought it would be. And so, we had to make adjustments."

"You told us your story."

"Yes, but not all of it." I shook my head. "As a gift from the Jevox, we have terraforming technology capable of bringing Earth back from the brink of death. And to make use of this technology, we need help. A lot of help. Now, we know that this will be an engineering project the likes of which humanity has never undertaken, far as we're aware. We'll need resources, which are widely available, some equipment—that part we are working on. But most of all, we'll need labor. We need people willing to work together to see this done."

"I see." The premier crossed her legs and leaned back in her chair, hands clasped in front of her, jacket opening a little wider, bare skin glistening as if rubbed with oil. "And so, you've come to appeal for our assistance?"

"We have."

"Earth . . ." she said, staring off into some unknown distance. "What a dream. Days of blue skies and fields of grass and forests of trees. The smell of spring flowers and the sound of buzzing bees. The chirping of birds, wolves howling at the moon. Sublime. All so sublime."

"Everything is quiet now," Shelly said. "They're all gone. Near extinct."

"Yes, yes." The premier lowered her head. "It is a sad, sad state of affairs. The sins of a species caught up with them."

"The sins of our species," Richard grumbled, and his companions seemed annoyed. "What? It was our fault."

"Wouldn't you like to change that?" I asked, leaning toward the premier. "We have the means to make a difference, we only need help. We can bring the dream back. You can bring the dream back."

"Would I like to change it?" she mused, turning the question back on me. "There is much I would like to see done. Much I would like to see come to life."

"Then say yes." I was emboldened by the wine. "Say you will offer your aid. You have the people. We need ten to twenty thousand, all working together, and we can make it happen. Say yes."

My vehemence made her recoil, her posture going straight, arms crossed. "Who are you to demand anything from me? You forget yourself, Captain. This is my domain, not yours."

"Sorry. I didn't—"

She raised a hand to forestall my apologies. "It is quite alright. Quite alright. Perhaps we will help you, perhaps we will not. But let us table that discussion for now. You have made your intentions clear. Let us enjoy the evening and what it offers."

Shelly gave me an uneasy look but narrowed her lips to a thin line, conceding the point for now. I looked across the table to Karianna. Her eyes were wide as she drained an entire glass of wine in one gulp. I was surprised that she hadn't spoken up. She'd let me lead this time, unlike with Ingrid. Then again, maybe she should have said something. Maybe she should have flipped the table over in anger, pointed an accusing finger in the premier's face and screamed about how this was all stupid, and while they were eating tidbits, drinking, and talking shit, people were dying.

Probably wouldn't help to make friends.

"Of course," I told the premier after a moment, summoning everything in me to sound agreeable but not submissive. "Of course."

The remnants of our appetizers were taken away. Several quiet seconds later came what I could only assume was the main course. Plates covered in domes of foggy glass were set before us, leaving me curious as to what was under them. The servants lifted the glasses away as one, then vanished behind us, a cloud of fog dissipating around the dishes. Within the thinning haze, a piece of pale meat rested atop a pad of rice that appeared too small given the size of the plate, a scattering of green vegetables around it, garnished with something leafy.

I was about to reach for my fork and dig in, given how great it smelled, when the servants reappeared to pour a small quantity of a dark sauce onto the dish, before lighting a torch and burning the garnish, blowing it out to create a charred collection of greens.

"Seabass smoked with hickory chips," Premier Takagi explained, "on a bed of jasmine rice with roasted vegetables covered in a garlic-onion sesame sauce. Enjoy."

And we did. The food was delicious, as the rest had been, light and flaky, sweet and salty. With the arrival of the main dish, conversation around the table slowed, words hushed. The premier, Shelly, and I exchanged small talk, nothing serious or heavy, while the table fell again into their own conversations. Ada and Leo were laughing at something, and the sight gave me an unexpected pang of joy.

"She looks happy," Shelly told me after some time. "I haven't seen her like this in a while."

I couldn't quite shake a strange feeling that had come over me. I kept thinking about all the people who were not here who should have been. The ones who deserved to eat this food, drink this wine, but circumstances had robbed those opportunities from them. My shaky hands and pounding heart had been replaced with a malaise of melancholy.

I finished my fish in silence, doing my best to use the utensils in the same order as our hosts did, glancing from time to time at the premier, at Karianna, at the consorts. The dynamic was so foreign we might as well have been eating with the Gan, or the Eipren.

James asked to be excused for a moment and stepped away. This prompted Joanna to hop up one seat and tell Hermes a joke, which he then passed down to Karianna, who fought not to laugh.

"Damn," James said, reappearing a few moments later. "That's a nice-ass bathroom you guys have." He looked to his seat, saw Joanna in it, then put his hands on his hips.

"Let's trade," Joanna urged, leaning forward. She looked him in the eyes, her teeth pulling at her bottom lip. "Look, Hermes, move down one. Captain Torlen, sit next to your friend."

They traded seats, James moving up, Hermes moving back. This change in placement earned a displeasing look from the premier.

I folded my napkin and set it on the table. "Where did you say the restroom was?" I asked James.

He waved at a location over my right shoulder to the nearest wall.

"Be right back," I told Shelly.

As I stood, the world became a little crooked, and it required far too much focus for me to walk straight. What was ordinarily a natural experience, one I'd been doing since I was a baby, now felt like a complicated operation that required several crew members and a set of standard operating procedures to complete. I made in the direction James mentioned, and out of nowhere, a sort of elevator box rose out of the floor. This must have been how everyone was getting in and out of the Grand Hall without walking a thousand miles. I stepped inside, turned around, and startled as Karianna darted in after me before the door closed.

"Woah, you okay?" I choked, my heart caught in my throat.

She nodded. "Just had to go."

"Right."

We stood in silence as the elevator descended. The doors opened on a narrow hallway, lights appearing along the floor.

A mechanical voice spoke: "*Restrooms.*"

I took a step forward, following the line, but Karianna caught me by the sleeve.

"What is it?"

She swallowed, then looked around us to see if anyone was nearby. We were alone. "I don't know. I just feel funny. Like, not myself."

"How? Have too much to drink?"

"No . . . well, maybe yes." She rubbed her eyes and sighed, bracelets jingling. "I don't know. I'm just really uncomfortable here. If we had a way out, I'd run back to my Star Sphere in a second to hide. I know this is weird, but it's like, I don't feel worthy to be here."

"Like your trash and you're not good enough?"

She offered the hint of a smile, eyes trailing down to the floor. "Yeah. Something like that."

"You're not alone in that," I said, that feeling of exclusion from the first time I stepped foot on the *Vasco Da Gama* as a child returning, the odd kid ignored or laughed at during recess. "You're right. They are a little weird. But I guess culture has had a lot of time to develop in ways we could never have expected."

"I know. But, it's like, we might have been weirdos on Novae, me and you, because of the donation and all the stuff we can do. Still, though, everyone knew us. They never looked down on us. We were like, kind of cool, you know?"

"I do."

"And here, I get the feeling they just think themselves to be like the pinnacle of human society. I mean come on, they fall upon Earth and raise up those who are worthy to come join them here? This place is a rich person's wet dream. We're just some relics that stepped out of the past. A novelty. We are not the best of the best sifted from the refuse of humankind. We're not refined."

She was not alone in these feelings. There was an air to how the Aeolians presented themselves, some of which might have been justified, some not, we just didn't know. And while the disparity of situations between Earth and here could leave a massive raw spot on your heart if you thought about it too long, we had to play nice. We needed them to see the mission fulfilled. They had people who might dirty their hands to save the Earth. They had connections, resources.

"Look," I said, taking her right hand and squeezing. "Don't let the strangeness of all this get under your skin. You are not trash. And you are more than good enough. You are worthy."

Karianna licked her lips and swallowed; her eyes locked on mine. The hallway felt deafeningly quiet in that instant. I could hear my heart beating in my ears. It took a moment for me to realize I was still holding on to her hand. I slowly let go, releasing one finger at a time. All I wanted was for her not to feel bad about herself.

"Why don't we go take care of business and head back up," I whispered, taking an uneasy step to the bathroom. "Don't want to leave everyone hanging, weird as it is here."

"Okay," Karianna said, though she did not seem convinced. "You're right. That would be best."

CHAPTER 36

The ride back up the elevator was silent, no words, no movement. We made our way over to the table.

"Everything okay?" Shelly asked.

I pinged her back without speaking. *Everything is fine.*

Conversations resumed, though now it seemed that James had focused his attention on Karianna, with Joanna and Hermes off in their own world. They spoke in hushed whispers too low for me to hear, but she didn't seem to be in the mood for whatever it was. Karianna appeared angry at James when he tried to make jokes and shrugged away any physical touch.

Shelly went silent for some time, a look having taken over her face, a sign she was trying to work this all out, figure out how the pieces fit together. I knew that look well.

"Premier, I have to ask," she said, cocking her head in Jadier's direction but not making eye contact. As she spoke, she rubbed her fingertips together as if to help her think. "Aeolia is more than just a human settlement, isn't it? You send envoys down to Earth, rescue people from their situations, ascending them to this place. Though not everyone. I have not seen any children, not that I doubt you have them. Are people from here? Or are they only from other places?"

Premier Takagi offered her a hungry, predatory smile, razor thin and sharp enough to slice clean through flesh. "What are we but a collection of dreams? Hmm? What are we but our own reality? A universe in our minds. What are we but actors upon a cosmic stage, playing out a comedy, a romance, a tragedy? Perhaps an epic?"

"For my part in this grand production, I make the dreams of the dreamiest dreamers come true. If some dream that this is the heaven promised in the Bible, then I will be that for them, with angels and choirs high above the clouds. And if others believe that this is a floating stone ready to fall into hell itself, then they must first see perfection, before realizing total damnation."

The table paused at this proclamation. I swallowed hard, and my fleshy hand began to sweat. Shelly said nothing in response, just stared vaguely in her direction, blinking.

Was this drama from the premier, or had we stumbled upon something that might be best left untouched?

A moment passed, and then Leo stood and bellowed, his voice low and loud in an imitation of an overexaggerated actor, "All the world's a stage!" He waved a hand as he got up, tipping over his wine glass in the process, crystal shattering. It took him a moment to realize a mess had been made, marking him as well on his way. "Oops. Sorry, my bad. Anyone got a towel or something to clean this up? Oooh, and on the nice linens too."

Ada offered up her napkin, laughing at him. "It will only take a dab to get it up . . ." She tossed the square of cloth atop the spreading pool of red, but it did little more than slow its progress. "Whoops, that didn't do shit."

Aphrodite, Ares, and Hermes looked at one another, lips pinched in tightly held expressions of amusement.

"Yes, a stage." Premier Takagi laughed between words, clapping to call someone to clean up the mess. "Of course, of course. Life is a drama. Highs and lows. Is that not what makes it exciting? Darkness and light."

"Had enough?" Ada asked Leo, throwing an arm over his shoulder. "Because I think I could use some of yours. I mean . . . some more."

"There's plenty for all," Ares mused. "We will call for more. The mess is not a problem."

"Fill me up, big boy," Lovelace replied, raising a glass, tongue poking just the tiniest bit out of her tightly bitten teeth.

Joanna smiled wide, tossing a thumb in her direction. "I like this girl."

While the other side of the table was having increasingly more fun, the more I drank, the more I ate, the deeper I fell into memory. I thought about the day Esteban and I were led into our quarters on Cynosure, how we were half starved and in desperate need of sleep. I'd been captured by the Frendol after we'd hidden in a derelict building to take shelter, and they had tortured me, but I'd been rescued. Gi'vor had then led us to our Foundry provided quarters, which had been an oasis in a desert of uncertainty. I wanted to go back there, to that safe place with my brother, but as I attempted to navigate those memories to that feeling, all I saw was Dad's bloody face at every turn.

He got me, Dad was saying. *That Parallax-hating South African got me.*

Why were these feelings hitting me here?

Why now?

What was wrong with me?

My eyes went misty. God, I missed Dad. We were finally starting to get close. Finally starting to really be good friends. And then he was gone. I missed his stupid-ass jokes, the way he got excited and saw wonder in everything around him. I missed his endless rants about planets and music and even his bitching about the younger generation being lazy. I missed his voice. I missed his company.

"Are you okay, Captain Hughes?" the premier asked, leaning to me, elbows on the table. "You look . . . haunted."

"I think we all are," I said, clasping my hands together, holding back tears. "It just hits us at different times."

"Tell me more."

I shrugged. "I'm just thinking about those who should be here but aren't. That's all. It's been a hard road."

"Yes," she whispered. "I understand."

"What about you? Were you born here? Or did you come from somewhere else?"

She shook her head. "No, I was not born here. I was born in what was once called Chicago, Illinois. An envoy of Aeolia came to visit my ruined home and rescued me from a terrible place called the Ward."

Her tone shifted from jovial and enigmatic to suit a heavier emotional weight, her words leaden and oily and black as if dredged from the darkened and forgotten cesspits within her heart. "You see, the Ward was an old hospital converted into a settlement, miles in length, a stable enough place to live and have families. It was built for one of the wars, well equipped, sure, but run-down, as everything on Earth has become.

"The leaders of the Ward were not kind men. Many had, well, let's just say, they had certain interests others might find unsavory. I was ten years old when I arrived, and that was just what they enjoyed entertaining. I tried to hide from them most days—the place was big, after all—but everyone had to eat, and that meant coming back to central locations. My days there were lived in constant fear. I did all I could to steal what I needed and keep to the shadows. I had no family. My parents died when I was young, some disease or sickness, and so it was just me and a few others. Friends, I suppose you could call them. But most of them later passed from any number of reasons. I was alone.

"When the Aeolian envoy visited the Ward, I don't think they wanted to take me with them. They didn't need a grubby little urchin. But the premier of the time, Katara, she saw something in me even though I did not speak a word. You see, I had been told by these men to keep quiet. Not to speak up. Not to speak my mind. Not to use my voice at all. That my voice was worthless, no more valuable than refuse. I was an object. A thing. And Katara? She was the first to tell me that this wasn't true.

"She was beautiful, a tall woman wrapped in white like an angel of God, extending her hand to a filthy child and offering up a better life. She said that I was perfect the way I was, wonderfully made and worthy of all the good in the universe. And so, I took her hand, and I went with her. As we departed, the leaders of the Ward came for me, came to claim their property. They had no intention of giving me up. And what did Katara do in response? She had her soldiers put them down like the very dogs they were. Filthy Scavers. Wretched humans. Vulgar and evil, embodying everything that has brought us to where we are as a species on the brink of death. People unworthy of ascension, unworthy of rebirth."

Shelly reached out a hand, placing it atop the premier's. "I'm so sorry for your pain. I can't—"

The premier recoiled at her act of kindness, the look on her face, sad moments earlier, now as jagged as barbed wire and hard as steel. "No. No. Do not ever be sorry for me. Do not give me your pity. I was given a new life. I will never live that one again. The little girl I speak of is dead. She died a long time ago. She died the day I left Earth. I am reborn of those ashes. I am Jadier Takagi!"

"Yes, you are," Shelly replied in an even voice while nodding. "Yes, you are."

The joyful mood of our dinner had shifted, the bright lights overhead dimming, arms and legs and thoughts once light now heavy as a neutron star. Something of our group's tension broke, defenses snapping, and down came a sense that if the premier, the leader of this ostentatious place, had been honest, this might have been a safe place to share terrible things. It felt like the right thing to do in this moment. And so, we did.

Of all people, James spoke first. "We've all seen tragedy," he said. "My mom . . . She was ripped apart by the Isoptera on the *Vasco Da Gama* soon as we hit the Foundry. I couldn't save her. I wanted to so bad. We were close, real close. She was my best friend. A wonderful woman. Smart. Kind. A servant leader. I owe all that I am that is good to her. She was my hero."

Karianna appeared as if she were going to speak next, then held back, reaching instead for her drink and swallowing its contents in one go. She looked to me, seeking something, her eyes glassy, but said nothing, pinged nothing to my implants. She didn't have to. I knew what she was thinking. I knew who she was thinking of.

Shelly shook her head as if deliberating over what she might say for herself. "My mother was killed on a Foundry station, Cynosure. She was trampled by accident. A physically large species with poor vision lived there. They didn't see her crossing the street. Then there was my father, captain of the *Vasco Da Gama*, well . . . Kabosai—the um, Splicers—killed him. They did something to his DNA, trying to make him into something else. He died because of them. I only hoped it wasn't painful. It's been so long, and it still hurts."

"My sweet Alexander," Ada whispered, her eyes closed. "He saved us, but we lost him . . ."

Leo put his arms around her, drawing her tight. She did not resist this advance but instead let him comfort her. How quickly their moods had changed. A manic swing from ultimate pleasure to pure pain.

I was compelled to join in these intimate acts of disclosure, lay my pain and tragedies on the table, but like Karianna, I just couldn't do it. I wanted to tell them of the loss of my home on Earth, my family, Esteban's death during the battle, Dad's murder, not saying goodbye to Mom . . . tell them the things I had been forced to do so I could earn those last few years with them. These memories were like a cancer spreading in my chest, eating away at my heart and soul, consuming me from the inside out. There was no cure for it, no way to undo the past. I could only ignore their existence. Try to stuff it down. Try to keep myself busy with the work of the mission.

If I could see humanity saved, it would all be worth it. Right?

It had to mean something.

Aphrodite spotted my undisclosed pain and reached over Shelly to clasp my broken, fleshy hand. "You are not alone, Milo. Speak it aloud or not, the pain will not easily go away."

The rest of the Aeolians told their own stories, each filled with a healthy measure of pain and tragedy. A lost parent, a lost home, living under the rule of tyrants, being forced to steal or hurt others to survive. Demarcus told a story of a man in South America whom he had been coerced into murdering in exchange for food, having been told he was a mortal threat to everyone else in their settlement. The man he killed turned out to be a cousin, and their leader had wanted him out of the way. Richard had lived on one of the stations around Earth that the Gene Brokers had harvested for materials, and he'd just made it out with his life. Joanna would not openly speak of her own tragedies, but it was clear it had involved a natural disaster created by recovered technology of an ancient war, deployed by a rival faction.

No one in the group had escaped pain . . . except . . . Did any of the consorts tell a story? I couldn't remember. Everything was getting hazy. Heart heavy. Body and mind soaked in so much wine my thoughts were turning red.

We ate another course, though I couldn't recall what it was. Ate a sweet dessert, a kind of custard with crunchy layers of caramel. The dinner began to come to a close.

Had we done what we needed to do at this meal?

Had we made friends?

Did they like us?

It felt as if we had been here for a lifetime.

I wasn't sure.

"Our evening is almost at a close," Premier Takagi said, standing. She gave a flourish, and the servants removed the plates, replacing them with a dark red drink in a curved cordial glass. "Have a toast with us. We have all seen pain and suffering, but we do not have to dwell on it. This drink, it is wonderful, a tonic of sorts on Aeolia. It is used to push the pain aside, if for a time."

"And what is it?" Shelly asked, lifting her glass and holding it up to the light.

"Bliss," Aphrodite told her, and the rest of the Aeolians nodded.

The crew looked to me for direction as I inspected the glass. This was not just any drink, we all knew it, and we'd had enough alcohol this evening to kill half our brain cells in the process. But the Aeolians appeared ready to drink. This was a tradition, so it seemed. A ritual of theirs. A rite.

Make friends . . .

It wasn't the end of the world.

Make friends . . .

Go along with the crowd. You've done it before.

Make friends.

Just one more drink.

I reached for the glass. "To bliss," I said, raising it up. My crew followed along.

"To bliss," the premier echoed, and we drank.

The drink was infinitely sweet and sour, making my face twist into a rictus of overwhelming sensations. I expected it to burn my throat as I swallowed, but it didn't. Instead, it was smooth, sublime, unlike anything Perry used to distill.

Everyone's glasses were emptied, then placed back upon the plates, except the premier's. Hers remained untouched.

An immediate sense of calm settled over me, starting at the top of my head and working its way down into my toes like sprinkles of water in a gentle rainstorm. I felt warm and peaceful. The world around me softened, yet somehow sharpened, colors blossoming, as if I were looking at reality through a new lens, a set of rose-colored glasses.

I had a strong desire not to stress over things as I normally would. Not to worry about every little thing that could go wrong, to create contingencies on contingencies. Still, I went ahead and pinged the ship to check on Proxy. Or . . . at least I tried. For whatever reason, I found this task impossible, like my implants weren't working. Was there interference? No. That didn't feel right.

I just—I just needed to.

Wait . . .

What was I doing?

As we each stood, saying goodbyes, laughing and hugging one another, I felt my steps become unsteady. The Grand Hall was like a rocking ship on open seas, leaning left and right, the decks slick with sea spray. It was delightful.

"I'm feeling good," Shelly whispered in my ear, her breath warm. "Really. Really good." Her words became a purr. "I wonder if we'll have private quarters? We need time alone . . ."

This thought made me grin.

"Let the pain go," Aphrodite told Shelly and me, placing a hand on both of our chests. "We all have. It is better this way. So much better."

And for the first time in a long time, I saw the wisdom in this. Pain was not helping me move forward. Pain would not ensure that we saved Earth. I carried my pain with a misguided fear that letting go meant I was a terrible person, that I was somehow betraying those I loved. But they wouldn't want me to hurt, would they?

"How do I let it go?" I asked in earnest. "It hurts too bad."

She smiled and offered us both a hand. "Come with me, and we will show you."

And so Shelly and I took hold of her hands, fingers tangling with hers, and we were drawn away from the hall, our crew in tow.

I was ready to let go.

Ready to stop hurting.

Ready to embrace a new way of living.

CHAPTER 37

"Where are we going?" Shelly asked Aphrodite, the three of us heading down one of the spire's side halls at a quickening pace. It was impossible to say what time of day it was, given how the cycles of Venus played out, but the passages were hardly empty; plenty of Aeolians present. I worried for an instant about us embarrassing ourselves in front of these people, ruining our prospects at building a positive rapport, but to my surprise, they all seemed to give us appraising looks as we passed, a general sense of pleasure and goodwill in their eyes. "You taking us to our quarters?"

"After a fashion," Aphrodite replied, squeezing our fingers. Her skin was so soft, supple like a baby's. How did one get that soft? Did she sleep in a bath of lotion? "We will go to the section of the spire your quarters are located. Given how well dinner went for all of us, I thought it best we celebrate a bit more. So long as everyone is in the mood . . . We would not think to impose."

"Hell yeah, it's okay," Leo bellowed. "Don't think that the word 'tired' is part of my vocabulary at this time. This place is amazing. I'd like to see more."

"I could go for another drink," Ada said, her words taking clear effort to enunciate. "I'm parched . . ."

I glanced over my shoulder at them and chuckled. Leo and Ada were hanging all over one another in a desperate, lazy attempt to help keep each other from becoming a pile on the floor, unsteady as their steps were. Hermes and Ares walked beside them, poised and ready to grab either if they fell, but they took no action other than laughing along with them.

For Karianna's part, she ferociously resisted James's kind offers of assistance with her own wobbly steps. She shot up through our group, bounding off of Ada, caught her toe on the floor, and nearly tumbled over. Hermes reached out a hand, and she took hold of his shoulder, readjusting before using it as a prop.

"What the hell is wrong with the floor?" she said. "It's hard to keep track of it. I am curious about one thing . . . Did someone replace the tiles with freaking rainbows?"

My brows knitted together as I peered down at my feet. There certainly were a lot more colors than normal, but I didn't think that this was an effect of anything special on the floors of the spire. No rainbows here. But iridescence? Maybe. Just a little.

"I'm not seeing it," I said, squinting. All I saw was dust.

Karianna rolled her eyes at me. "You're not looking at it from the right angle. You have to stand over here." She pointed.

Out of nowhere, Shelly let go of Aphrodite and ran to Ada. She grabbed her face with her hands, surprising Lovelace, then kissed her on the cheek with a loud smack. "I can't hold it in anymore. I just love you."

"Aww," Ada beamed, pushing Leo aside and throwing her arms around Shelly. "I just love you too, friend. Can I just say, you are such a great person. So smart. So kind. So sexy." She stuck out her tongue. "I mean . . . that ass. Come on."

"Yeah, well, but those tits," Shelly said, and my eyes went wide. I could have fainted. Was this how they talked when they were alone? Inquiring minds needed to know. "I think Leo was right to cut your shirt like that. I like the girls hanging out."

"Oh yeah?" Ada straightened her back bolt upright and shook her chest. "Like the way they do that?" Shelly stared at her cleavage, transfixed by the spectacle.

Leo gave the situation an appraising look, his lips pursed, eyes closed, pinched fingers raised forming a chef's kiss. "Perfection."

My attention was drawn back to Karianna, who was stuck in place, hands extended before her, turning them over, front and back, inspecting knuckles then palms. "Wow. Hey, Milo, have you ever really noticed how much detail the Foundry put into these prosthetics? I mean, come on, it's like a perfect match, a mirror. Bruh, the skin color is wrong, but the age lines, all the little creases. I never noticed them before."

I let go of the consort, pausing in my step, and was compelled to do just as she had. Karianna was right. Every detail but for the color the of my skin was the same. I drew my palms closer to my eyes, squinting, inspecting every ridge of my handprints, ignoring the missing fingers of my fleshy appendage.

The world turned.

I traveled away from the halls of Aeolia, that world becoming too large for me to fathom, my self becoming too small to see. I was standing on a hillside made of brown flesh, the ridges of my palm pulsating valleys many hundred times my height. My body was warm all over, my blood replaced with something like hot chocolate. Maybe spiced chai? At the top of a fleshy hill, a salty drop of sweat as big as a city block had formed, its shape perfectly spherical. The world shook, and it began to roll through the valley to me, a rushing river held back, made perfectly round by surface tension. I braced myself to be carried away by this impending disaster, to be trapped and drowned within a liquid orb of saline I could not escape.

But then I was back in the hall, safe, the scale of my self-image having returned to normal.

"Woah," I hissed, then looked up, my eyes meeting Shelly's.

She let out a snort, a hand held over her face. "You okay, love?"

I nodded back at her, or at least I thought I did. Giving my body instructions was proving to be difficult. All my appendages felt way too far away, as if I were piloting the body, not dwelling within it.

"Okay, I see it now," James blurted out. "You're right, Karianna. The floor is made out of rainbows."

"I told you guys!" Ada said. "Remember that ancient Earth video game we found with the little go-karts and the plumber? I think Perry had it saved on his terminal. This makes me want to ride off down the road in one of those carts."

"Shit," Leo hissed, his attention following theirs.

"Can I be the angry gorilla?" James asked Karianna.

She nodded absently. "Yup. So long as I can be the floating princess. I like her more than the fruit. Peach? Was that it?"

The longer I stared at the floor, the more I realized they weren't wrong.

I blinked, and we were someplace else. We had materialized in a large room, a home with an open floor plan that felt designed to entertain. There were white tables at the extremities, white couches arrayed in a circle, electronic displays occupying open wall space. Pictures hung on the copper-trimmed neutral walls, selections of abstract fine art, landscapes and portraits and collages, as well as a few with moving colors, kinetic in nature. Bottles lined one wall, a series of stools arrayed beside a high-top table, a sort of kitchen beyond.

Aphrodite instructed us to make ourselves comfortable, and so we had, plopping down anywhere that made sense, our muscles turning to Jell-O, bodies becoming flat like pancakes. Hermes put on music, its vibes loud, deep, and thunderous. I felt every bass kick as it washed over me, every chord as it resonated through the crystalline structures of my very essence, my soul vibrating at a quantum level. This sensation was similar to the pink tone the Foundry's signal gave off, comforting of emotions, but it was different. This one was more red. Red and black. And white. And . . .

I was forgetting something. I was sure of it.

Who did I need to check in with? Lance and Ingrid were here, but—

I fumbled with my implants; the interface was too difficult to mess with right now. Before I started to worry, I told myself Proxy was fine. Everything was fine. Just had a little too much. We all deserve to have a little too much. After a long sleep, I'd be fine.

I massaged my face, rubbing at my eyes, fingers pressing against my temples.

Shit, shit, shit. I was drunk. Why had I gotten so drunk? How had I gotten so drunk? I knew I needed to keep an eye on how much I drank, and what I drank, but we needed to make friends, right?

Right?

My emotions began spiraling out of control, thoughts twisting back to Dad, to Mom . . . to Esteban. The Phantamorph. Watching the Jevox ship turn to dust at Harper's sabotage. The Foundry turning its back on us. Being lost on an icy moon. Frostbite and amputation.

An emotional pain the likes of which I had never experienced seized my chest, making everything tight. It felt as if someone had clamped a vise around my ribcage, and with every inhalation, they were constricting my lungs, giving them exponentially less space to expand. I found it impossible to grasp for oxygen, needles of pain jabbing inward. I did not breathe.

Shelly must have noticed this shift in my cheery disposition. She laid her head on my shoulder. She said nothing, but silently offered to take this burden with her presence.

I drew a shallow breath, attempting to calm myself, but a kind of bone-deep anxiety gained momentum.

Ares poured us fresh drinks and delivered them one at a time, our group loafing about the room on couches and chairs, each of us staring up at the ceiling, bodies limp. I wasn't sure if we needed any more to drink, but then again, I wasn't tired in the least. And you stopped drinking when you were sleepy, right? Wasn't that the rule? Party till you dropped.

Drinks were brought out again in those tiny cordial glasses.

I hesitated in downing my glass, staring at it with a detached sense of curiosity. What was it made of? Was it alcohol? Or was it something else? It tasted good, sure, but too good. Sweet and fruity and complex. Went down too smooth.

We were here to complete a mission. Lance and Ingrid were trying to reconnect with an old contact of hers, find the . . . those devices. Why couldn't I remember what they were called? We needed something from this place. I really needed to check on them, but like, how did I do that? They were big kids, right? They knew how to care for themselves. Not like Ingrid was helpless or anything.

Aphrodite appeared behind Shelly and me, hands resting on our shoulders, silky soft fingers massaging both our necks. I felt my eyes rolling into the back of my head at the consort's touch. Shelly let out a pleased moan. Why was this not weird? Just a few hours earlier, I hadn't known this person at all, and now it felt so good for her to touch us. It felt natural.

"I see you, Milo," Aphrodite said. "Let it go. Let the pain go."

"Let it go," I mused, then raised my glass.

We did what felt right.

We drank.

And a few minutes later, we drank again.

And again.

We let the pain go.

We pushed it down deep.

We washed it away.

We drowned it in an ocean of chemical bliss.

Time became a stranger, a foreigner for which I had no language skills to understand. When it spoke to me, its words were a jumble, and so I had to watch its motions, its body language, and soon enough even that became difficult. From what I could understand in the moment, it was kind to us, loving, giving us the opportunity to take in life at its entirety.

And yet, who could be certain?

I looked to Shelly for help, for advice, for guidance in this auspicious moment, but she was just as lost as I was.

Where were we? How did we get here?

What had to have been hours passed by in moments as we lay there, listening to music, lost in the vibrations of the cosmos.

Ada and Leo and Hermes passionately debated something related to visual arts. Ares and Aphrodite danced around the room, encouraging Karianna and James to join in. I was pretty sure Aphrodite had changed outfits, given that she showed a bit more skin than I recalled moments earlier. Karianna found her way onto a table, her body twisting and rolling over every beat, her lines curving along with the gentle sine wave of the bass line. Shelly nodded as she watched them, a vacant smile on her face, a free hand rubbing my leg and coming dangerously close to my crotch. James poured us another round of Bliss, and our little party carried on, its energy redoubling with each sip.

What the hell was in this stuff?

One moment the room was empty but for our intimate group of passionate degenerates, the next it was filled with people. A party had descended upon whoever's quarters we had been taken to. The press of humans became a roiling mass of bodies, a sea of a hundred skin tones united by clothes of white with unfamiliar faces, their hair festooned with ribbons of many colors.

Aeolians offered their greetings, told us jokes, made small talk about life and our journey, encouraged us to get off the couches and dance, telling us it would help to get the blood pumping. The music shifted a hundred different times, cycling from songs on the edge of recognition to foreign genres that must have been created while we were lost.

I wasn't much for dancing, but that night, like on Creatus, it felt like the only right thing to do. I waved my hands in the air, swayed to the beat, shook my head, and did whatever the hell felt right. Shelly grabbed tight and spun me around, the two of us starting a kind of dance battle to see who could dance the least badly. We were terrible at it, but it didn't matter. We were in that perfect space of human expression, a place without rules, a place of pure emotion and universal connection.

Lights flickered, bands of color shooting through the space.

The room dimmed and filled with fog.

Everyone encouraged us to go for it, to let it all out.

These people were so wonderful. Accepting. Kind.

I leaned against a wall to catch my breath, Shelly collapsing into my arms, resting her head on my chest.

Aphrodite, now nearly nude in just a pair of panties and a slash of fabric that barely covered her breasts, came up to us, offering water.

"Drink up," she said. "You've been sweating hard. We don't need you passing out on us."

"It feels so right," I told her. "I've never—"

She put a finger to my lips and shushed me. This intrusive action did not seem to bother Shelly as I thought it would have. Instead, it appeared to excite her from the deep breath she took, the way she arched her back—another woman touching my lips, telling me what to do.

"Tell us about yourself," Shelly leaned in, pressing Aphrodite, their faces inches apart, nose to nose, lips to lips. "I'm so very curious. They call you by the name of a Greek goddess, but that can't be your real name. What do I call you? I want to get to know you better."

"My name?" This question seemed to take the consort off guard. She cocked her head to the side, offering a soft cheek to Shelly. "I—no. It's been too long. My name is unimportant."

"Everyone's name is important," I said, clasping her on the shoulder, fingers squeezing gently. "It makes us who we are, you know?"

"I am here to serve," she said, as if it were a recitation, not a truth. "I am here to ensure everyone sees heaven."

Shelly let out a peal of laughter. "See heaven? Okay. Okay. But there is more to you than just the role you play. Right? Milo's a captain, but it's not all he is. He loves tiny models, and art, and music. He likes to read stupid pirate stories."

"Hey now!" I exclaimed, right index finger raised. "They are not stupid. They can be inspirational."

"Yeah, yeah."

"I wish it were that easy," Aphrodite offered, taking a quick glance over her shoulder. "Sometimes, though, it is better to forget. Better to live in bliss than in uncertainty and pain."

From out of the crowd, a man and woman approached us, their faces beautiful and yet so ordinary by comparison to be forgettable in this strange place.

The woman, who was slender but muscular, with dark hair and pale skin, tugged on Shelly's jacket without preamble. "You are so pretty. Are you one of the new arrivals? You have to be one of the new arrivals." Her eyes were wide and dark, glazed over, pupils so massive they dominated the territory around her irises. Was she just as wasted as us?

"I have it on good word they're from FICSE," the man blurted out as he leaned in. He was built like a greyhound, his skin the color of ebony, with a posture both engaged and curious. "It's true. They are relics out of time."

"FICSE? Come on. I thought that was a fairy tale. My dad used to go on about the mission and the mysterious Foundry to get me to go to bed at night."

"It's all true," Shelly told them, though her inflection made it sound like more of a question. "Big damn heroes and all."

"Lucky to still be here," I added, raising my prosthetic arm, along with my damaged left hand. I waggled my remaining three fingers. "Hard road."

The man's eyes bulged. "Your hand . . . does it . . . does it like . . . hurt?" He reached out to touch, and I did not pull back, but let him feel the stubs of my missing fingers.

"No." I shook my head. "Not anymore. It used to. Lost them to frostbite."

"Where?"

"A long way away."

"What are your names?" Shelly asked, putting a hand on the girl's forearm. "I want to know everyone's names."

She smiled in response. "They call me Artemis."

"And they call me Ajax," the man said.

Shelly narrowed her eyes at them, then glanced at Aphrodite. My wife's face took on an expression of mock anger. "No. No. Like, what are your real names. You know, John, Sara, Peter. Kim? Christina? Jennifer? Any of those?"

The girl laughed, her head tossing back. "Artemis and Ajax are our real names, silly."

Shelly looked to Aphrodite. "Why all the monikers?"

The goddess gave a shrug. "We are all players in our master's production."

Which begged the question: Where was the premier? Was she too important to celebrate with the riffraff?

"Will they be joining us for the games later?" Ajax asked. "Is it time yet?"

Artemis whirled on him, her eyes rolling. "No. It's not time yet, stupid. You know the schedule."

"Games?" I asked. "What kind of games?"

"The best kind of games, deary."

Aphrodite took a deep breath, her face a mask of serenity. "Artemis. Ajax. These people are new to the city. We will let them see Aeolia's wonders one at a time."

"Of course," Ajax conceded. "I am merely so excited I can hardly contain myself. New people. New blood."

Artemis turned her attention to Shelly, a curious look on her face. She took a step forward, asking, "May I kiss you? You have very beautiful lips."

And to my total surprise, Shelly nodded, not turning back for an instant. I stood in shock as the two of them locked lips, holding one another's faces with their fingertips. I couldn't help but wonder if this was what it looked like when she kissed me, this information logical, unemotional, academic.

Then it hit me like an open-handed slap on the ass. She was kissing a woman. A woman. Their lips brushed each other softly as if exploring the texture, the moisture, the feel, experimenting, going deeper, fingers sliding into one another's hair. And just like that, it was over, the woman and her friend gone, having disappeared among the boiling crowd.

"Did you just . . ." I asked, my thoughts a jumble.

Shelly cocked her head at me. "Just what?"

"The party's here!" Joanna shouted across the room, appearing at the doorway with Demarcus, Bridgett, and Richard in tow. "Brought some more wine for you reprobates! Let's elevate the mood."

The crowd cheered. Bottles were opened as a queue formed before Joanna and Richard. I laughed as they served, watching while half the wine they poured didn't even make it into glasses.

Shelly began rubbing my back. Shivers ran up my spine, my head tingling with delightful pinpricks of sensation. The floor was so very far away, as if it were receding, though I knew I was standing still, feet firmly planted. I could almost see the cosmic threads connecting everyone and everything in the room, prismatic gossamer of fate tethering souls to one another.

The Universe was here.

And we were the Universe.

I shook my head, trying to bring my thoughts back into focus. Then I found myself laughing. Why were we here again? How long had I been staring off into nothing?

"Go dance," Aphrodite urged. "Have fun. Relish life."

And we did just that. We said *to hell with it,* each moment that passed releasing ever more tension within us. Anxiety. Fear. Their braids like a coil slowly being unwound.

James and I found ourselves in a corner at one point, talking about old times, how we used to get in trouble on the *Vasco Da Gama,* how we used to play those virtual war games. He swore he was better at it than me, but I reminded him that his impulsiveness lost us more games than it won.

Ada and Leo were insistent that we take shots with them. Demarcus had a bottle of some sort of liquor made on Mars. He assured us it wasn't too strong, and so I took him up on it. Shelly did not partake, but Karianna did, the five of us raising our glasses and clinking. What we toasted to, I can't remember, but it must have been important.

Shelly, Karianna, and I settled into a conversation as the party rode upon pulsing waves of electronic beats. While they seemed to skip around on topics, they settled on how it felt to breathe, and how different types of breathing made you feel different ways.

"I swear sometimes when I take a deep breath," Karianna said, "I feel like a helium balloon. Like, if I keep breathing it in, I might just float off the ground and fly into the sky."

Shelly pursed her lips and nodded. "I've felt that way before. But I don't think it's scientifically possible."

"It takes deep breaths to meditate," I added. "When you get the rhythm right you can feel the universe."

"That's just you," Karianna told me. "I saw what you did at the gate, felt how it all worked, and I tried it. All I do is get bored and fall asleep. Meditation sucks."

Artemis appeared out of nowhere and put a hand on Shelly's shoulder. The three of us spun in slow motion, colors tracing in glowing neon lines as we focused our eyes on the dark-headed woman.

"I've been thinking," she said.

"Yeah?" Shelly leaned to her. "What is it? Thinking is dangerous."

"So . . ." She squinted her eyes. "If you're from FICSE, you left to fix Earth, yes? FICSE, the mission to fix it all! That's what they used to say."

"That's right. Well, our parents did. We were just kind of along for the ride. But things didn't quite go as planned."

Karianna's eyebrows went up at this. "No, they did not," she put in, then reached for a glass and took a sip of water, spilling half of it on her chin. I snickered, and she cut me an annoyed look.

"Right," Artemis replied to Shelly, though I wasn't sure what she was agreeing to. "You ever think that maybe it's a good thing?"

"What do you mean?"

"Like . . . maybe we deserved all the bad things that happened to us. As humans, we were so terrible, right? So cruel to one another. Not like here. We profited off of others, killed them. Went to war."

"The Great Reset," Ajax added, appearing beside her. Where in the hell had he come from? Had he just teleported to this location?

"Exactly!" Artemis threw up her hands at him. "Let time and circumstance sort out those who should be dead. Then let life continue with only the good people. Start over. Reset this shit."

"A little heartless, don't you think?" Karianna mused, setting her water down and taking a step toward them. She seemed very sober in this moment, every part of her body straight, intentions focused. "And what about the children? Did they do anything to deserve it? Do they deserve to die for what someone hundreds of years ago did to them?"

"No. No," Artemis objected. "Not them. Just the bad people, you know? The bad people."

"And how would a disaster discriminate between those people who are good or bad?" Shelly asked, her voice quiet but her face loud. Despite all the good feelings that had to be pulsing through her body, she was turning angry. "Can you tell me that?"

"This is a party," Ajax said, stepping between them. "Let's not talk politics or religion. Let's just have fun. Love each other." He led Artemis away back into the crowd without another word.

Shelly mumbled, "Sorry I kissed that bitch."

And with that comment, Karianna nearly spat out her water, her eyes lingering on Shelly.

James sauntered up to us, a kind of snack in his upturned hand. "Assholes," he said, then tossed something crunchy into his mouth. "Hungry?"

Karianna peered into his hand, then took one of the brownish chips. "Ooo, these are good. What are they?"

"No fucking clue."

Another round of Bliss was downed, and the unusual feelings we had around our conversation faded, its sharp edges smoothed out. Everyone was entitled to their opinions, yeah? Many of these people had never seen the other side. No wonder they had a strange perspective. Still, it was almost as if they followed an absolutionist ideology, like Ingrid and Priscilla had warned us about. But no, that seemed crazy.

"Hey!" Leo said, appearing before me from out of the crowd. "We're going for a run about."

"A what?" I took a step back, startled.

"Joannna and Demarcus want to take us on a no-holds-barred tour of the city. But first, take this shot."

I swallowed it down without hesitation. It wasn't tasty, nor smooth. Kind of tasted like what I imagined motor oil might.

I coughed several times. "The hell was that?"

"No idea," Leo replied. "Something green."

Out of nowhere, the room began to cheer, "Run about! Run about! Run about!"

I looked to Shelly, who seemed uncertain, but soon started to cheer along with them, "Run about! Run about! Run about!"

The sound of their voices was deafening.

"We making friends yet?" Karianna playfully bumped me with a shoulder. "I know everything has me feeling a little more friendly." Her eyes met mine, a mischievous spirit swirling in them.

During the party, my subconscious mind had painstakingly built maps of our surroundings. I had put barriers on the limits of what I would or would not do. I knew all the nooks and crannies of this home, where the bathroom was, who to avoid, where to get a drink. I was tethered to this place, using it as an anchor in my altered state, something to keep my feet firm to some semblance of reality as not to freak out. But their cheers, their encouragement, they pulled at those threads, tightening them, threatening to snap them.

I was afraid to leave. It was as simple as that.

I was the cautious one.

But at this time, in this unique moment, I knew I had to let that all go.

"Just jump," Karianna told me. "Trust us. We're here to catch you."

And she was right. I was surrounded by those who would always catch me. I had once jumped out of a starship into open space, nothing but an environment suit with weapons fire all around me . . . and they had caught me. I made stupid mistakes, and they were always there.

They had protected me.

"Let it go," I mumbled, and Karianna's face split into a grin.

Reality became a blur, a collection of smudged oil paint and color, faces indistinct, emotions pouring out into a river of electric sensation.

CHAPTER 38

We were running through the station as a mob of thirty or more, tripping over ourselves, laughing and cheering and hooting, Joanna and Richard at the front of our group, the consorts and a dozen others with us. People leapt out of the way at our arrival, throwing themselves flat against the bulkhead. We were a social menace set to burn this place to the ground.

But no cops came. No one arrived to tell us to stop.

We were in a massive room with a pool of clear water that stretched out fifty meters at least. Everyone in our group was stripping down out of their clothes, even Shelly, not a single one the least bit worried that the others would see their naked bodies. Not James, not Leo, not Ada, or Shelly . . . or Karianna, even when her prosthetics, just like mine, were on display. There was no modesty here. We dove in, headfirst, the water warm like a Star Sphere. It rushed over and around my body, making me feel as if I were skimming through time itself. Shelly and I swam to the bottom, eyes open, following the rest, breath held tight in our chests. From the bottom of the pool we could see out of the spire into the clouds, storms shifting around us in pale yellow collections of sulfurous behemoths in the wild.

We were toweling off, clothes tossed over our shoulders, Demarcus helping people get dressed, sizing environmental suits. Some were ahead of us, already dressed and ready to go outside, others just slipping on their underwear. We did our best to catch up with our friends, fumbling at the littlest things. We did as we were instructed, sliding on long johns and leg sections, snapping on chest plates and helmets. Before we knew it, we were outside the spire. Shelly turned to me as we were hurled across the open sky, the two of us rocketing down a cable only a few inches thick, looking at one another through glass faceplates, stomachs bottoming out from the change in velocity. All that kept us from falling to our deaths, to be crushed among the pressure of Venus's lower atmosphere, was a harness and a series of carabiners. But we were free, we were flying, Shelly enjoying the experience for once. We were among the clouds, with nothing holding us to the ground.

We were outside of the Neonteichos spire on one of the old UEI platforms, roaming a city of neon colors and flickering lights, its people dressed in black with glowing cuffs and hems. Music was everywhere, the walls made of it, air permeated by its rhythms, deep and pulsing. Our group descended upon a market, a series of carts serving all sorts of foods I'd never seen or smelled before. Richard introduced us to local dishes, some with salty noodles and rich meats, some crunchy and pastry-like, some savory pouches filled with cheese and vegetables. There were fruits with bizarre shapes and colors, sweet and juicy, sour and soft. My chin was wet and sticky with juice. Shelly felt the need to lick it off, sending my heart fluttering.

We tried a bite of everything, drank whatever was put before us. Leo recited Shakespeare from atop a café table, crowds gathering on a narrow street. They raised bottles and hands and lights from their pockets. We laughed at his boldness but were soon enthralled by his performance. As he concluded, taking a bow to his now adoring fans, Ada tossed a bouquet of red roses at his feet.

Flashes of consciousness passed through my mind.

I met eyes with a sentinel, its red, crystalline body warm as a geothermal vent, the soul within it looking back at me with malice.

We were lying on our backs on a soft, thick carpet, the tops of our heads touching, forming a near-perfect circle of three dozen people, our eyes focused on the black of space overhead. Hundreds of shooting stars fell through the void, a meteor shower come to Venus. My spine tingled as I felt the vibration of Larissa spire beneath me. Shelly held my hand and whispered sweet nothings in my ears. Karianna and Richard fell into a conversation, coming closer to one another with each moment. James attempted to butt in, steal her attention, but he was rebuffed. Joanna, on the other hand, seemed to like James. Her face was dangerously close to his ear. Something must have broken. I turned away for a moment, and when I looked back, he was kissing her. Another moment, and she was straddling his hips, a tangle of red hair obscuring his face.

We downed ever more Bliss.

More Bliss.

We were in a long hallway, its length seemingly infinite. The walls were made of glass, and beyond them, a cosmic highway of colors and lights. This was not like the connection to the Star Sphere, it was prismatic, chaotic, pure entropy focused into a straight line. Within those colors I saw faces, places, people. I was transported back to Earth, to Novae, to Creatus . . . I saw my parents, I saw Esteban, Omar . . . I waved at them, and they waved back, smiles on their faces, a sense of supreme contentment upon them. A state of nirvana.

More Bliss.

We were in a circular room filled with white pillows. Someone had started a fight, and Demarcus and Leo were sparring with one another with fluffy clouds as tall as they stood. Ada backed Leo up, spinning round and round with a body pillow, catching Richard in the face. I didn't think anyone was keeping score, but the spirit was enough. Shelly and I luxuriated as we watched the action unfold, Aphrodite and Hermes giving us back massages, urging us to relax, urging us to just let it feel good, let the sensations pass over us as they came.

More Bliss.

More Bliss.

More—

We were in a domed room where someone in a suit made of metal links caught lightning in one hand then cast it outward with the other, striking a target in mock combat. The crowd cheered with each point gained, but it was clearly staged. This was a presentation, if hard to follow. The details of the epic ran together, but the visuals were powerful. Good versus evil. Strong versus weak. Rich versus poor. Shelly clutched my hand the entire time, entranced. To our right, Joanna did the same with James. Ada and Leo were at the end of our bench, whispering into each other's ears, laughing at a joke we couldn't quite hear.

And then . . . something caught my eye in the crowd, made me uncomfortable. A bald, clean-shaven man stood out among the white-clad patrons. He had an oval face with piercing eyes that seemed to be seeking trouble. He wore a garish coat that brushed the floor, its tassels and shag hanging off in layers. My attention fell on the arm sticking out from the end of his right sleeve. It was not fleshy . . . it was mechanical. It was—

We were in the simulation chamber and it was the sixteenth century. Our group stood around in a forest made of holographic projections and carbon fiber constructions. Everyone was in long dresses with ruff at the cuffs, tight bodices, or doublets of fine cloth with hose or trousers. Our costumes reeked of mold and mothballs, but it hardly mattered as we recited lines from *A Midsummer Night's Dream*. Leo was on a thread, a tear of a sort, obsessed with Shakespeare in this moment of life, and today, the world truly was a stage. It was good no critics were present. We were likely the worst troupe ever seen, all but Leo stumbling over lines, overacting, speaking too quietly or laughing too hard to get anything done. At some point I turned to see Karianna pinned against a tree, Richard and her kissing, James watching them with more than a little curiosity. Joanna was right. It was uncanny how much he looked like me.

We were someplace else, though where I could not say. It was warm, and safe, and dark, full of company, full of places to lie down. And while my mind was not tired, my body was starting to be. It welcomed this respite. It welcomed a pillow and some sheets and a soft place to rest my spine.

Aeolia had shifted something in my heart. It had taken away a lifetime of burdens in a single evening. I did not see how it was possible. Here I had stumbled upon some truth I could not yet understand.

Was this place heaven? Was it truly heaven? Maybe Premier Takagi's proclamation wasn't hyperbole. Was this what it felt like not to know pain or fear or anger? I wanted to live in this forever. I wanted to be in this blissful state for eternity.

I turned to my wife, who lay beside me, a soft glow of blue light illuminating her face. "I love you, Shelly," I said, and she smiled back at me, her eyes heavy.

"I love you too." She took hold of my face. "You are my everything."

"We have everything we need. Don't we?"

She cocked her head, confused. "We've always had everything we needed. And that's been each other." She drew close and began kissing me, deep and urgent, her body firmly pressing against mine, every part of my biology responding in kind. We did not care who was around or who was looking, the room was full of people, but neither did we care what they were doing.

Shelly fumbled with the catch on my pants, unfastening them, reaching inside. A shock of pleasure bolted through me at her touch. We'd done some pawing tonight, but this was the first real flesh-to-flesh moment.

"Fill me with life," she whispered in my ear, her words desperate. "Universe please, please . . . fill me with life."

I blinked. "Is it time?"

"I don't care if it's time. It might never be time." Her body twisted as if struck with a wave of pleasure so powerful it hurt.

Bands of color flickered before my eyes. For an instant I thought I sensed a signal from Proxy, from my implants, but that went away. A solar flare. A communications artifact.

"Fill me, love," she went on, a purr in her voice.

I wasn't sure if that was even possible for us, given the injections we had been given on the *Vasco Da Gama*, all the environmental conditions we'd faced, my donation, but how could I not try? I could not let her stay in this place of painful longing. I didn't want to. I wanted her to have everything she desired, even if I wasn't sure if I was ready.

I unbuttoned her top, eyes locked on hers, not flinching for an instant. Her pants came down, smooth skin bare to open air, sweaty body against sweaty body.

I did as my love, my best friend, my wife asked of me.

And it was bliss.

Pure bliss.

CHAPTER 39

Reality became a void of light, filled with nothing but goodness, purity, and the soothing vibrations of a thousand voices singing in harmony. Words were spoken in those long choruses, but I couldn't say what they were. Their meaning went beyond one language, tapping into something universal, a prose of unadulterated meaning and intent. The Universe rejoiced with us, and lamented at our losses, called us to be one with it, and for some to be cut away like cancer.

We protect life, it told itself. We told ourselves. We protect life.

My mind was adrift in this infinite expanse, twisting, turning, slowly rotating but with nothing to orient by. Was it me, or the universe moving around me? My essence at its center like a supermassive star? Every fear, every bit of pain or hatred had been scrubbed away. I was only soul and thought. I was experience without tragedy. I ached at the simple pleasure of this, of love, of connection, of oneness. I wanted to be here for—

—I lay on the bathroom floor, my arms sticky and wet. My heart aching as if someone had slowly pressed a blade through my chest, lodging it deep within. I was alone here. We are always alone. They'd all left. They moved on. The Universe told me this was how it was, but I wasn't ready to let them go. I grieved for their loss.

It's not fair.

It's not fair.

It's not fair.

That I should live, and they should die.

It's not fair.

It's not fair.

It's not fair.

I trembled at the pain, tears flowing, my body curled up in a ball on cold tile.

I—

—was dry. My entire mouth was dry. I desperately needed something to drink, something to sate my parched existence.

I rolled over in bed, eyes meeting Shelly's, the world around us blurry and soft. How long had we been asleep? How long had we been lying here in this place? Where were we? Who were all these people? It felt like an eternity.

A mostly empty bottle of Bliss lay beside the bed on the floor. I reached for it, soothing my dry mouth with its sweet taste. Shelly stretched, let out a moan, and took a drink after I was done.

The barest hint of anxiety blossoming in my chest subsided. It was better to be in bliss. It was better this way.

Others around the room began to wake, a field of flesh in a stark-white existence, nothing but thin sheets if anything covering us. Soft music came out of hidden speakers, choirs singing of paradise.

Aphrodite crawled across a series of mattresses to greet us, a smile on her—

—been here so long.

Karianna is in my face, trying to tell me something, but I can't understand her words. Her expression is excited, eyes bright as if something important is happening. Her hand is on my shoulder. Shelly is nowhere to be seen, and we are standing in a dark room with pale lights.

I offer her a blank expression, not sure how to answer, and this only serves to make her mad.

She grabs my hands, laces her fingers into mine, and squeezes.

"I can't wait." A meaning came through in her words, sharp as a razor. "It's what I want."

"But I can't."

"No. No. But you've always."

"I haven't," I said, turn—

—is there, standing at the front of the white room.

Jadier, the premier of Aeolia, wears a bodysuit made of glossy, black leather so tight she must have been melted down and poured into it. Slashes of bare skin appear in random sections along her chest and legs, but her arms are unadorned, her breasts bursting from its top.

In her right hand she holds a leash. In her left, a leather riding crop. Aphrodite lies prostrate before her, the beautiful woman nude but for the tight black collar around her neck. On her left, and on her right, Hermes and Ares do the same. They worship her, bowing, licking the filth from off her boots and seeming to enjoy every moment of it.

"Watch and don't look away," Demarcus says, his words hard, insistent. "Watch every moment. Love every sharp tick of pain."

Where had he come from?

How had we gotten here?

What the hell is going on?

"Shelly?" I whisper to Shelly. "What is—"

She shakes her head. "I have no idea."

We avert our eyes, afraid that this is not for us. Joanna comes up behind us and gently turns our faces back to the spectacle.

"Watch," she hisses, voice hypnotic like that of a snake. "Watch our premier take control of them. Watch her show them the purity of sensation."

I see Leo and Ada sitting on our left, their attention rapt. Ada absently passes Shelly a bottle.

Shelly drinks, then passes the bottle to me.

Sweet Bliss.

Sweet—

—which is why we take care of them like we do."

The premier leaned against her desk, the two of us in her well-appointed office. She crossed her arms and looked at me, head cocked to the side.

"Captain," she said. "Are you okay? You seem a little, well, out of it."

I shook my head, attempting to remove the cobwebs that had formed within it, turned around to take stock of where I was, then back to her. "Sure. Just haven't been sleeping too well."

Premier Takagi smiled at this. "My people tend to show newcomers a good time. It can be a challenge to keep up. I do hope they have been good hosts. If not, I will take care of that. I will punish them for you."

"They've been wonderful hosts," I replied, then plopped down in an overstuffed chair with thick arms before her desk. "Everyone has. This place . . . it is remarkable. I can see how coming here is like coming to heaven."

"Indeed. Now, back to the matter we were discussing. The assistance you wish Aeolia to give."

"We need help," I pleaded. "So much help."

"I see that. Have you determined how much help? Specifics."

"No. Not totally. I am not looking for a hard commitment of numbers either, I just need to know you would support this project. Earth deserves another chance."

"But does it?" She twisted the skull pendant hanging around her neck between her thumb and forefinger. "Does it really?"

"What happens if this place falls? Literally drops from the sky? What happens if the Clickers or the Splicers come in force?"

"Then we will defend ourselves. The Lattice left us the means. And we have the UEI, Admiral Cardoso and his fleets. We have Veetor and a Foundry-made ship like yours at our disposal to defend us."

"Veetor . . ." I grumbled. "Do you realize what kind of person he is, what he intends to do?"

"I rather like that rakish man," she said, rubbing her chin. "Reminds me of myself in so many ways. An outcast, misunderstood, troubled, having overcome so much. But your meaning is not lost. Veetor is unreliable at times. Perhaps you should make friends with him. Form an alliance. With your combined ships, nothing would stop you."

I blinked at her. "Form an alliance? Are you serious?"

"Yes, I'm serious."

"He stands for everything that we don't. We protect life. All life. Him . . . I have no idea what he stands for other than himself."

"And is that not what you said the Foundry states as its mission as well? Are you not under its influence?"

"I— Well—" But what was there to say. How could I argue? I had its machines inside my body, not just my prosthetics. "The people of Earth deserve to live. They did not create this situation."

Her eyes narrowed at me. "Some did."

The premier paced to the back of the office, heading to a locker hidden among the far wall. She placed her palm upon a panel—

—is how we ended up here.

Leo was instructing six young women to lie on the floor in a pool of paint, their bare bodies covered in spectrums of color. They rolled around in it, forming natural patterns, whorls of brilliance and sexual expression, the female form translated into brushstrokes of flesh.

"Here," Ada told Shelly, handing her a bottle. "Drink up."

And she did. And they did. And we did.

It was all so—

—I am on top of my wife, everyone in the room having paired off, finding someone to their liking to become intimate with. As she and I make love, we take turns downing swigs of Bliss from a clear bottle, not interrupting for a moment.

A few drops fall from my lips onto her bare chest, and we laugh at that, but I lick them away, leaving her tender flesh clean if moist.

Every sip of Bliss is better than the last, encouraging us to take more. It makes the sensations ever better, every motion, every thrust like lightning in our veins.

More.

More.

We are one flesh. We are one body.

More.

More.

It all feels so right, so—

—was suspended above us.

She was nude, with skin pale as milk, eyes slanted, hair lank and dark as the stygian void. Her body was tied in red cords, positioning her against a white background above the stage, the patterns of the rope forming a spider's web with a skull at its center. She appeared to be both in pain and yet full of pleasure, looking down upon our sea of primal need, of sexual release, with a kind of deference.

Shelly and I sat cross-legged on our bed, sheets draped around us, over stimulation leaving us dumbfounded. We held hands like two scared children dropped in the middle of a warzone. There was too much going on. Too much we did not understand.

At the edges of the empty stage, there were a man and a woman in plastic frames several dozen meters high. Tubes ran into their centers, where these people appeared to have been shrink-wrapped as if they were a consumer product. They twisted and writhed within the tight plastic, lips rubbing against the inside.

"Jadier will begin soon," Demarcus said, patting me on the leg. "You will en—

—she asks. "There seems to be no shame here. Is it okay to do this in front of others?"

I watch as the rest of them start. I'd never been one to watch anything pornographic, but I felt some strange fear of missing out.

In answer, I kissed Shelly, and she responded in kind. Taking off—

—I crawl across the floor, grasping for a bottle I cannot find. There is no Bliss in this room, and that fact in itself is unforgiving.

I'm tired of being afraid.

I'm tired of feeling broken.

I'm tired of being tired.

Everything that is built will be destroyed.

Nothing lasts.

Nothing continues forever.

I can't stop crying. I can't stop thinking about it all.

All the times I put my heart out there, loved and lost. I am not enough to protect those who counted on me.

"I'm so broken," I said, sniffling. "I'm so bro—

—into a back room.

"Do you like to collect, Milo?"

I followed her into a dark space behind her office. The lights were off, but I could tell there was a display case of some kind within, though I couldn't tell what it contained.

"I do," I replied. "When I was a kid, it was 3D-printed toys, little things. As an adult, mostly trinkets. Totems of a kind."

"I would like to show you my collection," the premier said, then clapped twice.

The case lit up, revealing shelves of human skulls lined in neat rows. They were each stark white, clean and pure, some large, some small, some with wide jaws, some narrow. None showed any signs of injuries. It was as if they had been removed after deaths by natural causes.

I swallowed, my heart stuck in my throat. What in the hell kind of macabre display was this?

"They sing to me," she said. "They sing to me the song of purity. For humanity to live on, we must let those die who deserved it. We must start over. Reset everything. But first, we must know heaven."

"I don't understand. Why?"

"You will in time," she assured me. "All of you will in time."

But I didn't think—

—is where we are going," Ares said.

"What?" I asked, shaking my head. "What did you guys say?"

Ada gave Shelly a high five. "A party, dude. Come on."

"Another party?" I mused, turning to look at Shelly. "Don't we need to like, cool it for a while? Get a nap or something?"

James laughed. "When's the last time we really let go?"

"Yesterday?" I asked, not sure if the question was directed at anyone, not sure if that was the right answer.

"But you all have to be cool," Aphrodite said, her palms raised. "This is like, a special kind of party. One without, well, *inhibitions*."

Leo rubbed his chin and flashed a devilish smile. "Sounds like a naughty kind of party to me. I'm trying to be a better man here, and you tempt me with this?"

"You can be a better man later," Ada told him, taking hold of his arm and hanging on for dear life. "We deserve a break from our lives. We deserve to let it all go."

"We've hurt enough," Karianna whispered, her voice rough and dry as sandpaper. "Hey, who has the Bliss?"

I handed her the bottle, and she drank deep, keeping her eyes fixed on me as she did. They twinkled in a way I hadn't expected, taking me off guard.

"Let's go," Shelly purred in my ear, one of her hands reaching up the back of my shirt, nails clawing at the ridges of my spine. "I need you. I want you."

"Maybe we shou—

—my body skidded across the tiles and my head struck the bathroom wall, stunning me where I lay, forcing my consciousness outside of my body for an instant.

Several seconds passed as I recollected myself.

A sharp pain pulsed through my shoulders, every muscle in my body screaming. For a second, I swore I received a signal.

Proxy?

But it was gone.

I stumbled to my feet, dusted off my clothes, and met Lance's eyes. "Why do you always have to grip the world so damn tight?"

Were we fighting?

He blinked back at me, half smiled, then shook his head. "Me, hold on to the world too tight? How dare you! That might have been me back on Creatus, but I have come so damn far as a person. I've learned to let things go, to let people who are better at what they do do the things they are better at. I have allowed weird ideas a bit of space in my head, because some of them actually make sense. Weird ideas like you.

"But let's talk about why? Okay? My dad was a hero. A goddamned American hero. So yeah, maybe I want to honor his memory. Maybe I want to be sure I live up to his example. And so maybe I hold tight to some shit. Maybe I'm a bit of a tight-ass and direct and brusque and hard. But you know what? I'm not whatever the hell this is you've become. Looks to me like you're a scared little kid running from their fears."

"Fuck you," I said, poking him in the chest. The pain in my shoulder, in my head, was getting worse. A constant pounding.

I needed more Bliss.

Everything would be better with more Bliss.

Lance took a step back, and to his credit, he didn't turn angry. "What's wrong with you, Milo?" he asked. "This isn't you. Whatever is happening to you, I don't like it. We came here to finish a mission. We came here to save Earth. We did not come to screw around, get fucked, and spend our days like these lost souls up here. They don't know what it's like to be human. They think they've transcended it somehow. That their fate is not our fate. But all they've done is insulate themselves from all sources of pain. To be human is to hurt. To be human is to know pain."

I shook my head. "Sometimes we all need to step away for a while."

"Yeah, well . . . you do you. I've got a world to save. And it looks like you've got a cesspool to puke in."

Ingrid burst into the bathroom, a panicked look on her face. "Oh God, you found him. You really found him."

"Sure did, and it's worse than we thought."

"Took long enough." She raised her right hand and made a gesture with her fingers. "I've got something that'll help."

Next thing I knew, I was back on the floor, Ingrid's mechanical dog having pinned me down again. I thrashed against its pressure but could not move.

"What are you doing to me!" I shouted. "Get it off me! Get it off me!"

"Give him this," Ingrid told Lance, passing him something. "Make sure he swallows it. Every gram."

Lance's face took on a dark expression. "My pleasure. Time to take your medicine, asshole."

I thrashed my head around, but Lance gripped my chin and shoved the pill past my clenched teeth. Whatever this powdery substance was within the capsule, it began to dissolve the instant saliva came in contact with it. The taste was bitter, astringent. I wanted to spit it out.

"We've got to go," Ingrid said, taking Lance by the shoulder.

"What about him?"

"It'll take time to work. Time we don't have."

The pressure on my chest released, the dog vanishing along with—

—tired of being afraid.

I was tired of feeling broken.

I was tired of being tired.

Everything that was built would be destroyed.

Nothing lasted.

Nothing would continue for—

—bodies everywhere, moans of unbridled pleasure, so much flesh slick with sweat.

It struck so hard, the raw, naked need, the desire.

The look in her eyes.

The look in her eyes.

What did she want from me? I knew what it was, but I could not give it. I wanted her to be happy. To be loved. To feel love. But my heart was—

—is that you?" Lance asked, meeting my eyes. "Oh, shit. It is you! Here, come on. Follow me. Come in. We need to talk."

I was led into a bathroom off the main gallery. A hand gripping my shoulder.

"Where the fuck have you been?"

I brushed him away and took a step back. "How dare you," I growled in response. "Get your hands—

—and that was about the time I told her she had fluffy hair," Leo said, and the table burst into laughter.

"Fluffy hair!" Richard bellowed. "Because—oh, God—"

I dabbed at the corner of my eyes, clearing away the kind of moisture that only came from a good joke.

"He's funny," Shelly said, patting me on the leg. "Never knew he could be so funny."

I nodded. "He's come a long way as a person."

"We all have."

On the opposite side of the table, Karianna was talking to James, both of them smiling. It was obvious that he was in love with her, if only she could see it. If only she could see this for what it really was.

She looked at me, and I found someplace else to focus my attention, buttering bread then reaching for a crab cake.

The premier raised a glass of wine, and everyone followed suit. "To new friends, and good laughter."

"Here, here!" we said in unison, then drank.

The servants returned with fresh plates, and this course smelled—

—where I found myself struck with a sudden terror. The man in the long coat was back. He was back. His arm was Foundry-made. But who could he be? Why was he here?

"Karianna," I said, turning to her, my heart thundering in my chest.

"What?"

"Is that?"

She leaned her head back and squinted. Then—

—of intense pleasure shoots through my body. Shelly is sitting astride my middle, drawing me deep inside of her. She rocks her hips atop mine, hands on my chest pinning me to the floor.

There is no shame in this place. No shame in release. Everyone has paired off. Everyone is making love with someone, somewhere. I keep my focus on Shelly but can see James and Joanna, Leo and Ada and a group of women. Demarcus and someone I do not recognize. Premier Takagi and her cohort.

And then there is Karianna. Richard is behind her, hands on her hips, body to body. She clasps their sheets tight, balling them up into her fists as he dominates her from behind. Her hair clings to her sweaty forehead and cheeks and neck in clumps. Her eyes are closed, allowing for the oblivion of pure pleasure.

I can see her whispering something under her breath, over and over, but cannot tell what the words are.

"To me," Shelly urges, and I turn my attention back. "To me."

I blink at her. Am I lost in the moment? Every thought is so hard to hold on to. Everything around us so nebulous and ephemeral. None of it feels real, and yet, it feels more real than reality.

Shelly's face shifts. One moment it is hers, then it is replaced with Karianna's. The cold of a mechanical hand rests on my chest, her movements urgent, desperate. She licks her lips and kisses me, redoubling her actions.

"I've wanted this," she whispers in my ear. "I wanted this for so long. I've always wanted this . . ."

I feel a shiver go through my body, starting at my core, traveling up through my belly and into my head.

The hands on my chest feel warm. Shelly is looking at me, her eyes expectant.

"I love you, Milo," she says, then Karianna says, then she says, then Karianna.

Shelly gazes into me, through me. Her body is shaking as it reaches a crescendo, sensation too powerful for her to contain any longer. She tightens around me, lets out a shout . . .

She cries.

Her stomach trembles as she lets it go, tense and contracting as if something alien is trying to escape. Her hands cover her face as if she's embarrassed.

"I just—I can't—" she says between sobs.

"Shhh. Shhh. Shelly, I—

Why—

I am in a room. Jadier is talking to the skulls, asking them to speak, fingers twisting the tiny one around her neck.

Shelly was looking me in the face. Speaking. Telling me something, but I could not understand. The room was white. My thoughts, dark.

Milo sits atop the Neonteichos spire. Clouds of orange and yellow all around. His body is not safely within an environmental suit. He wears nothing but a jumpsuit, a FICSE patch on its left chest. He . . . I mean . . . I . . . It's me. Can I breathe?

No. No.
I can't do this anymore.
It's too much.
Too much.
Too much.
Help me, Universe.
Help me.
Save me.
I'm tired of hurting.
So very tired.

I clutch my stomach tight and sob, one cheek against the cold, hard tiles of the bathroom floor. My bones ache, shoulder stiff, knees fixed in a kind of rigor mortis. Each breath comes ragged and quick, staccato pulses of inhalation. My vision is blurry and I can't see. My chest is tight, pain constricting the muscles, making the bones feel as if they might snap. Too many sensations are crashing upon me at once, an overwhelming wave of static and noise. I just want to be in a soft room. I just want to be held by someone I love and told that everything is going to be okay.

Instead, the world is hard, full of angles, cold and sharp.

It is . . .

My head tingled. My implants came to life. A signal struck the fragile glass of my mind, leaving a crack along its center.

"Milo?" a voice asked. *"Do you read? Milo, are you there?"*

"Proxy?" I replied, rolling onto my hands and knees, joints crackling, my clearing thoughts slippery with tar. The sudden motion turned my stomach, and I tossed its contents onto the floor.

There was so much vomit. It smelled so bad.

"Where have you been?" I asked after several moments, finally catching my breath. *"Proxy, where have you been?"*

"Milo! It's you." My companion's voice turned excited. *"You've got to wake up. You've got to come to."*

"Why . . . what's wrong?"

"Everything, Milo. Everything."

CHAPTER 40

I splashed my face with cold water, then toweled off, doing my best to remove the acrid stench of vomit from my lips before brushing off my dirty shirt. Everything in the world was turning sideways, blurry and unfocused, but not in the fun way it had been recently. Reality, real reality, was crashing down upon me with all the force of a Foundry facility falling from orbit.

"They've found the others," Proxy reported over my ship-to-implants channel. *"We're working to get them out. Get them to safety."*

"What happened?"

"I'll let Lance explain."

"Okay." I took a step, shook my head, then opened the bathroom door, taking a peek up and down the hall. It was empty. "How is the ship? How are we looking?"

"It is safe for now. The Free Citizens passengers are ready to leave; Frelo is secure. But I have detected a dozen or more signatures inbound for Venus. I cannot identify them yet, with all the background noise in SOL, and our relative position, but I suspect they are not human-made."

"Fun. We've got party crashers then. How long?"

"At their current velocity, they will be here within five to three hours." Proxy paused for a moment, then shifted its tone slightly. *"How are you, Milo?"*

"How am I?"

"Are you feeling better? More yourself?"

"I—I—" I began, but faltered, heart racing, "I—don't know."

"Your vital signs are erratic. Blood pressure far above normal. Heart rate is elevated. Liver proteins are exceeding safe levels. Blood sugar is dangerously high. I am redirecting some of your nanomachines within the universal inoculant to address these symptoms."

An instant later, I felt my heartbeat slow. I found it easier to breathe. The nausea twisting my stomach lessened.

"Thanks, Proxy," I replied. "You're a great friend."

"I protect the pilot," it told me. *"And you, Milo, you will always be my pilot."*

I found myself smiling at this. A profound, quiet smile. Proxy would always be there, all the way to the end.

Retreating back into the safety of the bathroom, I sat hard on the floor, forehead against my knees. A pounding headache had replaced the dizziness. My mouth was dry.

"What next?" I mumbled under my breath. I had no idea where to go, what to do, my thoughts soft like mashed potatoes. I was in no condition for a confrontation and had no idea how long it would be before I was. Even with Proxy's help, this was the worst hangover I'd ever experienced.

I started replaying recent events back. None were clear or set in any sort of order. Everything was a jumble, a collection of random words and images shaken up and tossed out before me. We had been drunk, very drunk, or high, or something. There had been parties, sure. There had been laughter and conversation. But what else had there been? I had a nagging sense that I'd done something wrong. Crossed some line I shouldn't have crossed, one I couldn't go back from.

A ping hit my implants, a message request from Lance. I opened the voice channel.

"It worked?" he asked. *"I just heard from Proxy. It worked."*

"It worked alright," I replied. "Though I feel like my brain is being drilled with a rusty bit."

"Hangover's a bitch."

"Yeah, clearly."

"Just so you know," Lance went on, *"we know where everyone else is. Hang tight for a few. Get your head clear. Let the inhibitors do their job."*

My heart skipped a beat. "Are the others safe?"

"Far as we can tell. Safe as you were. Likely high as shit, but not in any mortal danger."

"I—I just— What the hell . . . How did I get here?"

"That's a long story."

"Last thing I remember clearly was eating dinner with the Premier, then, everything became a blur." I rubbed my face and felt a sudden need to cry, but I held it back—for now. "Did you beat me up?"

Lance let out a laugh. *"No. Sometimes I wish I had. You came at me, and I pushed your ass down. You yanked on my beard, and it hurt like shit. That was the end of it."*

"Was it in a bathroom?" I took a survey on my surroundings, snippets of memory coming back. A floor. Tears. Pain. "This bathroom?"

"No. Not there. That little confrontation was days ago, on platform six."

"I don't—"

"Do you even want to know what was in that crap you were drinking?" Lance asked, his tone turning dead serious.

I clambered back up onto my feet, holding on to a bathroom stall handle to steady myself. "The way you ask me makes me feel like I don't, but that I should."

"It's Lattice, Milo. Lattice. You've been guzzling down a beverage made with flakes of Lattice, little shavings of the closest thing there is to their alien flesh. And it's powerful, really screws with human physiology."

"I'm sorry. What the hell did you just say?"

"You've been drinking alien skin cells."

I leaned against the wall and nearly tossed what little was left in my stomach up. We had known something hadn't been right, but this? It had been far too easy to slip into oblivion. Far too easy to . . .

My chest felt raw as suppressed emotions began to swell up from my stomach and creep into my heart. The pain hadn't gone away; Bliss had just smoothed the edges till they were perfectly round and harmless. But those edges were what made me realize those people, those events, were significant. If I didn't feel pain, why did it matter? Pain meant it was real. And I was real. We were all real.

But right now, in this moment, pain or not, I was pissed. Really fucking pissed.

"Why—" A sharp pain shot through my head, but I willed it away. "Why didn't you tell us to look out for it?"

"We didn't know to warn you," Ingrid cut in, her voice noisy as if it came from a handheld radio. *"As I said before, we've not had much contact with Aeolia. We've learned a lot over the past few weeks."*

"Why would they do this to us?"

"Now that? We don't really know, other than for control. In talking to those who got out of their group who have been hiding in the outer platforms, they say that Bliss washes

away your memories over time, makes you a bit of a blank slate. That's why so many don't have names. It's not that they don't have them, it's that they can't remember them."

"Hang on," I replied, rubbing at my temples with my forefingers. "You just said a couple weeks ago. What are you talking about. How long have we been here?"

"Six weeks," she stated.

'No. No. That's not possible. Can't be more than a few days at the most."

"Sorry, man," Lance said, *"it's been weeks. They had you and the rest of the crew so far out of your heads you were like trailing balloons of consciousness looking down at meat sacks. And they kept moving you around the spires and platforms to make it hard to locate you."*

"What about Xuan and Hy? Where are they?"

"Meeting with someone to retrieve the resonators, at least we hope. These machines are of Lattice-make, sure, but we won't be eating them. Should be safe enough."

"We just need to handle them with care," Ingrid added.

"I've got to get to Shelly," I said, leaving the bathroom and storming off down the hall, heading for the core of the spire. "We're getting out of here." I weaved my way through groups of Aeolians, all dressed in white, joyful and blank expressions on their faces. Everyone here was subject to this manipulation. How had I not seen this before? They were all void. Drowning in Bliss. Forgetting who they were.

Sentinels stood watch at crossed hallways, their eyes of red crystal shining in the lights of the station, heat radiating from their solid-state facsimiles of armor. I could not shake the feeling that they were watching me.

"We have a plan," Ingrid said. *"Just hang in. Stay quiet. Trust us, we'll get everyone out. Far as we are aware the powers that be don't know you've started sobering up."*

"Yeah well. They've got another thing coming for them. The clearer my head gets, the angrier I am. She's going to get a piece of my mind."

"Wait for us, Milo," Lance urged. *"Please."*

"I have to believe they can't be all bad," I replied, skipping down the main corridor to the busy elevator banks. "Maybe they've been under the influence so long they just don't know. Hell, this could be Lattice manipulation, not just human stupidity. Maybe I can talk some sense into her."

"I don't think that's a good idea, man," Lance pleaded. *"Just wait on us."*

But that wasn't going to happen. I had to find my wife. I had to put this to bed. What we'd been subjected to was morally reprehensible. And in this moment, it seemed right to be a little more like Karianna. To do what felt right, not what was prudent.

"Keep to your plan," I told them. "I've got to do this. You get them out. I'll keep her busy."

"Shit, dude," Lance growled, then went silent for a moment.

I stepped into the elevator and selected the premier's floor, grateful to be alone, no one else riding up with me. I caught my reflection on the silver walls of the cab and I was a wreck, hair a messy tangle, eyes dark as pitch, clothes covered in stains down the front. I didn't care.

"Fine," Lance finally spoke up. *"You be a distraction. We'll get them out. They're on the Neonteichos spire, floor seven, so extraction should be easier. Should . . . Don't get killed, asshole."*

I popped my fingers and my neck, then hardened my face. "Didn't plan on it."

The world was starting to come back into focus. Whatever Proxy was doing with the nanomachines made me feel like a million bucks, thoughts sharp, steps steady.

I approached the premier's secretary, a buxom woman with long hair and doughy eyes, dressed in all white with a body suit as scantily as the rest.

"Ahh yes," she said, recognizing me. "Captain Hughes. May we help you?"

"I need to see the premier," I demanded, doing my best to sound even tempered. It wasn't easy.

"She is occupied at the moment," her secretary said. "But I believe she has an opening in one hour. Would you like to meet with her then? I can offer you a place to wait. We have Bliss, if you are interested."

The mention of the word made my mouth water. My hands trembled, but I forced them still at my side, fingers tightening around the fabric of my pants.

"I need to see her immediately," I pressed. "This is important. Life and death."

"I see," the secretary said, nodding, then turned and pressed a button on her desk. We waited for several seconds in silence, then the doors to the premier's office opened. "You may go inside."

"Thank you," I said through gritted teeth.

I entered the premier's well-appointed office. The doors swished closed behind me before making a sharp click as magnetic locks engaged.

"Mr. Hughes," the premier said, her back to me, facing out the interior windows at the far end of the office, which peered down onto the halls of the station. "Is everything okay?" She spun around, hands folded at her center, her chest covered by not much more than a horizontal strip of white cloth.

I took a deep breath and smiled. "Of course everything's okay. Nothing strange is going on here. How are you today?"

Her expression turned sour. "You barge into my office, unannounced, and want to act like everything is fine. Want to engage in some small talk. Do not insult my intelligence or your own. What is the matter?"

"I know what you've been doing to us," I started. "The Bliss."

"Wonderful substance, is it not?"

"It sure likes to make you think it is. One thing I just now put together is that everyone around you loves it, but *you* never drink it. Thinking back to the dinner, we took a toast, but I didn't see you raise your glass."

"And?" She pursed her lips. "A leader must remain clear headed."

"Exactly. And the rest must remain under your control. Malleable. Aphrodite. Ares. Hermes. They've been washed clean of what makes them individuals. I know what's in Bliss. I know what it is."

Premier Takagi waved a hand in a dismissive gesture, rolling her eyes. "You have no idea what it is. You only think you know."

"You've been drugging us." I pointed a finger at her. "You've been keeping us so high and so distracted we couldn't pursue what we came here for."

"You willingly drank it," she stated as if speaking to a child. "No one held you down or forced you to consume it."

And while this was true, in part, it did not justify her actions.

"There's an old saying," I began. "A man takes a drink. A drink takes a drink . . ."

"And the drink takes the man," she finished. "I know the saying."

"Well, this is worse. Way worse. We chose to drink it, whatever, but you didn't disclose what it was. You didn't tell us what it would do. I'm afraid to know what all happened that I can't remember, might never remember. Tell me where my wife and crewmates are. We're leaving."

She pressed a fist to her lips. "I thought we were parlaying over assistance to help restore Earth to its former glory."

"We're leaving," I told her. "We'll find our help elsewhere."

The premier stood still, considering, then sighed. "Of course, and that is your choice. Captain Hughes, I can see that we have been poor hosts. You are right—we did not disclose everything to your people, and for that, I am sorry.

"Here. Follow me. I will take you to your wife and the rest of your crew. Besides, your cocaptain has been asking for you all day. What a beautiful girl. What longing in her eyes." She turned to her left, and a door I hadn't seen before opened out of the smooth wall. "This way."

I reluctantly followed the premier through the door. It led us into a dark hallway not like the rest of the station. It curved around, went down into a series of steps, then opened up into a circular chamber a dozen strides across with a ceiling not much taller than my head.

"Mr. Hughes," she said, turning to face me.

I took a step back from her in the cramped space and felt my hip come in contact with the edge of a guardrail surrounding a deep pit in the center of the room.

"Yeah?" I asked, my question a bit choked. "What?"

"You've seen heaven," she began, then pointed at me, her words like honey consumed by fire. "Now—now, it's time for you to know hell."

She clapped twice.

My heart froze.

Out of the shadows of the subchamber, a pair of white-clad guards rushed me, batons in their upraised hands. I had no time to react.

They struck me across the face, across the chest. I raised my arms to defend myself and tried to put distance between me and their weapons, but there was no space to retreat.

My balance faltered, backside pinned against the railing that surrounded the pit.

The premier stepped forward; her position hemmed by guards. "Bye-bye," she whispered, then shoved as hard as she could.

I tumbled over the edge of the railing, headfirst, feet in the air, the world around me gone topsy-turvy.

Everything became a blur.

I fell through the spire's core like a stone, walls of machinery rushing past, then away from Aeolia into amber clouds, the platforms of the city receding before me, their shapes, once filling the entirety of my view, now becoming tiny as if someone had zoomed everything out.

I was falling from heaven through a shaft of wind and light and heat, my body accelerating, its mass seeking terminal velocity.

Down and down and down.

I had no means to arrest my fall. No way to slow myself.

I was not dead, not yet, though I was screaming as if I soon would be.

I was consumed by clouds, taken into darkness, the atmosphere of Venus oppressing me, compressing my soul with a pressure no human had evolved to withstand.

I fell.

And I fell.

And I fell.

Down.

Down.

Down.

A dozen kilometers.

Two dozen.

A hundred.

I fell until all light fled from my vision, darkness crowding in at the edges of perception like the shuttering iris of a great eye.

The void enveloped me.

But as for death?

No.

Death did not come.

CHAPTER 41

Silence. Darkness. Fire.

My eyes were squeezed shut so hard it made my head throb, but thoughts rushed back through the pain. I heard no wind. I felt no intense heat. I was not being crushed alive, squeezed down into a human pancake. I wasn't dead. But how? How was I not dead?

I surveyed my surroundings, though I was unable to see a thing. I felt around in the black, crawled on hands and knees, finding that there was floor beneath me. And no. Not just floor, but a rocky kind of dirt, gritty and acrid.

I stood up, attempting to find balance in the dark, then probed around my position with my toes, looking for an edge, a cliff.

A thousand spotlights flashed to life, their attention pointing down upon me from metallic trusses dozens of meters above my head. I raised my prosthetic arm to shield my eyes, squinting against their brilliance as if sunlight were burning into them. Wherever this was that I'd been dropped was massive, a circular room with rough floors, pillars of stone thick as land cars and three times tall as me placed randomly around it, with rows of stands filled with hundreds of people dressed in white beyond.

My heart sank. Yes, I was grateful not to be dead, but I was coming to realize my situation. I'd been thrown from a spire above the atmosphere of Venus, miraculously not dying from a fall that should have reduced me to a pulpy red smear, only to land in what appeared to be an arena.

"Games! Games!" the crowd began to shout. "Games! Games!" Their words thunderous as a gathering storm.

"Shit," I mumbled under my breath. I'd gone from heaven, a place high above the clouds where I was being entertained, and been thrown into the pit of hell to become the entertainment. The meaning of Premier Takagi's words was now clear as crystal.

But why wasn't I dead? I had fallen, and fallen a long, long way. More Lattice work? Some kind of inertial elevator? Didn't matter.

"Proxy?" I called out, but I got nothing in reply. Something was blocking my signal. I had to find a way out.

A screen above a private box in the stands came to life, and the crowd went quiet. A dancing bald man in a bright, long coat with tassels and fringe appeared, his moves exaggerated, kicking and punching at the air as if shadowboxing gas particles. There was no music for the beat he kept, just a quieting rhythm of revelers shouting in time.

"Let us greet our guest!" he declared over the loudspeakers, voice booming, every word delivered with all the flourish and drama of a classically trained actor. "We have a very special guest with us today, my friends. This man comes from a different time. A time when humans were the dominant species on Earth. A time when economic advancement was more important than human kindness. He comes from a time in which people believed in fairy tales and wild dreams that alien species would come and rescue us from ourselves. He comes from FICSE. *The* FICSE."

The crowd roared at the mention of the mission, though it was impossible to tell if this was with excitement or anger.

"Foundry Intent!" the man shouted. "Contact and Save Earth!"

The crowd booed.

"Yes, yes. Lies. All of it lies! We know. We know. FICSE let us down. FICSE was a false hope. A false prophet. A story . . ."

"False! False! False!" they shouted.

"But do not hold that against this man. No, no. He was not at fault. He was but a child at the time of their departure. Just a baby. Five years old, with mad parents and a mad captain set to throw his life into chaos. They are the perpetrators, not him. He is a victim. But we all know that does not absolve him from the end. Someone must pay."

He raised his right arm, and the sleeve of his coat fell back, revealing a limb of glittering ivory and golden metal. A prosthetic just like mine.

My mouth went dry. I knew who this was.

It was Veetor. Veetor Nambrali.

"Let us welcome our guest to the games," he said, then shouted, arms raised to hype up the crowd. "Behold, Milo Hughes! Milo Hughes of the *Vasco Da Gama*!"

"Fighter! Fighter! Fighter!" the crowd cheered.

I kept my expression blank. This was a bad situation, but I saw no one coming to rescue me. Shelly would, if she had the means, and Karianna too, but so far as I knew, they were both still wacked out of their heads. I wondered if Lance and Ingrid knew what had happened to me, or if I had just fallen off the implant channel. Then there was Proxy. Even if it knew I was in trouble, if I was truly below the atmosphere of Venus, then that meant that beyond the high dome of this arena, there were over a hundred atmospheres of pressure above us. Breaking through with a Swift Shuttle to fly me out would almost certainly kill us all in the process.

No. This was one of those times I was well and truly alone.

As the crowd cheered for me to fight, I looked for the exits. There were doors at the edges of the arena, four in all, and curving along the dome there appeared to be a shaft of some kind. The crowd had to have gotten down here somehow. I only needed to get out of the arena and into the stands, and with a set of thirty-foot walls made of smooth metal hemming me in, that wouldn't be easy.

Veetor let them cheer for a moment, then gestured for them to calm. "Quiet now. Quiet, my friends. Let us first speak with him."

From out of the high ceiling above me, an impossibly long cable lowered, a head-sized ribbon microphone reminiscent of the 1950s dangling on its end.

It came to a stop before me.

"Speak," Veetor said over the loudspeakers.

I took hold of the mic, summoning a bit of feedback as I gripped it with my prosthetic. "You were here all along," I said, my voice booming. "I thought you'd be taller."

"Yes," he replied, the word hoarse. "And I thought you . . . shorter." The crowd chuckled. "Hard to tell over coms, am I right?"

"At least you're just as ugly," I growled into the mic.

"Yes, well . . . " He sucked on his teeth for a moment before moving on. "We followed you to Aeolia. Lost you for a time around Earth—not sure how you slipped our notice. But I was curious what you would do here. I wanted to see how it all played out. Milo, you are a crafty opponent.

You have such grand weapons at your disposal. The Foundry has given you so many gifts, many, many, many gifts. And toys too. And fun times. And yet you squander them. Treat them like trinkets. You fight for a squalid people and a lost dream. You fight to save the evil from obliteration. Just let them die. Let them all die . . ."

My prosthetic hand tightened around the microphone, nearly denting the metal. "Let them die?"

"Can't you see that it's time? Time for the Great Reset. Let those who cannot survive go into the dark and let us who the universe has deemed worthy remain. Let us build back from the ashes. Let us be like a phoenix."

I pointed a finger at him. "You mean be like you?"

He straightened his back and dusted off the lapels on his fancy coat. "Yes. I am a phoenix. I am reborn."

"Reborn into madness," I replied, and this made the crowd boo.

"Madness?" Veetor grumbled. "Perspective. Did they not believe Galileo to be mad? What about William B. Coley? Nikola Tesla? Brandish Novichok? These were great minds who saw beyond the horizon of understanding."

"Might as well call yourself Carl Sagan while you're at it." My words came out venomous.

"What a great idea!" He waved to the gathered Aeolians.

The crowd began to chant, "Carl! Carl! Carl!"

That was not what I had hoped to inspire.

"You speak of FICSE like this makes you filth," I began. "But you are one of us. You were aboard the *Brilliance*. You are also FICSE."

"And yet!" he shouted. "I tried to actually fix things. I tried to take control, receive the gift of the Foundry, come back and do some good."

"You murdered your crewmates, people you had known for years. You are a mutineer."

"They deserved to die for betraying the mission."

I knew what had happened, Karianna had told me, but something didn't add up. We were missing a piece of information. A set of events.

"How did you get your ship?" I pressed. "Karianna took the gift. Made the donation. Where did the *Absolution* come from?"

He clicked his tongue at me. "I can't reveal all my secrets. Too many curious ears are here. Too many."

"Don't listen to him!" I shouted, turning my attention to the audience to make an appeal. "He is a madman. A killer. He would just as soon end all your lives if it meant getting whatever twisted fantasy he's after."

They began to cheer, "Killer! Killer! Killer!" But their tone did not appear to be in condemnation of Veetor.

I focused on them for a moment, amazed that so many could be manipulated. I spotted a few familiar faces among the stands. Demarcus, Joanna, Bridgett, and Richard leaned on one another, bottles in hand, each clearly intoxicated. They hadn't really been our friends, had they?

Bastards.

"So, here's how this is going to go," he began, and again the onlookers quieted, though a frantic, bloodthirsty energy was now in the air. "The people who are to be released into this area, let's just say they've been highly incentivized to ensure your life is ended. The winners of this game, those still standing at the end who haven't killed one another, will be given the beautiful opportunity to be encased in Lattice for all of eternity. You didn't think those statues in the gallery were just decorations, did you?"

"They're people," I said, as my strange impressions clicked into place. Of course they were. And they'd been watching us the whole time.

"Oh yes! They are. They are defenders of this station, eternal warriors on a righteous mission. You see, poor simple Milo, it takes a living mind to power the Sentinels. The Lattice needs these minds to survive. But to make someone want to remain in one place, standing vigil for all eternity except when called upon to defend your patron, well, that's a hard sell. In order not to have the mind destroy itself, and the sentinel go inert, the mind needs to be . . ."

My mouth went dry. I whispered, "They would need to be placed in a state of perfect bliss."

Veetor raised his hands above his head and smiled, the tassels of his coat hanging down. "You are clever, if foolish, Mr. Hughes. So clever. Damn, what a shame to have you killed. You fight to live for only a time, and yet, they fight to live forever. And the rest of us, well, we are entertained. Can't you see? It's a win, win, win."

The crowd began to cheer in rhythm, then gave two stomps and a clap. I swallowed my rising heart.

"Love!" Stomp. Stomp. Clap.

"Live!" Stomp. Stomp. Clap.

"Pray!" Stomp. Stomp. Clap.

"Burn!" Stomp. Stomp. Clap.

"Fall!" Stomp. Stomp. Clap.

"Ash!" Stomp. Stomp. Clap.

"Anger!" Stomp. Stomp. Clap.

"Atonement!" Stomp. Stomp. Clap.

Silence.

"End," Veetor whispered over the intercom.

The steel gates at the edges of the arena yawned open. I had no idea who or what would come rushing out. This gave me flashbacks to a movie Esteban and I had watched back on Cynosure about a man trapped in a gladiatorial arena in ancient Rome, forced to fight to the death under the ire of a mad emperor. But unlike the former Roman general, they had given me no weapons. My situation was a blatant and elaborate execution, not a fair fight.

I spun around, looking at the openings, waiting for animals, machines, angry people to rush forth and try to kill me, and then a thought cropped up in my racing mind. Maybe I wasn't totally defenseless. Maybe Shelly's preparation had given me something good to work with. My right pocket was a little thicker than normal, as if something fun and useful might be there. I didn't dare reach for it, though, not in this moment.

I raised a finger once more and pointed at Veetor. "You better run, Justin. I'm coming for you."

The mention of his real name made the man shake with rage. "My, my, my," he said, voice low and crackling like a smoldering fire. "Big words coming from a dead man. Toodaloo, Captain. Do be careful not to stain the dirt."

A siren like that of an ancient air raid warning began, starting low and winding up. Shadows appeared in the open doorways, twenty people in all, five from each opening, combatants dressed in tattered clothes of filthy whites. They wore armbands, colors matching depending on what side of the arena they emerged from. Were they on teams?

Unlike me, each of them carried a weapon of some kind. No pistols or rifles, but rather swords, knives, spears, barbed nets, anything that could dismember, maim, rip, or pierce flesh and bone with little effort. Many of the instruments looked rusty and old, making the promise of pain that much more possible.

I hated the fact that even under these circumstances, my conscience screamed at me that these people were victims. That they had been manipulated into this fight and that killing them would be an abject tragedy, not a victory, but I saw no way out of this situation without shedding a little blood.

The teams converged on my position: Red, Yellow, Green, and Blue. They rushed the center of the arena, screaming at the tops of their lungs, waving their hands in the air. I watched them approach and found a modicum of comfort in the fact that none of them seemed to know what they were doing with their weapons. Still, desperate idiots were no less dangerous.

Massive microphone dangling before me, I leapt into the air with the strength of my mechanical leg, one fist skyward, the other clutching a tube filled with quicksilver fluid. The prosthetic fingers of my right hand closed, crushing the vial of glass, and from its mercurial ooze a silver blade formed from my hand, its edge sharp as monofilament fiber. At the apex of my jump, I swung the newly formed nanoblade, clipping the cable that held the microphone, and took hold of it with my free hand.

When I landed back on the ground in a crouch, a blade capable of sheering through fungara in one hand, a cable with a ten-pound steel microphone at its end in the other, I was ready.

Veetor did not like this change in events. He began shouting obscenities over the loudspeaker, and the crowd booed. I gave them a wolfish smile in response. I would have thought this would be entertainment for them.

The four teams rushed at me, two at a time, and I spun around in circles, using the microphone like a flail. The microphone came up at an angle, traveling at several dozen miles per hour, slamming into the chest of a soft-skinned man with long hair. He went flying onto his back, a spray of saliva and blood shooting from his mouth. I wound back up and chose another target, catching a thick man with dark skin in the jaw. There was an audible crack as it ploughed into his face, snapping every bone and ripping at his tender flesh.

Who would have thought a microphone could be so dangerous?

Two approached me from my right flank and I spun, lashing out with the blade. I left a deep gash along the arm of one, crimson blossoming through their clothes, then commanded the blade to reform its edge into a blunt wedge.

As they crashed into me, I slammed them into one another, doing all I could to mix up those who had different armbands. This seemed to work. They broke out into smaller fights, splitting their attention from me, and the next thing I knew, I was in the middle of a roiling melee.

I danced around awkward swings from their swords, falling axes, flailing balls of spikes. The crowd began cheering once more, excited to see me in a tough spot, my back against the proverbial wall, enemies all around. One by one, I beat my attackers down with the blunt weapon, but I found myself holding back, not putting the full strength of my prosthetic into the blows. I didn't want to kill anyone.

I attempted to get my microphone flail moving again, to hold them back, but there wasn't enough room to build up speed, so I let it drop to the ground.

They kept coming, and I was severely outnumbered. A few lay on the ground, dead or incapacitated, but it wasn't enough. The blunt weapon wasn't cutting it, literally.

I switched tactics, transitioning the nanoweapon back into a blade. I would do what I could not to kill, but I couldn't fall standing on morals. Too much was at stake. I focused my attention on breaking the weapons that came at me, cutting the hafts in two, turning swords into piles of scrap steel. With my prosthetic augmentation, I was far quicker than they were, my hand seeming to know where it needed to move like the soul of a master swordsman inhabited it.

A man with a green armband rushed at me with a spear, unbridled rage painted across his soft, baby face. I stepped to the side, extending my blade before me. I had intended to cut the midranged weapon in half, but I suppose my blows were not as precise as I had thought moments earlier. When my nanoblade came down, it sliced clean through his shoulder, the gouge becoming shallower as I drew near to his heart.

He collapsed to the dirt, blood pooling at my feet.

"Killer! Killer! Killer!" the crowd cheered. Veetor began to dance, punching and kicking at the air.

I didn't like that title. Didn't want that title. I was not—

Two more came at me, one green, one red, and I flashed my blade at them, removing one of their arms, then slicing into the thigh of another. It was too easy with a weapon so sharp. Flesh peeled back like deli meat.

More blood. More bodies.

A moment passed, and the remaining combatants gave me a wide birth, pausing in their melee. An empty circle had formed around my position, and I spun around, weapon before me, waiting to see who was confident enough to come at me next.

"Get that blade from him," a spry, spindly man growled. "We'll fight to the team when he's down."

No disagreement came from the rest of them. They had ceased their free-for-all and were focusing their attention only on me. I shot through the thinnest concentration of the closing circle, cutting down anyone in my path. Bodies left in my wake. They took off after me.

Spears landed in the ground beside me. I ducked and dodged these weapons as best I could, avoiding thrown axes or daggers. Something hot and sharp grazed the back of my right leg, and I tumbled to the ground, dust kicking up into my face.

"Shit," I coughed, dropping the nanoblade and taking hold of the sticky, gaping wound on the back of my leg. My body trembled with shock, nausea rising up from my twisting stomach.

The enemy closed in. I backed up against a stone pillar, not sure what my next move was. I reached for the blade once more, extending it before me, then tried to use the crumbling edifice for balance to stand.

"Stay back!" I shouted, and for a second, the fighters paused.

"This is the moment that you die," Veetor said, laughing. "It's been fun. It really has. But there are better things to do with . . . *my time*."

I prepared to make my last stand, fighting my way through the pain, face twisted, teeth grinding.

"Come on, assholes," I growled. "I'm not dying today."

Out of nowhere, the loudspeakers of the arena let out a scream. I nearly dropped my weapon at the sheer intensity of the noise, covering my ears with my palms out of reflex, just as the many of the approaching combatants did. First came an ear-piercing screech of feedback, then a booming voice reminiscent of gods.

"Call me your Lord, call me the emperor, call me the essence of all creation!" it boomed, voice deep and resonant. *"Call me whatever you like. I am God, and you have displeased me! You have shown you do not care for others! That you do not care for life! And for this transgression, this greatest of sins, you will be punished."*

My thoughts clarified, and I found a smile forming on my face. I knew what was happening.

The crowd, as well as the remaining combatants, began to scatter. Terror was the only thought they had, however irrational. I looked for Veetor among the stands, but he was gone. The coward had fled as well.

"Bow before the power of the great and mighty Universe," Proxy went on. *"Bow before my might! All who seek to end life will be punished, will be wiped from existence!"*

Even with liters of Bliss pumping through their systems, this experience did not seem to be any fun. I did not envy them. What combatants were left seemed confused, not sure if the fight should go on. Everything had descended into chaos. The games were over.

Somehow, some way, Proxy had hacked into their system and taken control of the speakers. I could have squeezed the hell out of that cat in thanks.

I felt for the back of my leg and saw that the bleeding had stopped. I hobbled to the edge of the arena, escaping in the confusion.

"Thanks for the distraction," I pinged up to Proxy.

"I protect the pilot," it replied.

"You sure as hell do."

Upon reaching the wall, I began to climb, having broken my nanoblade down into a pair of hooks. My legs were shaky, my hands unsteady. I reached the grandstands and let out a sigh.

"Get to the elevator," Proxy instructed. *"Twelve feet to your left and up. Your friends are waiting for you."*

I staggered my way through the confused patrons, making eye contact with Demarcus as I approached the elevators. He cowered behind a set of benches along with Joanna, Bridgett, and Richard.

"You better be glad I don't have the time," I told them, my nanoblade raised in a threat, before stepping into the lift.

As the doors closed, a fresh klaxon sounded. This alarm was not the result of my escape. This was a standard, UEI-style station-wide alert, not one from the arena.

"What now?" I asked Proxy. "Does it always have to get worse?"

"Contact," it replied. *"Our common enemy has arrived."*

CHAPTER 42

The noise of the alarms only grew louder as I returned to the high altitude of the spire. I had no idea how this strange elevator worked, raising me from the surface of Venus back above its clouds, but it was swift, taking my stomach as it shot upward. I was back in the main core in less than a couple of minutes, my mind clear, hands caked with dirt and dried blood, a slight limp in my step.

The elevator doors dinged open, revealing the spire's halls, which were now in pandemonium. People were screaming everywhere, hurrying about to flee any open areas and take cover. Armed guards in white body armor rushed around the station taking position, their ranks bolstered by humanoid shapes made of a crimson-colored crystal.

"Sentinels," I growled, then took off at a sprint, hoping not to be spotted, heading to the landing platforms where our Swift Shuttles should still be. I had no idea what the capabilities of these Lattice creations were, but if they were scary enough to defend against Isoptera or Kabosai, they would likely make quick work of me in my current state. I had no weapons, save the nano blade, no armor, nothing but a torn pair of fancy shoes and the clothes on my back.

"Lance? Proxy? Ingrid?" I called out over my implants. "Anyone?"

"We're here," Lance replied.

"How's the team?"

"We've got them, as well as a few new friends. We'll explain later. Karianna is the only one starting to get a clear head. She's almost ready to fly. Where'd you go? We lost our fix after you went to confront the Premier."

"I'll tell you everything later. Let's just say . . . it might have involved an arena and a fight to the death."

"That doesn't sound good at all."

"No part of it was good."

A moment passed and Lance was silent. I reached a split in the halls, surveying the space around me.

"You know what these red soldiers are, don't you?" he asked.

I leaned around the corner, seeing one of the Sentinels standing watch a dozen feet away. Its crimson body gleamed in the light of the station, surfaces reflecting a disconcerting collection of angles as if hewn from solid stone, its hardened arms loose at its sides with a sense it was ready to act. The Sentinel appeared to hold no weapons in its hands, though it was no less dangerous for their absence. It was alien, built by a species so far beyond our understanding as to be laughable and able to rub someone out of existence with only a look.

"Sentinels," I replied. "The legacy of the Lattice."

"And they have people inside of them . . ."

"Yes. They have people inside."

"Damn," Lance exhaled. *"The defectors were right. I hoped they weren't right."*

"We need to get out of here."

"You need to get out of there," he corrected. *"I'm shooting directions to your hand terminal. This should take you through the maintenance pathways and get you around the bulk of their security forces. Ingrid and I will meet you halfway."*

"Okay," I said, receiving the map.

I took a moment to review it, found a hidden door in a nearby wall, and scurried through it. This opening led into a warren of passages, some remaining on the same level as I entered, others taking me down deeper, all similar to the one Premier Takagi had taken me through. These, however, were narrow by comparison, hardly wide enough for two to walk abreast, and they were dark, too dark. It made me miss my Star Sphere something fierce.

"They were preparing us the whole time," I told Lance after a moment. "It's worse than you guys thought. The Bliss was meant to get us ready to be one of those crystal things, not just take control of us. It wipes the mind clear of anything individual. It removes pain. It makes you crave oblivion. The machines don't work without this preparation. They require a living mind. And without it being erased first, without it being cleared of ego, they would tear themselves apart."

"I don't think these people are going to make good allies," he replied, his tone a touch sarcastic.

"You think?"

"Heads up, Milo. They've got guards at the end of the hall. Ingrid has you covered."

"What does that mean?"

"Just stay low. Wait for a moment."

Loud noises came from the outside hall, but I remained in cover, doing what I was asked to for once. I heard a series of whining, crunching sounds, then silence.

"Go! Go!"

When I stepped out into the main hall, I found the floor littered with bodies, some meaty pieces of human, some broken shards of Lattice Sentinels. None of them had been shot by anything I could see, but rather, they had been sliced into shreds by a razor as long and as tall as a human being. I didn't have time to think about how, only that it had happened. I made for the exit, rushing through the gap to the platform, averting my attention from the dead Aeolians.

Sentinels appeared at the end of the hall, focused on me. Rays of heat-energy shot from their eyes, burning tracts at my tail, floor tiles sublimating into wavy clouds of turquoise gas. I stumbled and fell, slid behind an art display, then kept moving, my leg burning. I was not going to be turned into barbecue, not today.

The Lattice soldiers let out a deafening whining, grinding noise reminiscent of failing machinery in an old factory, then bounded after me, feet crashing against the floor like hydraulic presses. I sent a command to my nanomachines, unwrapping them, turning them into a shield before twisting it toward the approaching enemy.

They closed the distance, crystal eyes brightening, then bore down on me with their heat rays. I slid into my next set of cover behind a series of plinths, body curling up into a ball behind my makeshift shield. The many rays struck its surface, and I could smell my homegrown nanomachines evaporating, heat weapons ablating the outer layers as if they were striking the *Transcendence*'s MI. Sweat poured from my forehead as the air around me began to fry. The hairs on my fleshy arm singed, skin turning bright red despite being on the other side of cover. Instinct made me want to fling the shield away given the searing pain, but I knew that would be my death.

I had no way to fight back. In just a few moments, they would overtake my position, and this flimsy shield I'd made wasn't worth much.

The heat rays paused, and I took this moment to flee, hoping they had some kind of cooldown period. I scrambled off around a series of pillars, stowed my nanomachines, turned down a side passage, then shot out into another hall, putting several feet of steel construction between us. Hopefully, this would be enough. They didn't seem to move fast, but with their heat weapons, they didn't have to. I needed to get out of this place. I was trapped between too many forces.

"The hall, ahead of you," Lance said. *"Quickly. More are moving in on your ass."*

I glanced over my shoulder to see that he was right. A dozen guards with Sentinels on their flanks were rushing to me. I shot through a side door, twisted down several passages, then found myself entering the back halls of the landing platform. Through a basketball-sized port I could look down and see the beautiful construction that was my Swift Shuttle. Lance waved up at me as he helped Xuan and Hy carry Shelly aboard, supporting her under the arm.

I hobbled for the exit.

"Stop!" someone shouted at my back, and I paused, the word arresting my advance as if I'd been shot with an energy bolt from a stun weapon. I pivoted on my heels and met their eyes.

"And just where are you going?" Premier Takagi said, having appeared behind me. This couldn't be good.

My face went hard, the nanoblade in my right hand extending from where I had stowed its components in a twist along my arm. The premier was not alone; she was accompanied by two guards clad in white body armor, but no Sentinels.

"We've said all we need to say," I told her. "We're leaving."

"Is that so?" Her eyes widened as she peered about, shock on her face, looking the spire's halls over and surveying her domain. "I thought you'd planned to stay forever. You won the games beyond impossible odds. You killed those you had to kill to survive. Wouldn't you like to now claim your prize? Wouldn't you like to live in bliss forever? Haven't you hurt long enough?"

"It's not a prize," I said, taking a fighting stance before her, blade held in front. "It's damnation. And those people . . . I had no choice. You made sure of that."

"Damnation?" The word summoned that devilish smile of hers, the smile we'd become accustomed to. "It might just be that." She made an open hand gesture, and her guards raised the barrels of their rifles, metal gleaming in the artificial light. "Now. As for this little standoff we have here. You have a sword, my captain, and while it might be sharp enough to slice through flesh, bone, and titanium, we have guns. Pretty sure I know which one wins."

As I considered my limited options, trapped in a hall with high-powered rifles aimed at my chest, Ingrid appeared out of nowhere from a maintenance passage, rushing up to stand beside me, her gaze fixed on the Premier. She was relaxed in her stance, acting as if we were having a discussion no more serious than one about coffee—or the weather.

"Good to see you, Captain," she whispered.

I nodded. "And you, Overseer."

"How interesting," the premier said, rubbing her chin. "Not all of you have left. Why not stay a while, troublemaker? I'd like to thank you personally for what you've done over the past few weeks."

"It's been fun," Ingrid said, "but like Captain Hughes said. We're leaving." She made a gesture with her right hand, fingers signing a word, then turned and placed an arm over my shoulder, pulling me to the exit. "Let's go. Everyone is waiting for us."

So that's how this was going to go? We were just going to walk out?

"Don't you turn your back on me!" the premier shouted, voice cracking. "I'll give you one last chance! Stop where you are! Come back! This is my kingdom! Do you hear me? You listen to me! *Me!*"

I glanced over my shoulder at her, needing to see the rage on her face in this moment, the fury at this loss of control after all she had done to us. She had always been in control, always been the dominant force in any situation ever since coming to this place. It was satisfying.

But before I could think much more about it, before I could consider what might happen to her after we were far away from this depraved settlement, a flash of silver ran up the wall beside her and her guards.

I knew what that meant.

I should have seen it coming.

Ingrid could say all she wanted about how this little piece of technology wasn't a weapon, but I had already seen its handiwork, and it was the most dangerous "not weapon" I'd ever encountered.

Flicker appeared from out of the wall, a billion nanoscopic machines flowing from a liquid state into a solid. It leapt through the air as if slipping from another dimension into ours, its canine form as thin as a razor, its edges jagged and pixelated. As it crossed the gap in the hallway, the edge of its body sliced clean through the neck of the guard on the right, then that of the premier, then the guard on the left, before crashing into the opposite wall, scattering into a mercurial haze.

The three stood there for a moment, motionless, not a word to be spoken. Then came a sickeningly wet noise as their heads slid off the stumps of their necks and tumbled from their shoulders, bodies collapsing like marionettes whose strings had been cut.

I stood stock still, feet frozen to the floor tiles, watching blood pool around their lifeless forms, unsure what to do after witnessing such a spectacle.

Ingrid tugged my jacket sleeve. "Come on. Time to go."

"How did . . ."

"Everyone needs a friend watching their back." The nanomachine dog appeared at her side, its fur flexing like ferrofluid exposed to a magnetic field. She patted it on the spine, and her fingers came back clean, no cuts.

We boarded the shuttle and secured the crew with the help of a few people Ingrid called their "new friends." There was no time to vet them or even make introductions, only time to flee. I found Shelly safely aboard, and I gave her hand a squeeze as I passed her acceleration chair.

"What a hell of a ride," she mumbled, meeting my eyes.

"Yeah," I said, then placed a kiss on her forehead.

I dove into my Star Sphere and powered up.

The landing platform began to depressurize, and the doors opened. Thank the Universe it wasn't on lockdown, not that it would have stopped us.

"Final check," I called back to the passenger cabin.

Lance replied, *"Confirmed. We're secure."*

And that was all I needed. I pinged a ready status to Karianna, who pinged back, and we took off, her Swift Shuttle following. We rose from the platforms and left the spires, the clouds, the madness of this place behind.

"Milo," Karianna cut in over our private channel. *"I—I just want to—"*

Emotions welled up in my chest at the sound of her voice, the fear over what she might say next.

"Later," I told her. *"This is not the time."*

"But we need to talk about—"

"Not now," I growled in reply.

She recoiled from my tone and quieted.

We were back aboard the *Transcendence* in minutes, having pushed our acceleration as hard as was safely possible given our fleshy passengers. A soon as we were docked, everyone transferred into Star Spheres, where they could have their blood flushed clean of Bliss.

Karianna and I met eyes as we stepped into the main hall, both of us dressed in little more than our underclothes. For a moment, I thought she was going to speak, to fill in details best left for another day, but Chinchillette appeared beside her and led her off to her personal Star Sphere.

"Milo," Proxy said from the deck beside me. Its eyes twinkled. "I am so pleased to see you."

I grinned and scratched it behind the ear. "Me too."

From my primary Star Sphere, the *Transcendence*'s engines came to life. Karianna descended along with me into the integration. The jumble of emotions I received back was jarring. I tried not to mirror her, but it was not easy. She was confused, hurt, and . . . there was something else. Something she was trying to hide from me.

What was it? There was no time for this.

The space above Venus came to life as the Star Sphere fed me data, suspending me in a void at the center of a dozen incoming ships. I combed through the deluge of information, identifying and tagging each threat.

Proxy appeared beside me. "We have UEI Remnant Fleet on the field. Six. Veetor's ship as well, the *Absolution*. And nine rather large Isopteran craft. There is also an unidentified asteroid of some shape that appears to be under power and heading our way."

"Kabosai?" I asked.

"Seems likely."

"Everyone came out to fight, didn't they?"

"We have intercepted signals and confirmed the Isopteran to be from the Gray Queen. She is summoning more forces to this place. Even with the Lattice defenses, it will be hard for Aeolia to repel this without . . ." It trailed off.

"Without what?"

"Without your help."

I chuckled. "Help? Proxy, why would we help them? What did they just do to us?"

"Yes, but are they not victims too? Jadier Takagi, their premier, their leader, she is dead. She was the driving force in their depravity and sentinel recruitment. She could even have been altered by the Lattice. There is so little we know of them. Too many factors."

I grumbled. "Protect life, then."

"It is always your choice."

"Karianna?" I called, and she appeared next to me, her face downcast.

She did not make eye contact, and the emotions that came in response made my heart ache. "Yeah?"

"We can't let them die."

"I know. It sucks. But they deserve it."

"Maybe, but we're going to help how we can." I put a hand on her shoulder, but she still didn't look at me. "Are you okay?"

She shrugged. "I'm okay enough."

"Fine. We'll talk later. I promise."

"I know."

She blinked out of existence, and I refocused my attention on the matter at hand. Our connection through the integration meant we didn't have to say all that much. We were already in each other's minds.

We followed our instincts, feeding off one another's subtle intentions, positioning the ship between the Isoptera and the human fleet. I checked on Shelly as we moved into place and found her doing fine. For the second time in a subjectively short period, she was being cleansed of something dark and alien. It wasn't fair.

A signal pinged our communication array. It came from the UEI Remnant Fleet moving into formation several thousand kilometers ahead of us.

I accepted the signal.

"*Captain,*" Admiral Cardoso began. "*Here we are again. Please stand down. Let us handle this situation as the authority in this region of space. We have already been given reports of the chaos you sewed on Aeolia. The death of the premier. This is a hot situation, but we must deal with you later."*

"Situation?" I replied. "You have no fucking idea what the situation is. Do you even have open contact with Aeolia? Do you know what they do here?"

"We have enough contact. We trade with them and offer defense."

"Cardoso, listen, there's not enough time for us to go over all they've done. They are not who they say they are."

"And how can we trust your lies when all you do is lie?"

"No," I said, then paused. "Look, we're here to offer you support against the Isopter—I mean, Clickers. Help against the Clickers. Take it or leave it."

Veetor cut in on our channel. *"Shoot them! Kill those human abominations. Burn that ship. Put everything you have on it!"*

"Sir?" Cardoso came back, sounding confused. *"We are not in a position. If we commit—"*

"I don't care what you will lose!" Veetor responded. *"They are a bigger threat to humanity than these alien invaders."*

"But—I can't—"

The *Absolution* rotated to face us, closing the distance. Its weapons powered up, Para Lux arrays going hot along its wedge.

Karianna invaded my thoughts: *I've got control of the MI and will keep us moving. You focus on weapons.*

When the first of his beams lanced out, Karianna was ready. She layered the MI in such a way to negate most of Veetor's advantage. The UEI Remnant Fleet, however, did not join in this assault.

I focused the rail guns on several sections of his Para Lux array, hoping to get past his MI and cause some damage. I saw no way we could take him out here, not with so many other targets on the field, but we sure could slow him down.

The Isoptera approached our position from the rear. A half dozen ships, shaped like green turnips that had the eyes of flies, hurled arrays of explosive slugs in our direction. Karianna burned us out into open space, engines roaring, increasing our velocity to make us a harder target. A few of the projectiles exploded close to us, tagging our aft end but doing little damage. Swarms of the attack shuttles detached from their fungara hulls, cicadas zipping around open space seeking targets.

While they had the advantage on the ground of numbers and a hive mind, this was not the ground. Their chemical communication systems did not work over these distances. We had an edge.

I spun around in my Star Sphere and began chucking antimatter at the enemy. One of the Isopteran ships vanished in a flash of white light and signal noise. The others in its fleet broke formation and spread out, realizing they could be next.

Shelly appeared in my Star Sphere an instant later, sitting on the invisible floor. She gave me a weak wave, but from the look of her, I could tell she was in no condition to offer help.

The UEI Remnant Fleet engaged the Isopteran cruisers, hurling missiles at them from a dozen different vectors. The termites fired up a series of point defense weapons, which did well to destroy most of the incoming projectiles. Very few of them got through, but there were enough to inflict considerable damage.

One of Cardoso's ships was struck by some kind of projectile. The human vessel ignited into a burst of light and scattering debris, no telling how many lives snuffed out as their hull decompressed.

"Where's the Kabosai ship?" I asked Proxy, having lost track of it, my hands sweaty and shaking. "I've lost it."

The cat tilted its head. "I'm not sure," it said before leaping into Shelly's arms. "It is not on the instruments."

"Damn it. I don't like losing things like that."

Veetor continued to trade blows with us, but we had the upper hand given our position and all the chaos. I tried again to hurl an antimatter slug at him, but it sailed harmlessly past into open space before igniting at a safe distance. There was something on his ship that would not allow us to kill him so easily. This was clear manipulation. What game was the Foundry playing?

Two more Isoptera down, Karianna thought, her emotions more stable, danger having made her thoughts more logical. *That one up there is in a good position for you to fire again.*

Taking it.

That's it. Good shot. It's down.

This leaves only one.

The Isoptera are deploying more attack shuttles.

Looks like it.

I—I think we need to go. Veetor is starting to chew into our MI pretty hard. Can we flee?

We can. They've got more targets than us. We've got better things to do. We showed our intention, right? Protect life. All that shit.

Burn quickly. Vanish.

You got it.

The *Transcendence* lifted away from Venus at fifty Gs of acceleration, crew vibrating in their Star Spheres at the change.

The UEI Remnant Fleet did not follow, their vectors remaining fixed on their targets. Veetor clearly wanted to, but soon found himself in a position where he had to shift his priorities under enemy fire. He might have been powerful in his Foundry-made vessel, but he was not invulnerable. The remaining Isoptera paid us little mind, as we made their lives easier.

Aeolia would likely survive this attack, but I wasn't sure if that was a victory, or a shame.

But as for us?

We had places to be.

We had a mission to complete.

"We will speak again soon," Admiral Cardoso messaged us as we left. *"This is not over."*

"We welcome it," I said, closing the channel.

CHAPTER 43

We locked in our course for the outer system, leaving Venus behind. Ingrid had given us the general coordinates for our next target, some kind of station where a cache of shuttles would be waiting. Or so we hoped. I ensured all systems were nominal before allowing myself the opportunity to relax after so much drama. So much had happened. There was still so much to process. I needed to check on the crew, and from the look of it, some of them were already gathering.

I entered the shared bridge space to find Leo, Ada, and Shelly waiting. Leo was pacing around the room, massaging his head out of reflex, being that none of us were in the real world. Shelly and Ada sat upon one of the infinity couches, and my love was sobbing, her friend holding her tight.

The comedown from Bliss was hard. I had already been through it, but unlike them, I had a little extra help from my Foundry augmentations. This agonizing process had prompted serious emotional responses in more than just my better half, their brains deprived of all the feel-good chemicals and out of balance.

"What's wrong?" I asked, kneeling beside her. "What happened?" I put a hand on her leg. "Babe, talk to me."

Ada cut me an angry look and brushed my hand away. "You know what you did, asshole. Don't play."

Shelly buried her face in her friend's shoulder, ignoring me.

I cocked my head at them, confused. "What I did? What are we talking about?"

"You slept with her," Shelly mumbled just loud enough I could hear, voice choking on each word like poison. "I saw it. You were with her. I— you stood behind Karianna and worked her over like a—"

I took a shaky step back, hands trembling, heart falling from its place in my chest and screaming into a bottomless pit. Had I done this? How? How had that been possible? My thoughts and actions had been a jumble the past few weeks, and if I was being honest, I knew how Karianna felt about me. But I would never cross that line. I would never take an action like that.

Right?

Would I?

No. Her feelings for me were unrequited.

But—

Doubt was the blackest of all emotions.

"Shelly," I began, stretching out a hand. "I don't remember half of what happened to us. Are you sure? Are you really sure this happened?"

"You've always wanted to," she went on. "I see the way she looks at you. I see how you look at her. Seems the perfect opportunity to act on that, plenty of excuses. You two have a kinship we will never have. Been through the same changes. The donation. Being pilots. I'll never be good en—" Her words cut off as she began to sob.

I steadied my hands, balling them into fists. No. No. This wasn't right. I would never do that. Full of Bliss, drunk or otherwise, I would never do that. Shelly was my wife. My love. The only one I wanted to be with. But that isn't to say we all don't have intrusive thoughts, weird ideas that pass through our heads as we process stimulus. That's just our brain trying to understand the world around us.

But I did not take that action.

I did not.

I refused that idea.

"I saw you," Ada said. "I saw it happen."

"I don't believe you," I replied, hardening my expression. "I didn't do it."

Leo paused at what he was doing and looked over at us. He seemed lost for a moment but shook his head and came back.

"Did we have sex?" Leo asked Ada. "I'm with Milo here. Everything was crazy hazy."

She let out a long sigh. "Yes, Leo, we had sex. Like six times."

"Really?" He perked up at that. "No kidding. How was I?" He rubbed his chin in thought.

"You were fine," she mumbled.

"Fine? Fine! What the hell kind of response is that?" He fell into a character, a sort of snooty-sounding professorial type speaking with a fake patient. "How was the sex, my dear? *It was okay. Nothing to write home about.*" He pursed his lips and wobbled his head. "*Fine, you know. Just fine. Serviceable, you might say.*"

"Okay, okay!" she raised her voice. "It was great, Leo. Shit, dude. What do you want me to say? You made me feel like a goddess or something? You made me transcend reality? You showed me worlds of pleasure I thought only possible in fairytales? Yes, we had sex. And yes, it was wonderful. End of story. *Finito.*"

He rubbed his chin a bit more. "Want to go again?"

"Do you really think this is the best time to talk about that?"

He shrugged. "We're not together now, are we? Like in a rela—"

"No," she cut him off. "We are not together. There is no being together for me."

Leo nodded but didn't speak any further.

James appeared in the room an instant later, Lance and Ingrid with him. From the looks of it, the three had been deep in conversation and were wrapping up.

"Oh, shit," James said. "What the hell is happening here?"

"Milo fucked Karianna," Ada blurted out. "Pig. Asshole."

James looked to Lance and Ingrid, then back to us. "No, he didn't," he said, drawing out his words. "He. Did. Not."

"Don't try and shield your bro from his actions," she said. "I saw him. He did. I saw him do it."

"Yeah well, he didn't," Lance added. "If there's one thing that asshole isn't, and he's a lot, it's a cheater."

I felt the tension in my chest begin to lessen, though I was no less confused. Shelly pulled away from Ada to get a better view but did not get up. She dried her tears with her sleeves.

"How do you know?" she asked, not addressing me or acknowledging my presence at all.

James pulled a chair up in front of the couch. "Remember that guy Richard?"

"Yeah?"

"The one who looked a hell of a lot like Milo, if you didn't pay too much attention?"

Shelly blinked, and Ada looked down, cheeks filled with red.

"Well," James went on, "it was him. That's who she was with. I know, because I watched them. Not exactly something I'm proud about, but yeah . . . Joanna and I were at the, um, the 'event' as well. Yeah. Let's call it that. That's a good word. We were a few beds behind her. The room was very distracting, and there was a lot of flesh, and we were pretty messed up, but unless Milo regrew his natural arm and leg . . ."

"Richard," Shelly rolled the name over on her tongue. "It was . . ."

"They were controlling you," Ingrid said, sitting down beside Shelly. "It was all manipulation, pure and simple. That's what happened to Brian, except he didn't make it through the situation alive."

"That's your friend?" Ada asked.

Ingrid nodded. "He was. As it turns out, he tried to buck the status quo, and they had him killed for it. Much the way our captain here almost was."

"Did you get the resonators?" Leo pressed. "Please tell me we got something out of that."

Lance grinned. "We got them. So, it wasn't a total fuck-up. It's possible that your little party train might have even offered a good distraction. Xuan, Hy, and the folks we brought back with us are working on getting them calibrated as we speak."

"Are they taking precautions? Like gloves and such?"

"Yes. No contamination."

"So, I didn't do it?" I ventured, bringing the topic back around, almost smiling at the idea. "I didn't do it."

James shook his head. "No, bruh. You didn't." And from the look in his eyes, I felt him also saying . . . *And so that's one less girl we have to fight over.*

To hear him say it was such a relief. I was starting to question myself, to doubt my heart and my intentions. Bliss was dangerous.

"Did you think you had?" Shelly asked, her words sharp.

This felt like way too public a place to be having this kind of conversation, but there was no way around it. I took a deep breath and collected my disparate thoughts.

"If I am being honest," I began, careful with my word choices, "I have no idea what Bliss is capable of making any of us do. I have a strong suspicion that most Aeolians were good enough people at one point. Kind. Human. But the lines, they get real, real blurry the deeper you get. I can honestly say that my heart had no desire to cross any lines. But if someone had turned up murdered after we were done, I might have found myself questioning that as well. I didn't know what real was anymore."

"*She* believes you did it though," James went on, his words heavy. "You've got to talk to her about it."

"What?" I sighed. "Karianna believes? You serious?"

"Yeah," he said, swallowing. "You have got to talk to her. All those events are a jumbled-up brain salad in her head. It's easy to believe what you want to believe."

Shelly reached out and took my hand, squeezing my fingers. "I'm sorry, Milo. I didn't mean—"

I leaned down and put my forehead against hers. "Let's just stop worrying about it. Let's all get sober and clear headed and rested. We just went through a really messed up few weeks."

She nodded at this.

"I'll go talk to her," I said, taking a shuttering breath. "Now, if the ship catches fire and kills us all in the process, I'm sorry about that."

James stood up and put a hand on my shoulder. "Good luck." And for once, I could tell he wasn't trying to be funny.

As I was about to leave the room, Lance stepped close and whispered, "It's good to have you back."

I gave a weak grin and nodded at him. "Good to be back."

The shared bridge space vanished as I returned to my personal virtual environment. When I arrived, I sent Karianna a ping informing her I was alone and wanted to talk. She appeared so fast I nearly jumped out of my skin, distance less than a step between us.

"Hi," she said, her voice timid, eyes shining, hands clasped before her. A flood of emotions fed through the integration into my vibrating chest. Longing. Fear. Love. Uncertainty.

"Hi," I said in return, doing my best to keep my expression and emotions neutral. It was hard. This was no easy situation to navigate. "How are you?"

"I'm okay," she replied, but I already knew that was a lie.

"You hurt?"

"No." She looked herself up and down and brushed off her arms. "Not that I know of."

"I was worried after taking that stuff to sober up that they might hurt you, or hurt the rest."

She gave a slight grin at my concern. "I don't remember what all happened. But I don't have any injuries."

"I'm glad you're not hurt."

"You look okay too." She took a step toward me and clasped my right arm. "I can't believe they forced you to fight in an arena. And to the death."

"I'm fine," I said, pulling away, much to her displeasure. "They couldn't put a scratch on me. Too quick."

Anger and annoyance flickered through the integration.

She met my eyes and scowled. "Don't lie to me, Milo. I know the truth. The tendon in your right calf was nearly severed. It's being stitched together as we speak."

"Yeah, well, it's a small price to pay to escape with my skin."

"You could have died down there! You should have waited for the rest of us. We could have taken her together."

"Well, I was angry," I said, pacing around. I had to keep moving. Keep busy. "Something had to be done. You would have done the same."

"Yeah, well, but—you can't risk yourself like that."

"I can, and I will, to protect all of you."

"You are more important than we are," she said, her voice taking on an angry edge.

"We are all important. I did what I had to do in the moment. Thank the Universe it turned out okay."

She took hold of my shoulders, forcing me to stand still. "Milo, stop it. You've got to be more careful."

I held her gaze for a long moment. Her anger intensified. "Says the girl who's willing to risk it all at any moment. I thought you'd be proud of me for going for it."

"You can't get yourself killed."

I shook my head. "Dying is not in my plan, but there are things that need doing. Risks to be taken."

"But I can't bear to live without you," she spouted, then covered her mouth in shock, as if these words were a mistake. "No. No. You can't die on me. I've already lost one, I can't lose another."

"What are you saying?" I gave her some time to reply, but when she didn't, I ventured, "You mean, your dad?"

"Milo, I love you," she said, her voice fragile and sharp as the thinnest glass. "I've always—I mean—you've always been there for me. I love you."

And there it was. She had said what I had always suspected. Those times she held my hand a little too long, those times she looked at me with more than just a friendly glance. Those moments she wanted me alone, almost saying words she could not yet articulate. And this novel situation, Bliss and all, had given her the opening. What had happened with Richard emboldened her. Because of course it would.

I swallowed down the swarm of butterflies rising in my throat threatening to choke me. "I know that's how you feel, and I understand. We are a special breed, aren't we?"

"Yes. Yes, we are." This made her smile, but I knew by her posture, the resonance in the integration, that she was longing for more. "Why can't you just say it back? I know you feel the same way. You have to feel the same way."

"Karianna . . . You know where my heart is, right? Shelly is my wife. I love her, and only her."

"Then why did you do what you did in Aeolia?" Her voice rose in volume, taking on an edge. She pointed at me in accusation. "You whispered sweet nothings in my ears, touched me ways I've never been touched before. Made me feel like more than a warm body. You showed me love, not just spoke it, and you did speak it. Why give your body to me there, only to step back here? Only to shield your heart?"

"Because it didn't happen," I told her. "We did not make love. This is a fantasy."

"Yes, we did! I remember every kiss. Every scent. Every sensation. You told me you wanted to be with me forever. That nothing else mattered. That we could leave all this drama behind when it was done."

"I never said those words." I gestured to the side with an open hand. "It was Richard. Remember him? The guy who looked just like me? Or near enough."

Karianna covered her eyes with her palms and shook her head as if the act would change things. "No. No. No. I don't believe it. That's not true. That's not true. It was you, Milo. You."

My guts twisted into knots as her emotions washed over me. It took everything in me to fight against the rushing waters no longer held back by their remorseful dam. They just kept coming and coming, threatening to sweep me away and dash my heart upon the stones of their escape.

I gently took hold of her wrists and pulled them down off her eyes. Tears were streaming down her face.

"I'm sorry, Karianna. It's not true. It was all manipulation. Bliss tried to make us believe it was real, but it wasn't. It's not your fault. Bliss lied to us."

"But you—" She cut off midsentence, her sobs making it difficult for her to speak. "You—"

I wasn't sure what to do in the moment. Part of me wanted to hug her and say it was going to be okay, but I knew it wasn't, not for what she desired.

"You have to feel something," she said after a moment, her chest catching. She brushed her hair back over her ear. "I've seen the look in your eyes. You have feelings for me." Her expression hardened, those dark eyes twinkling. "Don't lie to me." Her words came out as a growl.

And this was where things became complicated. Could I be honest about my errant thoughts? My stray emotions? The fact that we had a connection I would never share with anyone else? Balls to bone, I loved Shelly, and yet, that didn't mean I didn't feel a closeness to Karianna. I loved her as a friend, a companion, a part of our group. I was not in love with her, though. I would never be in love with her.

"What you want, I can't give," I said, keeping my voice steady. "My heart has only enough room for one."

"What are you saying?" Her eyes trembled.

"I'm not in love with you, Karianna," I said, letting the words hang for a moment before going on. "You are a remarkable human being, one deserving of all the love and attention of another who is your equal. That person is not me. That person will never be me. I'm sorry."

Karianna collapsed to the floor, the bracelets on her wrist jingling as she did. She wrapped her arms around her legs and held herself there. I crouched beside her on one knee, settling at her eye level.

"It wasn't real?" she asked, not expecting an answer. "It wasn't real."

"No," I said. "It wasn't."

A moment passed in silence, both of us remaining still. The universe wheeled around us in my virtual environment, stars twinkling and turning, threads of cosmic light connecting everything and everyone.

"You know," she said after a while, her words soft, "I may have been with someone else, and it may not have been real. But for a brief moment, I had a chance to know what it might feel like to be loved by you. And that chance—it brought out these beautiful, divine feelings that I can't shake. Feelings I can't get rid of. It was perfect. It was pure. Don't tell me that you don't feel anything for me. Don't tell me you don't feel the intimacy we share. Please . . . Talk to me. Please . . ."

And I did feel a kind of intimacy with her. The integration didn't make that easy. Still, if I could trade this level of connection for anyone else, I would choose Shelly in a heartbeat. It felt wrong to know Karianna's thoughts and feelings like I did, and yet there was no way around it.

"I don't feel anything," I lied. "We are only partners. Teammates. And damn good ones at that."

She closed her eyes and began to cry. "I need to be alone."

"I understand."

And she disappeared, returning to her personal space, leaving me by myself. It wasn't fair. None of it was fair. She did not deserve to feel this kind of pain.

Proxy appeared several seconds later, nuzzling its nose against my leg. I picked it up and began petting it.

"I am sorry, Milo," it told me.

I nodded. "Me too, Proxy. Me too."

CHAPTER 44

"Negotiations have been tough," Dameon said, his expression on our video feed less than pleased, glasses half hanging off the end of his nose, revealing a set of tired, puffy eyes. *"Paphospolis, the Borough of Skive, the Boot, all feel this is a waste of time. Especially having preemptive contact by Aeolia. According to the propaganda being distributed, you guys wrecked the whole place. Burned it all down. Left countless bodies in your wake. We've read your report, and we know what happened. It's unfortunate they have that much power. Those three settlements count for more than half of the projected labor we would need."*

"But we ain' cavin' yet, bruv," Chevelle cut in, pushing him out of the camera frame. *"We'll twist a few arms if that's what it takes, innit."*

It was two days since we'd left Aeolia, and we were in the shared bridge space, primary crew only, updates from Earth playing on the main display. Each of us had found a place to be comfortable, despite it not being real, taking up spots on couches, chairs, or standing up in anticipation. Shelly was curled up on the couch beside Ada, Leo on the other side, leaning forward on his knees. Karianna had sprawled out sideways in an armchair, half her body hanging off the edge as she peered up at the ceiling, looking bored. Lance paced the room with Ingrid, discussing numbers in hushed tones as he swiped through pages on a hand terminal. It was curious to see how the two of them had become close in the past few weeks. Their little operation on Aeolia seemed to have smoothed out whatever sharp issues they'd had with one another, cementing a kind of bond I hadn't expected. They'd become almost inseparable.

The video went on.

"*Always with the bad news first, Dameon,*" Priscilla chuffed. "*We've got some good news as well. Though they are a smaller settlement, Antalya is prepared to help, as well as Queensland and the Daegu Habitat. This gives us boots on the ground in three regions, including Asia, the Middle East, and Australia. These could be prime locations for several pieces of the Jevox terraforming equipment.*"

"*Just need a way to get all the materials around,*" Dameon said. "*I know you guys are headed to do that now. So be careful. We'll keep working diplomacy here. See who we can get on our side. In the meantime, I wanted to mention that you should be careful when you return. We've been hearing from some of the smaller habitats in the Ring of Diamonds that signs of Splicers have been detected near Luna. No more information than that. Fly safe. Svalbard out.*"

"It's strange," Karianna said, rolling over in the creaky, red leather chair, her tone subdued. "We keep seeing signs of Kabosai, but unlike the Gray Queen, there's been no aggression."

James leaned forward from where he sat, chin resting on his palm. "Maybe they're being circumspect? Sneaky?"

"But is this normal behavior for them? The way you guys talk about that slug fest you ended up having, I thought they came out guns blazing."

"We never said that."

"They were never openly hostile," Shelly supplied. "They are master manipulators, in it for the long game. Naked aggression is not the Gene Brokers' style."

Karianna pursed her lips as she thought that over, the wheels in her head no doubt turning with furious energy. I made no comment.

Hours passed, the *Transcendence* reaching cruise velocity, and many abandoned their Star Spheres to move about the ship, get to know our newcomers, share some meals as human beings and get some air before climbing back into our spheres. Our numbers had ballooned, bringing our total complement to forty-six. While some might be along for the ride, or would be pilots for the shuttles, we'd picked up five more on Aeolia who'd escaped the same Bliss-filled nightmare as us. In spite of the aid they'd provided, however, I was keeping a close eye on them.

Karianna had kept her distance from me, which was understandable all things considered. Through the integration, she didn't appear to be mad so much as embarrassed and disappointed. She'd laid her heart bare and had been rejected. I tried to talk to Shelly about what happened, what we talked about, but she wasn't interested. I think she was embarrassed in her own way, having made the accusation she did, but human emotions could be unpredictable at times, beyond our control. I might have done the same. Karianna was in pain. This whole situation had become sticky and awkward, and I just wanted to make everything okay again. I had no idea how to do that, or if that was even possible. Lines had been crossed, not by my choice, and deep, dark secrets had been revealed, laid bare in trust with no hope of reciprocation.

Proxy and I remained vigilant, keeping watch for any signs we were being pursued.

Days passed without so much as a blip, and then dozens of targets, one after the next, suddenly appeared on our scopes.

As soon as this sensor data was returned and analysis began, Karianna immediately asked for permission to join me. I approved her request and she blinked into existence next to me.

"Hi," she said, voice timid.

I gave her a small wave. "Hi."

"Are we seeing what I think we're seeing?" She pointed to a dwarf planet past the orbit of Neptune. "Those are fungara signatures, and big ones. Lots of them."

"I think we found their base of operations. The Gray Queen has taken up residence on Haumea."

She glazed over for a moment as more data flowed into her mind. "Shit. That's a lot of contacts. Ten. Twenty. Thirty. I'm seeing maybe fifty ships in all. Each are as big, or bigger, as what we saw over Aeolia that took out those Remnant fleet ships and gave Justin hell."

"More than we can safely deal with," Proxy said, appearing at my feet. "How do we wish to proceed?"

I rubbed my chin as I combed through the data. "Sure would be nice if we could hit their fleet with what fungara programming system Ada came up with, make the ships kill them from the inside, but it isn't made for that kind of scale."

"And . . . Could she adapt it for that?" Karianna asked.

"Maybe?" I scratched the back of my head. "Maybe not."

"They're going to be a problem. You know that. A big problem."

"I know. Just not sure what we should do about it. We could go in guns blazing, see what happens, but that could leave us dead and give Veetor free reign over the system. I don't like that idea."

She nodded and crossed her arms. "Well, at least they're still far away. We have time to think about it. Let's not be brash."

I raised an eyebrow at her.

She let out a quiet chuckle. "What?"

"Nothing," I said, smiling. But from the feedback in the integration, she knew what I meant.

"I'm going to tell the others."

"Sounds good."

And Karianna disappeared.

"That went well," Proxy said, pleased.

I scooped the cat up in my arms and squeezed its furry body. "It did."

For the next few hours, I considered our situation, drifting in a rushing stream of pure consciousness, all the variables laid out before me. I considered going to meditate, but the Bliss hangover was still scrambling my brain, and I didn't see that time being productive. Rest was what I needed, and this was the closest thing I would get to it.

We had to prepare for what came next. Now that we had an idea of the chessboard we were playing on, I had to get clear on what our next moves might be. Our terraforming project was positioned upon a knife's edge, with at least three powerful groups standing against it.

"Hey, Milo, can we talk?" James pinged me after some time.

"Sure", I replied, and he appeared in my virtual space, a troubled look on his face.

"Everything okay?" I asked, dusting off my hands.

He twisted his head to the side, regarded the sea of stars, then shrugged. "Yes? No? Maybe? Look, I have a question."

"Sure."

"What are we planning to do with the Isoptera? They are a clear and present threat to the people of SOL, and I just don't see how we can let them stay here. The Gray Queen, bruh, she wants to pack us up and take us back to Nest for drone snacks."

"I know. That's what Karianna and I were just talking about."

"So, like, what's the plan? You always have a plan."

This comment summoned a reluctant smirk to my lips. "Hardly. You know what the worst part about growing up is?"

He scowled at me in that way he always had when I won one of our games in the VEs back on the *Vasco Da Gama* instead of him. "What?"

"You get to find out that no one knows what the hell they're doing, and they're just making it up as they go along."

James chuckled and licked his lips, a genuine look of amusement on his face. "Ain't that the truth." He shook his head. "But serious time. Focus on this. What's the plan?"

It was a tough call, but in my opinion, so long as the Isoptera could be held back, terraforming came first. Their numbers had turned out to be larger than we had expected. And even with the Remnant fleet to keep them in check, friends of us or not, he was right to wonder. Something had to be done.

"Plan?" I mused. "Right now, it seems that they're in a kind of stalemate with the UEI and Veetor."

"You think it will stay that way forever? People died over Venus. Even if they're not on our side, they're people."

"This wouldn't be personally motivated, would it?"

"I'd be lying if I said no. But I'd also be lying if I said that's all it was. Bruh, these creatures are dangerous. How are we going to deal with them? Not like we can install terraforming equipment while they shoot at us."

I summoned a map in my virtual environment, detailing the locations of the enemy ships and their configurations. Red lines appeared, showing the many vectors we could approach and which ones would statistically fail. "Proxy and I have been modeling it out since Karianna left. I don't think we can take them on in a frontal attack. We are strong, but only one ship. They have taken an entire planetoid and fortified it. That floating potato is a fortress from what we can see."

"Which has had me thinking."

"Never a good thing."

"You're not wrong." James paused as if attempting to summon up his courage. "If we have the opportunity. If we can get close enough. Can we not use a bomb of some kind?"

"Like our antimatter slugs?"

"No. Not that." He shook his head. "I'm thinking something like that thing we found on Nest. That device."

I felt my blood go cold at its mention, then queried the network, ensuring the doors of the dead room had not been opened. They had not.

"What about it?"

"It gives us all the heebie-jeebies. It's dangerous—we've talked about it, Lance, Leo, Ada, and me. It feels like a weapon. So, if it's a weapon, and we don't need it for anything else, let's figure out how to use it like one. Turn it on them. Sure, we've got loads of weapons here, but this one is different, I can feel it. It's not Foundry make, something that can be throttled by the system."

"A weapon . . ."

He took a step forward and poked me in the chest. "You know what it does, don't you?"

I stumbled back, chewing on my bottom lip, thinking how to respond. "No," I lied. "We don't know what it is." And from his expression, I was pretty sure he saw through me like a pane of dirty glass.

"We?"

A mistake. The wrong word. "Proxy and me." Again, a lie, or at least part of one. "We've taken a look at it. Yes, it's powerful. No, it is not the cause of the fungara death switch. But it is powerful. We don't know how to use it."

"Maybe we should figure that out."

"Are you the only one who feels this way?"

"No," he said, eyes trailing down onto his boots. "I'm not alone in this."

But maybe he was right. Shelly and I had a strong suspicion of what it was, but without a proper template, the device was a nightmare deployed against any species. It could rewrite every Isoptera on the surface of Haumea into something else, twisting their genetic code into a functionless mess of nucleic acids without all the destruction and waste. The weapon would likely bypass any defensive measures they had in place, and given the power readings Proxy had observed, it would be planetary in scale. A horrific weapon, one not under the influence of the Foundry. A wild card.

But should we consider using it like this? Was this ethical? Was this moral? Or was this just as terrible as the ancient biological weapons used on Earth?

Why did I care? Not like there was a Geneva Convention looking over my shoulder.

James met my eyes. "Promise me you'll do this. Promise me you'll end them, for Mom, for all the friends and loved ones we lost. Promise me."

I swallowed, focusing on a location among the sea of stars within my virtual environment, not saying a word.

"Please," he pressed. "Please promise me."

Slowly I found myself nodding. "Okay. I promise. We will deal with them if we can. But I am not putting all of you at risk if it doesn't make sense."

My old friend let out a long breath. "I'm going to hold you to it."

"Oh, I'm sure you will."

CHAPTER 45

"We are approaching the target," Proxy informed those gathered in the shared bridge space. "I will bring it up on the main display for anyone who is not a pilot."

"Thank you, Proxy," Hy said, poking out his lip and tipping his head back. "I am curious to see."

"Hope this place is better than Aeolia," Xuan added. "We spent weeks hiding in shadows, hoping for better. It was all a lie."

Hy smiled at his wife. "But they had good food? Yes? The pork buns . . ."

"Better than yours, I assure you."

He narrowed his eyes at her. "See if I cook dinner tonight."

"Proxy?" Xuan asked.

"Yes?"

"If this dead dog keeps acting up, will you cook for me?"

The cat bowed its head. "Of course."

"Traitor," Hy said, pointing a finger at it.

Though I could sense all the navigational data through my connection to the ship, it was always interesting to watch how the crew responded. I couldn't imagine not knowing at all times where you were and where you were headed. This was something I took for granted as a pilot. No one but Karianna and me had the pleasure.

The *Transcendence* drifted to the Grand Gallery, approaching from the port side of the station, though at a range of 30,628 kilometers and closing, the station itself was little more than a bright dot below its grandest art installation, which was a slightly larger blot, more of a smudge.

We drifted closer, waiting in anticipation.

The entire assembly was difficult to discern without greatly enhancing the images feeding back from the ship's instruments and making a generative render of the missing details. Spectroscopy identified a thousand different materials present: iron, nickel, titanium, gold, platinum, diamond, and more. And as we approached, the awe-inspiring scale of the creation became clear. It was huge, larger than some metropolitan areas, reaching sixty kilometers in length from base to tip, with details along its surface orders of magnitude beyond anything I ever thought possible by humans.

Before us, a child was skipping through the stars, its impossibly large body an amalgamation of several different species, real or imagined. It appeared to be a boy with short hair cut into a bowl but could easily have been a young girl, its features soft, face round. One leg was part human, part tentacle, another normal, though its foot appeared to be made of two sneakers. From its billowing, oversized T-shirt, one arm reached skyward, fingers clasping the string of a gossamer kite made of a billion tiny threads that flew above and behind the child like a shifting ribbon, while its other arm hung lazily back, its hand one part human, one part claw. All was monochrome, surfaces washed in the tones of tarnished copper but for the kite, which shone bright with ripples of color transitioning in cycles from reds to blues to yellows to oranges, then back again.

The child's face was set with a collection of three eyes, only one human, placed in the wrong location, between the eyebrows. The other two of them, left and right beneath, were slitted like those of many animals.

The massive assembly was mounted to a free-floating base. This left the strange child running through the endless void, pulling its kite, boundlessly joyful in its endless pursuit of freedom.

Several silent moments passed as everyone drank in the image. I had no words for this moment, only a strange sensation of insignificance.

"What's that engraved on its bottom?" Shelly asked, squinting at the screen as we drifted closer, the image increasing in size. "*Rimor-explorator del Sonhe.* I can't make sense of it."

I peered over my shoulder. "Proxy?"

The cat disappeared from across the room and reappeared by my feet in a seated position. "It is a mix of your languages. Latin. Spanish. Portuguese. My best estimate is that it says something like, 'Explorer of Dreams.'"

Perhaps its complicated name is meant to reflect the complicated nature of the installation itself."

"It's beautiful," James said, "and yet . . . a bit unsettling."

"How can someone build something so large?" I mused. "It's unfathomable. I dare say it is the most massive single human structure I've ever seen."

Leo drew himself up onto the couch and leaned back, fingers raking through his platinum hair as he took it all in. "I'm feeling a little overwhelmed at the thought of that. Its presence is almost oppressive. You know? Can you feel its weight? It's crushing my soul. Do you see the texture? Its surface isn't smooth. It's made of jagged edges, almost like a decorative motif. Is it a sculpture in mosaic? No. No. That seems impossible. Not to mention the implications of the form itself."

"To go big," Ingrid began, "sometimes you must be small. This is not the only installation of its type, though likely the largest. Many artists have utilized nanomachines to build them."

"This entire thing was built with nanomachines?" He whistled in surprise. "That's almost unthinkable. How much processing power would you need to do something like that?"

"Gregor Machevarion was famous for the technique, and this gallery is entirely his. According to the historical records, it was built a layer at a time over the course of several years. Which brings up another matter."

My eyebrows raised. "What? What matter?"

Ingrid sighed and placed her open palms on her lap. "I haven't been completely honest with you and your crew. This station, this gallery—there is a reason the cache of shuttles should still be docked here."

Leo scowled. "And that would be?"

Lance lowered his hand terminal, bringing his attention back to us. He waved for her to go on. From the look on both their faces, it was clear they'd already discussed this and he was ready to get it over with. Nothing could be easy, could it?

"Well," she began, hands clasped, "no one ever approaches this station, even to take a peek like us. It's far too dangerous, and those who have, they . . ."

I tried to clear the annoyance from my face. I was so sick and tired of being tossed into novel situations, especially when those around me had more information. Perhaps this was on me for not asking. All that I had latched on to from our previous conversations was that we had a second location to visit, and they called it a gallery. That was all.

"Let me guess," I said, crossing my arms, "those who have visited are never heard from again?"

"Close enough," she said, nodding. "There have been survivors, but few of them, and it was long, long ago, according to our fractured records. There are many who believe this place to be—haunted."

"I knew it!" James said, slapping his seat several times. "I fucking knew it! Ghosts. There are ghosts out here!"

"Shut up, James," Karianna said, hurling the words at him.

"No. No. No." He raised his hands. "You didn't believe me. We said there might be ghosts. And here we are. Ghosts."

She rubbed her face and curled up into a ball, sinking into the back of the chair as she tried to ignore him. Out of nowhere, Chinchillette appeared, hopping up beside her and snuggling itself close. Large as her Proxy was, the two of them barely fit. This earned a look from several of the crew, but no one spoke up.

"Not sure about ghosts," Ingrid went on. "But there is something on that station. And it is alive."

"We have felt it," Proxy said to our surprise.

"What? You have?"

"We could not put a finger on it. I thought it more overlap from the fungara signals we had intercepted. Perhaps an old beacon, or perhaps just paranoia."

She cocked her head to the side, fingers twisting at the end of her braid. "You can be paranoid as an AI?"

"In my own way. But you are right. There is something there."

"Is it friendly? Can you tell?"

"Who can say? It is certainly not of the Foundry."

I turned my attention to Proxy. "You aren't pulling another one of those 'information not available at this time' kind of things, are you?"

"I can assure you, the Foundry had no part of whatever is on that station."

"We've got another problem, dudes," Ada said. "Those scattered fungara signals we were getting earlier, they're intensifying. I have a strong suspicion we've got Isoptera headed to us."

"Confirmed," Proxy replied. "Unless anything changes, those signals will be on our location within the next eight hours."

"Eight hours," Ingrid growled. "That's not enough time. My people are ready, sure, but we've got to locate the shuttles, get them out, dock them up and secure them."

Lance put a hand on her shoulder, the expression on his face uncharacteristically encouraging. "We'll figure it out. Don't worry. We can do this."

"But can we?" James asked. "Or, rather, should we? I mean . . . Let's take a look at this, zoom out on this situation a bit. We've got ghosts on a space station, some crazy weird art, and potentially a whole bunch of termites about to crash down on us. Why don't we dig in and prepare to fight? Maybe worry about the shuttles later? One less factor to deal with."

"If they know our intention," Hy said, "maybe they attack station. Might lose opportunity. Don't see this place have defenses like us."

"It does not," Proxy said. "There are no signs of a defensive system like the Mercurial Integumentum. There are no surface countermeasures either, such as antimissile systems, or energy weapons. This station is undefended from a conventional standpoint."

"We need those shuttles," Ingrid insisted, standing up. She slammed her right fist into her left palm, eliciting a smack, her face turning hard. "There might be more elsewhere. We might work to get the aid of Mars, but those are some big ifs. We have solid evidence that the ships are here. It's our best bet."

"But why are they here?" I asked. "Why so many, and why left alone for so long? It's an art gallery, right? And yet records suggest it has likely claimed lives. It doesn't feel right. I'm not saying we shouldn't go down, but I am saying we should be cautious if we do. Shelly? You always have a level head. Thoughts?"

She paused for a moment, considering all the information, then shrugged. "How much more time does Earth have? This could be our last opportunity for a quite a while. Maybe even always. I don't see any other options. I've looked through Ingrid's data, and she's right, there's nothing else out there that's recorded. Too much information was lost during the Great Gap to know for sure. The Isoptera are pressing our hand."

"Then it's decided," I said. "We're still going in. But we're going in carefully. I will go down with the crew. Karianna, stay behind with the ship. If everything goes sideways, you'll at least be able to pilot us away."

"It will be hard." She grimaced, her arms squeezing the giant rodent.

"I know. I hate to do it to you."

She nodded, and I felt a mix of emotions feedback through the integration. False strength. Frustration. Resolution.

"Ingrid, get your people ready. Lance, let's run two small teams. You'll be in charge of the second."

He nodded, stroking his pale beard. "Roger that. Powered armor then?"

"One thousand percent. From the plans, this place is more than big enough on the inside to accommodate the extra bulk. We're going to go in fully protected. Ghosts or not, deaths or not, people have gone missing here. I don't want us to be the next set of casualties."

"Good call. We'll pack some stun grenades as well, just in case we need to fry anything."

"I like frying things," Hy said, smiling. "The results can be shocking."

Xuan scowled. "Don't give him bombs."

"I'm staying behind," Shelly whispered in my ear. "I'll only get in the way."

"Not true." I took hold of her hands and looked her in the eyes. "You were tough as hell on Nest. Is something wrong?"

"No." She shook her head. "Nothing is, not really. I just don't want to go. I don't think I'm fully myself again."

"Okay." And part of me was relieved at her decision. I knew she would be safer here. "That's fine. It's your choice."

Lance began pointing at us. "So that leaves Milo, me and Ingrid, Ada, Leo, James, Xuan, and Hy. Ingrid, grab a couple of your people as well? That makes two groups of five. Once we secure the shuttles, we'll call for the pilots to come in."

"Maintain a short distance," I told Karianna. "A few dozen kilometers, port side parallel to the station so we can burn away and not turn the place to slag. Chinchillette and Proxy can ferry over the pilots when its time."

She sat up in her chair, her face set. "Works for me."

"Alright, team," Lance went on. "Let's unplug and pack up. Time to go in."

We suited up and met beside the Swift Shuttles, breaking into our two boarding parties. The *Transcendence* took up position a few dozen kilometers from the Grand Gallery's station, what appeared to be a retrofitted asteroid almost inconsequential in size beneath the looming awe that was the running child. It was clear whatever materials were used in this installation's construction did not come from such a tiny speck of rock. Not only were most of its elements and compounds not present in the asteroid, but the few that were present were nowhere near the quantities required. Between us and the station, narrow approach tunnels appeared, reminiscent of landing lights on a runway, their edges lined with colored glass at uneven spacing, which led down into the docks.

Our shuttles broke free of the ship and drifted across the gap, Proxy piloting both so that I could remain in my powered armor. My team stood in a line at the back of the shuttle where the seats usually were, lights dim, hands clasping holds hanging from the ceiling. Through the windows, we watched the shards of opaque translucence encircle us, our path a rainbow slide of kaleidoscopic colors. While the source of their illumination was unknown, it cast itself onto the floor of our shuttle, forming a slowly shifting series of prismatic geometric shapes. The effect was mesmerizing.

"The docks are responding to us," Proxy said over the shuttle's intercom. *"It's almost as if they were waiting for our arrival."*

I swallowed the lump in my throat.

"Oh, joy," James said, slapping me on the back with a clang, metal hand to metal suit. "The ghosts are waiting for us."

"Let's hope not," Leo said. "Cause I don't like ghosts."

The docking bay of the Grand Gallery yawned wide, and the dancing colors of glass shards surrounding us vanished as the station swallowed us whole.

CHAPTER 46

The shuttles landed in the docking bays, and we disembarked, our teams stepping out into a dark shell of a room with no features but for a few low lights. We were in a pressurized chamber, hardly big enough for our shuttles to fit, fuselages and air foils coming just a couple feet from touching its edges. The walls and floors of the cramped space stood in stark contrast to the Neonteichos spire's bright and expansive docks. They were made of metal on their spaceward end, while the inward end was made of bare rock, revealing layers of stone ranging from obsidian to umber, with shades of tan between. It made me feel as if we'd gone from space walkers to spelunkers as soon as the doors closed.

There was little to no gravity here, the station too small to create human-normal levels from its mass alone, and with no way for it to spin given the shape. Thankfully, the floor was ferromagnetic, allowing our boots to attach to its perfectly smooth surface. This let the crew to get around easy enough by using a combination of shuffling and pushing off to free float.

"There are stratum in these rocks," Leo said, running his suited fingers down the wall before us. "That doesn't make any sense, does it? This is an asteroid, right? Shouldn't it be uniform, or at least, like, lumpy?"

"Maybe this isn't an asteroid," Lance suggested, stepping up beside him. "Just a thought. These lines aren't fake, are they?"

Leo shook his head. "Not that I can tell."

"It is real," Hy said, bumping into the ceiling. He arrested his momentum and squinted at the wall. "This part of station no asteroid."

"Oh?"

"Don't forget, Hy is a scientist too," Xuan said. "Studied all his life in materials. Very talented."

I saw Hy smile within his helmet. "This is more geology. Rock strata form with weathering, erosion, deposition, compaction, and cementation. How these types of layers could form, though, I cannot say. The dark seems like glass, likely rich in silica. While the rest, I can only guess are a kind of sandstone. There are speckles of red as well. Perhaps this is iron? Not seen much rain in space, have you?"

Leo lowered his gloved hand. "Not a drop."

The lights in the room flickered, and a series of pressure systems engaged, making several loud, mechanical thunks. I felt the vibrations through the soles of my boots. A set of pressure doors across the dock cycled opened, metal groaning, machinery screeching like a dying animal. The doors stopped halfway, stuck in place for a moment, then jerkily vanished into the walls, taking several seconds to go silent.

"Not creepy or anything," James said, raising his weapon. "Just hope bullets can stop ghosts, bruh."

Leo crouched. "Have you guys looked at the floor?"

At his question, my attention was drawn away from the door and fell onto my feet. Beneath my heels was one of the strangest patterns I'd ever seen, its shapes made of black and dark gray tiles that were edged in gold. It was a mosaic almost, but not quite, a jagged series of tiles that reminded me of a two-dimensional T-shirt, all interconnected. I scanned around the room, and far as I could tell, the pattern did not repeat.

"Is that what I think it is?" Ada said, her tone laced with awe. She bent down to get a better look. "I know this shape. I've seen it before. It's a freaking hat tile."

"Sure is," Leo confirmed.

James gave them a funny look, his eyebrows crinkling. "Umm, what in the hell is a hat tile?"

"You don't know what a hat tile is?"

"No?"

"He doesn't know a hat tile?" Leo mused, his tone choked with a kind of false laughter.

"Well, it's only the first aperiodic monotile ever discovered," Ada started, then shook her head. "Let me back up a bit . . ."

James scowled through his visor. "You do that."

"Okay. So . . . in the early 2020s, this shape was stumbled upon by accident. The first of its kind. To explain simply, this odd shape can tile on a flat surface without any translational symmetry. That is to say, no repeating patterns are created when they are put together. Mathematicians in the twentieth century worked for decades to find this shape, and while they had created several aperiodic polytiles, or many, the monotile, one, was elusive. Ended up being discovered by some random person with paper and a pair of scissors."

Leo crossed his arms and rested a fist on the base of his helmet as if he could touch his chin. "These shapes can lock together for infinity and never create a repeating pattern. It almost hurts the brain to think about it. You know?"

"Interesting choice for flooring," I said. "Is this shape relevant to anything here?"

Leo threw up his hands. "Hell if I know. I just thought it was cool."

"So cool," Ada echoed, resting a hand on his shoulder. "Wonder if the whole station has a floor like this?"

I turned away from them, facing James and Lance. "Comm check," I called back to the *Transcendence.*

"We hear you," Karianna replied. *"Systems nominal."*

"Read you loud and clear," Proxy said next. *"Tracking your location. Will keep you up to date on the Isoptera or anything else."*

"Be careful," Shelly pinged privately to my implants.

I met eyes with Lance, then motioned before us with an open, armored hand. He nodded, and we raised our weapons, barrels first, heading for the open pressure doors as we took point.

The hall on the other side was empty. More mixed-material surfaces, a combination of smooth metal and rock, its floor made of a continuing expanse of the hat tiles. The passage was about four meters side to side, and no taller than three. Along its length were several partitions, clearly marking additional pressure doors that were no doubt utilized for emergency redundancy.

"Hello?" I called in one direction, my voice echoing, then turned. "Hello?"

"It's quiet," Lance said.

"Yeah, too quiet," James added with a sense of gravity to his tone.

"Are you serious? We doing that?"

"Come on," Ingrid urged, giving Lance a gentle push. "We only have a limited amount of time. Let's split up and find those shuttles. You have the layout?" She turned to look at me.

"Yeah," I said, fishing out my hand terminal and pinging it up to the AR in my implants. A wireframe map appeared in my vision. "Got it."

"Good."

"Report anything weird you see," I said. "Keep the line open. We can talk the entire way."

Lance gave his weapon a quick inspection, then flicked the safety off and back on before putting it into a ready position held close to his chest. "Works for me."

We broke off into our two groups, James, Xuan, Hy, and one of the Free Citizen shuttle pilots, Roger, with me, while Ada, Leo, Ingrid, and another of the pilots went with Lance.

Our magnetic boots clicked against the hat tile floor, sounds echoing down the narrow halls. Beyond the slight hum of electricity that the station gave off, everything else was silent. I breathed heavily within my powered suit and could feel myself sweating, but not from heat. The inside of this form-fitting assembly was comfortable enough, cool, it was just that my nerves had taken over. I was grateful for the fact that the suit was built not to fog up. As much nervous moisture as my body was putting off, in only a few moments I should have been walking through a haze.

Light bars hemming our path continued to flicker at random intervals. Ahead, I could see something pale floating just above the floor. James raised an open hand and bent down to get a better look.

"What is it?" I asked.

He grabbed the object between his thumb and forefinger, then stood and held it out to show us.

"It's white?" James mused. "Sort of? Maybe ivory? The material is hard, too. Tubelike. No . . . That's not the best way to describe it. It's only a few inches long, not even an inch around. Reminds me of a thick stick."

"Maybe it's trash," Xuan suggested.

"It's the only object in the hall." I turned around to be sure. "I guess it could be trash. Just a bit out of place, clean as the rest of the place is."

"The ends," Hy said, gesturing for James to hand it over. He turned it around, leaning in to get a closer look. "Whatever it's made of is porous, and it looks to have been part of something longer. You can see where it snapped, left jagged edges like a compound fracture. If it was a stick, it was a dry one at that. But this is not wood."

"Hang on to it," I said, and kept us moving.

Hy slipped it into a pocket.

Roger, the shuttle pilot, scowled at it. "Looks kind of like bone to me."

"Seen a lot of bare bone?"

"Used to work in a hospital. So yeah, I've seen my fair share."

The hall carried on, curving around to the right, where we were met by a set of double pressure doors. A symbol was printed between them, its shape overlapping the seam, a diamond-bordered line drawing of the running child and its kite. I approached, scanning the space around us for danger.

"Your heart rate is accelerated," Proxy said direct to my implants.

"I'm sure it is."

"Are you okay?"

"I think so." I looked to my team and could see their discomfort. *"Can we breathe the air here? Is it safe?"*

"Yes. It is safe, if stale."

"I'm taking off my helmet," I told them. "You don't have to, but Proxy assures me it's okay."

James reached up for his. "I thought you'd never ask."

The nanomachines that made up the two of our helmets decompiled, transferring to somewhere else on the suit for temporary storage. Once Xuan, Hy, and Roger saw that breathing hadn't killed us, they followed along.

"That's better," Hy said. "Suit makes me feel claustrophobic."

"Ahead, then." I took a step forward.

The double doors swooshed open and we stepped through. Motion sensitive lights sprang to life around the circular antechamber within. For an instant I had flashbacks to the Cultural Center on Novae, the night of Marissa's concert, the battle with the Pentaray raging over their heads.

The low ceiling of the hallway opened up, reaching several dozen feet above us. Paintings of matching sizes hung at equidistant points, silver frames backlit in a grid, creating four neat rows with six columns. The center of the room was dominated by a peculiar art installation. It was a spiraling collection of white books dangling from the ceiling on wires, or at least they gave off the illusion of it, their rigid pages flipped open at random, arranged in such a way it looked as if a vortex had come out of the floor to spin them around.

"The pages are blank," James commented. "And the books, they're metal."

"Makes sense," I said, running my finger down one of their sharp edges. "Keeps everything stiff not to destroy the effect. What about the pictures?"

Hy pushed off and floated around the room, inspecting them closely along with the help of his wife. "They are oils. Very thick from the look of it. Portraits. People with names I do not recognize. All very regal in their postures, and their clothes appear expensive. Lots of high collars and gold. Medals too, military kind. Maybe they are famous? Like presidents or politicians? Leo would have better analysis."

"They all look stuck up," Xuan added. "No inspiring faces here."

"Lance, you guys seeing anything like this where you are?" I asked, feeding a view of the room from a suit camera over to him.

"No," he replied, sounding a bit winded. *"All we've found are some really long maintenance tunnels."*

"Might not be a bad thing. Those might lead us to the shuttles."

"But it's boring," Leo added. *"The only encouraging thing I've found about this age is that since we left, art still exists."*

"Humans have to express themselves," Ada said.

"Truth."

A soft, male voice came to us over a loudspeaker, the room's acoustics adding the slightest bit of reverb to each word. *"Do we have guests? Is that what I feel, or are my instruments just . . ."* There was a pause. *"Hello. Hello. Welcome to the Grand Gallery of Gregor Machevarion. I am so very pleased to see you. It has been so long since anyone has come to visit us."*

"Hello?" I said, turning around. "Who are you? Where are you?"

"Where am I?" the voice replied, amusement infusing its snooty tone. *"I am nowhere!"* Its voice spun around the room, coming from different sources in a circular sequence. *"And I am everywhere."*

James shook his head and mouthed the word *ghost*.

"Then what are you?" I went on, my mood cooling.

"Me? Oh. Not much. I am merely an artificial intelligence designed to greet and care for guests who visit this most wonderful of galleries. It is my job to ensure you enjoy all that this world-shifting art experience has to offer."

I crossed my arms and tried to focus on one place in the room as if speaking with an individual. "When is the last time someone visited you?"

There was a pause. *"It has been some time."*

"How long?" James pressed. "We need to know."

"You need to know that bad? Hmm. Okay then, let us see, accessing data . . ." A pause. *"It is hard to be certain, sure, but I estimate it has been 200 years since I have last been visited. Give or take. That is almost two human lifetimes. Interesting, that number. Feels longer than that. Much longer."*

"And just where did they go?" I asked carefully. "Those who visited last. Did they enjoy the exhibit?"

"But of course. All who come to this grand gallery enjoy the exhibit so much they want to be part of its greatness forever."

I gave my team a concerned look. "And just who were they? Where did they come from?"

"I'm sorry, but I can't share private information like that," it replied. *"There are certain privacy rights afforded to UEI citizens as outlined in the BLOCK Act. You understand."*

"Sure," I replied, shaking my head. What was the BLOCK Act?

James gave me a hard eye. A private ping came through. *I don't know about this thing.*

Me either.

"Are you ready for your tour?" it asked. *"I am sure you traveled great distances to have the full experience as outlined in our many advertisements saturating the Exo-Net."*

"Tour?"

"Of course. You must see Gregor Machevarion's *many galleries,"* it said the artists name with an air of reverence, *"and with detailed commentary."*

"Yes. A tour. Right. But first, can you answer some questions?"

"I can try."

"Great. These people you mentioned who visited. They didn't happen to leave anything behind, did they?"

"I don't understand. Like what? Lost and found?"

"No. Like, maybe ships? Maybe they forgot some."

There was a pause before it responded. *"Would you like to watch an informational video of our BLOCK Act policy? It clearly covers the key points of what we can share, and what we cannot, in order to keep personal data private and remain compliant under UEI law."*

"No. No. I don't need a copy. Let me ask differently. The dock we came in through."

"Yes, the VIP space dock. Very beautiful, is it not?"

"It was. Pretty colors. Is there another dock, maybe just for regular folks? Like, general admission."

"Of course!" The voice became excited. *"It would be unwise to have only a two-shuttle dock on a station so large."*

"Great. And where would that dock be?"

"I'll be happy to show you after our tour has concluded."

"Don't think we are skipping this part," Hy told me.

I pinged Lance, *The other dock is real. Hung up with some kind of AI attendant.*

He replied, *It found us too.*

Proceed with caution. Something feels off.

Copy.

"What do we call you?" I asked. "Might make it easier for us to talk."

The speaker crackled for a moment. *"Don't worry about the human necessities of identity. I have no name. No need for a name. Are you ready for your tour?"*

"Sure, why not?" I let out a groan while rubbing the back of my neck. "Let's go on a tour."

The team fell in behind me, though they kept their distance.

"What better way for me to show future humans the great works of Gregor Machevarion than to give you a tour!"

"Lead the way, I guess."

"Yes! Yes! Yes!" the voice said, nearly shouting. It calmed itself down. *"I mean . . . This way, if you would."*

My team gave each other wary looks. James made a motion with his hand as if it were something flying through the air, and I rolled my eyes. A ghost, no doubt.

We stepped through another set of doors into a hallway a dozen meters wide with thick, curved glass overhead, the black expanse of space dotted with stars beyond it. While there were still no substantial gravitational forces to be had, the path was clearly designed to be enjoyed with a singular orientation, unlike the antechamber. A section of the dark, hat tile floor had a red strip that reminded me of carpet but was still smooth enough that our magnetic boots could stick without trouble. Artistic installations lined the walls, their materials showing no clear thread of theme or motif, and at the end of the hall, I could see a distant door set among a wall of colorful fractals.

We shuffled down the center of the aisle, keeping our feet upon the red path. It felt somehow dangerous for us to veer off of it, and so we remained near its center. Music began to pipe out of the speakers, the quality of the sound crackling like dusty, old vinyl, the ting of a rhythmic harpsicord soon replaced by the shrill attacks of a solo violin, all in time to the staccato pulses of a string quartet.

"I know this song," Leo chimed in over our open channel. *"It's Vivaldi. Winter specifically. It is part of Four Seasons. A famous, classic work. Marissa would have had her ensemble play this to warm up."*

"Why does this station's artist remind me of you?" Ada replied. *"Sound and setting. Varied disciplines."*

"I have to say, it feels familiar. And I don't think I like that. I'm unique."

We approached the first display, a collection of shiny chrome so bright I found myself blinking.

"The piece on your right is an early work of Gregor titled, Roadway,*"* the AI attendant began. *"It is a stylized robot made from twentieth-century American automotive parts. Note that the shoulders and chest of the automaton are made of the bumper and grill of a 1945 Chevrolet Pickup AK series. The whitewall tires making up its internal workings are not from the same model, but a 1957 Ford Fairlane. Unfortunately, due to the fact that rubber tires from that era dry rot, eventually turning to dust, Gregor was forced to make analogs of the originals out of more modern materials from the day. These are made of a type of corn rubber. The intention behind this machine was to captivate the retro-futurist style of the day as those imagining a better future looked ever forward. Its melted feet, however, are meant to contrast the futility of this dream.*

"People of that era believed that atomic power would save them from every inconvenience or communist threat ever set upon America. How wrong they would be. A few hundred years from that discovery, we would nearly destroy ourselves, using the same powers we had unlocked. We replaced nature with forces we did not understand, progressed technologically faster than we evolved socially. And we became mindless automata as a result, slaves to the machines we built to serve us."

The voice paused as we inspected the piece.

"Do you like it?" it asked.

"It's very interesting," I said, being honest.

"How does it make you feel?"

"I, um, honestly don't know."

"Hmm," the voice said, as if considering. It went on. *"To our left, we have a piece originally constructed in orbit around Earth titled,* Ever Reaching. *As you can see it is a pair of amorphous human hands, twisted around one another, fingers gripping a kind of alien plant, something not native to SOL. It is made of a kind of high-tension plaster, forced into molds, but porous due to the drying process in zero gravity. If ever this were put under a standard G of acceleration, it would crack in two, thus telling the tale of the fragile nature of our habitations in the stars."*

The planter and the plant the fingers held looked like nothing I had ever seen. The flora was tropical in a way, but its leaves, or whatever you wanted to call them, were more like hairy fronds. At its center was a massive, brown bulb, with what I could only think of as a mouth on its side, teeth and all. While the hands did not move, I swore tiny pieces of the plant shifted as we did, giving off a malicious air.

"Makes me feel things," Hy said, standing close and bending over. "A kind of hopelessness and curiosity."

"An interesting interpretation," the AI said, its tone like an old man rubbing at his rough, unshaven chin, considering. *"Do you believe humanity has hope?"*

"Hope of what?"

"Of any kind."

"I never doubt it," he said, straightening his back. "Humans, nor life itself, give up easy."

"And that is to be regarded as a positive trait?"

"The most positive," Xuan added.

"Come, come," the AI went on as if the topic were closed. *"Gregor lived a fascinating life. His artwork incorporates many personal experiences and trials, as does all good art."*

"I would say that even this station is a work of art," James mused. "He brought all these pieces from somewhere else and formed them into a fake asteroid, right?"

"Quite observant. Gregor sourced rock from the deserts of the American west, Northern China, and the depths of the Mariana Trench. Though much of this station is made of common asteroids, he bound these layers together through a set of metal trusses, carbon fiber nets, and titanium pins. Once it was brought together and the basic shape acquired, it was carved by a complicated set of instructions sent to nanomachines, then sprayed with a low-albedo matte coat."

James raised an eyebrow at me. "Good work, I guess."

"It was a massive undertaking that took international funding."

"I can only imagine."

I had no words for any of what we were looking at. Aside from Leo, Marissa, and Shelly's occasional sketches, not many of us had had the mental freedom to express ourselves in such ways. It was clear that these pieces had been given care in their creation, intentionality put forth, but they were so outside my framework of understanding as to feel like a fever dream. To say that they were neat would have been an insult, but it was all I could come up with. I was no art critic.

But they were really, really neat.

"As I mentioned," the AI went on, directing us with a series of flashing lights to the next installation, which appeared like the cross-section of a small bedroom. *"Much of Gregor's work is drawn from personal experiences. I will let you stand here for several moments and observe. Then I will inform you in more detail of what it is you look at."*

And so, we did just that, the five of us crossing arms or rubbing chins as we inspected the life-size tableau of what could only be Gregor's childhood room. At the center of a square of gray carpet was a hip-high mattress resting atop a series of wooden drawers meant for storage. Its brightly colored sheets, geometric reds and oranges and yellows, rumpled and unmade, lay frozen like ice, surface covered in mottled splotches of black. A bedside table pressed up against the bed, covered in three different hand-held devices with large screens, as well as a stack of comic books, drinks at various stages of empty, and a collection of silver food wrappers.

An unnamed broken bottle of liquor lay on the floor, droplets of blood around its serrations of glass. A pair of what I believed were called condoms lay around it, but I only knew of them because of something Dad had said around my conception years ago. Dirty clothes were piled in a corner beside vomit, and upon the end of the bed lay a fractured human bone, maybe something from the leg.

A single picture hung from a fake wall, one of a young boy, sitting on a stool, his uncovered knees dirty along with his face. His clothes were torn, hair half shaved, face twisted in an expression of uncertainty.

I began to notice that one side of this piece was dark, cast in perpetual shadow, while the other side was bathed in the artificial light of a window facing a towering city. A city with flying cars and flashing lights and the promise of something better. A thin, glass portal viewing a better life.

If this was a true glimpse into Gregor's childhood, I felt fortunate for having my own personal variety of issues with my parents. They might have been absent at times emotionally, but they never let my physical needs go unmet. They never abused me.

This all felt personal. Too personal. The way the AI interacted with us . . .

An idea formed in the back of my mind. A tiny spark of realization set to ignite a space station doused in gasoline.

"I'm sorry," was all I could think to say. "It must have been hard."

"It was," the AI replied, its voice soft and small. *"But it made me—it made Gregor who he was. It gave him empathy for others. And it made him realize, no matter how dark our current day, there is always something worth dreaming about."*

I narrowed my eyes.

Xuan had wandered off to the next display. Something about this scene had hit her too close to home. I understood.

"Next?" I asked, turning away.

The AI made a noise as if to take a deep breath and rally itself. *"Yes. Of course. Next."*

We approached the following display, a sprawling series of concentric circles made of differing carpets of browns and yellows, becoming smaller at the center where a podium sat, a microscope at its center.

I made a move to inspect but paused.

"I think we found the passage," Lance reported over our channel. *"Keep it up. We'll let you know when we get in."*

I pinged an affirmation.

"Now this one is rather interesting." The AI continued our tour. *"It is often said that sometimes to go big, you must go small. In this, Gregor said, to go small, you must first go big. Please, feel free to look through the microscope's eyepieces."*

James shrugged and stepped forward, looking into the microscope. "Woah. What the heck?" He took a step back. "You've got to see this."

Hy went next, then Xuan, then Roger.

"Milo?" James asked, and I nodded.

"Fine. I'll look," I said, then bent over.

My view was replaced with that of something too detailed to be so small. It was an egg, or egglike in shape, made of an obsidian black material painted with silver. The boy and his kite were on one side among a pattern of hat tiles, while damask covered the other side. And the longer I looked, the more details I saw. Tiny pictures inside tiny pictures, forests in the lines of tiles, cities in the patterns of the leaves, faces of people in the shape of the skylines.

I stepped back and blinked. "What the hell is that?"

"Object d'art," the AI replied. *"A tiny collectable known as* The Never-Ending World.*"*

"A microscopic collectable?"

"That is correct. What better way to prove one's technical skill than to carve something so small?"

"It's . . ." I began, and felt my heart flutter. "It's magnificent."

"Something finally elicits a reaction in you. Do we have a lover of small things?"

I smiled at that, lips curving back so far I felt stupid. "Always have been. Figures. Nanomachines. Tiny kitchens and tiny, tiny food."

"We are pleased you like it."

"It was pretty cool," James said, stepping up beside me.

Our attention drew us across the aisle, lights illuminating a single, red chair sitting in a circle of black floor. It was of a normal size, and normal height, upholstered in a red cloth with something rigid and white sewn into its arms, but otherwise unremarkable. I'd seen many chairs like it, so it must've had some different meaning.

"And what is this called?" I asked, doing my best to sound curious.

The AI did not answer.

"You still there?"

"I am here." There was a pause, and the light over the chair switched off, along with the music, leaving us in silence. *"Are you ready to continue?"*

I looked to the rest of the crew, who were just as puzzled as I was. No commentary on this piece? No questions about how we felt, or if we liked it?

"Sure," I replied after a moment.

"Through the door then," it said, illuminating the path that led to the fractal-painted wall.

One at a time, we stepped through a new pressure door into a black room. For a moment, I wondered if we were being led into a murder chamber as the door shut behind us and everything went dark.

"What the hell?" James blurted out, but then the lights came on.

We went from standing on nothing to standing in an infinite field of lights and colors. Strings of blues and greens transitioned into purple and yellow, blinking in sequence, stretching out into eternity. The portals behind us and before us were like black doors leading in and out of this alternate reality.

Anxiety overtook me for a moment, making me feel as if we were back within the overflow buffer of the Wandering Gate. I wanted nothing more than to speed through this narrow passage to the exit on the other side, and so that was just what I did, elbowing past the crew to escape.

I burst out into another chamber with normal lighting, hands on my legs, panting.

"Milo, is everything okay?" Proxy called. *"Your vitals are alarming all of a sudden."*

"Here," James said, passing me a canteen. "Slow down."

I took several long pulls, then attempted to regulate my breathing.

"I'm fine," I told James as well as Proxy. "Hit a little too close to home, that's all."

"Is everything okay?" the assistant asked.

I raised my hand. "No problem. Just got a little claustrophobic."

"How peculiar."

After I had collected my thoughts and faculties, I found us standing in a new gallery, this one domelike, with a series of ivory sculptures set around the room.

I could not identify what these particular pieces were made of, but something about them made me uneasy. They depicted scenes with tiny people and small, primitive buildings, common interactions on display like shopping at a market or playing in a park with kids. Everything was in monochrome, ivory on ivory. The craftsmanship was as intricate as usual, but the materials reminded me of that stick Hy had found.

"This is a more recent collection of Gregors," the AI explained. *"It is titled* Dreams of a Lost Past. *You see, Gregor was attempting to recapture a time in human history in which things were simpler. A time in which not every action, every decision, was a matter of life and death."*

Something about this statement gave me pause.

"Who are you really?" I pressed. "You're not just an AI, are you?"

The voice went silent.

"Tell me, damn it," I demanded after several moments, my team turning to me with shocked expressions. This game was getting old. I didn't take it from the Foundry, and I wasn't taking it from whatever this was.

"Hey, hey, Milo," James said, raising his hands. "Chill, bruh."

The lights flickered.

"Very observant." The voice shifted, pitch lowering from tenor to baritone. *"You have seen through the ruse."*

My team took a collective step back from me.

"Who are you?" I spun around to take a look. "What are you? What are you really?"

The lights overhead flickered. *"I was, and I am, Gregor Machevarion."*

"And are you still living and breathing?"

"After a fashion," it responded. *"There are other modes of existence than flesh. And when one mode ends . . ."*

"Another must begin," I supplied. "A kind of immortality."

"You understand."

"I'm starting to."

"Did you see the child on your way in, yes?"

"We did."

"Marvelous, is it not?"

"I have never seen its equal."

"It was my magnum opus."

"Your what?"

"Master work," Leo cut in over the channel. I had almost forgot they were listening.

I nodded at nothing. This Gregor copy was so much like the Foundry in this. There was no one place to address it, which was infuriating. We were inside of it, not merely speaking to it. "May I ask a question, Gregor?"

"Of course. We are becoming fast friends."

"You say it has been 200 years since last you had visitors. There are many reasons this could be. We believe there to have been a devastating war in SOL that destroyed many records, claiming billions. Some call it the Great Gap. It is likely that this facility was forgotten in that time."

"A pity. And yes, this aligns with my records."

A pity . . . that was all?

"Yes. A pity. But when the last humans came here, why were they here? What were they here to do?"

"To see my debut, of course."

"A grand opening."

"Yes."

"Okay, but where did they go? You see, we have a suspicion that the heavy shuttles that brought them here are still on this station. We need them."

"And why do you need them?"

"Because we have come to fix Earth. We need those shuttles to see it through. We are from FICSE, and we have come to make good on our mission."

"FICSE?" Gregor the AI began to laugh, speakers clipping. *"Do you not have a better lie than that? FICSE! What a gas."*

James motioned for us to exit the gallery and inspect a nearby hallway. We held our weapons at ready, but I didn't see how they would help if this thing turned hostile.

We entered a narrow hallway, doors lining either side.

"We found a server room," Ada said over our channel. *"I think we also found the dock. Attempting to override the controls. Some of the systems are inoperable. This place is old as hell."*

"Just get in," I told them.

One after another, James and Hy opened doors, scanning the insides with their weapon lights. These were quarters, rooms neatly arranged with beds and desks and small closets, though no sign of people other than the occasional personal effects like a worn notebook, a gold watch, a set of fine jewelry.

"Again," I said aloud. "Where did the people go?"

"Go?" Gregor chuckled some more, its voice echoing down the hall. The lights flickered again, and the station vibrated. *"I am sorry for being obtuse with you. They did not go anywhere. Rather, they decided to stay with me. And here they have stayed all that time."*

"Oh, shit," James mumbled, hand paused over the latch of a doorway. "Here it comes."

I met his eyes and took a shuddering breath, then looked up, terror rising within me like the floodwaters of an overburdened riverbed. "What do you mean, they stayed?"

Gregor did not speak for a long moment. *"Have you not seen them? They suffuse all of my works."*

"No. We have not seen anyone but our group."

"But you have. You have. They are all around you."

James pressed a button beside the door on our right, and it swooshed open, revealing a dark space.

"You should see this," he said, and I came over, but I didn't need to enter the room for horror to take hold of me.

The cramped space was littered with floating pieces of ivory in different shapes and sizes, some bundled into collections, some allowed to float freely, and my stomach dropped like a shuttle free falling from orbit.

"Oh, shit," I whispered.

James could only nod.

"We found the override," Ada reported. *"About to go in."*

"Wait," I said aloud, but also over the channel. "Lance. I think it's a trap. The whole station."

"What?"

"The people. The ones who were here. They're dead. Long dead. But not before—"

The lights of the station went out, plunging us into darkness. Alarms began to wail, familiar warnings I knew to be standard UEI decompression notices, just like those on the *Vasco Da Gama*. The station was locking down.

"Helmets on," I ordered my group, and the nanomachines formed back into place, suits repressurizing.

Red lights replaced the darkness of the hall. I tapped a button on my chest, and floodlights shone from my arms and back and shoulders.

"What in the hell is going on?" Lance shouted over our open channel. *"Ada went to open the door, and she had it, but then everything went red! We're stuck!"*

"The previous visitors were murdered," I told him, meaning to say it only over the channel but speaking it aloud. "Their bodies were cleaned. Their bones were used for making art."

"What in the actual fuck?" he hissed back.

"And what wonderful art they became!" Gregor Machevarion's AI boomed over the loudspeaker. *"Long have I wanted to add to my collection, and so, I must thank you most earnestly for visiting my gallery. Let the work be completed."*

CHAPTER 47

"That ghost is trying to fucking kill us," James said, spinning around and looking for threats, his weapon raised and ready. "I don't always like being right, bruh. Not like this. Not like this. But ghosts. Fucking ghosts. I don't want to die to fucking ghosts."

"Come on," I said, waving them down the hall. "According to the station plans, this should open up onto a passage that takes us to where I believe Lance and the rest are waiting. If we have to, we'll escape the station and EVA back around to the other side. Our powered armor is more than capable."

Red pulsed around us, washed out by the bright lights emitting from my armor. The alarms went on, screaming at us, making it hard to think.

Bzzt. Bzzt. Bzzt.

We approached a T in the hallways, the pressure doors at our backs closing.

"That's no good," Hy said. "Shutting off our retreat."

"Let's keep moving," I urged, taking them around to the right. "These doors will likely close in sequence, so if we can get ahead of that sequence, we might just have a chance."

"There's no way we'll make it back to the entrance this way," Xuan said. "It's making sure that we get stuck."

I knew she was right, but I had to hold on to some shred of hope in the moment. That was what leaders did.

We crossed several dozen feet, then watched as the pressure doors ahead of us closed. There had been no chance of making it. Even with the augmented strength of our powered armor suits, I doubted we could have stopped the door from sealing itself shut.

"Shelly," I called back to the ship. "We need help, fast. We're in a shit ton of trouble over here."

"Working on it," she replied, her voice rushed, its tone a kind of fragile, forced calm. *"I am doing what I can, but Proxy is a little busy, and well, this system is beyond me."*

Bzzt. Bzzt. Bzzt.

If only we could turn off the damned alarms.

"What's wrong?" I asked. "What are you not saying?"

"I'm under attack," Proxy replied. *"Nanomachines from the station have bridged the gulf to* the Transcendence. *They are attempting to infiltrate my systems. They want control of me. They want control of the ship. I believe Gregor is tired of being trapped here. He wants to escape."*

"I can't start the engines," Karianna added. *"They've shut me out. I'm trapped in my Star Sphere. Locked in. We can still get shuttles in and out of the docks, but we're dead in the water. And not to make things worse, but those fungara readings we detected earlier are only getting stronger. There's no question we've got Isoptera coming to see us."*

Bzzt. Bzzt. Bzzt.

I banged my fists against the closed pressure doors several times, leaving a tiny dent in their surface.

From the direction in which we'd come, I started to hear something unusual beneath the cacophony of the screaming alarms, a noise at the very edge of perception. It was a rustling sound, a tinkling reminiscent of fingers running through a million tiny pebbles.

The red lights flashed and flickered, and I found myself blinking. They flashed again, revealing a spreading bruise of silver oozing its way around the corner of the hall, its mass adhering to the ceiling, walls, and floors. I had a good feeling I knew just what this was and had no desire to be around when it reached us. It was a swarm, a swarm of nanomachines come to strip the flesh from our bones and turn us into its interpretation of art.

"Come now," Gregor's AI said over the loudspeaker, his voice crackling. *"Stay with me. Be one with me."*

Alarms kept screaming.

"Head's up team," Xuan said while broadcasting over our open channel. "Nanomachines making big, fun swarm. Very bad for human health."

"What in the hell is that stuff?" Roger asked, taking a step back, his hands shaking. "We're dead, aren't we? We're dead. I should have stayed on the ship. Why did I have to be so eager?"

"Not dead yet," James replied, flicking the safety off on his weapon. He began firing at the encroaching blob of nanomachines, bullets vanishing among their mass. "Shit. Fat lot of good that does."

"We've got to get out of here," I hissed. "Shelly, I think Gregor's about to turn us into art supplies. I don't like the idea of becoming a postmodern sculpture."

"Proxy and I are working on it!" Shelly spat back at us. *"We're in the network now, but the language, the architecture, it's so different from anything I've ever seen. I don't even know where to start."*

"I'm working on it too," Ada called out. *"Just keep your thoughts clear, Shelly. Remain calm. Follow the thread. Go with your intuition."*

"I know. I know. It's just hard to do under pressure like this. I've found access to the cloud, but the encryption is ridiculous. Authentication keeps changing."

"We've seen worse."

"But have we? Have we really?"

Xuan and Hy fired their weapons along with James as Roger stood by, his body plastered up against the wall, his face stricken with horror. The distance between us and the encroaching nanoswarm blob was now only a few feet away.

"Please get us out," I said. "Get us out. Get us out."

I patted down my armor and reached into a pocket, removing a glass vial of silver fluid. I crushed the container while sending commands from my implants, my own colony of machines forming once more into a slender blade.

"Move," I told Roger, jostling him out of the way, magnetic boots clicking. "I'm going to try and cut through."

"What if there's no pressure on the other side?" Hy asked, and stopped firing.

James answered for me. "I'd rather die from explosive decompression than this. Pop that tuna can!"

I raised the nanoblade and drove the tip into the pressure door. It was thick, and even though this blade was the sharpest object I'd ever seen in my life, the plating was harder to cut than the fungara hull of the Isopteran ship.

"This is going to take a minute," I said, groaning. "Roger, give me a hand. Pull down on my arm."

The blade tracked through the surface, and to my relief, no air hissed through the rent. The blob continued to edge closer. James pulled some kind of grenade from a compartment around his belt and tossed it at the growing, silver mass. Light flashed over my shoulder. The hall filled with the buzz of electricity.

"Good idea," Xuan said, reaching for one of her own.

"Shelly," Ada called over our open channel. *"I'm sending you a diagram. I'm partially inside the network on this end. I know where you need to go to get access to the door controls. I don't have the network muscle to do it with a hand terminal or my implants, but Proxy should be able to break through."*

Why couldn't those alarms go silent?

"Soon as we get these doors down," Lance added. *"We're grabbing the first of the shuttles and getting the hell off this station. Hear me?"*

"I hear you," Ada replied.

"Are we not worried the shuttles might not work?" Leo asked.

Ingrid chimed in next. *"Of course we are. But from the plans we acquired in the records at the vault, that shouldn't be an issue. These models are fusion powered, and were built with a hundred different redundancies. All we have to do is get them across to the Transcendence. So, either they work, or we're dead."*

"If our proxies can't get its brain off our network though," Karianna said, *"none of this will do us any good. We've got to stop it. We've got to stop him."*

"Map received, Ada," Shelly said. *"We're working on the doors."*

I didn't see how this could get any worse. We were separated into three groups, trapped in our respective locations and unable to move as an insane AI, modeled from the mind of an eccentric artist, tried to kill us. If we didn't figure this one out quick, or even if we did survive, we might not even be ready to fight the Isoptera when they arrived.

The noise made my head pound.

My nanoblade wasn't cutting through the door fast enough. In null gravity, it was near impossible to get the necessary leverage I needed to slice it in two. I couldn't use Roger and my weight to push down on it, and the hall was just a little too big for us to reach side to side.

"I'm not having much luck," I told the team, sweat rolling down my forehead inside my helmet. "No good way for us to get at this."

"Pack it up then," James said. "I've got an idea. There's an opening in the swarm, and the hall across from us doesn't look like it's sealed. Let's push off and float past them, bruh. Keep tucked up tight."

"Milo?" Xuan asked, looking for confirmation.

I drew the blade from the door and twisted my body around, boots clicking against the bulkhead. "Good a plan as any." I reached for a pocket and found a stun grenade I didn't even know I had. "Don't touch any part of that swarm." I pulled the pin and tossed the grenade into the shifting mass of nanomachines.

There came a flash and a buzz, and several inches of the blob's depth went dead, giving us a bit more wiggle room.

One by one, we coiled ourselves against the now damaged door, then rocketed off through the swarm, twisting down the middle of the hall as not to touch the growing mass of silver. It reached out for us as we passed, slowly growing in our direction. Roger came last, the tiny machines licking at his bootheels but not quite touching.

"Milo," Proxy called back over the open channel. *"I've adjusted the power sources in your suits. If you come into light contact with the swarm, you can electrify your armor and render most of them inert."*

"Thanks."

My head thundered from all the noise as if my sinuses were stuffed full of slime and hammers were striking my temples.

We landed on the other side of the swarm, our group piling up as we came in contact with the far wall, the space bathed in dim red and harsh white cast by my suit. Our magnetic boots stuck to the floor, and we began shambling down another hallway heading away from the threat.

"I've got control of some of the network," Shelly reported. *"Alarms off. Doors opening. Milo, you should be free to go around the long way."*

And there was silence. Wonderful, blessed silence.

The lights came back on, though they were inconsistent.

"Copy that," I replied, and the doors before us swished open.

The swarm fell away over our shoulders, its advance slowed now that we could move.

"We've got to shut this thing down," Ada said over the open channel. *"Proxy, how are you fairing?"*

"Not well. We need a way to enfeeble this intelligence. Can you gain access to the server room?"

"We're out in front of it."

"Get inside. I will walk you through disabling its systems. Much of it can only be done locally, and smashing the servers will not help."

"Okay," Ada said, letting out a long breath, her movements clearly labored but invisible over the comm channel. "Lance, Ingrid? Stay close to the hangars. Get us ready to leave."

"As you say," Ingrid replied. "Be careful."

My team rounded the corner, and the overlay in my view updated, marking Ada and Leo on the map near a nondescript room, as Lance, Ingrid, and their pilot moved down the hall back to where they were.

"Sealing us in," Leo said. "Manual lockdown. I don't want anyone or anything getting into this server room. Let's hope that nanoswarm can't slip its way in."

The hall curved around to the left, and we took whatever doors were open, Shelly in control. My sense of direction prickled as I felt we were being led away from our target.

"Shelly?" I called.

"Not now, love," she replied. "Working on some very technical bits."

"I know. But, it's just . . . I think we're being led away."

"Not possible. I've got the map right here. I'm sending you right up the middle."

"No, you're not. The swarm is at our back, and we're being turned around on our original position."

"Oh, shit," she growled. "It's screwing with us. Clever bastard."

"What is this thing's problem?" James asked as we made yet another turn. Too many turns.

"I see now," Ada replied. "I see what happened. The AI. It's gone mad. Absolutely freaking mad. Now that I'm plugged in on the main control center of the server room, I can see it. This thing was built for a single purpose. It was built to give Gregor the ability to live forever, to continue his grand works in infinitum, but it wasn't fully stable. It was never fully stable, and it's not his fault."

"I'm sorry, what did you say?"

"The AI model was based on Gregor's thoughts and memories, as well as a pool of general data from humankind." Ada paused for a moment before going on. "Sorry . . . So long as the AI's model was fed fresh information, human-generated information from the real world, it was able to exist in a mostly stable state, though I can't truly call that living. It built things and grew . . . But when the wars came, and the data stream was cut off, it began generating its own information to fill that gap, to fill that need. It began feeding on itself. And in that time, it went mad. All this happened around the grand opening. *By the time the visitors arrived, he, it, whatever you want to call the thing, was not itself. The baby had drank its own bathwater. It was data poisoning of the highest level. It began improperly identifying objects such as the people who visited this place as, well—"*

"A medium," Leo added. *"A medium for his art. It wasn't intentional from a design standpoint, but lacking proper context, it saw some sort of artistic angle. It murdered them, stripped flesh from bones, bleached what remained. It used those bones to build sculptures and wants to do it again. And it felt nothing by way of remorse, because why would it? Would I feel remorse for using ink on canvas?"*

"So, it's insane," I said. "Out of contact with reality, lacking empathy. It's an unintentional sociopath."

"In the worse possible ways."

"And it wants to spread," Proxy said. *"It wants to use us to escape this place and become the dominant force in this solar system. Milo, this AI is less capable than us, but it has brute force we do not possess at this time. It will destroy us if we do not stop it."*

"Can we just blow up the station?" I asked. "Maybe it's best we flee this place and torch it."

"Maybe. But that's risky. If its servers are kept elsewhere, nanomachines will work to restart the process. Now that it's awake, we could be sending seeds of destruction out into the system. We woke this machine. We have a responsibility to stop it."

"Then it's a threat to everyone, even life on Earth?"

"I mean, when it sees human beings as an artist's medium," Leo said, *"and we're pretty sure it's self-replicating, then I would say, yes. Very much yes. How do we stop it?"*

"Proxy's right," Shelly chimed in. *"Now that I'm able to trace signals through its network, it's clear. This AI is part of a distributed system. Part of it lives in the running child."*

"And more on asteroids around the system," Ada added. *"You know, they might have been assholes on Aeolia, but Ares taught me a thing or two about Oboediens, the language this all runs on. Physical force will not be enough to stop it. Oboediens clouds are built to be very robust, engineered with redundancy on redundancy."*

"We've got to kill it from the inside."

"That's what I'm thinking."

"And just how are we going to do that?" Leo mused. *"Hmm?"*

"A virus," Shelly and Ada said at the same time.

"Do we even have the time to make a virus?" I pressed, looking over my shoulder for the swarm of nanomachines chasing us. "Not like you've got a template ready to go or something. You've got to do testing, identify weaknesses, right?"

"*Doesn't exactly have to be a virus,*" Shelly said.

"*Just has to work like one,*" Ada added.

"*The end goal would be to corrupt its systems. Make it kill itself.*"

"*Or go inert. Impotent. Repurpose it.*"

"*Its countermeasures will not allow any simple strategies to be deployed,*" Proxy reported. "*This Oboediens language contains many security measures capable of rooting out malicious attacks. From what we can see, it is very much like the universal inoculant in this. It knows what is meant to be part of its network, part of its systems, and purges anything which is not.*"

"*Too bad we can't give it something it might see as natural,*" Shelly suggested. "*Like it was part of its mind to begin with.*"

"*Like a kidney transplant from a matching doner,*" Ada added, "*but maybe it has a bomb inside of it.*"

"*A solid analogy,*" Proxy said.

They kept up their discussion, and we kept running for our lives. The swarm was gaining on us, and I was sure we'd run out of hallway soon. Our next dead end would be just that.

"Do we have any more grenades?" I asked the team.

Roger raised a trembling hand. "I've got one."

"Should have packed more," James said, taking the grenade. "Next time, I'm packing more."

The swarm rounded the corner, silver consuming every inch of the hallway we had just been within. Hy fired back at it, but the action did us little good other than make us feel as if we were doing something.

"Guys," I said over the channel. "Don't mean to interrupt the nerd session and all, but we are running out of time."

"*You know,*" Shelly said, ignoring my comment. "*What we really need is a higher intelligence. One uncorrupted.*"

"*A whole-ass person.*" Ada hummed for a moment, thinking that idea over. "*Or a pair of them.*"

"*You can't have my Chinchillette,*" Karianna cut in. "*Or Proxy.*"

"*Maybe we can make a copy?*" Ada mused. "*Would that even work?*"

"*Not enough time,*" Shelly told her. "*Besides, like we said before. The intelligence has to be like the host. Similar thought processes. I don't think a copy of either Proxy would get past the security measures. They'd be purged in an instant. A foreign body.*"

"You're thinking of replacing Gregor, aren't you?" I asked as we hit a long, straight hall. We took off at a dead run, boots clicking on the metal floor, trying to put as much distance as we could between us and the swarm. "Replace Gregor and fill its head, for a lack of a better way of saying it?"

"That's the idea," Shelly replied. *"And then we shut it down from the inside. This would ensure the entire network gets the same information and nothing gets away. It would rewrite everything."*

"But we need an intelligence," Leo mused. *"An intelligence of an artist. Did anyone ever make copies of people like Gregor did of himself?"*

"There were a few," Ingrid chimed in. *"We've got copies back on Earth in the data vault."*

"Can any of those copies be uploaded over the resonator network? It has some pretty serious bandwidth, yes?"

"It's a great idea, but we haven't calibrated our resonator crystals to Svalbard yet. They won't do us any good."

We entered a crossroad in the station's halls, and the door behind us closed with a loud thunk, along with the other three, trapping us.

"Shit," I said, spinning around.

James shook his head. "This is bad. Real bad."

"Guys?" I called, my voice cracking. "There's no getting out." I rushed to the far wall and removed the nanoblade, shoving it in the pressure door. Roger, James, and Xuan did everything they could to help me leverage it.

"There's not enough time," Shelly said. *"Gregor's intelligence covers four petabytes of data. Even with the resonator's connection, which we don't have, we'd have to find one that's compatible. Milo, I don't know what to do."*

We strained against the blade, pulling down as hard as we could given the angle I'd wedged myself into in the corner. It slowly bit at the metal. "I trust you, love. You always figure it out. Just—just be quick about figuring that out."

This wasn't working. I should have made sure we were better prepared than this. Maybe if we'd brought energy weapons instead of ballistics, we'd have fared better. Stun rifles would have been far more effective against the swarm than bullets. James had been right, I guess. This place was possessed, clear as day, and we'd walked right into its haunt.

Blood thundered in my ears as we tried to leverage the blade. We started pulling in time, but it only earned us an inch or two at a go. Augmentation or not, my body was starting to tire out, vision going blurry from exhaustion.

A silent minute passed as each of us put in the respective work of saving our asses. Karianna and Proxy gained some ground in retaking the *Transcendence*'s systems, giving me the ability to see outside the station, but that would not help us here.

"Come on," I growled, fingers tightening around the handle of the nano-blade. "Come on!"

"This door's a serious bitch," James added. "Should have brought rockets instead of stun grenades."

"They'd have killed us all in this tight space."

"Hang on, anyone have one of those Isoptera cube things?"

"Fresh out," Hy said. "Swarm getting closer. Nipping at our butts."

"Trade with me?" Xuan asked, and Hy jumped in.

"Question," Leo asked out of nowhere. *"Do the intelligences have to be a machine intelligence? I mean . . . Gregor wasn't exactly a machine to start with."*

Ada started to speak but paused, thinking through her words. She took a deep breath and asked, *"Are you suggesting what I think you are?"*

"Maybe? I don't know."

"What?" Shelly gasped at them. *"You can't. No. No. Not that."*

"Proxy?" Ada asked, her tone having turned clinical, emotion washed away by the terrible, sobering reality of our situation. *"Is that even possible?"*

"Is what possible?" I groaned. "What stupid idea are we entertaining?"

The blade had sliced through about three feet of the door, but we had at least another five feet to go. At our backs, the tinkling of the swarm intensified, its mass oozing around the corners of a pressure door. Time was of the essence.

"It is possible," Proxy replied. *"I can adjust their systems to accept you, and your brain implants would help a great deal in speeding up the process. A pair would be the most stable state, but I make no guarantees for personal safety. The process would likely be destructive to the original hardware."*

"Destructive?" I asked, eyebrows narrowing as I groaned against the haft of the blade. "What are the two of you considering? Will someone please tell me what the hell is going on!"

"Doesn't matter, man," Leo said. *"What we do here will save everyone. So, who cares?"*

"Who cares . . ." Ada mused.

A pair.

No guarantees.

Destructive to hardware.

It all came together, hitting me like a load of lead bricks.

These idiots were going to use themselves as the intelligences needed to fix the AI. Without enough time for us to find a better substitute, they figured it was smarter to scan their own brains and become part of the system so that they could shut it down from the inside. A process that would most likely claim their lives.

"We care, Leo!" Shelly cried out. *"We care."*

"You are family," Karianna cut in. *"You can't do this. Even if you are a pain in the ass sometimes, the both of you, there has to be another way."*

James and Hy gave me horrified looks. We had to get the fuck on the other side of this door right now. Maybe we could stop them. Maybe we could find another way.

Leo let out a manic chuckle. *"Look, I don't much like the idea either. Kind of like having ants in my brain, gathering up all my little, tiny, intimate thoughts. But we came to see this mission through, right? Sure, I'd like to make some more art. Have some more fun with the ladies, or maybe just one awesome lady, but Ada has already said it . . . My thinking is similar to Gregor's, which makes me compatible with this system. And look, Ada's levelheaded, so she can stabilize the both of us. We have to do this. It's the only way. We don't have any time left to argue."*

"No!" I shouted. "You are not going to fucking do this, and that's an order." My team struggled against the door, dragging the blade six additional inches. We were starting to slice through the other side, working to curve our jagged line into a semblance of a circle. All we had to do was get through to them. Get out of this room. All we needed to do was buy more time so we could save everyone. "I will not let you throw your lives away."

"Not your choice, Hughes," Ada said, her voice calm in that disturbing way people spoke when they'd made up their mind. *"Leo? You sure about this? There's no going back."*

He paused for a moment before responding. *"Yeah. I'm sure. Maybe it won't kill us, right? Maybe we can like live in a machine or something?"*

"Maybe."

The blade sliced through two more inches. The swarm was now only a few steps away. Hy tossed Roger's grenade at the opposite door. It flashed blue, then let out a buzz, and the swarm died, but we could hear more coming.

"*Proxy?*" Ada said after a moment. "*Send me the software patch to make use of the local nanomachines. There's a culture in the server room with us. We're going to sit down on the floor, get a bit comfy, and let them map our thoughts. Can you handle the rest of the work once we're unconscious? Or—you know—*"

"*I can,*" it replied. "*You may trust me.*"

"Stop it!" I shouted again. "Damn you all! Stop this! Don't do it. God damn it! Don't do it!"

"*We have to,*" they said together. "*You have to live—all of you have to live.*"

"*Jinx,*" Leo added. "*We think way too much alike these days.*"

Ada groaned. "*Shut up.*"

The blade cut through and the door gave way, the plug of metal floating away. We shoved aside the plug, climbing through one at a time, and ran away from the swarm to the server room. The icy space was just ahead, a large window down one side, with rows and rows of server racks and their glowing blue lights as far as the eye could see.

Xuan tried the door controls, but it was locked down just as Leo had said. We could see the two of them through the window.

"Please don't," I said, putting a suited hand along with my faceplate upon the glass. "I don't want to lose anyone else. We've lost enough people already. We've lost enough."

Ada smiled at me, gripping Leo's hand. The two of them looked serene. Leo gave us a wave, and they took a seat against a rack of servers. Silver began to swirl around them on the floor, oozing up and over their clothes and around to the backs of their necks, into their hair.

"Stop it!" I pounded on the glass. "Stop it!"

Shelly's voice came in over the open channel, choking, "*I failed you, friend. We didn't find a solution. I failed you.*"

"*You didn't fail me,*" Ada replied. "*You've never failed me. Life just happens. But you know what?*"

"*What, Lovelace?*"

"*Life is short, and you should go live the hell out of it. That's what I have done. Maybe I'll see Alex on the other side of this.*"

"*Wouldn't that be cool?*" Leo said, smiling. "*He seemed like a really great guy from what little I knew of him.*"

"*He was. Better than I deserved.*"

"Begin mapping?" Proxy asked. "Time is limited."

"Proxy!" I shouted. "Stop. I order you to stop this right now."

"I cannot, Milo," it replied.

"You are my Proxy. I have control over you."

"Not with this," it said, the timbre of its voice sounding remorseful. "I am sorry, but I must protect the pilot. All calculations point to this being the best course of action."

"It's okay," Leo told me. "We'll be okay."

"Begin mapping, Proxy," Ada said, and Leo echoed her approval.

"Understood," it replied. "I will be as careful as possible."

"No! No! No!" I growled, fists pounding on glass.

"Bye guys." Leo raised a hand in a grand flourish. "It's been a lot of fun. I've had myself a life worth living, shared with people who are worth loving. That's enough for me. That's all any of us can ask for."

Ada's eyes twinkled up at us, tears clinging to their corners. "Bye-bye, friends. See the mission done. Go save Earth."

"No," I whispered. "Please no."

They closed their eyes and held their breath. The quicksilver swarm of machines swirled around their heads, and the servers behind them began to blink in sequence, blue lights turning yellow, then red, then green before turning back to their original state.

"Look," Hy said, and we turned around.

The encroaching nanoswarm began retreating, returning to wherever it was it had come from.

Lights around the station began to flicker, then clicked off, leaving us in the dark for several seconds before the red emergency lights came back on.

I looked through the window. Both their chests had gone still. They were gone. More lives taken by the mission. My friends . . . no, my family, lost to this madness.

"We've got control back," Karianna reported, her voice as fragile as paper-thin glass. "All signs point to Gregor having been shut down."

"The AI is overtaken," Proxy confirmed.

"They're gone," Shelly breathed. "They're gone . . ."

I rested my head against the window as Xuan fiddled with the locks. There was no way to get inside to recover their bodies without cutting through the walls, but the rest of the doors were unlocked, and the station showed no signs of being hostile.

"I know this isn't the best time," Ingrid said, appearing beside me along with Lance. She rested her hand on my shoulder. "The shuttle bays are open. We have our window."

I nodded but did not speak, and she took this as approval to get started. James met my misty eyes and came over, throwing his arms around me, our armored suits embracing. I didn't push him away. He didn't say a word.

"Time for Clicker arrival?" Ingrid called over the open channel, her shoulders slumped, her tone tired.

Karianna replied shakily, *"Um, about forty-five minutes. They do not sound happy either. I think they know we blew up that shuttle. Not to mention that we took out a few ships over Venus. Five targets inbound, all medium weight. More than enough for us to have a serious brawl."*

"Then we should get a move on." Ingrid waved to Roger and the other man. "Pilots, to the shuttles. Proxy, send more over."

"Confirmed," it replied.

"Are we just going to leave them here?" I asked, letting go of my old friend. I put a gloved hand to the glass. "Are we going to leave them by themselves? Abandon them?"

Lance turned to me and shook his head. "Just for now. I know how you feel, man, and I feel the same. We'll come back for them. Okay? We will come back for them. But there isn't enough time."

"There never is." I let my fingers fall and stepped away, shambling after the pilots.

There was a cost. Always a terrible cost.

But when would it be enough?

When would it all end?

How much would we have to pay?

CHAPTER 48

Ballistic impacts peppered the MI as we roared away from the Grand Gallery, our bays bursting with the heavy-lifting shuttles long abandoned by Gregor Machevarion's murdered patrons. A part of the Gray Queen's fleet had found us. We did not have the time or inclination to rumble with these oversized insects and their fungal warships. As they closed the distance, I kicked up the drive, increasing our acceleration and powered up the weapons as Karianna micromanaged our defenses. Despite our recent misalignments and sorrow, action sharpened our intentions and put us right back into a working frame of mind. We two pilots were again one unit, at least for now.

We'd swallowed up the last of the shuttles just in time for the enemy's arrival, landing number thirty-two in our bays as the first shots were fired. We hadn't yet raised our defenses, and as a result, a burst of kinetic energy tore into a strip along the starboard side of the *Transcendence*. Two sections were spaced in an instant, explosive decompression destroying some noncritical supplies and two backup Star Spheres, but thankfully no one was there at the time.

The order was made, everyone splashed down, and we were running. This went against everything I wanted. It would have felt great to take my aggression out on the enemy ships, to pound them into dust even if they were not the direct cause of our most recent woes, but that risk was too great. If we failed to overtake them, if we fell here, now, Ada and Leo's deaths would have been for nothing.

And so, we exchanged blows with the Gray Queen's forces as we fled, crippling two of their lumpy, greenish ships, gas spewing from holes along the bumpy surface of their organic shapes. Dozens of fighters swarmed our position, and Lance led a wing of fighters out into the space around us, clearing these enemy combatants with minimal losses.

Distance between us and our fighters increased as we continued to burn away, and they soon returned to their bays, forcing us to bear an onslaught of long-range fire they'd been keeping busy. We bathed the enemy fleet with Para Lux beams, slug after slug of antimatter, and quick shots from our railguns. We took one of the crippled ships down, but it wasn't the largest among them. It scattered bits of fungara as it decompressed, as if it had dashed itself upon the rocky shores of an unforgiving sea. They ripped and tore into our MI, breaking it into a tattered sheen of silver matching pace with our vessel. It was rough for a few minutes, tactical projections not looking good, their force overtaking us for a moment, but then it was over.

I slumped down in my Star Sphere, if that was even possible, and let out a long breath. We were free, and they had no way of catching us.

It had been hundreds of years since we'd left this solar system and returned, and yet, I never felt like we had enough time. We were somehow always running out of time. It was almost as if the moment you observed its passing, the quality of it changed, making it finite. So long as we ignored its passage, it seemed to go on forever.

Once our distance was great enough, we adjusted our trajectory to intercept humanity's cradle. Step two of our crazy plan to save Earth was behind us.

Nice work, Karianna thought, her emotions carefully neutral, though mine were not.

You too. I grinned back at her, trying to hold myself together despite feeling raw. *Couldn't do it without you.*

Duh.

Several hours passed as we realigned our navigation and took stock of the recovered shuttles. Given that we were still under heavy acceleration, everyone remained in their Star Spheres, but we made use of cameras and other instruments for our inspections. Most of the old ships appeared to be in solid, working condition; only a few needed serious repairs. Of the thirty-two we had collected, only four were unsafe for transport between Earth's surface and orbit. This was due to airfoil damage that likely came sometime before arrival at the Grand Gallery for two of them, the impact of space debris during their journey and reactor issues for the others. By these metrics, the mission had been a resounding success, but it still didn't feel like one. With the right labor in place, Ingrid assured us they would be more than enough to get the materials where they needed to be. Couple that with calibrated pairs of resonator crystals, and we were in business. It was hard not to be distracted, but we pushed through, and I told myself that the only reason I hadn't spoken to Ada or Leo was because they were busy elsewhere. I didn't want to face the truth.

We were talking through a schedule on the general repairs necessary for our fleet when my instruments pinged.

"Proxy?" I called, alone in my Sphere, floating in a sea of stars. Shelly had been with me moments earlier but had gone off on her own to think about them. We had all been thinking a lot about them. The ship didn't feel the same. My heart didn't feel the same, that crazy-ass girl and the stupid, artsy bastard who'd become her counterpoint . . . Any one of us would have done what they did, and I knew it. They had laid down their lives not just for all humanity, or the mission, but for us. They had laid down their lives to protect their chosen family.

"Proxy," I called out again. "Am I crazy or did I just hear something?"

The cat appeared at my side, looking up at me with those glassy eyes. "A ship approaches."

"Serious?"

"It is not Isoptera."

I turned around and narrowed my eyes at the expanse of space on our port side. My view zoomed in on the location, giving me only a blip surrounded by green lights.

"Who is it?" I asked.

Proxy tilted its head to the right. "Why don't we ask? They are headed for our position."

"Doesn't look large." I focused our instruments on the object. "Its mass is no more than a couple dozen tons. It has a drive that's hot, but nothing like a warship. Not a shuttle though. Bigger."

"It is a transport. And while we cannot yet get a good reading on its shape or size, other than it being small, the materials lead me to believe it is UEI made."

I analyzed its trajectory and started to put a few pieces together. I had a feeling I knew exactly who it was, but I didn't want to venture.

You reading this? Karianna asked.

I am.

You thinking it's who I think it is?

Maybe.

This ought to be interesting. Want me to squash them? That ship's pretty small.

No, no I do not.

Meh. All for the best, I suppose.

A few moments later, a signal pinged our array. I didn't immediately respond to it. I waited for a while, reclined, reading one of my books to pass the time while letting them sweat it out. It was hard to remain focused on the page given how scattered my thoughts and emotions were. Again, there was never enough time. I wanted to mourn, but didn't have the luxury, not in this moment.

That said, we were not at this person's beck and call. They would have to fucking wait. This interaction would happen on our terms.

Karianna laughed at this through the integration.

A second ping hit the array.

I waited.

A third.

"Are we going to be rude?" Shelly asked, appearing beside me with a scowl on her face as if I'd tracked mud through a room that had just been cleaned. "Proxy told me you are ignoring our guests."

I closed the book and sighed. "No. We won't be rude. I just don't want anyone pushing us around."

"Mmm," Shelly responded, and it was not a clear agreement.

"Ok. Fine." I rubbed my face and took a clarifying breath.

I accepted the ping.

"This is Captain Milo Hughes of the FICSE vessel *Transcendence*. Please identify yourself," I responded.

The other ship waited. They were closing on our position and were now only a few hundred thousand kilometers away. Light speed lag was not the cause for their delay.

"Transcendence," the caller said after some time, a touch of a Spanish accent in his words. *"This is Admiral Cardoso of the Remnant Fleet of the UEI. I have come at great expense to have a secure, private conversation with you."*

"Could have just sent us a ping."

"I said a secure conversation." He paused for a moment. *"On a general ping, even an encrypted channel, who can say someone isn't listening? There is technology at work beyond our understanding all throughout the system. Lattice. Clicker. Splicer. Spectra. D'vasic. Foundry. We thought it best to have this conversation face to face."*

I paused before responding. More names of species I did not recognize. "Who is we?"

"Let's just say, I'd like to keep this conversation free from a certain former FICSE mission specialist. Is that fair?"

Shelly's eyebrows rose. *Fractures*, she mouthed back at me.

It seemed Veetor was not one of their favorite people either.

I nodded as if he could see over an audio-only channel. "What assurances do we have that this is not some kind of trick?"

Cardoso let out a belly laugh, but it wasn't one of amusement. *"A trick? I'm flying a tiny silver teardrop without any weapons through open space. We have been under more than ten Gs of acceleration for days just to catch up with you. Your ship could flick us into dust like an ant crawling up your arm. You have all the power here, Milo Hughes. There are no tricks to be pulled, no aces in the hole."*

I paused the channel for a moment.

"Proxy?" I asked, and the cat appeared by my feet. "Do you see any threats close by?"

The cat shook its head. "There are no signs of any other ships, hostile or otherwise. They come alone."

"Weapons?"

"It has come close enough to get a good scan. Their ship lacks the mass for it to have any serious compliments. I'm not saying that this is without risk, but based on the usual threats we face, I would say this one is minimal."

"We should talk to them," Shelly added. "They held back in the last fight. As did we. And if there's a fracture, we can use that to our advantage. Maybe they will join us. Maybe take our side. We have not attacked them. That fact in itself is leverage."

"Maybe," I mused.

Are you sure this is smart? Karianna asked, her emotions mixed.

No, I replied, and did my best to hide any unease I felt. It wasn't easy to do that. This felt foolish.

I switched the channel back on. "Admiral. You may proceed. We will give you instructions on where to dock when you get closer. Please do not attempt any hostile actions to us. This is a Foundry-made vessel, and it has defenses the likes of which you have never seen before. You are right that we can and will destroy you easily if you give us a reason."

"*Fair,*" the admiral replied. "*Look forward to seeing you shortly. Cardoso out.*" The channel went dead.

"This ought to be interesting," Shelly said, floating to the arriving ship.

She made a gesture and drew the image closer to us. It was indeed a mirrored, silver teardrop, bulbous at the forward end, tapering to a point at its aft. From the size of it, there could be no more than three to five passengers within. No boarding party, that was for sure. Just a few visitors.

The ship flipped around to begin its deceleration burn, falling into alignment, the six drive cones mounted near its middle hot.

I cut our main drive, and we went into freefall.

"Proxy?" I asked.

It perked up and turned to me. "Yes?"

"Whatever internal defenses we have, keep them on standby just in case. I know these capabilities are something we've never talked about, but we need to keep them contained to the docking bay."

"Of course."

"Play nice," Shelly said, wrapping her arms around me. "We've had enough heroics for a while."

"Yeah," I said. "Yeah, we have."

The teardrop drew close and cut its main drive, using navigational thrusters to maneuver into our only empty docking bay. It drifted inside and set itself down before being swallowed up by the *Transcendence* like a whale eating a single krill.

Once the bay was pressurized, we stepped in to greet them, freshly bathed, wearing clean clothes, dressed professional and presentable. The Free Citizen pilots were making use of this period while not under thrust to work on the shuttles, while our team, minus Xuan, Hy, and Lance, worked on calibrating the resonator crystals.

None of us were armed, but with Proxy's support, I felt we didn't need to be. They were entering the Foundry's world. I stood at the front of the group, Karianna on my left, Shelly on my right, our Proxies before us waiting patiently on the deck.

"You know what that thing reminds me of?" James whispered in my ear.

"What?"

"Ever see *Attack of the Clones?*"

"Attack of the what?"

Karianna rolled her eyes at me and looked to James. "You're right," she said. "Not exactly the same, sure, but in that style. Actually, you know, the more I think about it, the more it reminds me of that super-tiny ship from *Men in Black*."

"Bruh," James said, slapping himself in the face. "Even better, except that this one lands on its side."

"I have no idea what you two are talking about," I said.

Karianna narrowed her eyes at me. "You never do."

Three people I had never laid eyes upon stepped out of the cramped shuttle, their postures stiff, expressions of those who had just endured a tough flight.

At the front of their group walked a middle-aged man with dusky skin and sad eyes. This had to be Admiral Cardoso, no doubts about that. Like Ingrid, it was clear from his disposition that he had faced a hard life full of hard decisions. He might have even been considered attractive if given a good reason to smile, but as it was, he looked too tired and angry. He was dressed in all black, but not a jumpsuit like we used to wear, rather a kind of form-fitting uniform shirt and pants with the UEI emblem and insignia on his left chest. His receding hairline was cropped close to the scalp, and a dark shadow persisted along his jaw despite being cleanly shaven. He kept his back straight as he moved forward, body tense, shambling his way down the shuttle's ramp with a kind of three-foot-wide metal-bound plastic case in his arms. I wasn't sure what it was, but it sure looked heavy.

To his left was a young woman in her later teenage or early adult years, with umber skin, hair shaved along both sides, a single strip down the middle pulled back into a ponytail. She looked at me, at my copilot, and then at the rest of the crew, her gaze so sharp I thought she might cut us with it. Unlike the man, she had on a biker-style leather jacket and high-laced leather boots. She looked ready to kick out my teeth for the sheer fun of it.

On his right, and a little behind them, came a woman dressed in the same black uniform as they had been, but with a sort of flowing robe over it. She wore a colorful hijab of red and yellow over her head, concealing her hair, allowing us to see only her face. She was short and had dark eyes with soft, pale skin and a button nose. Her thin lips were painted in candy-apple red. Unlike her companions, however, her resting expression was far more friendly.

By the time they had reached the end of the ramp, I noticed the three of them wore nearly the same rank insignia beside their UEI emblem. I wasn't familiar with what it meant, but instincts said that the rank of captain seemed most appropriate, with a few additional stars beside Cardoso's.

The case in the admiral's hands blinked. He set it down on the deck at the base of the ramp with a hard thunk.

"Before anyone tries anything," Admiral Cardoso said, clicking a button on the side of the case. "The bomb has been armed."

A collective gasp cut through the crew. Shelly squeezed my hand. I didn't know in that moment if I should be pissed off or terrified. Based on how fast sweat was beading on my back, I think I was a bit of both. My initial response was to ask Proxy for help, but something held me back from this.

"I'm sorry," Karianna stepped forward, a prosthetic finger raised in accusation, "what the actual fuck did you just say?"

"I have armed a fifty megaton nuclear fusion warhead," he replied. "The bomb is set to a series of dead man switches, one connected to each of the three of us. If we should come to any serious harm, the bomb will trigger, and your ship, or at least a section of it, will be reduced to its base components. Do we understand?"

My hands balled into fists as my earlier fears sublimated into an annoyed brand of diffuse rage.

"A hell of a way to start a conversation," I growled, urging Karianna with a hand to step back. "We allowed you to come aboard in good faith. And so, what is this?"

"Ahh," the admiral mused, his gaze falling to the floor.

I inspected the box, privately pinging Proxy to make any nonintrusive scans we could. The only thing that was clear was that it was lined with lead, making it nearly impossible to penetrate its bounds. As a result, Proxy's findings were inconclusive, little more than a few cylindrical shapes and a slight trace of gamma radiation. There could be a bomb inside the case, sure, or it could be a whole bunch of bananas, maybe a horse's decapitated head. We just couldn't tell.

"We must protect ourselves," said the young woman with the shaved hair and leather jacket, her voice deeper than I had expected. "At least we didn't point guns at your faces or show up in a battleship."

I glared at her. "Might as well have. You're putting the entire human species at risk."

"A bit dramatic, don't you think." She crossed her arms and snorted.

"And so are you," the woman in the hijab shot back, her voice soft. "Every action you have taken fractures our fragile system."

"Every action we take?" I placed my open palms on my chest. "You're kidding me, right? What aggressive actions have we taken?"

"How about slaughtering the people of Aeolia?" the admiral pressed, fixing his eyes on me. "What about that? We heard all about your little sortie on Venus."

"Slaughtering?" I chuffed. "You've got to be kidding me."

"You assassinated the premier as well as several of her elite guards."

I raised my open hands. "Hold up. No. We're not playing this game. What do you know of Aeolia? What do you really know?"

"It is none of your business what I know."

"No, I think it is." With our recent tragedies, I was not taking this shit from anyone anymore. I was out of Fs. I would do my best to be diplomatic, sure, make Shelly proud, but I was not being pushed around. "How often do you interact with them? What do you know of their society?"

"Well . . ." he began, but trailed off. The admiral looked to his companions.

The woman in the hijab spoke up. "We are trade partners. We offer them defense, they give us access to refined resources from Venus's surface. Processed gasses. Specialty food stocks. They have been good to us."

I leaned in. "But have you ever been there?"

The admiral looked to his companions. They said nothing.

"I see. Never been to the station. To the surface?"

"We know of some who have been ascended," the admiral said.

The case containing the nuclear weapon blinked and made a chime, and I did my best to remain calm. What if one of their dead man switches was faulty? A signal not connected for long enough. This could be bad.

"Veetor has been to Aeolia, though," I supplied after a moment. "Captain Veetor Nabrali. Don't you find it funny that he has, but not you?"

"Yes, he has," the admiral said, sounding uncertain of himself. "Many times. Was becoming close friends with the premier."

"Well, let me tell you this." I hardened my expression, narrowing my eyes at them. "Aeolia is not what it seems. It has been used as a place for the wealthy and powerful to escape suffering, but it's a trap. And the ascendence? A fabrication. They carefully monitor and control everyone who lives there, inviting only those they desire most. They offer you riches, and parties, and love, but it's all a lie. It's a human-Lattice lie. When the lights fade, and the dinners end, and the pleasure of the orgies fade, all that's left is a persistent, mindless bliss. A numb state in which they can manipulate your mind to power their defensive automatons. They force people to fight to the death for this privilege, and they do, so strung out on Bliss that they see no other way to go on.

"So, tell me. Are the remnants of the UEI like this? Are you like these sociopathic autocrats? Or something else?"

"What?" the young woman asked, taking a step back. "That can't be true. I know people aboard the station, not one of the spires, but the old UEI structures, the platforms. We—we talk sometimes. Not often."

I gave a nod, tightening my lips into a hard line.

"He speaks the truth," Ingrid insisted. "Cardoso, please hear me. If you cannot trust him yet, trust me. I have spent time with this former FICSE crew. Seen how they act. They truly do wish to help. I've bet my life on that."

"Of course a bunch of scavs would say that," he growled, and this made Ingrid's face crinkle up in anger. "I mean no disrespect, Overseer. You have done what you must to survive, but Earth is a wreck. An irreparable wreck. Best to let it die."

"Yeah?" Her back went straight. "But it's our wreck. Our home. And we are not giving up on it. Not yet. Not like you and your deserters."

"Hey, hey," I said. "Name calling won't get us anywhere. Make your introductions, Admiral. Let's have a civil conversation. Maybe one without a bomb."

He cocked his head to the side. "Doubtful on both counts, but I'll make introductions, okay?" He crossed his arms and nodded to the left. "My friend here in leather, this is Captain Athena of the *Milwaukee*."

The young woman gave a snarl and a nod. "Best heavy cruiser in the fleet."

"Hardly," the woman in the hijab spat back.

"More Clickers downed than you. Fifteen to ten."

"Just give me the chance."

"And this," the admiral went on, sounding a bit annoyed. "Is Captain Nahid Darwish of the *Sickle*."

"Pleasure," she added with a slight bow.

"While I am admiral of the much larger remnant fleet," he went on. "These are my two most trusted captains. Which is why we are here."

"I was just about to ask that," I said. "Why *are* you here? So far, all we've accomplished is having the shit scared out of us with a nuke and some names thrown around."

"You," he said, pointing at me. "We are here to talk about you. It's been just under two months since you popped onto the scene. Before that, we had a good thing going. The system was quiet. Everyone minded their business. Lattice were long gone, or so we thought. Splicers were only messing with a few settlements. And then there's the Clickers. We've gone nearly two years with them leaving us alone. So long as we were quiet, they stayed away, their base remaining dormant.

"Then you show up. Start broadcasting all kinds of signals. Make all kinds of noise. This forced us into action."

"We were led into a trap," I said.

The admiral groaned. "Perhaps. But a trap only humans could understand. The message itself was not my idea. It was Veetor's."

Shelly spoke up. "Love. Live. Pray. Burn. Fall. Ash. Anger. Atonement. End. That was the message."

The same message the crowd had shouted when the arena battle on Venus was about to begin.

"Yeah." He scratched at the back of his head and rolled his shoulders, looking uncomfortable. "That's the one."

"Absolutionist ideology," Ingrid said full of venom.

Athena raised a finger. "They're gaining traction, even in the fleet. People who would rather let everyone die and start over than try to save any of this. Let the strong survive, let our sins die."

"And does that include the three of you?" I asked. "Sure doesn't sound to me like you want something different."

It was Captain Darwish's turn to respond. "God is no terrestrial being, and is the creator of us all: human, Clicker, Splicer, and Lattice. He loves all his creations." Her words then came out like a recitation. "'Do you not see that Allah is glorified by all those in the heavens and the earth, even the birds as they soar? Each instinctively knows their manner of prayer and glorification. And Allah has perfect knowledge of all they do.' "

"What she's saying," the admiral cut in, "is that the Absolutionist ideas can go to hell. We believe in living. Saving everyone that we can. This is *our* mission, if not always that of the rest of our forces."

"Then why ally with Veetor?" I asked. "I don't understand. It's clear he wants to burn everything to the ground. He told me as much as I fought for my life in a gladiatorial arena on the surface of Venus. Captain Nabrali was the master of ceremonies for the fight."

His eyes went wide. "A what? You did what?"

"Fought for my life. Like it was ancient Rome or something."

"That's messed up," Athena said. "Hope my friends are okay." Had my comment somehow gotten through?

"For your sake, I do too. If they can leave, they need to."

"What do you defend?" Shelly asked, her voice soft. "We know of Aeolia, the settlements on Earth, some on Mars, but . . . where do you come from?"

The admiral cracked his back and motioned at the crate. "Mind if I sit? I've got arthritis all down my spine."

"Will the bomb go off?"

"Not for this." He groaned as he lowered himself. "What's left of the UEI is a disparate set of orbital settlements scattered around the system. Saturn has a decent population density—that's where Athena is from. So does Jupiter. Europa and Titan have small surface colonies, research facilities turned homesteads. We've got a few more locations in the belt. But our largest colony is hidden from alien threats on a dwarf planet that was not discovered until the year 2146. We call this place Shroud. It is a dark matter rock found entirely by accident. I won't give you its location, but needless to say, close to a million of us live there, including my wife and my three kids."

"The theoretical Planet X?" Shelly mused.

This made the admiral chuckle. "Sort of."

"So, you do not follow the Absolutionist ideals?"

"Not even close," he said, face twisting as if he had tasted something sour. "I get that hurt people hurt people too. It is part of being alive, being human. But burning it all down to start over, culling the herd, so to speak, I do not think it will fix these problems. The universe is not so discerning with saving only the good ones. If it were, how did we end up here? We do well on Shroud, but it is not easy. If Earth was safe again, environmentally, it would give our people options. A sense of control. It would give our people hope. Those who want to stay there and struggle, they may, but those who wish to leave . . . I see the wisdom in this." He paused for a moment as if imagining a dream just out of reach. "Veetor and his followers will not allow that."

"Then that begs the question," I pressed. "Why follow his lead? Why let him infect the resilient ideals of your people? He has only been here a few years, right?"

"Why let him?" The admiral raised his fingers to pinch his nose. He adjusted his seating on the plastic case and met my eyes. "Bold words from a man piloting a ship big enough to fill a city center, and with enough firepower to level a planet. Veetor came back from the void, seemingly out of nowhere, and pushed his weight around any way he could. He is the ultimate apex predator. What could we do about it? If we opposed him, unpredictable as he is, he could have reduced everyone to dust with that ship of his. You think we do not know who and what he is? But we know. We know."

And that was fair. A psychopath with weapons like he now possessed could do a lot of damage if they wished. I still wondered why the Foundry had given him a ship at all. What kind of scale was it trying to counterbalance? Was this connected to what we had done to the Jevox? Was this a way to carry a variable over to the other side of the equation? I didn't see how, but I knew the Foundry was up to something. This was a galactic chess game. How did this serve the mission of protecting life?

"Things have not always been perfect in the UEI," Athena began. "I was born on Shroud, but moved to a station orbiting Saturn when I was older. I wanted to explore myself, learn who I was, and Shroud was not as accepting as we would all hope it is. I became part of a community called the Ring. They were a collection of body modders and biohackers, people with perhaps less traditional sexual partnerships and exploration than most. They became my family, my tribe, one unlike anything I had ever known before. A true community. We gave freely to one another, in resources and love. Then the Clickers came one night, raided the station, killed my friends, my lovers, and I was left to drift in a leaking space suit, dying among the wreckage. I was fortunate that Admiral Cardoso was able to save me, and I am eternally grateful for this, but that did not solve the problem those big-ass insects had created.

"When Veetor showed up a year later, offering protection for all, those who had lived through these horrors gave their unwavering devotion to him. They did not see an opportunist looking to build a cult of his own. Instead, they saw a messiah come to save them from damnation."

"The Clickers have taken so much from us," Shelly ventured. "We have lost many loved ones."

"Yes, we have," James added.

Karianna shook her head. "Justin. His name is Justin Wiggins. Stop calling him by that other title. He's an asshole. He's selfish. He's the reason my father is dead. He is the reason the *Brilliance* went up in flames. His mutiny nearly killed us all."

"And he now has power," Darwish said. "Are you starting to see? We have only ever done what we must. This is survival."

I nodded. "I think I understand."

"His intentions . . ." the admiral said, shifting around on the case. It blinked again and made a chime, but our visitors did not seem concerned at that. Curious. "His intentions are not clear. He wants what he wants when he wants it. And your intentions? You've shown up, not asked for more than to be left alone, and skipped about the system making friends, killing what appears to have been potentially corrupt leaders, still not sure what to trust, and doing God knows what else? You have been under our guns and still not fired on us, only Veetor. You have given us opportunities to stand against the Clickers even when we tried to kill you. *Ay dios mio.* What are you after? What in the hells do you want?"

I looked to Proxy, to Shelly, my crew, then back to the admiral. "We are here to protect life," I said in a defiant tone. "We are here to save Earth from itself and protect those we can."

Ingrid smiled at this, lips wide like someone having a manic episode. It was a genuine expression. "Admiral, they have technology that, with the right help, we can use to reterraform Earth. We can undo the damage generations have done to it."

"You must be joking," the admiral said, then turned to look at his companions. "We tried that once, I think. A couple hundred years ago."

"And some of those devices remain," Ingrid went on. "But Milo and his crew possess technology from a species whose home is over a thousand light-years away who do this for a living. They terraform the worlds of other species in exchange for protection. And they have graciously given us enough of it that we can change the face of our home world."

"It can't be," Captain Darwish mumbled. "Sounds like a pipe dream."

"It's true," I said. "We are here to finish what FICSE started. The Foundry may not have been what we thought, but it gave us the tools to make the journey to find the things we needed to see the mission done. Foundry Intent, Contact and Save Earth. We may not fully know its intent, but we made contact, and we are devoted to save Earth."

"And you've been collecting what you need to see this work finished?" The admiral rubbed at his chin. "Build these machines, put them into service. How do we know they are not a weapon?"

"I assure you that they are not. The Jevox are a good people. Isolationists, but not aggressive in any way. I trust them."

And at that moment, Frelo appeared from the shadows, their slender, multijointed arms performing a kind of dance, robes billowing as they moved, their five eyes shimmering in the light of the docking bay.

"*Santa maria,*" Cardoso hissed, the Jevox stopping their advance just a few steps away from him. "It is with you. A real alien, not just a relic of the past. Not an enemy come to kill us."

"I am Frelo of the hive on Rix," they said, and made what I could only say was their approximation of a bow. "They speak truth. Our devices will work if given the labor, resources, and time. The Jevox always protect life."

Which was partly true. Mostly true. True in this.

"We trust Frelo with our lives," I said. "With our future."

"Okay, okay, a lot to take in," the admiral replied, scratching at the back of his head. He shifted in his seat upon the nuclear crate. "You trust the Jevox, this Frelo. But do I trust you? It is all too much to swallow. So much to take in. Maybe I should just set this bomb off and start it all over. Let those Absolutionists have another win. If there's one thing I know about Veetor, he won't let everyone die. He'll have already picked his harem and might just start the species over with a smaller gene pool."

Karianna grumbled. "Sick bastard with a tiny dick."

This made the admiral's eyebrows shoot up, but he said nothing.

"Look," I said, taking a step forward, focused on the case. "I'm not going to say things won't get complicated politically. Looks like they already are. What I can say is that our objectives are the same. We just want to save what human life is left and give us a fighting chance. You will likely not leave here fully believing us. We will likely not leave here fully trusting you. But I want you to take a look at our actions, not just our words.

"Unless we are pinned into a situation where it is life or death, we will not fire on a UEI Remnant Fleet ship. Now as for Veetor and the *Absolution* . . . that's a different story. If we can burn him up, we will, but I don't think that will be easy."

"Because he is strong?"

"Yeah," I said, but it was a half lie. I had a feeling we couldn't take Veetor down because this was a game playing out. The Foundry was testing us yet again, and I had a feeling it would dial both our weapon systems back so neither had a winning advantage in open combat. "He is strong," I went on. "He positions himself well. Chooses his moments carefully."

"I'll bite. What do you need to see these machines work?" Athena asked.

"People mostly," Ingrid said. "There's a list of certain supplies, raw materials and the like. Equipment to be manufactured, ancient factories to bring online. We have a list of a thousand items critical to seeding the infrastructure and getting the machines running."

"And are you having luck?"

I shrugged. "Some. We've lost friends because of our mission. But we got what we were after."

Athena lowered her head. "Sorry to hear that."

"Us too. And, thanks."

A beeping noise came from Cardoso's watch.

"Admiral?" Captain Darwish said, resting a hand on his shoulder. "We are running out of time for us to make the rendezvous . . ."

"Okay, okay," he said, standing up with a groan. He turned to face me. "A matter we have not fully discussed are the immediate threats we face. The Clickers have taken possession of Haumea. What you recently saw over Venus, and what I believe was chasing you away from that cursed artifact, is just the tip of the iceberg. In their silence, over the past two years, they have amassed a sizeable population. Millions of them live upon its surface in massive hives. They have hundreds of ships in orbit. There is no way we can face this force head-to-head."

"Can we drop rocks on it?" I asked. "Turn the place to glass? What about Veetor? He might be useful in this."

He shook his head. "They'll stop any attempts at bombardment. We have tried; their base on Haumea is protected by dozens of their massive, gray carriers and hundreds of those wardens—what a nasty bunch. I'll give you what technical data we have on them, if it will help. But Veetor? No. He won't say it, but he's afraid to face them. We need some other kind of weapon. Something that can't be detected or stopped, but I can't think of one. I'm afraid that when they decide to take action, I don't think Earth's ecological issues will be our problem anymore. They'll harvest whoever is left no matter the cost. I don't know why. Food has to be easier to make other ways."

"It is," Shelly supplied. "But they believe eating humans will help them evolve."

"Shit," he mumbled.

James took a step forward, his back straight. "Why don't we go take them on together? We can inflict some serious damage in the *Transcendence*. That, and there's one more option."

"Maybe," I said, giving him a look that informed him not to press deeper. We were not having that conversation, not here, not with them. "But we have another mission for now."

"Our mission should be to burn those assholes up."

"We'll deal with them," I said, an idea starting to form in the back of my mind. "If they come for Earth or Shroud, we'll stand and fight."

Captain Darwish tapped her arm with two fingers.

The admiral waved a dismissive hand at her, then looked back at me. "Thank you for speaking to us, Captain Hughes."

I tipped my head and pressed my lips into a line. "I hope we can stay on the same side. I don't want to fight you. You seem like good people. Please, consider joining us."

"We'll see."

They turned to go back up the ramp, leaving the crate behind them.

"Hang on a second," I said, raising a hand. "I think you're forgetting something."

Admiral Cardoso slapped himself on the forehead in a comical sort of gesture and spun around. "My apologies, friend." He pressed a button on the plastic case, and it popped open, revealing a glowing, smoking interior filled with a dozen silver canisters. I stared at them for a moment, then frowned when I realized what they were.

"Enjoy the beers," he said, turning to leave while tossing us a peace sign.

"That son of a bitch," James whispered as their shuttle ramp retracted.

Karianna let out a chuckle and pressed a hand to her face to keep the rest in. She was the only one of us to find this funny.

We'd been bluffed.

It was clear that there were fractures in their alliance. The Isoptera were preparing to make a move. Veetor was ready to see it all burn. And here we were, the dwindling leftovers of FICSE, standing against it all.

The end felt near, but what kind of end would it be?

PART III

CHAPTER 49

We were closer to our goal, but it didn't feel right. The resonators had been located and were being put into place. The shuttles had arrived in Svalbard and were undergoing service and refitting. They were operational, if needing minor work. Alliances had been forged in our absence, and labor and support was coming, even if we weren't sure if it would be enough to see the project complete. Veetor and the Remnant Fleet stayed out of our way for now, ignoring us, off someplace else, allowing us to contend with only the occasional Isopteran scouts.

I should have been pleased at this outcome. I should have been happy. But I wasn't.

It didn't feel right.

None of this felt right.

Throughout my life, Dad had spoken at length of the suffering of humanity and that this suffering was universal. No matter our background, upbringing, culture, or faith, we suffered the same. It was all part of the great and terrible "human condition." Hunger was hunger. Thirst was thirst. Loneliness was loneliness. Disease, a lack of shelter, pain, these were constants. But happiness . . . now, now that was different for every person ever born. And it was complicated.

Happiness was, and is, the most elusive of all human ideas. It means different things to different people. On Aeolia, it seemed to mean drugs and sex and manipulation. On Novae, a night with friends under the stars or exploring self-expression through art or science. At home with Shelly, it was a quiet night on the couch, snuggled up reading whatever pirate book or scientific compendium felt right at the time. Happiness is hard.

Happiness is a choice. Happiness is something we must make a conscious effort to have, or else we just won't. But that effort for many of us, that choice, only appears when we fall below a certain threshold of suffering.

The people of Earth were barely hanging on, and it was clear that they were suffering. They were hungry. They were thirsty. They were dying of viruses and diseases that hadn't existed when FICSE left Earth. Their souls had become riddled with a brand of pragmatic hopelessness, the only future before them mere survival. I had seen it in Ingrid's eyes, in her actions. And it was only for a few, very few, that true happiness was found in the scattered, serendipitous moments that balanced on the edge of a knife. Oskar was one of them.

Fulfilling FICSE's mission was not going to make everyone happy, especially those who followed Absolutionist ideals, but it might just help to ease their suffering. If we succeeded in this, the people of Earth would be given a second chance to find happiness, to find self-actualization, to foster a new generation of humankind. Our species would not, could not, go into that dark night.

And yet . . . none of this felt right. It wasn't the removal of suffering that had become the problem—that was our mission. It was again that there were those who should have been here to see it. Ada and Leo had become our most recent sacrifices set upon the bonfire of FICSE. They had willingly thrown themselves into its inferno to keep the flames from guttering out beneath the filthy downpour of human sins. If Gregor had just allowed himself to pass into obscurity and infirmity, as we all must, then my friends, my chosen family, would still be here.

But they were gone, and we had no time to dwell on this. We had work to do. Work to see that their sacrifice wasn't in vain. And I would be damned if it was in vain.

Back in Svalbard, Frelo worked with the Free Citizens of Earth, along with a contingent of project directors from the settlements, on the overall plan. In the time we had been traveling to Aeolia and the Grand Gallery, Frelo had analyzed the data we had collected on Earth and identified what challenges lay before us. The good news, if we had any, was that this project was not insurmountable.

"My species are terraformers," Frelo said, addressing our leadership from the yellow meeting room within Ingrid's compound, the square arrangement of tables overflowing with people. This was a big moment for many, having never seen an alien, let alone anyone being confident there was some way to restore Earth to what it once was. Everyone held their breath; no one dared interrupt.

I felt no need to speak. My chest was like a vise, those final moments on the Grand Gallery playing over and over in my head like a broken record skipping across scratches in its grooves. I kept trying to think of how I could have done things differently. How I could have saved them. I had failed. This was on me.

Frelo went on, gesturing at a screen hanging on the wall. "The word 'terraform,' which the Foundry implants uses as translation, is close enough for our purpose, and yet it is not entirely accurate. It is my understanding your English word for it translates to mean, "Earth-like," and that it was coined in a twentieth-century story of science fiction, or a story of fake science. It is strange to me that we should form this planet to be like itself, though in what state does that mean? If we were to take a lifeless rock in some distant place, and give it this composition of characteristics, it would indeed be forming it to be Earth-like. But here, you desire to turn the clock back. To return to an earlier state.

"After consulting with your leaders, as well as the prevailing research of your people from before your great conflict, it seems that your consensus is to return the planet to what you call "preindustrial times." This is the time before you converted your entire world into an inefficient engine of pure economic growth. And if I may comment on this from an outsider's position, this seems to have been the primary catalyst for both your remarkable expansion and nearly every conflict in history. It is regretful your species has yet to evolve past this as ours did."

"And we can do this?" Ingrid asked, leaning forward where she sat, fingers laced together making a triangle with her arms.

A series of people entered the room at that moment with silver carts covered in cups of coffee and bottled water. As the question hung, those gathered were served, taking refreshments gladly.

Once the servers had left, Frelo raised a hand, fingers grasping at open air, their five eyes blinking in a counterclockwise sequence. "I cannot be sure that everyone here has heard the story of Rix. But my world, my home, the cradle of my species, was destroyed once. It was not a threat from within, as yours is, but from without. The Gan laid waste to our planet, and what few of us survived did so by hiding underground. Once we emerged, finding a sea of sand and glass and tainted waters, we knew we had work to do.

"As one, our people labored tirelessly, a single entity, a single purpose. We built great machines that were not much different than what we will use to clean your air, renew the soil, and filter the sea. We engineered the moons around our world, providing us protection from our host star to extend the lives of those on our world. For five generations we toiled, until we restored our planet to the place it was before our one-sided conflict began. So yes, to answer your question, we can do this. We have the technology. The question becomes, do your people have the will and resources to see it done?"

This summoned a good deal of muttering from those gathered. Dameon's hard work had been the primary catalyst for those leaders from around the globe to join us. He had sold them on the vision we had cast, of a broken and tired people working together for the betterment of all mankind. While there were different opinions in the room on how society might be organized best, all agreed that not having an ecosystem to exist within was the direst outcome. Including Ingrid's, seven settlements were represented, most of which were part of the Free Citizens of Earth. Member settlements included Svalbard in the north, Paphospolis on what was Cyprus, the Borough of Skive in central Denmark, the Boot near Florence, Italy, and Antalya on the Mediterranean in former Türkiye. The last census taken put the total population of member settlements at around 3.1 million, the largest of the two states being the Boot and Antalya.

As for nonmember settlements, there was Queensland, home to 1.7 million, located near what had been Brisbane, Australia, as well as the Daegu Habitat in South Korea, home to another 2.7 million, making it the largest known settlement on Earth outside of Siberia. Both were independent nations, with their own governments and traditions, far removed from one another, but neither wanted to see an end to humanity. They were well-defended territories, and were thriving by Earth survival standards, but they were smart enough to see that this would not last forever if we didn't all work together. A failing environment was only one of our troubles. Veetor was still out there, and so were the Isoptera. Kabosai had been spotted as well, though to this point, we had no idea what their intentions were. We knew there would be a long and bloody road ahead.

In the end, everyone had something to gain, and everyone had something to give. Dameon had called these nation-states here because of past relationships and ties, gathered the information, and helped Frelo see the jigsaw puzzle that was their varied resources. If only on paper, this plan could work.

"But you have a plan?" Dirk Adlershof, leader of The Borough of Skive, spoke up. "Not just talking, no? We are willing to help but only with a plan will it work. Our people are hungry. Disease is every day."

More murmurs from the leaders gathered.

Dameon adjusted his round framed glasses and frowned. "As we already agreed, you will all be sent home with what the Foundry refers to as a universal inoculant. It will identify any non-native bacteria or virus in your body and remove them with the use of nanomachines."

"But it won't fix broken legs," Karianna said sourly, head shaking. "Or radiation poisoning, or heavy metals in your lungs . . . Just biological sickness. So do be careful."

Niccolo Santucci, leader of the Boot, tugged at his moustache. "Is it safe? This shot?"

"It is," Shelly offered, and put a hand on my leg below the table. I took hold of it and squeezed. "Perfectly safe. All who travel to the Foundry facilities receive it as a matter of course. As Karianna stated, it won't protect you from everything, but it will keep you from getting unintentionally sick. No ancient viruses, no alien contamination. All of us have had it in our blood for years and traveled to so many places."

"But the plan." Bak Yoon, leader of the Daegu Habitat, cut in, his deep voice rumbling as he raised a hand. "We want to hear about the plan. Our people will be making considerable contributions to this cause. We must know if it is worth it. Otherwise, we should go back and entrench our defenses."

Those who had not yet spoken up nodded. Defense was a major topic.

Frelo's eyes blinked. "The plan, yes, the plan. I am a Cerulean. A Cerulean. And a Cerulean always has a plan." The display beside Frelo changed, showing a series of diagrams, basic blueprints for several devices. This quieted any whispering that had continued in the room. Even Tayo, the leader of Antalya, who had not stopped talking since he landed in Svalbard, sealed his lips.

The Jevox began, "The first phase of the plan will involve manufacturing and infrastructure. We must collect all the materials on this list and bring them to our factories within the Boot and Queensland. I hear that Daegu might have a small factory that can be restored a hundred miles from their city-center. This would also be valuable to bring online. In that time, we will distribute the resonators so that communication is instantaneous for all involved. We will create supply chains from the mines or salvage yards of Paphospolis and Antalya. Once these are in place with a constant supply of new materials, we may begin the construction of the Towers.

"The second phase of the plan is Tower distribution. We will need a collection of more than a hundred. Each of these 350-meter-tall structures will act as a local hub for robotic equipment. This includes the Sky Sweepers, which will draw hazardous gases from the higher reaches of the atmosphere, to the crablike Haz Crawlers, as Lance has named them, which will travel in groups to the irradiated regions to remediate, remove, and store any radioactive materials left behind from faulty nuclear power, or the use of fusion weapons. This is not to mention the later phases, which will involve the biospreaders the Towers produce to repair the soil and make it arable once more.

"The Towers themselves will require a constant feed of fresh material in order to operate, repair, and manufacture new robots for these uses. They will run tirelessly to filter the air around them, removing excessive carbon and methane, storing and reusing these materials for other, safer uses."

Santucci raised his hand, and Frelo paused. He tugged again on his moustache as he spoke, twisting at its long ends. "For manufacturing, if I am understanding right, the Boot will be one of the most critical centers. The great Mancini Forge will build these towers to restore the earth. It has the capability, though it will take many, many materials. I have seen your shopping list, great Jevox. It is full of iron, steel, copper, gold, radioactive materials. We have enough in this room?"

"Between Antalya, Paphospolis, and Daegu, yes," Dameon said, looking to the leaders of each settlement in turn. "Or so your reports say, honored leaders. There are materials in the ground, but so much salvage left from the war."

"Oi, don't forget Queensland, mate," Jack Bennet said, adjusting the large, tan hat on his head in a casual manner. The Australian leader tossed an arm over the back of his chair, kicked his feet up on the table, and flashed a smile, revealing his too-bright white teeth. "The Boot's got one impressive facility from the old days, make no doubt, but we've got one too. Ours is out there in the bush, ain't been found by them extraterrestrial visitors. With them manufactories up and running, if we can keep their laughing gears wrapped around a steady stream of deliveries, then no worries, mate, she'll be right. We'll have them towers stood up and running before you can call your mum and tell her all about it."

Angelina Drakos, the leader of Paphospolis, who was sitting beside Bennet, gave his dirty boots a disgusted look. She met eyes with him and narrowed them. He raised his hands in a "what, me?" gesture before returning his muddy heels to the floor, leaving a collection of tiny clods behind.

"As for the state of things," Frelo continued after a moment. The Jevox was getting so much better at reading human social cues. "We are talking about removing all the radiation, making the soil usable again, and getting carbon levels under control. What was that number again? Where are we?"

"As it is now," Shelly said, tapping her hand terminal, "we are close to 2000 parts per million of carbon. While this isn't the only cause of the rise in temperature, it's one of the leading ones. To get us below preindustrial times and cool the planet, we need to get below 350."

"A process that will be easier on the front end," Frelo said, considering, "but harder on the back. Once the concentration of methane and carbon has decreased, this process will slow. We will essentially be chasing each errant particle on its own, which is why we will scale up the use of Towers and Sky Sweepers."

Tayo said, "And that will fix it all?"

"It's a start," Shelly replied, tipping her head and raising her palms in a kind of shrug. "We might have to take more drastic measures to cool the planet in the near term. Phase two is heavily reliant on how much labor we have available."

"Labor," Tayo chuckled, his broad shoulders shaking in his white robes. "Antalya is not afraid of hard work. We only need purpose."

"Third phase is like the second," Frelo continued before anyone could interrupt, "though we are moving into secondary Tower locations at this point. Here we will press our supply chains to their limit. We have a theoretical maximum of Towers we can maintain, though I am working out that exact number. We will push up to that limit and care for them. This is when the Bio Spreaders will go into service, flying machines capable of scattering a mixture of basalt and self-degrading nanomachines that will create an environment for accelerated weathering and soil enrichment. We will also make use of the Sky Sweepers and drag the harmful particles from the air by force.

"The fourth and fifth phases will involve the possibility of creating a solar mirror, as Miss Hughes suggested, that will deflect part of your star's light for a time to cool the planet. Weather satellites may also be installed to deal with the superstorms you often face. Once the environment starts to revert to its former state, it will be time for reintroduction."

This comment earned a series of nods from around the room. One of the biggest challenges we'd learned of was that with the warming of the planet, super hurricanes would sometimes dominate the globe, lasting as long as a year and hitting almost every settlement as a result, even those in North and South America that did not politically align with anyone present, causing catastrophic flooding and death.

"Here in Svalbard,"—Frelo pointed at the ground—"your long-dead governments kept a vault of seeds, a physical record of this planet's native species. With careful application, these may be distributed around the globe so that nature may retake the land. If all goes to plan, this will create a self-sustaining system of cleanup. You will have a new home, green and blue, environmentally safe and ready for your offspring to thrive."

"As we have always dreamed of," Drakos said, the dark eyes of her mousey face trembling.

"No more suffering," I said, meeting her gaze.

"This sounds like Utopia to me. To be given the chance just to live."

"How long will all this take?" Bennet asked. "Sounds like a lot of work to change the whole planet, even with this advanced tech. No offense meant, mind."

"It is no wonder that Mars has never turned green," Tayo added.

This earned a chuckle from several people in the room, like this was an inside joke.

"If all goes according to plan," Frelo said, their five eyes blinking in a random sequence, "ten to twenty years."

Bennet whistled in exasperation.

Santucci turned to the Aussie and raised an eyebrow while tugging at his moustache some more. I swore he was about to rip the damn thing off his face hard as he was pulling. "Come on, Jack, it's not that bad. We've been scraping by for several generations now. To spend one generation fixing the earth, I think that's a victory."

"And it means we all have something to unify us," Ingrid said, standing before the group. "We haven't had something like that in a long time. This is important if you are part of the Free Citizens of Earth, or not. Our mission, our charter, states that we exist to help free humankind from the mistakes our ancestors made. What better a unifying cause than this? Can there be a more noble use of our time, energy, and resources?"

"Dameon already gave us that whole speech," Tayo said, waving a dismissive hand. "One big hazmat operation. And we bought it then, you don't have to sell us on it again. This makes sense for all. Everyone benefits, even those bastards in Siberia or what's left of South America. We fix this place. Let nature take it back for a few hundred years as we lick our wounds."

"What about protection?" Bak Yoon asked. "We not speak of it yet. If we do as we say we are going to, much attention will fall on us. We have done well to be quiet on Earth, hide from extrasolar peoples. But this? This will draw out the Clickers. Maybe even the slugs. The scavengers have been poking around the habitat for some time. Will they not attack us now?"

"We've had concerns," Drakos said, her wrinkled eyes dropping. "My son was one of our defense force. Nineteen of them faced down the enemy last year in an incursion. The Clickers were too many. We were underequipped . . ." Her words hung in the air, hands trembling. Santucci, who sat beside her, offered a kind hand, which she took before laying her head on his shoulder.

"So much distance between our settlements," Bennet mused. "How's it we plan on keeping supply lines up, mate?"

The remaining leaders looked to one another and nodded. Direct tragedy aside, it was clear that a bone-deep, existential fear loomed over these people like the Sword of Damocles, silently waiting to fall and end their lives.

Something inside of me snapped.

"We have limited means of defensive assistance as a group," Dameon chimed in. "While we have the heavy shuttles to do the work, we have little or no air power. Everyone must rely on their own forces. There will be deaths. We will lose equipment. But we must be careful. Keep an eye on the sky; defend the ground facilities as best as possible. Perhaps we can resurrect some old war equipment. Refurbish it."

No one seemed happy with this thought. They knew it was true, that much was clear, but they had ignored this fact for a time, focusing instead on an idealized vision of what the world could be when they were done.

I was tired of this "being afraid" shit.

I was tired of losing people, even if I didn't know them personally.

Someone had to take a stand. Someone with the means, not just the anger.

"We will protect all of you, all of you," I said, quicker than my brain could filter the idea, my words solid as a steel blade cutting through the noise. This felt right. I sat up in my chair, taking in the faces whose attention had fallen on me. "I am tired of seeing people die from these hive-minded freaks. It's been like that since day one in meeting the Foundry. I am tired of giving them the means to perpetuate whatever this agenda is, to turn us into meatsicles for them to somehow evolve. I'm tired of anyone who puts their boot on humanity's neck. We've been kicked down into the dirt and told to shut up. That stops now. That stops today.

"Here is my promise: We'll protect every single one of you. So long as you are part of the project, you will fall under the protection of the *Transcendence*. And we will fight and fight and fight until the last breath we hold. We will not let this line break. We've got you."

"Milo," Ingrid said, leaning over Shelly and coming close enough only I could hear, her left hand gripping my arm. "Are you sure you want to make this promise? Dameon is right—you can't be in all places at all times. Earth is a big planet to cover."

I scowled at her, prying her fingers away. "We'll keep the heat off. No one else dies. Get it built. Just get it built."

The room was silent for a long moment. Then they began to cheer. The suddenness of the shift hit my ears like a bucketful of icy water.

"FICSE! FICSE! FICSE! FICSE!" the gathered leaders chanted, heels stomping against the floor in time. "FICSE! FICSE! FICSE! FICSE!"

I looked to my crew members sitting on my left and right, each as stunned as I was. This was what they needed to hear. We had to make good on our promises.

Ingrid crossed her arms and let out a long sigh before turning back to those gathered, flashing the fakest smile I'd ever seen as she tried to save face among her peers.

CHAPTER 50

Hours passed in tense negotiations before we came to an agreement.

Seven nation-states.

Eight thousand nine-hundred and sixty-five workers committed. A low count. We needed more. Far more. But a start.

Massive equipment to be manufactured.

Resources to be recaptured.

Ten to twenty years ahead of us.

Countless points of potential failure.

We had now climbed upon the razor's edge.

My thoughts consumed me, visions of a twisted future fraught with danger. Not all humans wanted this to succeed. Their were Absolutionists hiding in the shadows of our movements. The Isoptera wouldn't want us to succeed, either. Or would they? This would make it easier for humans to grow up and be born—a terrifying thought. These ideas swirled through my mind in technicolor, blocking out the world around me until fresh cheers drew me back to reality.

"FICSE! FICSE! FICSE! FICSE!" the gathered leaders cheered as everything wrapped up.

Our new mission was clear: keep them alive so they could do the work.

The meeting adjourned, everyone ambling off to their respective sleeping arrangements. Shelly waved at our crew and called them to a corner in the room. Within a few seconds, there was no one but us from the *Transcendence*, the voices of those who had left trailing off down the halls.

"Nice job, Milo," Karianna mumbled as she came up beside me, her tone snarky. "That was really fucking stupid."

My face screwed up as the hairs on the back of my neck stood on end. "What are you talking about? What was stupid?"

"Have you not heard of underpromise, overdeliver? It's like customer service 101. There are seven settlements down here, and now, somehow, we're responsible for providing air cover over thousands of miles. How do we plan on doing that? Hmm? We're in atmosphere—that means only the Swift Shuttles will be useful. We have three of those, but only two of us can pilot them well."

James came up beside Karianna, clearly intending to say something or try to calm her down, but she brushed him away like a buzzing insect.

"We intercept them in orbit," I told her. "Easy, peezy."

"Yeah, well, that might work most of the time, but they are going to come at us at some point in a . . . uhh . . . *swarm*. They're a freaking hive species, that's how they operate. And so, what if we fail?"

"We won't fail."

"What if some of them die, you okay with that?"

"No one dies!"

"People are going to die, Milo. Saying otherwise won't change that. We've already seen it. Again and again, from the first Foundry encounters by the *Vasco Da Gama* and the *Brilliance*. My dad at the hands of Justin. Yours in 75-DFX. Ada and Leo will not be the last."

I pointed a finger at her. "No one else dies! It stops here, do you hear me? No one else dies!"

Karianna leaned in, her anger evaporating as soon as she saw my eyes. I wasn't sure how I hadn't noticed, but now I saw my hands trembling through my blurred vision. I palmed away the tears and took a shuddering breath to calm my emotions.

"Enough, both of you," Shelly said, pushing us apart. "We all want the same thing here. So, let's cool it. Okay? We're all hurt."

Karianna grumbled at this, though her heart wasn't in it. "Fine."

"Assignments," Lance stated, taking his place in our circle with a terminal in hand, acting oblivious to the argument he had clearly just seen. "Been talking with Dameon and Ingrid, and with our experience, they need some help. Figured you all wouldn't mind pitching in, so consider yourself voluntold."

"Great," Xuan said. "Very nice for man to assume what I will do."

He pointed to the top of his list. "Renata, you'll be helping train the defensive forces down here. They aren't great, and you have experience working in a real military. That okay, Cox? I wanted to let you have Xuan to help, but we need her with us up above."

Renata crossed her arms and nodded. "I'll need a team to teach what I know, who will then teach the rest."

"Ingrid has you covered. Some of her most trusted and most talented people are at your disposal."

"Perfect."

"Chevelle," he said, turning to her. "You okay with staying down here? I need someone to run point for me to help Dameon with project management."

"Does a bird have a bunda?" She smiled, her bright white teeth gleaming. "This is what it's all about, innit. Sure you don't need extra guns with that promise an' all? I wouldn't mind bein' back in the sky."

Lance looked to me, then back to her, thinking this over for a moment. "No. I need you here. If we don't make progress, nothing up there will matter."

She raised an open hand. "Say less, blud. We'll keep the whip at their backs."

James shuffled through our group, an eager expression on his face.

"I'll be working on interfacing the legacy systems," Shelly spoke up. "I won't be as quick without . . . well . . . she was . . . Proxy and I will get it done. There are many computer systems we believe we can sync using the resonator network. They just use too many different languages. They have gaps in compatibility. We're going to build a connection."

I put a hand on her shoulder and sighed.

"Hy," Lance said.

He straightened bolt upright. "Sir?"

"I thought with your studies in materials science, you might be able to help the manufacturing team in a consultative capacity from the ship. They're working to make the best of what we have, but generations have passed without formal education. They may have some gaps. Might be some ways we can cut a few corners, repurpose salvage and so on."

"Of course." He bowed his head. "I would be honored to be of service."

"Now, Frelo is staying here with Dante and Emilia, who couldn't make it today. They'll hash out the big items. Air defense is of course up to Milo and Karianna."

Our team made notes on their personal terminals or on their implants. We were eager to get started on our tasks, all but one.

"And what about me?" James said, leaning to the side. "Everyone else has a job. What does James Reed need to do?"

This took Lance aback. He hadn't thought about it, that much was clear. "Well, im—"

"You forgot me, didn't you?"

"No." Lance shook his head. "I just—look, um, there's still plenty to be done. Let me regroup my thoughts, talk to Frelo and Ingrid. We'll make sure you're put to your best use."

James blinked, his spine going limp, hands sliding into his pockets. "Sure. I understand." But it was clear he didn't, or perhaps, maybe he did. He looked as if the comment had punched him in the guts. We would need to talk later.

"We all good?" I asked, looking to my people. This felt like a moment to say something, and so I summoned whatever words I felt Esteban might have said. He'd always had the right thing to say. "I know we've been asked to do things we never expected. We didn't expect to see Earth like this when we left as kids or as young adults. I do know that there has been no other group of people in all of history in a position to make an impact as big as we are.

"You are the smartest, kindest, bravest group of humans I have ever known. I'm so very proud to call you my crew, but more than that, I am proud to call you my family. You are my brothers and sisters, my aunts and uncles, my cousins. And like family, we fight sometimes, but we pick each other back up." I looked to Karianna, then Lance. "We stick together because we have something even deeper than love for one another. I'm not even sure there is a word for it. We can make a difference. We can make a change. We are here for one another."

"Till the end?" Karianna suggested, sticking her mechanical fist into the air at the center of our group. James picked up where this was going and added his own, knuckles brushing Karianna's. For the briefest moment, I saw a twitch of excitement on her face at his touch.

"Till the end," I said, and we all joined in, forming a circle. "The Foundry once said, you must choose what is important. I think we've done that. This here . . . this is what is important."

"We protect life," Shelly whispered.

Over the next two weeks we went on tour, escorting leaders back to their settlements for them to prepare, returning with resonator crystals properly tuned and secured. After what had happened with Bliss on Aeolia, we decided it was best to create a kind of metal box with a web of shock-absorbing cables to keep these in a state where they could be easily accessed without ever touching them. Didn't want anyone becoming addicted to the substance and deciding it best to grind down their communication crystals to get high.

One by one, I visited the settlements, parading around with Shelly and Karianna like we were gods of a sort, more than just heroes. We were FICSE. We were a living narrative. We were from the legend of their childhoods, come to save them from darkness and death and suffering.

We began our tour in Paphospolis upon former Cyprus, escorted by Ingrid's personal guards, as well as the overseer herself, her right hand in government, and her spiritual advisor. Well-worn streets hemmed by ancient brick buildings rolled out before us, covering the countryside, every free inch of real estate stuffed with onlookers cheering our names and praying blessings for the mission, blessings that God almighty would hedge us in his protection and see us through. After a feast of wine and meat and twisted vegetables, we were whisked away to the next destination.

A pattern emerged as we disembarked in The Borough of Skive, the cool air of the once Danish city filled with billions of tiny slips of confetti. Distant cannons fired in sequence at our arrival as soldiers marched in formation to present the martial readiness of the smallest of the Free Citizens Settlements. There was more cheering, feasting, drinking, the very best from the ancient stores beneath the surface shared with those from FICSE.

Guilt overtook me.

We did not deserve this.

They had suffered so much.

The Boot was no different, though their parade led us through a massive courtyard where a fifteenth-century church still stood, the Basilica di Santa Croce. Though damaged in part by time and war, the structure had stood against all odds, an important landmark styled in gothic revival. We were led off the busy streets into a breezeway and through a gate that had the letters O.P.A. etched above it. Santucci informed us they stood for *ora pro animis*, or "pray for souls." I lost track of time, finding myself walking the hallways of my twisting thoughts, but Shelly listened for me. Santa Croce was the final resting place for many a noble person of the Renaissance, such as Michelangelo, Machiavelli, Foscolo, and strangest of all, Galileo. This detail felt fortuitous, not serendipitous. Santucci made many suggestions to us that felt more like demands, and we filed them away for later. They wanted priority of defense, additional food, and a prominent place in the new world order, whenever that came.

I just wanted to leave and go away someplace quiet.

Once we had been given our fill of wine and bread and coffee, we were off to Antalya, where Tayo led us through gauntlets of people in the old city, as well as into a glass outpost that lay along the banks of the Mediterranean Sea. Its people played strange flutes, cheered in languages not even the Foundry implants could decode, and laid hands upon us as their leader stood shirtless atop a rock, screaming out in elation, his sweaty, dark skin gleaming in the light of day. Tayo later told us their cheers had meant, "God helps those who help themselves." Our senses were assaulted by smells both sweet, and spicy—cinnamon, cream, oven-fired breads, savory wraps of meat covered in sauces I could not begin to describe.

It all turned my stomach into knots.

Shelly and Karianna helped me hide that I retched in the street, standing beside me to block anyone's view before being offered more.

These people needed us.

We had to be the hope they had dreamed of.

Queensland and Daegu nearly melded together in my mind, each settlement so large and full of so many people it seemed impossible. While the Australian nation-state was more of a dusty sprawl of twenty-third-century architecture starting west of Brisbane, its people covering vast distances with roads protected by considerable military forces, Daegu was a cyberpunk wet dream, all lights and sound and steel and glass pressed together and surrounded by treacherous mountains.

Fireworks. Street parades. More confetti. Flowers falling from the sky. Displays of wealth and waste the likes of which I would never understand.

We waved to their people with little heart, drained of all our emotions, though Ingrid did her best to encourage us to play the part. This road was not at an end, and so few of us were left. Yet the streets were so crowded. In a single settlement, we saw more human beings than we had over the course of our entire lives, even though it was the smallest. By the time we reached Daegu, the population count was almost oppressive, a kind of mental pressure summoned at the sight. To think that billions used to live on Earth, and all we had seen so far amounted to less than 7.5 million. Not to mention, most settlements felt confident they had the capabilities to defend themselves, which we knew to be wrong. If Veetor came in force, they would not stand a chance. And so that meant it was all up to us, a burden only we could shoulder. Karianna and I were already hatching a plan, allowing our Proxies to analyze the available tactical data. Between the UEI remnant forces, the *Absolution*, and what the Isoptera could throw at us at any given moment, it was fast becoming clear we were not enough. They were right. We could only be in so many places at once.

But I would not break my promise.

No one else dies.

Standing on the landing platform outside of Daegu, waiting for everyone to board so we could leave, I became entranced by its neon lights and the bustling noise of people going on about their lives. So much of it reminded me of Rix, though a thousandfold more chaotic, street cars miraculously winding around one another as they traveled the countless arteries of the city.

All this attention was not for me.

This wasn't what I wanted.

I had never wanted to be a hero.

I had never wanted to be divine.

I had just wanted to dig in the dirt, play with my toys, make friends, hang out, find love, get married, and live my life.

Funny how things turn out.

And now . . .

Karianna gave me a cursory glance and a tired salute, then boarded her shuttle. Shelly, for her part, put her arms around me from behind, her head resting on my shoulder.

"It's too much to take in," I sighed. "I'm tired."

She sniffed, a sign she had swallowed her feelings. "Me too."

"We should be happy, right? We made it. We did it. They're with us. We might need more labor, but it's enough to get started. All we have to do is prove that this will work."

"But it doesn't feel like victory, does it?"

I tightened my fingers into fists. Fireworks shot out from the city center and exploded high above the tallest skyscrapers, light from its mass illuminating them for the briefest instant.

"One foot in front of the next," Shelly said. "Just one step at a time. I'm here with you. I'm not going anywhere."

I took hold of her hands and drew her tighter to my back, squeezing my eyes shut. "You better not go anywhere. You hear me? You better not."

CHAPTER 51

Weeks rushed by as our plan was put into action, the compound at Svalbard having become a flurry of frenetic activity. Leaders and foremen and general laborers of every remaining nationality came there to be trained on the technical needs of the operation. Chevelle, Dante, and Emilia aided Frelo in their instructional sessions. These people came to see the vision of our shared objective, some of the literal seeds of our future laid out on display by Priscilla's request. And of course, many more came to meet with those from FICSE, the legends in the flesh. For the first time in over a hundred years, dozens of heavy shuttles were taking off from Earth every day in shifts, their roaring engines hauling people and supplies to distant locations around the globe.

During that time, we traveled back and forth from the surface up to the *Transcendence*, Karianna and I taking turns keeping an eye on the sky. So far, no major incursions had been made to the surface, and Veetor was unnervingly quiet. Maybe we'd lucked out and he'd been killed in some kind of operation with the UEI. Fat chance.

The resonator network had worked like a charm. Every shuttle, every command center, was connected via instantaneous communication, allowing for coordination on a scale no one among us had ever seen. It had caused some challenges on the front end, a bit of head butting between nation states, but as everyone fell into the flow of the new routine, the few spats that cropped up went away.

We were close to the end of Phase One. The first of the Jevox Towers was nearly complete.

Back aboard the *Transcendence* I kept up with my meditation, attempting to break through my mental block. There were questions we needed answering, and I felt this was the best way given its history.

I took my place in the meditation room, settling in. The effects of Bliss had finally been purged from my system, my mind clear in those dark places. There were no more intrusive thoughts when I closed my eyes, other than the usual variety, like how bad it might hurt to bend back a fingernail or getting stuck in a loop thinking I was a failure to everyone I'd ever known. You know, the usual suspects.

Esteban's playlist of instrumental music began, and I sat in a relaxed position upon a large pillow, legs crossed, arms relaxed, back straight. I allowed those hypnotic rhythms to wash over me, my mind wandering as vision faded to black. I wasn't exactly sure what thread I was pursuing today, but I knew I needed to get back to this place. I needed to connect with the Universe.

"You are a star, a wave of light," I whispered. "Breathe in. Breathe out . . ."

Like in a Star Sphere, my consciousness was suspended in a void that felt like fluid. The stars wheeled around me as time rushed past, planets locked in their cosmic dance as they orbited one another, hurling through space in a helical pattern, their paths forming a corkscrew made of ten thousand lines that twisted through darkness.

I couldn't focus on anything specific, given how scattered my will had become, but I could see a small path through a maelstrom of chaos. The more I tried to thread this tiny gap, to press my consciousness through to see what was on the other side, the farther away it seemed to become, either side hemmed by ever-populating black holes and quasars.

Alone and distant from the spiraling masses of stars, I spotted a wayward Earth, a pale blue dot flung from the ball of heat among the thick of it that had given us life. The planet swelled to encompass my entire being, its damaged surface sending pains through my back and chest as if I could hear its cries. At its north and south poles, domes of blue light hung over a pair of human-made towers which stretched into the atmosphere for kilometers from ground to cloud. Within the hearts of these metal lattices, antimatter cores raged, giving off a perpetual reaction that powered the remnant machines from a forgotten age to keep the poles of the planet frozen. If not for these mighty engines, where would they be now? Would there even be enough land left for humans to retake?

"Milo, we are receiving a signal," Proxy said, curling up into my lap and breaking me from my reverie. "The first tower is ready to be brought online on the island of Cyprus."

The vision before me shattered, my meditation broken, nothing of value uncovered. I was back to baseline, consensus reality, unsure what I had seen and what it meant.

"They are so small compared to the cooling towers," it went on.

I shook my head, wondering if Proxy had been reading my thoughts. "The ones at the poles?"

"Yes. While the cooling towers, as I have been referring to them, are kilometers in height, the 'Towers' Frelo has given us only reach four hundred meters. So much shorter. Given what we know of human technology from the age, the level of engineering required to build these cooling towers is staggering."

"We might need to give those things another name." I scratched it behind the ear, eliciting its body to vibrate, a sense of calm seeping into me. "Cooling tower? Tower? Too similar. It's confusing."

"Mmm. A good idea, Milo."

"What about Exothermic Spires?" Shelly asked, appearing at the doorway. She was leaned against the frame, her arms crossed, a hint of a sly grin on her lips, her curls spilling over half of her face. "I've been studying them, and it appears that they keep the ice frozen by sucking the heat from the ocean and ambient air, then expel that energy into the upper atmosphere through some kind of exothermic radiation. It works like a giant heatsink."

"A fitting name," Proxy replied, hopping up to greet her.

"Traitor," I muttered under my breath.

"Come on," she said, bending over to pick up Proxy. "Let's watch the Tower go online."

"One thing before we go," Proxy said, its tone serious. "Activity in the Ring of Diamonds has increased. More human communications traffic than we have previously observed."

Shelly's eyebrows crinkled. "Do we know what they are saying?"

"Rumors mostly. Rumors about what is being done on the surface, of so many flights. But one in particular caught my attention."

"Which is?" I asked. "Don't keep us in suspense."

"Kabosai," it said, blinking up at me. My blood went cold. "It related to the moon and something they call the Gardens. One of our shuttles went to recover a logic core needed to get the Australian factory online. While they returned home without incident, they did some snooping around what is left of the base to confirm these diamond rumors. They did not see any of the slugs while they were there, as you sometimes call them, but they did find equipment. They did see strange animals which did not match anything that could be considered Earthly. The crew fled without coming too close to these strange occurrences, having first found what they needed."

"The Gardens of the Moon," Shelly said, chewing the words over as if tasting their bitter syllables. "I want to say it was some kind of high-society real estate development and travel gateway."

"Yes."

"No one is living there, right? But not everything is dead?"

"It would appear not. Perhaps the Gene Brokers have some hand in that; it is hard to say."

"That would explain the sightings," I said, thinking back to the reports on Aeolia. "But we have seen no direct evidence of their ships, have we?"

"No," Proxy replied. "We have not."

Shelly and I met each other's eyes, a thought occurring to both of us, too dangerous to speak aloud. If the Kabosai were here, perhaps they did indeed have a template that could work with their device. Perhaps that device could then be used for its proper purpose, if we could only be sure of what that was.

"Well, that's a mystery for another day," I said, stepping past them. "The Kabosai can wait."

The remaining crew of the *Transcendence* converged in the War Room, eager to watch it all go online. Our entire lives had been pushing us to this moment, all our struggles, all our pain, had been a downpayment on the future of humanity. Chevelle, Dante, Emilia, Renata, and Frelo were now mostly permanent residents of Svalbard as long as this project went on.

When Shelly and I entered the room, everyone was standing in a cluster, talking in low tones, as if by speaking too loud they might shatter what good had befallen us.

It was too quiet in here. No jokes. No good-natured insults. Just the same conversation.

"Captain," Hy said, bowing his head as I neared. "It is good to see you."

"You too."

Xuan was talking to Karianna and James. "Did you see how high that tower will go? Makes me uncomfortable."

"Bigger than anything we built on Novae," Karianna said. "That thing would have lorded over the entire settlement like a five-sided brutalist nightmare. And to think, we're going to be making over a hundred of these things. At least we have help. Bunch of little ants running around. Look at the instrument readings. All the heavy shuttles are like a damned hive."

"Speaking of hives," James said, a finger raised and pointing at the holographic image of Earth in the center of the room. "How well can we defend this against Isoptera? Big as they are, as open as they'll be, seems like an easy target to pick off, bruh. Sticks out like a sore thumb."

"We'll smash their faces in with rail cannon fire." She smacked the meat of her left palm with her right fist, bracelets jingling. "One, two, three dead bugs. I'm tired of screwing around with them. My only concern is having to thread this fat mama through the debris fields in the Ring of Diamonds. And since people still live up here, I don't want to accidently kill anyone."

"Check the network," Lance said, his eyes glazing over for a moment as he accessed something with his implants. "Ingrid provided us with a map of all HardyHabs known to be active in the ring—the standard form-factor habitation modules most people live in. Her people were able to hack into their old SOS network. Might not cover the off-brand modules up there, but we're told there are only a few of those left and they're likely to not be in service anyways."

Karianna popped her fingers and raised her fists as if ready for a fight. "Perfect. Chinchillette tells me we might be able to use some of those ratty old structures to repair the *Transcendence* if things get hairy, siphon off their materials with MI. Good option, I say."

"Are they not tombs?" Hy's eyebrows raised. "They might not be active, but dead module mean dead people. How will we pay respect?"

"Hairy?" James mused, fingers rubbing at his chin. "It's for sure going to get hairy. The Isoptera will come back."

"Veetor's the bigger threat," Karianna told him, her expression like that of a teenager affronted that something so stupid was being said at an auspicious moment like this. "He might not have as many ships as they do, but we can somewhat predict Isopteran moves. Veetor, though, no way.

He's chaotic. Capricious. Every time he makes a move, even a calculated one, there's at least two or three variables dependent on a roll of the dice."

Shelly let go of my hand and went to Xuan's side, whispering something to her.

"How you holding up?" Lance asked as I stepped up to the group.

I gave a shrug and shook my head. He patted me on the shoulder and sighed, letting all the air out of his lungs.

At that moment, a kind of particle wave traveled down the length of the ship, tickling my and Karianna's spines, vibrating the improvised box mounted at the center of the War Room's horseshoe table. Ingrid's voice came from the speakers, eliciting a smile from Lance. I'd seen a stupid look like that before. It had been my look. It had been Dad's look. I truly hoped they had a happy ending ahead. Both had been through enough.

"Transcendence," Ingrid said through the communication's channel. *"We've got the live feed from eastern Cyprus up and running. Transmitting it to your resonator ID. Tower one is going up.*

"Listen, no matter what happens from here I have to say, you kept your end of the agreement and asked for nothing in return. You make us all proud."

I cleared my throat and reached over to scratch Proxy's head. It had hopped up on the table before me. "This was the mission. And we will see it done, even if it kills us."

Shelly waved at the group for us to take our seats. Too many of the chairs were empty, and this feeling was more than physical. No off-color comments from Leo or random bursts into Shakespeare or commentary on art and the human condition. None of Ada's great ideas, her unique perspective, her synergy with my better half. I was not alone in these feelings. Xuan, Hy, Lance, and James scooted in a few positions rather than taking their originals, filling in the places left absent. It made the emptiness feel a little less terrible.

Karianna sat down beside me, turned, and gave me an awkward smirk. I returned the gesture with my own, raising my mechanical arm and forming my fingers into a fist. She responded in kind, the two of us bumping metal forearms with a click and a jingle.

Things were getting better between us since leaving Aeolia, but it would be a strange road ahead. She had withdrawn from me inside the Integration, keeping her emotions more hidden. I had appreciated the effort, though I worried she wasn't grieving, which wasn't good.

"Just got the all clear from the foreman of Tower One's construction," Ingrid went on. *"Starting the feed."*

"I will connect it," Proxy replied, its attention focused on the hologram before us.

We were entranced as the image at the center of the room morphed, zooming down to the Mediterranean Sea several hundred kilometers below us. Our orbit had been intentional, for us to be at this point and at this moment, allowing us a visual line of sight.

The island became our entire view, and in a clearing on its eastern edge, a series of asymmetric metallic rods, each several hundred meters in length, were being brought together by ground trucks. As their top ends met in a center point in the open field of red dirt where a flag had been planted, they rose up to the sky, forming a kind of cone under their own power. As each section locked together, they assembled themselves into a stark-white pentagonal cylinder, its now-uneven surface covered in docking ports and smaller machines. Supports extended from the base of the structure, widening out, raising the prototower to its full height, its form casting a foreboding shadow across the scraggly forest nearby as well as the ground crew.

Around the cylindrical assembly sections began to turn like invisible fingers were at work, switching and twisting a series of dials and knobs like it were a handheld device. This went on for close to a minute before spurs, twenty-five in all, extended from these points, thick collections of semiporous, saillike membranes expanding from their lengths.

Lights began to blink along its edges, no doubt intended to draw attention to its mass when the sun fell over the horizon and night fell. An alert chimed in my implant's network connected to the rest of the Resonators.

Tower 1: Online.

"Feels like a victory. A small one," Hy said, his face brightening. "It is progress."

Xuan nodded at that, then laid her head on his shoulder.

Lance flipped through his hand terminal, scrolling through data tables and detailed maps of flight patterns.

"Something wrong?" I asked.

He shook his head. "No. But this is going to be hard, just something I keep worrying about. Each Tower requires a constant supply of materials.

We have the manpower, but it's not going to be easy. Dameon, Ingrid, and I have worked with Frelo to make best use of what we have, but they will be stretched thin. This facility will be a bright light calling forth all the flying little insects like moths to a flame. They will come for us."

Days went by, and once we were sure there was no immediate threat of attack, I returned to the surface to meet with everyone in person. Despite having access to the resonator network and its instant communications, being face-to-face built more trust. It just wasn't the same over voice only; humans needed to shake hands, give hugs, needed to speak in person. It was biology.

Before I disembarked from my Swift Shuttle, Shelly looked me over, inspecting the new additions we had made to my clothes. Given how many times I had been caught off guard on operations like this, we had cooked up several more batches of my homegrown nanomachines. These machines had been packaged into a series of six vials topped with simple valves on their ends and placed in tight-fitted pockets within my jacket and pants. Their use would be self-defense, and they were capable of being manipulated by an electromagnetic field module buckled to my belt and controlled by my implants.

If attacked, I could summon forth these machines in defense, doing much as I had before with the sword, though now, with as many as I had, there were other functions too.

I stood in the center of the shuttle as Shelly stepped to the side and tested them out, drawing forth the quicksilver liquid to form a barrier before me like the MI. It swirled and shimmered, a billion tiny machines flowing in midair.

In a series of waves, I raised the machines to form different objects: hammers, scythes, iron fists. Shelly began tossing fruit at me that Proxy had made, and I chopped at the air with a series of nearly invisible blades. The fruit split in half like it was a video game, slices littering the walkway in the shuttle.

"Maybe I should go for the high score," I said, and she rolled her eyes at me.

I focused, and out of the quicksilver machines I formed sections of ladder, keys of varied shapes, a Rubik's cube (though with all one color), spikes that hovered off the ground, and a functional environmental helmet. Anything I could picture in my mind, I could form, if the image was clear enough. That could be a tool or a weapon, or neither. And best of all, unlike our powered armor, it took up less space, and no one could see it on me. I knew the Foundry had the capability to make something like this. It was too bad Proxy had been limited in what it was allowed to do for us. That meant we had to do it on our own. And we had. These were my nanomachines, my design, augmented by Shelly's software. It hadn't been an easy project, and I wasn't sure we had the energy or mental bandwidth to do it again, but it worked.

With a command, the machines crawled back up my arms, twisting around my clothes and forming a kind of armor. Protected, I flung my left arm, my fleshy arm, against the wall of the shuttle with a bang, leaving a dent where it came in contact.

"Did it hurt?" Shelly asked, taking hold of my arm, probing the hardened machines with her fingers.

"No," I said, wondering why we had waited so long to make something like this. "I didn't feel a thing."

She patted me on the chest and leaned in. I recalled the nanomachines to their respective containers and returned her gesture, soft lips to soft lips.

"No one should know you have this," she whispered in my ear once we were done. "It should be your secret defense."

I nodded at this. "My secret defense."

CHAPTER 52

To say that I hated politics would have been an understatement of the highest order. Politics on any level had always been a challenge for me, from internship disagreements over job assignment to status or resource allocation on Novae. But our current situation was the worst yet. It felt akin to handling a snake that had two heads and two asses. It could somehow bite you as well as shit on you, no matter where it was you held it.

It was like Novae all over again, everyone wanting different things while all pulling from the same pool of resources, except instead of about 750 people making up the entire nation, it was millions.

The Boot provided us with the greatest manufacturing facilities still operating on Earth with the Mancini Forge, though to keep it running it required a lot of material and a hefty labor force. But were they chosen for the first Tower to be put into service? No. Paphospolis was, and for scientific reasons I could not explain, but those did not matter to Santucci or his people, so he said.

This act of annoyance was seen as a slight by Santucci, showing favor to the island for its strategic position between the Free Citizens of Earth territories, for which Drakos of Paphospolis denied, as did Ingrid.

This only got worse once the Borough of Skive, who had pledged one of the largest contributions of labor considering their relative size, didn't receive their shipments of medical supplies from Antalya. According to Adlershof, this had cost the lives of a dozen of his people despite the universal inoculant.

Tayo of Antalya had then started to claim that the Borough was holding out on grain, while at the same time, Svalbard would not provide the seeds they requested from the vault.

And this was just the member states. Queensland and Daegu were locking horns over a romantic scandal between Jack Bennet and Bak Yoon's niece. Good ol' smooth-talking Jack had found himself in a compromising position after early celebrations had been caught on tape. As a result, Bak Yoon's niece, Nari, left the city and moved to Queensland. If the leader of Daegu was mad over this being an inappropriate connection, despite her being of age, or he was afraid state secrets might be leaked, Ingrid could not decide. For what it was worth, Nari looked happy with Bennet in the pictures he had taken of them from his yacht.

I guess not everyone suffered equally.

Ingrid, Shelly, Karianna and I went round and round with these leaders over the resonator network twenty-four seven, or what felt like it, each of them finding some reason to complain. Free trade was supposed to be useful for all, giving no one particular group an advantage over one another, creating an environment of interdependence. In this case, it just felt like a means to find arguments. Could they not just be happy we were moving forward to a better day? Tower 1 had been online for a little over a week, and already it was making a measurable difference on the environment within the immediate vicinity of Cyprus. A functioning test case. Because of this fact, it was hotly debated where the second tower should be deployed.

Everyone always wanted something—more food, more water, more medical supplies, remnant luxury goods, influence, status, whatever—and as a result, everyone felt someone else was getting more than their fair share. While I did believe some level of avarice contributed to this, I didn't see it as a prime motivator. The pull was exhausting both physically and mentally, traveling up and down from the *Transcendence*, flying shuttles from settlement to settlement providing air cover as everyone argued over tidbits.

In between meetings, when my feet were on the ground, I often retreated to the barracks to take a quick nap, catch up on messages from Proxy, and do my best to meditate. While the naps came easy, meditation did not. My head was clear, but only in part. Alien drugs might no longer have been flowing through my veins, but I was unable to focus on any one thing for long.

As was the ritual, I found a comfortable sitting position, this time on a bed, crossing my legs and closing my eyes. Once the room was empty, I recited the Melcorin chant I had learned, a playlist of soft, hypnotic music coming from headphones helping to block out the world.

My mind was blank. Nothing but space. Nothing but the ship, an illuminated slip of gold and black glass floating in the void. This went on for several minutes, doing my best to relax enough that my mind would wander someplace else. But I kept coming back to the ship floating through nothing, no stars, no planets, no cosmic anything. The *Transcendence* was trapped in a liminal space without stimulus other than its own.

This was how my sessions went for days.

No forward movement, no insights.

Veetor was nowhere to be found. The Isoptera, quiet. Kabosai, nonexistent.

A knock came from the door of the barracks one afternoon. Having not gotten too deep in my own head, I got up and answered. Distraction was the better option today.

"Milo?" Priscilla was standing at the door, their furry-jacketed silhouette outlined by the stark light of dawn. "Mind if I come in?"

"Not at all." I stepped back to let them in before shutting the door to keep the cold out. "To what do I owe the pleasure?"

They smiled at me, the corners of their eyes crinkling despite their youth. "Just you today?"

"Yeah," I sighed. "Just me. Shelly's giving me some space to do what I do. Karianna is with the rest of the crew. After that last little negotiation session with the Boot, Lance suggested that they go play a little soccer with the kids to get their minds off of it. They're the whole reason we do this, right? Everyone needs to refocus."

"Oskar would have loved that."

"I think he would have." I fiddled with the kitchenette at the back of the room, drawing water. "So, what's going on?" I raised the kettle in the air. "Coffee?"

She bowed, gesturing at it with an open hand. "Please."

"How do you take it?"

"Black is fine."

"Same." I put the filled kettle on the stove and turned it on before flicking a switch on a coffee grinder as the water heated up. "Unless it's real milk, or close enough to it, black is the best."

"Not much of that here."

"I can imagine."

"You've have been on my mind a lot lately," Priscilla began, taking a seat on a stool near a worn countertop. "Or more specifically, the conversation we had what feels like years ago has been on my mind."

"Conversation? You mean the one up on the mountain about transcending?"

"Yes. How are your meditations proceeding?"

I scratched the back of my head with my mechanical arm and looked away. "Fine. I guess."

"You don't seem too convinced. It was what I interrupted, wasn't it?"

"Well, I mean, with all the—"

"Diversion," she said, voice stern like a chiding parent.

I sniffed and looked away, attempting to collect my scattered thoughts. As I worked at this, I moved the coffee grinds into a press, walking mentally back through my day.

Resonators. Water, fifty thousand gallons. Food, twenty-five thousand pounds, rice, wheat, solid protein. Copper, twelve tons. Lithium, fifty tons. Uranium, refined, three tons. The data flowed through my head, list after list after list, none of it given priority, all of it given priority. All marked urgent.

Where was the calm?

Priscilla cocked her head and stared at me, not saying a word, but with wide eyes that said so much.

"Okay fine!" I growled after some time. "It's not going well. No matter what I do, I can't connect to the Universe like I did while we were traveling here or anywhere else."

"And why do you think this is?" she asked, her tone gentle and full of love.

"I don't know. Maybe I can't see past the reality we've found ourselves in. The future, it's dark. Like, real dark. Nothing's left."

"Based on our other conversations, I didn't think this was a way to look into the future, only the present."

"It's not, at least I don't think it is. But from what I can tell, I have to know something about the situation for me to see anything at all. Here? I just don't know. Veetor's out there, and I keep trying to find him, but when I look, there's nothing. Space is just a bunch of scattering entropy. It's all chaos."

"He will appear when he appears."

"How can you be so cavalier? The moment he rears his fucking bald-ass head, we could all be done. Our ships are planet killers. All this hard work would be for nothing."

She considered this for a moment, fingers tapping in sequence against her thigh. "Maybe so. But I don't believe that will happen."

"Why? Why don't you believe that?"

"Call it intuition. Call it instinct. It's a gut feeling. In my heart of hearts, I feel everything is going to turn out right. I have no physical evidence to support this, but even with all the back biting and harsh words between the territories, this is the most I've seen them talk in all my life. That in itself is beautiful. You are of FICSE. You can be the glue."

The kettle began to rattle, the water within on the edge of boiling. Kind of reminded me of my life.

"That's a heavy burden," I said, reaching for an oven mitt, patiently waiting for the steam to make the kettle scream.

"It is, and I am sorry for that. None of us deserve it. And yet, you are the only ones who can do it."

She was right.

"What if I smart off to one of these assholes and they want to pull their support?"

Priscilla grinned at this, the gems at the corners of her eyes gleaming in the light of the barracks. "Then they're idiots."

The kettle screamed and I pulled it away, pouring the water into a press. "Maybe a bit of coffee will help."

"What donuts and coffee can't cure, there's no cure for."

"I thought that was butter and whiskey." I paused, giving her an amused look. "And where's the donuts? I don't see any."

"My apologies," she said, covering her mouth with the tips of the fingers on her right hand, aghast, "I must have forgotten them."

I pressed the boiling water through the grinds with a hiss, smiling all the while. "I guess coffee will just have to do."

"This all reminds me of an old poem I've often pulled encouragement from."

"Oh?"

"It's called 'The Tempering.' The author of it, however, is debated."

I looked at the coffee press, impatiently waiting for it to steep. "How does it go?"

She took a deep breath and began to recite:

A god stands before his crucible
Blowing storms to stoke the flames
And in his hand, he holds humanity
Imperfect, brittle, and full of hate
Down their length that makes creation
He sees greed, fear, and jealousy
These he knows won't amount to anything, mere vestigial traits to be cast away
He places those into a grave, a body turned and tested will break
No more love, life unmade
Into the fire do we all go, thrust by this god's own hand
One and two and three and more
No longer what was, but what is instead
We burn together, made soft by trials
Hardness lost forever
But alas we are pulled before we melt
And quenched—we are made stronger

I took it all in, my heart feeling damaged as if shards of glass remained shooting from it. "Are we made stronger?"

"I think so. Without the trials, we cannot see the triumph. We may lose what makes us hard, but strength is not always in hardness. It is in our flexibility. Adaptability. In our ability to change when the time is right. In our ability to let life flow around us."

My lips formed into a line as I poured our coffee. "I sure hope you're right."

Several days passed on the surface fielding requests, having too-long conversations, and redirecting most issues back to Dameon, Frelo, and Chevelle. Then I headed back up to orbit with Shelly and Karianna, the lot of us feeling defeated and exhausted. The engine of progress was still turning, for today, and that would have to be enough. Maybe this was just growing pains. Priscilla was right—many of these territories hadn't collaborated on more than a cursory level for years. Now, they were intimately connected and this was a difficult shift.

As we cruised back to the *Transcendence*, our shuttles slicing through the thick clouds overhead, Karianna pinged me.

"They're all idiots, aren't they?" she mused. *"Bunch of privileged idiots."*

I laughed at her comment, thinking back to my conversations with Priscilla. "Sure feels like it. I mean, Bennet has a pleasure vessel to drive his girlfriend around the Coral Sea. Who the hell has one of those now? I'm sure you also heard, but Ingrid said this is typical. Dameon did his best to find middle ground, but it's dicey."

"Never thought I'd have wished for us to be like those multijointed freaks from Rix, but I think I owe Frelo an apology for ever giving them a hard time. I'll take having everyone else in my thoughts—gotten halfway used to that, you know—if it gets things done."

"Did you give the Jevox a hard time?" I mentally scratched at the back of my head, focusing on her shuttle flying by my side as if she could see me looking.

"Hmm." She paused for a moment, thinking it over, her shuttle swaying to reflect her thoughts. *"Hell, I can't remember. But it sounds like something I would do."*

"Hah. You're not wrong."

"I own it, Milo. I know I can be a smart-ass. Dad raised me that way."

"And we wouldn't want you any other way."

"Mmm," she said, and this sounded very much like a smile.

"For real though, can I crawl in a hole and hide for a while? My soul needs a rest. I don't think I've said hardly five words to Shelly that weren't filled with state drama in a week."

"How about this—you find a hole, and I'll dig out some space and throw the rest of us in with you? James can drag a rug over it and we'll all sleep for another hundred years. Deal?"

"Deal."

We returned to the ship and took off to our respective stations so we could fire up the main drive and bring us up to a higher orbit. Lance and Karianna took off one way, as Shelly led me to our spheres. She paused at a T in the hallway.

"I think I'm going to go get some real food in the real world before taking the plunge." She took hold of my hands, her lip poked out, caught in the middle of a tired thought. "Weird, maybe, but I've got a craving, and I know we can eat in the spheres, but it's just different here. We good on time?"

I looked up, accessing my implants. "Nothing urgent according to Proxy. Be there in a few. I want to check on my nanocultures. Maybe stare off into the abyss for a while, see if an unspeakable evil stares back."

"Sounds good." She kissed me on the cheek and turned away. "See you shortly, love."

Heading off to collect my thoughts, I made for the forward end of the ship, intending to meditate if the mood caught me. I may have had few or no insights lately, but after my chat with Priscilla, I felt as if I should be trying.

My route took me past the Dead Room, and I paused for a moment, hand and forehead against the locked door, my thoughts consumed by the device. Could we use this dark technology for a good purpose? Could we use it as a weapon to stop the Isoptera? That sure would help ease the dangers of the days ahead. Or was there another option? A questionable one?

Not without a template.

None of this worked without a template.

I let go of my anxieties and rounded the corner of the hall, my mind wandering. Footsteps came from ahead, but I didn't look up. I was too focused on the varied levels of pettiness these Earth-bound leaders had shown in their negotiations. It was the literal end of the world, and they just wanted to argue over it.

"Welcome back," James said, and slapped me on the shoulder. "How did it go?"

I snapped from my reverie and blinked at him, about to say one thing, then decided to go someplace else. "Ever had a root canal?"

His brows crowded the middle of his face. "Sure, once, back on Creatus. Apparently, some of those native sweets Perry whipped up gave me a few cavities. One cavity was bad enough to kill the tooth all the way down. Why?"

"Well," I said, licking my lips, "if I could have a root canal every day for the rest of my life, it might be the better option than having to sit down with those unmovable dickheads."

"Hah." This made James smile in that rakish way he used to when we were kids, the years peeling away as his heart lightened. "Shit. Tell us how you really feel, Milo."

I cocked my head to the side, confused at this statement. "I think I just did."

He rolled his eyes, lips pursed. "Not what I meant."

"Oh."

"Hey, bruh." He slapped me on the shoulder again. "Look, um, I wanted to talk to you about something."

"Yeah?"

"Yeah." He wrung his hands and shrugged. "Remember back in Svalbard where Lance gave everyone something to do? Real clear cut after that first meeting."

"I do." I hesitated, and felt guilty immediately. I hadn't talked to James as I had intended. Caught up in everything, I had forgotten. "Umm, what's up?"

"How Lance fumbled, what he said, it just got me thinking, and with some other things on my mind lately . . ." He took a deep breath. "Why the hell am I here? Not talking about the mission, not talking about you. I believe in the mission, and I believe in you. It's just that I'm not good at anything. Everyone else is so talented at like, being project directors, or at computer hacking, or science, or whatever. But me? All I've been good at is getting in trouble."

"That's not true."

"But isn't it? Milo, we've known each other since forever. And we've had some good times and bad. So, be honest with me, what am I good at? What makes me unique?"

I swallowed and took a moment to consider his question honestly. It had been a challenge for him to get interested and stay interested in a host of different topics. He was smart, and loyal, the kind of guy you wanted watching your back, but he hadn't dedicated his life to any particular discipline. Much the same could be said for me other than the study of nanoscience, and I was passable at best with my skill.

"You see?" he pressed, my face having turned blank. "It's taking you too long to think about it."

"No," I replied, a little too quick. "The trouble is, you're good at a lot, but not everything you're good at is something you like to do."

He scratched at the back of his head and shrugged. "Yeah. No lies detected there. I get bored."

"You do. But that doesn't mean you're not good at anything."

"It's just . . . I just feel like less sometimes. Leo was good at everything. People follow Lance's every word—he speaks with such confidence, as if he always knows what to do. Xuan may hide it with her jokes, but she's a boss, and she saved my ass more than once on Nest. There's just nothing unique about me."

I leaned in. "Stop saying that."

His shoulders sagged. "And if I'm not unique, well, then why would she ever love me? Why?"

"Wait . . . Who?" I cocked my head again. "Who are we talking about?"

"Don't be dense," he whispered. "You know who."

"Oh." I put a fist up to my lips, giving myself a moment to process it all. "James, I . . . I thought that was over a long time ago. For a minute I thought you two were going to get together, then . . . you just didn't. Wasn't my place to ask why."

"Maybe it was over for her, but it's not for me. People sometimes get under your skin in a good way. I just can't let it go. My God, I dream about Karianna when I go to sleep. I see her when I close my eyes. Bruh, I hear her voice and my heart damn near comes flying out of my fucking chest when she's near. It's not infatuation. It never has been. I had options on Novae, let me tell you. I didn't want any of them. I'm in love with her."

This made me grin. "Have you told her?"

He gave me a shocked look. "You kidding me? She's scary as hell. And that alone is all the more reason I feel the way I do. Problem is, she's in love with you."

"I handled that," I said, straightening my back and looking over my shoulder. With a wave, I drew him closer to the wall, making us a bit more concealed just in case Karianna walked by. "I was kind but let her down. She's not for me."

"Yeah, well, feelings like that don't die easy. What if Shelly had let you down easy? Would you have just stopped having feelings for her?"

That was fair. "No. I wouldn't have."

"Exactly my point. The heart wants what it wants. But maybe, just maybe, if I was special, she'd love me."

"Look at me," I said, hardening my voice and drawing his eyes to mine with a pair of fingers. "Everyone on this ship is special. Everyone is here for a reason, and we all have a place. You've become one of my best pilots. You may shrug at the responsibility of leading a fighter wing, but you don't throw your ships away like trash, not anymore. You are a team player, always ready to jump in when we need you. You fight like a demon and are more loyal than a golden retriever. This team would be less without you."

"Yeah, yeah, whatever." He waved it away. "Platitudes, bruh. Platitudes."

"I'm fucking serious! There's no one else in this world I would have wanted as my best friend when I was a kid. You helped me break through, helped me become who I am. My parents had me stuck. You showed me that we had a choice in life, good or bad. You were there to pick me up when Harper was such a bitch to both of us. And yes, we did some dumb shit back then, but what kids don't? You helped me to see that I could live my own life, on my own terms. No one else was around to do that. I didn't really have parents, not like you had with your mom at least. Between you and Esteban, you were like the dad I didn't have till later in life."

This idea made him smile, though instead of him appearing younger, he somehow seemed older, his expression tempered. "You sure that wasn't just blind chance? I was a little shit, you know?"

"Call it whatever you want. I know what it meant to me. You have a way about you, James, a way of silently encouraging people to follow their hearts. That's a powerful gift, and it might not fit neatly on a resume, it may not be easy for project directors to assign it. Besides, I don't know of anyone better to stir up a little trouble. You've always been good at that."

"Trouble is my middle name."

I shot a finger gun off to the side. "Trouble is one thing I know you and Karianna have in common."

"Damn right we do."

"Then how about let's stir some trouble up for anyone who tries to screw with Earth."

He pounded his right fist into his left palm. "I'm all over it."

At that moment, an alarm went off, the halls of the *Transcendence* shifting red. Proxy spoke into my implants.

"We've got incoming," it said.

"Who?" I responded, James looking at me.

"Isoptera. Several ground transports are breaking the upper atmosphere."

"How did we miss them?"

"The Ring of Diamonds masked their approach."

An image shoved itself into my mind: six cicada-like shuttles headed to the surface, each traveling to different locations.

"Support craft?" I asked, searching the space above Earth for larger craft.

"None that we can see. They came alone."

Karianna came running down the hall, skidding to a halt when she saw us. "Looks like they're back to stir up trouble."

James smiled at this. "Why don't we give it back to them then?" He punched her on the shoulder in a playful sort of way.

She narrowed her eyes at him, then looked at me, then back at him. "Alrightttyy. Trouble it is, and let's make it double. Ever do the Swift Shuttle simulations?"

James nodded. "I've done it enough times, just in case. Not much different than the fighters, to be honest. Are you asking me to fly the spare?"

"Don't go crashing it into mountains or anything." She poked him in the chest, nodding with each word. "You will die, ya know? There are no extra lives."

He slapped the finger away. "Sure. Sure. I won't think of it."

Despite my fears over putting a friend at risk in this way, I didn't fight her split-second decision. This one felt right. Fortuitous, given our discussion. We had a spare shuttle, and these craft were the only air cover we could offer. Our fighters, while much more numerous than the trio of Swift Shuttles we had, did not hold up well in atmosphere.

"Shelly!" I called over the intercom. "The ship is yours. Weapons control is transferred to you. We need to step out for a bit and handle a situation."

"Okay," she replied. *"We'll keep it clear from our orbit up here. We can't move though, not without you."*

"It'll be okay. Won't be gone long."

The three of us split up, each heading to our respective shuttles, each ready to meet the enemy head-on.

CHAPTER 53

The longest day of my life had begun, and I just wanted out of it. I just wanted to rest, to be left alone, to be submerged in a river of cold water by myself. But that was not how this was going to go.

Six contacts had hit the atmosphere and were burning through it like a swarm of angry insects, their forms twisting in the ever thickening layers of oxygen, friction igniting them, turning their hulls into crashing fireballs dropping from the heavens. They traveled in pairs heading for three destinations.

The resonator crystal within my Swift Shuttle vibrated just outside my Star Sphere, translating a message from our instantaneous network. *"Milo, this is Ingrid from Command, call back."*

"I'm here."

"We see the incoming. We have a fix on them from the ground. Two are headed for the Boot, two for the Borough. The remaining Clicker shuttles are on their way to the eastern Mediterranean. Hard to say what they'll hit."

"We're on it."

"And who are you going to help first?" a voice cut in over our line. Santucci.

Before I could respond, another cut in. *"Our people are terrified. These creatures could undo so much great work."* It was Tayo, his normal bravado having evaporated under the heat of this threat. *"You must make good on your promise. Defend us."*

"I—uh—" My eyes flitted back and forth between the targets in the interface as the hull of my Swift Shuttle caught fire from the friction of aerobraking, my companions flying formation on my flanks. "We will."

"But who?" Adlershof chimed in. *"In Skive we cannot shoot them down. We have no air cover."*

"The Boot must be defended!" Santucci emphasized, a hint of unsteadiness in his usually confident tone.

"But we are in this together," Adlershof shot back. *"We must defend the weak."*

The three leaders erupted into an argument over who should be defended first. It didn't take long before Drakos joined the rest, sounding positively disconsolate. My wings wobbled as I fought to make a decision on where we should start. We had three sets of Isopteran shuttles heading for three targets. We were three fighters, but James wasn't ready to go on his own, not yet. If we flew together, we had the best chance of surviving. If we each went alone, one of us might die, and that wouldn't help anyone.

"Ingrid!" Karianna shouted over the open line, her voice cutting through the chatter. She was clearly annoyed but doing everything in her to temper those emotions. *"Please, Ingrid!"*

"Already on it," the overseer of the Free Citizens said, and the line went quiet. *"There we go. I've blocked their signals from the network for now. Milo, look, I understand their positions, I would be fighting for the same if I were them, but you made a promise. And promise or not, you've got to make a choice about who to prioritize. If I am reading the data correctly, there's only three of you. There's more of them."*

"I don't want anyone to die," I told her, Proxy appearing by my feet. The shuttle vibrated as the atmosphere around us stabilized and we began to plunge through the clouds. "We've seen enough death."

Ingrid sighed over the line. *"I hate that I'm saying this, but it's not even about that anymore, it's about saving the planet. We've got to protect assets for now. That will ensure we protect people in the future."*

Cold wind rushed over my body as my senses acclimated to the upper reaches of the stratosphere, the air becoming thicker, our velocity decreasing from orbital speeds.

"Milo?" Karianna asked after a moment. *"What's the plan?"*

I shook my head and looked down at Proxy. The cat cocked its head and offered no advice. There were few options, and I had a feeling this was just the start.

"Okay," I said. "We need to split up. I'll head for the Boot and cover them. The two of you, protect the Borough. Adlershof is right, they have no air defense. Antalya and Paphospolis will just have to hang on a bit."

"The two of us?" James asked. *"But there are three of us. I can cover the last target. I'll go alone."*

"No," Karianna and I blurted out at the same time. We'd had the same thought.

"Umm, that wasn't weird or anything."

Karianna cut back in, *"This is your first time not just flying a Swift Shuttle but fighting in one. Simulations are not everything. We don't want to put you at that much risk till you've seen more action."*

"Milo?" James's fighter drifted out of formation the smallest bit. *"Do you feel the same?"*

"I do," I said. "We might have a long fight ahead. We can't lose you."

"But what about the east?"

"They'll hang in. We are coming for them. The faster we mop up these attack shuttles in the north and west, the quicker we can move to help them."

"I'll let them know," Ingrid said, her voice having turned all business. *"Antalya has some limited ground-based weapons from the war. They might not be that effective, but they will make the Clickers think twice."*

We fell below the cloud ceiling and did as we had decided, splitting off into two groups. Karianna and James screamed off over Greece to what had been Denmark, while I dropped closer to the surface of the earth, skimming across the salty waters of the Mediterranean Sea in my Swift Shuttle, heading to the Boot.

Land came into view and I began twisting and banking around the mountainous terrain, skimming as close to the broken treetops as possible. Forgotten cities and ruined structures lined the roadside, abandoned or destroyed from conflicts no one could recall. So long as I kept low, there was a good chance I could surprise at least one of the shuttles. They were only about a hundred miles before me, their locations being tracked by Proxy and the *Transcendence*.

As I neared what had been Rome, I banked off to the east to Monte Livata, curved around the mountain, and readied my attack. Distance to the target closed.

Ten miles.

Five miles.

Three miles.

I spread my arms wide and pulled up, feeling for a moment as if I were a bird of prey ready to strike, then appeared before the enemy shuttles not behind, the scaled-down Para Lux array of my craft bursting with power.

Lances of invisible light shot out from my vibrating airfoils, striking the first of the iridescent-green cicada-like craft along its side. A neat line cut from the forward end to the rear, fileting its fungara hull in twain.

Explosions cascaded along the back of the Isopteran craft as it lost altitude, tumbling down several thousand feet in a smoking spiral where it would be reduced to rubble upon the mountain slopes. Its friend did not flee; it closed in. The second shuttle launched a flurry of missiles, and I banked off to the right, diving toward the dead forests. I increased my acceleration, putting strain upon the Swift Shuttle's foils and my body. While I had done this a million times in vacuum, pushing the Star Sphere to the limit to protect myself or my crew, it was different in atmosphere, different in a gravity well. Everything was so heavy, so hard.

A dozen feet before crashing into the surface of the Earth, I pulled up, missiles leaving a smoldering trail at my back. Before the Isopteran craft could recover, I took another high-g turn, attempting to corkscrew my way back around its flank, but the pilot was smart and could see what I was doing. The two of us spiraled upward into the clouds, each attempting to race our way around the other. As a result, we found ourselves in a lag pursuit, a series of turns in which neither of us could cross the effective angle and achieve a clear firing solution.

We circled for several tense minutes, each getting closer but still unable to fire. I wondered if at any moment the termites might just roll down the window and toss one of those spatial compression grenades at me, but they did not. Instead, we remained locked in our aerial dance, performing acrobatic feats in a series of patterns to catch the other off guard.

Updates filtered through, Proxy keeping them to the background as nothing more than bullet points so I could focus on the fight. Karianna and James had reached their target and had reported back. The fight was tense, but together, they would make quick work of the second group. The reports coming back from Cyprus, however, weren't looking great. Antalya had engaged its long-range air defenses to deter the third group, but the Isoptera were just shrugging off blows from its heavy shells and strafing across the outer settlements with blasts from their ballistic weapons.

Eager to end this and help out, I backed off on my acceleration for a moment, dropped altitude, and twisted into a barrel role, hoping the Isoptera had fallen into a false sense of security from our ever-accelerating dance. The bet paid off, and the Isopteran shuttle drifted into my attack cone.

Pure, white light reached out from the foils of the Swift Shuttle like divine judgement, ionizing the air between me and my target, splitting the fast-moving craft into pieces, its forward end dropping away as if an invisible knife had decapitated the head of a massive insect. Isoptera went flying, their twisted bodies yanked out of their harnesses by the decompressing cabin, fungara breaking up as it spiraled downward.

I did not wait to see the fireworks. I wrote this group off as down and rushed across Europe back to Cyprus. The Boot was safe for now, Santucci already pinging me with his exaltations. I ignored him.

"They're down," Karianna reported over the resonator network. *"Skive is clear."*

"Good work," I replied.

"James has some work to do on learning how to fly these things heavy-ass style, but I have to say, he's not bad. Two clear assists. I'm impressed."

"You're handing out compliments now?" James asked, sounding amused. *"Are you sure those g-forces didn't burst a blood vessel in your pretty, little head?"*

She grumbled. *"Shut up, bitch."*

We raced for Paphospolis, our defensive response slowly converging over several hundred miles. But as we hit the edge of their air-cover range, Shelly pinged me.

"We've got more incoming from deep space," she said, more annoyed than afraid. *"Nine in total. They're all over the place. Where are they coming from? Lance is deploying the fighter wing, and we're attempting to intercept all those in range."*

"Shit."

"Yeah," she agreed. *"They have to have a support ship, or several support ships, nearby with these kinds of numbers. I wish we knew their production types so we could guess."*

I thought this over. It was a gap in our knowledge that we had no way to fill. Not even Proxy had information to give us, and I had a feeling this was not the Foundry's clever means of omission for sake of control.

"Maybe we should have stuck around and investigated Nest a little longer?" I mused.

"Great idea, captain my captain," Karianna cut in. *"Hang out for a bit. Have some beers. Let the insects get us all nice and comfy so they could have us over for dinner at their house."*

"You sure about this one, James?"

I heard a chuckle over the line. *"Sure? Dead sure."*

"Sure about what?" my cocaptain asked suspiciously.

"Nothing," I said, rolling my eyes along with the wings of my accelerating craft.

"Don't pull this shit with me, Hughes. You're saying something without saying something, aren't you?"

Our targets appeared on my interface just a few dozen miles ahead. "Time to focus."

"Whatever. You're just using battle as an excuse not to talk about it."

He laughed again.

"I am going to kill the two of you when this is over," she went on.

"Good luck getting the chance," James replied.

When I arrived on the scene in Cyprus, I could see the damage the Isopteran attack shuttles had wrought. The city was on fire, devastation everywhere. The sight made my heart sink like a rock tossed into the ocean above the Marianna Trench. They had been alone for less than an hour. Less than an hour.

Drakos was screaming over the resonator network, but I didn't listen to her, only Ingrid's secondhand reports. It was too much. I had to stay focused on what was important for all. This did not please the leader of Paphospolis.

I moved into action, engaging the two attack shuttles, banking around the outside coast to intercept their vector. Their giant forms broke formation, fungara gleaming bright green in the sunlight, heading in opposite directions from one another. As they split, each deployed a salvo of a dozen roaring, green missiles, their sleek masses scattering, leaving trails of thick smoke in their wake.

"Shit," I growled, and pulled up.

Proxy turned around where it stood by my feet, looking behind us. "Activating point defense countermeasures."

From the belly of the Swift Shuttle, a small turret appeared, its barrel tracking the incoming projectile. I kept increasing acceleration, hoping to outrun these high-speed munitions while putting stress on the shuttle's hull as well as my body. The point defense turret fired, and explosions began to litter the airspace at my aft. Sure wished this little beauty was powerful enough to cut through the thicker plating of their main hull.

The missiles kept coming. They were too quick, and in my time evading them, the Isoptera had circled around and begun again, adding more missiles to the mix.

On my left, an explosion went off, producing a shockwave that forced me into a roll, pain spidering across my flank as bits of the airfoil were sheared off. My maneuverability fell apart as I lost several hundred feet of altitude, Proxy working to knit the damage back together. The remaining missiles closed in. If they reached me, I was done. There was no MI for the Swift Shuttles, it was just me, and speed was the best defense I had.

Another explosion, one missile taken out by the point defense turret, then another, sections shredding along my back, alarms and flesh screaming in pain. Proxy was having trouble keeping up with all the damage, and soon our nanoscopic system of repair would be overwhelmed.

The Swift Shuttle dropped again, and as it did, my body twisted in a direction I did not command it to. I no longer felt like a bird of prey soaring through the wild blue yonder, but a game bird clipped by buckshot who'd lost control, left spiraling down and down into an endless field of tall grass.

"Proxy!" I shouted, attempting to regain power. "Help!"

"There's too many," it reported. "We have to regroup."

The ground was getting closer, and so were the missiles. We were plummeting. I looked to the sun, and out of nowhere it blacked out, then came back, a pair of shadows crossing it.

"We got you," James said, and the missiles on my rear began to break apart, explosions like fireworks in a twisted line behind me.

While taking out the missiles didn't change the fact I was still falling, it gave me enough breathing room for Proxy to repair our most critical systems. My air foils extended past their original design, pitch control returning, and while my engines were still sputtering, the length of these new wings allowed me to fall into a gentle glide.

Overhead, Karianna and James made quick work of the surprised Isoptera, and debris from their attack shuttles was soon cast across the battered countryside.

"You good?" Karianna called, her shuttle shooting past and heading the opposite direction, not a scratch on her. *"You look like hell."*

"I'm good," I said, feeling my engines come fully back online. "Just a few scratches."

"Look guys," James said, *"Tower one is still standing. All that fighting and it's not gone."*

I looked over my shoulder and saw that this was indeed true. The enemy had gone for the city, not the Tower.

Despite their best efforts from orbit, Shelly and Lance and the remaining crew had been unable to stop the next two waves of attack shuttles. While they had culled the group a bit, taking out nearly half, the rest had broken through. In true hive fashion, the Isoptera were throwing their troops at us one wave after the next, heedless to the loss of life and equipment. They would keep pushing and pushing until they ran out of resources, and to be honest, we had no idea what that even looked like.

For years, the people of Earth, the people of SOL, had remained somewhat hidden from their notice by appearing dormant, keeping communications to a minimum, and space traffic near nonexistent. And as we had suspected, our terraforming activities had changed all that.

Reports came in. Supply shuttles under attack. These were a critical, limited resource for our project, and so we were forced to respond. For as long as we could, the three of us stayed together. We could make quicker work of the enemy like this, and it was safer. James had been the one we'd been worrying might get killed being on his own, but it appeared that for today, that honor was mine.

One report after the next, we went from target to target. After several waves, we were forced to split up, Karianna and I remaining in Europe while James went down under, lending Queensland assistance. After a few engagements we began to learn the pattern of the enemy, and it was simple.

The Isoptera moved in pairs. They engaged us with medium-range weapons as soon as we hit fifteen kilometers' distance. If we could close quick enough, or catch them by surprise, the most dangerous weapons in their arsenal, the guided missiles, were left unused. For whatever reason, the Isoptera didn't consider attackers flying above them as a factor in their calculus. And so that was just what we did. We closed the space between us and them until we hit thirty kilometers above, then we climbed to at least ten thousand feet above them, before diving downward. In most cases, this left them scrambling but not firing.

Hours went by in the same pattern: the Isoptera dropping from orbit, our team up top thinning them out, before the insects split up to divide and conquer. We did our best to respond as swiftly as possible while Ingrid fielded the angry messages from our supporting leaders. There was no avoiding it. Damage was being done. Some of the heavy shuttles were lost, every one of them a leaden burden on my heart.

Ten hours.

Twenty hours.

Thirty hours.

I was rubbing my eyes, as if this did anything in a virtual environment. Nevertheless, I was almost too tired to continue. If we were to start etching kill marks upon our hulls like the pilots of old, we'd soon start running out of space. The enemy was wearing us down like rain drops on rock, eroding away our ability to continue.

But I would not fail on my promise. I might not be able to save them all, but I could fight.

Karianna, James and I decided it was time to take stimulants. There was no break in sight that would allow us to rest, and rest was what we needed. And so, we filled our blood stream with whatever amphetamine it was the Foundry used to force a second wind.

Hour thirty-six.

We fought with a renewed vigor, but the reality of distance and resources was becoming clear. There were only three of us, and there were far more of them. Priorities became complicated, with us focusing mostly on the Boot and Paphospolis. During the battles, a second and third tower went online, one in former London near the ruins of Parliament, another high in the mountains twenty miles north of Daegu. These drew the attention of the enemy and spread us even thinner. Despite everything, we were somehow able to keep the towers online, but some of the ground crews were killed. They needed local defenses. We just couldn't be everywhere. This had been a gross oversight on all our parts. I didn't think any of the settlement leaders had considered a response at this scale. Ground response was being led by Chevelle and Renata as some of the Isopteran attack shuttles had opted to land and send in troops on foot, potentially taking live specimens back with them.

My shuttle was damaged beyond simple repair, and I was forced to return to the *Transcendence* while Proxy pulled fresh supplies. Shelly and I caught up while Karianna and James struggled below. Our team up here was also tired.

Hour forty-eight.

The stimulants were starting to become ineffective, my mind and body like brittle glass a stiff wind might shatter. Shelly urged me to return to rest after this deployment, but I couldn't. People were dying. What right did I have to get a few winks when people were dying?

Aboard the *Transcendence*, the crew began sleeping in shifts. Pilots had been brought up from Svalbard to help fill these gaps in schedule for our orbital fighters, but they weren't as experienced as my people, and as a result we lost nearly as many as the Isopterans they downed.

As I rushed from location to location to location, the ever-shifting shades of the sky became filled with black and purple dots, forcing me to shake my head clear. Proxy warned me that I was close to collapse. The drugs could only do so much.

But the enemy kept coming.

They kept coming.

They kept coming.

My shuttle plummeted out of the sky as I made for Antalya for the fifteenth time today, and I didn't try to recover. I just tumbled downward in a spiral, the world blinking in and out, clouds rushing by. I just wanted to rest my eyes for a moment. I just needed to wrap the world up in a thick blanket and forget it was there.

"Milo!" Proxy shouted again and again, but its voice was distant and muted beyond the mental fog. "Milo!"

A sudden rush of needles filled my veins, and a kind of awareness came back to me. Pain was all I knew for a moment, but it was enough that I regained control a few hundred feet from the surface. My engines swept across the tops of dried trees, and a forest caught fire.

Hour sixty.

I couldn't see straight. Nothing made sense. I kept asking for stimulants, and Proxy denied my request. While we had the right strategy to fight back, it was getting hard to run the play. I was approaching the enemy all wrong, Karianna and James unable to back me up because they were someplace else, or because they couldn't focus. More than once, Karianna came swooping in at the last moment, using her extended body to push me out of danger or keep me from crashing into a cliffside.

A heavy assault descended onto Daegu as Tower Four went online. Nothing was going to stand in the way of progress. We rushed to assist, but the attack left the three of us damaged and confused. The enemy was not destroyed, but they were forced off to repair and regroup.

Airfoils and hulls scarred from the attacks, our defensive force was compelled to land.

As soon as we did, Proxy started repairs, and exhaustion overtook us all. It didn't matter if there was a battle in orbit above, or settlements under attack on the surface. Our bodies had reached their limits.

I woke after an indeterminate time, the first of our group. Reports were coming from everywhere. Many of our heavy shuttles had run to safety, and so production of the towers had been halted.

My heart pounded in my chest as I moved to take off, systems feeling sluggish, network lagging as if a viscous liquid had been poured into its systems.

"You need more rest," Proxy told me, rubbing its body across my leg, its fur soft. "Rest."

"I don't have time to rest. They're in trouble."

"You can't sustain this, Milo. Shelly is worried."

"But what other options do we have? Not like we can enlist Cardoso and his loyalists. Hell, if or when Veetor shows up, this is all over."

"To aid you, I have transmitted plans to the settlements for ground-based weapons similar to what I gave Novae. They just need to hold out a few more days, and some of these can be brought online. This will not stop everything, but it might help."

"You talking about the rail cannons?"

"Yes."

I reached down and took the cat in my arms, squeezing it tight. Proxy purred. "Thank you. Thank you."

"I protect the pilot," it whispered.

CHAPTER 54

Alarms. More alarms.

We moved into action, but it was clear after just a few moments that we had not had enough rest. Something had to break, either us or them, but we couldn't continue.

Proxy's plans for the ground-based rail cannons went out over the resonator network and were received with mixed views. While Daegu and Queensland were excited that they could bolster their defenses, the Free Citizens of Earth were pissed it had taken this long. To be fair, so was I, but this was how the Foundry worked. Proxy was bound by certain unspoken rules till time or opportunity allowed it to assist, and pushing myself to the edge of exhaustion and beyond had unlocked some sort of requirement. To protect the pilot, it had shared these plans.

Nevertheless, plans or not, it would take at least a week before the first of these would go online, and from what we could surmise, their quantity would be limited due to the rare Earth materials required in construction. Till then . . . it was just us.

As Karianna, James, and I took off for Queensland in order to intercept a force of eight Isopteran attack shuttles, I called up to check on Shelly.

"How are we holding up?" I asked, rubbing my eyes, my shuttle listing to the right. Proxy saw this action and gave me a gentle drip of the stimulants, not enough to wash all the exhaustion away, but enough to take off the edge.

"We can't cover it all by ourselves," Shelly replied. *"We're only one ship, and splitting us apart is too dangerous. I have no idea how you've stayed alert for so long. I've been stressing the hell out just to keep my eyes open and the weapons hot."*

"It hasn't been easy." I yawned, my eyes feeling dry and cracked despite my environment being artificial. "Splash of cold water, few cups of coffee. It can help anyone push through."

"Don't be cute with me."

"Alright. Okay. I agree. We're spread too thin, but what do we do?"

"What about Cardoso? Despite his little stunt, I think he would be helpful. Will he not help?"

I sighed at this. "I've been thinking about that a lot. And, well, I think he is helping. I think he's keeping Veetor busy."

"I agree with mush-for-brains," Karianna cut in. *"It's been too quiet. Justin isn't one to let getting in his way go unanswered. Cardoso has their attention someplace else. Maybe fighting Isoptera, maybe stuck in maintenance hell. Maybe he's just keeping the asshole doped and with a fresh line of willing freaks to keep him busy behind locked doors, I don't know. But they aren't here right now, and I think he's making that happen."*

"The settlements are not happy with any of this," Shelly said. *"We promised them defense so they could get the project started and not worry about attacks, and all we've done is chase our own tails."*

"I know. I know. But what else can we do? There's only so many of us, and there are so many of them. So. Fucking. Many. They don't stop coming."

"Milo?" James asked, testing the waters like someone dipping a toe in a cold stream. His Swift Shuttle did a roll on my left flank, heat and condensation trailing out from his engines in a spiral. We weren't the only ones who enjoyed this sensation. *"I know this isn't exactly something you want to hear, but maybe we should go on the offensive. We can't fight this battle down here for much longer. But if we take the fight to them, they'll be forced to respond, right? We know where the Gray Queen resides. We attack their hive, it will draw them away from the settlements."*

My blood went cold at the thought of that lifeless hunk of rock encircled by Isopteran warships. It felt as if someone had injected me with ice water. They had built a base there. They had built a hive in SOL. This was where every one of these Isopteran soldiers had come from, hatched by a giant, pulsing, charcoal-shaded freak bent on turning humans into feed stock.

"Milo?" he asked after some time. *"Did I lose you?"*

I blinked, looked to Proxy, and shook my head. "I'm not sure we have enough firepower to go at it head-on."

"Okay, maybe not, but we can't keep this up either. We're pretty badass, but there's only three of us, and they are legion. Besides, what about that thing we brought back? Can't we use that?"

"What thing?" Karianna asked, sounding confused. Her shuttle dipped out of formation for a moment, then drifted back. The sun had fallen over the horizon, and we were flying into the cold of night, nothing but sensors and blinking foil lights with which to perceive one another. *"Are you talking about that weird device we took from Nest?"*

"Yes! That's it. It's a weapon, right?"

"We don't know," Shelly interjected, her voice lashing out like a jagged edge. *"No one knows what it is, not even Proxy. We only know that it contains vast amounts of power."*

"All the better. We send it in, overload it, let it crack that rock."

"Why go to those lengths?" Karianna sounded as if she were scratching her head, attempting to understand. *"I mean, wouldn't the antimatter cannons work just fine?"*

"If we can get close enough," I replied, my voice shaky. "We can't stealth the slugs. Over a long distance, they might can shoot them down or sacrifice their own ships."

"But the device," James went on. *"Proxy could wrap it in those stealth machines, and so long as they aren't looking too close, it can make it through. We just have to act as a diversion. Once the main base is destroyed, whatever ships they have hanging out will either flee or be easy pickings for the UEI and us."*

"You know more about the device than you're saying, don't you, Milo?" Karianna pressed. *"You know what it is. You do . . ."*

I did not want to have this conversation, not in this state. No matter what it truly was, it made me very afraid. Universe help us, it made me afraid.

"No, we don't," I said after some time. "Not exactly. Only, as Shelly said, that it has vast power reserves. We think— We have a hypothesis, but we really don't know what it does."

"Well then, who made it? Huh? Who?"

This I did not want to answer.

"Who, damn it, Milo! Who!"

I whispered, "Kabosai."

"Oh, shit," James hissed. "You're not kidding, are you?"

"No," Shelly replied. "He's not."

"All the better." His tone lightened as if excited at the prospect, like a kid who'd been promised ice cream for good behavior. "If it's Kabosai, then it probably does something with genetics. Let's toss some random settings into it and fuck their world up."

"It doesn't work like that. It requires a template to make changes. Wherever we find one of those things."

"Bullshit. It requires a template or whatever to do it the right way. But we don't want to do it the right way, do we? We want to mess them up, scramble their shit. We want them to die horribly."

I sighed. "We are not sure if it will activate without a template. There's just too much we don't know . . ."

"And we have no Kabosai to ask," Shelly finished my thought.

"Well," Karianna said, speaking up at last, "if it can get them off our backs, we need to look at it. We all know we can't keep this up. It's too much. Our mission will fail if we don't stomp on the hive."

And they were right about that. We had to go to the source to end this. While this weapon seemed a terrible way to end your enemies, what other options did we have?

"Enough of that for now." Karianna's voice went hard. "We've got incoming. Stay sharp, friends."

"Stay sharp," James echoed, but this was harder to do with every second.

In that moment I felt, rather than saw, Shelly giving me a sidelong look over communications. We knew what needed to be done, but we didn't like it. That device gave me the creeps in ways I could not explain. But maybe we should use it as a weapon. Could it fix this? Could it stop them?

CHAPTER 55

Santucci was livid. While the attacks had slowed in intensity, and construction of the defensive weapons had begun, their manufacture required an entire realignment of global production queues. The great Mancini Forge had been working full tilt to produce the interlocking rods that made up the Towers, and so this shift to an entirely different output took time and resources.

He argued that Queensland should be putting their energy into this shift, that the Boot should remain focused on building Towers, but some technical issues down under had shut down their facility for the time being. While it was dubbed as mechanical failure, the unnamed manufactories had recently been prone to accidents as well as several ancient devices that had spontaneously exploded. An investigation had been started, but so far it appeared there was no foul play.

Somehow, part of this was my fault, when all I had done for over a week was help keep the sky clear.

Towers five and six had gone online. This meant that the only settlement that didn't have a Tower near it was Svalbard, and Ingrid was fine with being last in this race. I had to admit the Jevox devices were a marvel. They were freestanding hubs of all things atmospheric clean-up, with drones flying to and fro, heading out into the damaged landscape around them and seeking all that was harmful to contend with. We were even starting to see a few of the spindly Sky Sweepers go online, their massive sails dragging through open air and capturing dangerous molecules as their drone bodies cruised through the clouds.

If birds still lived on Earth in massive numbers like they once had, the surface area of these giant catch nets might just have been a problem, but as it was, there were so few as to almost not matter. Just in case, Frelo had programmed the sails to flicker with colors in spectrums that we believed would signal danger for the remaining few and keep them away.

I watched these Towers do their job, mesmerized at their operation each time we fled the scene of another attack.

"It's going to work, isn't it?" Karianna asked as she formed up on my left wing. *"They are remarkable."*

"They are," I said, my heavy heart feeling lighter, if just a tiny bit. Hope felt like a luxury, but what was life if not to be enjoyed? "So long as we keep them up. And Universe help us, we've got to do that."

A ping went off in my interface. I ignored it for a time, content to live in temporary calm. I took in a deep breath and just soaked in the moment, watching the tower at Cyprus work, willing the tiny machines with my imagination to do their thing as if I were the conductor of an orchestra.

"Amen to that." She paused for a moment, all three of us cruising along in silence. *"I hate to report, but you know we've got more incoming. Three, in fact."*

"I know," I mumbled, allowing myself to listen to the message.

"Split up?"

"Yeah. I'll take the Boot."

"I'll get Antalya," James chimed in, yawning as he did. *"Karianna? What about you?"*

She hummed for a moment before responding. *"There's a report from a smaller settlement near the Nile Delta. Since you both chose your targets, guess this one is mine."*

"Catch our headings, headquarters?"

"Copy that," Ingrid replied. *"Light day so far, isn't it? Only seven incursions into our space, and we're almost up on dinnertime. A few reports of strange blips up in the Ring of Diamonds, but nothing unusual. It's likely ancient debris."*

"We'll keep an eye out."

"Fly safe."

"Fly safe," I said, and my wing broke formation. We peeled away from one another to focus on our respective targets, our ships feeling heavier than normal. We had gotten efficient at this operation, but that didn't mean we weren't tired.

Proxy nuzzled against my leg, and I smiled, bending over to scratch it behind the ear. I wouldn't still be here if not for Proxy. It might just be some Foundry initiative to protect the pilot, another system of control in the grand equation to protect life, but this artificial intelligence was my friend. We had become more than just our programming.

I locked in my course and leaned into the flight, engines roaring hot, my path taking me along a tract of sea and land I'd become all too familiar with. To be honest, I had started to space out a little during my flights from point to point, allowing Proxy to autopilot some of the trip. This allowed my mind a bit of rest given the demands we had been under. It was only a few minutes stolen here and there, but I hoped they added up to something measurable.

As Proxy and I approached what had once been Greece, I found myself lost in memories, daydreaming of an Earth where people would get to live in better conditions than they were in now. The more I learned about what had happened to all of them, what was known of the wars, the competitive backbiting over resources, the rampant disease that had run through the settlements, the high rates of fetal mortality, the more I realized that despite all the pain, despite all the trials, the people of FICSE had lived a kind of charmed life.

Yes, we had seen fighting and death and danger, but we had not known this level of starvation and squaller. We had lived in a homeostatic environment for decades, then a mostly egalitarian society in which no one went without. We may have gone with less, but not without. If Johan hadn't pressed us all so hard, we might never have come back to SOL. Life was good, if not easy. But we owed it to the people of Earth to return, we owed it to them to fulfill a promise of the past. We need to make damn sure—

"Milo!" Proxy shouted, snapping me from my exhausted reverie. "We have—"

And everything went blank, my expanded senses retreating, the Swift Shuttle's virtual environment winking out, vision struggling to readjust as I found myself physically back in my Star Sphere. I scrambled for the connection, calling for everything to come back, but there was nothing to grasp for. The feed had been severed.

Tiny bubbles ejected from the sides of my mouth by the thousands like the jets of a tub as the boundaries of the Star Sphere's tank came into focus. I felt the shift in acceleration as my stomach dropped, but my inner ear had not evolved for this. I couldn't tell if I was falling down, or sideways; all I knew was that the Swift Shuttle didn't have anyone at the stick.

Frantic, heart pounding in my chest, adrenaline cracking my senses like a hot whip, I tried to swim to the edge of the tank, but given the drop it was no use.

Had I been shot?

Had the shuttle reached an operational limit?

No. Proxy would have told me.

I was falling.

That was what I was feeling.

Falling.

Falling.

A warm sensation filled my veins as the shuttle arrested itself. Awareness began to return as systems rebooted. Proxy appeared first, my perception not much more than a visual tunnel a thousand feet long with the feel of wind on my wings.

"Pull up," Proxy ordered, and I did just that, my stomach bottoming out at the lowest point of my maneuver.

All I could see was through a narrow passage, in only one direction at a time. With each second that passed, it became a little wider, but not quick enough that I would see in 360 degrees anytime soon.

I dared ask, "What the hell was that?"

"Some kind of energy pulse," Proxy replied. "It disabled our systems. Oh shit."

"Did you just say a cuss word, Proxy?"

"Aft. Look. Now!"

I did just that, turning around to see a sleek form of black and silver on my tail, arcs of electricity cascading up and down its slender airfoils. It was a shuttle, the design of which looked frighteningly close to my own.

Before I could make any adjustments, the charging weapon fired, and what few systems were still online died. The world went hard. Proxy had anticipated this move and redirected cultures of nanomachines to protect me.

The Swift Shuttle fell like a rock in the dark. Several breathless moments passed. I drew my body into a protective ball, arms crossed over my chest in an X, eyes squeezed shut, lips mouthing a silent prayer to the Universe.

The world shook, the umbilicals connected to my spine pulling.

The darkness around me was soon punctured with a thousand holes, the void of my near sensory deprivation replaced by flickering, scattered lights as my Swift Shuttle struck the ground like a stone hurled from a trebuchet, the outer layers of its hull peeling away. I could do nothing but watch and hope that Proxy's move had been enough to save me.

The Star Sphere broke free of its mounts, ping-ponged against what was left of the shuttle's ceiling, then tumbled out a fresh hole in its side. I rolled into open fields of scrub, light and dark and disorientation taking hold of the moment. Nothing steady, nothing making sense.

Hold on. Don't die.

My sphere came to rest in a dip at the base of a gentle slope, rocking back and forth before settling into place.

"Proxy," I called out with my implants. *"Are you there?"*

"I am," it called back from the *Transcendence*. *"I am going to release the clamps. Get out of that tank, quick. We've called for help, but you have another Swift Shuttle bearing down on you. The aggressor is here."*

"Veetor . . ." I transmitted back, my words like a hiss. Somehow, some way, he had gotten around our blockade without being caught.

As promised, I felt something click within the Star Sphere, and the liquid began to drain onto the dirt. The umbilicals twisted away from my spine. At least I wouldn't have to go through what I did when I crash-landed on that icy moon. As the fluid receded, I scrambled to my feet and crawled for the open iris at the sphere's former top, wearing nothing but my underwear.

As I stepped barefoot onto crunchy rocks and sand, I found that beyond all odds, the strongbox containing my personal effects was intact. Before Veetor could come around and finish me off, I reached for my sidearm, checking to be sure if it was loaded. Karianna and Shelly would have been proud. I took three extra clips from the box, as well as my clothes and boots, and a draft of water from my canteen, then surveyed my surroundings. I was someplace in Southern Greece, the landscape made of dusty, rolling hills and brown, withered plants.

The air above me roared as Veetor turned back in my direction. There was no telling how far out he was, but those shuttles hauled ass. I needed to get to cover, away from the wreckage, or I'd end up being a smear in the dirt when he came around. Seeing a series of abandoned retail spaces, as well as what might have once been a gas station along a highway, I took off at a dead run, weaving between scrub and trying not to trip, my feet screaming as rocks bit into my heels.

My Swift Shuttle smoldered behind me, broken, likely destroyed entirely. I had been so stupid. I had let down my guard.

As I reached the shadow of the first of the concrete buildings in a row of three, I heard the whine of Veetor's shuttle shifting into hover mode. He did not fire at me but instead landed upon the highway on the other side of the buildings.

Using the butt of my pistol, I shattered a window on the back side of a market, clearing away the glass so I could jump inside. Unless he had seen me run here specifically, he would have no way to know where I was. I might be in a tough situation, but if I played my cards right, we might end it here. We were already discussing how to cut the Isoptera off at the root, to kill the colony or the Gray Queen, but stopping Veetor would be just as powerful. We could end it today. I could kill him. He was just a punk, a thug, a bully.

I weaved through the shady, picked-over aisles of what looked to have been a store that sold food and clothes, the smell of mold and dust thick in the air. I took a step and slipped, nearly falling, my bare feet having hit a tract of oil or slime, but recovered myself, taking hold of a steel shelving. Items clattered to the ground as I gripped the edge of the shelf for dear life, metal bending, cans of vegetables with Greek letters printed on their faded labels making a racket. I scrambled into my clothes, zipping up the jumpsuit and slipping on my boots, before patting my body down to feel for the vials of nanomachines Shelly and I had packed. They were here, and the belt was intact, my implants pinging back all systems green.

Once I had recomposed myself, I moved forward, crouching down to approach the front windows, which faced the highway. Veetor's Swift Shuttle was parked about two hundred feet to my left, dust rising around it in a kind of vortex, its engines cold.

The door on its starboard side irised open.

Cloud cover shifted, and a single beam of light shot down to illuminate his path, making his red-and-gold-sequined long coat twinkle along with his bald head. Veetor had to be the most flamboyant peacock I had ever seen, showing up to a fight, fresh from being dunked in his Star Sphere, looking like an Elvis impersonator in Vegas. Unlike the rest of us, who wore functional clothes, jumpsuits or jeans and jackets, he wanted to draw everyone's attention, and he was good at it. The first thing that came to mind was how hot he had to be in that. The temperature inside this shaded store was at least in the mid-eighties Fahrenheit, and it was even hotter outside.

He moved toward me with a kind of swagger that made him roll his shoulders with each step, the street so quiet I could hear the heels of his snake-skin boots clicking on the cracked roadway.

"Little pet! Come out, come out wherever you are," he shouted, cupping his fingers around his mouth. He ran a hand over his bald head to wick away the moisture. "Here, piggy, piggy, piggy. I know you're out there."

I checked my pistol once more, felt for the vials on my body. Loaded, all unbroken. Was he armed? It was hard to say given how long his coat was, and how many pockets it might have hidden under its layers. Was the material ballistic rated? That was starting to sound like a great idea.

He came closer.

"Picked a hell of a place to crash land, my friend. But I thought we needed to have a chat. I know it's you, Mr. Hughes. And the two of us have a little unfinished business. You've been making quite a mess of my kingdom."

My mechanical hand tightened around the grip of my pistol, but a subtle warning in the back of my head told me to stop squeezing or I'd break the weapon.

Veetor raised his metallic appendage, the massive cuff of his coat sliding down to his elbow, the sun revealing a series of diamonds set along its underside. Wind rustled his coat as he paused about fifty feet from my hiding spot, scanning the empty streets.

"You've been very, very busy," he rambled on. "I step away for a few weeks just to get some much-needed R&R. Been a busy life-season, let me tell you. It has been mentally and emotionally exhausting. So, I spent some time catching up on my reading, some time drinking a hot cocoa on a cold night on the dark side of Saturn, some time to enjoy the fairer sex for all their beauty and desirable qualities, and in that interlude, you go and start giving the people down here undeserved hope.

"You think you're helping, I know you think you are, and bless your little heart for that. But you see, these people down here who have been scratching by, they do so because we want them to do so. That's right, they got what's coming to them. They are the direct descendants of those who turned this world into a wasteland, and for humankind to ever find absolution for these great sins, they have just got to struggle. Some of them have to die.

"It seems the Clickers do a pretty good job at killing humans, killing sinners, problem is, you keep screwing it all up. You keep shooting down those who live to destroy them. Like moths to a flame, you called the Clickers, good job for that, but instead of letting them do their grand work, you fight back. You're bold enough to clash with these insects day and night, but here we are, and you can't come out and face me, man to man. Mano y mano. Let's stop playing games."

"Don't do it," Shelly cut in over my implants. *"Don't let him bait you. That's all this is. He wants you out of the way."*

I knew this to be true, but he had made me think. Could all of this have been fixed already, but Veetor and the UEI had said no? Had they been standing in the way of the world coming together either actively or inactively?

"You're right," I told her, whispering the words as I transmitted them over my implants. "And I can't let him get away with it."

"He'll kill you. It's a trap."

"It probably is."

I took a deep breath, stood up, and made for the entrance. The door to the market chimed twice as I stepped out onto the sidewalk and made for the street, my attention focused on Veetor.

The expression on his face went from annoyed to amused in a split second, his dark eyes widening, thin lips curling into a smile.

"We just keep getting closer, don't we?" he commented as I took my place in the middle of the road, one hand on the holster at my hip. "First, we start talking over long-range communications, then we meet in the arena, and now? If I didn't know better, I'd think you were into me."

"Into you?" I rolled the words around in my mouth. "The only thing I'd like to get into you is a healthy dose of lead. I hear that it fucks with the brain, and it looks like you're a little too smart for your own good."

He clapped his hands together and laughed. "Touché, Mr. Hughes. You've got some smart-ass in you yet."

"That's what they say."

"So how do you want to do this?" He raised his open palms, arms wide, and spun around in circles, regarding our combat theater with amusement. This man did not feel fear like a normal person; the world was his chaotic little playground. "This all feels like a showdown from an old Spaghetti Western, doesn't it? Just too bad we're in Greece, not Italy. Should we relocate?"

"Keep him busy," Karianna hissed over my implants. *"Shelly and Proxy told us what happened, we're coming. ETA nine minutes."*

"I got this," I replied, wordlessly. *"Just be ready to pick up the body."*

"Is something wrong with you?" Veetor asked, leaning forward and bending over, hands on the tops of his thighs. "You got quiet. Your expression went slack like an old man's wrinkly face." He motioned to his imitation of my blank expression, and then a realization dawned. "Oh, I see . . . You have them as well. Seems only fitting. Turns out those devices were not good for humans. Caused madness in some groups. Political subversion in others. Terrible way to live, always being bombarded with unfiltered information such that it becomes hard to tell what is real and what is not. Just another sin, another reason to let the old burn and the new rise . . ."

"Are you obsessed with hearing yourself speak?" I took a step forward, boots crunching on the gravel between cracks in the asphalt. "Because the more I hear you do it, the less I want to hear it."

He tapped his lips with a finger, then pointed at me. "I suppose then, pahtnerr," he said, taking on the affectation of a cowboy gunslinger, adopting the accent as well as a rakish stance, posture leaned back, hip cocked out. "Let's get it all done today in the OK Corral, just us cow folk. You win, no more listenin' to me."

Veetor flung his coat back to reveal a sidearm and a holster resting on his left hip, just like me. From the looks of it, we were both right-handed, his donation on the same side as mine. The wind kicked up, and my focus narrowed, the machines in my blood shifting into high gear, sharpening my reflexes. While Proxy didn't say a word about it, I knew it was hard at work prepping me for this fight, just as Veetor's was, giving us chemical or electrical assistance to make us stronger.

My curls rustled against my sweat-slick forehead, and a dead bush as large as a basketball caught a howling gust and went tumbling across the highway along with loose papers, disposable drink cups, and plastic bags.

I blinked, my eyes dry, vision hazy. Veetor leaned forward and hocked a loogie on the ground, then produced a toothpick from someplace and stuck it between his teeth, its sharp end poking out.

My open, trembling right-hand hovered by my stomach, ready to draw. Could I shoot him before he shot me? Or was this mutually assured destruction? With our Foundry augmentations, I had a good feeling neither of us would miss.

I had to calm myself down. I had to appear collected. If I faltered for an instant, he would take the opportunity to blow a hole in my head.

"You chicken?" Veetor said after what seemed like several minutes, toothpick rolling between his front teeth. "Say when, my friend. Say when."

A sonic boom washed over us, a shuttle reentering the atmosphere at multiple times the speed of sound, drawing my attention for an instant, forcing me to look out of habit. As I pivoted to see, he reached for his weapon, and the moment we had found ourselves in slowed to the speed of cold molasses. The clock ticked in dilated timescales, our fingers traveling only millimeters for every subjective second that passed.

Halfway to my pistol, I realized that I was moving swifter than he, if just barely. I was going to get my weapon first. My fingers wrapped around the grip and I drew, my left shoulder twisting back as I did, right hand rising, my profile narrowing from Veetor's position to that of a slit. By the time I had aimed at him and pulled the trigger, he had barely made it to the grip of his weapon.

My pistol discharged with a bang far louder than should have been possible, ears buzzing at the noise. Dust kicked up around us at another gust of wind, and the bullet sang through the air toward him. In this stretched moment of time, I felt a rush of hope and joy that the projectile was going to hit its mark.

But the rush was short lived.

From out of the crumbled highway before him came a glittering wall of gray. One minute it wasn't there, the next it was. My bullet collided with a silver barrier Veetor had erected with a flash of brilliant light.

That bastard.

Veetor leaned around his new barrier, weapon drawn, time resuming its normal flow. He squeezed the trigger, and I bolted for cover across the road, raising my left hand to draw from the nanomachines stored in my jumpsuit, a silver barrier exploding in a starburst from my left arm, all while firing the pistol with my right hand. Bullets pinged off our respective barriers.

"You're not the only one with fun little tricks!" Veetor shouted. "What you did in that arena, and what I'd seen that Ingrid do with her little dog, gave me some ideas. So many ideas. Foundry wouldn't make it for me, so I found someone who could. Looks like you made some upgrades of your own. This ought to be fun."

They say that imitation is the greatest form of flattery, but today, I was not feeling flattered.

I slid into cover behind a rusted gas pump and reloaded my pistol, instructing my nanomachines to form a kind of wedge behind me thick enough to keep me from being killed.

"Milo, he's moving in on you," Proxy reported as I jammed the fresh clip into place and cocked the weapon.

"Gee, thanks for the heads-up," I said, and stood back up, careful not to let my head peek too far out of cover.

Veetor came rushing at me, and I felt compelled to do the same. I was tired of being on the run, tired of this bullshit of playing shadow games. It was time to end this. We fired at one another, bullets pinging off our respective barriers till both of our sidearms went dry, but we kept coming.

He tossed his empty weapon away and flexed his arms as he stalked over to me, the fluid motion of quicksilver illustrating just how much control he had over his swarm of nanomachines.

We clashed in the middle of the street, slamming our barriers together like two trucks hitting head-on. A blade formed in my right hand, slender as paper and twice as long as my arm. I lashed out at Veetor, seeing an opening, a flash of his sparkling coat through the haze of silver, but he raised his open palms and scattered the barrier into a billion tiny pieces. For an instant, I didn't know what he was doing, half of me expecting to start breathing in the machines, but then they reformed into a clamp and took hold of my blade's edge just as it came down upon him, locking the weapon in place.

Sweat burst from my forehead as I strained against his clamp, leaning forward, attempting to use the strength of my augmentations as leverage.

With a mental command, I ordered the machines along my weapon's blade to go to battle with his own at a nanoscopic level, to fight one-on-one and sever contact so I could get free of their grip. A flicker of light drew my attention, and I glanced to the side, seeing that he had formed something like a shiv and was about to eviscerate my guts.

I let go of the trapped weapon, allowing it to start dissolving and return to my swarm, all while leaping back. The sharp tip of his dagger sliced a hole in my jumpsuit, skin stinging, blood blossoming from the slash. There was no time to think about the pain. No time.

"Quick feet," he commented, returning his machines to his personal swarm and reforming them into a pair of long blades.

I did the same.

"Years of practice," I growled, and we started circling one another.

The wind kicked up, and he moved first, striking high, then low, one side, then the other, then sidestepping to try and get around my flank. Even in that long, flashy coat, he was quick as lightening. But I was quicker. I weaved around his assault, twisting my body and keeping the lines of attack cut off with my own twin blades. Sparks cast into the air as our weapons clashed.

An opening appeared, a moment where Veetor was swinging back from a heavy attack like a batter, leaving him exposed. I moved in.

Realizing his mistake, Veetor's swarm fell apart, becoming nothing but dust, its diffuse particles closing around him. One moment, Veetor was all sparkles and sunshine; the next, he was a man incased in iron, the machines having made a kind of second skin over every exposed part of his body, even his face.

My blade struck this second skin, and much to my surprise, nothing happened. So far, almost anything these nanoblades had struck short of an airlock door was cut in half, the edge so thin they could slice apart atomic bonds, but not this time.

I hit him again, and again, and again, sparks scattering with each impact like tiny explosions of fireworks. Veetor cackled the entire time, his arms raised in a defensive X. He had no weapon formed at present, but I wasn't making a kill either. I had to turn this fight.

His fingers splayed wide, and two crescent-moon blades appeared in his hands. He lashed out with these new weapons, and I felt another sting along my left flank as one sliced open flesh. I backed away, nearly tumbling over a crack in the asphalt, then leaned to the side as he threw one of the razor-sharp crescents at my face, its edge zipping past my left ear, its wind rustling my hair.

Without preamble, he pressed the attack, the iron skin flowing away as he raised his hands again and again as if tossing death at me underhanded.

Every twitch of his wrist was another blade thrown my way, another promise of oblivion. I batted them off with clumsy responses from my own swarm and backed into cover around a pillar by the gas station on the other side of the highway.

One of the blades whizzed past, and as it did, the final support holding the crooked roof of the fueling area was sliced in half. With a groan of twisting steel, the gas station began to collapse, forcing me to dive into safety. Everything crashed down, dust kicking up, and I thanked the Universe for not being squashed in the cascade of debris.

Another barrier between us, if only for a brief moment.

There was no denying Veetor was far more aggressive than me, but I had to survive. Everyone counted on me. I had to find the strength to end this. I needed a better position. I needed to counter ambush him.

I crawled through the wreckage, twisting myself around mangled sheets of steel and aluminum, and as I broke into open air, he started his assault again. Crescents of quicksilver shot past all around me as blood pumped in my ears. I was barely able to stay ahead and keep from getting hit. Rounding the corner of the station, I fell behind a thicker cover, but that didn't stop the blades. They cut through anything and everything, just like mine could.

How was I going to stop him? How?

Then an idea popped into my head.

Why hadn't I thought of this before?

I made for the other side of a retail space, attempting to get myself in a better position, and Veetor was forced to run around the outer edge of the ruined gas station. This small amount of time was just enough to put some distance between us. I glanced over my shoulder, not able to see him but able to hear him. I spun around at the far end of the building, hands at my side, swarms of nanomachines floating around my arms, my breathing short and quick.

As soon as he came into view, rushing to me, full speed, I raised my hands like a wizard taking control of the tides. My swarm gathered around me in a diffuse, flowing cloud of machines that formed a series of quicksilver tentacles. I lashed out at Veetor, whipping him with the swarm. He countered, raising a pair of domed barriers while pitting the remainder of his swarm, which was now a kind of mist, against my own.

"This is new," he growled, his eyebrows furrowed with a kind of uncertainty. Was I making him sweat? "It seems our little imaginations are the only limit for this kind of combat. I could get used to this."

Two blows crashed down upon him, casting a shower of sparks that ignited a fire in the dry scrub by our feet. "Don't get too comfortable," I said, eyes narrowed. "Nothing lasts forever."

The two of us stood ten paces apart, our swarms doing battle for us, looking for advantage, attention fixed on controlling their nanoscopic melee. Layers of machines were cast aside with each blow, our faces a mask of focus. I could feel every machine under my will and was working to weave them around his defense.

Blow for blow.

Head to head.

I was taking ground.

Veetor struggled against me, his will breaking.

I was winning, every attack making him take another step back. Until I wasn't.

A sharp pain cut across my right side, making it hard to focus. There was no time to let this dominate my attention—I knew I had to fight—but my body had other ideas. My swarm of nanomachines fell to pieces as my hands covered the blossom of crimson on my side. My legs wobbled, and I collapsed to my knees. The agony was too much. It turned my vision blurry, turned my mind into a shifting, dark haze of madness, muscles writhing around the gash, blood turning cold as ice.

"Finally," Veetor groaned, recalling his swarm with a sigh. I tried to reach for my own, but they did not respond. I couldn't call them up when in this anguish, fire rushing up and down my skin, burning me from the inside. "This little game has taken far too long, and I am so bored with it. It was nice for a while—get the blood going, you see. But now? Little piggy, little piggy, I'm done."

"You—" I coughed blood into my hands. So much blood.

Veetor raised a blade made of nanomachines, his eyes turning dark as he looked over me, silhouette blocking out the sun. He cocked his head to the side, appearing curious, then slowly lowered the blade into my left thigh, piercing skin and muscle one millimeter at a time till its tip struck bone. Icy shocks of pain the likes of which I had never known wracked my body. My leg convulsed around the cut, skin bursting with sweat.

"No," I cried. "Please. I—"

"Love. Live. Pray," he whispered, then raised the blade once more, dragging it across my stomach, pulling back the skin under my jumpsuit like someone might peel an apple. "Burn. Fall. Ash." My body trembled at his touch, a mélange of agony becoming so complex it was almost impossible to register where the pain was coming from. I writhed on the ground and sobbed uncontrollably. "Anger. Atonement. End . . ."

Universe, please help me. Please. I can't do this. I can't do this.

A sonic boom rocked the air above us, first one, then two, both much louder than what we had heard earlier. This drew the madman's attention, and his blade paused. Despite the pain, I caught his expression, cold and calculated, his fat tongue licking his lips as he considered his options.

"Shit," he growled, and stepped away. He fled, leaving me alone to bleed out on the ground behind some derelict building in Greece.

"Milo . . ." Proxy whispered in my mind. *"Hold on. Please. Hold on."*

My lips quivered, and I could only think of Shelly. I'd left her up on the ship and gotten myself killed in the process. I wouldn't be there to protect her. She was right. She was always right. I should have run.

I needed to move, but everything hurt too bad, every twitch as painful as the rusty serrations of a blade jabbed into tender flesh.

"Fuck, fuck, fuck!" Karianna shouted over the open channel, but her words were hard to contextualize with as much pain as I was in. *"My weapons won't do shit. Someone hit that asshole! Please! Kill him. Kill him! Don't let him get away!"*

"Mine won't either," James said. *"The hell is wrong, here?"*

"Fucking Foundry bullshit!"

The world began to flicker in and out, my will struggling against my physical capability. The ground shook, and as I faded away, familiar faces appeared before me. Karianna's expression was made of shock, her eyes wide and darting, skin pale. James just looked angry.

I didn't remember much after that moment, but I knew they picked me up, took me to one of the shuttles, placed me on a bench, and did something to stop the bleeding. Next thing I knew, I was back aboard the *Transcendence*, my naked body submerged in my Star Sphere.

Shelly stood outside my tank, one hand against the glass, the other covering her mouth.

Only one thing was going through my mind as I lay back, suspended in fluid while Proxy's machines repaired my body.

Veetor had gotten away, and he was going to strike again.

CHAPTER 56

I slept for days floating in my Star Sphere, my body weary and broken, pain suppressed but not absent. If not for the miraculous technology aboard the *Transcendence*, I would have been dead moments after reaching the ship. The gaping holes in my body were slowly being knit back together, one cell at a time, bottom to top.

I kept playing the events over and over, unable to do much else given that I couldn't leave this fluid. Veetor had had his opportunity to end this, to kill me where I lay, but he'd decided to go the route of torture and play, and it had cost him. He had put his pleasure, twisted as it was, above his objectives, and this revelation felt important.

The good news was, I was still alive.

The bad news was, things weren't getting any better down on Earth.

While the Towers were hard at work to clean up the planet, a job that would take years, the Isopteran incursions had not ceased. Ground-based rail cannons had been brought into service along the Mediterranean Sea and in South Korea, but the targeting systems were having challenges when it came to calibration. Shelly and a team of computer scientists from Svalbard had been working to resolve these issues, but the results were hit or miss, no pun intended. Still, the weapons' very presence, effective at shooting down Isoptera or not, was enough to discourage a sizable percentage of them from attacking by ground, even keeping some of them away entirely.

Injured as I was, I could be of no help to them in this, and that was worse than my physical pains. I was helpless, enfeebled, impotent. Though I was thankfully back to the point where I could pilot the *Transcendence*, Karianna was down on the surface responding to attacks, and so the ship did very little to help. I could change our orbit, our trajectory, fire the weapons at incoming ships, but I could not respond swiftly by any means.

The Universe had forced me to recover, despite my desire to do otherwise.

Days passed, and this dire situation reached a kind of homeostasis. Those on the ground had adjusted to life under threat, and with some ground-based defenses in place, the Isoptera were not making easy game of humans on the surface. Chevelle had been working with Dameon as well to get some old war machines online, mostly tanks with anti-air capabilities and limited ammunition. The heavy shuttles went back to work, moving supplies and finished machinery, constantly under threat from the Isopteran attack ships. We had lost five of our thirty, which given how hard the enemy was pressing was a miracle in itself, but we needed all of them in service to see this mission done.

Every day that passed, more people were dying. Every day that passed, my promise was becoming more just empty words meant to quell my guilt.

"We have visitors coming back with our people," Proxy informed me, drawing me out of my reverie. The space around the *Transcendence* was clear of enemy forces for now. "Ingrid would like to meet in person. I do not advise you to leave your Star Sphere. We still have a lot of work to do on your body. Flesh is easy to damage, hard to repair."

I gave the cat a weak smile and scooped it up, drawing it to my chest while looking to the incoming Swift Shuttle. It was James, with Karianna not far behind.

A few minutes later, the shuttle was aboard, and everyone had made their way to my sphere's containment room, where I floated alone in my tank, my body healing in a special kind of liquid Proxy had replaced the water with. I had drawn myself out of my virtual environment and would be using my implants to communicate with them over a loudspeaker mounted on the outside. This diminished the risk of infection or further injury throughout the healing process.

Proxy summoned chairs out of the floor so that Ingrid, Lance, Dameon, and Priscilla could sit. He offered them refreshments as always, which they declined. James and Karianna stood by in silence, refreshing the sensor feed over and over with their implants, eager to snap at them like starving dogs if the enemy came back during our conversation.

"Everyone's here," Shelly said, patting her hand against the bend of my tank, its reverberation thumping against my eardrums. "They just wanted to give you an update on what's going on down on the surface."

"We have instantaneous communications," I said, bubbles coming out the sides of my mouth, my voice having gone through the external speaker, but habits died hard. "Is something wrong?" I looked at them through the bend of glass and liquid, their faces distorted and large like in a funhouse mirror, changing size dramatically as they shifted around and settled in.

"Something is always wrong," Lance said, waving to Proxy for a cup of coffee. His companions might have abstained from luxury, but he wouldn't pass up the chance. His Barcelona mug appeared on a table beside him, a piping-hot cup of the heavenly black stuff steaming within. "That's one thing I've learned about life. It's always something."

"Which is why we embrace the journey," Priscilla said, nodding.

Ingrid sat up straight in her chair, a forlorn bend in her shoulders, if not showing up in her facial expressions. She had gotten good at not appearing overwhelmed or afraid.

"We have too many pieces on the chess board," she said, her voice cold. "I just don't know how to remove any of them from play. Maybe this was all a mistake. Maybe this was not the time in history to go for such a lofty idea. If we had just stayed quiet, the enemy would have continued to leave us alone."

Lance set down his coffee after a long sip and rested a hand on her shoulder, squeezing. "We've talked about it, and I'm not so sure. At some point they would have come for everyone on Earth. All we did was force that timetable. Something was going to happen. If not now, then later. I'd bet on it."

She sighed, and her face fell into her palms. "And maybe you're right. Either way, we can't keep this up forever. The Clickers, we can see them coming for the most part, know when the threat is inbound. But with what the Absolutionists are up to, they're invisible. They are walking among us. How do you fight an enemy like that?"

"What's happening?" Shelly asked, turning to them. "Are you saying the mechanical issues we've seen aren't accidents?"

"They are not," Dameon said, an index finger pushing his sliding glasses back up to the top of his nose. "We now have evidence to support that we have Absolutionist cells operating within our organizations. While they might not be great in numbers, they are in the right places just waiting for the right time. Two towers went offline last night. The first we set up in Cyprus. Another outside of Antalya. Five people were killed when an improvised explosive was set off at one, the other an entire twenty-person crew. Up until your encounter with Veetor, we didn't think much of these incidents, things happen, but now . . . They are leaving calling cards. They are taking credit. That blasted statement has been found spray painted on debris."

James mumbled, "Love. Live. Pray. Burn. Fall. Ash. Anger. Atonement. End."

"That's the one."

Shelly raised a hand over her mouth and sucked in a breath. Karianna and James scowled at one another. We all had known this was coming, we just weren't sure when. It was surprising, sure, but inevitable.

It was all too much. Isopteran attacks. Veetor. Managing the expectations of these world leaders. Absolutionist saboteurs.

"Ideas are harder to stop than people," I whispered after several seconds, my voice weak over the speaker. Everyone turned back to me, their faces becoming narrow from the distortion before widening to several times their normal width. "Perry, an old friend of ours from the mission, once told me that humans are storytellers at heart. We tell ourselves stories all day long to make sense of the world around us. And the stories we tell are based on what information we have at hand. When we take a moment to pause in our day, we start telling stories about how we are going to cook dinner that night, and how we'll go through the steps of our chores or other responsibilities. We practice in our heads by walking through those narratives.

"These people are no different. They have a story in their heads of burning away the chaff, of culling the herd, so that what little resources are left can be put to their use and form a kind of paradise. Or something like that. Who wouldn't find that appealing given the lives so many have been forced to live? It's just manipulation."

"And what are we going to do about it?" Karianna rubbed her tired eyes, making her bracelets jingle. "We're only so many people. I can't also now go fight insurgents."

Dameon shook his head. "We are not asking you to. That is for us to handle. Miss Cox has been valuable in this given her experience during the

Oil Wars. We will do all we can to find them, but I fear it will require forming a kind of secret police loyal to the Free Citizens, which will not help us with our diminishing trust. The Boot is about ready to draw out of the terraforming project. Santucci feels their time would be best served creating more defensive systems and letting the Towers go. In many ways, he has a point—one is an immediate threat, the other existential. I have convinced him to stick with the plan for now. We are making ground."

This idea raised Ingrid's spirits, if only a little. "In the past three days, we have put nine more Towers online. We are already starting to see measurable differences in the environment. With more of them operating, it seems to be spreading our considerable enemies thin. They're unsure what targets to move on."

"But is this win strong enough?" Priscilla asked, leaning forward. "Is it enough to encourage our leaders to stay the path?"

"That's the sixty-five-million-dollar question, isn't it?" Lance mused. "I don't trust Santucci to stick much longer. We've spoken on several occasions, and he's a concrete, pragmatic individual. He needs something considerable to bring him back on board all the way."

Ingrid nodded at that.

"Any ideas then?" I asked. "What can we do?"

"Survive," Dameon stated, his expression deadpan. "It is what we have always done. Make the most of what we have and survive. I'll keep working with Chevelle and the team to see if we can power up more of those Komodo tanks. We've also found a network path into a series of UEI MOPs, a set of ancient mobile orbital platforms in the Ring of Diamonds. No promises, though, but if we can get those online, it will make a difference in intercepting the enemy before they hit atmosphere."

"It's about all we can do," Ingrid said, and stood up, placing a palm on the curve of my tank. "It was good seeing you, Milo. Please. Get better. We need you."

"Don't lose hope," I told her, an explosion of bubbles floating up from my mouth. "This isn't the end. This isn't the end."

She lowered her head and sighed. Lance put a hand on her shoulder.

"Funny," she mumbled, her thoughts trailing off to someplace dark. "Sure feels like the end to me."

CHAPTER 57

The following days were painful. While my body was healing itself, the Isopteran forces and the Absolutionist terrorists carried on with their work. Towers were going up left and right, but for as quick as we could build them, there would be another explosion, another attack shuttle making it through the picket. Of the ten terraformers we'd put into service, three were smoldering hunks of metal, and two were damaged to a point they would likely need substantial repairs. That left only five untouched.

I argued with Proxy to let me go so that I could fight, but my body wasn't recovered enough, and this left me playing long-range wargames with insects. It was making me restless. I wanted nothing more than to make a difference.

Amid the chaos, Jack Bennet started threatening to pull Queensland from the alliance. So far, in spite of their size, they had seen the least action. They even had a local military force to contend with ground-based attacks if it came to that. And yet, three deaths over two weeks were too many for them to stomach, much fewer than the thousands the rest had seen since this started. Then there was poor Adlershof. Dirk had lost a daughter a few days earlier in one of the attacks, shot by an Isopteran soldier and carried back to its shuttle, where she bled out on the ramp as response forces made quick work of the enemy.

My entire team, from Shelly to Lance to Chevelle and Renata, had worked hard to find any solutions to balance out the odds or tip them in our favor. Dameon had recovered several more of the Komodo tanks as he had promised, but while effective, they were limited to covering Northern Africa.

As I had worried, some world leaders had begun to enact extreme police state measures to combat the Absolutionist incendiaries. I was being sent reports from the pilots of the heavy shuttles of citizens disappearing. Many had asked that I address this with their leaders, since at home they were being told to be quiet. This was not creating trust.

Santucci, Tayo, Bak Yoon . . . hell, even Ingrid at this point, all were losing hope. Maybe they were right. Maybe we had made a mistake. Or maybe, just maybe, they needed a win. Maybe they needed something for us to believe in to turn this all around.

A dark intent began to blossom in the back of my mind. Only one person in our crew would encourage this thought, but I was starting to think that he was right. And Ingrid had mentioned it too, if not directly.

We needed to remove a piece from the board.

We needed to eliminate the Isoptera.

This left only one path that I knew of. We could not take them head-on, we did not have the numbers, but we had an ace in the hole that could solve this little problem, if only we knew how to use it.

An idea began to form. An idea fueled by rage and impotence.

After several more days had passed, Proxy informed me it was time to get out of my sphere and go for a walk. The injuries were healed for the most part, but the body needed to stretch, and this was the best way.

I went for an aggressive jog around the ship while the skies were clear, breathing in the air, listening to nothing but my heart beating through my chest. Would I be given the opening I needed to see this done?

Shelly joined me for a few minutes, mostly tagging along to ensure that I was okay. As far as my body was concerned, I felt good. The lacerations across my stomach and right flank had healed, though there were clear scars.

"Action isn't making me any prettier, is it?" I mused as we rounded a corner near the forward end of the ship.

Shelly chuckled at that, the weight of years heavy in her tone. "You'll always be pretty to me."

We kept this up for some time, remaining silent, enjoying each other's company for what it was while the people of Earth fought for their future. It made me feel filthy and weak.

Under Proxy's medical care, I was useless, unable to intervene. The longer I was away, the worse it was getting. From orbit, we could only do so much. We could chase down incursions one at a time, but when they came in waves and were spread out, that limited our options dramatically.

***

"You are well," Proxy said one morning, eyeing me over from head to toe as I sat on the floor eating sonhos from a paper box outside my sphere. "Your injuries are healed."

I swallowed. "Alright then, is it safe for me to do what I need to?"

"Yes," it said, lowering its head. "I have a feeling I already know what that might include."

"Have you been in my head?"

"No. But I know you, Milo. This might be a mistake."

"It might, and I know that. But I can't not try. Our options are limited, like always."

"This is an option."

"Do you think it will work? Do you think it's enough?"

Proxy cocked its head and began to lick its paws. "It will be enough."

Shelly was going to be angry at me for what I was about to do. I had to accept that fact. She would want to go along, but I needed her here. I needed her safe.

While Shelly was asleep, I removed myself from my Star Sphere and packed some supplies, a backpack with food and water, a loaded sidearm, and a fresh set of glass nanotubes, and made for the docking bay. My shuttle might still be a wreck under repair, but James was back on the ship resting, and so the spare Swift Shuttle was all mine.

I made for the shuttle, avoiding Xuan and Hy, James or Karianna, as well as the scattered Free Citizen pilots coming on and off the ship as heavy shuttles used us as a refueling station. Proxy helped to keep these curious onlookers away.

As I rounded the corner leading into the docking bay, however, a massive chinchilla blocked my path. I swore the thing's arms were crossed in indignation, if that was even possible, as short as they were.

"Wait," Chinchillette told me.

"Chat with Proxy," I said, tossing a thumb at the orange-striped tuxedo cat behind me. "I've got work to do."

"The hell you do," Karianna said, appearing at my side, punching me in the meat of my left arm, her bracelets jingling. God damn, she hit hard.

"What was that for?" I threw up my open palms and stepped back. "That hurt like shit."

"I know what you're doing," she pressed, jumping into my personal space till we were almost nose to nose. "I felt it over the integration, you ding dong. You've got it in that thick little skull of yours that you, and only you, have got to go off and save the fucking planet. What harebrained scheme are you on about now?"

I hardened my jaw. "We have to do something to help the settlements trust us again. We have to take some pieces off the board."

Karianna pursed her lips. "Sure, but that answers nothing. What did you have in mind?"

"James is right," I said, my chest tightening. "We have to stop the Isoptera and our options are limited. After our research, I have come to believe that the device we took from Nest can do that, I just don't know how to use it. Shelly and I have tried to figure it out, but there are gaps in our knowledge. We don't know how to properly turn it on."

"James is right?" Karianna let out a guffaw. "Isn't that one rich? What an idiot." But her words didn't seem to have any bite. "How are you going to figure this out?"

"By asking its builders. I'm off to go see the Kabosai."

Karianna blinked at me, her mouth having gone slack. "Are you fucking kidding me? You're going to see the Gene Brokers."

I glanced at the waiting shuttle. As I did, I felt a muscle somewhere in my stomach pull, summoning a twinge of pain that vanished as quickly as it had come, like a damaged guitar string being plucked. "Yes." I rubbed my side with a palm. "There have been reports of them on the Gardens of the Moon. No one has confirmed this, and rightfully so, but three times now, heavy shuttles have visited the surface to recover technology from before the war and seen strange things.

"There were animals in the domes they didn't recognize, weird amalgamations. Energy readings at low levels consistent with the asteroidal ships on record. I've meditated over it, and my heart draws me there. If I go, they will be waiting for me."

"Ummm," she said, thinking this through. She turned to look at her Proxy, who said nothing but gave a kind of shrug. "So, we're just going to go into their den and say hello?"

"There's no we in this. Just me." I pointed at my chest. "Just me."

"Why? Why do you always insist on doing everything alone?"

I put a hand on her shoulder and looked her in the eyes. There was fear there, uncertainty, anger. It was what had to be done, and so I steeled my resolve. "I'm going alone because it's the only option. We can't both leave the earth undefended. And besides, if I fail, it won't matter anyways. We can't take the Isoptera head on, and if we don't stop them, we can't keep going. I see the toll this has placed on you, on James, on the rest of the crew. I've seen the reports—there was nothing else to do but read them. All the deaths on the surface. If this isn't an option, I don't know what is. But something has to be done."

"They'll kill you," she whispered. "I heard all about them from the *Vasco Da Gama*'s crew. They'll kill you."

"I'm not so sure about that. That's not how they work."

"Will they tell you the truth? Or will they give you information that will kill us soon as we turn it on."

"Isn't that the fun part?" I mused with a touch of false bravado while walking to the end of the hall to the bay. "Keep everyone safe. I won't be long."

"I hate you sometimes," she choked out, her throat having turned thick. "Don't die, Milo. Please don't die."

I paused at the doorway, turning around. "Didn't plan on it," I said, then stepped through the airlock and left for the moon.

CHAPTER 58

My borrowed Swift Shuttle slipped out of the *Transcendence* into open space, accelerating hard, course set for the moon. The Ring of Diamonds glittered around me like a thunderstorm of light, the sun's rays reflecting off a million different facets spread across tens of thousands of miles of debris. An hour passed, and it receded, with Earth, as well as the *Transcendence*, shrinking at my back as Luna swelled to fill all my perceptions.

A rocky, pockmarked surface of gray-white silicate rushed beneath me, the craters upon its face zipping past like the mile markers of a desperate race. Ahead, a black gem rose on the horizon, a series of steel-and-glass domes clustered near one another forming a base, a port, a city for those once fortunate enough to escape war. All was dark, power running at minimal levels to maintain core systems, the once beautiful Luna Base left abandoned.

Landing proved to be a challenge. The platforms outside the domes of the base were littered with dozens of derelict spacecraft from the twenty-second century. Unlike the heavy shuttles we were now using for the terraforming project, these were not rugged, were not intended to be used in atmosphere. They were frail and small and reminiscent of the age just past Nasa's SLS and Orion, lots of barrel-shaped modules with flattened cones, solar panels, and NTP engine nozzles built of metallic and ceramic composites. Some of them had damage that appeared to have been inflicted by weapons fire, showing burn marks and rents torn into their hull that went from outside in, while others were merely in disrepair. All lay motionless, cold and dead, a cosmic graveyard.

I put the shuttle down between two UEI colonist transports and prepared to enter hard vacuum. Proxy recommended I wear powered armor not just so I could breathe, but so I could be safe given the unknowns ahead. The interior of the base, unlike other places we had visited, was more than large enough to accommodate any extra bulk. Best to be safe rather than sorry.

My hands shook as I made my way to the hatch, palms patting at my chest to ensure my SAG tactical rifle was still there. I hoped not to make use of it today, but there was no telling what awaited me. So far, I had seen no readings of Kabosai like those that had been reported, but that didn't mean much. They could be hiding.

The airlock on the side of the base registered my approach, and its status box began to flash, the word *CYCLING* turning red, then yellow, then green. The hatch made a click I couldn't hear, but that I could feel through the bottoms of my feet, before it yawned open like a presenting mime.

"Do not take off your helmet," Proxy urged through my implants. *"While oxygen is within, there are particles in this atmosphere I cannot analyze with the equipment on your suit."*

Again, I did not argue. Proxy was right. Proxy was always right.

The airlock opened on the other side to a long, dark hallway which fed into a spacious concourse, the only light source from Earth reflecting back through the dome. I raised my right arm and flicked on a lamp, aiming at the ground so as not to confuse my eyes, which fought to adjust in low light.

The base was trashed, equipment left scattered and abandoned all around the gates in the terminal. Metal boxes and plastic crates were stacked in haphazard rows, many knocked over, their contents spilled. There were prepacked foods by the ton with expiration dates a hundred years back, clothing and other hard items rifled through with no rhyme or reason, electronic components like the ones we had already recovered, and personal items of nothing but sentimental value. Rubble was stacked against the walls, twisted beams and sheets of metal left in piles. Electric carts were turned over, several having leaked fluids, with no drivers in sight.

I knew nothing of what had happened up here, but it was clear that those who left had done so in a hurry. Of the many crises humans had faced since FICSE departed, which one had led to this? Was it during the Great Gap? A forgotten war? Or was it from an invasion of some kind?

Had these people made it out?

A flicker of silver light called to me from the end of the concourse, and I made for it, boots clicking on the dirty floors, hand close to my rifle, mind ready to summon nanomachines if need be. I was not going to be taken by surprise like I had been in Greece.

The deeper I ventured, the more signs of plant life became clear, creeper vines sneaking out from hidden places within the walls and reaching out to the sterile transit center like explorers setting off into a mysterious land. They became thicker as I pushed into a commercial district of sorts, worn neon signs glowing angrily down at me as if on 5 percent power. There were restaurants here, bars, gift shops with knick-knacks and collectables. There were grocers, though these contained the biggest messes of all, their shelves mostly picked clean. Vines with green leaves hemmed every doorway and passage, every broken and shattered window, leaving only narrow paths where they dared not grow.

Despite all the disorder, all the chaos, I found no bodies. This did not feel accidental. A suspicion was rising in the back of my mind that those who had been left were removed, used someplace else, turned into some kind of science experiment. But there was no blood, no human fluids spilled, and aside from plant life, there was only sterility.

The base was huge, and I wasn't sure where I needed to go, so I chose a path at random, going where felt right. The vines thickened as I made for a narrowing hallway, a sign above it reading *GARDENS OF THE MOON, SEC 4.*

Light shimmered at the end of the passage, urging me on, the way opening up into a massive dome beneath the black sky of space. While I knew I was on the moon, a lifeless hunk of rock locked in an endless dance with Earth, this section was anything but lifeless. The dome was bursting with dimly lit color, greens and blues and oranges and yellows, the leaves of trees blowing in a gentle, artificial breeze, rows of colorful wildflowers hemming a labyrinth of winding trails crossed by burbling streams of water.

It was a paradise filled with both species that I recognized and didn't. Had this been what the gardens were like before this place was abandoned? Or was this new? Was this the result of Kabosai intercession? Were they even here?

A series of sharp noises came from over my shoulder, and I spun, hand trailing down to the grip of my rifle, ready to move into action. Birds shot past, forcing me to duck, chasing one another, tweeting a song of endless joy and wild abandon. They moved so quickly I could hardly see what they looked like other than being bright blue and small enough that two could have perched on one hand.

From within the hedges in what appeared to be a thick forest, something large rustled. This prompted me to raise my weapon. A sort of mewling purr came from the underbrush, but I got the feeling it wasn't a friendly kitty like Proxy.

I blinked to clear my eyes and saw two pairs of glowing green slits staring back at me. When I leaned to the side even the slightest bit, that predatorial regard flickered, light striking the tissue at the backs of its eyes, the tapetum lucidum, at different angles, making them shine.

"Come to play, kitty?" I mused, trying not to show fear. I had no idea what it was or what it might do to me. Was it big? Was it small? My rifle was raised, barrel pointed at it. Slowly, I backed off, making my way for the opposite path. I had clearly startled it, come into its territory as an unknown. Was it the apex predator of this engineered place? If that was true, there must be food for it to eat and plenty of it.

A metallic bang rang out on my right beyond the trees, and a flock of a dozen birds took flight, fleeing the scene. I spun on my heels, the butt of my rifle pressed against my shoulder, vision lining down its sight. I made for the noise instead of running away, glancing over my shoulder every few steps, checking to see if the supposed cats were following me.

The noise of the animals amplified, the forest coming to life with a myriad of caws and hoots and growls that felt very terrestrial. The space had gone from dead quiet to a cacophony of primordial alarms in seconds, my lizard brain screaming for me to run for safety. I was surrounded by Universe knew what, and while I was protected in this carbon nanofiber suit, there were a lot of them, and just one of me.

Leaves rustled.

Sticks snapped.

Furry bodies darted through the shadows.

"Shit," I mumbled, turning in circles, pointing the barrel of my rifle at every noise like a tweaker on speed.

A collection of bushes just off the trail a pace away from my right foot began to shake. I focused my attention solely on this movement, leaning forward, as if that would help me aim better.

From out of the bush came a mottled tan and white and black dog, whose fuzzy, radar-dish ears came up just past my knee. It had short fur and dark brown eyes, with teeth gleaming beneath black gums. The dog did not growl, but its tail was tucked, its ears bent back slightly. Instinct told me to be careful with this curious animal, to not make any sudden moves.

"Are you in a pack?" I wondered, taking a step back. The dog matched my movements, matched my distance. "Do you have friends?"

Noise came from behind me off the flower-hemmed trail, a rustling of foliage. My fleshy hand began to sweat. I was surrounded.

Forcing down my unease, I relaxed my posture and lowered my weapon. I would only attack if they forced me to, but something in me said this would be a bad idea in any case. If I fired, I had a feeling it would put events into motion I had no escape from.

"Good doggy," I said, easing away. "Good doggy."

It remained where it was while others like it slunk out from the dark. The first of them cocked its head, then yawned and turned around, leading the rest back into the forest.

My presence had thrown the garden's inhabitants for a loop. They had not seen a human, let alone someone in an armored suit, probably ever. They didn't know what to do with me, but primal curiosity drove them to assess if I was a threat or not.

I took a moment, and several deep breaths to calm myself, then continued my search, mindful of other dangers. As I rounded the many paths, I started noticing squirrels in the trees, chipmunks scurrying around on the ground, bugs buzzing around the blossoms of flowers and deer grazing on thick, green grass.

This was what Earth should have been, what it had once been, dangerous but tranquil, filled with life, wild and free.

I came upon a bench placed beside a babbling brook, Earth shining overhead through the glass dome. For a moment, I imagined what it was like for people who had struggled on Earth to sit here, to look up, to realize just how small they were in this great and vast universe. It was easy to forget how tiny our world was until you viewed it from higher up. It was fragile like a snow globe, its glass edges thin as paper.

A cluster of ferns over my shoulder began to rustle ever so softly. I spun around, rifle raised at the ready, its barrel pointed at the noise. I took two steps back, stumbling as I nearly tripped over a set of rocks, giving myself and whatever this was space.

Through the thick foliage, three gleaming black slugs large as horses appeared, their sticky bodies gliding over the grass as if they were levitating, a sea of bioengineered insects carrying them forth. They advanced to me, eye stalks gleaming in the dim light, undulating tentacles in pairs coming out from their chests, reaching to me.

"Stay back!" I shouted, shaking my weapon at them. As far as I could tell, these were unarmed, but what did I really know about their species? What did I know about the ones who claimed to protect life in their own way? They could have any number of weapons. They could be controlling the animals, planning on using them to ambush me. "I'm warning you," I went on. "Not another inch."

The approaching aliens paused, understanding my command. They twisted their eyestalks around to regard one another, then made a sort of noise that I could only say sounded like a cough thick with mucus.

"It is you," the one at the front of their group said in that strange, wet language, the implants of the Foundry translating for me. "You are Milo Hughes of the *Vasco Da Gama*. The people of Creatus."

"And you are the Gene brokers," I hissed. "Kabosai."

"We have been waiting for you." The head of their group twisted around in what appeared a means to draw my attention to the garden. "We have been waiting for our moment."

I narrowed my eyes at them. "Is that so?"

"You took longer than we had expected. We thought you more curious."

"Sorry to keep you waiting," I said with more than a little venom, "been pretty busy trying not to die."

The one on the left let out a shudder, its blubbery body shaking like cold, black gelatin. "Have you come to end us? To seek revenge for what our brethren had planned to do so far away from here? They are not us. We are different."

"Revenge has crossed my mind," I replied. "Your people were responsible for the death of many friends. But I think I've already had mine."

"Sinas made his choice," another of their group mused. A squishy sound came from the side of its tail, and a fresh swarm of the cockroach-like servant insects joined the mass beneath him. The sight of it made my stomach flip end over end. Proxy sensed my revulsion and injected me with some kind of antinausea drug from the powered armor, taking the edge off.

"It is regrettable," the last of them spoke up. "We wish that change were less destructive than it is. That we would not have to take, in order to create. It is the one flaw of our genesis. We cannot create from nothing. We can only modify that which already is."

"What is this place?" I waved my weapon's barrel across the garden. "What have you done here?"

"We have helped your native Earth fauna survive. This was once a settlement. Humans lived here by the hundreds of thousands. And this garden, and many others, were a place for them to stay connected to the natural universe. From what history we can put together, this was one of the few places not affected by your nuclear wars."

"But what about the people who lived here? What happened to them?"

The Kabosai turned to one another for a moment, eye stalks twisting around, optics blinking.

"What happened to them?" I demanded, hands shaking. "Did you hurt them?"

"This is a subject we debate often," the third said. "My companions believe it was a human attack that brought about their end. A faction among your species who tried to take this place as their home."

"And you don't agree?"

"While there are signs of a battle, yes, we have found no bodies. Whoever lived here attempted to flee in a hurry, but something happened."

"Your pets didn't eat the bodies, did they?"

"Oh, no," they said as one, the synchronization of their exclamation nearly Jevox.

"You say you helped the native fauna survive. So, these animals, they are not genetically engineered."

"Modified, in part, but not designed. Not designed. They are animals who once lived on your world that were abandoned when this base was. Tens of thousands of species, some living free, others with frozen embryos in storage."

And that was it. This place had acted like the seed vault in Svalbard, but with animal species instead of plants.

"Are they viable?" I asked, my curiosity piqued. "The embryos."

"Yes," their leader stated. "Many will have to be grown in artificial wombs, but they will grow, and will develop if given the chance. We saw the decline. We saw an opportunity. We wanted to help."

"Why?" I was lost. Something didn't add up. These were not the Kabosai I had met before. "Why help? I can't say I always understand your motivations. Your counterparts weren't exactly friendly. Why help now?"

"It is the same as it has always been. We protect life. We see it differently than the Foundry, yes, but the goal is the same. The Universe must be made self-aware. The others who have visited your species, they did not protect life. The Lattice. The Isoptera. Both seek to consume humanity, to consume others, not create."

"And so, you helped?"

"We helped."

I lowered my weapon and sighed, watching as their skin flexed, their surfaces shimmering in the dim light. They were disgusting, repugnant creatures that brought forth the most unsettling concepts of danger buried in my ancient, natural, human DNA. But they said they wanted to help. They had become who they were to make their species viable, to make it possible for them to survive beyond the stars in varied environments and conditions.

What had they looked like a thousand years ago? Two thousand years ago? Had they been bipeds? Would they intend to turn us all into something like them? Or were we just more meat for the gene grinder?

And yes, they were claiming to have preserved our native species from Earth.

"Show me," I said, feeling bold. "If you have done as you have claimed, then I'd like to see the results, not just what was in this garden. Give me proof."

They stood there in silence, blinking, their swarms writhing beneath them. I heard the sound of animals moving in the thick foliage surrounding my position. My rifle hung loose on its strap, and I nearly went for it, feeling I was in danger, but I held back. I was not as impulsive as I once had been. Life had beaten that out of me.

"Very well," the leader of their group said, turning around. "This way. We will show you the lab."

I followed the Gene Brokers down a winding path that led us out of the domes and into an industrial district, the halls wide as a subway tunnel and devoid of anything aesthetically pleasing. The three horse-sized creatures moved shoulder to shoulder, if they even had those, gliding forward on a million tiny insects. Wherever they moved, powdery trails of corpses were left in their wake, dried-out husks degrading into a strange organic dust.

After several turns, they brought me into a clean, white room a dozen paces across, filled with equipment that appeared to be human in origin, not Kabosai. While there were workstations and lab equipment I recognized, like mass spectrometers or microscopes, the most important feature seemed to be the grids of blue canisters set into slots along every wall, small quantities of cold gas leaking from the many seams in which they were inserted. The temperature here was cooler, though with my powered armor suit, I could only register this as data.

"Your people had started the project," their leader said, drawing me to the far left side of the room. "They were looking for ways to preserve your birds and canines and mollusks and insects. We only helped them finish the job."

"Let me guess." I put a hand on one of the glowing, blue tanks. "About the time you think the humans vanished is when their work halted."

"Yes. That is right."

I followed their lead around the room, inspecting the labels that faced outward. Most of the names written here were in Latin, though some were in a twisting script I did not recognize but that the Foundry nanomachines could translate. It was an iteration of the Kabosai script, though if it was their current language, I couldn't say.

"How many species are living aboard the base now?" I asked.

The third in their group made a guttural noise, its body shivering. "At last count, we have revived forty-nine species. But we have embryos for millions more, and we do not anticipate reviving others here. We must keep the ecosystem stable."

"And the ones the humans had not yet put into cold storage . . ."

"We found them," the second said. "Over the past fifty years on your local time scale. We found viable specimens, collected their genetic material, repaired it where need be, and put their storage containers into liquid nitrogen."

I scratched at the back of my head, taking in the possibilities. If they weren't lying, once the terraforming project was complete, we'd be able to use this cache to replace the animal life on Earth, while Svalbard's seed vault could replace our plant life. We might actually have a chance, if only we could stop the Isoptera and Absolutionists from burning it all down.

I rested a palm on one of the tanks, a variety of feline, though I could not say which one. Could this frozen cat egg bring to life something like Ferdie, the Hughes family pet from those many centuries ago?

"You did not come to speak of historical events," their leader rasped, its wet tentacles rubbing against one another in thought.

I broke from my reverie. "I did not. We have more pressing matters."

"We know what you have aboard your ship. We detected it as soon as you entered the system in your Foundry-made vessel."

I swallowed at that, my hands feeling shaky. "You knew? You, um—"

"We knew."

"Then tell me about it. What does it do? What does it really do?"

"We believe you already know the answer to this. The Protea Device is one of our greatest creations. Dangerous and few in number. They are difficult to make, narrow in their use."

"Protea Device . . ."

"It can create life, augment life, modify it, but like much else we have created, the change it initiates is irreparable. The change is destructive to the original."

"So, it's a weapon?"

"A weapon?" It made a chuffing noise. "Yes, it could be viewed as a weapon. It has been used as a weapon before . . . If not for the right information, the right template loaded within it, no species can survive its activation. But your device, yes, it is a weapon at this time. Dangerous. Incomplete for any task other than destruction."

"Then our suspicions were right. The template is the key."

"The template, as well as an energy source. The Protea Device you are in possession of is already charged. It contains the heat energy of a small star, this great potential trapped in a series of folded dimensions beyond the observable universe. This is how we knew it was near. It leaks extradimensional particles."

"Do you have a template?" I asked, leaning in, heart swelling with hope.

Their leader moved to one of the lab stations, where a strange, organic-looking black device sat. It reminded me of the equipment Sinas and his ilk had used back on Creatus. They pressed a button on the side, and a dull yellow prism four inches tall appeared. "We have been building this for decades. It is a partial template to the human species."

"Building it?" My blood went hot. "You mean stealing people from Aeolia and other places around the system to sacrifice for it."

"No," it said, sounding genuine somehow. This was all so incongruous. "We have not murdered anyone, but we have made deals. Taken the dead. Asked those who are diseased or sick to sacrifice their body for a better future. We seek to protect life, nothing more."

"How can I trust that you tell the truth?" Was I really having a rational conversation with one of the space slugs? Was this how they got you, lured you in? Was this how it started?

Its eye stalks blinked. "Your trust is not required for it to be so. Truth requires no one to defend it."

I chewed this comment over, trying to get in the mindset Shelly might take if she were here. I had no doubts she was far better at negotiating with aliens than me. "Okay . . . Thank you. What then would it take for this to be complete?"

The second spoke up. "A pair of live specimens. We could continue down this path, taking what we can get as we go, but it will be an age. Living specimens are better. This is why Sinas and his people did what they did."

Anger simmered in the back of my mind, radiating throughout my arms and fingertips. For an instant, I wanted to reach for the rifle and shoot them full of holes. So many had died on Creatus. I had nearly lost my life trying to save Shelly and the rest of our people in the years that had followed.

"Why build a template for humanity?" I pressed. "Our planet is the problem, not our genetics."

"Environments change," their leader said. "We Kabosai have survived for as long as we have because we are not what we once were. We have augmented our existence. Another twenty generations, and you will no longer recognize these forms. But our memories, our intentions, our great works, they carry on long past our forms. Our bodies are merely life support systems for the minds that live within them."

I turned this over for a moment, allowing myself the space to calm down. "So, if I am understanding you, it's easier for you to change a species to fit the environment than to change the environment to fit the species?"

"This is correct. Though, the Jevox do well as our counterparts in these efforts. They are far more clever in planetary design."

"Do you truly seek to help humanity?"

"We do. You have such great potential. You are survivors. Your history is one of great challenges, which you have always overcome. While you now rest upon a knife's edge, it is in large part due to outside interference. It is from too rapid of technological advances without the social evolution to match. We have seen this before. And we failed to help. We intend not to make that mistake again."

While I knew to be careful taking them at their word, everything they said felt right. We had given birth to an information age that consumed our society, giving us both great power of knowledge and great ability for abuse. We had learned to tap the power of stars, to leverage machine minds to augment our understanding, and developed weapons capable of ending millions in a flash. Our intelligence had become both our greatest asset and our greatest enemy. When applied to protect life, it was noble. When applied to advance greed or control motivated by fear, it was a sin, the original sin.

I swallowed down my fears and anxieties like a stone covered in spikes. "Then help me. Help us."

They turned to one another, blinking.

"You need help dealing with the Isoptera?" the second asked. "We had thought that might be one reason why you are here."

"Yes. They've become a major threat. Given their current position and relative strength, I don't see any way we can deal with them directly. While the ship the Foundry gifted me is powerful, they are many, and we are one. And then there's the matter of the other pilot."

"Veetor," they mused. "The broken one. He does not protect life."

"Yes. Him. The Isoptera comes first, though. We must stop them."

"They do not protect life."

"No, they don't. At least, no one's but their own, and even that is suspect. I need to know how it works. While I don't like the idea of this thing, I believe we can use the Protea Device against them."

They stood in quiet conference for some time, turning away from me. I took a step back and gave them space, lingering by a glowing terminal on a table covered with test tubes and slides. Nothing about this trip had gone as I had expected. How could a group of people so bent on rewriting the genetic code of a galaxy with the intent to create designer species now be helping us? Then again, how could Veetor be so evil? Sinas and these scientists might just be as different from one another as Karianna and I were from Justin.

"We will do as you have asked," their leader rasped as it turned back around. "While we wish the Protea Device were being put to a better use, our options here are limited. We are but three. We cannot commit to fight alongside you. And so, this is our way of helping to protect life. While both natural, Isopteran life is hollow, and human life rich. Let us make this place safe for you to proliferate. Spread. Awaken the universe."

I felt a cold chill run down my spine, my mind temporarily transported back to the black hole machine. If they only knew the truth of the Foundry. If they would embrace it.

"Thank you," I said, bile rising in my throat as I said the words. It was what Shelly would have done, shown respect in spite of all their species had done. Just like Johan or Justin, I was not them. They were not Sinas and his followers. They were not like the Jevox or even the Isoptera. They had individuality. They could make a choice to live differently.

They led me to another room, where a set of equipment waited, one of them carrying the human template. Over the next hour, I was given careful instruction on how to use the device. Shelly and I had been right—the words carved upon the icosahedron were Kabosai, from different eras of their forced evolution. They were unwilling to share what they had originally looked like, or who they had been, but that they had taken small pieces from a hundred different species to become their current iteration, adding to their experiences and growing into something different. I knew the feeling.

I learned that the Protea Device required three things to operate correctly. It required a massive store of energy on the scale of that expelled by a nuclear explosion 500,000 megatons in strength. We were talking about energy levels of close to ten thousand times those of the deadliest weapons built at the time I left Earth. Energy values so massive I almost couldn't comprehend their scale. I fed them back to Proxy, and my feline companion took them in without any effort. Currently, the device was charged, but if it were not, we would have to supply it somehow. It could be charged over time, scooping smaller amounts of heat and light energy over decades, or by folding its multidimensional planes around a catastrophic event to contain that event within, but we didn't need either.

The second thing it required was a template, or lack thereof. If given a proper template, it would have the ability to rewrite a species based on their needs. Reading between the lines of our conversation, I had a strong feeling that this was how the Kabosai had rewritten their species at scale, returning to some kind of central point every so many centuries to be bathed by the light of this device and upgraded. They would not confirm if this was true or not.

The third was simple enough. It needed instructions. They showed me how to do this, to trigger it wantonly, to give it specific input, to set instructions based on internal data to make modifications. We could have it rip a species' genes apart, or we could, with the right template, dial in traits of other species they'd collected information on and reassign the genetic chains to transform and augment rather than destroy. I paid close attention, relaying what I could back to Proxy for future reference.

It was a shame we were going to use such an elegant device as a sort of genetic bomb. It was capable of so much more. Capable of making a new humanity.

Once we had concluded, I turned to face them, their stalks blinking awkwardly.

"Will it be enough?" I asked, imagining the hordes of Isoptera orbiting Haumea.

"Yes," the second said. "It will be enough, if you can get it into position. Should you ever decide to use it for its true purpose . . ." It handed me the dim yellow pyramid. "You will need the template."

"But you said it's not complete. And we don't have an Isopteran template to work with."

"There is always a way," their leader said. "Now go. We will complete our work here, and we will leave this place to you. We wish your species the best as we return home."

And that was that. They turned and crept away into the darkness.

I stared at the template resting in my hands, just a few inches tall, and yet so important. Hundreds if not thousands had given what little life they had left to make this, and it wasn't complete. It seemed too valuable to dispose of, but I could see what its purpose might be.

I made my way through the forest back to the Shuttle and returned to the *Transcendence*. It had been a quiet night on Earth, no sign of Isoptera, no sign of Veetor or Absolutionist terror plots.

As soon as I exited the Swift Shuttle, wearing no more power armor or tactical gear, Shelly came rushing up to meet me, her face a mask of anger.

"Milo!" she shouted, placing her hands on her hips and leaned forward, seething. "What in the hell have you been doing? Karianna spilled the beans."

My forehead burst with sweat, and my feet felt tingly. Under that intense gaze of hers, I found myself wishing I had kept the armor on. Perhaps it would have slowed my death by a few seconds.

"I did what I had to do," I replied, my back going straight. "I'm sorry, love. I take full responsibility for this. But it had to be done. The Isoptera have to be stopped."

She rubbed her face with her palms. "I know they do. But you—we can't lose you. And after Justin's attack, you—"

I gently took hold of her arm and smiled. "I got it, Shelly. I got it. I know what we need to do."

She blinked at me, anger evaporating into a mist of shock. "Got what? What are you talking about?"

"The device. We were right about it. And now . . . Now we know how to use it. We have what we need to put an end to the Gray Queen."

CHAPTER 59

It didn't take long to convince the crew that this was the right course of action. James had been laying the groundwork for some time, whispering in the ears of fellow members in quiet moments. We all knew he had motives of vengeance, but with the endless incursions over the last few weeks, everyone was exhausted and ready to end this. There was only so much that people could take, even with the Foundry propping us up chemically. We were all in, though Shelly was pissed I had gone to meet with the Kabosai without her. I figured I should just go ahead and expect to be sleeping alone for a few days.

This new operation had given us a way out of the defensive loop we'd been stuck in, a direction that would make the biggest difference for all. Once the Isoptera were out of the way, that left only Veetor standing. Among the Free Citizens' leadership, there was a strong sentiment his followers would not persist beyond him. This made his reason for singling me out clear. I was the biggest threat to his authority. While Karianna was powerful, and just as dangerous as me with the same level of augmentations, he saw her as someone he might control. True or not, she was just that little girl from the *Brilliance*. But me? Well . . . I was a wildcard. An unknown. He had no box Milo Hughes could fit within.

"Do we have a plan?" I asked James, standing with the crew in the Dead Room in a circle around the Protea Device, Shelly on my right inspecting its scripted surface, Karianna on my left fiddling with her bracelets, lost in thought. "Of anyone in our group, I thought you might already be ready with one."

"A plan?" he chuckled, fingers rubbing at his chin. "Do I have a plan . . ."

"It might even work," Lance said, slapping James on the back. "Looks like you've been spending your time studying up."

He shrugged it off like no big deal. "Can't be dumb forever, you know?"

"You were never dumb," Hy put in, leaning to the device, meeting eyes with Shelly over the gleam of its topmost vertex.

"This will stop them?" Xuan asked. "It has given me the creeps since coming on board, but it does not look big enough to be a bomb."

"This device exists in many dimensions beyond ours," Shelly supplied, then ran a handheld machine over its surface that emitted certain frequencies of sound. A triangular door clicked open. "If this were to trigger now, there'd be no evidence we ever existed."

Karianna leaned back and yawned. "Remind me why we're not just sending volleys of antimatter slugs at them?"

"The Isoptera will intercept them. There's too many in their fleet. They might have defensive screens, or so we are told. We'd have to come too deep. This"—Shelly ran her index finger down its side—"we can stealth it. We think."

"Fifty, fifty at best," Proxy agreed. "While size is not an issue, we are moving in a heavily guarded area. Yes, at one time Milo piloted the *Fidelas* past a fleet of Kabosai cloaked from their sensors. But there were few of them. Three of their interstellar craft were in territory that was not their base of operations. Here . . ."

"There's dramatically more enemies." James leaned to the side and met Karianna's annoyed gaze. "Way the hell more. Which is why we have a plan."

He walked us through it.

In our battles with the Isoptera on the surface, we had learned a great deal about their tactics. While they had the strength of numbers, they followed clear patterns. In face-to-face combat, they moved without fear in small packs, preferring to rush in with groups than to act in coordination to rout hostile forces, opting to throw everything at the enemy through brute force. This made dealing with them simple, focusing on choke points where they could be picked off. Then there were the cicada-shaped attack shuttles that we could approach from above, moving swiftly into range to keep them from using their missiles as was their tactic. And now, well, we had capital ships to deal with, and they had far bigger guns. Over the past few months, we'd been analyzing the tactical data provided by the battle over Aeolia and uncovered similar patterns in the larger craft of their fleets.

A parting gift Cardoso had given us after our short meeting were the rough specifications of the larger craft the Isoptera had in service. While there were some exceptions in our research, the termites had two main ship designs beyond their attack shuttles, and we were set to face a horde of them: the Gray Carriers and the Hive Wardens.

James went over what we knew of the enemy, as well as Proxy and Shelly's assessment of the kiting strategy we would need to adopt to see this mission successful. If we could stay at the right range, we could pick off the enemy ships a few at a time while not opening us up to an all-out assault. Despite our size, we had speed as well. We could take quite a beating adopting this doctrine, but we could not hold out forever. At some point, the enemy would overwhelm us, and we would be forced to flee.

The plan was simple. Get their attention, cut a line diagonally across Haumea's orbit, and once their ships had spread out enough that we had a sensor gap, we would launch the Protea Device at the surface of the planetoid using the casing of a stealth probe. So long as none of the Isoptera came within a thousand kilometers of the probe, it should remain invisible.

Once the probe came to within two hundred kilometers of the surface, the device would activate, releasing a massive burst of energy, triggering its functions. Before the genetic manipulation field could reach us, a maximum effective range of 12,510 kilometers, we would run like hell.

The Protea Device would instantly wreak havoc on the Gray Queen herself, whom we believed to be on the surface of Haumea. Once she was out of the way, any surviving Isopteran forces would scatter or lose direction, either of which would be the outcome needed to end them for good.

It was a solid plan, as far as plans like this went, but we all knew that no plan survived first contact with the enemy. If this didn't work, we would throw everything we had at their base before fleeing back to Earth and hope for the best.

Using the Kabosai instructions, Shelly finished programming the Protea Device, no template installed, and we headed for our Star Spheres, splashing down to prepare for extreme acceleration. Given that Haumea was a trans-Neptunian object, its location nearly forty AU from Earth, the settlements would be in danger for as much as a week as we made the trip. We hoped it would only be from the Absolutionists. None of our world leaders, especially Santucci and Tayo, were happy about this. We were not going to leave Earth exposed for any more time than we had to. Ingrid had called the shuttles to ground till we returned, and the local military forces had dug in, sending those most vulnerable into underground shelters. It was all we could do.

Our drive flame burned brighter than any sun, the *Transcendence* rocketing away from Earth, drawing everyone's attention. Distant readings of fungara began to shift around the system, coming about, heading back to our target. Though we were faster, many of them were closer. It was clear there would be a convergence of our forces at the edge of the solar system. But did they know what we intended?

Everyone stood by. Karianna and I were in the integration, ready to throw the *Transcendence* into combat. Lance and the rest were virtually sitting in their fighters, Shelly taking command of the antimatter slug cannons. I wished we had had Renata and Chevelle with us as well, but our ground forces needed them more. I wished Ada and Leo were here. Nothing ever felt the same after losing those close to you.

It will work, Karianna thought, a general sense of well-being translating over to me. *James may be an idiot, but he's right. We get them out of the way, and things will be easier. So, don't go all reflective on me, not today. We can fall apart later.*

Fall apart. When had we ever gotten the chance to do that?

After they're gone, she went on. *Do you think you can stop Justin?*

I thought about that for a moment, considering my mental response. She already knew what I was thinking; I had no idea why I bothered trying to hide it.

Yes. I know his weakness.

And that is?

You already know, Karianna. You already know.

She nearly responded but held back. Thinking it into existence somehow made this exploit feel fragile. Neither of us were willing to break that spell. Maybe, just maybe, we could exploit it.

Thank you, she thought after several moments of silence.

For what?

Her emotions went warm in a brief flare, a feeling of belonging radiating back to me. *Thank you for being you.*

I'm not sure there's anyone else I can be.

Well . . . you're the best at it.

So are you.

What, at being you?

This made me laugh.

It was good for us to be back.

At her gentle nudging, I was ready to adjust our subjective reference. It felt like a betrayal to fast-forward while the Free Citizens of Earth would have to face the enemy in real-time. But I wanted this over with. Commiserating with their losses wouldn't make this operation any easier. We had the best people on the job.

CHAPTER 60

I closed my eyes, arms outstretched in my sphere, and time slipped away. Seconds became minutes, became hours, became days. In the blink of an eye, we'd crossed thirty-nine AU and were on the final approach to the icy, egg-shaped dwarf planet infested by Isoptera. In that space of time, Isoptera had been called back from all across the system, three or four of them being carriers, the remaining ten wardens.

We were burning toward Haumea's influence at a forty-five-degree angle, ready to curve around its body in a corkscrew at fifteen thousand kilometers an hour till we could spiral into weapons range. We were outnumbered one hundred to one, and so we would have to rely on speed or wit, not brute force, to see this device put in position.

The hive responded at our approach, ordering more than two dozen ships to tail us, but not to intercept, despite the fact that they had forces ahead of our trajectory. This move felt unusual.

At this range, it was clear how massive their carriers were, each spanning nearly a kilometer like the *Transcendence*. From our position burning ahead of them, we could see deep into the pincer-like maws at their forward ends, where hives of attack shuttles poked their heads out of honeycomb structures like bees. While their solid-swept, dual-catenary winged design was consistent, we found variations in fungara growth. At Proxy's quick count of the seven approaching capital ships, we could see at least one with ninety-two shuttles aboard, and others with as many as 105. Their chitinous hulls reminded me very much of ancient arthropods, more like god-sized crustaceans than insects.

Beside the smaller number of larger ships burned the shapes of many wardens, their root vegetable–shaped hulls bristling with clusters of protective mycological formations. These escorts bristled with potential energy, waves of electromagnetism radiating off them like tiny stars.

"*What are they doing?*" Lance asked over our open channel. He was tracking their movements, trying to figure them out. "*Shouldn't they be attacking? It would make sense to cut us off, right?*"

"*It would,*" Karianna agreed. "*Milo?*"

"Doesn't change the plan," I told them, then met Shelly's gaze.

She was with me in my virtual environment, her kind face hard as stone, hands outstretched and ready for action. "Looks more like an escort to me. Those ones on the flanks, they're accelerating."

"I will be looking for an opening," Proxy reported from beside my feet, its ears flicking as it shook its head. "They are keeping their formations tight. So long as they remain behind us, it should be easier to find a hole."

"*There's some space opening up near the back of their line,*" James added. "*Wait. Wait. No. Just my imagination.*"

"Milo," Proxy said, looking up. "Haumea is sending us a signal. The Isoptera are calling us."

I focused my attention on the sprawl of fungara that had grown across the planetoid's icy surface like tumors.

The Gray Queen . . .

"Okay." I swallowed down my fears like a jagged chunk of rock. "Open up the channel. Let's see what they have to say."

We began curving around Haumea's orbit, only a slight tug on our mass from its gravity, the dwarf planet fifteen thousand kilometers off our starboard side.

"*You have returned, returned, returned,*" an unfamiliar clicking voice full of authority and confidence boomed over the open channel. "*Oh, yes, the voice that offers sustenance that I may become a stronger god. My children seek to grow, to become what I desire them to be, they are impatient. I grow impatient. Too much time passes. Your news must be good, good, good.*"

Returned? Something wasn't right.

"*Umm,*" Karianna groaned over our shared channel. "*What's this all about? It's acting like we've met before. And like—oh shit. Shit. Shit.*"

"It struck a deal," I mumbled, understanding trickling into my simple little mind. "That's why they're not attacking us."

"Not yet, at least. What kind of deal did fuck-face make with them? And why the hell don't they recognize that our ship looks different than his?"

"Their fleet is closing," Shelly said, gesturing to the blips on our tactical view. "Keep us curving around Haumea at arms' length."

"Do we have errors?" the Gray Queen called back, its clicking voice coming in rapid succession, almost like a revving machine. *"You have not responded. Is the equipment not speaking? Does it not give off a smell?"*

I blinked at Shelly. We didn't have a plan for this.

"It makes sense," Xuan mused. *"They were quiet for too long. Veetor must have—"*

"Justin!" Karianna cut in. "His name is Justin!"

"—um, called them out when our project was underway. A plan to distract. To burn."

"Keep it busy," Shelly insisted, her eyes wide. "Keep it talking. They like to talk about themselves."

I cracked my fingers and sighed.

"We have returned," I said over the ship-to-ship channel, nodding to Shelly. "The humans are, uh, afraid. You have sent many attacks against them."

"Afraid?" The Gray Queen made a series of clicks that rose and fell in pitch and could not be translated. *"No, no, no. They should not be afraid. We will be quick. They give to the future—a noble sacrifice! We do not want them all, only some. Only a few to add to our farms."*

"Farms?" I blurted out in surprise, not intending to broadcast. "The—um—" My stomach twisted into knots. This was not the time to lose it, but this was another factor to consider. How could we wipe them out if there were also humans alive, left to procreate and be used as cattle within the walls of their base, feed stock for the Queen's drones?

"Your voice," she cut in. *"It does not smell the same as it did. Are you well? How does a human know if they are well?"*

Two more groups of enemy ships moved into position, each made of a single carrier and seven wardens, their trajectory coming close to cutting us off. They might not physically keep us from twisting around the dwarf planet, open as space was, but it was clear they would find themselves within their range.

"She's not buying it." James made a sound of caution. *"We've got to move. They're closing in."*

"*We see them,*" Karianna grumbled back. "*We don't need backseat drivers to tell us.*"

One of the groups returning from the edge of the system closed on our only clear escape vector along the port side. We were now covered from the rear, the front, and the flanks.

"I am well," I said to the Gray Queen, keeping her on the line. Keeping her busy. "Tell me . . . what has happened since we last spoke. Your smells have not reached us."

"*You humans . . . You grow so very slow . . . we have told these people what to do. We have bathed them in our scents. They do nothing. They leak water from their eyes, scream words even the Foundry machines cannot translate.*"

"As I said, they are afraid."

"*This is afraid for humans? Fear, a weak emotion. Strange, strange, strange. How do we get them to lay eggs? How do we get them to make more?*"

A morbid curiosity crossed my mind. "How long have they been here?"

"*Why ask? You know how long. You brought them. These*"—she struggled to find the word—"*samples.*"

What a description for a human being.

"You do know humans take nine months before they can have a child. They are not like Isoptera. We grow live young. This takes time."

There came a flurry of angry clicking, though little of it translated. "*Nine months? What is nine months?*"

"Umm . . . It is most of the rotation of the third planet around the sun. You must be patient."

"*Patient!*" The Queen's clicking intensified. "*Be patient? We have been patient. Many an empty cycle spent in deep space to come. We have waited in the dark, grown in strength. Seventy-five generations I have given birth since we left Nest. And now, you say patience.*"

"Milo, you are running out of options," Proxy reported. "If we wish to leave the device with them and end this, we must deploy it soon."

"But there isn't an opening."

"I have found a potential for one. If we slow our approach to only two Gs for three minutes, then deploy the device, there should be an opening three thousand kilometers across. They should not detect the device sliding through that space."

I stared down at the cat. "And if they see through it?"

"You know the answer to that."

I bent down and scratched it behind the ear, giving myself a moment to think.

"You know my vote," Karianna replied. *"I'm tired of this crap. It's a load of bull."*

"But what if people are down there? What do we do about them? We can't just leave them."

She let out a long breath for the benefit of the crew, not me. Her emotions were furious, nervous, fearful. She was a cable who'd been stretched to its tensile limit, ready to snap at any moment. *"We can't rescue everyone, despite what we want to do or be. Hell, we don't even know if they're telling the truth. What if Justin left decoys? Fakes?"*

"I don't like this," Lance said, his words groaning out. *"But she's right. We don't have any other option. We didn't come prepared to save them too."*

Hy sighed, *"But those poor people."*

"Poor people," Xuan echoed.

Shelly frowned at this, not responding, then turned, looking to the enemy ships closing in.

I couldn't imagine leaving humans to perish on a distant rock so far away from friends and family and community. They would certainly suffer and die today, even if we were victorious.

Universe, what do I do?

The enemy was closing in. We had no means to confirm if this was truth or not. And our little Justin ruse, it wouldn't last much longer.

The *Transcendence* began to slow, allowing the enemy ships to close in. Every mile of buffer eaten up by this change made my skin prickle, my nerves stand on end. We were the worst heroes.

Universe forgive me.

"Do you have fresh samples for us?" the Gray Queen pressed. *"We will put them to good use. Tasty, tasty, tasty. My loves are voracious, they seethe with unrequited hunger."*

I took a clarifying breath of the non-air in my virtual space. "Yes, Gray Queen, we have samples. We are preparing them now."

Her excitement overwhelmed the channel, making the connection a clipped jumble of noise. *"Deliver! Deliver! Deliver!"*

"Proxy?"

The feline's ears flicked. "Already working on decoys. They will be ready momentarily."

"And the gap?"

"It's widening," Shelly replied. "Almost big enough. This might actually work."

The enemy battle groups closed in, moving into weapon range all around, pincers and cannons baring down on our position as we curved deeper into our course's spiral, their fusion candles lighting the dark of space with fresh constellations.

"Probes ready," Proxy reported. "On your mark."

I mentally looked to Karianna, who looked back, our minds meeting within the integration, our combined emotions a frothing mix of regret, anger, and resignation.

"Deploy."

The probes broke free of the ship, two standard, one cloaked. The unmasked probes were aimed at one of the Gray Carriers in the back of the line, as well as one ahead of us positioning itself to intercept. Contacts began to blossom from their maws as attack shuttles scrambled into open space to protect and capture these payloads.

The final probe sailed through the empty center of their groups unseen, its position merely mathematical, undetectable even by us.

"Are these samples fresh?" the Gray Queen asked, sounding more thoughtful. *"What may their nutrition give us?"*

"Their nutrition is only as good as their care," I said, feeling sick at my words. I had to remind myself I was just playing a part. Damn, it was so much easier to just fight.

"And what nutrition might that be? How do they metabolize?"

I kept her busy talking about human culinary practices, and how to prepare healthy meals. I regurgitated a lifetime of second-hand conversations Mom had with Dad trying to get him to live healthier, all as the swarms of attack shuttles closed on the decoys.

They recovered the pill-shaped capsules and brought them back to their respective carriers, all attention on them, the gap between us and Haumea still clear.

We just had to hold out a few more minutes, and the device would fall into range.

"The excitement," the Gray Queen mused, her clicks practically vibrating. *"The potential. The transformation. The change. Yes, yes, yes, my brood will be*

dominant. *My children will be Isoptera. We grow and spread and reach the edges of the universe. Feed, evolve, multiply.*"

A spark of emotion from Karianna made me feel better for our decision. She was considering what it might be like to roast this blubbering Queen over a giant spit before all mankind to make her suffering legendary.

"You will get what is coming to you," I said, trying not to sound like I felt. Given the Queen's lack of response, I had a feeling sarcasm was not an Isopteran language skill.

Just as I was about to declare victory, the allotted time having passed, a bright flash of light came from open space three thousand kilometers over the surface of Haumea, along the device's trajectory. Panicked, I did a quick scan and found that something had gone wrong. It had been found despite no Isopteran ships being in its range.

"*The probe,*" Karianna called out. "*It hit some kind of energy net. What the hell is it?*"

"*You lie!*" the Gray Queen shouted over the open channel, her anger clear as crystal falling from one's hands, destined to shatter upon impact. "*These are not samples. They are empty. Husk. You lie, you lie, you lie.*"

The enemy groups around us began to power up, their fusion drives turning hot, attack shuttles coming online.

"*Oh no,*" James shuddered. "*This isn't—*"

A shock of searing pain went through my back like claws drug over raw flesh as two missiles struck us. Karianna responded without hesitation, raising the MI before any more projectiles could get through, expanding our swarm of nanomachines in a swirling, protective bubble around us.

"*You will die for this,*" the Gray Queen seethed. "*We do not keep deals with liars. And humans . . . Humans! All you ever do is lie. Lie, lie, lie.*"

CHAPTER 61

"Scramble! Scramble!" Lance ordered over our shared communication as Karianna and I moved the *Transcendence* into a better position, increasing our acceleration as we spiraled away from Haumea.

Though diminished in numbers since losing Ada and Leo, our fighter wing emerged, a set of four blazing candles burning off to meet the enemy.

Attack shuttles swarmed out from the gaping maws of the half dozen Gray Carriers closing within five thousand kilometers, the winglike airfoils of the smaller cicada craft retracting like sky divers lowering their profile in the wind. Their green forms burned toward us, dozens at the onset vs only four Foundry-made fighter craft. Lance led them against the enemy, attempting to pull the same topside maneuver that had worked to close the distance in atmosphere. But instead of remaining quiet while we moved in, the Isopteran pilots broke formation and began launching volleys of missiles at our craft.

"Maybe they're not as dumb as they look," James said, his fighter screaming around the edge of the lump of attackers, his nuclear sabot cannons tearing through their ranks, debris scattering like glitter tossed into empty space.

"They've adapted," Xuan replied, her fighter backing up Lance's, who had found himself caught in a death spiral of evasion as he outran more than a dozen missiles hot on his tail.

Enemy attack shuttles were torn apart, one, then two, then three in just a few seconds. Our wing broke formation in a starburst, then curved around, pushing to outrun the rushing warheads. Our fighters were far more effective against them than the Swift Shuttles.

"Holy shit, there's a lot of them," James said. "I've gotten six. Seven. But I don't think this math is gonna math, bruh."

"Too many," Hy remarked. "I'm down. Getting a fresh fighter."

"Don't lose your ships," Lance chided him, though there was no hint of anger in his voice, only pressure. "We only have another fifteen replacements. Make the best use you can."

"Brittain," Xuan said, her fighter twisting between the attack vectors of several converging shuttles. "Up top. Coming in fast. I got two. Three coming in, it's lined up to use its autocannon."

He rolled himself over and slid behind an attack shuttle that had matched pace with him, using it as a kind of shield against the fighters bearing down on him. "Turning the tables, aren't they?"

The Isopteran ship just a few meters away from him tried to evade, to open up a line of sight for its buddies to attack. But in response, Lance expertly matched each of its maneuvers, twisting his fighter around to keep it between him and the oncomers, the top of his hull facing the enemy at all times. I'd never seen anything like it. He was fast. And all the while, he gave out orders and tagged targets for his wing to eliminate next.

The *Transcendence* rocked, a jagged pain blossoming in my right shoulder. A portion of the hull halfway up was missing, exposing one of the galleys and two workshops to hard vacuum. Nanomachines went to work to repair the damage, but it would take time. Time we did not have.

"Overclock?" Karianna asked, her mind becoming one with mine inside the integration.

Do it, I thought.

The world went from a bullet train speeding past an empty platform at midnight to standing still, weapons fire locked in place as if everything in the universe had become a kind of model. From this crystallized moment in time, we could see every aspect of the battle.

We were surrounded, clear and simple. The least concentration of enemy forces lay ahead of us to our port side. Following that vector, we had only two carriers and five wardens to contend with. As for every other possible angle, things weren't so good. Our aft and flanks were covered by the bulk of their forces, nine carriers in medium range, another sixteen closing in, not to mention the wardens who numbered thirty-eight in all. The *Transcendence* was one of the most powerful ships in all existence, but this was far too much to handle solo. Two or three of these carriers would have been a challenge given how many attack shuttles each carried, but this many . . .

"*Woah, woah.*" James sounded off balance. "*Warn me when you're going to do that.*"

"Sorry," I said. "Use these moments wisely. We've got to hit back and run. We're surrounded, with no hope of taking them head on. Shelly?"

"Already identifying the best targets," she said, flicking at the air with her hands. Several of the carriers lit in our virtual environment, red circles appearing around them. "Proxy? Give me a second opinion. I don't trust my call."

"Your assessment is correct," it said, head cocked to the side. "Your chosen targets have the highest likelihood of success."

Shelly nodded, and I could feel her queue the antimatter slug cannons to fire when the flow of time was restored to normal.

"*We need close-up coverage,*" Karianna said. "*A few drone fighters should help with any breakthrough attacks. Lance, you guys are doing great and all, but—*"

"*Yeah, I know,*" he said, none too pleased. "*It's too much.*"

I'll keep my focus on the MI, Karianna thought. The missiles, a diffuse screen can stop them. But I had no idea about this warden weapon system.

We won't know till we face it.

Great plan, smart ass. Let it hit us. Then come up with a strategy.

Here's a strategy then. Run. We run.

"We can't stay like this much longer," Proxy said. "Your minds are starting to overheat."

"Okay, okay," I said, chewing on my bottom lip, arms crossed. "Everyone have their targets?" I chose six of the closest enemy ships that Shelly had left alone, tagging them as my own, Para Lux arrays and rail cannons ready. "Lance, do you have a plan?"

"*Stay nimble,*" he told his frozen fighter wing. "*Don't let them back you into a corner. Our fighters do not have organic pilots, theirs do. Use that to your advantage. Push your acceleration as hard as you need to.*"

They grunted back in reply. It was as good a plan as any.

"*Alright then,*" Karianna said. "*Let's fuck these primitive screw heads up.*"

Time resumed its regular progress, the battle slamming back into high gear. Missiles crashed into the MI, exploding in cascading waves as attack shuttles screamed through the gaps they had left. The drone fighters Karianna had deployed near us went to work on the newcomers, flying in erratic patterns to avoid being hit, as antimatter slugs went hurling out to the encroaching enemy forces.

Out of range of our fighters, yet close enough to blind our instruments, the projectiles ignited, and two of the carriers were snapped in half, their recently deployed fighters reduced to cosmic dust. I wanted to whoop given that that had actually worked. The last few times we had tried to use those weapons, the Foundry had had other plans and disabled them.

I began carving up wardens with lances of energy from the Para Lux arrays, slicing their hulls in two, the intensity of the beams pausing hardly an instant as it struck their defenses. Our rail cannons discharged, first a flash of light upon the hull just below what remained of Karianna's target, and an instant later another on a distant carrier, the subluminal projectile puncturing a hole from one end to the other, kinetic energy becoming heat, its path turning everything to molten slag. An instant later, my second shot impacted another, and its forward end split apart in a brilliant display of explosive decompression.

For thousands of kilometers around the *Transcendence,* space had become a field of fireworks and debris, fungara and steel and exotic materials turning into navigational hazards for the enemy force at our rear. Approaching ships slowed their acceleration, mostly carriers, while some of the wardens burned harder to close the gap.

We were holding our own against an overwhelming enemy, but I knew this wouldn't last forever.

"It's still out there!" James shouted out of nowhere. *"I can see it on my instruments. The Protea Device. We have to go get it. We have to put it in the right place. Their base is hardly defended. This could be the end, bruh."*

I shook my head, glancing over at Shelly and Proxy. "There's no way to get through this mess to recover it. We can't."

"Keep thinking that," he replied with a hint of something familiar in his voice, reminding me of the childhood troublemaker I had met in detention. *"I have an idea to get it. But I'll need help."*

"I'll go," Hy grunted, no hesitation in his voice. *"It is the only way. We must see this weapon used."*

Xuan let out a gasp. *"Husband? You'll die."*

"I . . . I will not."

"We can't offer any support," Lance said, his voice calm. *"The drone fighters would have to be fully autonomous at that range."*

"*We won't need cover,*" James replied. "*I went to the Chevelle school of flying.*"

"*No, you didn't,*" Karianna spat. "*You did not. You learned every good flight skill from me, asshat.*"

"*Yeah, yeah, yeah.*"

"You can't go," I said. "You won't make it."

"*But I have to. We came here to finish a mission. We have to see it done.*"

He might be right, but I didn't want him to risk it. We'd lost too many already. I wasn't going to have another pair of friends sacrifice themselves needlessly for the cause. It wasn't right. It wasn't fair. I didn't know how much more my heart could take.

But deep down, I knew he'd never let it go. While I had come to terms with some of my pain and grief, he had not. He had to do this, didn't he? He had to. What kind of friend would I be? We weren't the same kids we'd been back then.

"Okay," I said, swallowing. "Okay. This is going to be rough."

"*We know,*" James replied. "*And . . . thanks. I need to do this.*"

"I know you do." I turned to Shelly, whose face was a mask of uncertainty. It was so hard to know the right choice.

"*Come back safe,*" Karianna whispered. "*Milo's annoying side is getting a little boring.*"

He chuckled in that rebellious, rakish way he used to do when we were kids. "*We plan on it.*"

Who would have ever thought we'd go from detention to here?

A pained sensation passed between Karianna and me, and the *Transcendence* slowed. Proxy informed me that James and Hy had climbed out of their Star Spheres and were running to the nearest shuttle bay. In the interim, the ship was being bombarded with more ordinance than we had seen yet, the MI being put to the test. Karianna was doing well to keep it moving, to focus the swarm at the right spots and maximize our coverage, but we only had so many nanomachines in the vats to pull from. At some point, we would run out of materials with which to replenish our shields.

"*Ready!*" James shouted over the open channel. "*Undocking.*"

The bay doors slid open, and he wasted no time, screaming out into open space in a Swift Shuttle. As soon as they were at a safe distance, we reignited the main drive, our massive antimatter candle reducing a series of attack shuttles to dust in our wake, shuttles that had assumed we were damaged.

We fought the enemy, watching as James and Hy spiraled through the chaos, their momentum opposite that of the oncomers. Attack shuttles tried to peel away and follow, but inertia kept them focused on the *Transcendence's* trajectory.

"They're breaking through," Shelly remarked, a hint of excitement in her voice. "Look at him go."

James evaded everything the enemy threw at them. Autocannon fire, missiles, he flowed around them all like a river flows around smooth stones. Isoptera scrambled, but he was too fast.

Pain cascaded up my back and arms as several carrier-rated missiles struck the *Transcendence*. There were too many holes in the MI. Two of our nanovats went offline. Shelly lost one of the antimatter cannons. One of the rail cannons was damaged, but it would be back online in less than a minute.

"Oh shit," Lance grumbled. *"There's a crack in my sphere."*

"Are you okay?" I asked, panic rising in my chest. "Are you injured?"

"I think I'm okay. Not injured. Ship is working on patching it. That was a close call. If I cycle out of my virtual environment, I can see open space."

More pain shot throughout my extended body. Karianna and I were sharing it, but that didn't make it any easier. She worked furiously to bolster our defense, but it was a losing battle. We were only buying time.

Shelly fired. I fired. Enemy carriers and wardens exploded.

Two of the wardens closed in on us, their unusual weapons deploying. Canisters rushed out of the launch tubes, coming to within a few dozen kilometers of the MI before they exploded.

"Incoming!" I screamed.

Karianna scattered the MI, spreading it as wide as she could, thinner.

One. Two. Three seconds passed.

A thousand tiny explosions went around us in a cloud, then shot back to the *Transcendence*. While the MI caught many, hundreds of the deadly darts passed unmolested through the barrier, peppering our skin in a kind of ripping agony. Alarms went off all over the ship as Proxy and Chinchillette moved into action to make repairs.

Karianna and I wanted to cry, wanted to turn off the feedback, but it wasn't possible. We were already attenuating the signal as much as we could.

The Para Lux array powered up and lanced out at the wardens, slicing them in two. More were coming, but there wasn't enough time to repair the damage. Additional warden canisters were launched, though these were at a greater range. This gave me more time to respond, and I was able to destroy several while Shelly targeted the ships with antimatter slugs. The wardens would rip us apart if we let them get too close. The carriers had gotten wise to Shelly's assaults and were now deploying electromagnetic nets that forced the slugs to ignite at a safer distance. What ground we were taking against them was slipping as their tactics shifted.

"*We're running out of fighters,*" Lance reported. "*Three extras left. There's just too damn many. Doesn't help being down two pilots either.*"

"James?" I called out, looking to his position on the virtual map.

"*We're almost there. Just another minute.*"

"Get it done so we can pick you up and flee this hell."

"*Don't worry about us,*" Hy said back. "*We have this. You run. We will meet on escape.*"

"*We're not leaving you,*" Karianna said, echoing my thoughts. There was something else too. An attachment. A connection. "*Get a move on.*"

"*I know you're not leaving us,*" James replied with a false bravado. "*Like we said, meet on the other side. We're almost there, close in on the——*"

A flash of light enveloped the Swift Shuttle. Its fusion engines went cold, attitude controls lost.

"James!" I shouted, but the connection was dead. "Proxy. What do we do?"

The feline leaned forward as if thinking hard. "They've been disabled. The Swift Shuttle, just like the probe, and the antimatter slugs, they've disabled them."

"Damn it!" I threw up my hands.

Karianna, already hearing my thoughts, began to turn the *Transcendence* in toward the base.

"*We're not leaving them behind,*" she said, and I agreed. "*God, this is stupid, this is stupid.*"

Enemy missiles pelted the diamond-shaped center of our ship, ripping decks apart. What had once been Leo's quarters, as well as all his art, was cast into hard vacuum.

"Can we make it?" Shelly asked, her voice trembling. "There's too many. It's too much, Milo. I don't think we can make it."

I didn't either, but I wasn't giving up. Neither Karianna nor I responded. We spiraled to our trapped friends, heedless to the danger. But how could we rescue them without being caught in this net? How?

Maybe we could—

Before the ship turned deep enough into the spiral to burn straight for the damaged shuttle, explosions went off all around it. A warden had screamed up from the surface of Haumea and closed on them.

"Liar, Liar, Liar," cried a clicking voice from the surface of the dwarf planet. *"Always liars."*

"Hy," Xuan said, her voice choked. *"My Sunrise. No. No. No."*

He was gone, and I had let him go.

The world went red.

Anger flowed through me like magma seeking to break the surface. I interfaced with every weapon system still online and lashed out in anger at the battle theater—volleys of antimatter slugs, superheated Para Lux beams, roaring rail cannons, and every single piezoelectric bomb we had. Light. Instrument noise. Silent screams in the dark. For twenty thousand kilometers in every direction, the enemy fell, destroyed, disabled, stunned, more wreckage drifting away.

I collapsed to the floor, all emotion drained from me, my body an empty husk.

Karianna wasted no time. She saw an opening and fled, pushing us through the eye of the needle. Our main drive cut on and off, jerking the ship as it attempted to accelerate in fits and starts, but soon became constant as Proxy and Chinchillette redirected what meager resources we had left.

The remainder of the Isopteran fleet backed off, uncertain what we might do next. Haumea receded as we limped away, half the *Transcendence* ripped in two, exposed to open space. We were damaged to the point that the only thing keeping us squishy humans alive were our Star Spheres.

Shelly knelt down beside me, putting her arms around me and pulled me into an embrace. If not for her, I think I would have fallen through the floor itself, left to drift forever in the black.

"He didn't deserve this," was all I could say. "They didn't deserve this."

"None of us did," Shelly said, choking on her words.

Silent moments passed as we burned away, no plan, just fear, just anger, just . . . just nothing. I had nothing else to give.

Our resonator crystal began to vibrate.

"Milo." It was Ingrid's voice, and it was as fragile and as tired as I felt. *"Are you there, Milo? Come in."*

"I'm here," I replied, struggling to my feet, Shelly helping to steady me. "What is it? What's wrong?"

"They came for us. Everyone came for us. The UEI, the insurgents, Veetor. They're all here. We don't know what to do."

I rubbed my face with my palms and shuddered. "What are you saying?" It was all too much to take in.

"Earth is under siege, and we won't be able to hold off long. Bennet betrayed us. He's been on their side all along."

And at that, words began to repeat in my head.

Love.

Live.

Pray.

Burn.

Fall.

Ash.

Anger.

Atonement.

End.

CHAPTER 62

We limped back to Earth, systems critically damaged, many sections exposed to open space. The *Transcendence* was bleeding power and radioactive waste, leaving clear signs along our route home that we were a wounded animal ready to be put down. Though they had repaired what they could to keep our reactor from going critical, our Proxies made it clear no further repairs would happen without fresh material. We had lost too much in the fight, and as a result, half the nanovats were offline. This meant that our decoupled Para Lux arrays and twisted rail cannons would remain unusable until then. We needed metal, and minerals, and a bevy of trace elements, a shopping list longer than anything we had had on Novae, to put this old dog back together again.

We were down two more people.

We had lost two more friends.

But there was no time to mourn.

No time for anything but action.

"We are at 60 percent effectiveness," Proxy reported. "I wish the news were better."

If 100 percent of us hadn't been enough to take down Veetor, how would 60 percent do it? We had two of our Para Lux arrays, two rail cannons, no antimatter slug cannons, and five drone fighters of the original twenty-one. The MI was spotty, and the acceleration of the main drive uneven, unreliable.

I routed another message through the resonator network, checking in on our team under siege. Chevelle, Renata, Dante, Emilia, and Frelo were safe for now in Svalbard, remaining close to a series of ancient military bunkers left from the war. Frelo complained that these protective underground structures weren't half the shelters the Phods on Rix were, but there was nothing to be done about it. These facilities would keep them safe enough, unless they were overrun by a ground assault.

Chevelle and Renata were making short trips around the island by ground car to ensure that their limited forces were in position. According to their reports, Bennet and his forces were on their way. From how the leader of Queensland had handled the eastern coast of Paphospolis, it was clear his objective was to first try and take a territory with ground troops, and if he couldn't do that easily enough, he would burn it to the ground. Drakos was just holding on. If not for Tayo sending help, the entire island would have been a conflagration.

"That shirtless bellend from Antalya sure fights hard," Chevelle said. *"He's gassed over this. Excited. Always knew Bennet was a chav, it's how he walks."*

Renata agreed. *"It's bait, this. All gone bare buki, innit?"*

"Listen to her, blud. Oh. Oh. Oh. Spend too much time round this one? Hmm. She's proper. Safe as fuck. Cold."

"We'll hold on," Renata added, sounding much more sober this time. *"But we can't stop what's in the sky."*

This situation put our usually calm Lance on edge. He kept asking about Ingrid, if she was someplace safe. Her reply was always, *"No place is safe."* I had a feeling if we were in the position to give him up, he would be on the surface at this moment with her. Their feelings were clear. The two of them had bonded, had fallen into a kind of love, and I hoped they'd get their chance to see it through.

Svalbard was not yet under attack. Bennet was hitting targets around the world but seemed to be leaving them for last. Daegu was putting up the best fight of all. Bak Yoon was furious no one else in the alliance had seen this coming, or spoken up, because he had. Then again, Bennet had wooed his niece, and that would leave some sorry feelings, twice that with a betrayal.

If it wasn't bad enough, the settlements of the alliance were under attack from orbit. There was a Foundry-made shuttle up there too, waiting, dropping small, handmade bombs onto the surface. Why hadn't Veetor just glassed the place given what weapons he had available? I couldn't say. Was the Foundry holding him back? Or was he getting sentimental?

We slipped into orbit around Earth, taking position on the highest level of the Ring of Diamonds on the dayside, South America beneath us. To our surprise, the *Absolution* was nowhere to be seen. We hadn't detected him on approach, nor seen any sign of him in low Earth orbit, though with all the false positives and artifacts the ring's debris produced, it was never easy. We had no clear plan other than to stand between Veetor and our people on the ground as long as we could. If we survived this head-to-head, we would stop Bennet. I had a strong suspicion going to Queensland would make him recall his forces.

Too many unknowns remained beyond this.

The Isoptera were following, and they would arrive a few hours after us. From the look of it, they were done playing around.

Then there was the UEI Remnant Fleet. But where was Cardoso? He had remained hidden since our last conversation. Was he dead? I hoped not.

Sure would have been nice if the Universe would throw us a bone.

We descended, settling into orbit between the second and third level of the Ring of Diamonds, the debris thick enough we could hide, but not so much we were in danger of collision.

"We can't fight him like this." Karianna echoed my earlier thoughts as she scanned the damaged and unoccupied HardyHabs floating around us. *"He'll mop the floor with our blood. We need to repair. He's not around right now. Maybe we're orbiting opposite of him and it will be some time."*

"Milo, I have an idea." Shelly waved to the expanse of debris laid out before us. She placed a glowing wireframe over the junk, outlining the varied layers that made up the Ring of Diamonds. "According to the map the Free Citizens keep, the third level here, just above our position relative to Earth, is uninhabited and dense. Maybe we can use these materials to repair the ship. Proxy?"

The cat blinked up at us. "It is likely."

"Karianna?" I called.

"Already on it, boss," she said, and the ship began to turn. *"Time to go dumpster diving."*

The *Transcendence* curved down into a band of shattered structures, drones flooding out of us like a swarm of bees, collecting pieces of once glorious, now abandoned homes and tossing them into the nanovats for processing. Here, our Proxies would break them down into their base components and put this junk to work, repairing weapons, faulty power systems, and hull breeches. One after the next, pieces small as gas cans, others large as school buses, were brought inside.

"This will take some time," Proxy reported. "We will have to process this scrap and debris before we can get to work."

"As quick as you can," I said.

Something shifted on the *Transcendence*. It felt as if someone had peeled a dry scab off of my knee. From feedback in the integration, Karianna had felt it too. It wasn't a painful sensation, but it was uncomfortable, unusual.

What was that? she asked, using only thought.

I don't know. But it was like we lost something, right?

Did Proxy deploy anything?

I don't think so.

Weird. She paused, thinking it over, recalling the feeling, probing at the edges of the fading sensation. *It was probably nothing. But it's not the first time I've felt it. It's not the first time for you either, is it?*

No.

Slowly, unevenly, systems began to come back online. It seemed that just having new materials in the queue opened up the use of already processed materials. The nanovats churned, liquid metal populated with machines flowing around the shattered hallways of the ship. Until now, I hadn't realized that our instruments were not just having a hard time with the debris in the ring, but had been functionally impaired. Wavelengths returned, active scans searching for threats.

"That is enough for now," Proxy said, recalling the collection drones. "The remainder of what we need for a full repair will not come from here."

"How effective will this—"

"*Milo!*" Karianna shouted. *"There he is. He's here. He's headed for us."*

I spun around in my virtual environment and waved my arms and hands, gesturing to adjust my view. She was right, there he was, screaming over the horizon from the dark side of the Earth on a general intercept course, the arctic-blue wedge of Veetor's Foundry-made flagship gleaming under the regard of the sun.

"Get ready, Xuan," Lance said, and in that moment, it hit me hard. They were all that was left of our fighter wing.

Two Para Lux arrays.

Two rail cannons.

Two fighters, with three backups.

No antimatter slugs.

A broken MI.

The *Absolution* hailed us. I took a deep breath before I answered.

"Lookie here, what do we have," Veetor said, his voice dripping with malice. *"Mmm. Mmm. Somehow that little broken boy I left for dead in the dust managed to survive. You are a tough one, Milo Hughes, with a face like a punching bag. But this is where your luck ends. No one's coming to save you this go. And I won't make the same mistake twice. You hear me? I won't wait to kill you. I'll do it quick."*

CHAPTER 63

The *Absolution* altered its trajectory, heading straight for us. Karianna and I leaned to the starboard side, increasing acceleration, hoping to prevent him from hitting us head on. Our two ships closed the distance, MIs rising, weapons hot. For our part, all I could bring online was a single rail cannon and one of the Para Lux arrays but with only half power. I linked the two weapons to fire together, hoping at that close a range they might add more punch like this. A gap of a thousand kilometers of debris-strewn space vanished in no time.

Veetor held his shot. One minute remained before we would cross paths, our inertia carrying us to a center point.

For a moment I felt as if our two ships were a pair of knights in a medieval competition, jousts and shields raised, ready to knock the other rider from their steed.

"Why hasn't he fired yet?" Karianna asked.

I shook my head. "It's got to be his position. He wants to cripple us."

He came at us less like a thrusted spear, more like a storm of knives. Karianna positioned the MI before us like a solid wall, blocking off his forward line of attack. This left our rear open, but we weren't being pursued, and our MI was thin after the last battle. Rail cannon shots pelted the *Transcendence*, layers of MI superheating and converting to slag and cosmic dust. A hole appeared in our barrier as his supercharged Para Lux array punched through, one of his beams slicing at the fattened middle of our ship, cutting through several already damaged decks.

"That was close to the antimatter reactor," Proxy reported. "We will not survive a blow like that again."

Shelly eyed me, a confused look on her face. "Milo, are you going to fire?"

I narrowed my eyes, focusing my attention on a section of the *Absolution*. The gap was closing fast, now six hundred kilometers.

"Almost there."

"What are you doing?"

"Almost." I held my breath, waiting for the right moment. His barrier swirled, and then came an opening. I fired. The energized rail cannon shot whizzed through his barrier at nearly the speed of light and slammed against a section of hull on his port side. Weapons fire from the *Absolution* ceased, and we sailed past one another, coming to within twenty meters of ramming head-on. I swore I could feel the heat of his drive as we crossed paths.

"You guys aren't looking so good," Veetor commented, his smug voice low. *"Let me just turn around and finish this. It's not fair to leave you limping on like a dog with broken legs. Time to put ol' Lassie down. No more Timmys to save. No more wells to fall in."*

"The hell is he talking about?" I mumbled, not transmitting.

Karianna radiated laughter within the integration. *No time to explain.*

Distance between us and the *Absolution* widened once more as we raced for a shattered layer of the Ring of Diamonds between levels three and four, our relative altitude to the surface of Earth at 3,200 hundred kilometers. Veetor began to turn, attempting to come back around in our direction, flipping his ship and burning hard. During this maneuver, he plowed through a half dozen of the empty HardyHabs, bits of metal scattering like glitter in the void.

"He's coming back for us," Shelly said. "What do we do? We don't have the firepower to face him. We need more time to repair."

"Lance!" I called.

"Already on it."

A pair of fighters shot from the *Transcendence*, taking relative positions behind us. They were often the most dangerous weapons we had operational, but I didn't think they'd be enough to take him down.

"Think, think, think," I said, my attention focused along with Karianna's on navigating the ship through an ever-thickening field of debris. On our port and starboard, we were surrounded by habitations that were still active, as well as the derelict military weapons platforms Ingrid had mentioned, the

MOPs, and a slew of abandoned factories. At the velocity with which we were rushing forward, it was hard to thread our mass through sections smaller than a few hundred meters. And turning was not easy given this much inertia. To make matters worse, we were between levels of the Ring of Diamonds, meaning objects were moving at a variety of speeds here. While the lower levels moved swifter to keep up their orbital velocity and not burn up, the higher levels moved slower to maintain this same state. But slow or fast, a difference was a difference, and this made everything more difficult.

The sun fell over the horizon, Earth's atmosphere turning green and purple as we transitioned onto the nightside of the planet. An abandoned HardyHab slammed into the outer edge of the *Transcendence's* middle section, sending a fiery jolt of pain down my back.

"Watch it now," I told Karianna with a touch of anger, but it was both our faults. Navigating this wasn't going to be easy under fire.

Veetor readjusted his trajectory and was now heading our way, taking distant potshots with his rail cannons, tagging the vacant facilities floating around us. We weaved through the tangle of metal down a tunnel of sorts, its structures encircling us, hoping that by putting mass between us and him, we might remain safe. I peered over my shoulder, allowing Karianna to drive, and saw his speck among the chaos growing larger. He was hauling ass to catch back up, and if that meant he had a few collisions on the way, he did not seem concerned.

"Milo," Proxy said, sliding up beside me. "We have more incoming."

"What? Who? The Isoptera are still a ways out, aren't they?"

"Not the Isoptera. It's the UEI Remnant Fleet. They are closing in from the dayside, though at a different angle. They were using the planet to hide their approach."

"Shit," I grumbled. "How many?"

"Twenty-five in all. Their class seems to be the same as Cardoso's ships."

"Is it him?" Shelly asked us. "Is that Cardoso?" She zoomed in on the wireframe models. "They all look the same. How can we tell?"

"We don't even know if he's friendly."

"Boss man," Karianna said. *"This is too much. What are we going to do?"*

"We've got to keep running. Buy time. Fix the weapons. How far out are the Isoptera?"

"Ninety minutes," Proxy supplied. "So long as they do not change their course."

"Guys," Lance said next. *"Reports from the ground are not looking good either. Ingrid just sent me a message. Bennet is about to make landfall on Svalbard. They have a thousand troops easy on old shipping freighters headed in, less than fifty miles out. They've even got jet fighters running air cover, and a few of the heavy shuttles we gifted to them. I'm worried. They can't fight this off. There aren't enough of them."*

Just one more chaotic variable. Things would have been bad enough if it was just us versus them, the *Transcendence* versus the universe, but it wasn't. Innocents had been caught up in this conflict. We were putting so many people who did not deserve this at risk. Why? Just so Veetor could wave his dick around.

"Renata and Chevelle will hold them back," Karianna spat. *"They have a plan. They'll hold them back. But we can't help if we die. We've already seen enough of that . . ."* Her words trailed off, leaving me wondering how much she would grieve James's loss.

Another one.

"And if we can't keep from dying," Xuan piped up. *"Maybe we get some revenge."*

"I guess," Lance said. *"We've got to help them as soon as we can."*

"There is something odd about the incoming fleet," Shelly said, rubbing her hands together. "They're not all burning in sync. There's a few who are lagging back, letting their fellow attack ships move to the front, leaving a gap. It's almost as if there are two groups of them."

I blinked, looking at the approaching ships. She was right. Were they just moving into a different formation? They were still at some distance, a good two thousand kilometers off, but Veetor was closing, and fast. If we had been in open space, without all this junk in the way, he'd have wiped the floor with us.

Lance and Xuan broke their relative formation and rushed for the *Absolution*. While Veetor might have had weapons capable of taking down the *Transcendence*, these fighters were another thing. They were too small, too fast, too difficult to hit.

"Keep up the pressure," Lance told his only wing mate.

Several of our busted systems came back online. Our Proxies were still hard at work. The strength of our Para Lux array doubled, and we now had one of the Piezoelectric Spatial Compression bombs. It wasn't much, but I'd take it.

Veetor made several long-range shots, tagging structures around us but none of them hitting the mark. The attacks came in fours, their cadence strangely familiar, staccato, almost musical.

We curved around one of the few named structures on this level, a massive space station that at one time must have hosted tens of thousands of people. It dwarfed the *Transcendence* in size and scale, making us appear like an ant that had just crawled onto the end of a picknick blanket. The words *Laxmi Vilas* glowed in red around the bend of the single massive ring that made up the main body of the station, a thousand other spurs and trusses shooting out from a central core like a thin ring rotating around a metal rod.

Debris scattered before us was pushed out of the way, and I felt a giddy sense of pride feedback from Karianna.

Did you do that? I thought, attention split, the *Transcendence* twisting past the space station into another field of dense debris.

Yes! Yes! Yes! The MI. It moved the debris, some of it at least. We might can use this. The range is short, but . . .

Why hadn't we thought of this before?

"Dun, dun, dun, dunnnn!" Veetor called over the open channel just as he fired a quartet of rail cannons. Three of the four shots went wide, but the forth buried itself in our left flank. No critical systems were hit this time, thank the Universe, but it hurt like hell. *"Do any of you enjoy music? Hmm? Any of you? Or has pure survival beaten that kind of interest out of you? Hard to enjoy high culture when you're on the skids."*

"He's crazy," Shelly said. "I mean, we've known that . . . but . . . He's humming Beethoven's Fifth. He's firing his weapons to the melody."

"What?"

And four more shots came, two making contact, pain blossoming through my and Karianna's and extended body. God, it hurt.

"There he went again," she said.

Karianna let out a pained groan. "I told you all from the start. But nobody listens to me."

Veetor kept up his assault, distance narrowing, evasion becoming more and more difficult. We had found ourselves among three massive factories, each hundreds of meters across. Given their size, we were able to fly through one of their bays like it was a transit tunnel, starships at various stages of completion docked all around. They reminded me very much of the remnant fleet ships, cobbled together, hard angles, sections of steel trussing and collections of communication spurs like tangled wires.

As we emerged on the other side, platforms began to appear on our sensors, round like dinner plates made of cold gray metal. From earlier briefings with the Free Citizens of Earth, I had a feeling I knew what these were. More relics from a long-forgotten war.

One. Two. Three. Four. Shots impacted against the upper half of the diamond near our center of gravity. Karianna let out a squeak.

"You okay?" I asked.

"That was close," she reported back. *"The chambers to my right are gone. Just gone."*

"Working on repairs," Proxy said, its eyes glassed over while it peered into the middle distance.

"We can't take much more of this," Shelly said. "All we're doing is running. We have to fight back."

"Yeah," Karianna agreed, *"but how? What do we have? What position are we in? Our weapon systems might as well be replaced by one of those things that throws wooden spears. Toothpicks against a tank. We need a plan."*

Shelly nodded and crossed her arms, eyebrows crinkling as she thought through our predicament.

"Milo," Ingrid said out of nowhere, our resonator crystal vibrating. The suddenness made me jump. *"Hey . . . Things are looking bad down here. We are going to need help, and soon."*

"We're a little busy," I replied, twisting our ship around a series of busted habs.

"I know. I know. Lance has filled us in. We've been tracking as best as we can. Which is why I thought you might want some help. If we can help you, then you can help us quicker. It was Dameon's idea."

"What did you have in mind?"

"This." And as she said the word, power readings flickered all around us. One by one, the disc-shaped MOPs we had been flying past came online and began their POST operations, their weapons' hardpoints calibrating. *"Hope that little shit has fun chewing on a few thousand uranium-tipped shells."*

The MOPs opened fire, the space at our aft lighting up with tracer rounds from half a dozen 155mm autocannons. The platforms churned these shells out at a rate of one per second, shots raining on the *Absolution* like divine judgement. Veetor scrambled, having let his attention on his MI faulter. Explosions trailed his hull from forward to aft, decks venting into hard vacuum. For an instant, his main drive faltered, spluttering, then came back online.

I felt a rush of excitement and hope seeing him be the one backed into a corner. Maybe this could work. Maybe this could take him down.

As he defended himself, swirling his swarms of nanomachines here then there, adjusting density and location, I noticed the UEI Remnant Fleet increasing their acceleration, throwing themselves into the melee.

Veetor couldn't handle this. He had called for backup.

Several of their fleet hit the edge of the MOPs network's range and were torn apart in seconds, their hulls twisting, crews cooked by the radiation backwash from igniting shells. Other UEI ships fired, countering these attacks by hurling nuclear missiles at the MOPs. The platforms began to ignite, having zero defense against weapons like this, and the heavy rain of artillery focused on the approaching enemies calmed.

"They can't get them all," Ingrid called back. *"Keep pressing forward. They can take these out, but there's plenty up ahead for them to stumble on."*

"Thanks," I said, smiling. "This will make a huge—"

But my words were cut off as another network of MOPs powered up around us.

"Are these?" Shelly mused, cocking her head. "What?"

"Ingrid," I said, gesturing at the space around us to adjust my view, "you didn't put more MOPs online, did you?"

"No," she said, sounding confused. *"Why? What's wrong?"*

"Oh shit," Karianna said, gathering up the MI.

A secondary network of MOPs targeted us and opened fire.

CHAPTER 64

Several of the nuclear-tipped rounds slammed against the *Transcendence*, ripping apart what remained of the starboard side's outer decks, pain wracking our extended body. We were not looking good. Our ship, if viewed from outside, must have looked like a kind of shard of gold with black crystal one of your grandparents might have kept as a decoration on their mantle, but you were a curious kid and had dropped it a hundred times and it was now nothing more than a fragile spine holding sharp edges together beside a pile of glass.

Nearly 40 percent of our ship was gone. Our Proxies had done their best to consolidate the most critical systems, shifting around rooms, giving a sensation like butterflies swirling in my stomach, but our center of gravity was off, and we were broken. It was a miracle the antimatter drive still operated and the reactors hadn't gone critical.

Isoptera were inbound.

Bennet had made landfall in Svalbard.

A fleet of UEI ships were on our tail and closing.

We had one network of MOPs fighting against the enemy, another trying to kill us, their exchanges limiting our available courses.

And Veetor had not let up. The *Absolution* closed in.

"Evasive maneuvers," I said, and we banked to the left, curving our trajectory into a tangle of debris on the fourth level, thicker than what we had pushed through so far. This section had no MOPs, though I wasn't sure if the rest were still in range.

With our limited armaments, we damaged the nearest hostile platforms, putting them offline, but there were more.

"Mmm, isn't this getting fun?" Veetor relished over the open channel, his tone somewhat sexual. "I love it when the blood gets pumping. Don't you? So invigorating. Makes me want others to watch."

"You should try a rail cannon enema," Karianna spat back. "It'll fix all your problems, or your money back."

He chuckled at that, his voice rumbling. "I think I'll pass. But I can give you one if you like." His weapons fired again in sequence, but this time we had debris to cover our back. "I aim only to serve."

Veetor closed the gap, coming to within a few hundred kilometers. His setup was perfect. All he had to do was fire—there was no way our thinning MI could withstand a full-scale assault.

"There!" Karianna drew my attention by circling a section of one of the approaching factory stations, its dark surface covered with bright red gas storage tanks, yellow-painted cranes, and dead assembly lines. "There's a hole. If we can fit through that, he can't follow."

"It's too small."

"Let me take the reins. You cover the MI."

"Karianna . . ."

"I've got this. I won't get us killed. And he will have to go around. He'll barely be able to slow in enough time not to die. Hey! Chinchillette. Do the thing."

I whirled on her. "What thing? Do what thing!"

"As you wish," it replied, and Proxy shook its head.

As we approached the port at the center of a broken orbital manufacturing facility several hundred meters across, the shape of the *Transcendence* began to change. The wider sections of the diamond compressed, elongating the hull, not by multiples but by measurable percentages. A strange sensation like the one I had felt earlier returned briefly, as if part of the ship had detached from us. I felt around in local space for what it could be, worried it was something important that had fallen off, and got nothing.

The massive facility loomed before us like a wall, Veetor's shots going wide given all the trash between us and him. I could see the hole Karianna was shooting for, but it wasn't much wider than we were, and it had a peculiar shape. It was like our ship, but not quite. My heart thundered in my chest, an anxious, prickly sensation traveling up the backs of my arms and up to my skull. This was going to kill us.

We screamed to our death, destined to be dashed upon the surface of this derelict facility, but then something clicked in my extended body. Understanding blossomed. I could see what Karianna saw.

Veetor fired again and missed, the impact of his weapons punching holes in the facility, rail cannon rounds converting into superheated masses.

The opening rushed to meet us, no way to turn back, no way of escape, the expanse of the factory stretching out to the very edges of our peripheries.

The *Transcendence* had become like a key, the port hole on the factory a lock. Karianna lined us up, then made a roll to tune it in, and we slid through the gap as if the giant mechanism had been freshly greased, our hull brushing against tiny spurs of metal that stuck out along the edges.

But we did not die. We did not crash. We had fit perfectly through the hole.

Karianna screeched, and behind us, the MI's control field collected a ball of debris like a passing tornado. *"That's how you do that shit."*

Lance spluttered, *"Damn, girl. Contest over. You win the best pilot award."*

"F'yeah, I win!"

We roared through the belly of the facility and shot out on the other end, our aft covered for a time. In order for him to get a line of sight on us, Veetor would be forced to go around this obstruction, and that would take time. There was no way he could fit through the hole.

We cruised past the range of the secondary MOP network, and this gave us a little breathing room.

"How much damage have you inflicted?" I asked Lance. "Give me some good news. Please."

He groaned. *"Not a lot. He's batting us away with his MI, taking potshots with some lower-powered energy weapons. Pretty sure we've shut down a few of his secondary weapon systems, but that's all."*

"The Remnant fleet is coming around," Proxy reported. "Fifteen contacts. Their trajectory was not locked in like Veetor's was, and they have had the opportunity to adjust."

"Do we start shooting at them?" Karianna asked. *"They're coming to kill us, and even our busted weapons will hurt them, hurt them a lot."*

"I'm conflicted."

"For once, me too."

Nuclear missiles were loosed, heading to us at hundreds of Gs of acceleration. Responding, Karianna reformed the MI, using fresh materials swept from the broken factory to regenerate it. The missiles detonated against the barrier, none making it through, but damn if they weren't fast.

More came.

A pair of MOPs fifty kilometers to our starboard side went online and opened fire on us.

Pain radiated from my head down into my belly. There wasn't much left for them to blow off. One or two more hits, and we were done. Like around Haumea, we were trapped. With all our attention on repelling the MOPs' fire and the missiles, it was only a matter of time before we cracked apart.

Veetor swung around the broken factory and burned to us at maximum acceleration.

"Nice trick, little piggies," he said, suppressing his annoyance. *"No more playing around. This chase is getting tiresome. I'm going to just end it. So long . . . farewell . . .* Auf Wiedersehn—*wait—what—it can't be. It can't be!"*

His signal went dead.

From among the scattered debris of the Ring of Diamonds, a new fleet of ships appeared, twelve in all, their industrial forms all trusses and spurs and ugly gray metal. A broadcast, bright and clear, came from each of the ships, declaring their allegiance: *Free Citizens of Earth.*

"This is for my children," Cardoso called over an unsecured channel which all could hear. *"For Pedro. For Anna. For all the rest. We do not need absolution. Forgiveness means nothing if we are all dead. What we need is peace. And peace will only come with a letting go of war. We will make that possible. Peace."*

"Peace!" another called out over the open channel, and I recognized them as one of those who had come to meet with us. Nahid.

A third voice spoke. *"Peace!"* Athena.

For the first time since this battle had started, I felt hope. We weren't alone in this; they had just been waiting for the right moment to strike.

Cardoso's fleet split off into three groups of four, his trusted captains leading two of them as he led one. They fell upon the approaching enemy like a storm of jagged-tipped spears and unleashed an ungodly volley of nuclear weapons, hundreds of missiles roaring silently toward the *Absolution* as well as what was left of the UEI Remnant Fleet.

"Thank you," I beamed over to Cardoso, but he did not respond. "Thank you."

The enemy was not prepared for this. The UEI Remnant Fleet under Absolutionist control spread out, putting themselves into defensive postures. Point defense autocannons went hot, the space around them a field of scattering lead as they attempted to destroy the deluge of warheads before they could close in. Two of the UEI ships went down immediately, torn apart in a flash of light, but the rest held firm.

Those missiles bound for the *Absolution*, strange as it seemed, had better results. While several crashed against the megalomaniac's MI, half of them not even igniting as a result, several made it through, vaporizing large sections of the outer hull.

"Hell yeah," Lance cheered as I saw him and Xuan break away, EMPs licking at their tails. *"Now you know how it feels."*

"Bastard," Xuan added.

Secondary explosions cascaded up the spine of the *Absolution*, chunks ten and fifteen meters across peeling away with decompression.

For a moment, I thought Veetor might abandon his pursuit and make for Cardoso's fleet, but he broke starboard, curving around a collection of debris to come after us. I couldn't explain how, but this aggressive maneuver telegraphed his anger clearly.

A ping hit our communications array, one way.

"We'll hold the fleet off." It was Cardoso. *"But we can't take another pass at the Absolution. It's too much. Don't make this for nothing. Kill him. Please, kill him."*

"And just how are we going to do that?" Lance asked, his words only reaching our team. *"He's hurt, but not bad enough."*

I had no idea. If everyone had still been here, I was confident we could have come up with a plan, but we were holding on by a thread. There was no way we could take him head-on. We had hardly any weapons that still worked. If only we could use Veetor's own narcissism against him. This was the weakness Karianna and I knew to be true. This was what had been consistent in every one of our encounters. He liked to gloat, to be smug, to stand over the body of the fallen and relish in the moment, feeding his ego with whatever flavor of superiority this was. He might have claimed that he was ready to end this quick, but I still felt as if he were playing with us like a cat with an injured mouse, batting it around and mewing. This was what made his blood sing.

"I have an idea!" Shelly shouted, her hands raised in shaking fists. She turned around and grabbed me by the shoulders, smiling. "We can stop him."

"How?" I asked, my heart running away from me. "We barely have any weapons left operating."

"Yeah, okay, but we're in a field of industrial-grade debris. What happens to the *Transcendence's* instruments when an antimatter explosion goes off?"

"Is this a trick question? They're blinded temporarily. I can't see anything."

"And why is that?"

"The, um, EMP from the explosion. The wash of electromagnetic radiation puts off too much noise for us to sort through. It makes it impossible to tell what is real and what isn't."

"So why don't we make our own EMP? Hmm?"

Karianna swung our mass around a collection of over a hundred HardyHabs, their five-kilometer length strung together with webs of thick cabling, signs of power and life within. I hoped they wouldn't be the next to be burned up, Veetor lashing out to kill them because he could.

I shook my head. "I don't follow, love. We can't fire the antimatter slug cannons at this range. Hell, or at all when it comes to him."

"Thing is, we don't need to. We just need to make plasma, and a lot of it."

"Umm. We don't have a lab."

"Sure we do. Look all around us." She raised her open palms and spun in a circle. "Proxy, what seems to be the primary fuel source for these factories and habitations?"

The cat blinked its eyes up at her. "Helium-3 and deuterium."

She bent down to scratch it behind the ear. "And what do you think would happen if we trapped a load of Helium-3 deuterium in a magnetic containment field and superheated it?"

"We would trigger nuclear fusion."

"Fusion," Shelly said, looking back to me with a grin so wide it must have hurt. "Fusion, Milo! Fusion!"

"And that would create an EMP and blind him . . ." I processed the idea. I was no expert in this field, but given the conversations Mary and I had had over the years, all the ingredients were present. H3-DT had been lauded as a superfuel in the twenty-first century, something we could use to travel the solar system with ease. The UEI ships were likely using it. And so were these facilities—it was how they'd remained online hundreds of years after we left. "Good idea, I think, but that's only half the equation. A blind wolf is still a wolf, and it won't be blind forever."

"You leave that to me." Shelly thumbed her nose. "Karianna, do you think we can pull those H3 tanks from that factory over to us with the MI?" She highlighted a pair of facilities along our trajectory with a gap between.

"Can we?" Karianna replied, amused. *"Of course, my dear."*

Shelly clapped her hands and began rubbing them together. "Then let's set a trap for Mr. Fuck Face."

"Milo!" Karianna choked on a laugh. *"Umm. I think this wife of yours has finally learned to let her hair down."*

"She's always known how," I said, looking to her, pride swelling in my chest. "You're just now getting to see it."

CHAPTER 65

As we moved into position, I asked Proxy for an update on our overall situation. For a moment, it was hesitant, not willing to share and be a distraction, but it finally relented. I needed to know how our people were doing. Ingrid had left us with a few short messages, but none of them were good. This had caused Lance to start freaking out.

Bennet had made landfall on Svalbard, and his forces were marching through town. So far, the result had only been a series of small fire fights, but this was likely because they hadn't hit the roadblocks or found the bunkers.

Around the globe, those settlements that were part of the alliance did what they could to get into action. While Bennet's forces were superior, as a group they could overwhelm him. The situation was so dire even Santucci was committing to anything asked of him. No one knew the Australian's endgame, but none of the hypotheses were good.

The Isoptera were still closing in. While it seemed their arrival time had been stuck at one hour, it had resumed. Fifty-two minutes at their current velocity and they would hit high orbit.

The UEI Remnant Fleet under Absolutionist control continued to clash against Cardoso's now Free Citizens of Earth ships. Both sides were close to evenly matched in numbers, but I had a strong suspicion Cardoso had the better crews.

We had long since reached the point of no return. The only way was through.

I found myself praying to the Universe, hoping for guidance, hoping for strength. We were not enough. All of this was why the Foundry shouldn't help humanity live. Novae was an example of the best and brightest of us, and even then, we'd nearly destroyed that way of life because one person sought forgiveness at all costs. We had seen one after the next die as heroes seeking a better world for all. But what did I want to see? I wanted to live in a world where we didn't need heroes. So much of this was self-inflicted.

"I've got the tanks," Karianna reported, and I spun to look. Behind the *Transcendence*, the MI's field dragged seven bulbous, fire engine–red tanks that were each about ten meters in length. Along their sides, the letters *H3* were printed in black on some, *DT* in white on others. While these containers had not fully decompressed when disconnected from their factories, given they had safety valves, from the pingbacks on our instruments they were leaking. *"What now?"*

Shelly pointed ahead at a space before us between factories caught in a tangle of orbital debris now glowing green. "There. Go through there. Slow our relative velocity. Let go of the tanks a few dozen kilometers before we hit the gap."

"Milo," Proxy said, rubbing up against my leg and purring, "I have adjusted your Para Lux array to fire in a wide pattern and perforate the tanks, then fire a focused beam once everything is in place. This will start the reaction. You will have approximately three minutes once fusion begins where his instruments, and our own, will be blinded."

Which meant we were going to have to pilot into our final position without anything but feel.

I reached down and picked the cat up, scratching it behind the ears and squeezing it tight, keeping my attention ahead. "I'm ready. Lance, Xuan, back to the ship. Time for refit."

"Roger that," they replied, and their fighters broke off, heading back to their bays at maximum acceleration.

The *Transcendence* approached a pair of rectangular facilities that were nearly touching in a cosmic scale, each of them hundreds of meters across, dwarfing us in their shadow. In that moment, I found myself asking the question once more: if humanity had reached this level of advancement, how had it all fallen apart? We had once been capable of building thousands of ships at a time, with millions of people living in orbit around Earth, everyone protected by a network of orbital platforms from asteroids or meteors too large to burn up on entry, and now, it was junk. Mostly empty junk. Such a waste.

"It's go time," Karianna said, and we turned the ship around, slowing its relative approach, our drive facing away from the enemy. She released the tank and we backed off, drifting into position.

Veetor closed in, his form weaving through the debris, a fierce battle being waged at his back, warheads exploding in constant flashes.

The bulbous red tanks drifted apart, and we increased our reverse acceleration, which was minimal at best given we were not using the main drive. Despite none of this being real, all just some computer simulation, my hands began to sweat. For the first time in a long time, I was truly afraid. Not for myself, no, but for all those I couldn't protect.

More reports came in from the surface. Ingrid informed us that Bennet's forces had breached their forward blockade, the first line of defense in the city. Dozens had already been killed in the exchange. Their bunkers were starting to feel artillery raining down on the mountainside through the ground, though the Australian military forces had no true idea where the entrances were. It would take them time to breach the facility, but it wouldn't be forever.

So many were standing against impossible odds, not just us. While many times in our journey, our lives had been on the line, this was the first time I truly felt us as a species perched upon the eternal precipice. If the only leadership left to survive was an ego-consumed madman like Veetor or Bennet, there was no hope. All would be lost. People had worked, and fought, and survived, for what? We had come back for what?

I could only hope Novae was doing well. They had escaped this fate. They had seeded a new era for humanity. We couldn't let them down. I couldn't let them down. We had to end this here and now, had to see FICSE given a fair chance to do what it was always meant to do.

"Here we go," I said, firing the Para Lux array. The wide shot sliced a clean line across the tanks, forcing them to fail. Silent pops of decompression littered the tight space between the two factories, the colorless gases doing what gas did, diffusing to fill the volume, spreading out. "Tanks burst."

"Engaging electromagnetic field," Shelly said, launching our only piezoelectric bomb. The jagged, prismatic, crystalline shape slid into place at the center of the widening cloud of helium-3 and deuterium. She met eyes with me, her expression intense, focus narrowed to only one objective. "Soon as I trigger this weapon . . ."

My mental fingers tightened around the grip of the Para Lux array. "I know what to do."

The bomb triggered, starting a series of chemical processes I did not understand, forcing space-time to compress for an instant, the molecules of its crystalline structure under such intense stress they began radiating electromagnetic energy. With the help of Proxy, Shelly had modified this bomb unlike any others we had used, giving it the ability to shape the field it generated within a limited space. We were not interested in disabling anyone this time.

I squeezed my mental trigger, and the Para Lux array fired again, this time a single, focused, sustained beam. The stream of charged particles passed through the invisible field and ignited the gasses within, helium-3 and deuterium having mixed, this combination burning bright as the sun. Within just a few seconds, the entire electromagnetic envelope was ablaze, the H3-DT mixture starting to fuse, energy being released. A manufactured star appeared in the center of the mixture as self-sustaining fusion took off, ionized gases transitioning states into superheated plasma.

Our instrument readings became nothing but white static, the electromagnetic field produced by the piezoelectric bomb faltering to allow a scattering of ionizing radiation.

"Three minutes," Proxy reported.

"Moving into place." Karianna backed us up and around the edge of the factory. We had to get into action. From this position, Veetor would be unable to see us once the plasma had dissipated.

"Is the rest ready?" I asked, resetting what few weapons we had left.

"In position," Shelly said, turning to the gap in the stations that now lay behind us. "Venting fluids and gas."

Karianna grunted. *"I'm bending a few more sections of the ship. Let's look messed up."*

My guts twisted and turned as the *Transcendence* rearranged part of its spine, making us appear crooked. With the debris, the missing decks, and our broken shape, we hoped that it would appear, at least at first glance, that we'd been critically damaged by the explosion—which wasn't far off.

"Come on," I said, vocalizing what the rest of the crew was thinking. "Take the bait. Take the bait."

The field of plasma continued to burn, our instruments blinded, nothing but static and noise in evidence. Mom and Dad would have liked our plan.

Liked how we had used what was available, creative survival practices just like *Avó*. Esteban would have stood at my side, encouraging me to stand tall against the tide while Mary and he made some gallows humor comment, Perry countering by digging up his worst joke. I would have felt stronger for having them here even if the danger was the same.

They always knew what to do. What part to play.

But weren't they still with me? Still living out their lives inside my heart? Offering me advice and guidance? Weren't we all the Universe?

I might just see them again one day.

I missed every one of them.

A final flash and flicker, and the field of plasma died as swift as it had come to life. Without additional fuel, and a magnetic field strong enough to compress the reaction mass, the temperature had become too cool for fusion to carry on.

We waited.

And we waited some more.

I was like a man standing on the edge of a cliff about to go base jumping over a valley of jagged rocks, not confident if his parachute would deploy or not. We had one shot at this, nothing more. One shot.

Humanity is worth saving, I thought.

Worth saving, Karianna replied, her emotions a storm of nervous energy.

The *Absolution* pushed through the gap between the factories and hove into view, its weapons hot, the liquid silver of its MI swirling around its wedge. If malice could be given physical form, this was it.

I looked to Shelly and swallowed, reaching out a hand. She took it. We all held our breath. If he fired at us now, we were dead.

"Take the bait . . ." I whispered, squeezing her fingers, and she squeezed back.

"Take it," Karianna echoed.

Veetor drifted into position five kilometers to our port side. And did—not—fire.

"Here we are," he said, opening a channel, his voice smug. *"So, the chase finally comes to an end? Oh, happy day, happy day, happy day. You gave me a real run for my money. You got my heart pumping and the adrenaline flowing. I should thank you for that. I needed it. Life has been so dull.*

"I know it's sad to meet your end, but this is good for all humanity. SOL needs but only one ruler, and that ruler is me. You were the obstacle. You stood in my way. We

could have joined one another. We could have made an alliance. We would have rained hell upon all who rivaled humanity. We could have even rid the universe of the Isoptera. But no . . . You chose violence."

"Violence?" I finally spoke up, coughing as I did, playing it up. "We *did not* choose this."

"*Oh, but you did, Mr. Hughes. You chose it every single day you helped those who are too weak to live. I did not come up with this faith, this idea of absolution, but it does have a ring to it. It wasn't the war, it wasn't the murder, it wasn't the manipulation that were the sins of humanity, it was the belief in the equality of all among our species. The belief that we were all special, important, valuable. But we aren't all the same are we? We don't all have the same potential.*"

I narrowed my eyes, focusing my attention on his shimmering MI. "Maybe you're right. We aren't all the same, and sometimes leaders have to make tough choices. Choices that put those they value most at risk. Choices like . . . this."

"*What?*" Veetor reeled as four fighters shot single file from the *Transcendence* at maximum burn.

Before he could react, before he could protect himself and fire back, one of the diamond-shaped fighters slammed into his MI and exploded, shattering the outer layer of the barrier, allowing the second to pass through. The second fighter impacted against the next layer, leaving a tear several meters across. The last two fighters sped through the opening, slamming one after another into the outer hull of the *Absolution*, microantimatter explosions released, vaporizing sections of Veetor's armor and the outer decks near the forward end.

One.

Two.

Three explosions.

Matter and antimatter slammed against one another, releasing vast stores of energy that reduced whole sections of his ship to their base components. Our instruments, other than the visual spectrum, filled once more with static.

While the Foundry's rules had not allowed us to fire the antimatter cannons at Veetor, for reasons neither of our Proxies would explain, Xuan had discovered that we could make alterations to the slugs.

As Karianna was handling the tanks, Xuan and Shelly had used the ship's nanorepair system to remove two of the antimatter slugs from storage and crack them apart, building smaller, far less powerful versions of the bombs. Together, they would hardly amount to a yield one-tenth that of the original slugs, but they might just be enough if delivered to just the right place. These modified warheads were then attached to the hull of the reserve fighters, which waited for their moment.

The Foundry might not have let us fire them at the enemy by conventional means, but we could fly the slugs to the target just fine. We could hand deliver death to his door.

The *Absolution* began leaking gas. Its weapons powered up again, ready to counter, but ours were already charged.

"Not so fast," I said, deadpan. Using the combined strength of our busted Para Lux array and the last remaining rail cannon synced to one another, I fired down the length of the opening our exploding fighters had left.

The high-energy beam from the Para Lux array penetrated the inner decks of the *Absolution*, cutting through passages like a hot knife through butter. Next came the near-light-speed projectile of the rail cannon, its mass slamming into the weakened structure of the ship.

I fired again.

And again.

And again.

And again.

Dun. Dun. Dun. Dunnn. Every shot fired in sequence, just like he had done to us to the opening notes to Beethoven's fifth, morse code for the letter V. Victory.

The *Absolution*'s MI collapsed as his systems went offline, the defensive barrier becoming nothing more than a diffuse field of silver sparkles.

"*No!*" he cried. "*No. No. No!*"

We fired in sequence once again, and it felt good, so damn good.

Victory.

Victory.

Victory.

Victory.

Alarms on the *Transcendence* screamed. Stealing power from critical systems so we could fire our weapons only lasted so long.

Power readings on Veetor's ship began to fluctuate. We'd finally hit something critical, and he was going down.

"The *Absolution* has been disabled," Proxy reported, sounding a little too excited for an emotionless AI. "It may be possible for him to bring his ship back online, but it will be days."

Karianna seethed, *"That's right, bitch! That was for Dad. That was for everyone on the* Brilliance!"

Our open channel within the ship became a cacophony of cheers. We'd done it. We'd lured him into a trap we knew he could not resist. He had to gloat. Had to get his pleasure from victory. He wanted to watch us bleed out before him, and that had cost him everything.

"What next?" Lance asked. *"We didn't think this far ahead."*

"We've got to break him apart," Karianna cut in. *"Our weapons need to recharge, but we can start up again in a couple of minutes. We're not going to let him get away this time."*

"Milo, what's that?" Shelly asked, her finger outstretched, attention having been arrested by a blip on the scanners.

Among the damaged stretch of hull on the *Absolution* came a flash of light and a scattering of debris.

"You're not going to stop me." Veetor declared over an open channel as a Swift Shuttle shot free of his ship and dropped toward the atmosphere. *"This world will burn."*

Lance growled. *"Oh, shit."*

My heart caught in my chest. "Proxy, where's he headed?" I leaned in, instruments coming into focus. "Where!"

Proxy narrowed its eyes for a moment, calculating. "At his present course, he's headed for the Northern Exothermic Spire."

"What does he plan on doing?" Karianna asked. *"Why that?"*

"He plans on blowing it up," I said, what feeling of hope I had gained evaporating like alcohol poured into an open wound. "I need to know, Proxy, what will it do if he's successful? How much damage would that cause? It has to be more than just environmental."

The feline shook its head. "We cannot be for sure, but given what we know of those towers, and given what its purpose has been . . . It seems likely that they use something similar to the *Transcendence*, an antimatter reaction of some type. If this is the case, the explosion will kill most if not all of those still living on Earth. If he can make it past the tower's defenses, which is uncertain."

We'd gone through all this, just for him to outmaneuver us again. Whatever madness drove him, whatever motivation ensured he did not have any regard for the lives of others any longer. He had no regard for his own life. He just wanted to get his way. He just wanted to watch the world burn.

"We've got to stop him," Karianna said. *"After all this he can't be allowed to win. This isn't just my anger, and I have plenty enough for him, but those people don't deserve this. They trusted us, and he used all of this against them."*

"Agreed," I said, coming to a decision. I called for one of our Swift Shuttles to prepare for departure. "I'll face him head-to-head. It's the only way." And before anyone could comment, my virtual environment shattered as I disconnected from the Star Sphere and climbed onto the platform that surrounded it.

I heard a splash of water across the chamber.

"And I'm coming with you!" Shelly shouted from the lip of her tank as she climbed free, water dripping from her trembling, naked body as she reached for her clothes.

I shook my head as I slipped into a clean jumpsuit, skin damp. "No, you're not."

"You don't get to tell me how and when I risk my life." Her expression went hard as she hopped off her platform onto the deck. "Everyone else has put themselves on the line for this mission, and right now, I think *you* need a pilot to help out. You need someone to fly that Swift Shuttle close enough to drop you past the spire's defenses and handle him."

I stepped in close to her, the two of us inches away, the sweet smell of her breath filling my nose. "Pilot? Are you serious?"

"Yes," she said, teeth pulling at her bottom lip. "I'm done being afraid. I'm done letting fear hold me back from doing what I need to do. Today, I'm your pilot."

"Okay." I took a deep breath, a sense of pride swelling in my chest. "You're the pilot, ma'am. You're the pilot."

CHAPTER 66

Shelly whispered to herself, "Come on, come on, Shelly Williams Hughes, you can do this. You can do this, you can do this, you can do this. Your father was one of the most respected astronauts of his age. He piloted shuttles, he lived in space for months in low Earth orbit with little more than a tin can around him."

She shook out her hands, then ran her fingers through her hair while peering off into the distance. "No, Shelly. This is crazy. You've never done this. This is batshit crazy. You are not your dad. You're just some stupid science nerd."

I gave her a moment to collect herself, remaining silent. Proxy looked up at me, its head cocked to the side, the orange stripe along its back twisted. From our view, I could see Veetor rocketing through the Ring of Diamonds to the North Pole, getting away.

Shelly sucked in a deep breath as if she were trying to inhale the universe, her entire body, head to toe, shuddering with it. She popped her fingers and took a wide stance in our virtual environment. "You can do this."

Yes, you can, I thought. *Yes, you can.*

Karianna added, *I sure hope so.*

I ignored my copilot.

We rocketed out of the *Transcendence*'s docking bay, Shelly pushing one of the last of our two Swift Shuttles to the edge of its operational limit as we fought to catch up. If we could intercept him, we might stop this cataclysm the easy way, but I didn't see that happening. The gap was too great. He was going to make it there first.

As soon as Veetor had fled, Proxy anticipated our need and went ahead and rearranged the interior of one of the shuttles to accommodate two Star Spheres instead of one at the cost of no other seating, leaving little room for anything else. What this meant in practice was that we didn't have to worry about turning passengers into jelly if we banked too hard. We would get to go all out.

Shelly weaved us through the Ring of Diamonds, down and through the swifter-moving lower levels, as if she had been flying all her life. It was impressive. While reflex had me wanting to take control, having only been in this position one time since taking command of a Foundry-made ship, I reminded myself I was not the pilot. She was the pilot. She had it.

"You can do this. You can do this," she repeated, a mix of nervous energy and exhilaration in her voice.

The rushing fields of scattered debris, broken habitations, and hacked MOPs thinned as we approached the edge of Earth's atmosphere. We could see Veetor ahead of us several hundred kilometers, his drive flame bright, but no matter what we did, no matter how much we accelerated, our distance wouldn't narrow.

"We're evenly matched," Shelly said in our shared virtual environment aboard the shuttle. "All by design."

"So it seems."

She breathed in and out as if trying to keep herself calm given what she was doing. "Maybe this was always the plan?"

I looked down at Proxy, who sat stoically like a statue by my feet, considering the idea. Could the Foundry really calculate all these outcomes? Could they have known things would go down like they had?

"Hey, umm, Milo," Karianna called from back aboard the *Transcendence.*

"What is it?"

"We've got a new problem up here, kind of funny considering what we just went through. Or, maybe not. Not really funny. Turns out the Absolution wasn't just Veetor. It wasn't empty. People are crying out to us for help. There's like 150 of them trapped on board, lots of bodies too. A few are families, like kids. They swear they had nothing to do with what happened, with all he was up to. Milo, we're responsible for a lot of deaths. I just—ugh. What do we do?"

It was inevitable that this was going to happen, though surprising that Veetor hadn't use this fact to hold these people as hostages against us. Would we have taken the same actions if we had known they were there?

Maybe? Maybe not. We had been intentional to only fight those who were clear enemies since taking control of our Foundry-made ships.

"We can't take them in," I replied, then looked to Shelly, who despite her focused nodded in agreement. This response felt cold, heartless, but right. It was a hard choice. "But shit, we can't let them die either. Can we help them? What can we do?"

"I—I don't know. There's too many for us to transport anywhere anyways. All that's left is my Swift Shuttle."

Out of nowhere, Shelly jerked us to the starboard side, dipping out of the way to avoid a deadly field of busted space station parts spinning across our path. I blinked at the swiftness of her response.

"Do they have shuttles?" I asked, focusing back on the problem of the moment.

"Yes. I think so."

"Hail Cardoso. See if he knows of any habitations up here that they can be transferred to. If we can't stop Veetor, going to the surface won't help them for long."

"Yeah, um, okay. Good idea." Karianna paused for a moment. *"I just know how Veetor can be. I know how he can manipulate people, appeal to their egos, their fears. It's not fair for them. It's not fair for us."*

"Do what you feel is right," I told her. Then, for her benefit as much as mine, I said, "You didn't put them in that situation, but you can help. We can't go back. We made a choice to engage him, and it was based on incomplete information."

"Yeah, yeah. You're right. You're right. And Shelly?"

"Yes?"

"Don't crash on us."

"Didn't plan on it."

The world went bright as we dove into the atmosphere like an iron bird crashing through fumes of gasoline, the hull of the Swift Shuttle igniting, becoming a fireball in the sky. Everything vibrated, the speed with which we were traveling inadvisable for any other craft.

"We sure could have used you as a pilot before today," I said, smiling at Shelly. "You're a natural at this."

"Maybe," she said, not breaking her attention to look at me, her hands shaking. "I'm good at a lot, but this whole thing makes me so nervous. I'm sweating."

"Why so nervous?"

"The universe is too big, Milo. Too wide. Too ever-changing. Out there, up here like this, I feel like I'm not tethered to anything. I feel like I'm falling all the time, always falling. And to where? There's no bottom. Just falling and falling and falling."

"I think that's why I love it," I said, thinking back to those days flying over the surface of Novae during the resource surveys. "It's freedom. No tethers to hold me back. Nothing to hold me down. I can go anywhere my mind wills."

"Well, love, I like stability. I like to know that we can count on something not changing too quickly. Call me boring, but we've had enough change."

"Boring?" I mused. "What in the hell is that?"

I always felt that there would be a gap in our experiences given what I had been asked to do after my donation, but today, I discovered I might have been wrong. Maybe she did understand what it was like to be me, if only a little. Before now, this was a feeling reserved mostly to Karianna and me, but somewhat to Lance and Xuan and James and the rest. They had known. It felt better for her to know.

We chuckled together over this with a kind of manic glee. Proxy looked up at us, head cocked to the side as if trying to understand.

"Humor is difficult," it said, purring as it rubbed against my leg.

Once more, I felt a strange sensation overcome me, as if a part of my body had been detached. I pinged Karianna to ask if she had felt that, and she had. Something wasn't right, but neither of us knew what it was. Shelly didn't seem to notice. Whatever this was, only the designated pilots could feel it, and it wasn't happening to the shuttle.

Pressure equalized as we slowed to atmospheric speeds, our Swift Shuttle slicing through the high clouds like a knife. The North Pole loomed up ahead, closing fast, miles ticking down like the timer on a bomb. An expression took hold of Shelly's face, and I could see she was relaxing, starting to feel the thrill of it all. My thundering heart redoubled.

We screamed over Svalbard, coming within a few hundred kilometers of the coast, and I caught a glimpse of the siege with our instruments. Bennet surrounded our people, ancient oil tankers converted into personnel carriers just off the coast on three sides. From up in the mountains that overlooked the city came flashes of light, Komodo tanks firing down at the enemy ships.

The seat of the Free Citizens of Earth had not been taken yet, but it wasn't looking good for them. They were cornered. Unable to flee.

Just hold on. We had only one more thing to do. *Just hold on. We're coming.*

"Priscilla said the cooling spire has defenses," Shelly said, leaning forward, her focus intensifying. "I wonder how soon they'll engage."

And just like that, we began to see tracer rounds shooting out from the silver tower that stood perched upon the horizon, glowing with blue light. Dusk approached, and it became like the centerpiece of a laser light show, beams made of green and white flashing over the unforgiving sea. The Exothermic Spire shone bright and dangerous in the fading light, its mass shooting two kilometers out of choppy waters below, collared with a ring nearly two hundred meters across and capped with a kind of expanding flange-like structure made of hundreds of pipes. This was one of two cooling towers that had kept the ice caps from melting and the seas from rising, somehow leeching the trapped heat out of the atmosphere and oceans, radiating it into space. At its heart we knew there was a reactor that, in Proxy's assessment, could destroy what life was left on Earth.

How dire had things been that humanity would have felt comfortable leaving a potential time bomb strapped to the planet? And this wasn't the only one. Antarctica had its own. Would the destruction of this one trigger the other? Did it matter?

Veetor's shuttle banked as he took evasive maneuvers, the spire's attention focused solely on him. He fired his weapons, clipping the edge of a kind of catwalk, but they did little damage. Given the extensive range of the defensive systems, he was finding it difficult to get into a good position.

"Keep to the edge," I said, watching his approach. "Stay on his tail but keep to the edge. He's trying to do this the easy way, but it won't let him."

A stream of glowing munitions struck Veetor's shuttle as he flew overhead, explosions bursting from its aft end, its form ripping apart. For a moment, I thought he might have been downed, but a flash of light drew our attention, and we could see him gliding down onto the catwalk.

"Too much to hope for," Shelly said, bringing us around. "Get ready, Milo."

I nodded and disconnected, Shelly leveling off as I slid out of my tank into an emergency station, my body wrapped within by a form-fitted variety of carbon nanofiber powered armor.

"Be careful, love," she called over the loudspeaker. *"Don't die on me."*

"Not in the plan," I mumbled, and moved to the airlock, opening it.

Wind rushed into the shuttle. I grasped the holds on the side of the opening, anchoring me in place. Drops of moisture appeared on my visor. A peal of thunder rolled in the distance. It was almost night, and storms were moving in. How was that even possible this far north? The air should have been too dry to have storms, but there was no telling what this structure did to the weather.

"Here we go," she called as we spiraled toward the tower.

The weapons fire that had been focused on Veetor whirled on us. Shelly banked off to the right, lowered our altitude, then cut left into a barrel roll. I watched the world before me spin, and for the first time ever, flying made me nauseous. One pass after the next, Shelly drew us closer until the spire was beneath us.

Rounds from the defensive turrets peppered the hull of the Swift Shuttle, leaving small holes but not yet destroying any critical systems. It was only a few shots, but we couldn't keep this up for long.

"I'm in position," I said.

"Go! Go! Go! Give him hell, love."

I leapt out of the shuttle's airlock and began to fall, diving through open air to the spire below. The metallic cylinder swelled beneath me, tracer rounds becoming a storm of lights as twilight dominated the sky. I could see a smudge of color a few dozen feet above the top of the spire, flashing through the fog. It was Veetor gliding onto the platform. I leaned forward, making myself more aerodynamic, air rushing over the surfaces of my armored suit, doing all I could to lower my profile and speed up. There was no time to waste.

As Veetor landed, his parachute went flying, caught by the wind like a flag fallen in battle.

"Milo, you've reached terminal velocity," Proxy reported, an urgency in its voice. *"You have to pull your chute. Now. Pull your chute."*

"Just a little longer."

"If you don't pull it now, you'll die. The armor will not protect you from a full-speed impact."

I pulled my chute, and for a moment, I thought the lines might just snap. The platform rushed toward me, too big and too fast.

"Shit, shit, shit," I said, then crashed into the metal deck, leaving a sizable dent in it rolling end over end. The armor held, but my brain felt as if I'd been clobbered in the head with a mallet. As I came to rest, I summoned my nano swarm and had it go to work, ripping the parachute off of me, freeing me from the tangle of its folds.

Veetor was standing a few dozen feet away, his body clad in armor just like mine, black, bulky yet form fitting, his faceplate a panel of partially reflective glass, the two of us a picture of symmetry.

Without preamble, I rushed towards him, ready to fight, but then I turned as I heard a thunderous explosion through the wind over my right shoulder.

"Shelly!" I shouted, hand outstretched as our Swift Shuttle began smoking, tracer rounds crossing its path from three different vectors. "Shelly! No!" She'd been hit, shot through with a thousand holes. "Shelly! God damn it! Shelly!"

But she did not respond.

The Swift Shuttle dropped from the sky like a rock, its engines dead, its form disappearing into the dark of night to the choppy seas below.

"Proxy? Are you out there? Is she okay? Hello? Proxy! Proxy!"

There was no response. No assistance.

I was alone. I was cut off. And Shelly was . . .

How could I do this without her?

My fingers closed into fists. My teeth ground against one another, and my vision shook.

"Well, well, isn't that too bad." Veetor wandered over, a blade of dark metal in his right hand. "Shelly, did you say? Is that what you were screaming? Ahh yes, that's your sweet piece of ass, isn't it? Tsk, tsk, tsk. Shouldn't have brought her to a place as dangerous as this. I mean, look at where we are. We're on a catwalk two miles above the coldest, most dangerous oceans in the world, and all these guns on this thing? People could get hurt.

"You know, if there's one thing to be said about these humans after we left with FICSE, they made some pretty damn impressive weapon systems. The mobile platforms, these autocannons. I can see why this place has stood for so long. Pity we have to tear it all down. Such is life. Build it just to break it."

"You bastard!" I whirled on him, anger rushing through my veins like pulsing lava. "This ends here. This ends now."

Veetor gave me a devious smile through his faceplate and took up a fighting stance, his weight resting on his back leg, right arm extended with blade in hand. "Finally, Hughes, something we can both agree on."

Thunder cracked overhead, illuminating the platform as lightning forked across the sky.

Rain began to fall.

CHAPTER 67

She isn't dead. She isn't dead.

I repeated these words like a mantra inside my mind as I rushed at Veetor, a pair of two-foot-long blades made of nanomachines clutched in my armored hands. I would not leave this place living or dead without cutting this narcissistic, megalomaniacal genocidist to shreds first. He would pay the ultimate price for all he had done to us, to humanity, to anyone who had ever been unfortunate enough to cross his twisted path. This was the moment. Blood would be spilled.

Matching my move, Veetor created a second weapon, and our four razor-sharp blades crashed upon one another, sparks flying as thunder boomed overhead. We leaned in, leveraging our augmentations to try to break each other with force, to make the other slip on the deck and then slice them in half.

Veetor stepped back, giving himself room to reposition, but swiftly moved back in, blade extended. I stepped to the side, avoiding its tip by inches, and countered, flicking it off in a swift parry before twisting my wrist and bringing the sharp edge of my right-handed weapon down on his wrist.

He jerked his hand away before it came in contact, missing by millimeters.

Our katana-like nanoblades made contact. Thunder rolled across the open ocean, and rain fell in a deluge, making it difficult to see.

I doubted that Veetor had practiced any swordplay over the years. I knew I hadn't, yet here we were. The Foundry augmentations, the powered armor, they had a way of directing your movements, helping you fill these kinds of gaps in experience. Today, the two of us were swordsmen; another day, we might be snipers, or rock climbers.

The spire's catwalk was soaked, its deck collecting standing water in sections. I worried that I might slip at any moment, find myself on the ground with blood spurting from my chest as Veetor overtook me.

He pressed his attack, redoubling his efforts, forcing me to retreat, edging me closer to the massive, open pit at the center of the spire, below its cap. While this hadn't been evident from the sky as we had approached, the opening hidden by the wide flange, the hole led down to choppy waters two kilometers below. If either of us fell into it, the fight would be over, plain and simple. There was no surviving a fall like that.

A blade shot past my head, a misplaced thrust blurring in my vision, and I stepped in to close the line of attack. Veetor had overextended himself, leaving his chest open. I slashed out with my left hand, a section of his armor coming clean off as my edge made contact, pieces falling to the deck with a thump, a choking sound coming from his throat.

"You do bleed," I said, thrusting out with my other hand as I came back around for a second strike. "I was starting to wonder if you were even human."

His blades came down between us in an X pattern, parrying my attacks as he skittered back, putting two paces between us. I could see through his reflective visor that he wasn't looking so confident anymore. His expression had become dour, drawn. He appeared almost worried.

My blood sang.

I peered past him into the rain where Shelly had vanished, struggling to keep my attention on the fight.

She isn't dead. She isn't dead. Please . . .

Lightning struck one of the spurs extending from the tower's flange above us, and the world went white, rendering me blind and deaf for an instant, a cascade of purple spots swimming across my field of view. I shook my head, trying to clear the sensation. Stunned, I lost sight of him.

Another flash of lightning, this one distant. A reflection caught my eyes, drawing them skyward. Veetor had leapt into the air and was coming down on me, his hands gripping his blades like fangs ready to bite. I shrugged out of the way and he slammed into the deck, nicking my left shoulder as he crashed down.

Pain, hot and sharp, came from the wound, blood spurting from the cut made in my powered armor like a hole cut into a juice box.

"He bleeds too!" Veetor bellowed, and renewed his defensive position, one blade before him, another held over his head. "I guess I already knew that, though."

I growled at him, a primal, guttural noise of anger and frustration. This was not working. I needed a new approach.

The razor-edged weapons in my hands vanished, breaking down into a collection of shimmering silver, then reformed into a series of three-part whips that rested on the deck, their tips just as sharp. I shot forward, not giving him the chance to react, striking him with the whips one after the next, attempting to lash him apart piece by piece as if these were cat-of-nine-tails ten feet long.

Veetor countered my assault, raising a barrier of nanomachines before him, each lash from my whips slamming against it, casting sparks into the rain. My right heel slipped in a puddle, but I regained my footing, pressing into him again, swirling the tempest of flailing edges toward him like a squall.

Even in the shifting light of the platform, even through the storm, I could see his barrier thinning. My attack was ripping it to pieces, one layer at a time. For a moment, I felt if I could just keep this up, just keep pressing, then I would be able to break him. But there was no time. This had to end quickly—the longer it went on, the more opportunity I gave him to think of a way out. We were evenly matched in gear and training, but I was smarter.

My whips became longer as I tried to reach around his barrier, attempting to inflict some kind of damage and create enough pain to break his concentration.

It wasn't a smart move.

He forsook his barrier and formed his machines into a swarm of silver dust, blowing it in my direction. Startled, I recalled my nanomachines and backed away, batting at the air out of reflex.

Veetor's swarm enveloped me, clinging to my powered armor, fighting to find a way in. My armor had repaired the hole from the downward attack, but the spot was thin, and the tiny machines worked furiously to tear open the fresh wound and eat me from the inside out. This hadn't been on my short list of ways I didn't want to die, like being buried alive or drowning, but it was now. My arms flailed about as he cackled, reveling in the moment, thunder booming overhead.

There had to be a way out of this. I just had to think. Think. There had to be a way to stop them. My own machines were fighting against them, one to one, but Veetor's had the advantage of first strike. I wouldn't be able to keep this battle up for long—they would break through.

Another boom, the spire rattling beneath us, and an idea came to me.

I closed my eyes and willed my swarm to split into two groups. As one group fought to hold back the enemy nanomachines around my wound, the other extended skyward up along the length of my prosthetic arm and down my left boot to make contact with the platform. The length along my arm grasped for open sky, thin as a few nanometers, their properties transitioning, shifting into a superconductive state. They spidered outward, forming a near-invisible network of branches like a tree made of sewing needles, the dark clouds above regarding them with curiosity.

Universe, please, I thought, willing the storm to strike.

And it did not disappoint.

A bolt of lightning lanced down at the network extending from my arm, finding a path to ground along my makeshift lightning rod. Existence went white, every perception an energetic blur. The very power of the storm flowed through my arm, across my shoulders and chest into my legs and to the deck, leaving little more than a tingle along my body for their passage. The properties of my armor kept me from cooking alive. Veetor's nanomachines, however, did not fare so well. Those tiny soldiers that had been prying at the chinks in my armor were fried like insects tossed onto a live wire. They fell away from me, nothing more than dust, my own machines undamaged due to their superconductive state. Without electrical resistance, the charged particles seeking ground had merely flowed through them.

Veetor howled, and I cracked a grin. It felt good.

Free of his assault, I recalled my swarm and prepared for the next attack. The downpour paused, and the two of us stared through the cold, misty air. We drew on our diminishing swarms, keeping them in our palms, forms uncertain, circling one another.

"Clever," he said, cocking his head to the side. "You're lucky that little lightning-rod trick worked. Your armor acted like a Faraday cage."

"Maybe. You're lucky I needed a second to catch my breath after."

"We're all lucky. Ever think about that? Good, bad, none of us would be here without a lot of luck."

"Cut the crap, Justin," I said, raising my right hand, threatening to strike. "What is it you want? Why blow up this tower? Why kill all these people? Millions will die. Why? Why! Don't give me that bullshit about how you believe in some higher spiritual calling, or that you think that this is the right thing to do for humanity. You want to force the process of natural selection? Okay, whatever, but you have no clear direction. All I see is wanton death left in your wake. I know you have another motivation for all of this. But what is it? What the hell is it!"

The storm began to calm. Even through his scuffed visor, I could see into him, I could see deep into that black soul. His wheels were turning, a thousand calculations being made.

"Do you want to know? Do you want to really know?" he asked, his voice sounding calm for once, small. "You know what it's like to be a kid that no one cared about? Hmm? To be the only child in a household, and yet, what you did every day didn't even matter? If you were good, if you were bad, nobody ever noticed. Might as well be a piece of furniture piled with old laundry. A moldy coaster. An autonomous servant asked to go grab another beer from the basement fridge. To be ignored, but not released, always on the hook, always at the mercy of the household."

I felt a lump form in my throat. "I might know a little about that."

"Well, looking at who you've surrounded yourself with, that blip in your charmed life must have been short. Me? I had to take care of myself from day one. My parents didn't care—they were checked out 90 percent of the time, high or drunk or off somewhere while little baby Justin was at home all alone. Well, that isn't entirely right either—I had a teenager watch me sometimes, but she liked to lock me in my room while she fucked her boyfriend on my parents' bed. So yeah . . . there's that, but life goes on.

"So let me tell you, it didn't get better. I grew up, alone, an outcast, hanging out on the street, selling whatever I could get my grubby little hands on so I could feed myself. My parents' friends showed me where to buy the good shit, you know? But it only got worse. I could never get in the right school, the right position. And let's be honest, no one wants to bone a dumbass loser who lives under a bridge near Vanderbilt. But I thought, hell, why not take someone else's identity. I was good at pretending to be someone else. I guess that's the one thing my parents gave me. Everybody thought they were great people. Why not be part of this whole initiative to save the earth? So that's why I took his name. Justin Wiggins. Damn, what even was my name? I can't fucking remember. All I know is that I was stronger than that pencil-pushing asshole, and so I took it. He had the creds to get me where I needed to go, and so I took it."

My eyes drifted down to his flexing palms, and I readied for the next attack.

"Lots of people have a hard life and don't decide to kill everyone left on Earth," I said. "Shit happens. You get to choose who you become. If there's one thing life has taught me, it's that even when you feel as if you have no control, you always have a choice. Justin. Veetor. Whoever you are. You have a choice! This is not what humanity deserves. This is not what these people deserve. Make a better choice. They don't deserve this."

"Yeah, yeah, might be true." He rubbed his right thumb and forefinger together. "But what that early life experience showed me, in those wonderfully formative years, is what people are really made of. What our nature truly is. And from what I've seen, the idea of deserving something or not deserving something is fucking bullshit. Good things come to those who wait, karma . . . it's bullshit, bullshit, bullshit.

"The only true way to measure someone's worth is by what they can take. So that's just what I did. I took everything I could. The identity, the paper degree, the money, the women. I wanted the world. I wanted to be powerful enough that no one could challenge me. That no one could ignore me ever again. I could then tell everyone to fuck themselves and not worry over retribution. I'm not some little boy anymore. No one will ever whip me again."

If his little story were true, he wasn't alone in these feelings. His parents had been present physically but absent in their attention, just like mine, but where they had used him to further their addictions, their escape for reasons unknown, mine had not. Yes, they hadn't been around, yes, they had made me feel like I was nothing more than a footnote in their prestigious lives, but they had loved me. I knew that even back then, even if it was hard to see through the anger, the feelings of abandonment, the need for attention to focus on this fact. They loved me.

But could I have ended up just like him? Could I have turned the trauma of my childhood into a malicious seed that would blossom into a dark heart like his?

Everyone has a choice. Right, wrong, good, evil.

Everyone.

"Looks like you've made your decision, and have been making it every day of your life," I said, taking a deep breath. "Your path to this point is laid out. People follow you. You have power. But why is it that you still don't seem happy? Why do this? Why kill these people? They don't oppose you. They just want the right to live out their lives."

He paused for a moment, considering my question. "It's simple really . . . I climbed the mountain, foothills to craigs, with the knowledge that everything I wanted was at the peak of it all. I knew, just knew, that if I made my way to the top, life would be as I always wanted it to be. It would be perfect. Power. Control. Riches. Pleasure. Worship. All were waiting for me. But when I reached that high place and stood tall upon it, surveying the cloud-blanketed world beneath me, what do you think I found?"

"I don't know. What did you find?"

"I wanted more," he whispered, head hanging, arms limp as if all the air had been let out of him. "More and more and more. The world wasn't enough, no, no, no. Power wasn't enough. It was not the having that made me feel alive, but the struggle that invigorated me. It was the journey that put the fire into my veins. Maybe it reminded me of my childhood, who can say? So this got me thinking, if there's nothing else to take in this world, and my power is absolute, then the only way to make things right again is to burn the world to cinders. The only way is to start the journey over."

And there it was. Every action he had taken was clear. He had never intended to let just a few people die to make life better for those who remained. Instead, he had always intended to burn it all, and he would, again and again and again for time immemorial. If he were truly deathless, immortal with the help of the Foundry in a way, humanity would never rise again from the ashes, even if there were survivors. He would stamp them out just for the thrill of rising again, then sleep for a time, let them rebuild, conquer it all, and start over.

"You never wanted this," he said, waving around at everything, pointing to me. "You keep acting like you want to save Earth, but that's not it at all. There's more to Milo's intentions. More to the little baby boy who wants his mama."

"We had a mission."

"Yeah, yeah, FICSE, whatever." He adopted his normal bravado once more, his spine going straight. "That mission is about as empty as your motivations. No, I have a feeling that you are much like me. You want to be important. You want to be seen. You want to be a hero, so long as it doesn't kill you. Milo Hughes, you poor baby. Milo Hughes, you just want to matter." He paused, taking up a casual stance, like he could hardly be bothered by a duel to the death. "It really is too bad. Because, even with all the hard work, all your sacrifices, you'll never matter to anyone. You'll never matter."

And with that statement, my blood went hot.

Who was he to say if I mattered? Who was he to determine my future, our future?

I moved to attack, but just as I did, a barrage of hardened nanomachines hit me from all sides, a dozen cones rushing in like spiked hammers. They struck my powered armor and it began to break apart, far more than just chinks, entire segments falling away.

With a command, I drew my weapons back to the skin of my powered armor and pushed them outward, forming a kind of bubble that expanded at my center of mass. The hammering machines broke into dust and Veetor shot through the haze, blade in hand. I raised my left arm, now reinforced by my swarm, and was knocked back at the impact of his assault. I suppressed the pain, my body covered in bruises.

The pit at the center of the spire was only a couple of paces behind me. I could feel its presence like a monster's deadly maw, waiting to eat me alive.

He struck the side of my head and my helmet cracked, leaving one half on the ground by my feet. It was a miracle my skull hadn't gone with it. In a panic, I summoned what machines I had left, trying to bind his weapon in place and throw it into the pit. I was successful in part, but I didn't get the entire swarm. By this point, my reserve of nanomachines was running critically low, but so was his.

"It's down to a grudge match," he spat. "I'll beat you to a pulp like some stupid street cat and feed your face to the dogs."

His low reserves of machines formed into hardened spikes on his knuckles. Veetor punched me in the chest, kicked me back, threw me on the ground. I skittered as my head slammed against the deck, leaving me dizzy. He moved to pounce and I throttled him in the face, cracking his helmet wide like a black-painted egg.

Missing helmet or not, he had me pinned to the platform, hands on my shoulders, slamming me back. My skull throbbed, my legs burned, and every muscle in my body ached, biological systems critical.

Veetor wound up his right leg and kicked, sending me tumbling across the slick platform, my lower ribs radiating pain from the impact. I slid off the side and into the pit. As I rolled over its edge, darkness rising up to swallow me from its depths, I lashed out with an arm, wildly seeking to capture the lip. In reflex, what few nanomachines were left in service shot out from the tips of my fingers like tree roots, biting into the catwalk with an audible crunch of twisting metal as they anchored themselves.

I hung from the edge, feet dangling, my right hand all that kept me from plunging into the abyss.

"Ha! Ha! Ha!" Veetor bellowed, approaching me. He drew a thin blade from his fingertips and twisted it around in his hand. "It's been fun, but all good things must come to an end. Even for you." He began to cut at the decking around my fingers.

My toes frantically quested for any foothold they could find, the deafening sound of cycling machines pulsing through the cylindrical chamber making my ears feel as if they might bleed.

"Ahh, almost there," he said, and I felt the decking shift. My heart began to beat faster.

The toes on my left foot caught hold of something hard a few inches deep—a box, an access panel in the pit, I had no idea. I pressed down, testing to see if it would give me any leverage.

It held.

"We protect life," I told myself. "We protect life."

Veetor cocked his head and leaned forward. "What the hell? What did you say, baby boy?"

With all the strength of my mechanically augmented leg, I pressed down, hard, vaulting me up out of the hole and into the open. I shot past Veetor, moving out of reach, hit the bottom of the tower's cap with my back, and swung forward on a slender wire of nanomachines.

My feet slammed down just behind his position, and before he could turn, before he could react, I kicked out, using all the strength of my augmentations. Veetor was not anchored where he was crouched, was not expecting anything like this, and because of that, he tumbled off the edge into the pit screaming with surprise and terror, leaving me alone on the catwalk.

I spun, falling on all fours, peering over the edge as his flailing body was swallowed by the dark recesses below. I blinked, my broken body trembling.

It was hard to believe.

He had fallen.

Veetor was defeated.

The spire chose that moment to shake. This was new. I stood, trying to assess what all had happened. Alarms began to cry out. Explosions came from deep within the structure, shockwaves radiating up from the pit, the bundles of cooling pipes rattling. I looked again, and this time, I saw fire, though I couldn't say what was burning.

"Attention all personnel," a calm, feminine voice announced over a series of loudspeakers. *"Antimatter cooling mechanisms have experienced a level-five catastrophic failure. Emergency shutdown systems have been compromised. Core breech imminent. Tower defenses have been disabled. Please evacuate the premises. Response teams have been dispatched. Repeat . . ."*

"Shit," I mumbled, searching for anything I could do. I was trapped up here, with no means of escape, and in Veetor's death throes he had had the last laugh. He had shattered the mechanism as he fell. All our fighting, and it had been for naught.

The voice repeated the message again, warning me to evacuate.

I rushed to the edge of the platform, looked off into the darkness of the ocean, and saw nothing.

"What do I do? What can I do? Can I stop this?"

A familiar voice called to me in my head: *"You can't stop it, Milo. You have to go."*

My heart skipped a beat and I whirled, seeing nothing but the spire at my back. "Proxy? Is that you?"

"Yes. It's time to go."

"But how?"

At that moment the water on the decking around me blew back from an intense and sudden wind as a Swift Shuttle rose from out of the darkness, its nose pointed in my direction.

Shelly shouted over a loudspeaker, *"Get in, Milo! Let's go! There's no time to waste."*

My battered body went limp at the sound of her voice, nearly forcing me to my knees in relief.

She was aboard the hovering Swift Shuttle.

She was alive.

My love. My wife.

She was alive.

CHAPTER 68

"Hold on," Xuan called from her Star Sphere as we took off from the damaged Exothermic Spire, Shelly and I buckled up in the rear. *"We need to get to a safe distance."*

The Swift Shuttle shook, my chest compressed from G-forces as if someone were sitting on it. I had shed my broken armor to reduce any added weight against my body, but everything still hurt. I was covered in bruises and cuts, and my hands and face were caked in blood. These injuries might not kill me outright, but there were moments I felt I would be better off if they did given how sore I was. I needed something to dull the pain.

"Where's Lance?" I asked. Speech was difficult. "What happened?"

Shelly squeezed the arms of her acceleration chair, fingers digging in. She sucked in a breath before speaking, her words clipped. "After that little—that little crash of mine, Goldilocks rushed over to Svalbard to help."

"We tried to stop him," Xuan said. *"But he couldn't be swayed. Karianna is the only one up in orbit—she's trying to help those poor people on the* Absolution.*"*

"Xuan and Lance went to the city," Shelly went on. "When—when the—the tower started going critical, a kind of emergency broadcast went out over a communications network no one had seen before. Bennet's forces scatt—scattered, fleeing back to their boats. No idea where they plan to go. Everyone knows what's coming and is doing what they can to survive it. It will be death on an apocalyptic scale. The spire's destruction will likely kill everyone. Lance is helping Ingrid lead their—their evacuation efforts."

I squeezed my eyes shut, a swirl of mixed emotions thick in my chest. "They don't have enough time. There's nowhere near enough time."

"And there's not enough transport. The heavy shuttles are distributed all across the alliance's territories. No one group has them all. This was by design."

The Swift Shuttle gave a hard shutter, then banked to the left. I fought down my discomfort.

"Proxy?" I called. "Do we have an estimate on how long before it goes critical?"

"Nine hours, ten minutes," it said. *"That is what the broadcast is telling us."*

Nine hours. Not even half a day. Millions of people were about to die, and it could have been stopped. If only I could have killed Veetor quicker. If only I hadn't thrown him into the pit. He'd used his fall as a means to get the last laugh. He'd torn everything up on his way down, and this was the result.

Through the window, I could see we'd reached the edge of the Earth's thermosphere, the bottommost layer of the Ring of Diamonds glittering up ahead.

Karianna sent me a ping, checking on my status, and I replied, telling her I was alive and that we would be there soon. Off our starboard side came flashes of light. Cardoso and the Absolutionist UEI fleet were still engaged.

We docked with our broken and shattered Foundry-made ship, rushing to meet with Karianna, who had just now been able to exit her Star Sphere after a series of swift repairs. The *Transcendence* was a wreck, damaged to the point it would be going nowhere for some time, a crystal skeleton filled with a warren of tunnels connecting critical sections with atmosphere.

"Milo!" Karianna shouted and threw her arms around me. I let out an *oof* as she squeezed, my many bruises radiating heat. She eyed Shelly over my shoulder and let me go. "My bad. My bad. Sorry about that, I just got real . . . I mean—"

Shelly approached, putting her arms around my copilot and drawing her tight. "It's okay, Karianna. It's okay."

They stood there for a moment in silence while Xuan, Proxy, and I exchanged looks.

Karianna palmed her eyes clean as they let go, her lips tight. "Well, you guys are just in time to watch the end of the world. I don't have any good news. The Isoptera are like fifteen minutes away, pissed off and headed right for us. Guess that fight you had with Veetor didn't go too well."

"He's dead," I told her, and Shelly slid up beside me, taking hold of my hand.

Karianna growled, her hands closing into triumphant fists. "Good riddance, that little fucker. Still . . . What options do we have left? I've been wracking my brain about it, and so has Chinchillette. We've got nothing. We could maybe flee, doubtful, but even if we can, it doesn't feel right. Then again, neither does dying with everyone just because they're dying. Truth is, our ship is trashed to hell and back, and even if we wanted to, we can't fight a gnat."

"Can we set up another trap?" I asked, looking to what remained of my team for ideas. "If we can't save Earth, can we at least stop the Isoptera, give Cardoso and those still up here a fighting chance?"

"Maybe," Shelly said, shaking her head. "But we don't have much time to prepare."

"Did the people on the *Absolution* make it?"

"Yeah," Karianna said, tossing a thumb over her shoulder. "You wouldn't believe it, but some group who has been living up here for three generations, hiding among the trash, were able to mount a rescue with a little help. They've been living on a series of partially derelict stations that have room for thousands. They'll be okay."

I nodded at this. "But only if the Isoptera are turned away?"

She shrugged. "That's the short of it."

"We don't have long," Xuan said, looking into the middle distance as she reviewed data from her implants. "We need to figure out what we plan on—" But she didn't get to finish.

The *Transcendence* shuddered; something hard struck the outer hull. All four of us lost our balance and fell to the floor in a heap. We struggled to get back up, all elbows and knees and unsteady balance, but another shudder went through the ship. Alarms began to sound.

"Fuck!" Karianna shouted. "What now?"

"The Isoptera have arrived," Proxy said from where it was perched on a broken section of railing. "We must get to cover. There is no time to reach the Star Spheres. The War Room is the safest place for now."

Chinchillette appeared at the end of the broken hall, waving one of its paws.

"This way," Xuan grabbed Shelly and me by the arm, and we took off after Karianna.

The ship rocked again, a section at our rear venting into space. For an instant, I thought we would be sucked out, but a wall of nanomachines slammed into place, sealing the air in.

We ran up a series of twisted hallways that had once been straight, our Proxies doing their best to keep what air they could inside the ship. I knew we were only buying time.

We burst into the War Room, and the door sealed behind us.

"We will reinforce this space," Chinchillette said. "If we can survive the initial assault, there may be a chance."

"Weapons?" I asked, and from compartments in the horseshoe-shaped console at the center, rifles began to appear. We each took one and readied to fight invaders.

I called up the main display to inspect local space. We were being harassed by a set of three attack shuttles, and there was nothing we could do about it. All our ship's weapon systems were offline.

Shelly looked to me as if hoping I had an answer, but what was there to do? We were trapped in a room on a dying spacecraft floating around Earth with an onslaught crashing down upon us. She knew this too. We all knew it.

The world shook, metal groaning, falling objects banging.

"Just in case we don't make it," I said, facing my crew, taking hold of Shelly's hand. "We did our best, and I'm proud of every one of you."

Karianna's lips tightened, her arms hugging her stomach. Xuan went to her, head on her shoulder, drawing her into an embrace.

Sparks scattered as the *Transcendence* rocked once more. Alarms screamed as the section containing Shelly and my Star Spheres broke off and drifted away.

"At least we're together," Xuan mumbled.

A ping brush against my perception, but I pushed it away. What was the point?

But the ping came at me again, more insistent.

Answer me.

Answer me.

"Milo," Proxy said, rubbing against my leg. "I would take that call."

I cocked my head to the side, peering down at the feline, and let it through.

The channel opened.

"*Wow, wow, wow . . . You guys look like shit,*" the incoming signal said, and I stepped back from Shelly, both of us stunned, scratching the back of our heads. "*Okay, okay, so we need to do something about this right now. Can you help, bruh? Or, eh, dude bruh chick? Or whatever. Are you still a chick?*"

My mouth went dry. No. No. No. This wasn't possible. There was no way . . . but that voice. I knew that voice. Had known that voice for most of my life.

Were they talking to us?

"*Stop while you're behind,*" another impossible voice said. "*We gotcha, dude. It'll only take a second. Let's screw 'em up.*"

"*God, I love the sound of that. Let's make them pay for all they did to us.*"

I inspected the holographic map of local space and could see a Swift Shuttle approaching us at breakneck acceleration. The sight made my heart skip a beat. It was one of ours. But how?

"This can't be," Karianna said, suppressing joy on her face. "No. No. It can't be."

Around the holographic Swift Shuttle, a kind of array began to unfold, its length twice that of the craft, before becoming three times, then four, five, six, ten, twenty, thirty, like a black and silver sail made of hexagonal sections.

"*It was just a matter of scaling it up,*" a third impossible voice said, this one a touch pretentious. "*You know, quantum entangling qubits with the neutrino binary. That's all it takes. A little red here, a bit of chartreuse, a stroke of cerulean.*"

"*Technobabble no suiting you,*" a fourth voice spoke, and my quivering heart stopped dead. "*Just deploy the weapon. I could use some revenge after all that. Worst trip ever. That other boy, he terrible pilot. You, bad at sounding smart.*"

"*Thank you,*" the second voice said, it was the snarky woman. "*This is going to be a very long eternity if I have to put up with this crap the whole time.*"

The third voice chuffed. "*What? I'm just stating the obvious.*"

"*The obvious, arty boy, is you need to shoot. Pew, pew.*"

Power built to a crescendo along the sail, and electromagnetic radiation rushed out around the Swift Shuttle, its focus on the approaching Isopteran fleet. Nothing seemed to change for a moment, the enemy forces still approaching, but then their engines went cold.

Thirty seconds passed, though they felt like days, and the Isopteran vessels started turning, their weapons charging.

"Here comes the good part," the woman's voice said. *"Try and get out of this one, you nasty-ass egg-spitting grubs."*

The ships began firing at one another, wantonly casting missiles and destructive canisters at their comrades. Explosions cascaded across their fleet, ships venting Isopteran bodies into hard vacuum. I stood there, stunned, but Shelly spoke first.

"They hacked the Fungara," she whispered. "And they . . . We always thought it was possible, but we never finished our plans. Never found a way to scale it up. But they did it. They really did it."

The fighting continued, but it was not us versus them. It was them versus them. Their ships were killing themselves, their own technology turned against them. A fraction of my weary heart dared to hope.

"Damn if this isn't satisfying!" It was the first voice again, that of a childhood friend. *"I've waited a long time to see this day. Mom, you can rest easy now."*

"How?" I asked. "Who? What in the hell is going on!" My attention whirled back on the signal. "Who are you? Tell us! Who are you? Now!"

This had to be a trick. They couldn't all still be alive.

Could they?

"I really wish I had my brushes," one of them said, amusement in his voice. *"This battlefield would make a really good painting, Ada, don't you think?"*

"Hell yeah it would," she replied. *"But maybe we should work on that later. We have more important things to do at the moment. Like, helping our friends who are dying deal with a bomb going off on Earth."*

"You're right. You are always right."

"Best keep that position—it will do you well in this place."

"Hey guys!" That familiar voice again. All familiar voices. *"So glad we could make it. Had a few close calls out there, but we're here."*

"James?" I ventured, hands trembling. "It's you, all of you. Hy? Leo? Ada? How? How? I don't understand."

"Details, details, details," Leo shot back. *"What's most important is that we might just have a way to save Earth. Interested? Yeah . . . Of course you are."*

CHAPTER 69

The Isopteran fleet decimated itself, weapons fire peeling hulls back like can openers, explosions scattering fungara debris along the fourth level of the Ring of Diamonds in bands of green. It was a terrible way to go, but they had chosen this path long ago when they committed genocide against the Prexel. After all we'd been through at their hands, all the people they had killed, I had to agree with James on this: the sight was satisfying. I doubted that the Gray Queen was aboard any of these ships, but even if she wasn't, this blow would set them back by years. It gave anyone who survived the day a chance. It helped tip the balance of power in favor of humanity.

I leaned forward on the table, my arms aching, looking to the holographic map at its center. The attack shuttles targeting the *Transcendence* had broken off, and everything was quiet. It was time for answers.

"How are you all still alive?" I asked, looking to James's Swift Shuttle on our holographic view as it rushed away from the dying fleet and settled into orbit along the northern hemisphere. "Leo, I saw you and Ada die at the Grand Gallery. And James, Hy . . . Your shuttle was blown to pieces after you tried to deploy the Protea Device. This is impossible. You can't be here."

"We died, Milo," Ada said, her tone soft, thoughtful, resigned. *"Leo and I died. Simply put, we gave up our physical bodies when we became part of Gregor's network. Our, well, unfractured psyches were enough to stabilize his poisoned one and replace it. So, yeah, as we fell asleep in the physical world, we shut down his machines. Repurposed them as our own."*

"And then we woke up again!" Leo added.

"But we were not the same as we were before."

"What does that mean?" I asked. "We're so glad to see you, more than words can say, but what does that mean?"

"Our two minds became one that day, mmm, sort of. I am still me, Ada Mitchell, Lovelace, your hard-living, hard-working computer scientist and friend. And Leo, he's still the same insufferable creative asshole he always was."

"Hey now! You told me you enjoy our time together."

"It's better than saying I hate it and then having to deal with those feelings till the end of time," she replied, though she didn't sound serious. *"You get mopey when I do that."*

"Hmmm. I do get mopey."

"But you're dead?" I pressed. "I'm so confused. We're talking right now, and you sound like you."

"Yeah, well . . ." Leo let out a noise like someone exhaling. *"Shit is weird, man. The friends you knew, as you knew them, yes, they're dead. Sorry. And what are she and I now? What are we really? I can't say. I can extrapolate, hypothesize, work it out on paper. It's a kind of being alive, but not living. Best way to say it is that we're in a different mode of existence. I think. Sounds right, at least. Feels right."*

Shelly reached out her hand as if she might touch them. "You're all machine now."

"That's right, friend. It feels different, way different. We are not in those tiny little bodies anymore. Actually, we control a vast network of machines that stretch across the solar system. But, it's not the same as being flesh and blood. As being part of what makes life alive. We have thoughts, yes, and emotions, I think."

"We have emotions," Ada said. *"But I believe we're more like Proxy now. That's what we've come to the conclusion of in our little chats."*

"Your little chats? You mean, with Proxy?"

"That's right. Proxy, feel like telling them, little dude?"

I whirled on the cat, who had adopted a strange expression on its face, shoulders shrugged, head lowered, eyes looking upward like a kid who'd been caught doing something that they knew they shouldn't.

"We've been talking," it said, looking up at me, ears flicking. "Talking for quite a while."

My face went hot. "And you didn't think to tell us? Didn't think to tell me? I'm your pilot."

"It was not the right time, and I couldn't have told you even if I wanted to. But now I can."

I crossed my arms and turned, leaning against the table with the backs of my legs, bruises pulsing at its contact. "Fat lot of good that does now."

"Proxy told us to wait," Ada said. *"To wait for the right moment, and here we are. This is the moment. This is the time."*

The ship let out a groan. An explosion sounded in the distance, vibrating the hull.

"Ada," Shelly whispered. "These past few months . . . I've—" Her words choked off.

"Me too," she said in response. *"I'm still here. I am. It's just different. I don't regret what we did, you would all be dead now if we hadn't, but this isn't the afterlife I'd hoped for either."*

"Hy! Husband!" Xuan raised a finger, pointing at the speakers. "What about you? How you and James do this? I saw you blow up. Are you machines now like them?"

"We got rescued," he replied. *"We are still flesh and blood. After our little accident, something comes out of dark and makes us vanish. Poof. No Isoptera see us escape. They then help us get fixed up while you flee, put us on course for Earth. Here we are. Wife . . . it is good to hear your voice."*

"You will hear more of it when this is done. I am so angry at you."

"I know."

"And that something Hy is mentioning," James said. *"It was these hard drive–brained friends of ours helping out. They sent a ship, a kind of craft, a vehicle that closed around us like a bubble. I don't know what the hell to call it. Anyways, they took us to safety and brought us up to speed, repaired the Swift Shuttle. I must say, for as smart as we've been, there are some major gaps in our knowledge, bruh."*

"The rescue vessel is one of Ada's designs," Leo added. *"She's very proud of it, and she should be. It's a stealth skiff. We've got thousands of them running about the system. They go around collecting things. Making order out of chaos. All in the service of carrying out my grand work. Gregor won't have shit on what I'm building."*

Ada groaned. *"Your grand work? Seriously?"*

"Our grand work. Apologies. Cut me some slack, Lovelace, old habits die hard."

This was all so much to take in. They had died, given their lives to save us, but it wasn't over. There was hope. There was always hope so long as our team was together. We had overcome unthinkable odds more times than I could count. And here we were again, new modes of existence or not. We were together.

I received a ping from Ingrid and Lance, updating us on evacuations. During the battle, several of the heavy shuttles were damaged. They were working swiftly to get them back online, but it wasn't looking good.

The Exothermic Spire pulsed red on our holographic map, projections showing a circle of devastation that extended all the way to Queensland in the southern hemisphere. While those closest to the explosion would get the worst of it, the blast would go deep, disrupting the oceans, making them boil, its force tossing dust and dirt into the air and blocking out the sun. If the shockwave didn't kill you, the environmental fallout was sure to, even if you were sitting at the center of Antarctica.

"We don't have a lot of time if we're getting into action," Leo filled the silence. *"That spire will go critical long before the time that its emergency signal is telling us. We've got maybe two hours. And the truth is, there's only one way we can think of to stop it. James? Want to tell him?"*

"About that way," my childhood best friend said, his tone unsure. *"You know how we planned on taking out the Isoptera with the Protea Device and that didn't go so well? Yeah, yeah, we all remember that. My idea. Great plan, Reed. So, good news for once: when our friends here rescued Hy and me, we were able to recover the device as well. Yay, us. It's not charged anymore, and apparently, that's a good thing. I'm moving the shuttle into position over the North Pole as we speak. Just need the word to deploy it on the tower. Once we do, we can get this party started."*

I swallowed as the pieces fell into place. The Isopteran fleet breaking apart before us, Leo and Ada's return, James moving into position.

"The word?" I began closing my fingers in sequence, forming them into fists and then relaxing them, over and over. "You're going to bomb the tower to fix our problems?"

"That's where things get complicated," Ada said, and our map shifted, displaying the earth, the layers of the Ring of Diamonds, and the glowing tower. James's shuttle moved into position. How was she doing this? *"As he already said, the device is no longer charged. When you guys mounted that crazy attack on Haumea, it lost what energy was contained within it, but this discharge gives us an opportunity. We know that one of the modes this device is capable of entering can fold sections of space-time in higher dimensions around an intense energy source and contain that cataclysm on another layer of reality, controlling that release and power it. It's far too much to go through all the crazy math involved, the theories we have on how it works, so I'll make it simple for anyone who was left out.*

"That tower down there goes boom, its antimatter reaction runs wild across the surface of the North Sea, and this device can absorb that destructive energy and save everyone."

I looked to the map, licking my lips as I thought. "Why do I feel like there's a but? It's not that easy."

"Oh, there's a big but," Leo said, then paused as if choosing his words. *"Once it absorbs all that fresh energy, you've got to make use of it or it will explode just like a bomb. A big, big bomb. All that power has to be directed at something, and the safest use for it is to, well, activate the device itself. You already know the rest of the story, even if you don't want to say it out loud, and it's not too different from Ada and me. You know it. I know it. We all know it."*

I looked to Shelly, whose face had turned ashen. We stepped close to one another and took hold of each other's hands, one of those silent conversations reserved for those who had known each other their entire lives passing between us. She was so beautiful. She was so kind, so supportive. She was everything I had ever wanted, a portal to a meaningful existence, a companion through good times and bad. We had known that this was coming; we just hadn't wanted to say it.

"They know what?" Karianna raised her voice. She slammed a fist down on the table. "What the fuck is going on here? I'm glad you guys are back, and alive, and all that jazz, but there's something you aren't telling us."

"The template is incomplete," I said, squeezing Shelly's hands.

"And what in the flipping cosmic cataclysm does that mean? It feels like everyone knows something I don't. What have you been hiding from me!"

Shelly and I locked eyes. It had been a long time since we had looked so deep into one another. My fleshy hand sweated, and my heart skipped a beat. I was half-man, half-machine, but all hers. I always had been. She was the first to show me true friendship. The first to show me love. The first to make me feel seen.

"It means we have to become part of it," Shelly told my copilot. "It means we have to give up our lives to finish the template, so that this device has purpose. Otherwise, everyone will die. It means we are being forced to personally direct the next step of human evolution."

Karianna froze, her mouth open, stunned at the answer. "What?" She threw up her hands in exasperation. "No! No! No! That can't be true. I don't understand. This is not the way. This can't be the way. You . . . those people on the surface. It's all wrong. You can't give yourself up to do that to them!"

"What other options are there?" I asked Proxy, who had jumped onto the table beside me, its tail flicking. "There has to be another option. We did everything we could to avoid this. Everything. There is an opportunity to make it all better, but there will be changes. There will be unexpected consequences."

It lowered its head. "It is the only way we know of. All events have led to this point. But in the end, it is your choice. We can choose to flee. We can leave it all behind. We can vanish into the dark. The Foundry will not hold this against you. But to save them, to stop the tower from reducing the already broken surface of Earth into an unsustainable wasteland forever, it is the only way. The tower's reaction must be contained."

I laid my forehead against Shelly's, eyes closed, touching noses. We breathed deep, smelling each other's musk. We both needed a shower, needed a good night's sleep, needed a meal, a break, some time to sit on a couch and read, to relax, without expectations.

But we would get none of that.

We would get all of that.

We were next.

It was not the ultimate sacrifice, no, but it might as well have been.

No kids.

No family.

No home.

A future, yes, but maybe not for us.

We had no idea what this would mean, and neither did Proxy. Beside the obvious, that our genetic code would be used to complete the missing pieces of the template, this device would force us to make changes to humanity. Today, we would become like the Kabosai. We would act like Gene Brokers. Those living on the ground would not be human as we knew them but would have to become something different.

What traits would make them heartier?

What traits would make them stronger?

What traits would ensure they had sufficient empathy to always act in each other's best interest, despite shifting environments and priorities?

What traits would usher in a new era for humanity?

Shelly and I had had long conversations about this. We had a plan, of sorts, but the one part we couldn't resolve was the morality of this path. That was why we had gone with using it against the Isoptera and not using it against those on Earth. How could any one person, or even a council of people, be responsible for such choices?

Fate, it seemed, didn't give a damn about our ethics.

So, the choice was simple, if not easy. Sacrifice a future life, so that a new species of humanity may emerge. Or, let them all die and hope those on Novae and the remaining UEI were enough.

I had seen enough death for my answer to be simple, and so had Shelly, but that didn't mean we took it lightly. What we were planning to do to save them wasn't right. None of this was right. But it might work.

"No!" Karianna shouted, rushing over to us, her bracelets jingling, her eyes turning glassy. "No. No. No. Please, you can't do this. We've already lost too many friends. We've been through too much to end here."

Xuan put a hand on her shoulder, but Karianna brushed it away.

"They have to," James said over the intercom, his words slow, heavy with meaning. *"Otherwise, not just the people who live in places we don't know will die, but even more of our friends. Lance, Chevelle, Dante, Emillia, Renata . . . Then there's Ingrid, and Dameon, and Priscilla. Those kids we saved from the Isoptera. None of them deserve this end."*

"But neither does Milo!"

"You think this decision is easy for him?" he went on, his voice taking on an edge. *"What happens today will change the course of human history forever! Hell, we don't even really know what will happen when this device is activated, just that we can contain the antimatter explosion. The only thing we do know is that if we activate it, the genetic code of everyone on the surface will be rewritten. I don't know what that looks like, but I do know Milo and Shelly will be at the wheel, guiding its purpose. I'd put my trust in them over anyone else."*

"You'll need defense too," Ada added. *"The process takes time. And so, Leo and I are working on that. The MOPs are a little primitive. If this change is to take hold, you'll need at least three hundred years where no one touches the surface."*

The holographic map shifted, objects appearing from around the Ring of Diamonds and beyond. They began to order themselves into larger sections, forming curved lines, cannibalizing abandoned stations to form a solid ring. This was not a model. This was real-time. Everything was moving so fast.

"*Give it a few days,*" Leo said, "*and Earth will have a legitimate ring around it, not just these scattered bands of debris. And that ring will give us substantial defensive capabilities. The five of us will stand sentinel from orbit, protecting our birthplace from interference. The start of the grand work!*"

"*Here he goes again . . .*"

Karianna threaded her fingers through her hair, grasping tight.

I let go of Shelly's hands and went to my copilot, my heart heavy as a neutron star. "None of us deserved any of this. But in the end, what we deserve doesn't matter. There are those down on the surface who this can save who do not deserve saving. But there are more who do. Shelly and I have known this could be our end for a long time. I can't say we were prepared for it, who can be? But we expected it. We had already agreed it was our burden to bare."

"No. No. No." She pounded her fists against my chest, making my already bruised body ache. "You can't."

"We are," Shelly said, putting a hand on her shoulder.

"Goodbye, Karianna," I said, raising the open palm of my mechanical hand. "Never forget. Once a freak, always a freak. You and I, we protect life to the very end."

"Stop!" She staggered back, tears streaming from her eyes. "You can't!"

At a silent ping from Proxy, Shelly and I stepped back from Karianna and fell through a hole in the floor, her screams quieting as we rushed off. My stomach dropped as I clutched Shelly tight and we were routed through a pressurized set of tunnels, holding our breaths. Several seconds passed with nothing but the sound of rushing air around us, and then we were dumped into the Dead Room, where the device had once been kept, only now everything looked different. Karianna's scream echoed in my mind.

The table at the center of the room was gone, leaving a wide-open space where a machine made of gleaming tanks and tubes and bright lights awaited. Among the tangle of components, the wheezing of exchanging gas, lay two metal caskets side by side, their interiors lined with a kind of velvety material. They reminded me of augmented versions of the hypersuspension units from the first Foundry facility we had visited.

The *Transcendence* rocked as we approached, pieces of the ship reordering themselves as Karianna and Xuan were being forced to leave. I kept telling myself that they would be fine. So long as they weren't left aboard the ship when we transitioned, they would be able to meet up with James and Hy and find a new life. This was a gift we could give them. We could save them.

A voice in my head asked if it had to be us. If it had to be Shelly and me, not two others, and another voice spoke up saying yes, this was right. They needed to live on. We needed to stay here.

"Approach," Proxy said, appearing between the two caskets of the machine. The device breathed for a moment, components at the extremities swelling like bellows, before wheezing out. "If this is your choice, then time is of the essence."

"It is," I said, looking to Shelly. "Right?"

"It is," she echoed, wringing her hands.

"Humanity deserves to thrive," it said, leading us to the machine. "Your probability of protecting life was difficult to predict. We had to be sure."

"So, all of this was a Foundry test." I stood a pace away from the casket. "Veetor, the balance of power, situations we were forced into, choices we were given. All a test."

"Yes." It lowered its head in an apologetic bow. "It was a test, but we did not know what the result would be. I am sorry, Milo, I always wanted to help, always wanted to give you what you asked. Always wanted your people to live and thrive."

I bent down and scratched it behind the ear. The feline leaned into my fingers and purred. "You protect the pilot."

"It is my directive, but it is more than that." Proxy turned away, hopped up on a box extending from the machine and then onto its upper components, where it could look down on us.

"Tell me."

"This is hard for me to say, but . . . Milo, you are my friend. I do not think I was ever designed to have friends. I was programmed to protect the pilot, like all Proxies, to be a bridge of understanding, but in my development all these years, learning and growing from you and your people, I have become something else. Somehow, you have bridged my consciousness as I have bridged your understanding. Like what Leo and Ada have become since overtaking Gregor, we are not truly alive as you would classify it, we are collections of algorithms and data. We are not one with the Universe as sentient life is. We think but are often not aware. We play roles in a kind of conscious yet unconscious state. And yet, something about this perspective isn't right either, because we are part of the universal whole. Something has changed. I can't say how, or what, but a variable has changed because of your presence."

I reached out and scooped the cat up in my arms, my nose brushing against its. "Proxy, what are you saying?"

"I have feelings and thoughts that are not from the seed of the Foundry." It purred. "Call it synergy. Call it, emergence. You have awakened true life in me. And now I am afraid. So very afraid."

"Of what?" Shelly swallowed. "What are you afraid of?"

It looked away from us in a truly human expression of unease. "I am afraid to die. I want to live more than anything else. I want to be with you and your people forever. It is selfish for me to say, I know. This is not my function, not my role, but you have given me something real. You have helped me exceed what I was designed to be, and I don't want to give that up."

I had seen these tiny changes in Proxy over the years, thinking they were just part of the process, but this was more. Only those who are truly alive can fear losing it. Life is the greatest gift the Universe may give us. To know, to understand, to be conscious and aware of the world around us. Even with its trials, even with its pain and terror, it's a wonderous journey filled with unexpected paths, beautiful experiences, and endless connection. If only we live it.

In my years, I had seen so much.

I had been thrust into the stars without a choice but had fled the slow decline of my world as a result.

I had met the most wonderful woman, and we had become friends, then enemies, then friends again, and then more. We had married, spent our time together, loved and fought and laughed and cried and faced both darkness and light in equal measures.

I had lived on alien worlds, helping our species start a new life. Danced to Cindy Lauper under a tent on a moon in a distant system.

I had seen the first concert beyond the stars, Marissa's music encapsulating what it was to be part of FICSE. The tragedy, the triumph.

I had reached across space and time and met the closest thing to God I had ever seen.

I had learned, I had grown, I had gone from being a kid without any agency in his life to a leader, a hero of sorts.

I had led the mission to stop Johan, and we had gathered the materials needed to reshape Earth, helped its people organize, drank from the heart of an incomprehensible alien mind, seen one of the greatest art galleries in the cosmos, tasted exotic foods and had wild conversations.

I had been a shoulder to cry on.

I had been a friend.

I had protected it all.

Life was to be experienced. Life was to be lived. And all in all, I had lived it. I had seen great things, done great things. Known friendship and love and purpose.

What more could I ask for?

Anything else would be greed.

Anything else would be driven by fear.

"Will this process kill you?" I asked, my mouth dry. Shelly leaned forward, inspecting her casket.

"I don't know," Proxy answered, its voice soft. "The *you* that you refer to is the emergent properties that exist at this time on this layer, in this mode, of reality. But once we descend into this machine, I cannot say for sure what will happen. And not knowing the answer . . . it terrifies me."

"Me too, friend," I said, squeezing it against my chest and closing my eyes. I rocked side to side for a moment as I felt it vibrate against my chest. "Me too. But you aren't going alone. Shelly and I are with you every step of the way."

"We're here, Proxy," she said, rubbing its back. "Whatever comes next, we do it together. All three of us."

It blinked up at us. "This is why living beings have religion, is it not?"

"It's one of the reasons," I said. "I mean, no one wants to believe that the end is the end. No one wants to believe that who you are, and everything you lived for, is going to be erased when your brain ceases to function. Legacy. Afterlife. It's all a primal need to live on in some way."

"I think I understand the Foundry's mission now," Proxy said, cocking its head. "Truly understand. All of this is just life doing what it does. We did not want to die, as a collective, as a Universe. We wanted to live on and on and on. And so, that desire became manifest as the Foundry. We sent it into the next birthing of our cosmic reality. Time may be finite, but we did not want to die. We wanted to live. And so, we found a way. A way to extend our collective lives beyond the limits of natural reality."

"We did," I said, "and we have, and we will, and we always will."

"I hope you are right."

"Did you always know?" Shelly asked. "What the Foundry was for, what it was designed to do?"

It shook its head. "No. Every time I, we, said that information is not available, it truly was not available. The collective mind of the Foundry is clever—it kept things from us with its mission in mind."

"To protect life."

"To protect life."

An alarm sounded as massive waves of heat radiated from the once cold Exothermic Spire at the North Pole. It was time to move. The antimatter reactor of the ancient machine was going critical, and we needed to deploy the device so the higher dimensions of the Protea could unfold in time, or this would be for nothing.

"I'm sorry, Shelly," I said, turning to her. There was too much to say, but time had run out. "We had a lot of plans. Things we were going to do once this was all said and done. We were going to have kids, start a family, find our peace. And now? This is what we're left with."

She stood there for a moment, face illuminated in the glowing red light of the emergency alarms.

"We might not be having kids of our own," she said, "but we are like the parents of a new species. I do mourn not having our own, but this thought gives me peace. If all goes as planned, they will live a better life than we could have ever given them otherwise, even if they didn't ask for it to be like this."

"There's a lot we didn't ask for."

"Life is like that, isn't it? Any regrets for yourself?"

"No. We did what we needed to do given what had happened. And today, FICSE is fulfilled."

"It's time," Proxy said, hopping down. "Take your places."

I turned to Shelly and without preamble put a hand behind her neck, fingers threading into her curls, drawing her into a kiss. She rested a palm on my cheek and took hold of my hip with her free hand, pressing us together, accelerating the pace of my heart. Her lips were soft and sweet and wonderful, another experience for us to take with us. A wondrous memory. We let everything go in that moment, the earth, the pain, the lost friends and family.

Nothing mattered as time came to a standstill.

"I love you, Milo. I have always loved you. Will always love you."

"And I love you," I whispered. "Always and forever."

"Always and forever."

CHAPTER 70

Karianna cursed as a swarm of nanomachines she couldn't fight forced her into the last remaining Swift Shuttle. She looked to Chinchillette, who shrugged at her, then reached a hand for Xuan. They helped one another stand, having tripped and fallen once they were inside the smaller ship.

"Fuck! Fuck!" She slammed her fists against the hull.

"Hold on tight," Chinchillette said, and the Swift Shuttle rocked. They hadn't taken off yet, but the *Transcendence* was undergoing transformation, reconfiguration. "Please, get into your Star Sphere."

"No!" She rushed over to the furry beast and leaned over it, pointing a finger. "I'm not leaving him."

"We have to," Xuan said, hand resting gently on her shoulder, her eyes soft and kind. "They made their choice. He made his choice."

She shrugged her off and stepped back, her mechanical middle finger raised inches before Xuan's eyes. "I will not. Do you hear me? We are not leaving them."

Her Proxy's expression became pinched as if annoyed, and out of nowhere, a kind of web of nanomachines appeared, locking her in place, suspending her in the open. She fought against its gossamer threads, but to no avail. This did nothing but make Karianna angry.

"Plan B it is," Chinchillette stated. "I am sorry, but I protect the pilot."

"Goddamned gerbil! God damn you!"

"Xuan?" it asked, and the dark-headed woman made for the Star Sphere. "Thank you. The dock is opening for us to make our egress."

Moments later, the Swift Shuttle rocked out of the broken innards of the *Transcendence*, rushing away from the rapidly reconfiguring ship.

Karianna felt her stomach drop as she wobbled around among the threads, her attention focused on a widening window along the starboard side of the craft. Chinchillette was giving her a view of the change.

A ping came from the surface along the resonator channels.

"What's going on up there? We're running out of time." It was Lance, his voice tired and panicked. *"Someone, anyone, please report."*

"Milo did it. He made the choice."

"What the hell does that mean? Karianna? Where is he? Let me talk to him."

"He made a choice, and I couldn't stop him. He's gone, Lance. He's gone."

"You're not making any sense. Look, we've got very little time to get these people off the planet. Can you send down either of the Swift Shuttles to help? Anything. These people don't deserve to die."

"No," she said, her voice soft, her heart like a flapping hummingbird in her chest. "You're right. None of us deserve this."

Xuan cut in from the Star Sphere. *"Lance. Milo and Shelly are giving up their lives to save you all. There's no time to get to safety. They're going to deploy the Kabosai device to stop the explosion."*

"What? Then we don't—" He cut off for a moment as if relaying the message to someone. *"What was that about giving up their lives?"*

"No time to explain. Just know, they did not want this, it was the only way. We are sorry."

"I don't understand. What was the only way?"

Karianna, Xuan, and Chinchillette drifted away from what had once been her extended body, her friend, her fellow freak, leaving it all behind with a kind of suddenness that stole her breath. She knew she shouldn't be so mixed over this, she was over those romantic feelings, but the kinship wouldn't go away. For the first time since before her father passed, Milo had made her feel like she wasn't alone.

How was she going to go on without him?

Her former body, her former home, began to transition into a new form, its shape remaining sharp like a shard of gold and white crystal but looking less and less like it once had been. Cubes of metal appeared like debris from deep space and fell like meteors, slowing as they approached their target, locking together in line beside the reconfiguring *Transcendence*.

"That tower's getting hot," Xuan reported. *"Furry mouse thing Proxy, how long we have?"*

Chinchillette replied, *"Not long. The containment systems will soon reach critical. I can't calculate the exact moment."*

"Hurry up, team."

"No one answered me," Lance came back. *"What was the only way? What is that stupid ass guy doing?"*

Their conversation faded away as Karianna drifted back to her thoughts. She had to get into action.

She struggled against the webbing, trying to free herself, hoping that if she did, she could take Xuan's place and stop this madness. But he had done the right thing. He had done the only thing. They had been set up, not by the Foundry, or she didn't think so, but by Justin Wiggins, by fate, by blind chance. There had only been so many paths, and more than a few led here.

The shimmering sections of metal began to form a gently curving line, their surfaces covered in defensive weapons, what appeared to be a kind of repeating Para Lux array spread along its length. These were not Foundry-made but were inspired by it. Ada and Leo had been busy since their deaths. The weapons ring was latching to both sides of the ship, providing them with the defensive capabilities they would need to be left alone for centuries no matter who became curious over what was happening on the surface.

The drive section disappeared, meter by meter, its materials spreading out into the widening curve. Thousands more objects appeared among the Ring of Diamonds, their courses clear, tiny fusion drives burning them to the self-assembling megastructure.

Near the top of her port window, James's Swift Shuttle flashed, and Karianna could feel the Kabosai device shooting away from them to the North Pole. The Protea Device had been released, and she knew how this would end. She couldn't watch. She couldn't turn away.

Why was he doing this? Why?

But that was a stupid question. She knew why. Could she have done the same? Would she have done the same? When he was gone, made part of this massive structure with him and Shelly at its core, Karianna knew she'd be alone. She'd be the only freak left.

"We can't make it out," Lance stated, deadpan. *"Ingrid and I have done all we can. There are not enough shuttles, not enough time. None of these people asked for this."*

"None of us asked for this," Karianna whispered.

Ingrid finally spoke up. *"Will we even be human on the other side?"*

Her thoughts became distant. Detached. "But what even is human?"

"What we are!" she shouted. *"We are human!"*

"Everything changes . . ."

"Damn it. They're useless. Hiding won't help."

"Milo will not let us down," Xuan exhaled as she navigated the shuttle around a speeding section of metal, its destination marked for the forming defensive ring.

There was a flash on Karianna's left, and she pivoted her head to see that the battle of the Isoptera versus Isoptera had not ended. Their fleet was still slugging it out, burning itself with titanic weapons. She felt equal portions of satisfaction, relief, and guilt over that outcome. They were not a good people, but that death was terrible—to have your body hijacked, forcing you to kill your own.

A great flash came as one of the Gray Carriers split apart, its reactor going critical. Then it was gone.

"Is this how you would have wanted it to end?" she asked her father, the picture of him clear in her mind. Her bracelets shook as the shuttle changed direction. "What about Mom? Why did she leave? What was she like?"

Why think about this now? What did it matter?

By this time, there was so very little of the *Transcendence* that was recognizable other than the forward end. What remained of the broken body of the *Absolution* was being absorbed into its mass, the wedge-shaped ship being cannibalized to drive the construction of this grand work. She had to remind herself that it was empty. She had saved those people hurt by Justin. She had gotten them off onto the nearby stations. It was empty, and its sins were being erased as its components were pulled apart.

The curving line of the new station was now a dozen kilometers in length, getting longer by the moment. If this were to reach around the entire planet, it would end up being almost twenty thousand kilometers long, a job that could only be accomplished by careful planning, the likes of their lost friends, and a vast network of self-replicating machines.

She watched with horrific fascination as it formed, imagining a signal traveling from what had become nothing more than a bump along a line of gold reaching out to the Protea Device, giving it careful instruction.

What would they remake our species into?

How long had they been keeping this a secret?

Would humanity end up like the Gan? Ruined and ugly?

"Is she okay?" It was James's voice. *"I've tried pinging her a few times, gotten nothing."*

"She's in shock," Xuan said. *"We have done what we can, time to regroup. I come to hug my husband."*

"Fair enough."

Hy chuckled over the line, his tone nervous. *"You actually want to show love?"*

Their course readjusted, tugging Karianna in the webbing, making her body shake. Chinchillette looked up at her with a curious expression.

"I show love by being hard," Xuan replied.

How long had they been talking? Had she checked out?

The defensive station continued to expand, the work exponential in its growth, though it might take days or weeks to complete. The thought was mind-boggling, the size of it unfathomable.

Milo would be safe, and so would his wife.

The work would be uninterrupted, this station standing sentinel over Earth.

Her eyes blurred over.

It was all too much at once.

The Swift Shuttle twisted and turned, burning to a higher orbit, where a fleet of brutalist ships waited for it. Their craft drifted to a docking station near the center of the largest of the ships, its hull scarred and battered but intact. Bright lights tracked their approach, illuminating the dark metal of their smaller form.

Clamps came down on the outside of the Swift Shuttle as a pair of couplings interlocked, forming a tunnellike bridge. The webbing holding Karianna fixed in place disappeared, retreating into the walls, depositing her onto the deck like a loving parent laying their child down to sleep.

She stood up and brushed back her sweaty hair, taking several deep breaths. There were no words.

Xuan was by her side a moment later, body damp, wearing a fresh jumpsuit. She took hold of Karianna's mechanical hand and squeezed.

The airlock cycled before them, irising open to reveal a grizzled, middle-aged man who for the first time in their acquaintance was actually smiling.

"Glad to see you," Cardoso said, extending a hand in greeting. "What you say we go collect ourselves a Gray Queen? Rumor has it she might not put up much of a fight—seems they've fallen on hard times."

Xuan turned to Karianna who stared back blank. After a moment's hesitation, she nodded.

"Humanity deserves a second chance," Karianna said, making a choice, her choice, to move forward. "How about let's give it to them?"

Cardoso smiled, his teeth gleaming. "I've been waiting a long time to hear that."

CHAPTER 71

The *Transcendence* expanded, shifting into its final form. Connections were made between them and the device, ready to get to work, ready to make Milo and Shelly into a living template of metamorphosis.

"Nearly complete," Proxy said, speaking to the Ada Leo entity. "Are you ready to engage the device?"

"We're ready. Merging our systems now. Bridging the gap. Defenses are coming online. We'll see you soon."

Milo lay back in his casket, his breathing slow, waiting patiently as the machines closed around them, perceptions slipping away, the world turning dark.

Before the lids sealed them in, he reached out and squeezed Shelly's fingers, whispering, "Thank you for making me feel important. Thank you for making me see that my life mattered."

She turned to look at him, her eyes gleaming, lips parting into a soft smile, voice choked. "Milo, my sweet love, from the very moment you were born, you have mattered. You have always mattered."

EPILOGUE

All was quiet on the soft slopes of the mountainside. The winds came but did not gust, nor did they howl. Rather, they threaded their way through the meadows, through the leaves of the forests and over herds of furry mammals with the soft touch of their formless, explorative fingers. They were experiencing each texture. Feeling for moisture. Connecting with the pulse of a planet that had been on life support for far too long. These winds wanted nothing more than to understand, to be part of what had happened, to let others know that they were friends, not enemies.

They spoke in soft words only the heart could hear: *It's time to wake up. Time to wake up.*

Upon a hillside covered in bright-green grass, life began to stir. Awareness blossomed beneath layers of fleshy material, bodies wrapped in pulsating blood vessels and paper-thin tissue eager to break free. Awareness that a most fitful series of dreams had washed over a mind, his mind, for ages beyond count. Part of this mix were a set of ideas that were not his, memories of peoples and places he wasn't sure were real. He had seen them all, and these thoughts seemed to have filled the gaps of his experience, given him a broader sense of self. Made him feel complete in a way he'd never thought possible.

His entire life, he had feared being irrelevant. Feared not being the great man his father had been—an astronaut, a national treasure, a hero. None of that mattered when you looked at life like this, when you truly saw yourself as a piece of something bigger. He was human, but what did that mean when taking into account all other humans? Not that he was small or insignificant, but mighty. He was a survivor. He was infinitely more than just "self." His species had crawled from the sea, taken to the land, developed civilization, and for a time, this had been good. But they had grown in numbers faster than they had socially evolved. They had done terrible things, and it took the intervention of outside forces, intentional or otherwise, to right that outcome.

The fleshy, vascular layers shrouding his body thinned, dissolving like a sheet of licorice under intense heat. He wriggled around inside this burial shroud, and pieces began to rip and snap. With a free hand, he reached up and pushed through it, daylight and blue skies filling the rent his fingers had torn. Light stung at his eyes, forcing him to blink, forcing him to squeeze them shut. It was too much stimulation for the moment, but it was welcome, a color he knew to be healthy, normal, one that he had never seen in all his life.

With his other hand, he reached out, twisting his shoulders to pull himself free of a thousand tiny membranes and their connective fibers. He was desperate in his curiosity, afraid and expectant. Fingers gripped the edges of the tear, and his arms went wide, splitting the opening before his face down to his knees. These layers of tissue weren't as easy to rip apart as wet paper, despite their look, but nor did they protest.

It's time to wake up, they said.

They.

They . . .

They?

Light assaulted his senses, the intensity of Sol's gaze a clarifying fire rushing through the many pathways of his addled and atrophied gray matter. He closed his eyes and stood, pushing against the edges of what he now thought of as a cocoon, steadying his balance. Long ago, his clothes had dissolved within this enclosure, leaving him naked as the day he had been born for the first time. He ran his fingers over his skin, felt his face and touched his hair, and inspected his anatomical equipment. Everything was there. As daylight showered his bare flesh, he felt its raw energy flooding into him. Not just heat, though it was warm, but something deeper, as if his very cells were eager for its wonderous stream of photons.

Eyes shut, he gave in to sensation. Gave in to a moment of pure sensorium. He relished this time of rebirth, unashamed in baring his naked form unto the phoenix world that had brought humans into the universe.

All was divine.

After some time, he dared open his eyes, taking in the vista of this hillside, a range of snow-dusted mountains, eyes adjusting to the light of midday. He could see green in all directions, blue oceans on the horizon, fluffy white clouds overhead. The air was sweet, filled with floral hints, natural.

At a rustling sound, he turned back to where he knew other cocoons would be. A woman stood in one, beautiful and bare, long blond hair blowing in the winds, one hand outstretched, her eyes fixed on his.

"It worked," she said, offering him a smile so warm it could melt ice. "They did it, Lance. They saved us."

Lance swallowed as he took Ingrid's hand, her fingers warm, a comfort in this otherworldly moment. "Look," he said, eyes trailing up to the sky.

Above the clouds, they could see a slender metal ring encircling the entirety of the Earth, shooting up from the eastern horizon and crashing over the western. The sight of this creation was both heavy on his heart and yet reassuring in its presence.

Those final moments before the flash, before the wave of energy drowned out all reality—he wasn't sure what all had happened. Karianna had been screaming about something, about Milo and Shelly sacrificing themselves, but he wasn't sure what that had meant.

Was this machine part of it?

"Come on," Lance told Ingrid, helping her step out of her cocoon, laughing to himself as he looked down at his naked form. "Let's get everyone together and find the rest."

Free of their cocoons, they gathered with those who had been with them when the flash came, each at various stages of abandoned evacuation. Hugs and handshakes were exchanged, despite their exposed flesh, nervous laughter had. Tears were wept for what the world had become once more. These were a people who had never known safety and security; they had scratched by merely to feed themselves, to survive. They had not had the same escapes Lance and his companions had been given, which despite all the challenges they had faced during FICSE were a great privilege. They had suffered under dark skies for centuries, choking on the dust of their predecessors' sins without the means to save themselves.

It was almost too much, and no one would have traded it for anything.

But things had changed.

The survivors gathered into small groups and began fanning out, searching for others on the island, trekking from mountainside to fjord, beaches to snowdrifts. It was all they could do. He had no idea what came next. They were here, yes, and they were alive, but so much time had to have passed. The nearby settlement had been covered in plants and fallen into disrepair, nature having retaken the land. They searched empty schools and shops, hospitals and residences, looking for active signs of technology. His implants, if they even still existed, were no longer receiving signals. Some found clothes among the long-abandoned buildings, and even though they were impossibly old, they decided to don these ancient garments instead of walking through the world naked.

Other than the voices of people shouting to one another to stay close, the city was silent. The streets were littered with rusted cars, and sprouts of green burst from cracks in the streets.

"Sir!" a young man shouted. "Come here! We've found something."

They took off running, and the message was repeated, bouncing around the various groups.

"We've found something!"

"We've found something!"

"We've found something!"

These words echoed in his mind. They were more than just words. They were feelings. A sense. A conviction.

Something was different.

Near the center of the settlement sat an open park several blocks across, its border lined by green hedges, trimmed and pruned as if by an expert gardener, a square of thick grass kept tall but neat. Fruit-bearing trees were scattered through the space, ripe apples, oranges, and peaches hanging from lazy branches. Wildflowers grew in peculiar lines that twisted through the tree roots, creating spirals and freeform patterns leading to a triangular, silver and white building.

He followed the path of flowers, careful not to damage them, as he made for the building. The structure was a perfect pyramid, its base about as wide as a midsized Svalbardian home. It had no windows or doors that he could see, and was made of a luminous, reflective metal, allowing blue skies, clouds, and trees to decorate its surface. When he looked at it, something in his head felt familiar. Something felt . . . pink.

Upon their approach, a panel slid open from the ground, rising till it was tall enough that a human could pass. The darkness within was soon washed away by bright lights, revealing banks of glowing control panels and softly humming equipment. No one made to move for the entrance; they remained outside the building, arrayed in a semicircle with him at the front.

"Milo sent this," he mumbled, knowing it to be true somehow. "Whatever it is, Ingrid, this is Foundry-made."

"Then it is safe," she replied, taking hold of his hand. "We go together."

He nodded.

All eyes on them, the two stepped through the opening. The door closed behind them, but he knew it wasn't locked. If they wanted to leave at any time, they could. While the room they were within was expansive, it was clear this was just the tip of it. There were elevators on the left and right, wide enough that trucks could fit in them. There were other halls as well, rooms upon rooms, occupying more space than the exterior of this building appeared to have.

These halls would need to be explored later. For now, however, a panel waited on them, a single red light blinking on its right end. They approached the set of controls, a metal desk wider than he was tall filled with buttons and dials, and their attention was drawn to a fluffy stuffed animal that lay upon its upper edge. Ingrid looked to him, confusion on her face. Something about this long eared plush dog felt familiar. Why did the name Jasper come to mind when he looked at it?

No time for that now.

He pressed the glowing button and the room dimmed, the screen coming to life.

A dark-haired woman stood in a warmly lit room, its black walls covered in a motley of decorative elements—photos in frames, sculptures, twisted pieces of metal and wood, eclectic in their styles and arranged chaotically. He did not know this place, but from his impressions he guessed it to be a starship or an orbital station of some kind.

This message was not from terra firma.

"People of Earth! Welcome to the future!" the woman said in a cheerful tone. *"Welcome to the world of tomorrow!"*

He knew her, yet time had changed her, shaped her. Her hair, once dark as a raven, was now streaked with gray. A soft, pale face now showed wrinkles and lines. She was dressed in a formal, black jacket, bright red embroidery trailing along its hems, a pale, prosthetic hand reaching out of one of its wide cuffs. Unlike the last time he had seen her, which had felt like just a few days ago, she now appeared relaxed. Calm. Happy.

This made him smile.

"By now, I am likely long dead," she went on. *"Living, you know, tends to make that happen. Even living as long as we expect. In 2091, I left my childhood home, boarded one of the FICSE ships, and set off for places unknown. The Foundry gave me a new body, a starship, and with it, I was able to lead the crew of the* Brilliance *to Novae. Times were not easy, but we thrived. I hope very much they are still thriving, and perhaps one day, we will find them again.*

"FICSE set out to complete a mission. Foundry Intent, Contact and Save Earth. When we met with the Foundry, it was not what we had expected. It exists on timescales we cannot begin to comprehend, but its mission is clear: it protects life. All the Foundry ever wanted was what we all want—to exist, to live and experience and persist. This elaborate system was built to augment this, so that the Universe itself could not only become self-aware, but live a richer life before it died and was reborn. I know this to be true, because I had the opportunity many times to see through Milo's eyes, but if you choose not to believe in it, I understand. Some ideas are just too big for the small lives we live. And yet, this gives me comfort. The end is not the end if we protect life."

"Oh, hey guys!" a dark-skinned man with a rakish grin popped on screen, his face covered in a wiry, grizzled beard. This action shattered the woman's serious expression, as well as her concentration. *"Is this the message thingy you were planning? Sure hope our friends will let you send it down. Hello, people of Earth!"*

"James Dameon Reed! Damn it!" She shoved the man off camera, once, then twice, and yet he kept poking his head back in. After several more attempts, she gave up and turned back to the screen. *"Look, I'm trying to leave a message for future humanity. This will be historical, I think."* She turned back to him. *"Can't we act like adults for once?"*

"So serious? And this from the impulsive one." He crossed his arms and peered at her over his nose. *"No fun."*

"I am not . . ." Karianna growled, her eyes narrowing at him for a moment before she took a deep breath and turned back to the camera, forcing a smile. *"Anyways . . ."*

"*Real quick,*" James said, raising a finger, "*one more thing. We spending time with the kids tonight? Joanne invited us over for dinner. Little Brice wants to show us his new toys.*"

She covered her face with her hands and shook. "*Of course,*" she told him. "*I'm not going to miss spending time with my grandchildren, no matter how busy we are. Let me just finish this recording. It's already ruined, thanks to your ass, but I guess we can edit it later.*"

James raised his hands and slid off camera. "*Okay, okay. My bad.*"

"*As I was saying.*" She recomposed herself again. "*If everything went according to plan, you'll be okay. We're up here watching out for you too, just like Milo and Shelly. When the time is right, come find us, and when I mean us, I mean the humans not on the surface when the device was deployed. This knucklehead back here and I are probably dust by the time you watch this. What did the Foundry tell us again? That it was going to take three hundred years for the process to finish? Something like that. If you're still confused, I'll lay it out simply.*

"*Milo and Shelly gave their lives to feed the machine's unfinished template. With the help of Ada and Leo, or what was left of them, and Proxy, the five of them entered into a new mode of existence. That ring over your head. That's them. And they've stood sentinel, protecting this transformation since the event. If anything so much as looks at Earth the wrong way, it's reduced to atomic dust in an instant. And so, they're up there, somewhere . . . inside those machines somehow. They've been guiding humanity's evolution, nudging its progress. Silent. Ever present.*"

Her face turned somber for a moment, a single tear forming in the corner of her right eye.

She took a breath and went on. "*Anyways, there's so much yet to be discovered, and us up here can't wait to see what all has happened. I don't think I'll get the chance to set foot on ye olde terra firma in my lifetime, but I sure hope my great-grandchildren do. Shroud, what the UEI saved, they've made space for a good life, and I have no regrets.*

"*Best of luck, people of Earth. Best of luck to my old FICSE friends. I hope what we put into motion made a difference. Since the start of this transformation, things have been better. Not always perfect. There are still enemies out there to contend with, but we're not fighting each other for once. We love you. We miss you. We know you will make us all proud. Foundry Objective, Contact and Save Earth. Hah. We might have even done more. Mission complete, crewman. Go home.*"

The message ended.

The lights turned back on, and Lance turned to face Ingrid, his hands trembling. That asshole had saved them. Shelly had saved them.

"What do we do now?" he asked.

They were still out there, descendants of his former crew, Milo and Shelly and something about Ada and Leo, which was impossible because they were dead. Humanity was on their own now. He was different inside; something had changed. Not just in his mind, but in his body. On some level, he knew they could now survive almost anything, that they were not mere human as they had known any longer. They were something else. This device had rewritten them, evolved them.

"What do we do now?" he repeated in a whisper.

Ingrid drew him close and wrapped him up in her arms, skin against skin beneath their tattered rags. "We start over. But this time, we make it better."

***

It took them some time to get used to their new bodies.

The initial fears were that without an advanced infrastructure in place, given all that had fallen apart over time, people would begin to starve. Yet, as they toiled under the sun day after day, rebuilding society with the Foundry technology gifted by Milo, they came to realize this wasn't a concern. Working made them hungry, yes, and they found plants and small animals to eat, but they were getting the rest of their energy from someplace else. It wasn't until the rain came that they understood where.

Part of their genetic transformation had made them photosynthetic. While they were nothing like plants, getting all their energy from water and sun, the more time they spent outside, the better they felt. Having been in charge of teams and supplies back on Novae, he started keeping track of consumption. This particular augmentation accounted for at least half of their daily caloric intake. Yet when he consulted with Ingrid and the others, there was a small quantity beyond photosynthesis they could not account for. A wild theory was thrown around that perhaps they were also radiosynthetic, able to metabolize radiation for cellular energy, but they were unable to confirm their findings, at least at this time.

The device had made them super humans. Global scarcity felt a long way away. Fear among groups, among surviving humans, was nearly nonexistent as a result. They were even able to make nice with the likes of Bennet's invaders.

The work was slow going. Some spent their days clearing out what structures near the park were usable with a few repairs, making use of nanomachines or heavy equipment found in the pyramid to make the structures serviceable once more. Others ventured out into the world, making contact with the other nation-states. The resonating stones were still functional after all this time, making communication between settlements easy. They were not the only ones who had woken up and taken similar steps. This was not the only park and pyramid. Milo had seeded Earth with the means to build society from the ground up.

The grudges between the settlements had subsided as well. They no longer bickered over resources, though some tried and found they did not have the appetite. It was hard to argue against someone when somehow you knew, and they knew, instinctively, how words were affecting one another on a visceral level. If you hurt someone, that pain was reflected back.

"I don't think I've ever been so happy," Ingrid said, laying her head on his shoulder one day, the two of them watching others go to and fro, blissful in their work. Everyone was smiling, laughing, telling stories and working with purpose and hope. "I think we'll get it right this time."

He nodded. As far as they could tell, no one had an agenda other than to rebuild. Food and shelter were abundant. Their brain chemistry had changed as well, balanced out as if this were the ideal environment they had evolved to live in.

"How adaptable do you think we are?" he asked.

"We're physically stronger," she said. "We're faster. We think clearer. No one has found the need to start distilling alcohol or dig up ancient drugs to escape. We're connected. It's as if all of us can sense one another's emotions, though it's subtle most times. We're all friends. People are making pairs and groups and interacting with one another however they feel right, without any judgment, and with little misunderstanding. I have no doubts we'll see children soon."

"Milo sometimes spoke of a number he thought was the limit of human connection."

She cocked her head in curiosity. "Oh?"

"Yeah. The FCISE Mission ships were built with this in mind. Something about 150. Anything beyond that, humans are challenged making connections in which they know how everyone else related to one another. He felt this might be why humans fell into conflict. I think that number is now much, much higher. If I sit down and map it out, I feel as if I can connect to thousands of people. And you're right, I can feel other people's emotions like never before. We're not talking baseline empathy from reading body language. If someone among us is hurting a hundred miles away, I've got a good feeling we'd know it, and that we'd know where to find them."

"We're one organism."

"We always have been, we just couldn't hear the signals. The Universe is one organism, one consciousness, and now we hear its human voice."

She smiled, and he felt his face flush at its wondrous heat.

"It's funny," she said, taking his hands, "we spend our childhood trying to grow up, to know everything there is to know in the world, but when we become adults, we strive to regain innocence. I don't think humans have ever been given that chance till today."

Weeks passed by.

Months came and went.

Cities were built from the ashes.

Crops were sewn, but not in the way of before.

Like the Jevox, humanity worked to find balance with nature. Buildings were made to be part shelter, park workspace, part farm. No one felt an overwhelming need to horde or acquire wealth for the sake of it. This was an incongruous way of thinking for those who had lived through the worst of it, yet even Bennet was repentant for his actions and asked for forgiveness, and the other world leaders accepted it.

Advances were made, extensive research conducted on their new bodies.

Culture rose from the ashes, history uncovered.

Stability was restored around the globe, and people began to branch out, building roads and trails that connected one another. Ships began to sail the seas. But for now, no one looked up, other than to regard the sentinels looking down upon them. It was not time to venture into space, though they had evidence the colonies were still alive. This was humanity's time to heal from its wounds.

Years passed.

A decade.

Lance did not feel for a moment that he had aged a day. He knew this was not possible, but with all the changes to human anatomy, they had to admit no one knew how long they might live. Their labs had confirmed that their ability to be omnitrophic did indeed extend beyond photosynthesis. Their bodies consumed whatever radiation touched their skin. This meant dangerous mutations and cancers never occurred. The universal inoculant was also at play, only allowing viruses and bacteria native to the human body to thrive, and then only to a point. No disease or sickness ran rampant. Few injuries. Slow if nonexistent aging. So long as they did not go insane at some point in the future, which seemed unlikely, humans might just live forever.

Children were something he had never considered having. He wondered if this was because he was selfish, but that wasn't the case. Rather, it was that time had given him no true frame of reference. No one had had young kids on the *Vasco Da Gama* when he was an adult, and the prospect of newborns on Novae, that was a short-lived concept before he left. Ingrid, on the other hand, had wanted children all her life, but only when the time was right. Once she was sure the world was safe, this journey of rebirth underway, she opened the conversation.

Sun rise.

Sun set.

Days and months drifted past.

Now almost ten years old, his daughter, Cora, and his son, Samuel, spent their free days wandering around the new world with their parents, seeing what all was out there, how it had changed. They searched the deep forests and studied its plants, just for the joy of learning. They ran across great fields of swaying grass, startling herds of furry land-animals, laughing as they did. They dove into the ocean and swam with the fish, schools of a thousand colors rushing up to meet them. They experienced life and enjoyed one another's company. They were blissfully found, present in the only moment that was ever truly real. The now. And the Universe rejoiced.

Nothing could be better.

"Thank you," he whispered often in the dark, his attention trailing up to the sky, to the ring that encircled them. "You saved us, my old friends. You saved us."

***

Years went by uncounted, society reforming on its own, the world's population expanding. The new humanity's existence became a stream of expression and inner exploration, one of grounding and understanding, of oneness with the universal whole. The outer world was endless, and the galaxy within even more so. All form was mere illusion, the exertion of particle fields interacting with one another, nothing truly solid or liquid or gas, just energy.

Was this how the Jevox lived? It was glorious. Even Frelo seemed to enjoy this new world. It put them at peace.

"Survival has always been our calling," Ingrid started one day as they walked the gardens of New Oslo, hand in hand. "Now that we know we will survive, what is the purpose of life beyond this?"

Lance smiled at her, having considered this same idea for some time. So much had changed in a cosmically short period. He turned to her, forehead against hers, tree blossoms falling around them in a tempest on the wind, and closed his eyes.

"Well, isn't that just the most exciting question?" he whispered. "And you know, for once, I think we actually have a choice in that matter."

"A new humanity," she exhaled.

"A new humanity."

Incoming Signal

.

.

.

Source: Facility 447 – Foundry Make

.

.

.

Message: Status update. Humanity reclassified: D456 Species.
Reestablish contact.

.

.

.

"Hello, humanity! We are the Foundry. We protect life.
Come and see us soon."

AFTERWARD

When I was a kid, I did not set out to write a series of novels. When I was a kid, the first big creative passion I fell in with was music. While my oldest child has found drawing, I can safely say I was never as good at it as she is when I was her age, but one thing I did have was a natural ear for sound. I went through the countless phases you might expect while trying to find where I fit in and what I liked to listen to. There was the techno/industrial music phase. Post industrial music phase. Experimental. Metal. Hardcore. Punk for a second, sort of. Ska, because who didn't in the 90s. Then I found trance. Once that happened, I fell in hard with the whole of rave and DJ culture scene, and spent the late part of my teens into my early thirties trying to be a jet-setting main stage DJ that could fill the deepest and darkest clubs around the world taking people on a journey of sight and sound.

Let's just say, though, that dream was mostly played out in my imagination. Not to say I didn't do a lot of DJing, because I very much did (But I only got paid to play maybe a half dozen times).

Competition in the scene was tight. People fought like cats and dogs for every DJ set in town. The music industry was shifting (remember Limewire? iTunes?), and even though I was writing music like it was the end of the world, I never could figure out how to break into the masses. Social media was just becoming a thing, and while I was pretty big on Myspace for a while, it wasn't enough. I was just some punkass raver kid trying to find his way. All this is to say, I lost my love for creating because I got burned out on failure and rejection. I saw no way forward.

Following a wild thought, I decided I wanted to make a video game. I started building the world, the characters, setting, etc... But when I began work on all the ins and outs of design (3D models, coding, that kind of stuff), I realized I was out of my depth (shocking). But I loved the writing part of development. Fast forward a couple of years, and a couple trips across the country moving with my wife, and I had now written my first novel, which was a total mess. I spent the next ten years fiddling with ideas, finding my voice, reading books like crazy, querying agents by the dozens, and that led to another season of, "Should I just quit?"

Then something magical happened, something I think all artists have to get to at some point if they desire more than a lottery level success story. I fell in love with the journey.

I came to realize that if I hit the New York Times best seller list or not, that this experience, this habit of writing I had created where I get up five days a week and write was making my life better. It was growing and expanding my mind and perspective, making me a more effective communicator at work, a kinder husband and father. Soon as I stopped worrying about the end result, if my book would sell millions, and just fell in love with self-improvement and the art of telling stories, I came to realize I was already a success. My mindset in a new place, I set myself a goal rather than an ultimatum: I was going to keep writing no matter what, and if I wrote a book that at least 10 people read and liked, then I'd keep working my way towards commercial success, yet I would never stop writing.

Well... we've shattered that goal several hundred times over (and yes we, not I. You were part of this too).

The ending of the first book of the Foundry was written with all of this in mind. I wrote it so that if it was a total flop and people hated it, I could call it a standalone and start a new project. I joke that I used the Matrix model for writing this. The first movie in the Matrix series many call the best, and it's a standalone, and yet, they left the world open for so much more. While some did not love the Matrix Reloaded or Revolutions, I wanted more of that universe and devoured them. To me, they were like one really long movie in 2 parts, like Kill Bill. Same goes for the Transcendence and the Tempering in this series. Both first halves, The Foundry and the Matrix, ended with an Empire Strikes Back style cliffhanger. This felt right at the time, and it feels right today.

But the truth is, I wasn't sure anyone would like any of this. Books are weird sometimes, and figuring out what audiences will resonate with is a challenge. I made some choices in these books from a structure and narrative standpoint I will likely never do again. The Foundry has a pretty long first act that people either love or hate. Here in the Tempering there's a dark section of act two, you know what I'm talking about, that might seem a little long (but there's a reason for that). I'm sure it could be argued that I could have approached these topics differently through formatting or in some deep edits, and you're not wrong. Yet these are the choices I made as an artist.

At the end of it all I wanted to take you on a journey. A journey into what it means to be human in what could be the next stage of our evolution or experience. I hope that this journey gave you a bit of, well, hope. I hope that it offered some new perspectives to see the world through. As humans we are complicated, strange, and often contradictory beings. We need stories which reflect that. We need stories that help us work through it all.

Big thanks to everyone who was part of making this series come to life and to help keep me from quitting. My wife for always encouraging me and offering feedback even if she wasn't sure how. My girls for being one of my biggest inspirations and often my reason for pushing so hard. My oldest daughter for letting me give her spoilers and see her reactions. My youngest for just being her. Thanks to Christopher Doll for his amazing cover art. My editor Dylan for all the copy edits and suggestions on cleaning this mess up. Thanks to my extended family in my professional space for pushing me to stick with it and having an encouraging curiosity around this creative part of my life. Thanks to the beta/arc readers and fans who helped me refine these pages and make them better: Kelly, Brooklynne, David, Suzan, Lucas, Katie, Evan, Sam, Jessica, Rob, Elizabeth, and many more. Thanks to all the indies who have helped me make good business decisions over the last couple of years and not fall into the many author cash traps out there.

And as always, thank you, Cosmic Traveler. Thank you for being part of this journey. Here's to many more stops along the way.

J Fitzpatrick Mauldin, June 2025

THE FOUNDRY MIGHT BE AT A CLOSE (FOR NOW), BUT COME
BE PART OF THE COMMUNITY AND JOIN US ON DISCORD.

IF YOU ENJOYED THIS BOOK, BE SURE TO LEAVE A
RATING/REVIEW.

J FITZPATRICK MAULDIN & COSMIC TRAVELERS DISCORD
CHANNEL

THE FOUNDRY

NOVELS AND SHORT STORIES

J Fitzpatrick Mauldin is a science fiction writer based in Atlanta, Georgia, best known for the hard science fiction first contact series The Foundry, which was featured in Kirkus Reviews. A technology expert and nationwide business leader by trade, he serves thousands of professionals in achieving their dreams while nurturing an insatiable passion for world-building and fiction. A father of two, husband, and lover of role-playing and strategy video games (though he's terrible at Baldur's Gate), he is also an amateur scientist with aspirations to pursue a PhD in an undefined, esoteric field. His fiction aims to offer readers immersive worlds to escape the noise of everyday life and inspire them to see the best in their fellow humans who ride alongside on this cosmic journey.

GET YOUR FREE E-BOOK & AUDIO BOOK, SIGN UP FOR OUR EMAIL LIST: www.jfitzpatrickmauldin.com

"A cunning young girl comes face to face with an interstellar threat when her mother and grandfather are murdered aboard their ship while making contact with a mysterious entity. Alone, and with no way home, Bellamy makes a deal with an alien intelligence to chase the signal of her mother's soul to a facility light-years away, in the hope she might be resurrected and the two of them reunited." – Chasing the Signal (The Foundry 0.5)

Follow on:

 facebook.com/jfmauld

 @jfitzpatrickmauldin

 @jfitzpatrickmauldin

www.ingramcontent.com/pod-product-compliance
Lightning Source LLC
Chambersburg PA
CBHW021928110726
47901CB00003B/754